Official 1982 National Football League Record Manual

63rd Season

NATIONAL FOOTBALL LEAGUE
Pete Rozelle, Commissioner
AMERICAN FOOTBALL CONFERENCE
Lamar Hunt, President
NATIONAL FOOTBALL CONFERENCE
George Halas, President

A National Football League Book

Distributed by Dell Distributing

A National Football League Book.
Compiled by the NFL Public Relations Department and Seymour Siwoff.
Edited by Fran Connors, AFC Director of Information.
Statistics by Elias Sports Bureau, Inc.
Produced by NFL Properties, Inc., Creative Services Division.
Cover Photograph of San Francisco 49ers quarterback Joe Montana by Peter Read Miller.

Another National Football League book from Dell you will enjoy:
NFL Report '82 (season preview annual)

Printed in the United States of America.

NATIONAL FOOTBALL LEAGUE
410 Park Avenue, New York, N. Y. 10022 (212) 758-1500

Commissioner: Pete Rozelle
Executive Director: Don Weiss
Treasurer: Bill Ray
Counsel to Commissioner: Jay Moyer
Director of Operations: Jan Van Duser
Director of Public Relations: Jim Heffernan
Director of Information: Joe Browne
Director of Broadcasting: Val Pinchbeck, Jr.
Director of Security: Warren Welsh
Assistant Director of Security: Charles R. Jackson
Director of Personnel: Joel Bussert
Administrative Coordinator: Peter Hadhazy
Supervisor of Officials: Art McNally
Assistant Supervisor of Officials: Jack Reader
Assistant Supervisor of Officials: Nick Skorich
Director of Special Events: Jim Steeg
Assistant Director of Special Events: Maxine Isenberg
Special Projects Manager: Bill Granholm
Director of Player Relations: Buddy Young
Auditor: Tom Sullivan
Director of Office Services: Wayne Rosen
Officiating Assistant: Stu Kirkpatrick

AMERICAN FOOTBALL CONFERENCE
President: Lamar Hunt, Kansas City Chiefs
Assistant to President: Al Ward
Director of Information: Fran Connors

NATIONAL FOOTBALL CONFERENCE
President: George Halas, Chicago Bears
Assistant to President: Joe Rhein
Director of Information: Dick Maxwell

CONTENTS

1981 PRESEASON STANDINGS

AMERICAN FOOTBALL CONFERENCE

EASTERN DIVISION

	W	L	T	Pct.	Pts.	OP
Miami	4	0	0	1.000	106	54
New England	4	0	0	1.000	93	68
N.Y. Jets	3	1	0	.750	104	55
Buffalo	2	2	0	.500	85	78
Baltimore	0	4	0	.000	64	88

CENTRAL DIVISION

	W	L	T	Pct.	Pts.	OP
Cincinnati	2	2	0	.500	95	85
Pittsburgh	2	2	0	.500	100	97
Cleveland*	2	3	0	.400	106	121
Houston	1	3	0	.250	57	92

WESTERN DIVISION

	W	L	T	Pct.	Pts.	OP
Denver	2	2	0	.500	62	84
Oakland	2	2	0	.500	73	80
San Diego	2	2	0	.500	98	99
Kansas City	1	3	0	.250	33	63
Seattle	1	3	0	.250	93	98

Includes Hall of Fame Game

NATIONAL FOOTBALL CONFERENCE

EASTERN DIVISION

	W	L	T	Pct.	Pts.	OP
St. Louis	3	1	0	.750	85	65
Washington	3	1	0	.750	66	49
Dallas	2	2	0	.500	90	88
N.Y. Giants	2	2	0	.500	73	92
Philadelphia	2	2	0	.500	85	54

CENTRAL DIVISION

	W	L	T	Pct.	Pts.	OP
Green Bay	3	1	0	.750	97	66
Chicago	2	2	0	.500	62	84
Detroit	1	3	0	.250	85	95
Minnesota	1	3	0	.250	70	100
Tampa Bay	1	3	0	.250	67	85

WESTERN DIVISION

	W	L	T	Pct.	Pts.	OP
New Orleans	3	1	0	.750	78	83
Los Angeles	2	2	0	.500	117	119
San Francisco	2	2	0	.500	86	93
Atlanta*	2	3	0	.400	93	88

AFC PRESEASON RECORDS —TEAM BY TEAM

EASTERN DIVISION

BALTIMORE (0-4)
23	New Orleans	24
17	N.Y. Giants	20
7	Washington	13
17	Seattle	31
64		88

BUFFALO (2-2)
14	Detroit	21
10	Cleveland	13
31	Cleveland	20
30	San Diego	24
85		78

MIAMI (4-0)
20	Minnesota	6
24	Denver	14
31	Detroit	27
31	Kansas City	7
106		54

NEW ENGLAND (4-0)
34	Los Angeles	21
17	Tampa Bay	16
23	Oakland	21
19	Washington	10
93		68

N.Y. JETS (3-1)
33	Denver	7
20	Atlanta	21
37	N.Y. Giants	24
14	Philadelphia	3
104		55

*Hall of Fame Game
(OT) Denotes Overtime*

CENTRAL DIVISION

CINCINNATI (2-2)
24	Tampa Bay*	17
30	Detroit	20
21	Chicago	24
20	Denver	24
95		85

CLEVELAND (2-3)
24	Atlanta*	10
31	Pittsburgh	35
13	Buffalo	10
20	Buffalo	31
18	Green Bay	35
106		121

HOUSTON (1-3)
13	Philadelphia	10
7	New Orleans	27
17	Tampa Bay	27
20	Dallas	28
57		92

PITTSBURGH (2-2)
35	Cleveland	31
20	Philadelphia	36
14	Dallas	24
31	N.Y. Giants	6
100		97

WESTERN DIVISION

DENVER (2-2)
7	N.Y. Jets	33
14	Miami	24
17	Green Bay	7
24	Cincinnati	20
62		84

KANSAS CITY (1-3)
10	Washington	16
13	Chicago	0
3	St. Louis	16
7	Miami	31
33		63

OAKLAND (2-2)
17	Atlanta	16
14	Green Bay	34
21	New England	23
21	San Francisco	7
73		80

SAN DIEGO (2-2)
10	St. Louis	12
31	San Francisco	28
33	Los Angeles	29
24	Buffalo	30
98		99

SEATTLE (1-3)
24	San Francisco (OT)	27
21	St. Louis	30
17	San Francisco	24
31	Baltimore	17
93		98

NFC PRESEASON RECORDS —TEAM BY TEAM

EASTERN DIVISION

DALLAS (2-2)
17	Green Bay	21
21	Los Angeles	33
24	Pittsburgh	14
28	Houston	20
90		88

N.Y. GIANTS (2-2)
23	Chicago	7
20	Baltimore	17
24	N.Y. Jets	37
6	Pittsburgh	31
73		92

PHILADELPHIA (2-2)
10	Houston	13
36	Pittsburgh	20
36	New Orleans	7
3	N.Y. Jets	14
85		54

ST. LOUIS (3-1)
12	San Diego	10
30	Seattle	21
16	Kansas City	3
27	Chicago	31
85		65

WASHINGTON (3-1)
16	Kansas City	10
27	Minnesota	13
13	Baltimore	7
10	New England	19
66		49

Hall of Fame Game
(OT) Denotes Overtime

CENTRAL DIVISION

CHICAGO (2-2)
7	N.Y. Giants	23
0	Kansas City	13
24	Cincinnati	21
31	St. Louis	27
62		84

DETROIT (1-3)
21	Buffalo	14
20	Cincinnati	30
27	Miami	31
17	New Orleans (OT)	20
85		95

GREEN BAY (3-1)
21	Dallas	17
34	Oakland	14
7	Denver	17
35	Cleveland	18
97		66

MINNESOTA (1-3)
6	Miami	20
13	Washington	27
20	Atlanta	19
31	Los Angeles	34
70		100

TAMPA BAY (1-3)
17	Cincinnati	24
16	New England	17
27	Houston	17
7	Atlanta	27
67		85

WESTERN DIVISION

ATLANTA (2-3)
10	Cleveland*	24
16	Oakland	17
21	N.Y. Jets	20
19	Minnesota	20
27	Tampa Bay	7
93		88

LOS ANGELES (2-2)
21	New England	34
33	Dallas	21
29	San Diego	33
34	Minnesota	31
117		119

NEW ORLEANS (3-1)
24	Baltimore	23
27	Houston	7
7	Philadelphia	36
20	Detroit (OT)	17
78		83

SAN FRANCISCO (2-2)
27	Seattle (OT)	24
28	San Diego	31
24	Seattle	17
7	Oakland	21
86		93

1981 NFL STANDINGS

AMERICAN FOOTBALL CONFERENCE

EASTERN DIVISION

	W	L	T	Pct.	Pts.	OP
Miami	11	4	1	.719	345	275
N.Y. Jets*	10	5	1	.656	355	287
Buffalo*	10	6	0	.625	311	276
Baltimore	2	14	0	.125	259	533
New England	2	14	0	.125	322	370

CENTRAL DIVISION

	W	L	T	Pct.	Pts.	OP
Cincinnati	12	4	0	.750	421	304
Pittsburgh	8	8	0	.500	356	297
Houston	7	9	0	.438	281	355
Cleveland	5	11	0	.313	276	375

WESTERN DIVISION

	W	L	T	Pct.	Pts.	OP
San Diego	10	6	0	.625	478	390
Denver	10	6	0	.625	321	289
Kansas City	9	7	0	.563	343	290
Oakland	7	9	0	.438	273	343
Seattle	6	10	0	.375	322	388

NATIONAL FOOTBALL CONFERENCE

EASTERN DIVISION

	W	L	T	Pct.	Pts.	OP
Dallas	12	4	0	.750	367	277
Philadelphia*	10	6	0	.625	368	221
N.Y. Giants*	9	7	0	.563	295	257
Washington	8	8	0	.500	347	349
St. Louis	7	9	0	.438	315	408

CENTRAL DIVISION

	W	L	T	Pct.	Pts.	OP
Tampa Bay	9	7	0	.563	315	268
Detroit	8	8	0	.500	397	322
Green Bay	8	8	0	.500	324	361
Minnesota	7	9	0	.438	325	369
Chicago	6	10	0	.375	253	324

WESTERN DIVISION

	W	L	T	Pct.	Pts.	OP
San Francisco	13	3	0	.813	357	250
Atlanta	7	9	0	.438	426	355
Los Angeles	6	10	0	.375	303	351
New Orleans	4	12	0	.250	207	378

*Wild Card qualifiers for playoffs.

San Diego won AFC Western title over Denver on the basis of a better division record (6-2 to 5-3). Buffalo won a Wild Card playoff berth over Denver as the result of a 9-7 victory in head-to-head competition.

FIRST ROUND PLAYOFFS
AFC . . . . Buffalo 31, New York Jets 27, December 27 at New York
NFC . . . . New York Giants 27, Philadelphia 21, December 27 at Philadelphia
DIVISIONAL PLAYOFFS
AFC . . . . San Diego 41, Miami 38 (OT, 13:52), January 2 at Miami
Cincinnati 28, Buffalo 21, January 3 at Cincinnati
NFC . . . . Dallas 38, Tampa Bay 0, January 2 at Dallas
San Francisco 38, New York Giants 24, January 3 at San Francisco
CHAMPIONSHIP GAMES
AFC . . . . Cincinnati 27, San Diego 7, January 10 at Cincinnati
NFC . . . . San Francisco 28, Dallas 27, January 10 at San Francisco
SUPER BOWL XVI . . . . San Francisco (NFC) 26, Cincinnati (AFC) 21, January 24 at
Pontiac Silverdome, Pontiac, Michigan
AFC-NFC PRO BOWL . . . . . AFC 16, NFC 13, January 31 at Aloha Stadium, Honolulu, Hawaii

AFC SEASON RECORDS—TEAM BY TEAM

BALTIMORE (2-14)

29	New England	28
3	*Buffalo	35
10	Denver	28
28	*Miami	31
17	Buffalo	23
19	*Cincinnati	41
14	*San Diego	43
28	Cleveland	42
10	Miami	27
14	*N.Y. Jets	41
13	Philadelphia	38
24	*St. Louis	35
0	N.Y. Jets	25
13	*Dallas	37
14	Washington	38
23	*New England	21
259		533

BUFFALO (10-6)

31	*N.Y. Jets	0
35	Baltimore	3
14	*Philadelphia	20
24	Cincinnati (OT)	27
23	*Baltimore	17
31	*Miami	21
14	N.Y. Jets	33
9	*Denver	7
22	*Cleveland	13
14	Dallas	27
0	St. Louis	24
20	*New England	17
21	*Washington	14
28	San Diego	27
19	New England	10
6	Miami	16
311		276

CINCINNATI (12-4)

27	*Seattle	21
31	N.Y. Jets	30
17	*Cleveland	20
27	*Buffalo (OT)	24
10	Houston	17
41	Baltimore	19
34	*Pittsburgh	7
7	New Orleans	17
34	*Houston	21
40	San Diego	17
24	*Los Angeles	10
38	*Denver	21
41	Cleveland	21
3	*San Francisco	21
17	Pittsburgh	10
30	Atlanta	28
421		304

CLEVELAND (5-11)

14	*San Diego	44
3	*Houston	9
20	Cincinnati	17
28	*Atlanta	17
16	Los Angeles	27
7	Pittsburgh	13
20	*New Orleans	17
42	*Baltimore	28
13	Buffalo	22
20	Denver (OT)	23
15	San Francisco	12
10	*Pittsburgh	32
21	*Cincinnati	41
13	Houston	17
13	*N.Y. Jets	14
21	Seattle	42
276		375

DENVER (10-6)

9	*Oakland	7
10	Seattle	13
28	*Baltimore	10
42	*San Diego	24
17	Oakland	0
27	*Detroit	21
14	Kansas City	28
7	Buffalo	9
19	*Minnesota	17
23	*Cleveland (OT)	20
24	Tampa Bay	7
21	Cincinnati	38
17	San Diego	34
16	*Kansas City	13
23	*Seattle	13
24	Chicago	35
321		289

HOUSTON (7-9)

27	Los Angeles	20
9	Cleveland	3
10	*Miami	16
17	N.Y. Jets	33
17	*Cincinnati	10
35	*Seattle	17
10	New England	38
13	Pittsburgh	26
21	Cincinnati	34
17	*Oakland	16
10	Kansas City	23
24	*New Orleans	27
27	*Atlanta	31
17	*Cleveland	13
6	San Francisco	28
21	*Pittsburgh	20
281		355

KANSAS CITY (9-7)

37	Pittsburgh	33
19	*Tampa Bay	10
31	*San Diego	42
20	Seattle	14
17	New England	33
27	*Oakland	0
28	*Denver	14
28	Oakland	17
20	San Diego	22
13	*Chicago (OT)	16
23	*Houston	10
40	*Seattle	13
10	Detroit	27
13	Denver	16
7	*Miami	17
10	Minnesota	6
343		290

MIAMI (11-4-1)

20	St. Louis	7
30	*Pittsburgh	10
16	Houston	10
31	Baltimore	28
28	*N.Y. Jets (OT)	28
21	Buffalo	31
13	*Washington	10
27	Dallas	28
27	*Baltimore	10
30	New England (OT)	27
17	*Oakland	33
15	N.Y. Jets	16
13	*Philadelphia	10
24	*New England	14
17	Kansas City	7
16	*Buffalo	6
345		275

NEW ENGLAND (2-14)

28	*Baltimore	29
3	Philadelphia	13
21	*Dallas	35
21	Pittsburgh (OT)	27
33	*Kansas City	17
24	N.Y. Jets	28
38	*Houston	10
22	Washington	24
17	Oakland	27
27	*Miami (OT)	30
6	*N.Y. Jets	17
17	Buffalo	20
20	*St. Louis	27
14	Miami	24
10	*Buffalo	19
21	Baltimore	23
322		370

N. Y. JETS (10-5-1)

0	Buffalo	31
30	*Cincinnati	31
10	Pittsburgh	38
33	*Houston	17
28	Miami (OT)	28
28	*New England	24
33	*Buffalo	14
3	*Seattle	19
26	N. Y. Giants	7
41	Baltimore	14
17	New England	6
16	*Miami	15
25	*Baltimore	0
23	Seattle	27
14	Cleveland	13
28	*Green Bay	3
355		287

OAKLAND (7-9)

7	Denver	9
36	Minnesota	10
20	*Seattle	10
0	Detroit	16
0	*Denver	17
0	Kansas City	27
18	*Tampa Bay	16
17	*Kansas City	28
27	*New England	17
16	Houston	17
33	Miami	17
21	*San Diego	55
32	Seattle	31
30	*Pittsburgh	27
6	*Chicago	23
10	San Diego	23
273		343

PITTSBURGH (8-8)

33	*Kansas City	37
10	*Miami	30
38	*N. Y. Jets	10
27	*New England (OT)	21
20	New Orleans	6
13	*Cleveland	7
7	Cincinnati	34
26	*Houston	13
14	*San Francisco	17
21	Seattle	24
34	Atlanta	20
32	Cleveland	10
24	*Los Angeles	0
27	Oakland	30
10	*Cincinnati	17
20	Houston	21
356		297

SAN DIEGO (10-6)

44	Cleveland	14
28	*Detroit	23
42	Kansas City	31
24	*Seattle	10
31	*Minnesota	33
43	Baltimore	14
17	Chicago (OT)	20
22	*Kansas City	20
17	*Cincinnati	40
23	Seattle	44
55	Oakland	21
34	*Denver	17
27	*Buffalo	28
24	Tampa Bay	23
23	*Oakland	10
478		390

SEATTLE (6-10)

21	Cincinnati	27
13	*Denver	10
10	Oakland	20
14	*Kansas City	20
10	San Diego	24
17	Houston	35
0	*N. Y. Giants	32
19	N. Y. Jets	3
24	Green Bay	34
24	*Pittsburgh	21
44	*San Diego	23
13	Kansas City	40
31	*Oakland	32
27	*N. Y. Jets	23
13	Denver	23
42	*Cleveland	21
322		388

*Denotes Home Game
(OT) Denotes Overtime

NFC SEASON RECORDS—TEAM BY TEAM

ATLANTA (7-9)

27	*New Orleans	0
31	Green Bay	17
34	*San Francisco	17
17	Cleveland	28
13	Philadelphia	16
35	*Los Angeles	37
41	*St. Louis	20
24	*N.Y. Giants (OT)	27
41	New Orleans	10
14	San Francisco	17
20	*Pittsburgh	34
31	*Minnesota	30
31	Houston	27
23	Tampa Bay	24
16	Los Angeles	21
28	*Cincinnati	30
426		355

CHICAGO (6-10)

9	*Green Bay	16
17	San Francisco	28
28	*Tampa Bay	17
7	*Los Angeles	24
21	Minnesota	24
7	*Washington	24
10	Detroit	48
20	*San Diego (OT)	17
10	Tampa Bay	20
16	Kansas City (OT)	13
17	Green Bay	21
7	*Detroit	23
9	Dallas	10
10	*Minnesota	9
23	Oakland	6
35	*Denver	24
253		324

DALLAS (12-4)

26	Washington	10
30	*St. Louis	17
35	New England	21
18	*N.Y. Giants	10
17	St. Louis	20
14	San Francisco	45
29	*Los Angeles	17
28	*Miami	27
17	Philadelphia	14
27	*Buffalo	14
24	Detroit	27
24	*Washington	10
10	*Chicago	9
37	Baltimore	13
21	*Philadelphia	10
10	N.Y. Giants (OT)	13
367		277

DETROIT (8-8)

24	*San Francisco	17
23	San Diego	28
24	Minnesota	26
16	*Oakland	0
10	Tampa Bay	28
21	Denver	27
48	*Chicago	17
31	*Green Bay	27
13	Los Angeles	20
31	Washington	33
27	*Dallas	24
23	Chicago	7
27	*Kansas City	10
17	Green Bay	31
45	*Minnesota	7
17	*Tampa Bay	20
397		322

GREEN BAY (8-8)

16	Chicago	9
17	*Atlanta	31
23	Los Angeles	35
13	*Minnesota	30
27	N.Y. Giants	14
10	*Tampa Bay	21
3	*San Francisco	13
27	Detroit	31
34	*Seattle	24
26	*N.Y. Giants	24
21	*Chicago	17
3	Tampa Bay	37
35	Minnesota	23
31	*Detroit	17
35	New Orleans	7
3	N.Y. Jets	28
324		361

LOS ANGELES (6-10)

20	*Houston	27
17	New Orleans	23
35	*Green Bay	23
24	Chicago	7
27	*Cleveland	16
37	Atlanta	35
17	Dallas	29
17	San Francisco	20
20	*Detroit	13
13	*New Orleans	21
10	Cincinnati	24
31	*San Francisco	33
0	Pittsburgh	24
7	N.Y. Giants	10
21	*Atlanta	16
7	*Washington	30
303		351

MINNESOTA (7-9)

13	Tampa Bay	21
10	*Oakland	36
26	*Detroit	24
30	Green Bay	13
24	*Chicago	21
33	San Diego	31
35	*Philadelphia	23
17	St. Louis	30
17	Denver	19
25	*Tampa Bay	10
20	*New Orleans	10
30	Atlanta	31
23	*Green Bay	35
9	Chicago	10
7	Detroit	45
6	*Kansas City	10
325		369

NEW ORLEANS (4-12)

0	Atlanta	27
23	*Los Angeles	17
7	N.Y. Giants	20
14	San Francisco	21
6	*Pittsburgh	20
14	*Philadelphia	31
17	Cleveland	20
17	*Cincinnati	7
10	*Atlanta	41
21	Los Angeles	13
10	Minnesota	20
27	Houston	24
14	*Tampa Bay	31
3	St. Louis	30
7	*Green Bay	35
17	*San Francisco	21
207		378

N.Y. GIANTS (9-7)

10	*Philadelphia	24
17	Washington	7
20	*New Orleans	7
10	Dallas	18
14	*Green Bay	27
34	*St. Louis	14
32	Seattle	0
27	Atlanta (OT)	24
7	*N.Y. Jets	26
24	Green Bay	26
27	*Washington (OT)	30
20	Philadelphia	10
10	San Francisco	17
10	*Los Angeles	7
20	St. Louis	10
13	*Dallas (OT)	10
295		257

PHILADELPHIA (10-6)

24	N. Y. Giants	10
13	*New England	3
20	Buffalo	14
36	*Washington	13
16	*Atlanta	13
31	New Orleans	14
23	Minnesota	35
20	*Tampa Bay	10
14	*Dallas	17
52	St. Louis	10
38	*Baltimore	13
10	*N.Y. Giants	20
10	Miami	13
13	Washington	15
10	Dallas	21
38	*St. Louis	0
368		**221**

ST. LOUIS (7-9)

7	*Miami	20
17	Dallas	30
40	*Washington	30
10	Tampa Bay	20
20	*Dallas	17
14	N.Y. Giants	34
20	Atlanta	41
30	*Minnesota	17
21	Washington	42
10	*Philadelphia	52
24	*Buffalo	0
35	Baltimore	24
27	New England	20
30	*New Orleans	3
10	*N.Y. Giants	20
0	Philadelphia	38
315		**408**

SAN FRANCISCO (13-3)

17	Detroit	24
28	*Chicago	17
17	Atlanta	34
21	*New Orleans	14
30	Washington	17
45	*Dallas	14
13	Green Bay	3
20	*Los Angeles	17
17	Pittsburgh	14
17	*Atlanta	14
12	*Cleveland	15
33	Los Angeles	31
17	*N.Y. Giants	10
21	Cincinnati	3
28	*Houston	6
21	New Orleans	17
357		**250**

TAMPA BAY (9-7)

21	*Minnesota	13
10	Kansas City	19
17	Chicago	28
20	*St. Louis	10
28	*Detroit	10
21	Green Bay	10
16	Oakland	18
10	Philadelphia	20
20	*Chicago	10
10	Minnesota	25
7	*Denver	24
37	*Green Bay	3
31	New Orleans	14
24	*Atlanta	23
23	*San Diego	24
20	Detroit	17
315		**268**

WASHINGTON (8-8)

10	*Dallas	26
7	*N.Y. Giants	17
30	St. Louis	40
13	Philadelphia	36
17	*San Francisco	30
24	Chicago	7
10	Miami	13
24	*New England	22
42	*St. Louis	21
33	*Detroit	31
30	N. Y. Giants (OT)	27
10	Dallas	24
14	Buffalo	21
15	*Philadelphia	13
38	*Baltimore	14
30	Los Angeles	7
347		**349**

*Denotes Home Game
(OT) Denotes Overtime

1981 ATTENDANCE BREAKDOWN

	Games	Attendance	Average
AFC Preseason	10˙	478,920	47,892
NFC Preseason	10	529,701	52,970
AFC-NFC Preseason, Interconference	37	1,969,838	53,239
NFL Preseason Total	57	2,978,459	52,254
AFC Regular Season	86	5,127,069	59,617
NFC Regular Season	86	5,333,046	62,012
AFC-NFC Regular Season, Interconference	52	3.146.875	60,517
NFL Regular Season Total	224	13,606,990	60,745
AFC First Round Playoff	1		
(Buffalo-New York Jets)		59,067	
AFC Divisional Playoffs	2		
(San Diego-Miami)		74,233	
(Buffalo-Cincinnati)		59,032	
AFC Championship	1		
(San Diego-Cincinnati)		59,579	
NFC First Round Playoff	1		
(New York Giants-Philadelphia)		70,952	
NFC Divisional Playoffs	2		
(Tampa Bay-Dallas)		63,510	
(New York Giants-San Francisco)		58,657	
NFC Championship	1		
(Dallas-San Francisco)		61,061	
Super Bowl XVI at Pontiac, Michigan	1		
(San Francisco-Cincinnati)		81,270	
AFC-NFC Pro Bowl at Honolulu, Hawaii	1	50,402	
Postseason Total	10	637,763	63,776
NFL All Games 1981	291	17,223,212	59,186

PAID ATTENDANCE

Year	League	Reg. Season Games	Reg. Season Attendance	Average	Post-season Games	Post-season Attendance	Super Bowl	
1981	NFL	224	13,606,990	60,745	10	637,763	XVI	81,270
1980	NFL	224	13,392,230	59,787	10	624,430	XV	75,500
1979	NFL	224	13,182,039	58,848	10	630,326	XIV	103,985
1978	NFL	224	12,771,800	57,017	10	624,388	XIII	79,641
1977	NFL	196	11,018,632	56,218	8	534,925	XII	75,804
1976	NFL	196	11,070,543	56,482	8	492,884	XI	103,438
1975	NFL	182	10,213,193	56,116	8	475,919	X	80,187
1974	NFL	182	10,236,322	56,244	8	438,664	IX	80,997
1973	NFL	182	10,730,933	58,961	8	525,433	VIII	71,882
1972	NFL	182	10,445,827	57,395	8	483,345	VII	90,182
1971	NFL	182	10,076,035	55,363	8	483,891	VI	81,023
1970	NFL	182	9,533,333	52,381	8	458,593	V	79,204
1969	AFL	70	2,843,373	40,620	3	167,088		
	NFL	112	6,096,127	54,430	3	162,279	IV	80,562
1968	AFL	70	2,635,004	37,634	2	114,438		
	NFL	112	5,882,313	52,521	3	215,902	III	75,377
1967	AFL	63	2,295,697	36,439	1	53,330		
	NFL	112	5,938,924	53,026	3	166,208	II	75,546
1966	AFL	63	2,160,369	34,291	1	42,080		
	NFL	105	5,337,004	50,829	1	74,152	I	61,946*
1965	AFL	56	1,782,384	31,828	1	30,361		
	NFL	98	4,634,021	47,286	2	100,304		
1964	AFL	56	1,447,875	25,855	1	40,242		
	NFL	98	4,563,049	46,562	1	79,544		
1963	AFL	56	1,208,697	21,584	2	63,171		
	NFL	98	4,163,643	42,486	1	45,801		
1962	AFL	56	1,147,302	20,487	1	37,981		
	NFL	98	4,003,421	40,851	1	64,892		
1961	AFL	56	1,002,657	17,904	1	29,556		
	NFL	98	3,986,159	40,675	1	39,029		
1960	AFL	56	926,156	16,538	1	32,183		
	NFL	78	3,128,296	40,106	1	67,325		
1959	NFL	72	3,140,409	43,167	1	57,545		
1958	NFL	72	3,006,124	41,752	2	123,659		
1957	NFL	72	2,836,318	39,393	2	119,579		
1956	NFL	72	2,551,263	35,434	1	56,836		
1955	NFL	72	2,521,836	35,026	1	85,693		
1954	NFL	72	2,190,571	30,425	1	43,827		
1953	NFL	72	2,164,545	30,064	1	54,577		
1952	NFL	72	2,052,126	28,502	2	97,507		
1951	NFL	72	1,913,019	26,570	1	57,522		
1950	NFL	78	1,977,753	25,356	3	136,647		
1949	NFL	60	1,391,735	23,196	1	27,980		
1948	NFL	60	1,525,243	25,421	1	36,309		
1947	NFL	60	1,837,437	30,624	2	66,268		
1946	NFL	55	1,732,135	31,493	1	58,346		
1945	NFL	50	1,270,401	25,408	1	32,178		
1944	NFL	50	1,019,649	20,393	1	46,016		
1943	NFL	50	969,128	19,383	2	71,315		
1942	NFL	55	887,920	16,144	1	36,006		
1941	NFL	55	1,108,615	20,157	2	55,870		
1940	NFL	55	1,063,025	19,328	1	36,034		
1939	NFL	55	1,071,200	19,476	1	32,279		
1938	NFL	55	937,197	17,040	1	48,120		
1937	NFL	55	963,039	17,510	1	15,878		
1936	NFL	54	816,007	15,111	1	29,545		
1935	NFL	53	638,178	12,041	1	15,000		
1934	NFL	60	492,684	8,211	1	35,059		

*Only Super Bowl which did not sell out.

AMERICAN FOOTBALL CONFERENCE OFFENSE

	Balt.	Buff.	Cin.	Clev.	Den.	Hou.	K.C.	Mia.	N.E.	N.Y.J.	Oak.	Pitt.	S.D.	Sea.
First Downs														
Rushing	274	315	361	364	306	241	315	306	306	318	296	318	379	295
Passing	95	127	124	131	91	103	160	123	124	122	108	137	127	103
Penalty	158	163	210	196	181	124	132	157	166	170	166	156	224	166
	21	25	27	37	34	14	23	26	16	26	22	25	28	26
Rushes	441	524	493	474	515	466	610	535	499	571	493	554	481	440
Net Yds. Gained	1850	2125	1973	1929	1895	1734	2633	2173	2040	2341	2058	2372	2005	1594
Avg. Gain	4.2	4.1	4.0	4.1	3.7	3.7	4.3	4.1	4.1	4.1	4.2	4.3	4.2	3.6
Avg. Yds. per Game	115.6	132.8	123.3	120.6	118.4	108.4	164.6	135.8	127.5	146.3	128.6	148.3	125.3	99.6
Passes Attempted	479	503	550	624	485	441	410	498	482	507	545	461	629	524
Completed	265	253	332	348	289	258	224	271	254	283	267	247	368	307
% Completed	55.3	50.3	60.4	55.8	59.6	58.5	54.6	54.4	52.7	55.8	49.0	53.6	58.5	58.6
Total Yds. Gained	3379	3661	4200	4339	3992	3119	2917	3385	3904	3279	3356	3457	4873	3727
Passer Tackled	37	16	35	61	61	40	37	30	45	30	53	27	19	37
Yds. Lost	321	146	205	353	461	342	277	236	321	224	437	231	134	300
Net Yds. Gained	3058	3515	3995	3986	3531	2777	2640	3149	3583	3055	2919	3226	4739	3427
Avg. Yds. per Game	191.1	219.7	249.7	249.1	220.7	173.6	165.0	196.8	223.9	190.9	182.4	201.6	296.2	214.2
Net Yds. per Pass Play	5.93	6.77	6.83	6.00	6.47	5.77	5.91	5.96	6.80	5.69	4.88	6.61	7.31	6.11
Yds. Gained per Comp.	12.75	14.47	12.65	12.47	13.81	12.09	13.02	12.49	15.37	11.59	12.57	14.00	13.24	12.14
Combined Net Yds. Gained	4908	5640	5968	5915	5426	4511	5273	5322	5623	5396	4977	5598	6744	5021
% Total Yds., Rushing	37.69	37.68	33.06	32.61	34.92	38.44	49.93	40.83	36.28	43.38	41.35	42.37	29.73	31.75
% Total Yds., Passing	62.31	62.32	66.94	67.39	65.08	61.56	50.07	59.17	63.72	56.62	58.65	57.63	70.27	68.25
Avg. Yds. per Game	306.8	352.5	373.0	369.7	339.1	281.9	329.6	332.6	351.4	337.3	311.1	349.9	421.5	313.8
Ball Control Plays	957	1043	1078	1138	1061	947	1057	1063	1026	1108	1091	1042	1129	1001
Avg. Yds. per Play	5.1	5.4	5.2	5.2	5.1	4.8	5.0	5.0	5.5	4.9	5.4	5.4	6.0	5.0
Avg. Time of Poss.	26:28	30:24	30:52	30:59	32:27	27:56	31:01	30:14	27:51	31:21	28:20	30:17	29:17	26:59
Third Down Efficiency	33.3	43.3	45.2	40.9	37.0	32.5	40.5	38.2	37.0	41.4	37.9	41.1	48.9	37.3
Had Intercepted	23	20	12	27	21	23	22	21	34	14	28	19	18	15
Yds. Opp. Returned	281	333	143	347	405	289	247	288	570	212	339	226	377	257

16

Ret. by Opp. for TD	1	0	1	1	4	0	1	0	1	0	0	0	1	1
Punts	78	80	73	70	86	79	70	83	75	81	98	84	63	68
Yds. Punted	3071	3175	3272	2884	3478	3137	2697	3386	2951	3290	4238	3641	2540	2652
Avg. Yds. per Punt	39.4	39.7	44.8	41.2	40.4	39.7	38.5	40.8	39.3	40.6	43.2	43.3	40.3	39.0
Punt Returns	12	35	29	50	51	41	50	45	50	50	52	53	31	32
Yds. Returned	56	292	205	369	441	325	528	458	199	337	380	412	378	293
Avg. Yds. per Return	4.7	8.3	7.1	7.4	8.6	7.9	10.6	10.2	6.4	6.7	7.3	8.2	12.2	9.2
Returned for TD	0	0	0	0	0	0	0	1	0	0	1	0	0	0
Kickoff Returns	84	57	49	72	47	72	52	54	65	58	71	53	70	69
Yds. Returned	1651	1085	1056	1537	801	1722	1043	1228	1190	1151	1411	1096	1422	1278
Avg. Yds. per Return	19.7	19.0	21.6	21.3	17.0	23.9	20.1	22.7	18.3	19.8	19.9	20.7	20.3	18.5
Returned for TD	0	0	0	0	0	2	0	1	0	0	0	0	0	0
Penalties	106	114	109	109	99	93	97	71	89	112	101	97	128	106
Yds. Penalized	913	1001	896	971	833	825	924	541	742	936	867	840	947	823
Fumbles	27	33	25	38	26	33	36	26	32	38	42	39	39	41
Lost	14	18	12	26	18	21	24	10	16	17	20	22	22	23
Out of Bounds	2	2	3	1	2	2	2	3	2	2	2	3	4	4
Own Rec. for TD	1	0	0	0	0	0	0	0	0	1	0	0	0	0
Opp. Rec. by	14	17	18	20	23	13	21	15	17	15	19	16	18	27
Opp. Rec. for TD	0	0	1	0	0	0	3	1	0	0	2	0	0	2
Total Points Scored	259	311	421	276	321	281	343	345	322	355	273	356	478	322
Total TDs	33	38	51	32	39	34	38	39	40	40	33	47	61	40
TDs Rushing	11	13	19	11	12	11	22	18	23	11	11	21	26	14
TDs Passing	21	25	30	21	27	21	12	18	17	26	18	25	34	21
TDs on Ret. and Rec.	1	0	2	0	0	2	4	3	0	3	4	1	1	5
Extra Points	29	37	49	31	36	32	37	37	37	38	27	38	55	37
Safeties	1	1	0	1	0	0	0	1	0	1	3	0	0	0
Field Goals Made	10	14	22	17	17	15	26	24	15	25	14	12	19	15
Field Goals Attempted	18	24	32	33	30	22	36	31	24	36	24	17	26	24
% Successful	55.6	58.3	68.8	51.5	56.7	68.2	72.2	77.4	62.5	69.4	58.3	70.6	73.1	62.5

AMERICAN FOOTBALL CONFERENCE DEFENSE

	Balt.	Buff.	Cin.	Clev.	Den.	Hou.	K.C.	Mia.	N.E.	N.Y.J.	Oak.	Pitt.	S.D.	Sea.
First Downs	406	298	324	299	268	325	316	296	328	291	316	323	365	371
Rushing	162	113	126	119	103	138	112	124	160	112	104	114	114	175
Passing	214	154	167	157	142	162	177	160	148	155	178	181	216	173
Penalty	30	31	31	23	23	25	27	12	20	24	34	28	35	23
Rushes	607	516	465	516	467	549	507	492	644	465	524	500	491	588
Net Yds. Gained	2665	2075	1881	2078	2005	2411	1747	2032	2950	1867	1832	1869	1825	2806
Avg. Gain	4.4	4.0	4.0	4.0	4.3	4.4	3.4	4.1	4.6	4.0	3.5	3.7	3.7	4.8
Avg. Yds. per Game	166.6	129.7	117.6	129.9	125.3	150.7	109.2	127.0	184.4	116.7	114.5	116.8	114.1	175.4
Passes Attempted	491	474	548	469	497	502	567	509	439	505	537	544	571	502
Completed	301	267	316	275	267	295	291	297	243	275	289	302	313	294
% Completed	61.3	56.3	57.7	58.6	53.7	58.8	51.3	58.3	55.4	54.5	53.8	55.5	54.8	58.6
Total Yds. Gained	4228	3243	3757	3512	3168	3554	3821	3645	3052	3522	4011	4108	4695	3394
Passer Tackled	13	47	42	29	36	33	27	38	20	66	52	40	47	36
Yds. Lost	100	373	349	223	295	239	195	314	175	518	370	325	384	260
Net Yds. Gained	4128	2870	3408	3289	2873	3315	3626	3331	2877	3004	3641	3783	4311	3134
Avg. Yds. per Game	258.0	179.4	213.0	205.6	179.6	207.2	226.6	208.2	179.8	187.8	227.6	236.4	269.4	195.9
Net Yds. per Pass Play	8.19	5.51	5.78	6.60	5.39	6.20	6.10	6.09	6.27	5.26	6.18	6.48	6.98	5.83
Yds. Gained per Comp.	14.05	12.15	11.89	12.77	11.87	12.05	13.13	12.27	12.56	12.81	13.88	13.60	15.00	11.54
Combined Net Yds. Gained	6793	4945	5289	5367	4878	5726	5373	5363	5827	4871	5473	5652	6136	5940
% Total Yds. Rushing	39.23	41.96	35.56	38.72	41.10	42.11	32.51	37.89	50.63	38.33	33.47	33.07	29.74	47.24
% Total Yds. Passing	60.77	58.04	64.44	61.28	58.90	57.89	67.49	62.11	49.37	61.67	66.53	66.93	70.26	52.76
Avg. Yds. per Game	424.6	309.1	330.6	335.4	304.9	357.9	335.8	335.2	364.2	304.4	342.1	353.3	383.5	371.3
Ball Control Plays	1111	1037	1055	1014	1000	1084	1101	1039	1103	1036	1113	1084	1109	1126
Avg. Yds. per Play	6.1	4.8	5.0	5.3	4.9	5.3	4.9	5.2	5.3	4.7	4.9	5.2	5.5	5.3
Third Down Efficiency	51.4	33.0	42.5	36.8	33.8	43.4	36.5	37.9	43.5	34.7	36.4	39.1	42.3	48.6
Intercepted by	16	19	19	15	23	18	26	18	16	21	13	30	23	21
Yds. Returned by	210	352	318	165	342	330	406	254	195	432	97	376	224	397
Returned for TD	0	0	1	0	0	0	1	0	0	2	1	1	1	3

Punts	55	72	78	101	94	74	87	80	70	88	78	81	77	48
Yds. Punted	2337	2900	3286	3928	3802	2872	3565	3109	2935	3789	3173	3266	3237	1817
Avg. Yds. per Punt	42.5	40.3	42.1	38.9	40.4	38.8	41.0	38.9	41.9	43.1	40.7	40.3	42.0	37.9
Punt Returns	33	31	34	45	31	35	45	46	47	46	30	42	34	44
Yds. Returned	153	168	358	514	149	305	286	293	360	388	253	416	220	402
Avg. Yds. per Return	4.6	5.4	10.5	11.4	4.8	8.7	6.4	6.4	7.7	8.4	8.4	9.9	6.5	9.1
Returned for TD		0	2	0	0	1	0	0	1	0	0	0	0	0
Kickoff Returns	67	88	52	49	63	68	60	68	59	47	45	80	61	43
Yds. Returned	1177	1528	1253	1068	1415	1326	1218	1296	1201	1007	1156	1612	1268	864
Avg. Yds. per Return	17.6	17.4	24.1	21.8	22.5	19.5	20.3	19.1	20.4	21.4	25.7	20.2	20.8	20.1
Returned for TD	0	0	0	1	0	0	0	0	0	0	0	1	1	0
Penalties	104	108	112	102	106	83	104	89	102	104	100	104	93	101
Yds. Penalized	944	877	960	826	935	763	886	740	838	949	870	787	690	776
Fumbles	43	38	31	28	35	34	30	42	20	36	31	32	38	28
Lost	27	18	16	19	15	17	15	21	13	23	20	18	17	14
Out of Bounds	3	3	2			1	1	4	1	2	1	2	6	2
Own Rec. for TD									1		1		1	
Opp. Rec.	23	22	22	20	17	16	10	24	21	18	26	12	18	14
Opp. Rec. for TD	0	0	1	2	2	2	0	0	0	1	1	0	0	0
Total Points Scored	388	390	297	343	287	370	275	290	355	289	375	304	276	533
Total TDs	46	48	35	42	36	42	33	34	39	35	45	38	30	68
TDs Rushing	20	25	10	15	19	20	10	17	16	17	14	12	7	30
TDs Passing	25	22	22	24	15	18	23	16	22	13	28	24	21	37
TDs on Ret. and Rec.	1	1	3	3	2	4		1	1	5	3	2	2	1
Extra Points	41	45	33	38	33	39	33	29	38	34	40	38	30	65
Safeties					1	2					1			
Field Goals Made	23	19	18	17	12	25	14	19	27	15	21	12	22	20
Field Goals Attempted	29	26	33	30	20	39	21	27	42	27	34	21	26	31
% Successful	79.3	73.1	54.5	56.7	60.0	64.1	66.7	70.4	64.3	55.6	61.8	57.1	84.6	64.5

NATIONAL FOOTBALL CONFERENCE OFFENSE

	Atl.	Chi.	Dall.	Det.	G.B.	L.A.	Minn.	N.O.	N.Y.G.	Phil.	St.L.	S.F.	T.B.	Wash.
First Downs	318	278	321	340	308	305	343	280	253	332	300	317	269	334
Rushing	116	126	137	167	104	142	91	126	92	157	135	110	95	136
Passing	176	126	158	150	174	134	217	124	140	150	141	183	159	173
Penalty	26	26	26	23	30	29	35	30	21	25	24	24	15	25
Rushes	495	608	630	596	478	559	391	546	481	559	519	560	458	532
Net Yds. Gained	1965	2171	2711	2795	1670	2236	1512	2286	1685	2509	2213	1941	1731	2157
Avg. Gain	4.0	3.6	4.3	4.7	3.5	4.0	3.9	4.2	3.5	4.5	4.3	3.5	3.8	4.1
Avg. Yds. per Game	122.8	135.7	169.4	174.7	104.4	139.8	94.5	142.9	105.3	156.8	138.3	121.3	108.2	134.8
Passes Attempted	563	489	439	436	514	477	709	441	506	476	477	517	473	525
Completed	311	222	241	228	286	235	382	238	251	258	253	328	239	307
% Completed	55.2	45.4	54.9	52.3	55.6	49.3	53.9	54.0	49.6	54.2	53.0	63.4	50.5	58.5
Total Yds. Gained	3986	2728	3414	3475	3576	3008	4567	2778	3009	3249	3269	3766	3565	3743
Passer Tackled	37	35	31	52	52	50	29	41	47	22	48	29	19	30
Yds. Lost	287	266	245	337	387	451	234	359	368	205	405	223	136	277
Net Yds. Gained	3699	2462	3169	3138	3189	2557	4333	2419	2641	3044	2864	3543	3429	3466
Avg. Yds. per Game	231.2	153.9	198.1	196.1	199.3	159.8	270.8	151.2	165.1	190.3	179.0	221.4	214.3	216.6
Net Yds. per Pass Play	6.17	4.70	6.74	6.54	5.63	4.85	5.87	5.02	4.78	6.11	5.46	6.49	6.97	6.25
Yds. Gained per Comp.	12.82	12.29	14.17	15.24	12.50	12.80	11.96	11.67	11.99	12.59	12.92	11.48	14.92	12.19
Combined Net Yds. Gained	5664	4633	5880	5933	4859	4793	5845	4705	4326	5553	5077	5484	5160	5623
% Total Yds., Rushing	34.69	46.86	46.11	47.11	34.37	46.65	25.87	48.59	38.95	45.18	43.55	35.39	33.55	38.36
% Total Yds., Passing	65.31	53.14	53.89	52.89	65.63	53.35	74.13	51.41	61.05	54.82	56.41	64.61	66.45	61.64
Avg. Yds. per Game	354.0	289.6	367.5	370.8	303.7	299.6	365.3	294.1	270.4	347.1	317.3	342.8	322.5	351.4
Ball Control Plays	1095	1132	1100	1076	1044	1086	1129	1028	1034	1057	1044	1106	950	1087
Avg. Yds. per Play	5.2	4.1	5.3	5.5	4.7	4.4	5.2	4.6	4.2	5.3	4.9	5.0	5.4	5.2
Avg. Time of Poss.	29:34	31:55	32:08	31:35	29:23	29:26	28:54	31:19	28:09	31:42	30:39	31:38	27:33	31:23
Third Down Efficiency	41.0	35.5	40.6	39.3	34.3	34.5	36.7	40.4	34.3	44.4	38.5	44.0	32.3	43.3
Had Intercepted	24	23	15	23	24	32	29	27	20	22	24	13	14	22
Yds. Opp. Returned	301	385	124	274	475	361	384	479	252	357	312	297	179	391

	1	2	3	4	5	6	7	8	9	10	11	12	13	14
Ret. by Opp. for TD	0	2	0	1	2	2	1	3	1	3	1	2	0	1
Punts	88	114	81	64	84	89	88	66	97	64	69	93	82	73
Yds. Punted	3543	4531	3284	2784	3330	3735	3646	2672	4198	2580	2883	3858	3375	2923
Avg. Yds. per Punt	40.3	39.7	40.5	43.5	39.6	42.0	41.4	40.5	43.3	40.3	41.8	41.5	41.2	40.0
Punt Returns	50	45	45	52	40	49	39	41	64	58	43	48	38	49
Yds. Returned	383	518	235	450	306	676	303	426	502	422	453	344	244	507
Avg. Yds. per Return	7.7	11.5	5.2	8.7	7.7	13.3	7.8	10.4	7.8	7.3	10.5	7.2	6.4	10.3
Returned for TD	0	1	0	1	0	3	0	2	0	0	1	0	0	2
Kickoff Returns	62	64	53	61	58	68	67	70	57	43	75	45	46	67
Yds. Returned	1419	1214	981	1164	1066	1244	1328	1523	1120	832	1625	909	912	1673
Avg. Yds. per Return	22.9	19.0	18.5	19.1	18.4	18.3	19.8	21.8	19.6	19.3	21.7	20.2	19.8	25.0
Returned for TD	0	1	1	0	1	1	1	0	0	0	0	1	0	0
Penalties	90	121	103	111	84	117	109	109	108	113	106	92	89	98
Yds. Penalized	940	996	839	990	687	916	865	899	897	855	877	752	779	940
Fumbles	31	37	45	41	31	34	39	40	38	33	33	26	27	32
Lost	17	17	20	20	17	15	21	20	16	17	20	12	14	19
Out of Bounds	1			0	0	1	0	2	1	2	3	1	1	2
Own Rec. for TD		1	0	2	0	0	3	0	0	0	0	0	3	0
Opp. Rec. by	21	22	16	15	24	16	19	17	17	21	17	21	14	15
Opp. Rec. for TD	3	0	1	0	0	1	1	0	3	2	0	1	1	0
Total Points Scored	426	253	367	397	324	303	325	207	295	368	315	357	315	347
Total TDs	52	31	40	46	37	36	37	24	32	44	37	43	38	42
TDs Rushing	15	13	15	26	11	17	8	16	11	17	20	17	13	19
TDs Passing	30	14	24	18	24	15	27	8	16	25	15	20	20	19
TDs on Ret. and Rec.	7	4	1	2	2	4	2	0	5	2	2	6	5	4
Extra Points	51	29	40	46	36	36	34	24	31	42	36	42	36	38
Safeties	0	3	0	0	0	0	3	0	0	1	0	0	0	0
Field Goals Made	21	12	27	25	22	17	21	13	24	20	19	19	17	19
Field Goals Attempted	33	23	35	35	24	26	25	25	38	31	32	29	28	30
% Successful	63.6	52.2	77.1	71.4	91.7	65.4	84.0	52.0	63.2	64.5	59.4	65.5	60.7	63.3

NATIONAL FOOTBALL CONFERENCE DEFENSE

	Atl	Chi	Dall	Det	G.B.	L.A.	Minn	N.O.	N.Y.G.	Phil	St.L	S.F.	T.B.	Wash.
First Downs	303	290	286	279	326	285	299	303	291	266	328	280	320	310
Rushing	94	120	106	93	140	125	117	127	106	102	134	113	123	133
Passing	172	144	162	158	168	128	163	161	156	137	171	144	174	152
Penalty	37	26	18	28	18	32	19	15	29	27	23	23	23	25
Rushes	459	521	468	469	546	585	540	504	553	476	509	464	551	532
Net Yds. Gained	1666	2146	2049	1623	2098	2397	2045	1916	1891	1751	2428	1918	2172	2161
Avg. Gain	3.6	4.1	4.4	3.5	3.8	4.1	3.8	3.8	3.4	3.7	4.8	4.1	3.9	4.1
Avg. Yds. per Game	104.1	134.1	128.1	101.4	131.1	149.8	127.8	119.8	118.2	109.4	151.8	119.9	135.8	135.1
Passes Attempted	565	525	511	475	505	439	481	471	544	507	495	514	541	452
Completed	322	233	236	261	284	204	265	287	294	248	282	273	317	214
% Completed	57.0	44.4	46.2	54.9	56.2	46.5	55.1	60.9	54.0	48.9	57.0	53.1	58.6	47.3
Total Yds. Gained	3927	3527	3717	3596	3353	3057	3599	3578	3318	3050	3547	3135	3297	3310
Passer Tackled	29	31	42	47	36	43	33	27	44	40	32	36	23	32
Yds. Lost	239	279	347	373	266	330	271	241	384	354	252	290	157	265
Net Yds. Gained	3688	3248	3370	3223	3087	2727	3328	3337	2934	2696	3295	2845	3140	3045
Avg. Yds. per Game	230.5	203.0	210.6	201.4	192.9	170.4	208.0	208.6	183.4	168.5	205.9	177.8	196.3	190.3
Net Yds. per Pass Play	6.21	5.84	6.09	6.17	5.71	5.66	6.47	6.70	4.99	4.93	6.25	5.17	5.57	6.29
Yds. Gained per Comp.	12.20	15.14	15.75	13.78	11.81	14.99	13.58	12.47	11.29	12.30	12.58	11.48	10.40	15.47
Combined Net Yds. Gained	5354	5394	5419	4846	5185	5124	5373	5253	4825	4447	5723	4763	5312	5206
% Total Yds. Rushing	31.12	39.78	37.81	33.49	40.46	46.78	38.06	36.47	39.19	39.37	42.43	40.27	40.89	41.51
% Total Yds. Passing	68.88	60.22	62.19	66.51	59.54	53.22	61.94	63.53	60.81	60.63	57.57	59.73	59.11	58.49
Avg. Yds. per Game	334.6	337.1	338.7	302.9	324.1	320.3	335.8	328.3	301.6	277.9	357.7	297.7	332.0	325.4
Ball Control Plays	1053	1077	1021	991	1087	1067	1054	1002	1141	1023	1036	1014	1115	1016
Avg. Yds. per Play	5.1	5.0	5.3	4.9	4.8	4.8	5.1	5.2	4.2	4.3	5.5	4.7	4.8	5.1
Third Down Efficiency	33.5	29.6	35.5	36.7	44.8	33.3	38.1	45.0	37.7	42.8	39.8	38.8	39.1	41.3
Intercepted by	25	18	37	24	30	17	16	17	17	26	21	27	32	24
Yds. Returned by	494	345	482	286	495	237	120	214	222	266	281	448	648	249
Returned for TD	3	3	0	1	1	0	0	0	1	0	1	4	4	2

Punts	96	98	80	81	69	94	84	69	105	76	69	83	73	80
Yds. Punted	4050	3985	3293	3471	2738	3856	3415	3045	4160	3096	2852	3433	3006	3338
Avg. Yds. per Punt	42.2	40.7	41.2	42.9	39.7	41.0	40.7	44.1	39.6	40.7	41.3	41.4	41.2	41.7
Punt Returns	59	66	38	39	50	52	46	36	61	34	37	57	52	50
Yds. Returned	577	594	231	299	511	481	399	282	561	246	276	664	668	388
Avg. Yds. per Return	9.8	9.0	6.1	7.7	10.2	9.3	8.7	7.8	9.2	7.2	7.5	11.6	12.8	7.8
Returned for TD	2	1	0	0	0	0	1	0	1	0	0	1	1	1
Kickoff Returns	67	44	71	70	70	60	62	50	50	60	55	67	64	69
Yds. Returned	1286	937	1508	1257	1183	1443	1260	966	959	1334	1163	1389	1332	1275
Avg. Yds. per Return	19.2	21.3	21.2	18.0	16.9	24.1	20.3	19.3	19.2	22.2	21.1	20.7	20.8	18.5
Returned for TD	0	0	0	0	0	2	0	0	0	0	0	0	0	0
Penalties	97	119	104	95	108	118	115	118	111	91	98	108	79	108
Yds. Penalized	804	961	837	872	907	1018	991	1089	876	813	845	866	650	921
Fumbles	43	33	43	29	42	37	27	31	38	38	35	36	32	32
Lost	21	22	16	15	24	16	19	17	17	21	17	21	14	15
Out of Bounds	4	3	3	2	2	2	1	5	2	3	3	2	2	1
Own Rec. for TD	0	0	0	0	0	0	0	0	0	0	0	0	0	0
Opp. Rec.	17	17	20	20	17	15	21	20	16	17	20	12	14	19
Opp. Rec. for TD	0	0	0	1	3	0	0	0	0	0	1	1	0	3
Total Points Scored	355	324	277	322	361	351	369	378	257	221	408	250	268	349
Total TDs	43	39	34	38	45	39	46	46	27	26	50	30	27	43
TDs Rushing	10	13	16	14	21	19	15	17	10	11	20	10	16	17
TDs Passing	30	23	17	22	18	17	26	26	14	12	29	16	10	21
TDs on Ret. and Rec.	3	3	1	2	6	3	5	3	3	3	1	4	1	5
Extra Points	41	37	31	37	43	37	42	45	27	23	48	29	27	38
Safeties	1	1	0	0	0	1	1	1	1	0	0	1	2	1
Field Goals Made	18	17	14	19	16	26	17	19	22	14	20	13	25	17
Field Goals Attempted	29	29	29	22	24	33	27	25	33	28	26	23	33	24
% Successful	62.1	58.6	48.3	86.4	66.7	78.8	63.0	76.0	66.7	50.0	76.9	56.5	75.8	70.8

AFC, NFC, AND NFL SUMMARY

	AFC Offense Total	AFC Offense Average	AFC Defense Total	AFC Defense Average	NFC Offense Total	NFC Offense Average	NFC Defense Total	NFC Defense Average	NFL Total	NFL Average
First Downs	4394	313.9	4526	323.3	4298	307.0	4166	297.6	8692	310.4
Rushing	1675	119.6	1776	126.9	1734	123.9	1633	116.6	3409	121.8
Passing	2369	169.2	2384	170.3	2205	157.5	2190	156.4	4574	163.4
Penalty	350	25.0	366	26.1	359	25.6	343	24.5	709	25.3
Rushes	7096	506.9	7331	523.6	7412	529.4	7177	512.6	14,508	518.1
Net Yds. Gained	28,722	2051.6	30,043	2145.9	29,582	2113.0	28,261	2018.6	58,304	2082.3
Avg. Gain	—	4.0	—	4.1	—	4.0	—	3.9	—	4.0
Avg. Yds. per Game	—	128.2	—	134.1	—	132.1	—	126.2	—	130.1
Passes Attempted	7138	509.9	7155	511.1	7042	503.0	7025	501.8	14,180	506.4
Completed	3966	283.3	4025	287.5	3779	269.9	3720	265.7	7745	276.6
% Completed	—	55.6	—	56.3	—	53.7	—	53.0	—	54.6
Total Yds. Gained	51,588	3684.9	51,710	3693.6	48,133	3438.1	48,011	3429.4	99,721	3561.5
Passer Tackled	507	36.2	526	37.6	514	36.7	495	35.4	1021	36.5
Yds. Lost	3988	284.9	4120	294.3	4180	298.6	4048	289.1	8168	291.7
Net Yds. Gained	47,600	3400.0	47,590	3399.3	43,953	3139.5	43,963	3140.2	91,553	3269.8
Avg. Yds. per Game	—	212.5	—	212.5	—	196.2	—	196.3	—	204.4
Net Yds. per Pass Play	—	6.23	—	6.20	—	5.82	—	5.85	—	6.02
Yds. Gained per Comp.	—	13.01	—	12.85	—	12.74	—	12.91	—	12.88
Combined Net Yds. Gained	76,322	5451.6	77,633	5545.2	73,535	5252.5	72,224	5158.9	149,857	5352.0
% Total Yds. Rushing	—	37.63	—	38.70	—	40.23	—	39.13	—	38.91
% Total Yds. Passing	—	62.37	—	61.30	—	59.77	—	60.87	—	61.09
Avg. Yds. per Game	—	340.7	—	346.6	—	328.3	—	322.4	—	334.5
Ball Control Plays	14,741	1052.9	15,012	1072.3	14,968	1069.1	14,697	1049.8	29,709	1061.0
Avg. Yds. per Play	—	5.2	—	5.2	—	4.9	—	4.9	—	5.0
Third Down Efficiency	—	39.7	—	40.0	—	38.6	—	38.2	—	39.1

Interceptions	21.8	609	22.3	312	23.6	331	21.2	297	19.9	278
Yds. Returned	317.3	8885	326.5	4571	341.9	4787	308.1	4314	292.7	4098
Returned for TD	1.1	30	1.4	19	1.4	20	0.8	11	0.7	10
Punts	80.0	2240	82.6	1157	82.3	1152	77.4	1083	77.7	1088
Yds. Punted	3276.9	91,754	3409.9	47,738	3381.6	47,342	3144.0	44,016	3172.3	44,412
Avg. Yds. per Punt	41.0	—	41.3	—	41.1	—	40.6	—	40.8	—
Punt Returns	43.6	1220	48.4	677	47.2	661	38.8	543	39.9	559
Yds. Returned	372.9	10,442	441.2	6177	412.1	5769	304.6	4265	333.8	4673
Avg. Yds. per Return	8.6	—	9.1	—	8.7	—	7.9	—	8.4	—
Returned for TD	0.4	11	0.6	8	0.6	9	0.2	3	0.1	2
Kickoff Returns	61.0	1709	61.4	859	59.7	836	60.7	850	62.4	873
Yds. Returned	1238.6	34,681	1235.1	17,292	1215.0	17,010	1242.1	17,389	1262.2	17,671
Avg. Yds. per Return	20.3	—	20.1	—	20.3	—	20.5	—	20.2	—
Penalties	102.9	2881	104.9	1469	103.6	1450	100.9	1412	102.2	1431
Yds. Penalized	867.5	24,291	889.3	12,450	873.7	12,232	845.8	11,841	861.4	12,059
Fumbles	34.4	962	35.4	496	34.8	487	33.3	466	33.9	475
Lost	18.1	508	18.2	255	17.5	245	18.1	253	18.8	263
Out of Bounds	2.3	63	2.5	35	2.1	29	2.0	28	2.4	34
Own Rec. for TD	0.1	3	0.0	0	0.1	1	0.2	3	0.1	2
Opp. Rec.	18.1	508	17.5	245	18.2	255	18.8	263	18.1	253
Opp. Rec. for TD	0.8	22	0.9	13	0.9	13	0.6	9	0.6	9
Total Points Scored	330.8	9262	320.7	4490	328.5	4599	340.9	4772	333.1	4663
Total TDs	39.4	1104	38.1	533	38.5	539	40.8	571	40.4	565
TDs Rushing	15.8	441	14.9	209	15.6	218	16.6	232	15.9	223
TDs Passing	21.1	591	20.1	281	19.6	275	22.1	310	22.6	316
TDs on Ret. and Rec.	2.6	72	3.1	43	3.3	46	2.1	29	1.9	26
Extra Points	37.2	1041	36.1	505	37.2	521	38.3	536	37.1	520
Safeties	0.6	17	0.6	8	0.6	8	0.6	9	0.6	9
Field Goals Made	18.6	521	18.4	257	19.7	276	18.9	264	17.5	245
Field Goals Attempted	28.3	791	27.5	385	29.6	414	29.0	406	26.9	377
% Successful	65.9	—	66.8	—	66.7	—	65.0	—	65.0	—

CLUB LEADERS

	Offense	Defense
First Downs	S.D. 379	Phil. 266
Rushing	Det. 167	Det. 93
Passing	S.D. 224	L.A. 128
Penalty	Clev. 37	Mia. 12
Rushes	Dall. 630	Atl. 459
Net Yds. Gained	Det. 2795	Det. 1623
Avg. Gain	Det. 4.7	N.Y.G. 3.4
Passes Attempted	Minn. 709	L.A. & N.E. 439
Completed	Minn. 382	L.A. 204
% Completed	S.F. 63.4	Chi. 44.4
Total Yds. Gained	S.D. 4873	Phil. 3050
Passer Tackled	Buff. 16	N.Y.J. 66
Yds. Lost	S.D. 134	N.Y.J. 518
Net Yds. Gained	S.D. 4739	Phil. 2696
Net Yds. per Pass Play	S.D. 7.31	Phil. 4.93
Yds. Gained per Comp.	N.E. 15.37	T.B. 10.40
Combined Net Yds. Gained	S.D. 6744	Phil. 4447
% Total Yds., Rushing	K.C. 49.93	S.D. 29.74
% Total Yds., Passing	Minn. 74.13	N.E. 49.37
Ball Control Plays	Clev. 1138	Det. 991
Avg. Yds. per Play	S.D. 6.0	N.Y.G. 4.2
Avg. Time of Poss.	Den. 32:27	—
Third Down Efficiency	S.D. 48.9	Chi. 29.6
Interceptions	—	Dall. 37
Yds. Returned	—	T.B. 648
Returned for TD	—	S.F. & T.B. 4
Punts	Chi. 114	—
Yds. Punted	Chi. 4531	—
Avg. Yds. per Punt	Cin. 44.8	—
Punt Returns	N.Y.G. 64	Clev. 30
Yds. Returned	L.A. 676	N.Y.J. 149
Avg. Yds. per Return	L.A. 13.8	Sea. 4.6
Returned for TD	L.A. 3	
Kickoff Returns	Balt. 84	Balt. 43
Yds. Returned	Hou. 1722	Balt. 864
Avg. Yds. per Return	Wash. 25.0	G.B. 16.9
Returned for TD	Hou. 2	—
Total Points Scored	S.D. 478	Phil. 221
Total TDs	S.D. 61	Phil. 26
TDs Rushing	Det. & S.D. 26	Buff. 7
TDs Passing	S.D. 34	T.B. 10
TDs on Ret. and Rec.	Atl. 7	Mia. 0
Extra Points	S.D. 55	Phil. 23
Safeties	Three with 3	—
Field Goals Made	Dall. 27	Cin. & N.Y.J. 12
Field Goals Attempted	N.Y.G. 38	N.Y.J. 20
% Successful	G.B. 91.7	Dall. 48.3

CLUB RANKINGS BY YARDS

Team	Offense			Defense		
	Total	Rush	Pass	Total	Rush	Pass
Atlanta	7	18	5	14	2	25
Baltimore	22	22	18	28	26	27
Buffalo	8	13	9	7	17	4
Chicago	26	11	27	19	20	14
Cincinnati	2	17	3	12	9	22
Cleveland	4	20	4	16	18	15
Dallas	5	2	15	20	16	21
Denver	14	21	8	6	13	5
Detroit	3	1	17	4	1	13
Green Bay	23	26	14	9	19	10
Houston	27	23	23	24	24	17
Kansas City	17	3	25	17t	3	23
Los Angeles	24	8	26	8	23	2
Miami	16	10	16	15	14	19
Minnesota	6	28	2	17t	15	18
New England	9t	15	6	25	28	6
New Orleans	25	7	28	11	11	20
New York Giants	28	25	24	3	10	7
New York Jets	15	6	19	5	7	8
Oakland	21	14	21	21	6	24
Philadelphia	12	4	20	1	4	1
Pittsburgh	11	5	13	22	8	26
St. Louis	19	9	22	23	25	16
San Diego	1	16	1	27	5	28
San Francisco	13	19	7	2	12	3
Seattle	20	27	12	26	27	11
Tampa Bay	18	24	11	13	22	12
Washington	9t	12	10	10	21	9

t—Tie for position

1981 TEAM & INDIVIDUAL STATISTICS

1981 TEAM AND INDIVIDUAL LEADERS

SCORING
 INDIVIDUAL: 121 points—Ed Murray, Detroit; Rafael Septien, Dallas
 TEAM: 478 points—San Diego Chargers

RUSHING
 INDIVIDUAL: 1,674 yards—George Rogers, New Orleans
 TEAM: 2,795—Detroit Lions

PASSING
 INDIVIDUAL: 98.5 rating points—Ken Anderson, Cincinnati
 TEAM: 93.4 rating points—Cincinnati Bengals

PASS RECEIVING
 INDIVIDUAL: 88 receptions—Kellen Winslow, San Diego

INTERCEPTIONS
 INDIVIDUAL: 11—Everson Walls, Dallas
 TEAM: 37—Dallas Cowboys

PUNTING
 INDIVIDUAL: 45.4-yard average—Pat McInally, Cincinnati
 TEAM: 44.8-yard average—Cincinnati Bengals

PUNT RETURNS
 INDIVIDUAL: 13.4-yard average—LeRoy Irvin, Los Angeles
 TEAM: 13.8-yard average—Los Angeles Rams

KICKOFF RETURNS
 INDIVIDUAL: 29.7-yard average—Mike Nelms, Washington
 TEAM: 25.0-yard average—Washington Redskins

SCORING

POINTS

Kickers
- **NFC:** 121—Ed Murray, Detroit
  - 121—Rafael Septien, Dallas
- **AFC:** 115—Jim Breech, Cincinnati
  - 115—Nick Lowery, Kansas City

Non-kickers
- **AFC:** 114—Chuck Muncie, San Diego
- **NFC:** 102—Wendell Tyler, Los Angeles

TOUCHDOWNS
- **AFC:** 19—Chuck Muncie, San Diego (19-rush)
- **NFC:** 17—Wendell Tyler, Los Angeles (12 rush, 5-pass)

EXTRA POINTS
- **AFC:** 55—Rolf Benirschke, San Diego (61 attempts)
- **NFC:** 51—Mick Luckhurst, Atlanta (51 attempts)

FIELD GOALS
- **NFC:** 27—Rafael Septien, Dallas (35 attempts)
- **AFC:** 26—Nick Lowery, Kansas City (36 attempts)

MOST POINTS, GAME
- **AFC:** 30 points—Kellen Winslow, San Diego vs. Oakland, November 22 (5-TD)
- **NFC:** 20 points—Joe Danelo, New York vs. Seattle, October 18 (2-XP, 6-FG)

TEAM LEADERS
- **AFC:** BALTIMORE: 60, Curtis Dickey; BUFFALO: 79, Nick Mike-Mayer; CINCINNATI: 115, Jim Breech; CLEVELAND: *79, Matt Bahr; DENVER: 87, Fred Steinfort; HOUSTON: 77, Toni Fritsch; KANSAS CITY: 115, Nick Lowery; MIAMI: 109, Uwe von Schamann; NEW ENGLAND: 82, John Smith; NEW YORK: 113, Pat Leahy; OAKLAND: 69, Chris Bahr; PITTSBURGH: 74, David Trout; SAN DIEGO: 114, Chuck Muncie; SEATTLE: 60, Steve Largent.
- **NFC:** ATLANTA: 114, Mick Luckhurst; CHICAGO: 49, John Roveto; DALLAS: 121, Rafael Septien; DETROIT: 121, Ed Murray; GREEN BAY: 101, Jan Stenerud; LOS ANGELES: 102, Wendell Tyler; MINNESOTA: 97, Rick Danmeier; NEW ORLEANS: 78, George Rogers; NEW YORK: 103, Joe Danelo; PHILADELPHIA: 101, Tony Franklin; ST. LOUIS: 93, Neil O'Donoghue; SAN FRANCISCO: 81, Ray Wersching; TAMPA BAY: 75, Bill Capece; WASHINGTON: 95, Mark Moseley.

*Includes 18 points with San Francisco

TEAM CHAMPIONS
- **AFC:** 478—San Diego
- **NFC:** 426—Atlanta

AFC SCORING—TEAM

	TD	TDR	TDP	TD Misc.	PAT	PAT Att.	FG	FG Att.	SAF	TP
San Diego	61	26	34	1	55	61	19	26	0	478
Cincinnati	51	19	30	2	49	51	22	32	0	421
Pittsburgh	47	21	25	1	38	46	12	17	0	356
New York Jets	40	11	26	3	38	40	25	36	1	355
Miami	39	18	18	3	37	39	24	31	1	345
Kansas City	38	22	12	4	37	38	26	36	0	343
New England	40	23	17	0	37	40	15	24	0	322
Seattle	40	14	21	5	37	40	15	24	0	322
Denver	39	12	27	0	36	39	17	30	0	321
Buffalo	38	13	25	0	37	38	14	24	2	311
Houston	34	11	21	2	32	34	15	22	0	281
Cleveland	32	11	21	0	31	32	17	33	1	276
Oakland	33	11	18	4	27	33	14	24	3	273
Baltimore	33	11	21	1	29	33	10	18	1	259
AFC Total	565	223	316	26	520	564	245	377	9	4,663
AFC Average	40.4	15.9	22.6	1.9	37.1	40.3	17.5	26.9	0.6	333.1

NFC SCORING—TEAM

	TD	TDR	TDP	TD Misc.	PAT	PAT Att.	FG	FG Att.	SAF	TP
Atlanta	52	15	30	7	51	52	21	33	0	426
Detroit	46	26	18	2	46	46	25	35	0	397
Philadelphia	44	17	25	2	42	44	20	31	1	368
Dallas	40	15	24	1	40	40	27	35	3	367
San Francisco	43	17	20	6	42	43	19	29	0	357
Washington	42	19	19	4	38	42	19	30	0	347
Minnesota	37	8	27	2	34	37	21	25	3	325
Green Bay	37	11	24	2	36	37	22	24	0	324
St. Louis	37	20	15	2	36	37	19	32	0	315
Tampa Bay	38	13	20	5	36	38	17	28	0	315
Los Angeles	36	17	15	4	36	36	17	26	0	303
N.Y. Giants	32	11	16	5	31	32	24	38	0	295
Chicago	31	13	14	4	29	31	12	23	1	253
New Orleans	24	16	8	0	24	24	13	25	0	207
NFC Total	539	218	275	46	521	539	276	414	8	4,599
NFC Average	38.5	15.6	19.6	3.3	37.2	38.5	19.7	29.6	0.6	328.5
League Total	1,104	441	591	72	1,041	1,103	521	791	17	9,262
League Avg.	39.4	15.8	21.1	2.6	37.2	39.4	18.6	28.3	0.6	330.8

NFL TOP 10 SCORERS —TOUCHDOWNS

	TD	TD Rush	TD Pass	TD Misc.	TP
Muncie, Chuck, San Diego	19	19	0	0	114
Tyler, Wendell, Los Angeles	17	12	5	0	102
Johnson, Pete, Cincinnati	16	12	4	0	96
Sims, Billy, Detroit	15	13	2	0	90
Jenkins, Alfred, Atlanta	13	0	13	0	78
Riggins, John, Washington	13	13	0	0	78
Rogers, George, New Orleans	13	13	0	0	78
Watson, Steve, Denver	13	0	13	0	78
Andrews, William, Atlanta	12	10	2	0	72
Springs, Ron, Dallas	12	10	2	0	72

NFL TOP 10 SCORERS — KICKING

	PAT	PAT Att.	FG	FG Att.	TP
Murray, Ed, Detroit	46	46	25	35	121
Septien, Rafael, Dallas	40	40	27	35	121
Breech, Jim, Cincinnati	49	51	22	32	115
Lowery, Nick, Kansas City	37	38	26	36	115
Luckhurst, Mick, Atlanta	51	51	21	33	114
Leahy, Pat, New York Jets	38	39	25	36	113
Benirschke, Rolf, San Diego	55	61	19	26	112
von Schamann, Uwe, Miami	37	38	24	31	109
Danelo, Joe, New York Giants	31	31	24	38	103
Franklin, Tony, Philadelphia	41	43	20	31	101
Stenerud, Jan, Green Bay	35	36	22	24	101

AFC SCORING—INDIVIDUAL

KICKERS	PAT	PAT Att.	FG	FG Att.	TP
Breech, Jim, Cincinnati	49	51	22	32	115
Lowery, Nick, Kansas City	37	38	26	36	115
Leahy, Pat, New York Jets	38	39	25	36	113
Benirschke, Rolf, San Diego	55	61	19	26	112
von Schamann, Uwe, Miami	37	38	24	31	109
Steinfort, Fred, Denver	36	37	17	30	87
Smith, John, New England	37	39	15	24	82
Bahr, Matt, S. F.-Cleveland	34	34	15	26	79
Mike-Mayer, Nick, Buffalo	37	37	14	24	79
Fritsch, Toni, Houston	32	34	15	22	77
Trout, David, Pittsburgh	38	46	12	17	74
Bahr, Chris, Oakland	27	33	14	24	69
Herrera, Efren, Seattle	23	25	12	17	59
Wood, Mike, Baltimore	29	33	10	18	59
Alvarez, Wilson, Seattle	14	15	3	7	23
Jacobs, Dave, Cleveland	9	10	4	12	21
Cox, Steve, Cleveland	0	0	0	1	0

NON-KICKERS	TD	TDR	TDP	TD Misc.	TP
Muncie, Chuck, San Diego	19	19	0	0	114
Johnson, Pete, Cincinnati	16	12	4	0	96
Watson, Steve, Denver	13	0	13	0	78
Jackson, Billy, Kansas City	11	10	1	0	66
Campbell, Earl, Houston	10	10	0	0	60
Cribbs, Joe, Buffalo	10	3	7	0	60
Dickey, Curtis, Baltimore	10	7	3	0	60
Largent, Steve, Seattle	10	1	9	0	60
Winslow, Kellen, San Diego	10	0	10	0	60
Butler, Ray, Baltimore	9	0	9	0	54
Harris, Franco, Pittsburgh	9	8	1	0	54
Walker, Wesley, New York Jets	9	0	9	0	54
Brown, Theotis, St. Louis-Seattle	8	8	0	0	48
Butler, Jerry, Buffalo	8	0	8	0	48
Casper, Dave, Houston	8	0	8	0	48
Collinsworth, Cris, Cincinnati	8	0	8	0	48
Franklin, Andra, Miami	8	7	1	0	48
Nathan, Tony, Miami	8	5	3	0	48
Pruitt, Mike, Cleveland	8	7	1	0	48
Barkum, Jerome, New York Jets	7	0	7	0	42
Burrough, Ken, Houston	7	0	7	0	42
Collins, Anthony, New England	7	7	0	0	42
Joiner, Charlie, San Diego	7	0	7	0	42
Smith, Jim, Pittsburgh	7	0	7	0	42
Brooks, James, San Diego	6	3	3	0	36
Chandler, Wes, N.O.-San Diego	6	0	6	0	36
Hasselbeck, Don, New England	6	0	6	0	36
Leaks, Roosevelt, Buffalo	6	6	0	0	36
Morgan, Stanley, New England	6	0	6	0	36
Newsome, Ozzie, Cleveland	6	0	6	0	36
Cappelletti, John, San Diego	5	4	1	0	30
Doornink, Dan, Seattle	5	1	4	0	30
Harper, Bruce, New York Jets	5	4	1	0	30
Hooks, Roland, Buffalo	5	3	2	0	30

	TD	TDR	TDP	TD Misc.	TP
Kreider, Steve, Cincinnati	5	0	5	0	30
Long, Kevin, New York Jets	5	2	3	0	30
Lytle, Rob, Denver	5	4	1	0	30
McKnight, Ted, Kansas City	5	5	0	0	30
Odoms, Riley, Denver	5	0	5	0	30
Ross, Dan, Cincinnati	5	0	5	0	30
Stallworth, John, Pittsburgh	5	0	5	0	30
Swann, Lynn, Pittsburgh	5	0	5	0	30
Canada, Larry, Denver	4	3	1	0	24
Chandler, Bob, Oakland	4	0	4	0	24
Cunningham, Sam, New England	4	4	0	0	24
Griffin, Archie, Cincinnati	4	3	1	0	24
Jensen, Derrick, Oakland	4	4	0	0	24
Lewis, Frank, Buffalo	4	0	4	0	24
Logan, Dave, Cleveland	4	0	4	0	24
Marshall, Henry, Kansas City	4	0	4	0	24
McMillan, Randy, Baltimore	4	3	1	0	24
Pruitt, Greg, Cleveland	4	0	4	0	24
Ramsey, Derrick, Oakland	4	0	4	0	24
Smith, Sherman, Seattle	4	3	1	0	24
Thornton, Sidney, Pittsburgh	4	4	0	0	24
Vigorito, Tommy, Miami	4	1	2	1	24
Woodley, David, Miami	4	4	0	0	24
Alexander, Charles, Cincinnati	3	2	1	0	18
Bradshaw, Morris, Oakland	3	0	3	0	18
Carr, Roger, Baltimore	3	0	3	0	18
Cavanaugh, Matt, New England	3	3	0	0	18
Cefalo, Jimmy, Miami	3	0	3	0	18
Cunningham, Bennie, Pittsburgh	3	0	3	0	18
Delaney, Joe, Kansas City	3	3	0	0	18
Feacher, Ricky, Cleveland	3	0	3	0	18
Ferguson, Vagas, New England	3	3	0	0	18
Hadnot, James, Kansas City	3	3	0	0	18
Jones, Johnny, New York Jets	3	0	3	0	18
Malone, Mark, Pittsburgh	3	2	1	0	18
McCullum, Sam, Seattle	3	0	3	0	18
McNeil, Freeman, New York Jets	3	2	1	0	18
Parros, Rick, Denver	3	2	1	0	18
Preston, Dave, Denver	3	3	0	0	18
Sievers, Eric, San Diego	3	0	3	0	18
Tatupu, Mosi, New England	3	2	1	0	18
Upchurch, Rick, Denver	3	0	3	0	18
Whittington, Arthur, Oakland	3	1	2	0	18
Christensen, Todd, Oakland	2	0	2	0	*14
Bradshaw, Terry, Pittsburgh	2	2	0	0	12
Brammer, Mark, Buffalo	2	0	2	0	12
Calhoun, Don, New England	2	2	0	0	12
Curtis, Isaac, Cincinnati	2	0	2	0	12
Dierking, Scott, New York Jets	2	1	1	0	12
Dixon, Al, Kansas City	2	0	2	0	12
Grogan, Steve, New England	2	2	0	0	12
Harris, Duriel, Miami	2	0	2	0	12
Harris, John, Seattle	2	0	0	2	12
Harris, M.L., Cincinnati	2	0	2	0	12

Scoring

	TD	TDR	TDP	TD Misc.	TP
Hawthorne, Greg, Pittsburgh	2	2	0	0	12
Hill, Calvin, Cleveland	2	0	2	0	12
Hill, Eddie, Miami	2	1	1	0	12
Holston, Michael, Houston	2	0	2	0	12
Hughes, David, Seattle	2	0	2	0	12
Jones, Bobby, New York Jets	2	0	1	1	12
McCall, Reese, Baltimore	2	0	2	0	12
McCauley, Don, Baltimore	2	0	2	0	12
Miller, Cleo, Cleveland	2	2	0	0	12
Moore, Nat, Miami	2	0	2	0	12
Pollard, Frank, Pittsburgh	2	2	0	0	12
Ray, Darroll, New York Jets	2	0	0	2	12
Rose, Joe, Miami	2	0	2	0	12
Smith, J.T., Kansas City	2	0	2	0	12
Smith, Ron, San Diego	2	0	2	0	12
van Eeghen, Mark, Oakland	2	2	0	0	12
Verser, David, Cincinnati	2	0	2	0	12
Westbrook, Don, New England	2	0	2	0	12
Wilson, Marc, Oakland	2	2	0	0	12
Anderson, Ken, Cincinnati	1	1	0	0	6
Armstrong, Adger, Houston	1	0	1	0	6
Augustyniak, Mike, New York Jets	1	1	0	0	6
Barber, Mike, Houston	1	0	1	0	6
Barnett, Buster, Buffalo	1	0	1	0	6
Barnwell, Malcolm, Oakland	1	0	1	0	6
Bauer, Hank, San Diego	1	0	1	0	6
Blount, Mel, Pittsburgh	1	0	0	1	6
Boyd, Dennis, Seattle	1	0	1	0	6
Branch, Cliff, Oakland	1	0	1	0	6
Breeden, Louis, Cincinnati	1	0	0	1	6
Brown, Curtis, Buffalo	1	0	1	0	6
Buruss, Lloyd, Kansas City	1	0	0	1	6
Carson, Carlos, Kansas City	1	0	1	0	6
Chester, Raymond, Oakland	1	0	1	0	6
Coleman, Ronnie, Houston	1	1	0	0	6
Davis, Russell, Pittsburgh	1	1	0	0	6
Dixon, Zachary, Baltimore	1	0	1	0	6
Easley, Kenny, Seattle	1	0	0	1	6
Egloff, Ron, Denver	1	0	1	0	6
Ferguson, Joe, Buffalo	1	1	0	0	6
Franklin, Cleveland, Baltimore	1	1	0	0	6
Grossman, Randy, Pittsburgh	1	0	1	0	6
Hardman, Cedrick, Oakland	1	0	0	1	6
Hargrove, Jimmy, Cincinnati	1	1	0	0	6
Howard, Thomas, Kansas City	1	0	0	1	6
Jodat, Jim, Seattle	1	1	0	0	6
Johns, Paul, Seattle	1	0	1	0	6
Johnson, Andy, New England	1	0	1	0	6
Johnson, Gary, San Diego	1	0	0	1	6
Johnson, Greggory, Seattle	1	0	0	1	6
Jones, Willie, Oakland	1	0	0	1	6
Kenney, Bill, Kansas City	1	1	0	0	6
Kozlowski, Mike, Miami	1	0	0	1	6
Krieg, Dave, Seattle	1	1	0	0	6

	TD	TDR	TDP	TD Misc.	TP
Landry, Greg, Baltimore	1	0	0	1	6
Lee, Ronnie, Miami	1	0	1	0	6
Moser, Rick, Pittsburgh	1	0	1	0	6
Moses, Haven, Denver	1	0	1	0	6
Newton, Tom, New York Jets	1	1	0	0	6
Owens, Burgess, Oakland	1	0	0	1	6
Paul, Whitney, Kansas City	1	0	0	1	6
Pennywell, Carlos, New England	1	0	1	0	6
Pinney, Ray, Pittsburgh	1	0	1	0	6
Plunkett, Jim, Oakland	1	1	0	0	6
Renfro, Mike, Houston	1	0	1	0	6
Roaches, Carl, Houston	1	0	0	1	6
Rome, Stan, Kansas City	1	0	1	0	6
Rucker, Reggie, Cleveland	1	0	1	0	6
St. Clair, Mike, Cincinnati	1	0	0	1	6
Scales, Dwight, San Diego	1	0	1	0	6
Scott, Willie, Kansas City	1	0	1	0	6
Sipe, Brian, Cleveland	1	1	0	0	6
Spani, Gary, Kansas City	1	0	0	1	6
Thomas, Rodell, Seattle	1	0	0	1	6
Tullis, Willie, Houston	1	0	0	1	6
Watts, Ted, Oakland	1	0	0	1	6
Walker, Fulton, Miami	1	0	0	1	6
White, Charles, Cleveland	1	1	0	0	6
Williams, Clarence, San Diego	1	0	1	0	6
Willis, Chester, Oakland	1	1	0	0	6
Wright, James, Denver	1	0	1	0	6
Zorn, Jim, Seattle	1	1	0	0	6
Buttle, Greg, New York Jets	0	0	0	0	*2
Gordon, Larry, Miami	0	0	0	0	*2
Robinson, Johnny, Oakland	0	0	0	0	*2
Taylor, Hosea, Baltimore	0	0	0	0	*2
Williams, Ben, Buffalo	0	0	0	0	*2

*Indicates safety.

NFC SCORING—INDIVIDUAL

KICKERS	PAT	PAT Att.	FG	FG Att.	TP
Murray, Ed, Detroit	46	46	25	35	121
Septien, Rafael, Dallas	40	40	27	35	121
Luckhurst, Mick, Atlanta	51	51	21	33	114
Danelo, Joe, New York Giants	31	31	24	38	103
Franklin, Tony, Philadelphia	41	43	20	31	101
Stenerud, Jan, Green Bay	35	36	22	24	101
Danmeier, Rick, Minnesota	34	37	21	25	97
Moseley, Mark, Washington	38	42	19	30	95
O'Donoghue, Neil, St. Louis	36	37	19	32	93
Corral, Frank, Los Angeles	36	36	17	26	87
Wersching, Ray, San Francisco	30	30	17	23	81
Capece, Bill, Tampa Bay	30	32	15	24	75
Ricardo, Benny, New Orleans	24	24	13	25	63
Roveto, John, Chicago	19	20	10	18	49
Yeprernian, Garo, Tampa Bay	6	6	2	4	12
Nielsen, Hans, Chicago	8	8	0	2	8
Thomas, Bob, Chicago	2	3	2	3	8

NON-KICKERS	TD	TDR	TDP	TD Misc.	TP
Tyler, Wendell, Los Angeles	17	12	5	0	102
Sims, Billy, Detroit	15	13	2	0	90
Jenkins, Alfred, Atlanta	13	0	13	0	78
Riggins, John, Washington	13	13	0	0	78
Rogers, George, New Orleans	13	13	0	0	78
Andrews, William, Atlanta	12	10	2	0	72
Springs, Ron, Dallas	12	10	2	0	72
Montgomery, Wilbert, Philadelphia	10	8	2	0	60
Anderson, Ottis, St. Louis	9	9	0	0	54
House, Kevin, Tampa Bay	9	0	9	0	54
Brown, Ted, Minnesota	8	6	2	0	48
Huckleby, Harlan, Green Bay	8	5	3	0	48
Lofton, James, Green Bay	8	0	8	0	48
Payton, Walter, Chicago	8	6	2	0	48
Senser, Joe, Minnesota	8	0	8	0	48
Solomon, Freddie, San Francisco	8	0	8	0	48
Davis, Johnny, San Francisco	7	7	0	0	42
Ellis, Gerry, Green Bay	7	4	3	0	42
Hipple, Eric, Detroit	7	7	0	0	42
Jackson, Alfred, Atlanta	7	0	6	1	42
Rashad, Ahmad, Minnesota	7	0	7	0	42
Washington, Joe, Washington	7	4	3	0	42
Cain, Lynn, Atlanta	6	4	2	0	36
Carmichael, Harold, Philadelphia	6	0	6	0	36
Carpenter, Rob, Hou.-N.Y.Giants	6	5	1	0	36
Dorsett, Tony, Dallas	6	4	2	0	36
Giles, Jimmie, Tampa Bay	6	0	6	0	36
Monk, Art, Washington	6	0	6	0	36
Perkins, Johnny, New York Giants	6	0	6	0	36
Cosbie, Doug, Dallas	5	0	5	0	30
Francis, Wallace, Atlanta	5	1	4	0	30
Green, Roy, St. Louis	5	1	4	0	30
Johnson, Butch, Dallas	5	0	5	0	30
Krepfle, Keith, Philadelphia	5	0	5	0	30

	TD	TDR	TDP	TD Misc.	TP
Morris, Wayne, St. Louis	5	5	0	0	30
Patton, Ricky, San Francisco	5	4	1	0	30
Scott, Freddie, Detroit	5	0	5	0	30
Wilder, James, Tampa Bay	5	4	1	0	30
Wilson, Wayne, New Orleans	5	1	4	0	30
Young, Charle, San Francisco	5	0	5	0	30
Campfield, Billy, Philadelphia	4	1	3	0	24
Clark, Dwight, San Francisco	4	0	4	0	24
Coffman, Paul, Green Bay	4	0	4	0	24
Dennard, Preston, Los Angeles	4	0	4	0	24
Guman, Mike, Los Angeles	4	4	0	0	24
Hill, David, Detroit	4	0	4	0	24
Hill, Tony, Dallas	4	0	4	0	24
Jefferson, John, Green Bay	4	0	4	0	24
Russell, Booker, Philadelphia	4	4	0	0	24
Smith, Charles, Philadelphia	4	0	4	0	24
Thompson, Leonard, Detroit	4	1	3	0	24
Thompson, Ricky, Washington	4	0	4	0	24
Williams, Doug, Tampa Bay	4	4	0	0	24
Baschnagel, Brian, Chicago	3	0	3	0	18
Bruer, Bob, Minnesota	3	0	3	0	18
Evans, Vince, Chicago	3	3	0	0	18
Hill, Drew, Los Angeles	3	0	3	0	18
Irvin, LeRoy, Los Angeles	3	0	0	3	18
Kane, Rick, Detroit	3	2	1	0	18
Lott, Ronnie, San Francisco	3	0	0	3	18
Miller, Junior, Atlanta	3	0	3	0	18
Owens, James, Tampa Bay	3	3	0	0	18
Pearson, Drew, Dallas	3	0	3	0	18
Seay, Virgil, Washington	3	0	3	0	18
Shirk, Gary, New York Giants	3	0	3	0	18
Suhey, Matt, Chicago	3	3	0	0	18
Tilley, Pat, St. Louis	3	0	3	0	18
Watts, Rickey, Chicago	3	0	3	0	18
White, Sammy, Minnesota	3	0	3	0	18
Anderson, Marcus, Chicago	2	0	2	0	12
Arnold, Walt, Los Angeles	2	0	2	0	12
Bell, Theo, Tampa Bay	2	0	2	0	12
Bright, Leon, New York Giants	2	2	0	0	12
Brown, Cedric, Tampa Bay	2	0	0	2	12
Danielson, Gary, Detroit	2	2	0	0	12
DuPree, Billy Joe, Dallas	2	0	2	0	12
Eckwood, Jerry, Tampa Bay	2	2	0	0	12
Galbreath, Tony, Minnesota	2	2	0	0	12
Giammona, Louie, Philadelphia	2	1	1	0	12
Giaquinto, Nick, Mia.-Washington	2	0	2	0	12
Gray, Earnest, New York Giants	2	0	2	0	12
Gray, Mel, St. Louis	2	0	2	0	12
Harrell, Willard, St. Louis	2	1	1	0	12
Harrington, Perry, Philadelphia	2	2	0	0	12
Henry, Wally, Philadelphia	2	0	2	0	12
Hicks, Dwight, San Francisco	2	0	0	2	12
Holmes, Jack, New Orleans	2	2	0	0	12
Johnson, Kenny, Atlanta	2	0	0	2	12

Scoring	TD	TDR	TDP	TD Misc.	TP
LaFleur, Greg, St. Louis	2	0	2	0	12
Lawrence, Amos, San Francisco	2	1	0	1	12
LeCount, Terry, Minnesota	2	0	2	0	12
Lomax, Neil, St. Louis	2	2	0	0	12
Martin, George, New York Giants	2	0	0	2	12
Mitchell, Stump, St. Louis	2	0	1	1	12
Montana, Joe, San Francisco	2	2	0	0	12
Nelms, Mike, Washington	2	0	0	2	12
Parker, Rodney, Philadelphia	2	0	2	0	12
Taylor, Billy, New York Giants	2	2	0	0	12
Theismann, Joe, Washington	2	2	0	0	12
Williams, Dave, Chicago	2	0	2	0	12
Young, Rickey, Minnesota	2	0	2	0	12
Ahrens, Dave, St. Louis	1	0	0	1	6
Barnes, Benny, Dallas	1	0	0	1	6
Bell, Todd, Chicago	1	0	0	1	6
Brown, Greg, Philadelphia	1	0	0	1	6
Bryant, Cullen, Los Angeles	1	1	0	0	6
Childs, Henry, Los Angeles	1	0	1	0	6
Coleman, Monte, Washington	1	0	0	1	6
Colzie, Neal, Tampa Bay	1	0	0	1	6
Cooper, Earl, San Francisco	1	1	0	0	6
Curry, Buddy, Atlanta	1	0	0	1	6
Dennis, Mike, New York Giants	1	0	0	1	6
Earl, Robin, Chicago	1	0	1	0	6
Easley, Walt, San Francisco	1	1	0	0	6
Fencik, Gary, Chicago	1	0	0	1	6
Fisher, Jeff, Chicago	1	0	0	1	6
Friede, Mike, New York Giants	1	0	1	0	6
Groth, Jeff, New Orleans	1	0	1	0	6
Hall, Alvin, Detroit	1	0	0	1	6
Hardy, Larry, New Orleans	1	0	1	0	6
Harper, Roland, Chicago	1	1	0	0	6
Harris, Al, Chicago	1	0	0	1	6
Harris, Joe, Los Angeles	1	0	0	1	6
Hofer, Paul, San Francisco	1	1	0	0	6
Holloway, Randy, Minnesota	1	0	0	1	6
Hood, Estus, Green Bay	1	0	0	1	6
Ivery, Eddie Lee, Green Bay	1	1	0	0	6
Jackson, Louis, New York Giants	1	1	0	0	6
Jackson, Terry, New York Giants	1	0	0	1	6
Jones, Gordon, Tampa Bay	1	0	1	0	6
Jones, James, Dallas	1	1	0	0	6
King, Horace, Detroit	1	0	1	0	6
Kotar, Doug, New York Giants	1	1	0	0	6
Kuykendall, Fulton, Atlanta	1	0	0	1	6
Lee, Mark, Green Bay	1	0	0	1	6
LeMaster, Frank, Philadelphia	1	0	0	1	6
Logan, David, Tampa Bay	1	0	0	1	6
Margerum, Ken, Chicago	1	0	1	0	6
Marsh, Doug, St. Louis	1	0	1	0	6
Martin, Robby, Detroit	1	0	0	1	6
Merkens, Guido, New Orleans	1	0	1	0	6
Middleton, Terdell, Green Bay	1	0	1	0	6

	TD	TDR	TDP	TD Misc.	TP
Mistler, John, New York Giants	1	0	1	0	6
Mullady, Tom, New York Giants	1	0	1	0	6
Nichols, Mark, Detroit	1	0	1	0	6
Obradovich, Jim, Tampa Bay	1	0	1	0	6
Oliver, Hubert, Philadelphia	1	1	0	0	6
Olkewicz, Neal, Washington	1	0	0	1	6
Payton, Eddie, Minnesota	1	0	0	1	6
Perry, Leon, New York Giants	1	0	1	0	6
Porter, Tracy, Detroit	1	0	1	0	6
Pridemore, Tom, Atlanta	1	0	0	1	6
Reece, Beasley, New York Giants	1	0	0	1	6
Ring, Bill, San Francisco	1	0	1	0	6
Saldi, Jay, Dallas	1	0	1	0	6
Stief, Dave, St. Louis	1	0	1	0	6
Swanke, Karl, Green Bay	1	0	1	0	6
Thompson, Vince, Detroit	1	1	0	0	6
Walker, Rick, Washington	1	0	1	0	6
Warren, Don, Washington	1	0	1	0	6
Washington, Mike, Tampa Bay	1	0	0	1	6
Whitehurst, David, Green Bay	1	1	0	0	6
Williams, Joel, Atlanta	1	0	0	1	6
Wilson, Mike, San Francisco	1	0	1	0	6
Young, Dave, New York Giants	1	0	1	0	6
Hannon, Tom, Minnesota	0	0	0	0	*4
Clarke, Ken, Philadelphia	0	0	0	0	*2
Dutton, John, Dallas	0	0	0	0	*2
Martin, Harvey, Dallas	0	0	0	0	*2
Plank, Doug, Chicago	0	0	0	0	*2
Williams, Walt, Minnesota	0	0	0	0	*2
Wilkes, Reggie, Philadelphia	0	0	0	0	**1
Wingo, Rich, Green Bay	0	0	0	0	**1

*Indicates safety.
**Scored extra point on pass reception.

FIELD GOALS

BEST PERCENTAGE
  NFC: .917—Jan Stenerud, Green Bay (22 made, 24 attempts)
  AFC: .774—Uwe von Schamann, Miami (24 made, 31 attempts)
MADE
  NFC: 27—Rafael Septien, Dallas (35 attempts)
  AFC: 26—Nick Lowery, Kansas City (36 attempts)
ATTEMPTS
  NFC: 38—Joe Danelo, New York Giants
  AFC: 36—Pat Leahy, New York Jets
        36—Nick Lowery, Kansas City
AVERAGE YARDS MADE
  NFC: 38.3—Ed Murray, Detroit
  AFC: 35.2—Chris Bahr, Oakland
LONGEST
  NFC: 55—Joe Danelo, New York Giants vs. New Orleans, September 20
  AFC: 54—Efren Herrera, Seattle vs. Green Bay, November 1

AFC FIELD GOALS—TEAM

	Made	Att.	Pct.	Long
Miami	24	31	.774	46
San Diego	19	26	.731	52
Kansas City	26	36	.722	52
Pittsburgh	12	17	.706	48
N.Y. Jets	25	36	.694	49
Cincinnati	22	32	.688	51
Houston	15	22	.682	50
New England	15	24	.625	50
Seattle	15	24	.625	54
Buffalo	14	24	.583	46
Oakland	14	24	.583	51
Denver	17	30	.567	49
Baltimore	10	18	.556	48
Cleveland	17	33	.515	39
AFC Totals	245	377	—	54
AFC Average	17.5	26.9	650	—

NFC FIELD GOALS —TEAM

	Made	Att.	Pct.	Long
Green Bay	22	24	.917	53
Minnesota	21	25	.840	45
Dallas	27	35	.771	47
Detroit	25	35	.714	53
San Francisco	19	29	.655	48
Los Angeles	17	26	.654	44
Philadelphia	20	31	.645	50
Atlanta	21	33	.636	47
Washington	19	30	.633	49
N.Y. Giants	24	38	.632	55
Tampa Bay	17	28	.607	51
St. Louis	19	32	.594	47
Chicago	12	23	.522	43
New Orleans	13	25	.520	46
NFC Totals	276	414	—	55
NFC Average	19.7	29.6	.667	—
League Totals	521	791	—	55
League Average	18.6	28.3	.659	—

AFC FIELD GOALS—INDIVIDUAL

	1-19	20-29	30-39	40-49	50 & Over	Totals	Avg. Yds. Att.	Avg. Yds. Made	Avg. Yds. Miss	Long
von Schamann, Uwe, Miami	0-0 1.000	9-9	11-12 .917	4-10 .400	0-0 —	24-31 .774	34.5	32.0	43.3	46
Benirschke, Rolf, San Diego	2-2 1.000	7-7 1.000	5-8 .625	3-4 .750	2-5 .400	19-26 .731	35.6	33.4	41.6	52
Lowery, Nick, Kansas City	0-0 —	5-5 1.000	13-15 .867	7-9 .778	1-7 .143	26-36 .722	38.3	34.8	47.2	52
Herrera, Efren, Seattle	0-0 —	6-7 .857	3-3 1.000	2-5 .400	1-2 .500	12-17 .706	34.8	31.4	42.8	54
Trout, David, Pittsburgh	3-3 1.000	5-6 .833	1-2 .500	3-5 .600	0-1 .000	12-17 .706	32.9	28.5	43.4	48
Leahy, Pat, N.Y. Jets	0-0 —	11-13 .846	6-8 .750	8-12 .667	0-3 .000	25-36 .694	36.4	34.4	37.7	49
Breech, Jim, Cincinnati	0-0	9-11 .818	7-9 .778	5-11 .455	1-1 1.000	22-32 .688	35.3	33.3	39.7	51
Fritsch, Toni, Houston	0-0 —	3-4 .750	4-4 1.000	7-13 .538	1-1 1.000	15-22 .682	38.9	31.5	41.3	50
Smith, John, New England	0-0 —	7-7 1.000	2-6 .333	5-7 .714	1-4 .250	15-24 .625	37.3	33.7	43.3	50
Bahr, Chris, Oakland	0-0 —	6-8 .750	2-4 .500	3-7 .429	3-5 .600	14-24 .583	37.6	35.2	41.0	51
Mike-Mayer, Nick, Buffalo	0-0 —	4-6 .667	5-7 .714	5-10 .500	0-1 .000	14-24 .583	37.0	35.1	39.6	46
Bahr, Matt, S.F.-Clev.	3-3 1.000	5-7 .714	5-10 .500	2-5 .400	0-1 .000	15-26 .577	33.3	29.7	38.2	47
Steinfort, Fred, Denver	0-0 —	6-9 .667	5-11 .455	6-8 .750	0-2 .000	17-30 .567	35.0	33.4	37.1	49
Wood, Mike, Baltimore	2-2 1.000	2-3 .667	3-5 .600	3-7 .429	0-1 .000	10-18 .556	35.4	31.0	40.9	48
Alvarez, Wilson, Seattle	0-0 —	3-3 1.000	0-0 —	0-4 .000	0-0 —	3-7 .429	34.3	23.3	42.5	28
Jacobs, Dave, Cleveland	0-0 —	2-3 .667	2-6 .333	0-1 .000	0-2 .000	4-12 .333	36.3	30.5	39.1	35
Cox, Steve, Cleveland	0-0 —	0-0 —	0-0 —	0-0 —	0-1 .000	0-1 .000	53.0	0.0	53.0	0
AFC Totals	10-10 1.000	90-106 .849	74-109 .679	61-115 .530	10-37 .270	245-377 .650	36.0	33.1	41.4	54
League Totals	22-24 .917	182-213 .854	162-231 .701	134-256 .523	21-67 .313	521-791 .659	36.1	33.5	41.1	55

NFC FIELD GOALS — INDIVIDUAL

	1-19	20-29	30-39	40-49	50 & Over	Totals	Avg. Yds. Att.	Avg. Yds. Made	Avg. Yds. Miss	Long
Stenerud, Jan, Green Bay	2-2 1.000	7-8 .875	9-9 1.000	2-3 .667	2-2 1.000	22-24 .917	33.0	32.6	37.0	53
Danmeier, Rick, Minnesota	1-1 1.000	5-6 .833	11-12 .917	4-6 .667	0-0 —	21-25 .840	33.7	33.1	36.8	45
Septien, Rafael, Dallas	1-1 1.000	11-11 1.000	8-9 .889	7-12 .583	0-2 .000	27-35 .771	35.1	32.0	45.8	47
Wersching, Ray, San Francisco	2-2 1.000	7-7 1.000	4-7 .571	4-7 .571	0-0 —	17-23 .739	33.3	31.8	37.5	48
Murray, Ed, Detroit	1-1 1.000	5-5 1.000	9-14 .643	7-11 .636	3-4 .750	25-35 .714	38.5	38.3	39.1	53
Thomas, Bob, Chicago	0-0 —	1-2 .500	1-1 1.000	0-0 —	0-0 —	2-3 .667	28.7	31.0	24.0	37
Corral, Frank, Los Angeles	0-0 —	6-9 .667	5-6 .833	6-11 .545	0-0 —	17-26 .654	35.1	33.7	37.7	44
Franklin, Tony, Philadelphia	0-0 —	5-5 1.000	7-9 .778	7-13 .538	1-4 .250	20-31 .645	39.5	36.1	45.8	50
Luckhurst, Mick, Atlanta	1-2 .500	7-7 1.000	8-12 .667	5-11 .455	0-1 .000	21-33 .636	35.2	32.7	39.7	47
Moseley, Mark, Washington	1-1 1.000	7-8 .875	6-8 .750	5-12 .417	0-1 .000	19-30 .633	36.1	32.4	42.4	49
Danelo, Joe, N.Y. Giants	1-1 1.000	7-9 .778	7-9 .778	6-11 .545	3-8 .375	24-38 .632	38.8	35.4	44.7	55
Capece, Bill, Tampa Bay	0-0 —	5-7 .714	3-5 .600	5-10 .500	2-2 1.000	15-24 .625	37.1	36.9	37.4	51
O'Donoghue, Neil, St. Louis	2-2 1.000	8-8 1.000	4-6 .667	5-11 .455	0-5 .000	19-32 .594	37.0	30.4	46.5	47
Roveto, John, Chicago	0-1 .000	6-7 .857	2-3 .667	2-7 .286	0-0 —	10-18 .556	33.0	29.5	33.4	43
Ricardo, Benny, New Orleans	0-0 —	5-5 1.000	3-9 .333	5-10 .500	0-1 .000	13-25 .520	37.8	34.9	40.8	46
Yepremian, Garo, Tampa Bay	0-0 —	0-0 —	1-1 1.000	1-3 .333	0-0 —	2-4 .500	41.0	38.0	44.0	44
Nielsen, Hans, Chicago	0-0 —	0-1 .000	0-1 .000	0-0 —	0-0 —	0-2 .000	28.0	0.0	28.0	0
NFC Totals	12-14 .857	92-107 .860	88-122 .721	73-141 .518	11-30 .367	276-414 .667	36.2	33.8	40.9	55
League Totals	22-24 .917	182-213 .854	162-231 .701	134-256 .523	21-67 .313	521-791 .659	36.1	33.5	41.1	55

RUSHING

INDIVIDUAL CHAMPIONS
  NFC: 1674—George Rogers, New Orleans
  AFC: 1376—Earl Campbell, Houston
YARDS PER ATTEMPT
  AFC: 5.3—Tony Nathan, Miami (147 attempts, 782 yards)
  NFC: 4.9—Wilbert Montgomery, Philadelphia (286 attempts, 1402 yards)
TOUCHDOWNS
  AFC: 19—Chuck Muncie, San Diego
  NFC: 13—John Riggins, Washington
        13—George Rogers, New Orleans
        13—Billy Sims, Detroit
ATTEMPTS
  NFC: 378—George Rogers, New Orleans
  AFC: 361—Earl Campbell, Houston
LONGEST
  AFC: 82 yards—Joe Delaney, Kansas City vs. Houston, November 15 (TD)
  NFC: 79 yards—George Rogers, New Orleans vs. Cleveland, October 18
        (TD)
MOST YARDS, GAME
  AFC: 193 yards—Joe Delaney, Kansas City vs. Houston, November 15 (29
        attempts)
  NFC: 185 yards—Billy Sims, Detroit vs. Denver, October 11 (28 attempts)
TEAM LEADERS
  AFC: BALTIMORE: 779, Curtis Dickey; BUFFALO: 1097, Joe Cribbs; CIN-
        CINNATI 1077, Pete Johnson; CLEVELAND: 1103, Mike Pruitt; DEN-
        VER: 749, Rick Parros; HOUSTON: 1376, Earl Campbell; KANSAS
        CITY: 1121, Joe Delaney; MIAMI: 782, Tony Nathan; NEW ENGLAND:
        873, Anthony Collins; NEW YORK: 623, Freeman McNeil; OAKLAND:
        828, Kenny King; PITTSBURGH: 987, Franco Harris; SAN DIEGO:
        1144, Chuck Muncie; SEATTLE: 583, Theotis Brown.
  NFC: ATLANTA: 1301, William Andrews; CHICAGO: 1222, Walter Payton;
        DALLAS: 1646, Tony Dorsett; DETROIT: 1437, Billy Sims; GREEN BAY:
        860, Gerry Ellis; LOS ANGELES: 1074, Wendell Tyler; MINNESOTA:
        1063, Ted Brown; NEW ORLEANS: 1674, George Rogers; NEW YORK:
        822, Rob Carpenter; PHILADELPHIA: 1402, Wilbert Montgomery; ST.
        LOUIS: 1376, Ottis Anderson; SAN FRANCISCO: 543, Ricky Patton;
        TAMPA BAY: 651, Jerry Eckwood; WASHINGTON: 916, Joe Washington.
TEAM CHAMPIONS
  NFC: 2795—Detroit
  AFC: 2633—Kansas City

AFC RUSHING—TEAM

	Att.	Yards	Avg.	Long	TD
Kansas City	610	2,633	4.3	82t	22
Pittsburgh	554	2,372	4.3	50	21
New York Jets	571	2,341	4.1	43	11
Miami	535	2,173	4.1	46	18
Buffalo	524	2,125	4.1	35	13
Oakland	493	2,058	4.2	60	11
New England	499	2,040	4.1	43	23
San Diego	481	2,005	4.2	73t	26
Cincinnati	493	1,973	4.0	39t	19
Cleveland	474	1,929	4.1	26	11
Denver	515	1,895	3.7	37	12
Baltimore	441	1,850	4.2	67t	11
Houston	466	1,734	3.7	43	11
Seattle	440	1,594	3.6	43	14
AFC Total	7,096	28,722	—	82t	223
AFC Average	506.9	2,051.6	4.0	—	15.9

NFC RUSHING—TEAM

	Att.	Yards	Avg.	Long	TD
Detroit	596	2,795	4.7	51	26
Dallas	630	2,711	4.3	75t	15
Philadelphia	559	2,509	4.5	41	17
New Orleans	546	2,286	4.2	79t	16
Los Angeles	559	2,236	4.0	69t	17
St. Louis	519	2,213	4.3	44t	20
Chicago	608	2,171	3.6	39	13
Washington	532	2,157	4.1	32	19
Atlanta	495	1,965	4.0	35	15
San Francisco	560	1,941	3.5	28	17
Tampa Bay	458	1,731	3.8	59	13
New York Giants	481	1,685	3.5	35	11
Green Bay	478	1,670	3.5	34	11
Minnesota	391	1,512	3.9	38	8
NFC Total	7,412	29,582	—	79t	218
NFC Average	529.4	2,113.0	4.0	—	15.6
League Total	14,508	58,304	—	82t	441
League Average	518.1	2,082.3	4.0	—	15.8

NFL TOP 10 RUSHERS

	Att.	Yards	Avg.	Long	TD
Rogers, George, New Orleans	378	1674	4.4	79t	13
Dorsett, Tony, Dallas	342	1646	4.8	75t	4
Sims, Billy, Detroit	296	1437	4.9	51	13
Montgomery, Wilbert, Philadelphia	286	1402	4.9	41	8
Anderson, Ottis, St. Louis	328	1376	4.2	28	9
Campbell, Earl, Houston	361	1376	3.8	43	10
Andrews, William, Atlanta	289	1301	4.5	29	10
Payton, Walter, Chicago	339	1222	3.6	39	6
Muncie, Chuck, San Diego	251	1144	4.6	73t	19
Delaney, Joe, Kansas City	234	1121	4.8	82t	3

AFC RUSHING—INDIVIDUAL

	Att.	Yards	Avg.	Long	TD
Campbell, Earl, Houston	361	1376	3.8	43	10
Muncie, Chuck, San Diego	251	1144	4.6	73t	19
Delaney, Joe, Kansas City	234	1121	4.8	82t	3
Pruitt, Mike, Cleveland	247	1103	4.5	21	7
Cribbs, Joe, Buffalo	257	1097	4.3	35	3
Johnson, Pete, Cincinnati	274	1077	3.9	39t	12
Harris, Franco, Pittsburgh	242	987	4.1	50	8
Collins, Anthony, New England	204	873	4.3	29	7
King, Kenny, Oakland	170	828	4.9	60	0
Nathan, Tony, Miami	147	782	5.3	46	5
Dickey, Curtis, Baltimore	164	779	4.8	67t	7
Parros, Rick, Denver	176	749	4.3	25	2
Franklin, Andra, Miami	201	711	3.5	29	7
Preston, Dave, Denver	183	640	3.5	23	3
McNeil, Freeman, New York Jets	137	623	4.5	43	2
Hadnot, James, Kansas City	140	603	4.3	30	3
McMillan, Randy, Baltimore	149	597	4.0	42	3
Brown, Theotis, St.L.-Seattle	156	583	3.7	43	8
Pollard, Frank, Pittsburgh	123	570	4.6	29	2
Brooks, James, San Diego	109	525	4.8	28t	3
Jensen, Derrick, Oakland	117	456	3.9	33	4
Jackson, Billy, Kansas City	111	398	3.6	31	10
Harper, Bruce, New York Jets	81	393	4.9	29t	4
Leaks, Roosevelt, Buffalo	91	357	3.9	31	6
White, Charles, Cleveland	97	342	3.5	26	1
Ferguson, Vagas, New England	78	340	4.4	19t	3
Augustyniak, Mike, N.Y. Jets	85	339	4.0	12	1
Dierking, Scott, New York Jets	74	328	4.4	15t	1
Anderson, Ken, Cincinnati	46	320	7.0	25	1
Alexander, Charles, Cincinnati	98	292	3.0	16	2
Dixon, Zachary, Baltimore	73	285	3.9	41	0
Woodley, David, Miami	63	272	4.3	26	4
Davis, Russell, Pittsburgh	47	270	5.7	28	1
Long, Kevin, New York Jets	73	269	3.7	19	2
Cunningham, Sam, New England	86	269	3.1	12	4
Cappelletti, John, San Diego	68	254	3.7	30	4
Smith, Sherman, Seattle	83	253	3.0	21	3
Hooks, Roland, Buffalo	51	250	4.9	19	3
Newton, Tom, New York Jets	73	244	3.3	13	1
Brown, Curtis, Buffalo	62	226	3.6	13	0
Whittington, Arthur, Oakland	69	220	3.2	13	1
Calhoun, Don, New England	57	205	3.6	33	2
Thornton, Sidney, Pittsburgh	56	202	3.6	17t	4
Tatupu, Mosi, New England	38	201	5.3	43	2
McKnight, Ted, Kansas City	54	195	3.6	26	5
Doornink, Dan, Seattle	65	194	3.0	11	1
Hawkins, Frank, Oakland	40	165	4.1	19	0
Miller, Cleo, Cleveland	52	165	3.2	13	2
Griffin, Archie, Cincinnati	47	163	3.5	23	3
Bradshaw, Terry, Pittsburgh	38	162	4.3	16	2
Reed, Tony, Denver	68	156	2.3	10	0
Sipe, Brian, Cleveland	38	153	4.0	22	1
van Eeghen, Mark, Oakland	39	150	3.8	11	2

Rushing

	Att.	Yards	Avg.	Long	TD
Wilson, Marc, Oakland	30	147	4.9	18	2
Armstrong, Adger, Houston	31	146	4.7	18	0
Hill, Eddie, Miami	37	146	3.9	24	1
Zorn, Jim, Seattle	30	140	4.7	20	1
McCutcheon, Lawrence, Buffalo	34	138	4.1	12	0
Hughes, David, Seattle	47	135	2.9	15	0
Todd, Richard, New York Jets	32	131	4.1	19	0
Pruitt, Greg, Cleveland	31	124	4.0	15	0
Fuller, Steve, Kansas City	19	118	6.2	27	0
Vigorito, Tommy, Miami	35	116	3.3	30t	1
Canada, Larry, Denver	33	113	3.4	11	3
Taylor, Billy, N.Y. Giants-N.Y. Jets	38	111	2.9	14	2
Lytle, Rob, Denver	30	106	3.5	18	4
Jodat, Jim, Seattle	31	106	3.4	15	1
Bennett, Woody, Miami	28	104	3.7	12	0
Cavanaugh, Matt, New England	17	92	5.4	11	3
Coleman, Ronnie, Houston	21	91	4.3	30	1
Kenney, Bill, Kansas City	24	89	3.7	21	1
Jones, Bert, Baltimore	20	85	4.3	17	0
Marshall, Henry, Kansas City	3	69	23.0	34	0
Malone, Mark, Pittsburgh	16	68	4.3	19	2
Hargrove, Jimmy, Cincinnati	16	66	4.1	27	1
Bledsoe, Curtis, Kansas City	20	65	3.3	13	0
Hawthorne, Greg, Pittsburgh	25	58	2.3	16	2
Upchurch, Rick, Denver	5	56	11.2	37	0
Krieg, Dave, Seattle	11	56	5.1	29	1
Fouts, Dan, San Diego	22	56	2.5	13	0
Willis, Chester, Oakland	16	54	3.4	15t	1
Franklin, Cleveland, Baltimore	21	52	2.5	8	1
Grogan, Steve, New England	12	49	4.1	24t	2
Largent, Steve, Seattle	6	47	7.8	15	1
Schonert, Turk, Cincinnati	7	41	5.9	19	0
DeBerg, Steve, Denver	9	40	4.4	11	0
Ivory, Horace, Seattle	9	38	4.2	7	0
Plunkett, Jim, Oakland	12	38	3.2	13t	1
McCauley, Don, Baltimore	10	37	3.7	8	0
Wilson, Tim, Houston	13	35	2.7	7	0
Riddick, Robb, Buffalo	3	29	9.7	12	0
Ferguson, Joe, Buffalo	20	29	1.5	16	1
Adkins, Sam, Seattle	3	28	9.3	13	0
Williams, Clarence, San Diego	20	26	1.3	6	0
West, Jeff, Seattle	3	25	8.3	27	0
Hill, Calvin, Cleveland	4	23	5.8	9	0
Lane, Eric, Seattle	8	22	2.8	5	0
Kreider, Steve, Cincinnati	1	21	21.0	21	0
Morgan, Stanley, New England	2	21	10.5	11	0
Howell, Steve, Miami	5	21	4.2	9	0
Newsome, Ozzie, Cleveland	2	20	10.0	14	0
Lewis, Kenny, New York Jets	6	18	3.0	7	0
Morton, Craig, Denver	8	18	2.3	5	0
Stallworth, John, Pittsburgh	1	17	17.0	17	0
Brammer, Mark, Buffalo	2	17	8.5	11	0
Moore, Jeff, Seattle	1	15	15.0	15	0

	Att.	Yards	Avg.	Long	TD
Smith, Jim, Pittsburgh	1	15	15.0	15	0
Orosz, Tom, Miami	1	13	13.0	13	0
Reaves, John, Houston	6	13	2.2	13	0
Landry, Greg, Baltimore	1	11	11.0	11	0
Wright, James, Denver	1	11	11.0	11	0
Verser, David, Cincinnati	2	11	5.5	9	0
Stoudt, Cliff, Pittsburgh	3	11	3.7	10	0
Bass, Don, Cincinnati	1	9	9.0	9	0
Colquitt, Craig, Pittsburgh	1	8	8.0	8	0
Bauer, Hank, San Diego	2	7	3.5	4	0
Watson, Steve, Denver	2	6	3.0	6	0
Moser, Rick, Pittsburgh	1	4	4.0	4	0
Garrett, Mike, Baltimore	2	4	2.0	3	0
Miller, Terry, Seattle	2	4	2.0	2	0
Moore, Nat, Miami	1	3	3.0	3	0
Pennywell, Carlos, New England	1	3	3.0	3	0
Roberts, George, San Diego	1	2	2.0	2	0
Nielsen, Gifford, Houston	6	2	0.3	4	0
Butler, Jerry, Buffalo	1	1	1.0	1	0
Johnson, Andy, New England	2	1	0.5	5	0
Anderson, Kim, Baltimore	1	0	0.0	0	0
Jones, Johnny, New York Jets	2	0	0.0	5	0
McDonald, Paul, Cleveland	2	0	0.0	2	0
Williams, Mike, Kansas City	2	0	0.0	3	0
Ramsey, Chuck, New York Jets	3	0	0.0	0	0
Chandler, Wes, San Diego	5	−1	−0.2	9	0
Carson, Carlos, Kansas City	1	−1	−1.0	−1	0
Feacher, Ricky, Cleveland	1	−1	−1.0	−1	0
Robinson, Matt, Buffalo	1	−2	−2.0	−2	0
Stabler, Ken, Houston	10	−3	−0.3	4	0
Ryan, Pat, New York Jets	3	−5	−1.7	−1	0
Dixon, Al, Kansas City	1	−5	−5.0	−5	0
Kush, Rod, Buffalo	1	−6	−6.0	−6	0
Luther, Ed, San Diego	3	−8	−2.7	−1	0
Franklin, Byron, Buffalo	1	−11	−11.0	−11	0
Jackson, Harold, New England	2	−14	−7.0	−5	0
Grupp, Bob, Kansas City	1	−19	−19.0	−19	0
Strock, Don, Miami	14	−26	−1.9	9	0
McInally, Pat, Cincinnati	1	−27	−27.0	−27	0

t indicates touchdown
Leader based on most yards gained.

NFC RUSHING—INDIVIDUAL

	Att.	Yards	Avg.	Long	TD
Rogers, George, New Orleans	378	1674	4.4	79t	13
Dorsett, Tony, Dallas	342	1646	4.8	75t	4
Sims, Billy, Detroit	296	1437	4.9	51	13
Montgomery, Wilbert, Phil.	286	1402	4.9	41	8
Anderson, Ottis, St. Louis	328	1376	4.2	28	9
Andrews, William, Atlanta	289	1301	4.5	29	10
Payton, Walter, Chicago	339	1222	3.6	39	6

Rushing	Att.	Yards	Avg.	Long	TD
Tyler, Wendell, Los Angeles	260	1074	4.1	69t	12
Brown, Ted, Minnesota	274	1063	3.9	34	6
Washington, Joe, Washington	210	916	4.4	32	4
Ellis, Gerry, Green Bay	196	860	4.4	29	4
Carpenter, Rob, Hou.-N.Y. Giants	208	822	4.0	35	5
Riggins, John, Washington	195	714	3.7	24	13
Eckwood, Jerry, Tampa Bay	172	651	3.8	59	2
Springs, Ron, Dallas	172	625	3.6	16	10
Patton, Ricky, San Francisco	152	543	3.6	28	4
Cain, Lynn, Atlanta	156	542	3.5	35	4
Suhey, Matt, Chicago	150	521	3.5	26	3
Bussey, Dexter, Detroit	105	446	4.2	23	0
Bryant, Cullen, Los Angeles	109	436	4.0	20	1
Guman, Mike, Los Angeles	115	433	3.8	18	4
Morris, Wayne, St. Louis	109	417	3.8	14	5
Owens, James, Tampa Bay	91	406	4.5	35t	3
Huckleby, Harlan, Green Bay	139	381	2.7	22	5
Wilder, James, Tampa Bay	107	370	3.5	23t	4
Kane, Rick, Detroit	77	332	4.3	20	2
Cooper, Earl, San Francisco	98	330	3.4	23	1
Oliver, Hubert, Philadelphia	75	329	4.4	39	1
Davis, Johnny, San Francisco	94	297	3.2	14	7
Perry, Leon, New York Giants	72	257	3.6	23	0
Easley, Walt, San Francisco	76	224	2.9	9	1
Evans, Vince, Chicago	43	218	5.1	25	3
Thompson, Vince, Detroit	35	211	6.0	30	1
Williams, Doug, Tampa Bay	48	209	4.4	29	4
Galbreath, Tony, Minnesota	42	198	4.7	21	2
Bright, Leon, New York Giants	51	197	3.9	25	2
Holmes, Jack, New Orleans	58	194	3.3	11	2
Hofer, Paul, San Francisco	60	193	3.2	12	1
Jones, James, Dallas	34	183	5.4	59t	1
Tyler, Toussaint, New Orleans	36	183	5.1	42	0
Jackson, Wilbur, Washington	46	183	4.0	14	0
Middleton, Terdell, Green Bay	53	181	3.4	34	0
Theismann, Joe, Washington	36	177	4.9	24	2
Mitchell, Stump, St. Louis	31	175	5.6	43	0
Hipple, Eric, Detroit	41	168	4.1	18	7
Kotar, Doug, New York Giants	46	154	3.3	18	1
Harrington, Perry, Philadelphia	34	140	4.1	16	2
Wilson, Wayne, New Orleans	44	137	3.1	13	1
Murray, Calvin, Philadelphia	23	134	5.8	20	0
Young, Rickey, Minnesota	47	129	2.7	13	0
Jaworski, Ron, Philadelphia	22	128	5.8	26	0
Russell, Booker, Philadelphia	38	123	3.2	17	4
Thomas, Jewerl, Los Angeles	34	118	3.5	40	0
Campfield, Billy, Philadelphia	31	115	3.7	13	1
Ring, Bill, San Francisco	22	106	4.8	16	0
Harper, Roland, Chicago	34	106	3.1	11	1
Haden, Pat, Los Angeles	18	104	5.8	16	0
Lomax, Neil, St. Louis	19	104	5.5	22t	2
Giaquinto, Nick, Miami-Wash.	20	104	5.2	20	0
White, Danny, Dallas	38	104	2.7	17	0
Giammona, Louie, Philadelphia	35	98	2.8	9	1

	Att.	Yards	Avg.	Long	TD
Montana, Joe, San Francisco	25	95	3.8	20t	2
Bell, Ricky, Tampa Bay	30	80	2.7	8	0
Jensen, Jim, Green Bay	27	79	2.9	15	0
Thompson, Leonard, Detroit	10	75	7.5	21	1
Forte, Ike, New York Giants	19	74	3.9	15	0
McClendon, Willie, Chicago	30	74	2.5	17	0
Ivery, Eddie Lee, Green Bay	14	72	5.1	28	1
Jackson, Louis, New York Giants	27	68	2.5	9	1
Mayberry, James, Atlanta	18	66	3.7	11	0
Green, Roy, St. Louis	3	60	20.0	44t	1
Metcalf, Terry, Washington	18	60	3.3	12	0
LeCount, Terry, Minnesota	3	51	17.0	38	0
Whitehurst, David, Green Bay	15	51	3.4	15	1
Nichols, Mark, Detroit	3	50	16.7	30	0
Lawrence, Amos, San Francisco	13	48	3.7	14	1
Solomon, Freddie, San Francisco	9	43	4.8	16	0
Simms, Phil, New York Giants	19	42	2.2	24	0
Newsome, Timmy, Dallas	13	38	2.9	7	0
Rogers, Jimmy, New Orleans	9	37	4.1	15	0
Cosbie, Doug, Dallas	4	33	8.3	15	0
Atkins, Steve, Green Bay-Phil.	12	33	2.8	21	0
Newhouse, Robert, Dallas	14	33	2.4	6	0
Clark, Dwight, San Francisco	3	32	10.7	18	0
Pearson, Drew, Dallas	3	31	10.3	25	0
Dennard, Preston, Los Angeles	6	29	4.8	21	0
Elliott, Lenvil, San Francisco	7	29	4.1	9	0
Manning, Archie, New Orleans	2	28	14.0	15	0
Groth, Jeff, New Orleans	2	27	13.5	28	0
King, Horace, Detroit	7	25	3.6	7	0
Scott, Freddie, Detroit	7	25	3.6	10	0
Robinson, Bo, Atlanta	9	24	2.7	5	0
Danielson, Gary, Detroit	9	23	2.6	11t	2
Jefferson, John, Green Bay	2	22	11.0	15	0
Redwine, Jarvis, Minnesota	5	20	4.0	8	0
Brunner, Scott, New York Giants	14	20	1.4	23	0
Williams, Dave, Chicago	2	19	9.5	15	0
Claitt, Ricky, Washington	3	19	6.3	11	0
Cromwell, Nolan, Los Angeles	1	17	17.0	17	0
Moroski, Mike, Atlanta	3	17	5.7	14	0
Lewis, Leo, Minnesota	1	16	16.0	16	0
Hill, Drew, Los Angeles	1	14	14.0	14	0
Dils, Steve, Minnesota	4	14	3.5	7	0
Matthews, Bo, New York Giants	4	14	3.5	6	0
Kramer, Tommy, Minnesota	10	13	1.3	8	0
DuPree, Billy Joe, Dallas	1	12	12.0	12	0
Margerum, Ken, Chicago	1	11	11.0	11	0
Love, Randy, St. Louis	3	11	3.7	4	0
Wonsley, Otis, Washington	3	11	3.7	7	0
Baschnagel, Brian, Chicago	1	10	10.0	10	0
Erxleben, Russell, New Orleans	2	10	5.0	26	0
House, Kevin, Tampa Bay	2	9	4.5	8	0
Kemp, Jeff, Los Angeles	2	9	4.5	7	0
Carano, Glenn, Dallas	8	9	1.1	11	0
Francis, Wallace, Atlanta	1	8	8.0	8t	1

Rushing	Att.	Yards	Avg.	Long	TD
Stief, Dave, St. Louis	1	8	8.0	8	0
Bell, Theo, Tampa Bay	1	7	7.0	7	0
Harrell, Sam, Minnesota	1	7	7.0	7	0
LeMaster, Frank, Philadelphia	1	7	7.0	7	0
Smith, Ron, Philadelphia	1	7	7.0	7	0
Stauch, Scott, New Orleans	2	6	3.0	5	0
Strong, Ray, Atlanta	3	6	2.0	3	0
Harrell, Willard, St. Louis	5	6	1.2	4	1
Dickey, Lynn, Green Bay	19	6	0.3	13	0
Walker, Rick, Washington	1	5	5.0	5	0
Davis, Tony, Tampa Bay	2	5	2.5	3	0
Jackson, Alfred, Atlanta	2	5	2.5	5	0
Smith, Charles, Philadelphia	2	5	2.5	5	0
Pastorini, Dan, Los Angeles	7	5	0.7	13	0
Gray, Mel, St. Louis	1	4	4.0	4	0
Harmon, Clarence, Washington	1	4	4.0	4	0
Torkelson, Eric, Green Bay	1	4	4.0	4	0
Fusina, Chuck, Tampa Bay	3	3	1.0	7	0
Komlo, Jeff, Detroit	6	3	0.5	5	0
Daykin, Tony, Atlanta	1	2	2.0	2	0
Garrett, Alvin, New York Giants	1	2	2.0	2	0
Senser, Joe, Minnesota	1	2	2.0	2	0
Thompson, Aundra, Green Bay	1	2	2.0	2	0
Hart, Jim, St. Louis	3	2	0.7	4	0
Avellini, Bob, Chicago	5	2	0.4	2	0
Bartkowski, Steve, Atlanta	11	2	0.2	5	0
Benjamin, Guy, San Francisco	1	1	1.0	1	0
Carmichael, Harold, Philadelphia	1	1	1.0	1	0
Wilson, Dave, New Orleans	5	1	0.2	9	0
Pisarcik, Joe, Philadelphia	7	1	0.1	10	0
Blanchard, Tom, Tampa Bay	1	0	0.0	0	0
Childs, Henry, Los Angeles	1	0	0.0	0	0
Connell, Mike, Washington	1	0	0.0	0	0
Phipps, Mike, Chicago	1	0	0.0	0	0
Sciarra, John, Philadelphia	1	0	0.0	0	0
Siemon, Jeff, Minnesota	1	0	0.0	0	0
Merkens, Guido, New Orleans	2	−1	−0.5	2	0
Perkins, Johnny, New York Giants	2	−1	−0.5	10	0
White, Sammy, Minnesota	2	−1	−0.5	1	0
Jones, June, Atlanta	1	−1	−1.0	−1	0
Birdsong, Carl, St. Louis	1	−2	−2.0	−2	0
Henry, Wally, Philadelphia	1	−2	−2.0	−2	0
Rutledge, Jeff, Los Angeles	5	−3	−0.6	4	0
Myers, Tommy, New Orleans	2	−3	−1.5	6	0
Caster, Richard, New Orleans	1	−3	−3.0	−3	0
Hill, Tony, Dallas	1	−3	−3.0	−3	0
Scott, Bobby, New Orleans	3	−4	−1.3	−1	0
Monk, Art, Washington	1	−5	−5.0	−5	0
Neal, Dan, Chicago	1	−6	−6.0	−6	0
Parsons, Bob, Chicago	1	−6	−6.0	−6	0
James, John, Atlanta	1	−7	−7.0	−7	0
Swider, Larry, Tampa Bay	1	−9	−9.0	−9	0

t indicates touchdown
Leader based on most yards gained.

PASSING

INDIVIDUAL CHAMPIONS (RATING POINTS)
- **AFC:** 98.5—Ken Anderson, Cincinnati
- **NFC:** 88.2—Joe Montana, San Francisco

ATTEMPTS
- **AFC:** 609—Dan Fouts, San Diego
- **NFC:** 593—Tommy Kramer, Minnesota

COMPLETIONS
- **AFC:** 360—Dan Fouts, San Diego
- **NFC:** 322—Tommy Kramer, Minnesota

COMPLETION PERCENTAGE
- **NFC:** 63.7—Joe Montana, San Francisco (488 attempts, 311 completions)
- **AFC:** 62.6—Ken Anderson, Cincinnati (479 attempts, 300 completions)

YARDS
- **AFC:** 4802—Dan Fouts, San Diego
- **NFC:** 3912—Tommy Kramer, Minnesota

YARDS PER ATTEMPT
- **AFC:** 8.61—Steve Grogan, New England (216 attempts, 1859 yards)
- **NFC:** 8.45—Eric Hipple, Detroit (279 attempts, 2358 yards)

TOUCHDOWN PASSES
- **AFC:** 33—Dan Fouts, San Diego
- **NFC:** 30—Steve Bartkowski, Atlanta

TOUCHDOWN PERCENTAGE
- **AFC:** 6.1—Ken Anderson, Cincinnati (479 attempts, 29 touchdowns)
- **NFC:** 5.6—Steve Bartkowski, Atlanta (533 attempts, 30 touchdowns)

MOST INTERCEPTIONS
- **AFC:** 25—Brian Sipe, Cleveland
- **NFC:** 24—Tommy Kramer, Minnesota

LOWEST PERCENTAGE INTERCEPTED
- **AFC:** 2.1—Ken Anderson, Cincinnati (479 attempts, 10 intercepted)
- **NFC:** 2.5—Joe Montana, San Francisco (488 attempts, 12 intercepted)

LONGEST
- **AFC:** 95 yards—Craig Morton, Denver vs. Detroit, October 11
   (to Steve Watson)—TD
- **NFC:** 94 yards—Eric Hipple, Detroit vs. Chicago, October 19
   (to Leonard Thompson)—TD

TEAM CHAMPIONS (RATING POINTS)
- **AFC:** 93.4—Cincinnati
- **NFC:** 87.8—San Francisco

AFC PASSING — TEAM

	Att.	Comp.	Pct. Comp.	Gross Yards	Tkd.	Yards Lost	Net Yards	TD	Pct. TD	Long	Had Int.	Pct. Int.	Avg. Yds. Att.	Avg. Yds. Comp.	Rating Points
Cincinnati	550	332	60.4	4200	35	205	3995	30	5.5	74t	12	2.2	7.64	12.65	93.4
San Diego	629	368	58.5	4873	19	134	4739	34	5.4	67t	18	2.9	7.75	13.24	89.1
Denver	485	289	59.6	3992	61	461	3531	27	5.6	95t	21	4.3	8.23	13.81	86.8
Seattle	524	307	58.6	3727	37	300	3427	21	4.0	80t	15	2.9	7.11	12.14	81.8
New York Jets	507	283	55.8	3279	30	224	3055	26	5.1	49	14	2.8	6.47	11.59	80.9
Pittsburgh	461	247	53.6	3457	27	231	3226	25	5.4	90t	19	4.1	7.50	14.00	78.9
Houston	441	258	58.5	3119	40	342	2777	21	4.8	71t	23	5.2	7.07	12.09	74.6
Buffalo	503	253	50.3	3661	16	146	3515	25	5.0	67t	20	4.0	7.28	14.47	74.3
Baltimore	479	265	55.3	3379	37	321	3058	21	4.4	67t	23	4.8	7.05	12.75	72.2
Cleveland	624	348	55.8	4339	40	353	3986	21	3.4	62	27	4.3	6.95	12.47	71.0
Miami	498	271	54.4	3385	30	236	3149	18	3.6	69t	21	4.2	6.80	12.49	70.3
Kansas City	410	224	54.6	2917	37	277	2640	12	2.9	64t	22	5.4	7.11	13.02	64.4
New England	482	254	52.7	3904	45	321	3583	17	3.5	76t	34	7.1	8.10	15.37	61.8
Oakland	545	267	49.0	3356	53	437	2919	18	3.3	66t	28	5.1	6.16	12.57	58.3
AFC Total	7138	3966	—	51,588	507	3,988	47,600	316	—	95t	297	—	—	—	—
AFC Average	509.9	283.3	55.6	3,684.9	36.2	284.9	3400.0	22.6	4.4	—	21.2	4.2	7.23	13.01	75.7

NFC PASSING — TEAM

	Att.	Comp.	Pct. Comp.	Gross Yards	Tkd.	Yards Lost	Net Yards	TD	Pct. TD	Long	Had Int.	Pct. Int.	Avg. Yds. Att.	Avg. Yds. Comp.	Rating Points
San Francisco	517	328	63.4	3766	29	223	3543	20	3.9	78t	13	2.5	7.28	11.48	87.8
Dallas	439	241	54.9	3414	31	245	3169	24	5.5	73t	15	3.4	7.78	14.17	84.4
Atlanta	563	311	55.2	3986	37	287	3699	30	5.3	70t	24	4.3	7.08	12.82	77.3
Tampa Bay	473	239	50.5	3565	19	136	3429	20	4.2	84t	14	3.0	7.54	14.92	77.1
Washington	525	307	58.5	3743	30	277	3466	19	3.6	79t	22	4.2	7.13	12.19	75.1
Philadelphia	476	258	54.2	3249	22	205	3044	25	5.3	85t	22	4.6	6.83	12.59	74.2
Green Bay	514	286	55.6	3576	52	387	3189	24	4.7	75t	24	4.7	6.96	12.50	73.5

Detroit	436	228	52.3	3475	44	337	3138	18	4.1	94t	23t	5.3	7.97	15.24	70.5
Minnesota	709	382	53.9	4567	29	234	4333	27	3.8	63	29	4.1	6.44	11.96	69.4
St. Louis	477	253	53.0	3269	48	405	2864	15	3.1	75	24	5.0	6.85	12.92	64.3
N.Y. Giants	506	251	49.6	3009	47	368	2641	16	3.2	80	20	4.0	5.95	11.99	62.2
New Orleans	441	238	54.0	2778	41	359	2419	8	1.8	55	27	6.1	6.30	11.67	53.9
Chicago	489	222	45.4	2728	35	266	2462	14	2.9	85t	23	4.7	5.58	12.29	53.3
Los Angeles	477	235	49.3	3008	50	451	2557	15	3.1	67t	32	6.7	6.31	12.80	51.9
NFC Total	7042	3779	—	48,133	514	4180	43,953	275	—	94t	312	—	—	—	—
NFC Average	503.0	269.9	53.7	3438.1	36.7	298.6	3139.5	19.6	3.9	—	22.3	4.4	6.84	12.74	70.0
League Total	14,180	7745	—	99,721	1021	8168	91,553	591	—	95t	609	—	—	—	—
League Avg.	506.4	276.6	54.6	3561.5	36.5	291.7	3269.8	21.1	4.2	—	21.8	4.3	7.03	12.88	73.0

NFL TOP 10 INDIVIDUAL QUALIFIERS

	Att.	Comp.	Pct. Comp.	Yards	Avg. Gain	TD	Pct. TD	Long	Int.	Pct. Int.	Rating Points
Anderson, Ken, Cincinnati	479	300	62.6	3754	7.84	29	6.1	74t	10	2.1	98.5
Morton, Craig, Denver	376	225	59.8	3195	8.50	21	5.6	95t	14	3.7	90.6
Fouts, Dan, San Diego	609	360	59.1	4802	7.89	33	5.4	67t	17	2.8	90.6
Montana, Joe, San Francisco	488	311	63.7	3565	7.31	19	3.9	78t	12	2.5	88.2
White, Danny, Dallas	391	223	57.0	3098	7.92	22	5.6	73t	13	3.3	87.5
Bradshaw, Terry, Pittsburgh	370	201	54.3	2887	7.80	22	5.9	90t	13	3.8	83.7
Zorn, Jim, Seattle	397	236	59.4	2788	7.02	13	3.3	80t	9	2.3	82.3
Todd, Richard, New York Jets	497	279	56.1	3231	6.50	25	5.0	49	13	2.6	81.8
Bartkowski, Steve, Atlanta	533	297	55.7	3829	7.18	30	5.6	70t	23	4.3	79.2
Dickey, Lynn, Green Bay	354	204	57.6	2593	7.32	17	4.8	75t	15	4.2	79.1

	Att.	Comp.	Pct. Comp.	Yards	Avg. Gain	TD	Pct. TD	Long	Int.	Pct. Int.	Rating Points
Anderson, Ken, Cincinnati	479	300	62.6	3754	7.84	29	6.1	74t	10	2.1	98.5
Morton, Craig, Denver	376	225	59.8	3195	8.50	21	5.6	95t	14	3.7	90.6
Fouts, Dan, San Diego	609	360	59.1	4802	7.89	33	5.4	67t	17	2.8	90.6
Bradshaw, Terry, Pittsburgh	370	201	54.3	2887	7.80	22	5.9	90t	14	3.8	83.7
Zorn, Jim, Seattle	397	236	59.4	2788	7.02	13	3.3	80t	9	2.3	82.3
Todd, Richard, New York Jets	497	279	56.1	3231	6.50	25	5.0	49	13	2.6	81.8
Jones, Bert, Baltimore	426	244	57.3	3094	7.26	21	4.9	67	20	4.7	76.8
Ferguson, Joe, Buffalo	498	252	50.6	3652	7.33	24	4.8	67t	20	4.0	74.1
Woodley, David, Miami	366	191	52.2	2470	6.75	12	3.3	69t	13	3.6	69.7
Stabler, Ken, Houston	285	165	57.9	1988	6.98	14	4.9	71t	18	6.3	69.5
Sipe, Brian, Cleveland	567	313	55.2	3876	6.84	17	3.0	62	25	4.4	68.3
Kenney, Bill, Kansas City	274	147	53.6	1983	7.24	9	3.3	64t	16	5.8	63.8
Grogan, Steve, New England	216	117	54.2	1859	8.61	7	3.2	76t	16	7.4	63.0
Cavanaugh, Matt, New England	219	115	52.5	1633	7.46	5	2.3	65	13	5.9	60.0
Wilson, Marc, Oakland	366	173	47.3	2311	6.31	14	3.8	66t	19	5.2	58.8

AFC Non-Qualifiers

	Att.	Comp.	Pct. Comp.	Yards	Avg. Gain	TD	Pct. TD	Long	Int.	Pct. Int.	Rating Points
McDonald, Paul, Cleveland	57	35	61.4	463	8.12	4	7.0	46	2	3.5	95.8
Nielsen, Gifford, Houston	93	60	64.5	709	7.62	5	5.4	44	3	3.2	92.3
Krieg, Dave, Seattle	112	64	57.1	843	7.53	7	6.3	57t	5	4.5	83.3
Schonert, Turk, Cincinnati	19	10	52.6	166	8.74	0	0.0	36	0	0.0	82.3
DeBerg, Steve, Denver	108	64	59.3	797	7.38	6	5.6	44	6	5.6	77.6
Fuller, Steve, Kansas City	134	77	57.5	934	6.97	3	2.2	53	4	3.0	73.9
Adkins, Sam, Seattle	13	7	53.8	96	7.38	1	7.7	31t	1	7.7	71.3
Strock, Don, Miami	130	79	60.8	901	6.93	6	4.6	52	8	6.2	71.1
Reaves, John, Houston	61	31	50.8	379	6.21	2	3.3	51t	2	3.3	67.6

Malone, Mark, Pittsburgh	88	45	51.1	553	6.28	3	3.4	30	5	5.7	58.4
Plunkett, Jim, Oakland	179	94	52.5	1045	5.84	4	2.2	42	9	5.0	56.7
Landry, Greg, Baltimore	29	14	48.3	195	6.72	0	0.0	34	2	3.4	56.2
Thompson, Jack, Cincinnati	49	21	42.9	267	5.45	1	2.0	21	2	4.1	50.1
Ryan, Pat, New York Jets	10	4	40.0	48	4.80	1	10.0	18	1	10.0	49.2
Luther, Ed, San Diego	15	7	46.7	68	4.53	1	6.7	25	1	6.7	32.0
Owen, Tom, New England	36	15	41.7	218	6.06	1	2.8	28	4	11.1	31.8
Humm, David, Baltimore	24	7	29.2	90	3.75	0	0.0	20	2	8.3	8.1

Less than 10 attempts

Chandler, Wes, San Diego	2	0	0.0	0	0.00	0	0.0	0	0	0.0	0.0
Collins, Anthony, New England	1	0	0.0	0	0.00	0	0.0	0	0	0.0	0.0
Cribbs, Joe, Buffalo	1	1	100.0	9	9.00	1	100.0	9t	1	100.0	0.0
Hadnot, James, Kansas City	1	0	0.0	0	0.00	0	0.0	0	0	0.0	0.0
Hill, Eddie, Miami	1	1	100.0	14	14.00	0	0.0	14	0	0.0	0.0
Jackson, Harold, New England	1	0	0.0	0	0.00	0	0.0	0	0	0.0	0.0
Johnson, Andy, New England	9	7	77.8	194	21.56	4	44.4	66t	1	11.1	0.0
Kreider, Steve, Cincinnati	3	1	33.3	13	4.33	0	0.0	13	0	0.0	0.0
Largent, Steve, Seattle	1	0	0.0	0	0.00	0	0.0	0	0	0.0	0.0
Leaks, Roosevelt, Buffalo	1	0	0.0	0	0.00	0	0.0	0	0	0.0	0.0
Marshall, Henry, Kansas City	1	0	0.0	0	0.00	0	0.0	0	1	100.0	0.0
Mike-Mayer, Nick, Buffalo	1	0	0.0	0	0.00	0	0.0	0	0	0.0	0.0
Muncie, Chuck, San Diego	1	1	100.0	3	3.00	1	100.0	3t	0	0.0	0.0
Nathan, Tony, Miami	1	0	0.0	0	0.00	0	0.0	0	0	0.0	0.0
Parsley, Cliff, Houston	2	2	100.0	43	21.50	0	0.0	31	1	100.0	0.0
Reed, Tony, Denver	1	0	0.0	0	0.00	0	0.0	0	0	0.0	0.0
Robinson, Matt, Buffalo	2	0	0.0	0	0.00	0	0.0	0	0	0.0	0.0
Stoudt, Cliff, Pittsburgh	3	1	33.3	17	5.67	0	0.0	17	0	0.0	0.0
West, Jeff, Seattle	1	0	0.0	0	0.00	0	0.0	0	0	0.0	0.0
Winslow, Kellen, San Diego	2	0	0.0	0	0.00	0	0.0	0	0	0.0	0.0

t indicates touchdown.

NFC PASSING—INDIVIDUAL QUALIFIERS

	Att.	Comp.	Pct. Comp.	Yards	Avg. Gain	TD	Pct. TD	Long	Int.	Pct. Int.	Rating Points
Montana, Joe, San Francisco	488	311	63.7	3565	7.31	19	3.9	78t	12	2.5	88.2
White, Danny, Dallas	391	223	57.0	3098	7.92	22	5.6	73t	13	3.3	87.5
Bartkowski, Steve, Atlanta	533	297	55.7	3829	7.18	30	5.6	73t	23	4.3	79.2
Dickey, Lynn, Green Bay	354	204	57.6	2593	7.32	17	4.8	70t	15	4.2	79.1
Theismann, Joe, Washington	496	293	59.1	3568	7.19	19	3.8	75t	20	4.0	77.3
Williams, Doug, Tampa Bay	471	238	50.5	3563	7.56	19	4.0	79t	14	3.0	76.5
Simms, Phil, New York Giants	316	172	54.4	2031	6.43	11	3.5	84t	9	2.8	74.2
Jaworski, Ron, Philadelphia	461	250	54.2	3095	6.71	23	5.0	80	20	4.3	74.0
Hipple, Eric, Detroit	279	140	50.2	2358	8.45	14	5.0	85t	15	5.4	73.3
Kramer, Tommy, Minnesota	593	322	54.3	3912	6.60	26	4.4	94t	24	4.0	72.8
Hart, Jim, St. Louis	241	134	55.6	1694	7.03	11	4.6	63	14	5.8	68.9
Haden, Pat, Los Angeles	267	138	51.7	1815	6.80	9	3.4	58t	13	4.9	64.4
Manning, Archie, New Orleans	232	134	57.8	1447	6.24	5	2.2	67t	11	4.7	64.0
Lomax, Neil, St. Louis	236	119	50.4	1575	6.67	4	1.7	55	10	4.2	60.1
Evans, Vince, Chicago	436	195	44.7	2354	5.40	11	2.5	85t	20	4.6	51.0
NFC Non-Qualifiers	Att.	Comp.	Pct. Comp.	Yards	Avg. Gain	TD	Pct. TD	Long	Int.	Pct. Int.	Rating Points
Phipps, Mike, Chicago	17	11	64.7	171	10.06	2	11.8	43t	0	0.0	137.3
Pisarcik, Joe, Philadelphia	15	8	53.3	154	10.27	2	13.3	44t	2	13.3	89.3
Rutledge, Jeff, Los Angeles	50	30	60.0	442	8.84	3	6.0	64	4	8.0	75.6
Benjamin, Guy, San Francisco	26	15	57.7	171	6.58	1	3.8	27t	1	3.8	74.4
Danielson, Gary, Detroit	96	56	58.3	784	8.17	3	3.1	45	5	5.2	73.4
Whitehurst, David, Green Bay	128	66	51.6	792	6.19	7	5.5	46t	5	3.9	73.0
Dils, Steve, Minnesota	102	54	52.9	607	5.95	1	1.0	44	2	2.0	66.0
Carano, Glenn, Dallas	45	16	35.6	235	5.22	1	2.2	55	1	2.2	51.7
Komlo, Jeff, Detroit	57	29	50.9	290	5.09	1	1.8	46	3	5.3	49.6
Wilson, Dave, New Orleans	159	82	51.6	1058	6.65	1	0.6	50	11	6.9	46.1
Moroski, Mike, Atlanta	26	12	46.2	132	5.08	0	0.0	22	1	3.8	45.9

Player	Att	Comp	Pct	Yds	Avg	TD	TD%	Long	Int	Int%	Rating
Brunner, Scott, New York Giants	190	79	41.6	978	5.15	5	2.6	43	11	5.8	42.7
Avellini, Bob, Chicago	32	15	46.9	185	5.78	1	3.1	72t	3	9.4	36.4
Flick, Tom, Washington	27	13	48.1	143	5.30	0	0.0	33	2	7.4	33.4
Scott, Bobby, New Orleans	46	20	43.5	245	5.33	1	2.2	31	5	10.9	28.3
Campbell, Rich, Green Bay	30	15	50.0	168	5.60	0	0.0	27	4	13.3	27.5
Pastorini, Dan, Los Angeles	152	64	42.1	719	4.73	2	1.3	46	14	9.2	22.9
Wilson, Wade, Minnesota	13	6	46.2	48	3.69	0	0.0	22	2	15.4	16.4

Less than 10 attempts

Player	Att	Comp	Pct	Yds	Avg	TD	TD%	Long	Int	Int%
Baschnagel, Brian, Chicago	1	1	100.0	18	18.00	0	0.0	18	0	0.0
Brown, Ted, Minnesota	1	0	0.0	0	0.00	0	0.0	0	1	100.0
Clark, Dwight, San Francisco	1	0	0.0	0	0.00	0	0.0	0	0	0.0
Corral, Frank, Los Angeles	1	0	0.0	0	0.00	0	0.0	0	0	0.0
Easley, Walt, San Francisco	1	1	100.0	5	5.00	0	0.0	5	0	0.0
Ellis, Gerry, Green Bay	2	1	50.0	23	11.50	0	0.0	23	0	0.0
Fusina, Chuck, Tampa Bay	1	1	100.0	2	2.00	1	100.0	2t	0	0.0
Guman, Mike, Los Angeles	1	1	100.0	7	7.00	1	100.0	7t	0	0.0
House, Kevin, Tampa Bay	1	0	0.0	0	0.00	0	0.0	0	0	0.0
James, John, Atlanta	3	2	66.7	25	8.33	0	0.0	14	0	0.0
Jones, June, Atlanta	6	2	33.3	25	4.17	0	0.0	19	1	16.7
Kemp, Jeff, Los Angeles	2	1	50.0	20	10.00	0	0.0	20	0	0.0
Merkens, Guido, New Orleans	2	1	50.0	8	4.00	1	50.0	8t	0	0.0
Myers, Tommy, New Orleans	1	0	0.0	0	0.00	0	0.0	0	0	0.0
Parsons, Bob, Chicago	2	0	0.0	0	0.00	0	0.0	0	0	0.0
Payton, Walter, Chicago	2	0	0.0	0	0.00	0	0.0	0	0	0.0
Pearson, Drew, Dallas	2	2	100.0	81	40.50	1	50.0	59	0	0.0
Scott, Freddie, Detroit	1	0	0.0	0	0.00	0	0.0	0	0	0.0
Skladany, Tom, Detroit	3	3	100.0	43	14.33	0	0.0	19	0	0.0
Solomon, Freddie, San Francisco	1	1	100.0	25	25.00	0	0.0	25	0	0.0
Springs, Ron, Dallas	1	0	0.0	0	0.00	0	0.0	0	1	100.0
Washington, Joe, Washington	2	1	50.0	32	16.00	0	0.0	32	0	0.0

t indicates touchdown.

PASS RECEIVING

INDIVIDUAL CHAMPIONS
  AFC: 88—Kellen Winslow, San Diego
  NFC: 85—Dwight Clark, San Francisco
YARDS
  NFC: 1358—Alfred Jenkins, Atlanta
  AFC: 1244—Frank Lewis, Buffalo
        1244—Steve Watson, Denver
YARDS PER RECEPTION
  AFC: 23.4—Stanley Morgan, New England (44 receptions, 1029 yards)
  NFC: 21.0—Kevin House, Tampa Bay (56 receptions, 1176 yards)
TOUCHDOWNS
  AFC: 13—Steve Watson, Denver
  NFC: 13—Alfred Jenkins, Atlanta
LONGEST
  AFC: 95 yards—Steve Watson, Denver vs. Detroit, October 11 (from Craig
        Morton)—TD
  NFC: 94 yards—Leonard Thompson, Detroit vs. Chicago, October 19 (from
        Eric Hipple)—TD
MOST RECEPTIONS, GAME
  NFC: 15—William Andrews, Atlanta vs. Pittsburgh, November 15 (124
        yards)
  AFC: 13—Kellen Winslow, San Diego vs. Oakland, November 22 (144
        yards)
MOST YARDS, GAME
  AFC: 210—Nat Moore, Miami vs. New York Jets, October 4 (7 receptions)
  NFC: 179—James Lofton, Green Bay vs. Atlanta, September 13 (8
        receptions)
        179—Alfred Jenkins, Atlanta vs. New Orleans, November 1 (5
        receptions)
TEAM LEADERS
  AFC: BALTIMORE: 50, Randy McMillan; BUFFALO: 70, Frank Lewis; CIN-
        CINNATI: 71, Dan Ross; CLEVELAND: 69, Ozzie Newsome; DENVER:
        60, Steve Watson; HOUSTON: 40, Ken Burrough; KANSAS CITY: 63,
        J. T. Smith; MIAMI: 53, Duriel Harris; NEW ENGLAND: 46, Don Has-
        selbeck; NEW YORK: 52, Bruce Harper; OAKLAND: 52, Derrick Ram-
        sey; PITTSBURGH: 63, John Stallworth; SAN DIEGO: 88, Kellen
        Winslow; SEATTLE: 75, Steve Largent.
  NFC: ATLANTA: 81, William Andrews; CHICAGO: 41, Walter Payton; DAL-
        LAS: 46, Tony Hill; DETROIT: 53, Freddie Scott; GREEN BAY: 71,
        James Lofton; LOS ANGELES: 49, Preston Dennard; MINNESOTA:
        83, Ted Brown; NEW ORLEANS: 38, Jack Holmes; NEW YORK: 51,
        Johnny Perkins; PHILADELPHIA: 61, Harold Carmichael; ST. LOUIS:
        66, Pat Tilley; SAN FRANCISCO: 85, Dwight Clark; TAMPA BAY: 56,
        Kevin House; WASHINGTON: 70, Joe Washington.

NFL TOP 10 PASS RECEIVERS

	No.	Yards	Avg.	Long	TD
Winslow, Kellen, San Diego	88	1075	12.2	67t	10
Clark, Dwight, San Francisco	85	1105	13.0	78t	4
Brown, Ted, Minnesota	83	694	8.4	63	2
Andrews, William, Atlanta	81	735	9.1	70t	2
Senser, Joe, Minnesota	79	1004	12.7	53	8
Largent, Steve, Seattle	75	1224	16.3	57t	9
Lofton, James, Green Bay	71	1294	18.2	75t	8
Ross, Dan, Cincinnati	71	910	12.8	37	5
Jenkins, Alfred, Atlanta	70	1358	19.4	67	13
Lewis, Frank, Buffalo	70	1244	17.8	33	4
Joiner, Charlie, San Diego	70	1188	17.0	57	7
Washington, Joe, Washington	70	558	8.0	32	3

NFL TOP 10 PASS RECEIVERS BY YARDS

	Yards	No.	Avg.	Long	TD
Jenkins, Alfred, Atlanta	1358	70	19.4	67	13
Lofton, James, Green Bay	1294	71	18.2	75t	8
Lewis, Frank, Buffalo	1244	70	17.8	33	4
Watson, Steve, Denver	1244	60	20.7	95t	13
Largent, Steve, Seattle	1224	75	16.3	57t	9
Joiner, Charlie, San Diego	1188	70	17.0	57	7
House, Kevin, Tampa Bay	1176	56	21.0	84t	9
Chandler, Wes, New Orleans-San Diego	1142	69	16.6	51t	6
Clark, Dwight, San Francisco	1105	85	13.0	78t	4
Stallworth, John, Pittsburgh	1098	63	17.4	55	5

AFC PASS RECEIVING — INDIVIDUAL

	No.	Yards	Avg.	Long	TD
Winslow, Kellen, San Diego	88	1075	12.2	67t	10
Largent, Steve, Seattle	75	1224	16.3	57t	9
Ross, Dan, Cincinnati	71	910	12.8	37	5
Lewis, Frank, Buffalo	70	1244	17.8	33	4
Joiner, Charlie, San Diego	70	1188	17.0	57	7
Chandler, Wes, N.O.-S.D.	69	1142	16.6	51t	6
Newsome, Ozzie, Cleveland	69	1002	14.5	62	6
Collinsworth, Cris, Cincinnati	67	1009	15.1	74t	8
Pruitt, Greg, Cleveland	65	636	9.8	33	4
Stallworth, John, Pittsburgh	63	1098	17.4	55	5
Smith, J. T., Kansas City	63	852	13.5	42	2
Pruitt, Mike, Cleveland	63	442	7.0	21	1
Watson, Steve, Denver	60	1244	20.7	95t	13
Butler, Jerry, Buffalo	55	842	15.3	67t	8
Harris, Duriel, Miami	53	911	17.2	55	2
Ramsey, Derrick, Oakland	52	674	13.0	66t	4
Preston, Dave, Denver	52	507	9.8	37	0
Harper, Bruce, New York Jets	52	459	8.8	24	1

Pass Receiving

	No.	Yards	Avg.	Long	TD
McMillan, Randy, Baltimore	50	466	9.3	31	1
Nathan, Tony, Miami	50	452	9.0	31	3
Walker, Wesley, New York Jets	47	770	16.4	49	9
Butler, Ray, Baltimore	46	832	18.1	67t	9
Hasselbeck, Don, New England	46	808	17.6	51	6
McCullum, Sam, Seattle	46	567	12.3	36t	3
Brooks, James, San Diego	46	329	7.2	29t	3
Johnson, Pete, Cincinnati	46	320	7.0	33	4
Morgan, Stanley, New England	44	1029	23.4	76t	6
Smith, Sherman, Seattle	44	406	9.2	28	1
Muncie, Chuck, San Diego	43	362	8.4	32	0
Branch, Cliff, Oakland	41	635	15.5	53	1
Cunningham, Bennie, Pittsburgh	41	574	14.0	30	3
Burrough, Ken, Houston	40	668	16.7	71t	7
Cribbs, Joe, Buffalo	40	603	15.1	65t	7
Jackson, Harold, New England	39	669	17.2	45	0
Barkum, Jerome, New York Jets	39	495	12.7	40t	7
Renfro, Mike, Houston	39	451	11.6	43	1
Johnson, Andy, New England	39	429	11.0	36	1
Marshall, Henry, Kansas City	38	620	16.3	64t	4
Carr, Roger, Baltimore	38	584	15.4	43	3
Odoms, Riley, Denver	38	516	13.6	28	5
Curtis, Isaac, Cincinnati	37	609	16.5	68	2
Kreider, Steve, Cincinnati	37	520	14.1	46	5
Dickey, Curtis, Baltimore	37	419	11.3	50	3
Harris, Franco, Pittsburgh	37	250	6.8	26	1
McCauley, Don, Baltimore	36	347	9.6	31	2
Campbell, Earl, Houston	36	156	4.3	17	0
Hughes, David, Seattle	35	263	7.5	22	2
Swann, Lynn, Pittsburgh	34	505	14.9	44	5
Reed, Tony, Denver	34	317	9.3	33	0
Casper, Dave, Houston	33	572	17.3	52t	8
Brammer, Mark, Buffalo	33	365	11.1	24	2
Vigorito, Tommy, Miami	33	237	7.2	31t	2
Upchurch, Rick, Denver	32	550	17.2	63	3
Logan, Dave, Cleveland	31	497	16.0	40t	4
Feacher, Ricky, Cleveland	29	654	22.6	48	3
Cefalo, Jimmy, Miami	29	631	21.8	69t	3
Smith, Jim, Pittsburgh	29	571	19.7	46t	7
Dixon, Al, Kansas City	29	356	12.3	48	2
Brown, Theotis, St. Louis-Seattle	29	328	11.3	51	0
Armstrong, Adger, Houston	29	278	9.6	48	1
Jensen, Derrick, Oakland	28	271	9.7	21	0
Alexander, Charles, Cincinnati	28	262	9.4	65t	1
Rucker, Reggie, Cleveland	27	532	19.7	49	1
Holston, Michael, Houston	27	427	15.8	50t	2
Doornink, Dan, Seattle	27	350	13.0	80t	4
White, Charles, Cleveland	27	219	8.1	21	0
King, Kenny, Oakland	27	216	8.0	30	0
Chandler, Bob, Oakland	26	458	17.6	45	4
Moore, Nat, Miami	26	452	17.4	52	2
Collins, Anthony, New England	26	232	8.9	22	0
Dierking, Scott, New York Jets	26	228	8.8	23	1
Parros, Rick, Denver	25	216	8.6	26	1

	Att.	Yards	Avg.	Long	TD
Rose, Joe, Miami	23	316	13.7	50	2
Hadnot, James, Kansas City	23	215	9.3	20	0
Whittington, Arthur, Oakland	23	213	9.3	22	2
Bradshaw, Morris, Oakland	22	298	13.5	29t	3
Sievers, Eric, San Diego	22	276	12.5	32	3
Delaney, Joe, Kansas City	22	246	11.2	61	0
McCall, Reese, Baltimore	21	314	15.0	65t	2
Sawyer, John, Seattle	21	272	13.0	30	0
Jones, Johnny, New York Jets	20	342	17.1	47t	3
Griffin, Archie, Cincinnati	20	160	8.0	17	1
Scales, Dwight, San Diego	19	429	22.6	60t	1
Coleman, Ronnie, Houston	19	211	11.1	24	0
Pollard, Frank, Pittsburgh	19	156	8.2	26	0
McNeil, Freeman, New York Jets	18	171	9.5	18	1
Augustyniak, Mike, New York Jets	18	144	8.0	15	0
Egloff, Ron, Denver	17	231	13.6	40	1
Rome, Stan, Kansas City	17	203	11.9	23	1
Dixon, Zachary, Baltimore	17	169	9.9	41	1
Hill, Calvin, Cleveland	17	150	8.8	23	2
Newton, Tom, New York Jets	17	104	6.1	13	0
Jones, Bobby, New York Jets	16	239	14.9	36t	1
Miller, Cleo, Cleveland	16	139	8.7	17	0
Moses, Haven, Denver	15	246	16.4	30	1
Jessie, Ron, Buffalo	15	200	13.3	44	0
Hardy, Bruce, Miami	15	174	11.6	21	0
Gaffney, Derrick, New York Jets	14	246	17.6	39	0
Lee, Ronnie, Miami	14	64	4.6	11	1
Barber, Mike, Houston	13	190	14.6	35	1
Harris, M. L., Cincinnati	13	181	13.9	42	2
Chester, Raymond, Oakland	13	93	7.2	15	1
Long, Kevin, New York Jets	13	66	5.1	18	3
Tatupu, Mosi, New England	12	132	11.0	41	1
Williams, Clarence, San Diego	12	108	9.0	15	1
Cunningham, Sam, New England	12	92	7.7	12	0
Hill, Eddie, Miami	12	73	6.1	16	1
Burke, Randy, Baltimore	10	153	15.3	24	0
Hooks, Roland, Buffalo	10	140	14.0	37	2
Cappelletti, John, San Diego	10	126	12.6	25	1
Hawkins, Frank, Oakland	10	109	10.9	35	0
Barnwell, Malcolm, Oakland	9	190	21.1	61t	1
Johns, Paul, Seattle	8	131	16.4	34	1
Christensen, Todd, Oakland	8	115	14.4	30	2
Thornton, Sidney, Pittsburgh	8	78	9.8	30	0
McKnight, Ted, Kansas City	8	77	9.6	23	0
Carson, Carlos, Kansas City	7	179	25.6	53t	1
Dawson, Lin, New England	7	126	18.0	42	0
Westbrook, Don, New England	7	122	17.4	32	2
Calhoun, Don, New England	7	71	10.1	20	0
van Eeghen, Mark, Oakland	7	60	8.6	13	0
Lane, Eric, Seattle	7	58	8.3	22	0
Leaks, Roosevelt, Buffalo	7	51	7.3	13	0
Brown, Curtis, Buffalo	7	46	6.6	10	1
Verser, David, Cincinnati	6	161	26.8	73t	2
McInally, Pat, Cincinnati	6	68	11.3	20	0

Pass Receiving

	Att.	Yards	Avg.	Long	TD
Lytle, Rob, Denver	6	47	7.8	14t	1
Franklin, Cleveland, Baltimore	6	39	6.5	10	0
Jackson, Billy, Kansas City	6	31	5.2	10	1
Scott, Willie, Kansas City	5	72	14.4	26	1
Toler, Ken, New England	5	70	14.0	23	0
Piccone, Lou, Buffalo	5	65	13.0	16	0
Tice, Mike, Seattle	5	47	9.4	14	0
McCutcheon, Lawrence, Buffalo	5	40	8.0	17	0
Wilson, Tim, Houston	5	33	6.6	11	0
Jodat, Jim, Seattle	4	52	13.0	26	0
McGrath, Mark, Seattle	4	47	11.8	16	0
Ferguson, Vagas, New England	4	39	9.8	20	0
Barnett, Buster, Buffalo	4	36	9.0	16	1
Davis, Russell, Pittsburgh	4	34	8.5	19	0
Hawthorne, Greg, Pittsburgh	4	23	5.8	12	0
Bennett, Woody, Miami	4	22	5.5	10	0
Manning, Wade, Denver	3	49	16.3	34	0
Pennywell, Carlos, New England	3	49	16.3	22t	1
Brooks, Billy, San Diego-Houston	3	37	12.3	21	0
Canada, Larry, Denver	3	37	12.3	20	1
Bledsoe, Curtis, Kansas City	3	27	9.0	17	0
Wright, James, Denver	3	22	7.3	14	1
Grossman, Randy, Pittsburgh	3	19	6.3	14t	1
Moore, Jeff, Seattle	3	18	6.0	10	0
Franklin, Andra, Miami	3	6	2.0	3t	1
Sweeney, Calvin, Pittsburgh	2	53	26.5	32	0
Fulton, Danny, Cleveland	2	38	19.0	27	0
Smith, Tim, Houston	2	37	18.5	25	0
Murphy, James, Kansas City	2	36	18.0	22	0
Franklin, Byron, Buffalo	2	29	14.5	16	0
Grogan, Steve, New England	2	27	13.5	16	0
Sherwin, Tim, Baltimore	2	19	9.5	11	0
Lewis, Kenny, New York Jets	2	14	7.0	8	0
Howell, Steve, Miami	2	9	4.5	5	0
Malone, Mark, Pittsburgh	1	90	90.0	90t	1
DeRoo, Brian, Baltimore	1	38	38.0	38	0
Adams, Willis, Cleveland	1	24	24.0	24	0
Willis, Chester, Oakland	1	24	24.0	24	0
Holohan, Pete, San Diego	1	14	14.0	14	0
Raible, Steve, Seattle	1	12	12.0	12	0
Studdard, Dave, Denver	1	10	10.0	10	0
August, Steve, Seattle	1	9	9.0	9	0
Cavanaugh, Matt, New England	1	9	9.0	9	0
Oden, McDonald, Cleveland	1	6	6.0	6	0
Moser, Rick, Pittsburgh	1	5	5.0	5t	1
Bauer, Hank, San Diego	1	4	4.0	4t	1
Boyd, Dennis, Seattle	1	3	3.0	3t	1
Williams, Mike, Kansas City	1	3	3.0	3	0
Pinney, Ray, Pittsburgh	1	1	1.0	1t	1
Todd, Richard, New York Jets	1	1	1.0	1	0
Hargrove, Jimmy, Cincinnati	1	0	0.0	0	0
Huff, Ken, Baltimore	1	−1	−1.0	−1	0

t indicates touchdown
Leader based on most passes caught.

AFC TOP 25 PASS RECEIVERS BY YARDS

	Yards	No.	Avg.	Long	TD
Lewis, Frank, Buffalo	1244	70	17.8	33	4
Watson, Steve, Denver	1244	60	20.7	95t	13
Largent, Steve, Seattle	1224	75	16.3	57t	9
Joiner, Charlie, San Diego	1188	70	17.0	57	7
Chandler, Wes, New Orleans-San Diego	1142	69	16.6	51t	6
Stallworth, John, Pittsburgh	1098	63	17.4	55	5
Winslow, Kellen, San Diego	1075	88	12.2	67t	10
Morgan, Stanley, New England	1029	44	23.4	76t	6
Collinsworth, Cris, Cincinnati	1009	67	15.1	74t	8
Newsome, Ozzie, Cleveland	1002	69	14.5	62	6
Harris, Duriel, Miami	911	53	17.2	55	2
Smith, J. T., Kansas City	852	63	13.5	42	2
Butler, Jerry, Buffalo	842	55	15.3	67t	8
Butler, Ray, Baltimore	832	46	18.1	67t	9
Hasselbeck, Don, New England	808	46	17.6	51	6
Walker, Wesley, New York Jets	770	47	16.4	49	9
Ramsey, Derrick, Oakland	674	52	13.0	66t	4
Jackson, Harold, New England	669	39	17.2	45	0
Burrough, Ken, Houston	668	40	16.7	71t	7
Feacher, Ricky, Cleveland	654	29	22.6	48	3
Pruitt, Greg, Cleveland	636	65	9.8	33	4
Branch, Cliff, Oakland	635	41	15.5	53	1
Cefalo, Jimmy, Miami	631	29	21.8	69t	3
Marshall, Henry, Kansas City	620	38	16.3	64t	4
Curtis, Isaac, Cincinnati	609	37	16.5	68	2

NFC PASS RECEIVING — INDIVIDUAL

	No.	Yards	Avg.	Long	TD
Clark, Dwight, San Francisco	85	1105	13.0	78t	4
Brown, Ted, Minnesota	83	694	8.4	63	2
Andrews, William, Atlanta	81	735	9.1	70t	2
Senser, Joe, Minnesota	79	1004	12.7	53	8
Lofton, James, Green Bay	71	1294	18.2	75t	8
Jenkins, Alfred, Atlanta	70	1358	19.4	67	13
Washington, Joe, Washington	70	558	8.0	32	3
Tilley, Pat, St. Louis	66	1040	15.8	75	3
White, Sammy, Minnesota	66	1001	15.2	53	3
Ellis, Gerry, Green Bay	65	499	7.7	46t	3
Carmichael, Harold, Philadelphia	61	1028	16.9	85t	6
Solomon, Freddie, San Francisco	59	969	16.4	60t	8
Rashad, Ahmad, Minnesota	58	884	15.2	53	7
House, Kevin, Tampa Bay	56	1176	21.0	84t	9
Monk, Art, Washington	56	894	16.0	79t	6
Coffman, Paul, Green Bay	55	687	12.5	29	4
Cain, Lynn, Atlanta	55	421	7.7	28	2
Scott, Freddie, Detroit	53	1022	19.3	48	5
Perkins, Johnny, New York Giants	51	858	16.8	80	6
Cooper, Earl, San Francisco	51	477	9.4	50	0
Anderson, Ottis, St. Louis	51	387	7.6	27	0
Dennard, Preston, Los Angeles	49	821	16.8	64	4
Montgomery, Wilbert, Phil.	49	521	10.6	35	2
Metcalf, Terry, Washington	48	595	12.4	52	0

Pass Receiving

	Att.	Yards	Avg.	Long	TD
Wilder, James, Tampa Bay	48	507	10.6	38	1
Hill, Tony, Dallas	46	953	20.7	63t	4
Springs, Ron, Dallas	46	359	7.8	32t	2
Giles, Jimmie, Tampa Bay	45	786	17.5	81t	6
Tyler, Wendell, Los Angeles	45	436	9.7	67t	5
Young, Rickey, Minnesota	43	296	6.9	22	2
Shirk, Gary, New York Giants	42	445	10.6	46	3
Payton, Walter, Chicago	41	379	9.2	30	2
Jefferson, John, Green Bay	39	632	16.2	41	4
Margerum, Ken, Chicago	39	584	15.0	41	1
Pearson, Drew, Dallas	38	614	16.2	42t	3
Smith, Charles, Philadelphia	38	564	14.8	45	4
Holmes, Jack, New Orleans	38	206	5.4	19	0
Jackson, Alfred, Atlanta	37	604	16.3	49	6
Young, Charle, San Francisco	37	400	10.8	29	5
Carpenter, Rob, Hou.-N.Y. Giants	37	281	7.6	37	1
Campfield, Billy, Philadelphia	36	326	9.1	29t	3
Baschnagel, Brian, Chicago	34	554	16.3	72t	3
Green, Roy, St. Louis	33	708	21.5	60	4
Hill, David, Detroit	33	462	14.0	34	4
Suhey, Matt, Chicago	33	168	5.1	15	0
Miller, Junior, Atlanta	32	398	12.4	37	3
Dorsett, Tony, Dallas	32	325	10.2	73t	2
Waddy, Bill, Los Angeles	31	460	14.8	46	0
Wilson, Wayne, New Orleans	31	384	12.4	55	4
Thompson, Leonard, Detroit	30	550	18.3	94t	3
Francis, Wallace, Atlanta	30	441	14.7	36	4
Merkens, Guido, New Orleans	29	458	15.8	50	1
Warren, Don, Washington	29	335	11.6	32	1
Sims, Billy, Detroit	28	451	16.1	81t	2
Thompson, Ricky, Washington	28	423	15.1	57	4
Bright, Leon, New York Giants	28	291	10.4	36	0
Watts, Rickey, Chicago	27	465	17.2	42t	3
Gray, Mel, St. Louis	27	310	11.5	41t	2
Hofer, Paul, San Francisco	27	244	9.0	22	0
Huckleby, Harlan, Green Bay	27	221	8.2	39t	3
Patton, Ricky, San-Francisco	27	195	7.2	31t	1
Seay, Virgil, Washington	26	472	18.2	60	3
Johnson, Butch, Dallas	25	552	22.1	55	5
LeCount, Terry, Minnesota	24	425	17.7	43t	2
Eckwood, Jerry, Tampa Bay	24	213	8.9	33	0
Hardy, Larry, New Orleans	23	275	12.0	27	1
Tyler, Toussaint, New Orleans	23	135	5.9	18	0
Gray, Earnest, New York Giants	22	360	16.4	45	2
Bryant, Cullen, Los Angeles	22	160	7.3	39	0
Bell, Theo, Tampa Bay	21	318	15.1	58t	2
Groth, Jeff, New Orleans	20	380	19.0	54	1
Jones, Gordon, Tampa Bay	20	276	13.8	44	1
Arnold, Walt, Los Angeles	20	212	10.6	24	2
King, Horace, Detroit	20	211	10.6	41	1
Krepfle, Keith, Philadelphia	20	210	10.5	26	5
DuPree, Billy Joe, Dallas	19	214	11.3	33t	2
Morris, Wayne, St. Louis	19	165	8.7	21	0
Friede, Mike, New York Giants	18	250	13.9	43	1

	Att.	Yards	Avg.	Long	TD
Kane, Rick, Detroit	18	187	10.4	40	1
Galbreath, Tony, Minnesota	18	144	8.0	23	0
Guman, Mike, Los Angeles	18	130	7.2	14	0
Williams, Dave, Chicago	18	126	7.0	18t	2
Bussey, Dexter, Detroit	18	92	5.1	16	0
Cosbie, Doug, Dallas	17	225	13.2	28	5
Hill, Drew, Los Angeles	16	355	22.2	45	3
Rogers, George, New Orleans	16	126	7.9	25	0
LaFleur, Greg, St. Louis	14	190	13.6	27t	2
Mullady, Tom, New York Giants	14	136	9.7	21	1
Harrell, Willard, St. Louis	14	131	9.4	62t	1
Perry, Leon, New York Giants	13	140	10.8	24	1
Caster, Richard, N. Orleans-Wash.	12	185	15.4	31	0
Childs, Henry, Los Angeles	12	145	12.1	39	1
Owens, James, Tampa Bay	12	145	12.1	35	0
Giaquinto, Nick, Miami-Wash.	12	93	7.8	25	2
Middleton, Terdell, Green Bay	12	86	7.2	27	1
Walker, Rick, Washington	11	112	10.2	24	1
Harmon, Clarence, Washington	11	98	8.9	23	0
Nichols, Mark, Detroit	10	222	22.2	59	1
Miller, Willie, Los Angeles	10	147	14.7	20	0
Earl, Robin, Chicago	10	118	11.8	24	1
Oliver, Hubert, Philadelphia	10	37	3.7	27	0
Anderson, Marcus, Chicago	9	243	27.0	85t	2
Henry, Wally, Philadelphia	9	145	16.1	44t	2
Wilson, Mike, San Francisco	9	125	13.9	27t	1
Easley, Walt, San Francisco	9	62	6.9	21	0
Kotar, Doug, New York Giants	9	32	3.6	11	0
Harrington, Perry, Philadelphia	9	27	3.0	12	0
Parker, Rodney, Philadelphia	8	168	21.0	55t	2
Norris, Ulysses, Detroit	8	132	16.5	34	0
Mistler, John, New York Giants	8	119	14.9	31	1
Thompson, Aundra, G.B.-N.O.	8	111	13.9	25	0
Bell, Ricky, Tampa Bay	8	92	11.5	22	0
Saldi, Jay, Dallas	8	82	10.3	18	1
Williams, Brooks, N. Orleans-Chi.	8	82	10.3	16	0
Martini, Rich, New Orleans	8	72	9.0	15	0
Taylor, Billy, New York Giants	8	71	8.9	39	0
Smith, Ron, San Diego-Phil.	7	168	24.0	42	2
Brenner, Hoby, New Orleans	7	143	20.4	34	0
Moore, Jeff, Los Angeles	7	105	15.0	35	0
Elliott, Lenvil, San Francisco	7	81	11.6	19	0
Jackson, Wilbur, Washington	7	51	7.3	16	0
Bruer, Bob, Minnesota	7	38	5.4	10	3
Spagnola, John, Philadelphia	6	83	13.8	28	0
Marsh, Doug, St. Louis	6	80	13.3	20	1
Riggins, John, Washington	6	59	9.8	22	0
Giammona, Louie, Philadelphia	6	54	9.0	19	1
Jones, James, Dallas	6	37	6.2	16	0
Mitchell, Stump, St. Louis	6	35	5.8	16	1
Stief, Dave, St. Louis	5	77	15.4	29	1
Combs, Chris, St. Louis	5	54	10.8	13	0
Jensen, Jim, Green Bay	5	49	9.8	16	0
Young, Dave, New York Giants	5	49	9.8	15	1

Pass Receiving

	No.	Yards	Avg.	Long	TD
Thomas, Jewerl, Los Angeles	5	37	7.4	13	0
Ramson, Eason, San Francisco	4	45	11.3	16	0
Obradovich, Jim, Tampa Bay	4	42	10.5	16	1
Thompson, Vince, Detroit	4	40	10.0	17	0
Porter, Tracy, Detroit	3	63	21.0	27t	1
Donley, Doug, Dallas	3	32	10.7	17	0
Floyd, John, St. Louis	3	32	10.7	16	0
Lewis, Gary, Green Bay	3	31	10.3	15	0
Ring, Bill, San Francisco	3	28	9.3	21	1
Jackson, Louis, New York Giants	3	25	8.3	19	0
Shumann, Mike, San Francisco	3	21	7.0	8	0
McCrary, Gregg, Washington	3	13	4.3	12	0
Forte, Ike, New York Giants	3	11	3.7	6	0
Lawrence, Amos, San Francisco	3	10	3.3	5	0
Mayberry, James, Atlanta	3	4	1.3	6	0
Davis, Johnny, San Francisco	3	−1	−0.3	3	0
Lewis, Leo, Minnesota	2	58	29.0	52	0
Harris, Ike, New Orleans	2	33	16.5	20	0
Nixon, Fred, Green Bay	2	27	13.5	19	0
Callicutt, Ken, Detroit	2	24	12.0	16	0
Harrell, Sam, Minnesota	2	23	11.5	17	0
Cobb, Mike, Chicago	2	20	10.0	11	0
Banks, Gordon, New Orleans	2	18	9.0	12	0
Mikeska, Russ, Atlanta	2	16	8.0	11	0
Matthews, Bo, New York Giants	2	13	6.5	11	0
Rogers, Jimmy, New Orleans	2	12	6.0	9	0
Harper, Roland, Chicago	2	10	5.0	8	0
Ivery, Eddie Lee, Green Bay	2	10	5.0	8	0
McClendon, Willie, Chicago	2	4	2.0	4	0
Newhouse, Robert, Dallas	1	21	21.0	21	0
Cobb, Garry, Detroit	1	19	19.0	19	0
Harris, Al, Chicago	1	18	18.0	18	0
Carter, Gerald, Tampa Bay	1	10	10.0	10	0
Strong, Ray, Atlanta	1	9	9.0	9	0
Pittman, Danny, New York Giants	1	8	8.0	8	0
Murray, Calvin, Philadelphia	1	7	7.0	7	0
Stauch, Scott, New Orleans	1	7	7.0	7	0
Zanders, Emanuel, Chicago	1	7	7.0	7	0
Cassidy, Ron, Green Bay	1	6	6.0	6	0
Lafary, Dave, New Orleans	1	5	5.0	5	0
Peets, Brian, San Francisco	1	5	5.0	5	0
Wonsley, Otis, Washington	1	5	5.0	5	0
Atkins, Steve, Green Bay	1	2	2.0	2	0
Swanke, Karl, Green Bay	1	2	2.0	2t	1
Bostic, Jeff, Washington	1	−4	−4.0	−4	0
Russell, Booker, Philadelphia	1	−5	−5.0	−5	0

t indicates touchdown.
Leader based on most passes caught.

NFC TOP 25 PASS RECEIVERS BY YARDS

	Yards	No.	Avg.	Long	TD
Jenkins, Alfred, Atlanta	1358	70	19.4	67	13
Lofton, James, Green Bay	1294	71	18.2	75t	8
House, Kevin, Tampa Bay	1176	56	21.0	84t	9
Clark, Dwight, San Francisco	1105	85	13.0	78t	4
Tilley, Pat, St. Louis	1040	66	15.8	75	3
Carmichael, Harold, Philadelphia	1028	61	16.9	85t	6
Scott, Freddie, Detroit	1022	53	19.3	48	5
Senser, Joe, Minnesota	1004	79	12.7	53	8
White, Sammy, Minnesota	1001	66	15.2	53	3
Solomon, Freddie, San Francisco	969	59	16.4	60t	8
Hill, Tony, Dallas	953	46	20.7	63t	4
Monk, Art, Washington	894	56	16.0	79t	6
Rashad, Ahmad, Minnesota	884	58	15.2	53	7
Perkins, Johnny, New York Giants	858	51	16.8	80	6
Dennard, Preston, Los Angeles	821	49	16.8	64	4
Giles, Jimmie, Tampa Bay	786	45	17.5	81t	6
Andrews, William, Atlanta	735	81	9.1	70t	2
Green, Roy, St. Louis	708	33	21.5	60	4
Brown, Ted, Minnesota	694	83	8.4	63	2
Coffman, Paul, Green Bay	687	55	12.5	29	4
Jefferson, John, Green Bay	632	39	16.2	41	4
Pearson, Drew, Dallas	614	38	16.2	42t	3
Jackson, Alfred, Atlanta	604	37	16.3	49	6
Metcalf, Terry, Washington	595	48	12.4	52	0
Smith, Charles, Philadelphia	564	38	14.8	45	4

INTERCEPTIONS

INDIVIDUAL CHAMPIONS
  NFC: 11—Everson Walls, Dallas
  AFC: 10—John Harris, Seattle
YARDAGE
  NFC: 239—Dwight Hicks, San Francisco
  AFC: 227—Darroll Ray, New York
TOUCHDOWNS
  NFC: 3—Ronnie Lott, San Francisco
  AFC: 2—John Harris, Seattle
  2—Darroll Ray, New York
LONGEST
  AFC: 102 yards—Louis Breeden, Cincinnati vs. San Diego, November 8 · (TD)
  NFC: 101 yards—Tom Pridemore, Atlanta vs. San Francisco, September 20 (TD)
TEAM LEADERS
  AFC: BALTIMORE: 3, Larry Braziel & Bruce Laird; BUFFALO: 5, Mario Clark; CINCINNATI: 5, Ken Riley; CLEVELAND: 4, Clarence Scott; DENVER: 5, Steve Foley; HOUSTON: 3, Carter Hartwig & Greg Stemrick; KANSAS CITY: 7, Eric Harris; MIAMI: 4, Glenn Blackwood; NEW ENGLAND: 3, Tim Fox & Rick Sanford; NEW YORK: 7, Darroll Ray; OAKLAND: 3, Lester Hayes & Odis McKinney; PITTSBURGH: 6, Mel Blount & Jack Lambert; SAN DIEGO: 5, Willie Buchanon; SEATTLE: 10, John Harris.
  NFC: ATLANTA: 7, Tom Pridemore; CHICAGO: 6, Gary Fencik; DALLAS: 11, Everson Walls; DETROIT: 9, Jim Allen; GREEN BAY: 6, Maurice Harvey & Mark Lee; LOS ANGELES: 5, Nolan Cromwell; MINNESOTA: 4, Tom Hannon & Willie Teal; NEW ORLEANS: 4, Dave Waymer; NEW YORK: 4, Beasley Reece; PHILADELPHIA: 5, Brenard Wilson; ST. LOUIS: 7, Ken Greene; SAN FRANCISCO: 9, Dwight Hicks; TAMPA BAY: 9, Cedric Brown; WASHINGTON, 7, Mark Murphy.
TEAM CHAMPIONS
  NFC: 37—Dallas
  AFC: 30—Pittsburgh

AFC INTERCEPTIONS—TEAM

	No.	Yards	Avg.	Long	TD
Pittsburgh	30	376	12.5	50t	1
Kansas City	26	406	15.6	46t	1
Denver	23	342	10.5	65	0
San Diego	23	224	9.7	39	1
New York Jets	21	432	20.6	67	2
Seattle	21	397	18.9	82t	3
Buffalo	19	352	18.5	53	0
Cincinnati	19	318	16.7	102t	1
Houston	18	330	18.3	38	0
Miami	18	254	14.1	39	0
Baltimore	16	210	13.1	49	0
New England	16	195	12.2	49	0
Cleveland	15	165	11.0	45	0
Oakland	13	97	7.5	34	1
AFC Total	278	4098	—	102t	10
AFC Average	19.9	292.7	14.7	—	0.7

NFC INTERCEPTIONS—TEAM

	No.	Yards	Avg.	Long	TD
Dallas	37	482	13.0	96	0
Tampa Bay	32	648	20.3	82t	4
Green Bay	30	495	16.5	53	1
San Francisco	27	448	16.6	72	4
Philadelphia	26	266	10.2	35	0
Atlanta	25	494	19.8	101t	3
Detroit	24	286	11.9	60t	1
Washington	24	249	10.4	52t	2
St. Louis	21	281	13.4	47	1
Chicago	18	345	19.2	92t	3
Los Angeles	17	237	13.9	94	0
New York Giants	17	222	13.1	32t	1
New Orleans	17	214	12.6	54	0
Minnesota	16	120	7.5	28	0
NFC Total	331	4787	—	101t	20
NFC Average	23.6	341.9	14.5	—	1.4
League Total	609	8885	—	102t	30
League Average	21.8	317.3	14.6	—	1.1

NFL TOP 10 INTERCEPTORS

	No.	Yards	Avg.	Long	TD
Walls, Everson, Dallas	11	133	12.1	33	0
Harris, John, Seattle	10	155	15.5	42t	2
Hicks, Dwight, San Francisco	9	239	26.6	72	1
Brown, Cedric, Tampa Bay	9	215	23.9	81t	2
Thurman, Dennis, Dallas	9	187	20.8	96	0
Allen, Jim, Detroit	9	123	13.7	34	0
Ray, Darroll, New York Jets	7	227	32.4	64t	2
Pridemore, Tom, Atlanta	7	221	31.6	101t	1
Lott, Ronnie, San Francisco	7	117	16.7	41t	3
Greene, Ken, St. Louis	7	111	15.9	47	0
Harris, Eric, Kansas City	7	109	15.6	43	0
Downs, Michael, Dallas	7	81	11.6	25	0
Murphy, Mark, Washington	7	68	9.7	29	0

AFC INTERCEPTIONS—INDIVIDUAL

	No.	Yards	Avg.	Long	TD
Harris, John, Seattle	10	155	15.5	42t	2
Ray, Darroll, New York Jets	7	227	32.4	64t	2
Harris, Eric, Kansas City	7	109	15.6	43	0
Blount, Mel, Pittsburgh	6	106	17.7	50t	1
Lambert, Jack, Pittsburgh	6	76	12,7	31	0
Clark, Mario, Buffalo	5	142	28.4	53	0
Barbaro, Gary, Kansas City	5	134	26.8	34	0
Foley, Steve, Denver	5	81	16.2	24	0
Shell, Donnie, Pittsburgh	5	52	10.4	25	0
Green, Gary, Kansas City	5	37	7.4	16	0
Buchanon, Willie, San Diego	5	31	6.2	18	0
Riley, Ken, Cincinnati	5	6	1.2	6	0
Breeden, Louis, Cincinnati	4	145	36.3	102t	1
Blackwood, Glenn, Miami	4	124	31.0	39	0
Romes, Charles, Buffalo	4	113	28.3	35	0
Burruss, Lloyd, Kansas City	4	75	18.8	46t	1
Scott, Clarence, Cleveland	4	46	11.5	26	0
Simpson, Bill, Buffalo	4	42	10.5	42	0
Gradishar, Randy, Denver	4	38	9.5	16	0
Williams, Reggie, Cincinnati	4	33	8.3	14	0
Thomas, J. T., Pittsburgh	4	18	4.5	16	0
Thompson, Bill, Denver	4	14	3.5	14	0
Easley, Kenny, Seattle	3	155	51.7	82t	1
Stemrick, Greg, Houston	3	94	31.3	38	0
Hartwig, Carter, Houston	3	78	26.0	36	0
Lynn, Johnny, New York Jets	3	76	25.3	67	0
Darden, Thom, Cleveland	3	68	22.7	45	0
Laird, Bruce, Baltimore	3	59	19.7	24	0
Swenson, Bob, Denver	3	53	17.7	32	0
Shaw, Pete, San Diego	3	50	16.7	23	0
Washington, Anthony, Pittsburgh	3	46	15.3	35	0
McKinney, Odis, Oakland	3	38	12.7	34	0
Kozlowski, Mike, Miami	3	37	12.3	29	0
Braziel, Larry, Baltimore	3	35	11.7	27	0
Rhone, Earnest, Miami	3	35	11.7	16	0
Sanford, Rick, New England	3	28	9.3	21	0
Fox, Tim, New England	3	20	6.7	20	0
Mehl, Lance, New York Jets	3	17	5.7	10	0
Blackwood, Lyle, Miami	3	12	4.0	11	0
Hayes, Lester, Oakland	3	0	0.0	0	0
Lowe, Woodrow, San Diego	3	0	0.0	0	0
Williams, Mike, San Diego	3	0	0.0	0	0
Harris, Bo, Cincinnati	2	92	46.0	49	0
Schroy, Ken, New York Jets	2	58	29.0	39	0
Jackson, Michael, Seattle	2	51	25.5	33	0
Kay, Bill, Houston	2	47	23.5	30	0
Perry, Vernon, Houston	2	46	23.0	34	0
Edwards, Glen, San Diego	2	45	22.5	39	0
Kyle, Aaron, Denver	2	40	20.0	40	0
Clayborn, Ray, New England	2	39	19.5	39	0
Brudzinski, Bob, Miami	2	35	17.5	19	0
Glasgow, Nesby, Baltimore	2	35	17.5	31	0
Buttle, Greg, New York Jets	2	34	17.0	22	0

	No.	Yards	Avg.	Long	TD
Harden, Mike, Denver	2	34	17.0	38	0
Simpson, Keith, Seattle	2	34	17.0	21	0
Flint, Judson, Cleveland	2	33	16.5	33	0
Owens, Burgess, Oakland	2	30	15.0	30t	1
Paul, Whitney, Kansas City	2	30	15.0	25	0
James, Roland, New England	2	29	14.5	21	0
Bingham, Gregg, Houston	2	20	10.0	17	0
Reinfeldt, Mike, Houston	2	18	9.0	16	0
Manumaleuga, Frank, Kansas City	2	17	8.5	12	0
Robertson, Isiah, Buffalo	2	15	7.5	15	0
Matthews, Clay, Cleveland	2	14	7.0	8	0
Gregor, Bob, San Diego	2	11	5.5	11	0
Smith, Ed, Baltimore	2	11	5.5	8	0
Hatchett, Derrick, Baltimore	2	8	4.0	8	0
Johnson, Ron, Pittsburgh	2	8	4.0	8	0
Brazile, Robert, Houston	2	7	3.5	7	0
Springs, Kirk, New York Jets	2	5	2.5	5	0
Brown, Dave, Seattle	2	2	1.0	2	0
Butler, Keith, Seattle	2	0	0.0	0	0
Smith, Dennis, Denver	1	65	65.0	65	0
Anderson, Kim, Baltimore	1	49	49.0	49	0
Buben, Mark, New England	1	49	49.0	49	0
Johnson, Gary, San Diego	1	41	41.0	36	1
Fuller, Mike, Cincinnati	1	31	31.0	31	0
Cole, Robin, Pittsburgh	1	29	29.0	29	0
King, Linden, San Diego	1	28	28.0	28	0
Ham, Jack, Pittsburgh	1	23	23.0	23	0
Kush, Rod, Buffalo	1	19	19.0	19	0
Washington, Ted, Houston	1	19	19.0	19	0
Woodruff, Dwayne, Pittsburgh	1	17	17.0	17	0
Hawkins, Mike, New England	1	16	16.0	16	0
Manor, Brison, Denver	1	16	16.0	16	0
Blinka, Stan, New York Jets	1	15	15.0	15	0
Bess, Rufus, Buffalo	1	12	12.0	12	0
Horn, Bob, San Diego	1	12	12.0	12	0
Watts, Ted, Oakland	1	12	12.0	12	0
Duhe, A. J., Miami	1	11	11.0	11	0
Razzano, Rick, Cincinnati	1	11	11.0	11	0
Zamberlin, John, New England	1	11	11.0	11	0
Krauss, Barry, Baltimore	1	10	10.0	10	0
Nelson, Shane, Buffalo	1	9	9.0	9	0
Browning, Dave, Oakland	1	8	8.0	8	0
Martin, Rod, Oakland	1	7	7.0	7	0
Jones, Leroy, San Diego	1	6	6.0	6	0
Cherry, Deron, Kansas City	1	4	4.0	4	0
Bolton, Ron, Cleveland	1	3	3.0	3	0
Green, Bubba, Baltimore	1	3	3.0	3	0
Haynes, Mike, New England	1	3	3.0	3	0
O'Steen, Dwayne, Oakland	1	2	2.0	2	0
Evans, Larry, Denver	1	1	1.0	1	0
Goode, Don, Cleveland	1	1	1.0	1	0
Wilson, J. C., Houston	1	1	1.0	1	0
Winston, Dennis, Pittsburgh	1	1	1.0	1	0
Ambrose, Dick, Cleveland	1	0	0.0	0	0

Interceptions

	No.	Yards	Avg.	Long	TD
Bessillieu, Don, Miami	1	0	0.0	0	0
Cameron, Glenn, Cincinnati	1	0	0.0	0	0
Davis, Mike, Oakland	1	0	0.0	0	0
Duncan, Frank, San Diego	1	0	0.0	0	0
Holmes, Jerry, New York Jets	1	0	0.0	0	0
LeClair, Jim, Cincinnati	1	0	0.0	0	0
Lee, Keith, New England	1	0	0.0	0	0
Logan, Dave, Cleveland	1	0	0.0	0	0
Pinkney, Reggie, Baltimore	1	0	0.0	0	0
Shoate, Rod, New England	1	0	0.0	0	0
Walker, Fulton, Miami	1	0	0.0	0	0
Williams, Ben, Buffalo	1	0	0.0	0	0

t indicates touchdown
Leader based on most interceptions.

NFC INTERCEPTIONS—INDIVIDUAL

	No.	Yards	Avg.	Long	TD
Walls, Everson, Dallas	11	133	12.1	33	0
Hicks, Dwight, San Francisco	9	239	26.6	72	1
Brown, Cedric, Tampa Bay	9	215	23.9	81t	2
Thurman, Dennis, Dallas	9	187	20.8	96	0
Allen, Jim, Detroit	9	123	13.7	34	0
Pridemore, Tom, Atlanta	7	221	31.6	101t	1
Lott, Ronnie, San Francisco	7	117	16.7	41t	3
Greene, Ken, St. Louis	7	111	15.9	47	0
Downs, Michael, Dallas	7	81	11.6	25	0
Murphy, Mark, Washington	7	68	9.7	29	0
Harvey, Maurice, Green Bay	6	217	36.2	53	0
Washington, Mike, Tampa Bay	6	156	26.0	34	1
Fencik, Gary, Chicago	6	121	20.2	69t	1
Colzie, Neal, Tampa Bay	6	110	18.3	82t	1
Lee, Mark, Green Bay	6	50	8.3	25	0
Cromwell, Nolan, Los Angeles	5	94	18.8	94	0
Butler, Bobby, Atlanta	5	86	17.2	41	0
Johnson, Cecil, Tampa Bay	5	84	16.8	36	0
Wilson, Brenard, Philadelphia	5	73	14.6	26	0
Henderson, Reuben, Chicago	4	84	21.0	39	0
Reece, Beasley, New York Giants	4	84	21.0	32	0
Thomas, Pat, Los Angeles	4	80	20.0	64	0
Waymer, Dave, New Orleans	4	54	13.5	31	0
Lavender, Joe, Washington	4	52	13.0	30	0
Williamson, Carlton, San Fran.	4	44	11.0	28	0
White, Stan, Detroit	4	37	9.3	16	0
Young, Roynell, Philadelphia	4	35	8.8	33	0
Hannon, Tom, Minnesota	4	28	7.0	28	0
Teal, Willie, Minnesota	4	23	5.8	15	0
Wehrli, Roger, St. Louis	4	8	2.0	6	0
Hood, Estus, Green Bay	3	59	19.7	41t	1
Jackson, Terry, New York Giants	3	57	19.0	32t	1
Murphy, Mark, Green Bay	3	57	19.0	50	0
Coleman, Monte, Washington	3	52	17.3	52t	1
Green, Roy, St. Louis	3	44	14.7	29	0
Johnson, Kenny, Atlanta	3	35	11.7	23	0

	No.	Yards	Avg.	Long	TD
Cobb, Garry, Detroit	3	32	10.7	17	0
Wright, Eric, San Francisco	3	26	8.7	26	0
Knoff, Kurt, Minnesota	3	24	8.0	20	0
Cumby, George, Green Bay	3	22	7.3	17	0
Waters, Charlie, Dallas	3	21	7.0	21	0
Douglass, Mike, Green Bay	3	20	6.7	13	0
Irvin, LeRoy, Los Angeles	3	18	6.0	18	0
Perry, Rod, Los Angeles	3	18	6.0	10	0
Wattelet, Frank, New Orleans	3	16	5.3	16	0
Anderson, John, Green Bay	3	12	4.0	8	0
Currier, Bill, New York Giants	3	2	0.7	2	0
Edwards, Herman, Philadelphia	3	1	0.3	1	0
Peters, Tony, Washington	3	0	0.0	0	0
Myers, Tommy, New Orleans	2	70	35.0	54	0
Chesley, Al, Philadelphia	2	66	33.0	35	0
Green, Hugh, Tampa Bay	2	56	28.0	50	0
Blackmore, Richard, Philadelphia	2	43	21.5	25	0
Kelley, Brian, New York Giants	2	43	21.5	27	0
Jones, Earl, Atlanta	2	42	21.0	39	0
LeMaster, Frank, Philadelphia	2	28	14.0	22	0
McNeill, Fred, Minnesota	2	26	13.0	14	0
Kaufman, Mel, Washington	2	25	12.5	25	0
Olkewicz, Neal, Washington	2	22	11.0	12	1
Glazebrook, Bob, Atlanta	2	21	10.5	18	0
McCoy, Mike C., Green Bay	2	20	10.0	16	0
Fantetti, Ken, Detroit	2	18	9.0	17	0
Swain, John, Minnesota	2	18	9.0	18	0
Wilkes, Reggie, Philadelphia	2	18	9.0	11	0
Lewis, David, Tampa Bay	2	12	6.0	10	0
Breunig, Bob, Dallas	2	8	4.0	8	0
Schmidt, Terry, Chicago	2	4	2.0	4	0
Fisher, Jeff, Chicago	2	3	1.5	3	0
Wilson, Steve, Dallas	2	0	0.0	0	0
Logan, Randy, Philadelphia	2	−1	−0.5	0	0
Bell, Todd, Chicago	1	92	92.0	92t	1
Hall, Alvin, Detroit	1	60	60.0	60t	1
Harris, Al, Chicago	1	44	44.0	44t	1
Favron, Calvin, St. Louis	1	42	42.0	42	0
Wingo, Rich, Green Bay	1	38	38.0	38	0
Curry, Buddy, Atlanta	1	35	35.0	35t	1
Ray, Ricky, New Orleans	1	33	33.0	33	0
Brown, Guy, Dallas	1	28	28.0	28	0
Butz, Dave, Washington	1	26	26.0	26	0
Williams, Joel, Atlanta	1	25	25.0	25	0
Barnes, Benny, Dallas	1	24	24.0	24	0
McColl, Milt, San Francisco	1	22	22.0	22	0
Kuykendall, Fulton, Atlanta	1	20	20.0	20t	1
Youngblood, Jim, Los Angeles	1	20	20.0	20	0
Johnson, Charles, St. Louis	1	19	19.0	19	0
Nairne, Rob, New Orleans	1	18	18.0	18	0
Collier, Tim, St. Louis	1	17	17.0	17	0
Williams, Eric, St. Louis	1	17	17.0	17	0
Ahrens, Dave, St. Louis	1	14	14.0	14t	1
Holt, John, Tampa Bay	1	13	13.0	13	0

Interceptions

	Att.	Yards	Avg.	Long	TD
Kovach, Jim, New Orleans	1	13	13.0	13	0
Oldham, Ray, Detroit	1	10	10.0	10	0
Van Pelt, Brad, New York Giants	1	10	10.0	10	0
Baker, Al, Detroit	1	9	9.0	9	0
Flowers, Larry, New York Giants	1	9	9.0	9	0
Haynes, Mark, New York Giants	1	9	9.0	9	0
Richardson, Al, Atlanta	1	9	9.0	9	0
Harris, Joe, Los Angeles	1	7	7.0	7	0
Hunt, Byron, New York Giants	1	7	7.0	7	0
Redd, Glen, New Orleans	1	7	7.0	7	0
Junior, E. J., St. Louis	1	5	5.0	5	0
Griffin, Jeff, St. Louis	1	4	4.0	4	0
Bordelon, Ken, New Orleans	1	3	3.0	3	0
Nelms, Mike, Washington	1	3	3.0	3	0
Robinson, Jerry, Philadelphia	1	3	3.0	3	0
Brantley, Scot, Tampa Bay	1	2	2.0	2	0
Blair, Matt, Minnesota	1	1	1.0	1	0
Parrish, Lemar, Washington	1	1	1.0	1	0
Taylor, Lawrence, New York Giants	1	1	1.0	1	0
Bradley, Luther, Detroit	1	0	0.0	0	0
Gaison, Blane, Atlanta	1	0	0.0	0	0
Gary, Russell, New Orleans	1	0	0.0	0	0
Gray, Hector, Detroit	1	0	0.0	0	0
Johnson, Charlie, Philadelphia	1	0	0.0	0	0
Lewis, D. D., Dallas	1	0	0.0	0	0
Martin, Saladin, San Francisco	1	0	0.0	0	0
Musser, Neal, Atlanta	1	0	0.0	0	0
Phillips, Ray, Philadelphia	1	0	0.0	0	0
Poe, Johnny, New Orleans	1	0	0.0	0	0
Reynolds, Jack, San Francisco	1	0	0.0	0	0
Sciarra, John, Philadelphia	1	0	0.0	0	0
Spivey, Mike, New Orleans	1	0	0.0	0	0
Turner, Keena, San Francisco	1	0	0.0	0	0
Walterscheid, Lenny, Chicago	1	0	0.0	0	0
Hunter, James, Detroit	1	−3	−3.0	−3	0
Singletary, Mike, Chicago	1	−3	−3.0	−3	0

t indicates touchdown
Leader based on most touchdowns.

PUNTING

INDIVIDUAL CHAMPIONS (AVERAGE)
AFC: 45.4 — Pat McInally, Cincinnati (72 punts, 3272 yards)
NFC: 43.5 — Tom Skladany, Detroit (64 punts, 2784 yards)
NET AVERAGE
NFC: 37.3 — Tom Skladany, Detroit (64 total punts, 2385 net yards)
AFC: 36.1 — Jeff West, Seattle (66 total punts, 2385 net yards)
      36.1 — Pat McInally, Cincinnati (73 total punts, 2636 net yards)
LONGEST
AFC: 75 yards — Rich Camarillo, New England vs. Oakland, November 1
NFC: 75 yards — Carl Birdsong, St. Louis vs. Philadelphia, December 20
MOST PUNTS
NFC: 114 — Bob Parsons, Chicago (4531 yards)
AFC: 96 — Ray Guy, Oakland (4195 yards)
TEAM CHAMPIONS (AVERAGE)
AFC: 44.8 — Cincinnati
NFC: 43.5 — Detroit

AFC PUNTING — TEAM

	Total Punts	Gross Yards	Long	Gross Avg.	TB	Blk.	Opp. Ret.	Ret. Yards	In 20	Net Avg.
Cincinnati	73	3272	62	44.8	11	1	42	416	17	35.6
Pittsburgh	84	3641	74	43.3	16	0	34	358	25	35.3
Oakland	98	4238	69	43.2	16	0	45	514	23	34.7
Cleveland	70	2884	66	41.2	12	2	30	253	11	33.2
Miami	83	3386	61	40.8	11	0	45	286	21	34.7
New York Jets	81	3290	65	40.6	13	0	31	149	27	35.6
Denver	86	3478	67	40.4	5	0	46	388	20	34.8
San Diego	63	2540	61	40.3	7	1	31	168	16	34.9
Buffalo	80	3175	71	39.7	12	0	34	220	16	33.9
Houston	79	3137	62	39.7	3	0	47	360	17	34.4
Baltimore	78	3071	57	39.4	2	0	44	402	11	33.7
New England	75	2951	75	39.3	13	0	35	305	14	31.8
Seattle	68	2652	56	39.0	2	0	33	153	16	36.2
Kansas City	70	2697	57	38.5	4	0	46	293	9	33.2
AFC Total	1088	44,412	75	—	127	4	543	4265	243	—
AFC Average	77.7	3172.3	—	40.8	9.1	0.3	38.8	304.6	17.4	34.4

NFC PUNTING — TEAM

	Total Punts	Gross Yards	Long	Gross Avg.	TB	Blk.	Opp. Ret.	Ret. Yards	In 20	Net Avg.
Detroit	64	2784	74	43.5	5	0	39	299	21	37.3
New York Giants	97	4198	62	43.3	12	0	61	561	19	35.0
Los Angeles	89	3735	67	42.0	3	0	52	481	19	35.9
St. Louis	69	2883	75	41.8	8	0	37	276	18	35.5
San Francisco	93	3858	65	41.5	15	0	57	664	14	31.1
Minnesota	88	3646	73	41.4	11	0	46	399	17	34.4
Tampa Bay	82	3375	62	41.2	6	2	54	668	17	30.8
Dallas	81	3284	56	40.5	7	0	38	231	19	36.0
New Orleans	66	2672	60	40.5	6	0	36	282	11	34.4
Philadelphia	64	2580	64	40.3	6	0	34	246	18	34.6
Atlanta	88	3543	62	40.3	5	1	59	577	13	32.2
Washington	73	2923	57	40.0	5	0	50	388	13	33.4
Chicago	114	4531	55	39.7	7	0	66	594	31	33.3
Green Bay	84	3330	72	39.6	9	2	50	511	16	30.7
NFC Total	1152	47,342	75	—	105	5	677	6177	246	—
NFC Average	82.3	3381.6	—	41.1	7.5	0.4	48.4	441.2	17.6	33.8
League Total	2240	91,754	75	—	232	9	1220	10,442	489	—
League Average	80.0	3276.9	—	41.0	8.3	0.3	43.6	372.9	17.5	34.1

NFL TOP 10 PUNTERS

	Net Punts	Gross Yards	Long	Gross Avg.	Total Punts	TB	Blk.	Opp. Ret.	Ret. Yds.	In 20	Net Avg.
McInally, Pat, Cincinnati	72	3272	62	45.4	73	11	1	42	416	17	36.1
Guy, Ray, Oakland	96	4195	69	43.7	96	15	0	45	514	23	35.2
Skladany, Tom, Detroit	64	2784	74	43.5	64		0	39	299	21	37.3
Colquitt, Craig, Pittsburgh	84	3641	74	43.3	84	16	0	34	358	25	35.3
Jennings, Dave, New York Giants	97	4198	62	43.3	97	12	0	61	561	19	35.0
Swider, Larry, Tampa Bay	58	2476	62	42.7	60	4	2	39	409	13	33.1
Cox, Steve, Cleveland	68	2884	66	42.4	70	12	2	30	253	11	34.2
Corral, Frank, Los Angeles	89	3735	67	42.0	89	3	0	52	481	19	35.9
Birdsong, Carl, St. Louis	69	2883	75	41.8	69	8	0	37	276	18	35.5
Camarillo, Rich, New England	47	1959	75	41.7	47	9	0	20	209	12	33.4

AFC PUNTING — INDIVIDUAL

	Net Punts	Gross Yards	Long	Gross Avg.	Total Punts	TB	Blk.	Opp. Ret.	Ret. Yds.	In 20	Net Avg.
McInally, Pat, Cincinnati	72	3272	62	45.4	73	11	1	42	416	17	36.1
Guy, Ray, Oakland	96	4195	69	43.7	96	15	0	45	514	23	35.2
Colquitt, Craig, Pittsburgh	84	3641	74	43.3	84	16	0	39	358	25	35.3
Cox, Steve, Cleveland	68	2884	66	42.4	70	12	2	34	253	11	34.2
Camarillo, Rich, New England	47	1959	75	41.7	47	9	0	20	209	16	34.2
Roberts, George, San Diego	62	2540	61	41.0	63	7	1	31	168	12	33.4
Orosz, Tom, Miami	83	3386	61	40.8	83	11	0	45	286	16	35.4
Ramsey, Chuck, New York Jets	81	3290	65	40.6	81	13	0	31	149	21	34.7
Prestridge, Luke, Denver	86	3478	67	40.4	86	5	0	46	388	27	35.6
Parsley, Cliff, Houston	79	3137	62	39.7	79	3	0	47	360	20	34.8
Cater, Greg, Buffalo	80	3175	71	39.7	80	12	0	34	220	17	34.4
Garrett, Mike, Baltimore	78	3071	57	39.4	78	2	0	44	402	11	33.9
West, Jeff, Seattle	66	2578	56	39.1	66	2	0	32	153	16	36.1

	Net Punts	Gross Yards	Long	Gross Avg	Total Punts	TB	Blk	Opp. Ret	Ret. Yds	In 20	Net Avg
Grupp, Bob, Kansas City	41	1556	57	38.0	41	1	0	26	165	5	33.4
Non-Qualifiers											
Gossett, Jeff, Kansas City	29	1141	55	39.3	29	3	0	20	128	4	32.9
Hubach, Mike, New England	19	726	56	38.2	19	2	0	12	95	2	31.1
Hartley, Ken, New England	9	266	41	29.6	9	2	0	3	1	0	25.0
Bahr, Chris, Oakland	2	43	32	21.5	2	1	0	0	0	0	11.5
Garcia, Frank, Seattle	2	74	41	37.0	2	0	0	1	0	0	37.0

Leader based on gross average, minimum 40 punts.

NFC PUNTING — INDIVIDUAL

	Net Punts	Gross Yards	Long	Gross Avg	Total Punts	TB	Blk	Opp. Ret	Ret. Yds	In 20	Net Avg
Skladany, Tom, Detroit	64	2784	74	43.5	64	5	0	39	299	21	37.3
Jennings, Dave, New York Giants	97	4198	62	43.3	97	12	2	61	561	19	35.0
Swider, Larry, Tampa Bay	58	2476	62	42.7	60	4	1	39	409	13	33.1
Corral, Frank, Los Angeles	89	3735	67	42.0	89	3	0	52	481	19	35.9
Birdsong, Carl, St. Louis	69	2883	75	41.8	69	8	0	37	276	18	35.5
Miller, Jim, San Francisco	93	3858	65	41.5	93	15	0	57	664	14	31.1
Coleman, Greg, Minnesota	88	3646	73	41.4	88	11	0	46	399	17	34.4
White, Danny, Dallas	79	3222	60	40.8	79	7	0	38	231	19	36.1
Runager, Max, Philadelphia	63	2567	64	40.7	63	6	0	34	246	18	34.9
James, John, Atlanta	87	3543	62	40.7	88	5	1	59	577	13	32.6
Stachowicz, Ray, Green Bay	82	3330	72	40.6	84	9	0	50	511	16	31.4
Erxleben, Russell, New Orleans	66	2672	60	40.5	66	6	2	36	282	11	34.4
Connell, Mike, Washington	73	2923	57	40.0	73	5	0	50	388	13	33.4
Parsons, Bob, Chicago	114	4531	55	39.7	114	7	0	66	594	31	33.3
Non-Qualifiers											
Blanchard, Tom, Tampa Bay	22	899	58	40.9	22	2	0	13	259	4	27.3
Septien, Rafael, Dallas	2	62	33	31.0	2	0	0	0	0	0	31.0
Franklin, Tony, Philadelphia	1	13	13	13.0	1	0	0	0	0	0	13.0

Leader based on gross average, minimum 40 punts.

PUNT RETURNS

INDIVIDUAL CHAMPIONS (AVERAGE)
NFC: 13.4—LeRoy Irvin, Los Angeles (46 returns, 615 yards)
AFC: 13.2—James Brooks, San Diego (22 returns, 290 yards)

YARDAGE
NFC: 615—LeRoy Irvin, Los Angeles (46 returns)
AFC: 528—J. T. Smith, Kansas City (50 returns)

RETURNS
NFC: 54—Wally Henry, Philadelphia (396 yards)
AFC: 50—J. T. Smith, Kansas City (528 yards)

FAIR CATCHES
NFC: 20—Jeff Fisher, Chicago (63 chances)
AFC: 13—Ted Watts, Oakland (48 chances)
      13—Mike Fuller, Cincinnati (36 chances)

LONGEST
NFC: 94 yards—Mark Lee, Green Bay vs. New York Giants,
                November 11 (TD)
AFC: 87 yards—Tommy Vigorito, Miami vs. Pittsburgh,
                September 10 (TD)

TOUCHDOWNS
AFC: Tommy Vigorito, Miami vs. Pittsburgh, September 10 (87 yards)
      Ted Watts, Oakland vs. Pittsburgh, December 7 (52 yards)
NFC: LeRoy Irvin, Los Angeles vs. Chicago, September 28 (55 yards)
        vs. Atlanta, October 11 (75 yards)
        vs. Atlanta, October 11 (84 yards)
      Mike Nelms, Washington vs. San Francisco, October 4 (58 yards)
        vs. New England, October 25 (75 yards)
      Jeff Fisher, Chicago vs. Tampa Bay, September 20 (88 yards)
      Mark Lee, Green Bay vs. New York Giants, November 11 (94 yards)
      Robby Martin, Detroit vs. Minnesota, December 12 (45 yards)
      Stump Mitchell, St. Louis vs. Washington, September 20 (50 yards)

TEAM CHAMPIONS (AVERAGE)
NFC: 13.8—Los Angeles (49 returns, 676 yards)
AFC: 12.2—San Diego (31 returns, 378 yards)

AFC PUNT RETURNS—TEAM

	No.	FC	Yards	Avg.	Long	TD
San Diego	31	10	378	12.2	42	0
Kansas City	50	7	528	10.6	62	0
Miami	45	17	458	10.2	87t	1
Seattle	32	6	293	9.2	34	0
Denver	51	5	441	8.6	39	0
Buffalo	35	7	292	8.3	25	0
Pittsburgh	50	9	412	8.2	33	0
Houston	41	4	325	7.9	40	0
Cleveland	50	6	369	7.4	40	0
Oakland	52	16	380	7.3	52t	1
Cincinnati	29	19	205	7.1	34	0
New York Jets	50	13	337	6.7	46	0
New England	31	7	199	6.4	26	0
Baltimore	12	7	56	4.7	11	0
AFC Total	559	133	4673	—	87t	2
AFC Average	39.9	9.5	333.8	8.4	—	0.1

NFC PUNT RETURNS—TEAM

	No.	FC	Yards	Avg.	Long	TD
Los Angeles	49	8	676	13.8	84t	3
Chicago	45	24	518	11.5	88t	1
St. Louis	43	2	453	10.5	50t	1
New Orleans	41	7	426	10.4	36	0
Washington	49	4	507	10.3	75t	2
Detroit	52	9	450	8.7	45t	1
New York Giants	64	5	502	7.8	55	0
Minnesota	39	10	303	7.8	18	0
Atlanta	50	19	383	7.7	53	0
Green Bay	40	10	306	7.7	94t	1
Philadelphia	58	8	422	7.3	52	0
San Francisco	48	10	344	7.2	39	0
Tampa Bay	38	3	244	6.4	56	0
Dallas	45	5	235	5.2	17	0
NFC Total	661	124	5769	—	94t	9
NFC Average	47.2	8.9	412.1	8.7	—	0.6
League Total	1220	257	10,442	—	94t	11
League Average	43.6	9.2	372.9	8.6	—	0.4

NFL TOP 10 PUNT RETURNERS

	No.	FC	Yards	Avg.	Long	TD
Irvin, LeRoy, Los Angeles	46	6	615	13.4	84t	3
Brooks, James, San Diego	22	6	290	13.2	42	0
Fisher, Jeff, Chicago	43	20	509	11.8	88t	1
Groth, Jeff, New Orleans	37	6	436	11.8	36	0
Johns, Paul, Seattle	16	4	177	11.1	34	0
Nelms, Mike, Washington	45	1	492	10.9	75t	2
Mitchell, Stump, St. Louis	42	0	445	10.6	50t	1
Smith, J. T., Kansas City	50	7	528	10.6	62	0
Vigorito, Tommy, Miami	36	12	379	10.5	87t	1
Anderson, Larry, Pittsburgh	20	8	208	10.4	33	0

AFC PUNT RETURNS—INDIVIDUAL

	No.	FC	Yards	Avg.	Long	TD
Brooks, James, San Diego	22	6	290	13.2	42	0
Johns, Paul, Seattle	16	4	177	11.1	34	0
Smith, J. T., Kansas City	50	7	528	10.6	62	0
Vigorito, Tommy, Miami	36	12	379	10.5	87t	1
Anderson, Larry, Pittsburgh	20	8	208	10.4	33	0
Manning, Wade, Denver	41	4	378	9.2	39	0
Hooks, Roland, Buffalo	17	2	142	8.4	25	0
Watts, Ted, Oakland	35	13	284	8.1	52t	1
Fuller, Mike, Cincinnati	23	13	177	7.7	34	0
Roaches, Carl, Houston	39	4	296	7.6	40	0
Harper, Bruce, New York Jets	35	9	265	7.6	46	0
Hall, Dino, Cleveland	33	6	248	7.5	40	0
Montgomery, Cleotha, Cleveland	17	0	121	7.1	17	0
Smith, Jim, Pittsburgh	30	1	204	6.8	28	0

Punt Returns

Non-Qualifiers	No.	FC	Yards	Avg.	Long	TD
Morgan, Stanley, New England	15	4	116	7.7	26	0
Lewis, Will, Seattle	15	2	100	6.7	23	0
Matthews, Ira, Oakland	15	2	92	6.1	26	0
Sohn, Kurt, New York Jets	13	3	66	5.1	14	0
Shula, Dave, Baltimore	10	7	50	5.0	11	0
Upchurch, Rick, Denver	9	1	63	7.0	15	0
Piccone, Lou, Buffalo	9	2	57	6.3	13	0
James, Roland, New England	7	2	56	8.0	18	0
Haynes, Mike, New England	6	1	12	2.0	6	0
Chandler, Wes, San Diego	5	3	79	15.8	30	0
Walker, Fulton, Miami	5	1	50	10.0	17	0
Franklin, Byron, Buffalo	5	3	45	9.0	15	0
Simmons, John, Cincinnati	5	6	24	4.8	11	0
Riddick, Robb, Buffalo	4	0	48	12.0	22	0
Collins, Anthony, New England	3	0	15	5.0	15	0
Tullis, Willie, Houston	2	0	29	14.5	16	0
Blackwood, Glenn, Miami	2	2	8	4.0	6	0
Anderson, Kim, Baltimore	2	0	6	3.0	6	0
Whittington, Arthur, Oakland	2	1	4	2.0	4	0
Johnson, Greggory, Seattle	1	0	16	16.0	16	0
Bessillieu, Don, Miami	1	1	12	12.0	12	0
Kozlowski, Mike, Miami	1	1	9	9.0	9	0
Bauer, Hank, San Diego	1	0	7	7.0	7	0
Schroy, Ken, New York Jets	1	1	5	5.0	5	0
Hicks, Bryan, Cincinnati	1	0	4	4.0	4	0
Edwards, Glen, San Diego	1	0	1	1.0	1	0
Jones, Bobby, New York Jets	1	0	1	1.0	1	0
Shaw, Pete, San Diego	1	0	1	1.0	1	0
Kyle, Aaron, Denver	1	0	0	0.0	0	0
Phillips, Irvin, San Diego	1	0	0	0.0	0	0
Williams, Mike, San Diego	0	1	0	—	0	0

t indicates touchdown
Leader based on average return, minimum 16 returns.

NFC PUNT RETURNS—INDIVIDUAL

	No.	FC	Yards	Avg.	Long	TD
Irvin, LeRoy, Los Angeles	46	6	615	13.4	84t	3
Fisher, Jeff, Chicago	43	20	509	11.8	88t	1
Groth, Jeff, New Orleans	37	6	436	11.8	36	0
Nelms, Mike, Washington	45	1	492	10.9	75t	2
Mitchell, Stump, St. Louis	42	0	445	10.6	50t	1
Lee, Mark, Green Bay	20	1	187	9.4	94t	1
Hicks, Dwight, San Francisco	19	4	171	9.0	39	0
Martin, Robby, Detroit	52	8	450	8.7	45t	1
Woerner, Scott, Atlanta	33	16	278	8.4	38	0
Payton, Eddie, Minnesota	38	8	303	8.0	18	0
Bright, Leon, New York Giants	52	0	410	7.9	55	0
Henry, Wally, Philadelphia	54	8	396	7.3	52	0
Solomon, Freddie, San Francisco	29	6	173	6.0	19	0
Jones, James, Dallas	33	2	188	5.7	17	0
Bell, Theo, Tampa Bay	27	0	132	4.9	13	0

Non-Qualifiers	No.	FC	Yards	Avg.	Long	TD
Nixon, Fred, Green Bay	15	4	118	7.9	17	0
Smith, Reggie, Atlanta	12	3	99	8.3	53	0
Fellows, Ron, Dallas	11	1	44	4.0	10	0
Holt, John, Tampa Bay	9	3	100	11.1	56	0
Garrett, Alvin, New York Giants	8	2	57	7.1	18	0
Sciarra, John, Philadelphia	4	0	26	6.5	10	0
Metcalf, Terry, Washington	4	0	15	3.8	13	0
Johnson, Kenny, Atlanta	4	0	6	1.5	4	0
Hill, Drew, Los Angeles	2	0	22	11.0	12	0
Jackson, Terry, New York Giants	2	0	22	11.0	21	0
Colzie, Neal, Tampa Bay	2	0	12	6.0	12	0
Whitaker, Bill, Green Bay	2	0	1	0.5	1	0
Banks, Gordon, New Orleans	2	0	0	0.0	0	0
Cassidy, Ron, Green Bay	2	4	0	0.0	0	0
Johnson, Johnnie, Los Angeles	1	2	39	39.0	39	0
Pittman, Danny, New York Giants	1	1	13	13.0	13	0
Harrell, Willard, St. Louis	1	1	8	8.0	8	0
Walterscheid, Lenny, Chicago	1	0	6	6.0	6	0
Donley, Doug, Dallas	1	0	3	3.0	3	0
Plank, Doug, Chicago	1	1	3	3.0	3	0
Poe, Johnnie, New Orleans	1	0	2	2.0	2	0
Gray, Johnnie, Green Bay	1	1	0	0.0	0	0
Pridemore, Tom, Atlanta	1	0	0	0.0	0	0
Reece, Beasley, New York Giants	1	2	0	0.0	0	0
White, Sammy, Minnesota	1	0	0	0.0	0	0
Merkens, Guido, New Orleans	1	1	−12	−12.0	−12	0
Greene, Ken, St. Louis	0	1	0	—	0	0
Hannon, Tom, Minnesota	0	1	0	—	0	0
Nord, Keith, Minnesota	0	1	0	—	0	0
Porter, Tracy, Detroit	0	1	0	—	0	0
Thurman, Dennis, Dallas	0	1	0	—	0	0
Wilson, Steve, Dallas	0	1	0	—	0	0
Baschnagel, Brian, Chicago	0	3	0	—	0	0
Seay, Virgil, Washington	0	3	0	—	0	0

t indicates touchdown
Leader based on average return, minimum 16 returns.

KICKOFF RETURNS

INDIVIDUAL CHAMPIONS (AVERAGE)
  NFC: 29.7—Mike Nelms, Washington (37 returns, 1099 yards)
  AFC: 27.5—Carl Roaches, Houston (28 returns, 769 yards)
YARDAGE
  NFC: 1292—Stump Mitchell, St. Louis (55 returns)
  AFC: 949—James Brooks, San Diego (40 returns)
RETURNS
  NFC: 60—Drew Hill, Los Angeles (1170 yards)
  AFC: 40—James Brooks, San Diego (949 yards)
LONGEST
  NFC: 99 yards—Eddie Payton, Minnesota vs. Oakland, September 14 (TD)
  AFC: 96 yards—Carl Roaches, Houston vs. Cincinnati, October 4 (TD)
TOUCHDOWNS
  AFC: Carl Roaches, Houston vs. Cincinnati, October 14 (96 yards)
        Willie Tullis, Houston vs. Los Angeles, September 6 (95 yards)
        Fulton Walker, Miami vs. Buffalo, October 12 (90 yards)
  NFC: Amos Lawrence, San Francisco vs. Los Angeles, November 22
        (92 yards)
        Eddie Payton, Minnesota vs. Oakland, September 14 (99 yards)
TEAM CHAMPIONS (AVERAGE)
  NFC: 25.0—Washington (67 returns, 1673 yards)
  AFC: 23.9—Houston (72 returns, 1722 yards)

AFC KICKOFF RETURNS — TEAM

	No.	Yards	Avg.	Long	TD
Houston	72	1722	23.9	96t	2
Miami	54	1228	22.7	90t	1
Cincinnati	49	1056	21.6	78	0
Cleveland	72	1537	21.3	48	0
Pittsburgh	53	1096	20.7	35	0
San Diego	70	1422	20.3	47	0
Kansas City	52	1043	20.1	48	0
Oakland	71	1411	19.9	47	0
New York Jets	58	1151	19.8	42	0
Baltimore	84	1651	19.7	46	0
Buffalo	57	1085	19.0	36	0
Seattle	69	1278	18.5	36	0
New England	65	1190	18.3	32	0
Denver	47	801	17.0	31	0
AFC Total	873	17,671	—	96t	3
AFC Average	62.4	1262.2	20.2	—	0.2

NFC KICKOFF RETURNS—TEAM

	No.	Yards	Avg.	Long	TD
Washington	67	1673	25.0	84	0
Atlanta	62	1419	22.9	52	0
New Orleans	70	1523	21.8	57	0
St. Louis	75	1625	21.7	67	0
San Francisco	45	909	20.2	92t	1
Tampa Bay	46	912	19.8	40	0
Minnesota	67	1328	19.8	99t	1
New York Giants	57	1120	19.6	41	0
Philadelphia	43	832	19.3	43	0
Detroit	61	1164	19.1	36	0
Chicago	64	1214	19.0	56	0
Dallas	53	981	18.5	33	0
Green Bay	58	1066	18.4	52	0
Los Angeles	68	1244	18.3	50	0
NFC Total	836	17,010	—	99t	2
NFC Average	59.7	1,215.0	20.3	—	0.1
League Total	1,709	34,681	—	99t	5
League Average	61.0	1,238.6	20.3	—	0.2

NFL TOP 10 KICKOFF RETURNERS

	No.	Yards	Avg.	Long	TD
Nelms, Mike, Washington	37	1099	29.7	84	0
Roaches, Carl, Houston	28	769	27.5	96t	1
Lawrence, Amos, San Francisco	17	437	25.7	92t	1
Walker, Fulton, Miami	38	932	24.5	90t	1
Tullis, Willie, Houston	32	779	24.3	95t	1
Smith, Reggie, Atlanta	47	1143	24.3	52	0
Verser, David, Cincinnati	29	691	23.8	78	0
Brooks, James, San Diego	40	949	23.7	47	0
Mitchell, Stump, St. Louis	55	1292	23.5	67	0
Wilson, Wayne, New Orleans	31	722	23.3	57	0

AFC KICKOFF RETURNS—INDIVIDUAL

	No.	Yards	Avg.	Long	TD
Roaches, Carl, Houston	28	769	27.5	96t	1
Walker, Fulton, Miami	38	932	24.5	90t	1
Tullis, Willie, Houston	32	779	24.3	95t	1
Verser, David, Cincinnati	29	691	23.8	78	0
Brooks, James, San Diego	40	949	23.7	47	0
Murphy, James, Kansas City	20	457	22.9	46	0
Hall, Dino, Cleveland	36	813	22.6	48	0
Whittington, Arthur, Oakland	25	563	22.5	47	0
Montgomery, Cleotha, Clev.-Oak.	17	382	22.5	38	0
Anderson, Larry, Pittsburgh	37	825	22.3	35	0
Harper, Bruce, New York Jets	23	480	20.9	42	0

Kickoff Returns

	No.	Yards	Avg.	Long	TD
Franklin, Byron, Buffalo	21	436	20.8	33	0
Dixon, Zachary, Baltimore	36	737	20.5	46	0
Sohn, Kurt, New York Jets	26	528	20.3	31	0
Williams, Kevin, Baltimore	20	399	20.0	35	0
Collins, Anthony, New England	39	773	19.8	30	0
Manning, Wade, Denver	26	514	19.8	31	0
Anderson, Kim, Baltimore	20	393	19.7	30	0
Lewis, Will, Seattle	20	378	18.9	36	0
Ivory, Horace, N.E.-Seattle	16	300	18.8	32	0
Non-Qualifiers					
Willis, Chester, Oakland	15	309	20.6	43	0
Barnwell, Malcolm, Oakland	15	265	17.7	26	0
Riddick, Robb, Buffalo	14	257	18.4	25	0
Johnson, Greggory, Seattle	13	235	18.1	25	0
White, Charles, Cleveland	12	243	20.3	32	0
Hooks, Roland, Buffalo	11	215	19.5	36	0
Harden, Mike, Denver	11	178	16.2	23	0
Carson, Carlos, Kansas City	10	227	22.7	48	0
Lane, Eric, Seattle	10	208	20.8	27	0
Toler, Ken, New England	9	148	16.4	32	0
Chapman, Clarence, Cincinnati	8	171	21.4	29	0
Chandler, Wes, San Diego	8	125	15.6	30	0
Matthews, Ira, Oakland	7	144	20.6	39	0
Brown, Curtis, Buffalo	7	140	20.0	30	0
Hawthorne, Greg, Pittsburgh	7	138	19.7	30	0
Bessillieu, Don, Miami	7	114	16.3	30	0
Griffin, Archie, Cincinnati	6	119	19.8	28	0
Bledsoe, Curtis, Kansas City	6	117	19.5	26	0
Shaw, Pete, San Diego	6	103	17.2	24	0
Lewis, Kenny, New York Jets	5	108	21.6	30	0
Burruss, Lloyd, Kansas City	5	91	18.2	22	0
Johns, Paul, Seattle	5	81	16.2	20	0
Lytle, Rob, Denver	5	80	16.0	24	0
Shula, Dave, Baltimore	5	65	13.0	16	0
Vigorito, Tommy, Miami	4	84	21.0	25	0
Sanford, Rick, New England	4	82	20.5	27	0
Christensen, Todd, Oakland	4	54	13.5	19	0
Williams, Clarence, San Diego	4	47	11.8	23	0
Pruitt, Greg, Cleveland	3	82	27.3	30	0
Moser, Rick, Pittsburgh	3	76	25.3	29	0
Dombroski, Paul, K.C.-New Eng.	3	66	22.0	24	0
Jackson, Billy, Kansas City	3	60	20.0	23	0
Johnson, Andy, New England	3	53	17.7	19	0
Cherry, Deron, Kansas City	3	52	17.3	22	0
Gregor, Bob, San Diego	3	47	15.7	20	0
Dirden, Johnnie, Pittsburgh	3	45	15.0	22	0
Dufek, Don, Seattle	3	45	15.0	17	0
Wilson, Tim, Houston	3	41	13.7	23	0
Armstrong, Adger, Houston	3	36	12.0	18	0
Miller, Cleo, Cleveland	3	35	11.7	22	0
Hunt, Daryl, Houston	3	19	6.3	11	0
Thompson, Aundra, San Diego	2	44	22.0	25	0
Calhoun, Don, New England	2	38	19.0	22	0
Smith, Ron, San Diego	2	32	16.0	20	0

	No.	Yards	Avg.	Long	TD
Griffin, Ray, Cincinnati	2	31	15.5	17	0
Piccone, Lou, Buffalo	2	31	15.5	16	0
Wilson, J. C., Houston	2	27	13.5	14	0
Stephens, Steve, New York Jets	2	21	10.5	14	0
Lee, Keith, New England	2	20	10.0	16	0
Canada, Larry, Denver	2	19	9.5	13	0
Brown, Thomas, Cleveland	2	17	8.5	10	0
Sievers, Eric, San Diego	2	4	2.0	4	0
Rourke, Jim, Kansas City	2	0	0.0	0	0
Riley, Avon, Houston	1	51	51.0	51	0
Kozlowski, Mike, Miami	1	40	40.0	40	0
Glasgow, Nesby, Baltimore	1	35	35.0	35	0
Fuller, Mike, Cincinnati	1	34	34.0	34	0
Beaudoin, Doug, San Diego	1	31	31.0	31	0
Henderson, Wyatt, San Diego	1	26	26.0	26	0
Giaquinto, Nick, Miami	1	22	22.0	22	0
Sims, Marvin, Baltimore	1	22	22.0	22	0
Hill, Kenny, Oakland	1	21	21.0	21	0
Harris, Duriel, Miami	1	20	20.0	20	0
Bauer, Hank, San Diego	1	14	14.0	14	0
Delaney, Joe, Kansas City	1	11	11.0	11	0
Hill, Eddie, Miami	1	11	11.0	11	0
Simmons, John, Cincinnati	1	10	10.0	10	0
Davis, Russell, Pittsburgh	1	8	8.0	8	0
Rudolph, Ben, New York Jets	1	8	8.0	8	0
Sawyer, John, Seattle	1	8	8.0	8	0
Egloff, Ron, Denver	1	7	7.0	7	0
Hasselbeck, Don, New England	1	7	7.0	7	0
Hawkins, Frank, Oakland	1	7	7.0	7	0
Johnson, Eddie, Cleveland	1	7	7.0	7	0
Williams, Mike, Kansas City	1	7	7.0	7	0
Bess, Rufus, Buffalo	1	6	6.0	6	0
Jones, Johnny, New York Jets	1	6	6.0	6	0
Miller, Matt, Cleveland	1	6	6.0	6	0
Matthews, Bill, New England	1	5	5.0	5	0
Rose, Joe, Miami	1	5	5.0	5	0
Malone, Mark, Pittsburgh	1	3	3.0	3	0
Ryan, Jim, Denver	1	2	2.0	2	0
Preston, Dave, Denver	1	1	1.0	1	0
Thornton, Sidney, Pittsburgh	1	1	1.0	1	0
Dinkel, Tom, Cincinnati	1	0	0.0	0	0
Foote, Chris, Baltimore	1	0	0.0	0	0
Freeman, Steve, Buffalo	1	0	0.0	0	0
Hamilton, Ray, New England	1	0	0.0	0	0
Kemp, Bobby, Cincinnati	1	0	0.0	0	0

Fair Catch: Rick Razzano, Cincinnati
t indicates touchdown
Leader based on average return, minimum 16 returns.

NFC KICKOFF RETURNS—INDIVIDUAL

	No.	Yards	Avg.	Long	TD
Nelms, Mike, Washington	37	1099	29.7	84	0
Lawrence, Amos, San Francisco	17	437	25.7	92t	1
Smith, Reggie, Atlanta	47	1143	24.3	52	0
Mitchell, Stump, St. Louis	55	1292	23.5	67	0
Wilson, Wayne, New Orleans	31	722	23.3	57	0
Payton, Eddie, Minnesota	39	898	23.0	99t	1
Garrett, Alvin, N.Y.G.-Wash.	18	401	22.3	35	0
Rogers, Jimmy, New Orleans	28	621	22.2	44	0
Henry, Wally, Philadelphia	25	533	21.3	43	0
Williams, Dave, Chicago	23	486	21.1	42	0
Hall, Alvin, Detroit	25	525	21.0	36	0
Moorehead, Emery, Chicago	23	476	20.7	56	0
Martin, Robby, Detroit	25	509	20.4	34	0
Owens, James, Tampa Bay	24	473	19.7	34	0
Hill, Drew, Los Angeles	60	1170	19.5	50	0
Bright, Leon, New York Giants	25	481	19.2	41	0
Jones, James, Dallas	27	517	19.1	33	0
Non-Qualifiers					
Metcalf, Terry, Washington	14	283	20.2	36	0
Lee, Mark, Green Bay	14	270	19.3	31	0
Nord, Keith, Minnesota	14	229	16.4	27	0
Newsome, Timmy, Dallas	12	228	19.0	27	0
Campfield, Billy, Philadelphia	12	223	18.6	32	0
Nixon, Fred, Green Bay	12	222	18.5	25	0
Holt, John, Tampa Bay	11	274	24.9	40	0
McCoy, Mike C., Green Bay	11	221	20.1	36	0
McDole, Mardye, Minnesota	11	170	15.5	22	0
Ring, Bill, San Francisco	10	217	21.7	29	0
Woerner, Scott, Atlanta	10	210	21.0	27	0
Pittman, Danny, New York Giants	10	194	19.4	34	0
Fellows, Ron, Dallas	8	170	21.3	31	0
Green, Roy, St. Louis	8	135	16.9	28	0
Huckleby, Harlan, Green Bay	7	134	19.1	27	0
Harrell, Willard, St. Louis	7	118	16.9	29	0
Lott, Ronnie, San Francisco	7	111	15.9	20	0
Fisher, Jeff, Chicago	7	102	14.6	23	0
Wonsley, Otis, Washington	6	124	20.7	27	0
Middleton, Terdell, Green Bay	6	100	16.7	30	0
Frazier, Leslie, Chicago	6	77	12.8	15	0
Davis, Gary, Tampa Bay	5	81	16.2	21	0
Nichols, Mark, Detroit	4	74	18.5	26	0
Wilson, Mike, San Francisco	4	67	16.8	22	0
Coffman, Paul, Green Bay	3	77	25.7	52	0
Stauch, Scott, New Orleans	3	65	21.7	29	0
Cronan, Peter, Seattle-Washington	3	60	20.0	21	0
Davis, Tony, Tampa Bay	3	51	17.0	21	0
Dennis, Mike, New York Giants	3	51	17.0	17	0
Groth, Jeff, New Orleans	3	50	16.7	21	0
Love, Randy, St. Louis	3	46	15.3	25	0
Gaison, Blane, Atlanta	3	43	14.3	24	0
Jones, Arrington, San Francisco	3	43	14.3	22	0
Newhouse, Robert, Dallas	3	34	11.3	15	0
King, Horace, Detroit	3	33	11.0	14	0

	No.	Yards	Avg.	Long	TD
Sully, Ivory, Los Angeles	3	31	10.3	22	0
Merkens, Guido, New Orleans	2	38	19.0	20	0
Seay, Virgil, Washington	2	36	18.0	19	0
Baschnagel, Brian, Chicago	2	34	17.0	23	0
Griffin, Jeff, St. Louis	2	34	17.0	26	0
Jackson, Wilbur, Washington	2	34	17.0	17	0
Wilson, Steve, Dallas	2	32	16.0	17	0
Russell, Booker, Philadelphia	2	28	14.0	20	0
Gray, Johnnie, Green Bay	2	24	12.0	19	0
Callicutt, Ken, Detroit	2	23	11.5	12	0
Mayberry, James, Atlanta	2	23	11.5	15	0
Brock, Stan, New Orleans	2	18	9.0	12	0
McLaughlin, Joe, New York Giants	2	9	4.5	5	0
Williams, Brooks, Chicago	1	35	35.0	35	0
Reece, Beasley, New York Giants	1	24	24.0	24	0
Hicks, Dwight, San Francisco	1	22	22.0	22	0
Grant, Darryl, Washington	1	20	20.0	20	0
Giammona, Louie, Philadelphia	1	19	19.0	19	0
Wilder, James, Tampa Bay	1	19	19.0	19	0
Meisner, Greg, Los Angeles	1	17	17.0	17	0
Galbreath, Tony, Minnesota	1	16	16.0	16	0
Atkins, Steve, Philadelphia	1	15	15.0	15	0
Jensen, Jim, Green Bay	1	15	15.0	15	0
Thomas, Jewerl, Los Angeles	1	15	15.0	15	0
Young, Rickey, Minnesota	1	15	15.0	15	0
Claitt, Rickey, Washington	1	14	14.0	14	0
Murray, Calvin, Philadelphia	1	14	14.0	14	0
Obradovich, Jim, Tampa Bay	1	14	14.0	14	0
Ramson, Eason, San Francisco	1	12	12.0	12	0
Guman, Mike, Los Angeles	1	10	10.0	10	0
Banks, Gordon, New Orleans	1	9	9.0	9	0
Fisher, Bob, Chicago	1	9	9.0	9	0
Peters, Tony, Washington	1	5	5.0	5	0
Jefferson, John, Green Bay	1	3	3.0	3	0
Penaranda, Jairo, Los Angeles	1	1	1.0	1	0
Blair, Matt, Minnesota	1	0	0.0	0	0
Braggs, Byron, Green Bay	1	0	0.0	0	0
Brantley, Scot, Tampa Bay	1	0	0.0	0	0
Clarke, Ken, Philadelphia	1	0	0.0	0	0
Cosbie, Doug, Dallas	1	0	0.0	0	0
Davis, Johnny, San Francisco	1	0	0.0	0	0
Harrell, James, Detroit	1	0	0.0	0	0
Lee, Larry, Detroit	1	0	0.0	0	0
Pankey, Irv, Los Angeles	1	0	0.0	0	0
Patton, Ricky, San Francisco	1	0	0.0	0	0
Anderson, Marcus, Chicago	1	−5	−5.0	−5	0

Fair Catch: John Mistler, New York Giants
t indicates touchdown
Leader based on average return, minimum 16 returns.

AFC FUMBLES — TEAM

	Fum.	Own Rec.	Fum. *O.B.	Yds.	TD	Opp. Rec.	Yds.	TD	Tot. Rec.
Cincinnati	25	10	3	−5	0	18	28	1	28
Denver	26	6	2	1	0	23	5	0	29
Miami	26	13	3	−21	0	15	40	1	28
Baltimore	27	11	2	10	1	14	3	0	25
New England	32	14	2	−8	0	17	44	0	31
Buffalo	33	13	2	0	0	17	42	0	30
Houston	33	10	2	−18	0	13	6	0	23
Kansas City	36	10	2	−4	0	21	260	3	31
Cleveland	38	11	1	−39	0	20	21	0	31
New York Jets	38	19	2	7	1	15	4	0	34
Pittsburgh	39	14	3	−35	0	16	39	0	30
San Diego	39	13	4	−22	0	18	40	0	31
Seattle	41	14	4	8	0	27	94	2	41
Oakland	42	20	2	14	0	19	83	2	39
AFC Totals	475	178	34	−112	2	253	709	9	431
AFC Average	33.9	12.7	2.4	−8.0	0.1	18.1	50.6	0.6	30.8

*Fumbled out of bounds.

NFC FUMBLES — TEAM

	Fum.	Own Rec.	Fum. *O.B.	Yds.	TD	Opp. Rec.	Yds.	TD	Tot. Rec.
San Francisco	26	11	3	0	0	21	83	1	32
Tampa Bay	27	10	3	−37	0	14	29	1	24
Atlanta	31	13	1	−21	1	21	160	3	34
Green Bay	31	14	0	−28	0	24	92	0	38
Washington	32	11	2	−8	0	15	23	0	26
Philadelphia	33	14	2	−25	0	21	85	2	35
St. Louis	33	10	3	−7	0	17	7	0	27
Los Angeles	34	16	3	−6	0	16	44	1	32
Chicago	37	19	1	−14	0	22	56	0	41
New York Giants	38	21	1	−13	0	17	41	3	38
Minnesota	39	15	3	−3	0	19	87	1	34
New Orleans	40	18	2	57	0	17	30	0	35
Detroit	41	19	2	−20	0	15	24	0	34
Dallas	45	22	3	−58	0	16	72	1	38
NFC Totals	487	213	29	−183	1	255	833	13	468
NFC Average	34.8	15.2	2.1	−13.1	0.1	18.2	59.5	0.9	33.4
League Totals	962	391	63	−295	3	508	1542	22	899
League Average	34.4	14.0	2.3	−10.5	0.1	18.1	55.1	0.8	32.1

*Fumbled out of bounds.

AFC FUMBLES — INDIVIDUAL

	Fum.	Own Rec.	Yds.	Opp. Rec.	Yds.	Tot. Rec.
Alexander, Charles, Cincinnati	0	1	0	0	0	1
Alzado, Lyle, Cleveland	0	0	0	1	0	1
Ambrose, Dick, Cleveland	0	0	0	2	0	2
Anderson, Ken, Cincinnati	5	2	−20	0	0	2
Anderson, Kim, Baltimore	2	3	−1	0	0	3
Anderson, Larry, Pittsburgh	1	0	0	0	0	0
Armstrong, Adger, Houston	2	0	0	0	0	0
Augustyniak, Mike, New York Jets	3	0	0	0	0	0
Baker, Jesse, Houston	0	0	0	1	0	1
Banaszak, John, Pittsburgh	0	0	0	1	0	1
Barbaro, Gary, Kansas City	0	0	0	1	0	1
Barkum, Jerome, New York Jets	0	3	0	0	0	3
Barnwell, Malcolm, Oakland	2	0	0	0	0	0
Bass, Don, Cincinnati	0	0	0	1	0	1
Baumhower, Bob, Miami	0	0	0	3	10	3
Beamon, Autry, Cleveland	0	0	0	1	5	1
Bell, Mike, Kansas City	0	0	0	1	0	1
Bennett, Woody, Miami	1	1	0	0	0	1
Bess, Rufus, Buffalo	0	1	0	1	4	2
Bessillieu, Don, Miami	1	1	0	1	0	2
Bingham, Gregg, Houston	0	0	0	1	0	1
Blackwood, Glenn, Miami	0	0	0	1	5	1
Bledsoe, Curtis, Kansas City	4	1	0	0	0	1
Bolton, Ron, Cleveland	0	0	0	2	0	2
Borchardt, Jon, Buffalo	0	1	0	0	0	1
Bradley, Henry, Cleveland	0	0	0	1	0	1
Bradshaw, Terry, Pittsburgh	7	3	−23	0	0	3
Brammer, Mark, Buffalo	3	1	0	0	0	1
Braziel, Larry, Baltimore	1	0	0	1	0	1
Breeden, Louis, Cincinnati	0	0	0	1	10	1
Brock, Pete, New England	0	1	0	0	0	1
Brooks, James, San Diego	7	2	0	0	0	2
Brown, Curtis, Buffalo	4	0	0	0	0	0
Brown, Dave, Seattle	0	0	0	1	8	1
Brown, Theotis, St. Louis-Seattle	8	3	0	0	0	3
Brown, Thomas, Cleveland	0	0	0	1	0	1
Browner, Ross, Cincinnati	0	0	0	1	0	1
Browning, Dave, Oakland	0	0	0	1	0	1
Bryan, Bill, Denver	1	0	0	0	0	0
Buben, Mark, New England	0	0	0	1	31	1
Buchanon, Willie, San Diego	0	0	0	4	0	4
Burrough, Ken, Houston	1	2	0	0	0	2
Burruss, Lloyd, Kansas City	1	0	0	1	4	1
Bush, Blair, Cincinnati	0	1	12	0	0	1
Busick, Steve, Denver	0	0	0	2	3	2
Butler, Jerry, Buffalo	2	0	0	0	0	0
Butler, Keith, Seattle	1	0	0	0	0	0
Buttle, Greg, New York Jets	0	0	0	2	0	2
Calhoun, Don, New England	1	0	0	0	0	0
Camarillo, Rich, New England	1	1	0	0	0	1
Campbell, Earl, Houston	10	2	0	0	0	2
Canada, Larry, Denver	1	1	0	0	0	1

Fumbles

	Fum.	Own Rec.	Yds.	Opp. Rec.	Yds.	Tot. Rec.
Cancik, Phil, Kansas City	0	0	0	1	0	1
Cappelletti, John, San Diego	3	0	0	0	0	0
Carson, Carlos, Kansas City	1	1	0	0	0	1
Carter, David, Houston	0	1	0	0	0	1
Carter, Rubin, Denver	0	0	0	1	0	1
Cavanaugh, Matt, New England	2	0	0	0	0	0
Chandler, Bob, Oakland	2	1	22	0	0	1
Chandler, Wes, New Orleans-San Diego	1	1	51	0	0	1
Chavous, Barney, Denver	0	0	0	1	0	1
Christensen, Todd, Oakland	0	0	0	1	0	1
Christopher, Herb, Kansas City	0	0	0	1	0	1
Clark, Mario, Buffalo	0	0	0	2	5	2
Clayborn, Ray, New England	0	0	0	2	4	2
Cole, Robin, Pittsburgh	0	0	0	1	0	1
Coleman, Ronnie, Houston	2	0	0	0	0	0
Collins, Anthony, New England	8	2	0	0	0	2
Collinsworth, Cris, Cincinnati	3	1	0	0	0	1
Condon, Tom, Kansas City	0	1	0	0	0	1
Courson, Steve, Pittsburgh	0	2	0	0	0	2
Cribbs, Joe, Buffalo	12	1	0	0	0	1
Cronan, Peter, Seattle	0	1	0	0	0	1
Cunningham, Bennie, Pittsburgh	0	1	0	0	0	1
Cunningham, Sam, New England	2	0	0	0	0	0
Curtis, Isaac, Cincinnati	1	1	0	0	0	1
Darden, Thom, Cleveland	0	0	0	2	0	2
Davis, Russell, Pittsburgh	3	2	0	0	0	2
DeBerg, Steve, Denver	2	0	0	0	0	0
Delaney, Joe, Kansas City	9	0	0	0	0	0
Dickey, Curtis, Baltimore	8	0	0	0	0	0
Dierking, Scott, New York Jets	2	1	0	0	0	1
Dixon, Zachary, Baltimore	1	0	0	0	0	0
Dobler, Conrad, Buffalo	0	1	0	0	0	1
Donaldson, Ray, Baltimore	0	1	0	0	0	1
Doornink, Dan, Seattle	3	1	0	0	0	1
Dorris, Andy, Houston	0	0	0	1	0	1
Duhe, A.J., Miami	0	0	0	1	0	1
Dunn, Gary, Pittsburgh	0	0	0	1	1	1
Dykes, Donald, New York Jets	0	1	0	0	0	1
Easley, Kenny, Seattle	0	1	21	3	4	4
Edwards, Eddie, Cincinnati	0	0	0	1	0	1
Edwards, Glen, San Diego	1	1	0	2	−3	3
Egloff, Ron, Denver	2	0	0	1	6	1
Evans, Larry, Denver	0	0	0	1	0	1
Ferguson, Joe, Buffalo	2	0	0	0	0	0
Ferguson, Vagas, New England	1	1	0	0	0	1
Fields, Joe, New York Jets	1	0	−15	0	0	0
Foley, Steve, Denver	0	0	0	1	0	1
Fouts, Dan, San Diego	9	2	−22	0	0	2
Franklin, Andra, Miami	5	1	0	0	0	1
Franklin, Byron, Buffalo	2	0	0	0	0	0
Franklin, Cleveland, Baltimore	2	0	0	0	0	0
Fuller, Mike, Cincinnati	1	0	0	1	0	1
Fuller, Steve, Kansas City	4	1	−6	0	0	1
Gaines, Greg, Seattle	0	0	0	1	0	1
Gastineau, Mark, New York Jets	0	0	0	2	0	2

	Fum.	Own Rec.	Yds.	Opp. Rec.	Yds.	Tot. Rec.
Geisler, Jon, Miami	0	1	0	0	0	1
Glasgow, Nesby, Baltimore	0	0	0	2	0	2
Glassic, Tom, Denver	0	1	0	0	0	1
Golic, Bob, New England	0	0	0	1	0	1
Gordon, Larry, Miami	0	0	0	1	0	1
Grant, Will, Buffalo	0	1	0	0	0	1
Green, Bubba, Baltimore	0	0	0	1	0	1
Green, Gary, Kansas City	0	0	0	1	0	1
Green, Jacob, Seattle	0	0	0	1	0	1
Griffin, Ray, Cincinnati	0	0	0	1	0	1
Grogan, Steve, New England	5	2	−8	0	0	2
Guy, Ray, Oakland	1	0	0	0	0	0
Hadnot, James, Kansas City	4	1	0	0	0	1
Hall, Dino, Cleveland	5	0	0	0	0	0
Ham, Jack, Pittsburgh	0	0	0	3	0	3
Hamilton, Ray, New England	1	0	0	0	0	0
Hannah, John, New England	0	2	0	0	0	2
Harden, Mike, Denver	0	0	0	1	0	1
Hardman, Cedrick, Oakland	0	0	0	1	52	1
Hardy, Bruce, Miami	1	0	0	0	0	0
Hardy, Robert, Seattle	0	0	0	2	3	2
Hargrove, Jimmy, Cincinnati	1	0	0	0	0	0
Harper, Bruce, New York Jets	7	2	0	0	0	2
Harris, Eric, Kansas City	0	0	0	2	20	2
Harris, Franco, Pittsburgh	6	0	0	0	0	0
Harris, John, Seattle	1	0	0	3	0	3
Harris, M. L., Cincinnati	1	0	0	2	3	2
Hartwig, Carter, Houston	0	0	0	1	0	1
Hasselbeck, Don, New England	2	0	0	0	0	0
Haslett, Jim, Buffalo	0	0	0	1	0	1
Hawkins, Frank, Oakland	1	1	0	0	0	1
Hawkins, Mike, New England	0	0	0	2	0	2
Hawthorne, Greg, Pittsburgh	1	0	0	0	0	0
Hendricks, Ted, Oakland	0	0	0	1	0	1
Henderson, Wyatt, San Diego	0	0	0	3	0	3
Herkenhoff, Matt, Kansas City	0	1	0	0	0	1
Hicks, Bryan, Cincinnati	0	0	0	2	3	2
Hill, Calvin, Cleveland	1	0	0	0	0	0
Hill, Eddie, Miami	2	0	0	0	0	0
Holloway, Brian, New England	0	1	0	0	0	1
Holmes, Jerry, New York Jets	0	0	0	1	0	1
Hooks, Roland, Buffalo	1	0	0	0	0	0
Horn, Rod, Cincinnati	0	0	0	1	0	1
Howard, Thomas, Kansas City	0	1	0	1	65	2
Howell, Steve, Miami	0	1	0	0	0	1
Hughes, David, Seattle	4	1	0	0	0	1
Humiston, Mike, Buffalo	0	1	0	0	0	1
Ilkin, Tunch, Pittsburgh	0	1	0	0	0	1
Ivory, Horace, Seattle	1	0	0	0	0	0
Jackson, Billy, Kansas City	1	0	0	0	0	0
Jackson, Charles, Kansas City	0	0	0	3	33	3
Jackson, Harold, New England	1	0	0	0	0	0
Jackson, Michael, Seattle	0	1	0	1	0	2
Jackson, Monte, Oakland	0	1	0	0	0	1
Jackson, Robert L., Cleveland	0	0	0	2	0	2

Fumbles	Fum.	Own Rec.	Yds.	Opp. Rec.	Yds.	Tot. Rec.
Jackson, Tom, Denver	0	0	0	1	0	1
James, Roland, New England	1	0	0	1	0	1
Jensen, Derrick, Oakland	0	1	0	0	0	1
Jodat, Jim, Seattle	4	0	0	1	0	1
Johns, Paul, Seattle	1	0	0	0	0	0
Johnson, Andy, New England	1	0	0	0	0	0
Johnson, Eddie, Cleveland	0	0	0	1	0	1
Johnson, Gary, San Diego	0	0	0	1	0	1
Johnson, Greggory, Seattle	2	1	0	3	31	4
Johnson, Jesse, New York Jets	0	0	0	1	0	1
Johnson, Ken, Buffalo	0	1	0	1	0	2
Johnson, Pete, Cincinnati	4	1	0	0	0	1
Joiner, Charlie, San Diego	2	0	0	0	0	0
Jones, Bert, Baltimore	3	1	0	0	0	1
Jones, Bobby, New York Jets	0	1	61	0	0	1
Jones, Johnny, New York Jets	2	2	0	0	0	2
Jones, Ken, Buffalo	0	2	0	0	0	2
Jones, Leroy, San Diego	0	0	0	1	5	1
Jones, Ricky, Baltimore	0	1	0	0	0	1
Jones, Rulon, Denver	0	0	0	1	0	1
Jones, Willie, Oakland	0	0	0	1	9	1
Justin, Kerry, Seattle	0	0	0	1	43	1
Kelcher, Louie, San Diego	0	0	0	1	0	1
Kennard, Ken, Houston	0	0	0	1	0	1
Kenney, Bill, Kansas City	4	0	−2	0	0	0
King, Kenny, Oakland	10	2	0	0	0	2
Klecko, Joe, New York Jets	0	0	0	2	0	2
Kohrs, Bob, Pittsburgh	0	0	0	1	0	1
Kozlowski, Mike, Miami	0	0	0	1	25	1
Krauss, Barry, Baltimore	0	0	0	2	0	2
Kreider, Steve, Cincinnati	2	0	0	0	0	0
Kremer, Ken, Kansas City	0	0	0	2	0	2
Krieg, Dave, Seattle	4	0	0	0	0	0
Kush, Rod, Buffalo	1	0	0	3	5	3
Kyle, Aaron, Denver	0	0	0	4	1	4
Laakso, Eric, Miami	0	1	0	0	0	1
Laird, Bruce, Baltimore	0	0	0	1	3	1
Lambert, Jack, Pittsburgh	0	0	0	2	38	2
Landry, Greg, Baltimore	2	1	11	0	0	1
Lane, Eric, Seattle	0	1	0	0	0	1
Largent, Steve, Seattle	2	0	0	0	0	0
Laslavic, Jim, San Diego	0	0	0	1	38	1
Latimer, Don, Denver	0	0	0	1	0	1
Lawrence, Henry, Oakland	0	2	0	0	0	2
Leaks, Roosevelt, Buffalo	1	0	0	0	0	0
LeClair, Jim, Cincinnati	0	0	0	1	0	1
Lewis, Frank, Buffalo	1	1	0	0	0	1
Lewis, Will, Seattle	5	1	0	0	0	1
Little, David, Pittsburgh	0	0	0	1	0	1
Long, Kevin, New York Jets	2	1	0	0	0	1
Lowery, Nick, Kansas City	0	1	0	0	0	1
Lyons, Marty, New York Jets	0	0	0	1	0	1
Lytle, Rob, Denver	1	0	0	0	0	0
Macek, Don, San Diego	0	1	0	0	0	1
Malone, Mark, Pittsburgh	2	0	0	0	0	0

	Fum.	Own Rec.	Yds.	Opp. Rec.	Yds.	Tot. Rec.
Manning, Wade, Denver	3	0	0	0	0	0
Manumaleuga, Frank, Kansas City	1	0	0	0	0	0
Marsh, Curt, Oakland	0	0	0	1	0	1
Marshall, Henry, Kansas City	2	0	0	0	0	0
Martin, Rod, Oakland	0	1	0	2	0	3
Marvin, Mickey, Oakland	0	0	0	1	0	1
Matthews, Bill, New England	0	0	0	1	0	1
Matthews, Clay, Cleveland	0	0	0	2	16	2
Matthews, Ira, Oakland	5	2	0	0	0	2
Matuszak, John, Oakland	0	0	0	1	0	1
McClanahan, Randy, Oakland	0	0	0	3	0	3
McCullum, Sam, Seattle	1	0	0	0	0	0
McCutcheon, Lawrence, Buffalo	1	0	0	0	0	0
McDonald, Paul, Cleveland	4	0	0	0	0	0
McGee, Tony, New England	0	0	0	1	0	1
McKinney, Odis, Oakland	0	0	0	1	0	1
McKnight, Ted, Kansas City	2	0	0	0	0	0
McMillan, Randy, Baltimore	1	0	0	0	0	0
McNeal, Don, Miami	0	0	0	1	0	1
McNeil, Freeman, New York Jets	5	0	0	0	0	0
Mehl, Lance, New York Jets	0	0	0	1	0	1
Mike-Mayer, Nick, Buffalo	0	1	0	0	0	1
Millen, Matt, Oakland	0	0	0	1	0	1
Minor, Vic, Seattle	0	1	0	0	0	1
Montgomery, Cleotha, Cleveland	2	1	0	0	0	1
Montoya, Max, Cincinnati	0	1	0	0	0	1
Morgan, Stanley, New England	2	2	0	0	0	2
Morton, Craig, Denver	2	0	0	0	0	0
Moses, Haven, Denver	1	0	0	0	0	0
Muncie, Chuck, San Diego	9	4	0	0	0	4
Nathan, Tony, Miami	2	2	0	0	0	2
Neil, Kenny, New York Jets	0	1	0	0	0	1
Newton, Tom, New York Jets	2	0	0	0	0	0
Nielsen, Gifford, Houston	3	1	−15	0	0	1
Norman, Joe, Seattle	0	0	0	2	0	2
Odoms, Riley, Denver	1	0	0	0	0	0
Orosz, Tom, Miami	0	1	0	0	0	1
Orvis, Herb, Baltimore	0	0	0	2	0	2
O'Steen, Dwayne, Oakland	0	1	0	2	0	3
Owen, Tom, New England	1	0	0	0	0	0
Owens, Burgess, Oakland	0	0	0	2	22	2
Parker, Ervin, Buffalo	0	0	0	1	0	1
Parrish, Don, Kansas City	0	0	0	3	0	3
Parros, Rick, Denver	6	1	0	0	0	1
Paul, Whitney, Kansas City	0	0	0	1	47	1
Perry, Vernon, Houston	0	0	0	1	0	1
Phillips, Irvin, San Diego	1	0	0	1	0	1
Piccone, Lou, Buffalo	0	1	0	0	0	1
Plunkett, Jim, Oakland	3	1	−6	0	0	1
Pollard, Frank, Pittsburgh	5	0	−12	0	0	0
Pratt, Robert, Baltimore	1	1	0	0	0	1
Preston, Dave, Denver	4	0	0	0	0	0
Prestridge, Luke, Denver	1	0	0	0	0	0
Pruitt, Greg, Cleveland	3	0	0	0	0	0

Fumbles	Fum.	Own Rec.	Yds.	Opp. Rec.	Yds.	Tot. Rec.
Pruitt, Mike, Cleveland	5	2	0	0	0	2
Ramsey, Chuck, New York Jets	2	1	−39	0	0	1
Ramsey, Derrick, Oakland	2	1	0	0	0	1
Ray, Darrol, New York Jets	1	0	0	2	4	2
Reaves, John, Houston	2	0	−2	0	0	0
Reed, Tony, Denver	1	0	0	0	0	0
Reinfeldt, Mike, Houston	0	0	0	2	0	2
Renfro, Mike, Houston	2	1	12	1	0	2
Rhone, Earnest, Miami	0	0	0	1	0	1
Riddick, Robb, Buffalo	1	0	0	0	0	0
Riley, Avon, Houston	0	0	0	1	6	1
Riley, Ken, Cincinnati	0	0	0	1	0	1
Robinson, Johnny, Oakland	0	0	0	1	0	1
Robinson, Matt, Buffalo	1	0	0	0	0	0
Robinson, Mike, Cleveland	0	0	0	1	0	1
Rome, Stan, Kansas City	0	1	13	0	0	1
Romes, Charles, Buffalo	1	0	0	2	11	2
Rose, Joe, Miami	0	0	0	1	0	1
Ross, Dan, Cincinnati	3	1	3	0	0	1
Rudnay, Jack, Kansas City	1	0	−28	0	0	0
St. Clair, Mike, Cincinnati	0	0	0	1	12	1
Salaam, Abdul, New York Jets	0	0	0	1	0	1
Sanford, Lucius, Buffalo	0	0	0	1	0	1
Sanford, Rick, New England	0	0	0	3	2	3
Scales, Dwight, San Diego	1	0	0	0	0	0
Schonert, Turk, Cincinnati	1	0	0	0	0	0
Schuh, Jeff, Cincinnati	0	0	0	1	0	1
Schumacher, John, Houston	0	1	0	0	0	1
Scott, Clarence, Cleveland	0	0	0	3	0	3
Shaw, Pete, San Diego	0	0	0	1	0	1
Shell, Donnie, Pittsburgh	0	0	0	2	0	2
Shiver, Sanders, Baltimore	0	0	0	1	0	1
Shoate, Rod, New England	1	0	0	2	7	2
Shula, Dave, Baltimore	2	2	0	0	0	2
Shull, Steve, Miami	0	0	0	2	0	2
Sievers, Eric, San Diego	1	0	0	1	0	1
Simmons, John, Cincinnati	1	1	0	0	0	1
Simonini, Ed, Baltimore	0	0	0	1	0	1
Simpson, Bill, Buffalo	0	0	0	1	0	1
Simpson, Keith, Seattle	0	0	0	1	0	1
Sipe, Brian, Cleveland	10	4	−39	0	0	4
Skaugstad, Daryle, Houston	0	0	0	2	0	2
Small, Gerald, Miami	0	0	0	2	0	2
Smerlas, Fred, Buffalo	0	0	0	1	17	1
Smith, Dennis, Denver	0	0	0	2	0	2
Smith, Jim, Pittsburgh	1	1	0	0	0	1
Smith, J. T., Kansas City	2	1	19	0	0	1
Smith, Sherman, Seattle	3	2	0	0	0	2
Sohn, Kurt, New York Jets	5	2	0	0	0	2
Spani, Gary, Kansas City	0	0	0	2	91	2
Springs, Kirk, New York Jets	1	1	0	1	0	2
Stabler, Ken, Houston	7	2	−13	0	0	2
Stallworth, John, Pittsburgh	4	0	0	0	0	0
Stensrud, Mike, Houston	0	0	0	1	0	1
Still, Art, Kansas City	0	0	0	1	0	1

	Fum.	Own Rec.	Yds.	Opp. Rec.	Yds.	Tot. Rec.
Sullivan, Gerry, Cleveland	0	1	0	1	0	2
Sutherland, Doug, Seattle	0	0	0	1	0	1
Swann, Lynn, Pittsburgh	1	1	0	0	0	1
Sweeney, Calvin, Pittsburgh	1	0	0	0	0	0
Swenson, Bob, Denver	0	0	0	3	0	3
Tatupu, Mosi, New England	2	1	0	2	0	3
Taylor, Hosea, Baltimore	0	0	0	1	0	1
Thomas, J. T., Pittsburgh	0	0	0	1	0	1
Thomas, Rodell, Seattle	0	0	0	2	5	2
Thompson, Bill, Denver	0	0	0	2	0	2
Thompson, Donnell, Baltimore	0	0	0	1	0	1
Thornton, Sidney, Pittsburgh	6	1	0	0	0	1
Todd, Richard, New York Jets	5	2	0	0	0	2
Toews, Loren, Pittsburgh	0	1	0	0	0	1
Toler, Ken, New England	0	1	0	0	0	1
Trout, David, Pittsburgh	0	0	0	1	0	1
Tuiasosopo, Manu, Seattle	0	0	0	3	0	3
Valentine, Zack, Pittsburgh	0	1	0	1	0	2
Verser, David, Cincinnati	2	0	0	0	0	0
Vigorito, Tommy, Miami	1	0	0	0	0	0
Villapiano, Phil, Buffalo	0	0	0	1	0	1
Walker, Fulton, Miami	4	2	0	0	0	2
Watson, Steve, Denver	0	2	0	0	0	2
Watts, Ted, Oakland	3	2	1	0	0	2
West, Jeff, Seattle	1	0	−13	0	0	0
White, Charles, Cleveland	8	3	0	0	0	3
White, Mike, Seattle	0	0	0	1	0	1
White, Sherman, Buffalo	0	0	0	1	0	1
Whittington, Arthur, Oakland	4	0	0	0	0	0
Wilkerson, Doug, San Diego	0	1	0	0	0	1
Williams, Ben, Buffalo	0	0	0	1	0	1
Williams, Clarence, San Diego	2	0	0	0	0	0
Williams, Kevin, Baltimore	4	1	0	0	0	1
Williams, Reggie, Cincinnati	0	0	0	3	0	3
Willis, Chester, Oakland	1	1	0	0	0	1
Wilson, J. C., Houston	1	0	0	0	0	0
Wilson, Marc, Oakland	8	2	−3	0	0	2
Wilson, Tim, Houston	2	0	0	0	0	0
Winslow, Kellen, San Diego	2	2	0	0	0	2
Woodcock, John, San Diego	0	0	0	2	0	2
Woodley, David, Miami	9	2	−21	0	0	2
Woodring, John, New York Jets	0	1	0	1	0	2
Woodruff, Dwayne, Pittsburgh	1	0	0	1	0	1
Woods, Mike, Baltimore	0	0	0	1	0	1
Wright, James, Denver	0	1	1	0	0	1
Wright, Louis, Denver	0	0	0	1	−5	1
Yarno, John, Seattle	0	1	0	0	0	1
Zamberlin, John, New England	0	0	0	1	0	1
Zorn, Jim, Seattle	2	0	0	0	0	0

Touchdowns: Greg Landry, Baltimore; Mike St. Clair, Cincinnati; Thomas Howard, Whitney Paul, and Gary Spani, Kansas City; Mike Kozlowski, Miami; Bobby Jones, New York Jets; Cedrick Hardman and Willie Jones, Oakland; and Greggory Johnson and Rodell Thomas, Seattle, 1 each.

NFC FUMBLES—INDIVIDUAL

	Fum.	Own Rec.	Yds.	Opp. Rec.	Yds.	Tot. Rec.
Allen, Jim, Detroit	0	0	0	1	0	1
Allerman, Kurt, Green Bay	0	0	0	1	0	1
Anderson, John, Green Bay	0	0	0	4	22	4
Anderson, Marcus, Chicago	1	0	0	0	0	0
Anderson, Ottis, St. Louis	13	3	0	0	0	3
Andrews, William, Atlanta	12	0	0	0	0	0
Ane, Charlie, Green Bay	0	1	0	1	0	2
Ard, Billy, New York Giants	0	1	0	0	0	1
Atkins, Steve, Green Bay	1	0	0	0	0	0
Audick, Dan, San Francisco	0	2	0	0	0	2
Baker, Charles, St. Louis	0	1	0	0	0	1
Banks, Gordon, New Orleans	2	1	0	0	0	1
Barnes, Benny, Dallas	1	0	0	2	72	2
Bartkowski, Steve, Atlanta	4	3	−1	0	0	3
Baschnagel, Brian, Chicago	2	2	0	0	0	2
Bell, Ricky, Tampa Bay	1	1	0	0	0	1
Bell, Theo, Tampa Bay	1	0	0	0	0	0
Bell, Todd, Chicago	0	1	0	0	0	1
Blackmore, Richard, Philadelphia	0	0	0	1	0	1
Blair, Matt, Minnesota	1	0	0	2	0	2
Blanchard, Tom, Tampa Bay	1	2	0	0	0	2
Bolinger, Russ, Detroit	0	2	0	0	0	2
Bostic, Jeff, Washington	0	1	0	0	0	1
Bradley, Luther, Detroit	0	0	0	1	0	1
Brahaney, Tom, St. Louis	0	1	0	0	0	1
Brenner, Hoby, New Orleans	1	0	0	0	0	0
Bright, Leon, New York Giants	3	4	0	0	0	4
Brock, Stan, New Orleans	0	2	0	0	0	2
Brooks, Perry, Washington	0	0	0	2	0	2
Brown, Cedric, Tampa Bay	1	0	0	1	0	1
Brown, Greg, Philadelphia	0	0	0	2	7	2
Brown, Ted, Minnesota	3	2	0	1	0	3
Bruer, Bob, Minnesota	1	0	0	0	0	0
Brunner, Scott, New York Giants	6	2	−3	0	0	2
Bryant, Cullen, Los Angeles	1	0	0	0	0	0
Bunting, John, Philadelphia	0	0	0	1	16	1
Bunz, Dan, San Francisco	0	0	0	2	0	2
Bussey, Dexter, Detroit	3	0	0	0	0	0
Cain, Lynn, Atlanta	3	2	0	0	0	2
Callicutt, Ken, Detroit	0	0	0	1	0	1
Campbell, Gary, Chicago	0	0	0	1	0	1
Campfield, Billy, Philadelphia	3	2	1	0	0	2
Carano, Glenn, Dallas	3	0	−6	0	0	0
Carmichael, Harold, Philadelphia	3	1	0	0	0	1
Carpenter, Rob, Houston-N.Y. Giants	3	0	0	0	0	0
Carson, Harry, New York Giants	0	0	0	1	2	1
Cassidy, Ron, Green Bay	1	0	0	0	0	0
Caster, Richard, New Orleans	2	0	0	0	0	0
Chesley, Al, Philadelphia	0	0	0	2	11	2
Childs, Henry, Los Angeles	1	0	0	0	0	0
Cobb, Garry, Detroit	0	0	0	3	0	3
Cobb, Mike, Chicago	0	1	0	0	0	1

	Fum.	Own Rec.	Yds.	Opp. Rec.	Yds.	Tot. Rec.
Coffman, Paul, Green Bay	1	0	0	1	0	1
Coleman, Monte, Washington	0	0	0	1	2	1
Coleman, Greg, Minnesota	0	1	0	0	0	1
Collins, George, St. Louis	0	1	0	0	0	1
Colzie, Neal, Tampa Bay	1	0	0	1	0	1
Connell, Mike, Washington	2	2	−8	0	0	2
Cooper, Earl, San Francisco	3	1	0	0	0	1
Cosbie, Doug, Dallas	1	0	0	0	0	0
Cromwell, Nolan, Los Angeles	0	1	0	2	4	3
Cumby, George, Green Bay	0	0	0	2	70	2
Curcio, Mike, Philadelphia	0	0	0	1	0	1
Currier, Bill, New York Giants	0	0	0	1	0	1
Danielson, Gary, Detroit	2	0	0	0	0	0
Davis, Gary, Tampa Bay	1	0	0	0	0	0
Davis, Johnny, San Francisco	1	0	0	0	0	0
Dawson, Mike, St. Louis	0	0	0	2	0	2
Dennard, Preston, Los Angeles	1	1	0	0	0	1
Dickerson, Anthony, Dallas	0	0	0	2	0	2
Dickey, Lynn, Green Bay	8	3	−26	0	0	3
Dierdorf, Dan, St. Louis	0	1	0	0	0	1
Dils, Steve, Minnesota	3	2	0	0	0	2
Donovan, Pat, Dallas	0	1	0	0	0	1
Dorney, Keith, Detroit	0	1	0	0	0	1
Dorsett, Tony, Dallas	10	2	0	0	0	2
Doss, Reggie, Los Angeles	0	0	0	1	0	1
Douglass, Mike, Green Bay	0	0	0	3	0	3
Downs, Michael, Dallas	0	0	0	1	0	1
Dusek, Brad, Washington	0	0	0	1	0	1
Easley, Walt, San Francisco	2	2	0	0	0	2
Eckwood, Jerry, Tampa Bay	3	2	0	0	0	2
Edwards, Herman, Philadelphia	0	0	0	1	4	1
Elias, Homer, Detroit	0	2	0	0	0	2
Elliott, Lenvil, San Francisco	2	0	0	0	0	0
Ellis, Gerry, Green Bay	5	1	0	0	0	1
Ellis, Ray, Philadelphia	0	0	0	1	0	1
English, Doug, Detroit	0	0	0	3	20	3
Erxleben, Russell, New Orleans	1	0	0	0	0	0
Evans, Vince, Chicago	13	2	−10	0	0	2
Fahnhorst, Keith, San Francisco	0	0	0	0	0	2
Fanning, Mike, Los Angeles	0	0	0	1	0	1
Fantetti, Ken, Detroit	0	0	0	1	0	1
Faumina, Wilson, Atlanta	0	0	0	1	0	1
Favron, Calvin, St. Louis	0	0	0	1	5	1
Fencik, Gary, Chicago	0	0	0	1	0	1
Fisher, Jeff, Chicago	3	0	0	1	0	1
Flick, Tom, Washington	2	1	0	0	0	1
Flowers, Larry, New York Giants	0	0	0	1	0	1
Forte, Ike, New York Giants	1	0	0	0	0	0
Fowler, Amos, Detroit	0	2	−10	0	0	2
Francis, Wallace, Atlanta	1	1	0	1	0	2
Gaison, Blane, Atlanta	0	0	0	1	0	1
Galbreath, Tony, Minnesota	2	0	0	0	0	0
Garrett, Alvin, New York Giants	1	0	0	0	0	0
Gay, William, Detroit	0	0	0	1	0	1

Fumbles

	Fum.	Own Rec.	Yds.	Opp. Rec.	Yds.	Tot. Rec.
Giammona, Louie, Philadelphia	2	0	0	0	0	0
Glazebrook, Bob, Atlanta	0	0	0	1	22	1
Gofourth, Derrell, Green Bay	0	1	0	0	0	1
Gray, Earnest, New York Giants	1	0	0	0	0	0
Gray, Johnnie, Green Bay	0	0	0	1	0	1
Green, Curtis, Detroit	0	0	0	1	0	1
Green, Hugh, Tampa Bay	0	0	0	1	0	1
Green, Roy, St. Louis	2	0	0	0	0	0
Greene, Ken, St. Louis	0	0	0	1	0	1
Greer, Curtis, St. Louis	0	0	0	4	2	4
Grimm, Russell, Washington	0	1	0	0	0	1
Grooms, Elois, New Orleans	0	0	0	1	20	1
Guman, Mike, Los Angeles	2	0	0	0	0	0
Haden, Pat, Los Angeles	5	1	−5	0	0	1
Hairston, Carl, Philadelphia	0	0	0	1	0	1
Hall, Alvin, Detroit	1	0	0	0	0	0
Hannon, Tom, Minnesota	0	0	0	1	31	1
Hardy, Larry, New Orleans	2	2	0	0	0	2
Harper, Roland, Chicago	1	0	0	0	0	0
Harper, Willie, San Francisco	0	0	0	1	0	1
Harrell, Willard, St. Louis	0	1	2	0	0	1
Harrington, Perry, Philadelphia	1	0	0	0	0	0
Harris, Al, Chicago	0	0	0	3	5	3
Harris, Joe, Los Angeles	0	0	0	2	21	2
Harris, Leotis, Green Bay	0	1	0	0	0	1
Harrison, Dennis, Philadelphia	0	0	0	3	0	3
Hart, Jim, St. Louis	4	0	−9	0	0	0
Hartenstine, Mike, Chicago	0	0	0	1	4	1
Harvey, Maurice, Green Bay	1	1	0	2	0	3
Hawkins, Andy, Tampa Bay	0	0	0	1	3	1
Haynes, Mark, New York Giants	0	0	0	1	0	1
Heath, Jo-Jo, Philadelphia	0	0	0	1	0	1
Henderson, Reuben, Chicago	0	0	0	1	0	1
Henry, Wally, Philadelphia	4	1	0	0	0	1
Herron, Bruce, Chicago	0	0	0	1	0	1
Hicks, Dwight, San Francisco	1	1	0	3	80	4
Hill, David, Detroit	1	0	0	0	0	0
Hill, Drew, Los Angeles	1	1	0	0	0	1
Hill, Tony, Dallas	1	0	0	0	0	0
Hipple, Eric, Detroit	14	4	−10	0	0	4
Hofer, Paul, San Francisco	1	0	0	0	0	0
Holloway, Randy, Minnesota	0	0	0	1	45	1
Holt, John, Tampa Bay	1	0	0	0	0	0
House, Kevin, Tampa Bay	2	0	0	0	0	0
Huckleby, Harlan, Green Bay	3	0	0	0	0	0
Hudson, Nat, New Orleans	0	1	14	0	0	1
Hughes, Ernie, New York Giants	2	2	0	0	0	2
Hunter, James, Detroit	1	0	0	1	0	1
Irvin, LeRoy, Los Angeles	3	2	0	1	14	3
Jackson, Alfred, Atlanta	0	1	0	0	0	1
Jackson, Louis, New York Giants	1	0	0	0	0	0
Jackson, Rickey, New Orleans	0	0	0	1	0	1
Jackson, Terry, New York Giants	0	0	0	1	0	1
Jackson, Wilbur, Washington	2	0	0	0	0	0
Jacoby, Joe, Washington	0	1	0	0	0	1

	Fum.	Own Rec.	Yds.	Opp. Rec.	Yds.	Tot. Rec.
Jaworski, Ron, Philadelphia	3	3	−2	0	0	3
Jenkins, Alfred, Atlanta	3	0	0	0	0	0
Jensen, Jim, Green Bay	1	0	0	0	0	0
Johnson, Cecil, Tampa Bay	1	0	0	0	0	0
Johnson, Charles, St. Louis	1	0	0	0	0	0
Johnson, Charlie, Philadelphia	0	0	0	2	0	2
Johnson, Johnnie, Los Angeles	0	0	0	5	5	5
Johnson, Kenny, Atlanta	1	0	0	2	55	2
Jones, Arrington, San Francisco	1	0	0	0	0	0
Jones, Cody, Los Angeles	0	0	0	1	0	1
Jones, Ed, Dallas	0	0	0	3	0	3
Jones, James, Dallas	4	2	0	0	0	2
Jones, Melvin, Washington	0	1	0	0	0	1
Jones, Terry, Green Bay	0	0	0	2	0	2
Kane, Rick, Detroit	2	0	0	0	0	0
Kelley, Brian, New York Giants	0	0	0	2	0	2
Kenn, Mike, Atlanta	0	1	0	0	0	1
Kenney, Steve, Philadelphia	0	2	0	0	0	2
King, Angelo, Dallas	0	1	0	1	0	2
King, Gordon, New York Giants	0	1	0	0	0	1
Knoff, Kurt, Minnesota	0	0	0	1	0	1
Kollar, Bill, Tampa Bay	0	0	0	3	0	3
Komlo, Jeff, Detroit	2	2	0	0	0	2
Koncar, Mark, Green Bay	0	1	0	0	0	1
Kovach, Jim, New Orleans	0	0	0	1	0	1
Kramer, Tommy, Minnesota	8	3	0	0	0	3
Kuykendall, Fulton, Atlanta	0	0	0	1	0	1
Lafary, Dave, New Orleans	0	1	0	0	0	1
Laughlin, Jim, Atlanta	0	0	0	1	0	1
Lawrence, Amos, San Francisco	3	0	0	0	0	0
LeCount, Terry, Minnesota	0	0	0	1	0	1
Lee, Mark, Green Bay	0	0	0	1	0	1
LeMaster, Frank, Philadelphia	0	0	0	2	47	2
Leonard, Jim, Tampa Bay	1	0	−6	0	0	0
Leopold, Bobby, San Francisco	0	0	0	2	0	2
Lewis, David, Tampa Bay	0	0	0	1	0	1
Lewis, D. D., Dallas	1	0	−2	0	0	0
Lofton, James, Green Bay	0	1	0	0	0	1
Logan, David, Tampa Bay	0	0	0	1	21	1
Logan, Randy, Philadelphia	0	0	0	1	0	1
Lomax, Neil, St. Louis	6	0	0	0	0	0
Lorch, Karl, Washington	0	0	0	2	0	2
Lott, Ronnie, San Francisco	1	0	0	2	0	2
Love, Randy, St. Louis	0	1	0	1	0	2
Manning, Archie, New Orleans	3	0	0	0	0	0
Margerum, Ken, Chicago	0	1	0	0	0	1
Marion, Frank, New York Giants	0	0	0	1	3	1
Marsh, Doug, St. Louis	1	0	0	0	0	0
Martin, Doug, Minnesota	0	0	0	1	0	1
Martin, George, New York Giants	0	0	0	3	28	3
Martin, Harvey, Dallas	0	0	0	1	0	1
Martin, Robbie, Detroit	3	2	0	0	0	2
Mayberry, James, Atlanta	1	0	0	0	0	0
Mays, Stafford, St. Louis	0	0	0	1	0	1
McCarren, Larry, Green Bay	1	0	0	0	0	0

Fumbles

Fumbles	Fum.	Own Rec.	Yds.	Opp. Rec.	Yds.	Tot. Rec.
McCoy, Mike C., Green Bay	1	1	0	0	0	1
McDole, Mardye, Minnesota	1	1	0	0	0	1
McMichael, Steve, Chicago	0	1	0	0	0	1
McNeill, Fred, Minnesota	0	0	0	1	11	1
Mendenhall, Mat, Washington	0	0	0	2	0	2
Merkens, Guido, New Orleans	1	1	0	2	0	3
Merrill, Casey, Green Bay	0	0	0	3	0	3
Metcalf, Terry, Washington	6	1	0	0	0	1
Middleton, Terdell, Green Bay	2	1	0	0	0	1
Milot, Rich, Washington	1	0	0	1	18	1
Mitchell, Stump, St. Louis	3	0	0	0	0	0
Montana, Joe, San Francisco	2	0	0	0	0	0
Montgomery, Wilbert, Philadelphia	6	2	0	0	0	2
Moore, Derland, New Orleans	0	0	0	1	0	1
Moriarty, Tom, Atlanta	0	0	0	1	0	1
Morriss, Guy, Philadelphia	2	0	−8	0	0	0
Mullady, Tom, New York Giants	1	0	0	0	0	0
Mullaney, Mark, Minnesota	0	0	0	1	0	1
Murphy, Mark, Green Bay	0	0	0	2	0	2
Murphy, Mark, Washington	0	0	0	3	0	3
Murphy, Phil, Los Angeles	0	0	0	1	0	1
Myers, Tommy, New Orleans	1	1	0	0	0	1
Nafziger, Dana, Tampa Bay	0	0	0	1	0	1
Nairne, Rob, New Orleans	0	0	0	2	0	2
Neal, Dan, Chicago	2	0	−4	0	0	0
Neill, Bill, New York Giants	0	0	0	1	0	1
Nelms, Mike, Washington	2	0	0	0	0	0
Nelson, Lee, St. Louis	0	0	0	2	0	2
Newsome, Timmy, Dallas	1	0	0	0	0	0
Nichols, Mark, Detroit	1	0	0	0	0	0
Nixon, Fred, Green Bay	2	0	0	0	0	0
Nord, Keith, Minnesota	2	1	0	0	0	1
O'Donoghue, Neil, St. Louis	0	0	0	1	0	1
Oliver, Hubert, Philadelphia	1	0	0	0	0	0
Osborne, Jim, Chicago	0	0	0	2	7	2
Owens, James, Tampa Bay	1	1	0	0	0	1
Page, Alan, Chicago	0	0	0	1	0	1
Pankey, Irv, Los Angeles	0	2	0	0	0	2
Parrish, Lemar, Washington	0	0	0	1	0	1
Pastorini, Dan, Los Angeles	4	1	−2	0	0	1
Patton, Ricky, San Francisco	3	0	0	0	0	0
Payton, Eddie, Minnesota	5	1	0	0	0	1
Payton, Walter, Chicago	9	3	0	0	0	3
Pearson, Drew, Dallas	4	0	0	0	0	0
Pelluer, Scott, New Orleans	0	0	0	1	0	1
Perkins, Johnny, New York Giants	2	0	0	0	0	0
Perry, Leon, New York Giants	4	2	2	0	0	2
Peters, Tony, Washington	0	1	0	0	0	1
Petersen, Kurt, Dallas	0	2	3	0	0	2
Pittman, Danny, New York Giants	2	1	0	0	0	1
Plank, Doug, Chicago	0	0	0	4	6	4
Poe, Johnnie, New Orleans	0	0	0	1	10	1
Pollard, Bob, St. Louis	0	0	0	1	0	1
Pridemore, Tom, Atlanta	0	0	0	3	24	3
Puki, Craig, San Francisco	0	0	0	2	0	2

	Fum.	Own Rec.	Yds.	Opp. Rec.	Yds.	Tot. Rec.
Quillan, Fred, San Francisco	1	0	0	0	0	0
Radford, Bruce, St. Louis	0	0	0	1	0	1
Rafferty, Tom, Dallas	2	1	−30	0	0	1
Rashad, Ahmad, Minnesota	1	1	0	0	0	1
Redwine, Jarvis, Minnesota	1	0	0	0	0	0
Reece, Beasley, New York Giants	1	3	3	2	4	5
Riggins, John, Washington	1	0	0	0	0	0
Ring, Bill, San Francisco	1	0	0	1	0	1
Robinson, Jerry, Philadelphia	0	0	0	2	0	2
Rogers, George, New Orleans	13	1	0	0	0	1
Rogers, Jimmy, New Orleans	3	1	0	0	0	1
Russell, Booker, Philadelphia	3	0	0	0	0	0
Saldi, Jay, Dallas	0	1	0	1	0	2
Saul, Rich, Los Angeles	0	1	0	0	0	1
Schmidt, Terry, Chicago	0	0	0	1	0	1
Sciarra, John, Philadelphia	3	2	−16	0	0	2
Scott, Bobby, New Orleans	1	1	0	0	0	1
Sendlein, Robin, Minnesota	0	0	0	1	0	1
Senser, Joe, Minnesota	3	2	0	0	0	2
Shirk, Gary, New York Giants	1	0	0	0	0	0
Shumann, Mike, San Francisco	1	0	0	0	0	0
Siemon, Jeff, Minnesota	1	0	−3	1	0	1
Simmons, Roy, New York Giants	0	2	0	0	0	2
Simms, Phil, New York Giants	7	2	−15	0	0	2
Sims, Billy, Detroit	9	3	0	0	0	3
Smith, Charles, Philadelphia	2	0	0	0	0	0
Smith, Don, Atlanta	0	0	0	3	2	3
Smith, Doug, Los Angeles	1	0	0	0	0	0
Smith, Lucious, Los Angeles	0	0	0	1	0	1
Smith, Reggie, Atlanta	4	1	0	0	0	1
Smith, Wayne, Detroit	0	0	0	1	4	1
Solomon, Freddie, San Francisco	3	2	0	0	0	2
Sorey, Revie, Chicago	0	1	0	0	0	1
Spagnola, John, Philadelphia	0	1	0	0	0	1
Springs, Ron, Dallas	3	3	11	1	0	4
Stalls, Dave, Tampa Bay	0	0	0	1	0	1
Stauch, Scott, New Orleans	1	1	0	0	0	1
Stokes, Tim, New York Giants	0	1	0	0	0	1
Strong, Ray, Atlanta	1	1	0	2	0	3
Stuckey, Jim, San Francisco	0	0	0	1	0	1
Studwell, Scott, Minnesota	0	0	0	3	0	3
Suhey, Matt, Chicago	3	3	0	0	0	3
Sully, Ivory, Los Angeles	1	1	0	1	0	2
Swain, John, Minnesota	0	0	0	1	0	1
Taylor, Billy, New York Giants	2	0	0	0	0	0
Taylor, James, New Orleans	0	1	0	0	0	1
Taylor, Lawrence, New York Giants	1	0	0	1	4	1
Theismann, Joe, Washington	7	1	0	0	0	1
Thielemann, R. C., Atlanta	0	2	0	0	0	2
Thomas, Jewerl, Los Angeles	1	1	0	0	0	1
Thomas, Norris, Tampa Bay	0	0	0	2	5	2
Thompson, Arland, Green Bay	0	1	0	0	0	1
Thompson, Leonard, Detroit	1	1	0	0	0	1
Thompson, Vince, Detroit	1	0	0	0	0	0
Thurman, Dennis, Dallas	0	0	0	1	0	1

Fumbles

	Fum.	Own Rec.	Yds.	Opp. Rec.	Yds.	Tot. Rec.
Tilley, Pat, St. Louis	1	0	0	0	0	0
Titensor, Glen, Dallas	0	0	0	1	0	1
Turner, Keena, San Francisco	0	0	0	3	0	3
Tyler, Toussaint, New Orleans	4	0	0	0	0	0
Tyler, Wendell, Los Angeles	11	4	1	0	0	4
Van Horne, Keith, Chicago	0	1	0	0	0	1
Van Note, Jeff, Atlanta	1	1	−20	0	0	1
Van Pelt, Brad, New York Giants	0	0	0	2	0	2
Waddy, Bill, Los Angeles	2	0	0	0	0	0
Walker, Rick, Washington	0	1	0	0	0	1
Walls, Everson, Dallas	0	0	0	1	0	1
Walterscheid, Lenny, Chicago	0	0	0	2	3	2
Warren, Frank, New Orleans	0	0	0	1	0	1
Washington, Joe, Washington	8	0	0	0	0	0
Washington, Mike, Tampa Bay	0	0	0	1	0	1
Waters, Charlie, Dallas	0	1	0	0	0	1
Wattelet, Frank, New Orleans	0	0	0	1	0	1
Watts, Rickey, Chicago	3	2	0	0	0	2
Waymer, Dave, New Orleans	0	0	0	2	0	2
Whitaker, Bill, Green Bay	0	0	0	1	0	1
White, Danny, Dallas	14	8	−34	0	0	8
White, James, Minnesota	0	0	0	2	0	2
White, Jeris, Washington	0	0	0	2	3	2
White, Sammy, Minnesota	1	0	0	0	0	0
White, Stan, Detroit	0	0	0	1	0	1
Whitehurst, David, Green Bay	4	1	−2	0	0	1
Wilder, James, Tampa Bay	3	1	0	0	0	1
Wilks, Jim, New Orleans	0	0	0	2	0	2
Williams, Doug, Tampa Bay	9	3	−31	0	0	3
Williams, Eric, St. Louis	0	0	0	2	0	2
Williams, Joel, Atlanta	0	0	0	2	57	2
Williamson, Carlton, San Francisco	0	0	0	2	3	2
Wilson, Dave, New Orleans	4	3	−8	0	0	3
Wilson, Mike, San Francisco	0	1	0	0	0	1
Wilson, Otis, Chicago	0	0	0	3	31	3
Wilson, Steve, Dallas	0	0	0	1	0	1
Wilson, Wade, Minnesota	2	1	0	0	0	1
Wilson, Wayne, New Orleans	1	0	0	1	0	1
Woerner, Scott, Atlanta	0	0	0	1	0	1
Wonsley, Otis, Washington	1	0	0	0	0	0
Wright, Eric, San Francisco	0	0	0	2	0	2
Yakavonis, Ray, Minnesota	0	0	0	1	0	1
Yeates, Jeff, Atlanta	0	0	0	1	0	1
Young, Rickey, Minnesota	4	0	0	0	0	0
Zanders, Emanuel, Chicago	0	1	0	0	0	1

Touchdowns: Kenny Johnson, Atlanta and George Martin, New York Giants, 2 each. Alfred Jackson and Joel Williams, Atlanta; Benny Barnes, Dallas; Joe Harris, Los Angeles; Randy Holloway, Minnesota; Beasley Reece, New York Giants; Greg Brown and Frank LeMaster, Philadelphia; Dwight Hicks, San Francisco; and David Logan, Tampa Bay, 1 each.

ALL-PRO TEAMS

1981 PFWA ALL-PRO TEAM
Selected by Professional Football Writers Association.

OFFENSE

Alfred Jenkins, Atlanta	Wide Receiver
James Lofton, Green Bay	Wide Receiver
Kellen Winslow, San Diego	Tight End
Anthony Munoz, Cincinnati	Tackle
Marvin Powell, New York Jets	Tackle
Randy Cross, San Francisco	Guard
John Hannah, New England	Guard
Mike Webster, Pittsburgh	Center
Ken Anderson, Cincinnati	Quarterback
Tony Dorsett, Dallas	Running Back
Billy Sims, Detroit	Running Back
Rafael Septien, Dallas	Kicker
Mike Nelms, Washington	Kick Returner
LeRoy Irvin, Los Angeles	Punt Returner

DEFENSE

Fred Dean, San Francisco	Defensive End
Joe Klecko, New York Jets	Defensive End
Gary Johnson, San Diego	Defensive Tackle
Randy White, Dallas	Defensive Tackle
Jack Lambert, Pittsburgh	Middle Linebacker
Jerry Robinson, Philadelphia	Outside Linebacker
Lawrence Taylor, New York Giants	Outside Linebacker
Mel Blount, Pittsburgh	Cornerback
Ronnie Lott, San Francisco	Cornerback
Gary Barbaro, Kansas City	Safety
Nolan Cromwell, Los Angeles	Safety
Pat McInally, Cincinnati	Punter

1981 NEA ALL-PRO TEAM
Selected by Newspaper Enterprise Association.

OFFENSE

Alfred Jenkins, Atlanta	Wide Receiver
James Lofton, Green Bay	Wide Receiver
Kellen Winslow, San Diego	Tight End
Anthony Munoz, Cincinnati	Tackle
Marvin Powell, New York Jets	Tackle
Randy Cross, San Francisco	Guard
John Hannah, New England	Guard
Mike Webster, Pittsburgh	Center
Ken Anderson, Cincinnati	Quarterback
Tony Dorsett, Dallas	Running Back
Billy Sims, Detroit	Running Back
Nick Lowery, Kansas City	Kicker

DEFENSE

Ed Jones, Dallas	Defensive End
Joe Klecko, New York Jets	Defensive End
Doug English, Detroit	Defensive Tackle
Randy White, Dallas	Defensive Tackle
Jack Lambert, Pittsburgh	Middle Linebacker
Bob Swenson, Denver	Outside Linebacker
Lawrence Taylor, New York Giants	Outside Linebacker
Mark Haynes, New York Giants	Cornerback
Ronnie Lott, San Francisco	Cornerback
Gary Barbaro, Kansas City	Safety
Nolan Cromwell, Los Angeles	Safety
Tom Skladany, Detroit	Punter

1981 ASSOCIATED PRESS ALL-PRO TEAM

OFFENSE

Alfred Jenkins, Atlanta.. Wide Receiver
James Lofton, Green Bay .... Wide Receiver
Kellen Winslow, San Diego .... Tight End
Anthony Munoz, Cincinnati .... Tackle
Marvin Powell, New York Jets .... Tackle
John Hannah, New England .... Guard
Herbert Scott, Dallas .... Guard
Mike Webster, Pittsburgh.. Center
Ken Anderson, Cincinnati.. Quarterback
Tony Dorsett, Dallas .... Running Back
George Rogers, New Orleans...................................... Running Back
Rafael Septien, Dallas .... Kicker
LeRoy Irvin, Los Angeles .... Kick Returner

DEFENSE

Fred Dean, San Francisco .... Defensive End
Joe Klecko, New York Jets .... Defensive End
Gary Johnson, San Diego............................ Defensive Tackle
Randy White, Dallas....................................... Defensive Tackle
Charlie Johnson, Philadelphia .... Nose Tackle
Bob Swenson, Denver .... Outside Linebacker
Lawrence Taylor, New York Giants .... Outside Linebacker
Jack Lambert, Pittsburgh .... Inside Linebacker
Mel Blount, Pittsburgh .... Cornerback
Ronnie Lott, San Francisco .... Cornerback
Nolan Cromwell, Los Angeles...................................... Safety
Gary Fencik, Chicago.. Safety
Pat McInally, Cincinnati .... Punter

1981 ALL-NFL TEAM

Selected by Associated Press, Newspaper Enterprise Association, and Professional Football Writers Association.

OFFENSE

Alfred Jenkins, Atlanta (AP, NEA, PFWA) .... Wide Receiver
James Lofton, Green Bay (AP, NEA, PFWA) .... Wide Receiver
Kellen Winslow, San Diego (AP, NEA, PFWA) .... Tight End
Anthony Munoz, Cincinnati (AP, NEA, PFWA) .... Tackle
Marvin Powell, New York Jets (AP, NEA, PFWA) .... Tackle
John Hannah, New England (AP, NEA, PFWA) .... Guard
Randy Cross, San Francisco (NEA, PFWA) .... Guard
Herbert Scott, Dallas (AP) .... Guard
Mike Webster, Pittsburgh (AP, NEA, PFWA) .... Center
Ken Anderson, Cincinnati (AP, NEA, PFWA) .... Quarterback
Tony Dorsett, Dallas (AP, NEA, PFWA) .... Running Back
Billy Sims, Detroit (NEA, PFWA) .... Running Back
George Rogers, New Orleans (AP) .... Running Back
Rafael Septien, Dallas (AP, PFWA) .... Kicker
Nick Lowery, Kansas City (NEA) .... Kicker
LeRoy Irvin, Los Angeles (AP, PFWA) .... Kick Returner
Mike Nelms, Washington (PFWA) .... Punt Returner

DEFENSE

Joe Klecko, New York Jets (AP, NEA, PFWA) .... Defensive End
Fred Dean, San Francisco (AP, PFWA) .... Defensive End
Ed Jones, Dallas (NEA) .... Defensive End
Randy White, Dallas (AP, NEA, PFWA) .... Defensive Tackle
Gary Johnson, San Diego (AP, PFWA) .... Defensive Tackle
Doug English, Detroit (NEA) .... Defensive Tackle
Charlie Johnson, Philadelphia (AP) .... Nose Tackle
Jack Lambert, Pittsburgh (AP, NEA, PFWA) .... Middle Linebacker
Lawrence Taylor, New York Giants (AP, NEA, PFWA) .... Linebacker
Bob Swenson, Denver (AP, NEA) .... Linebacker
Jerry Robinson, Philadelphia (PFWA) .... Linebacker
Ronnie Lott, San Francisco (AP, NEA, PFWA) .... Cornerback
Mel Blount, Pittsburgh (AP, PFWA) .... Cornerback
Mark Haynes, New York Giants (NEA) .... Cornerback
Nolan Cromwell, Los Angeles (AP, NEA, PFWA) .... Safety
Gary Barbaro, Kansas City (NEA, PFWA) .... Safety
Gary Fencik, Chicago (AP) .... Safety
Pat McInally, Cincinnati (AP, PFWA) .... Punter
Tom Skladany, Detroit (NEA) .... Punter

1981 ALL-AFC TEAM
Selected by United Press International.

OFFENSE

Frank Lewis, Buffalo . . . . Wide Receiver
Steve Watson, Denver . . . . Wide Receiver
Kellen Winslow, San Diego . . . . Tight End
Anthony Munoz, Cincinnati . . . . Tackle
Marvin Powell, New York Jets . . . . Tackle
John Hannah, New England . . . . Guard
Doug Wilkerson, San Diego . . . . Guard
Mike Webster, Pittsburgh . . . . Center
Ken Anderson, Cincinnati . . . . Quarterback
Joe Delaney, Kansas City . . . . Running Back
Chuck Muncie, San Diego . . . . Running Back
Nick Lowery, Kansas City . . . . Kicker

DEFENSE

Mark Gastineau, New York Jets . . . . Defensive End
Joe Klecko, New York Jets . . . . Defensive End
Bob Baumhower, Miami . . . . Defensive Tackle
Fred Smerlas, Buffalo . . . . Defensive Tackle
Randy Gradishar, Denver . . . . Middle Linebacker
A. J. Duhe, Miami . . . . Outside Linebacker
Ted Hendricks, Oakland . . . . Outside Linebacker
Mel Blount, Pittsburgh . . . . Cornerback
Gary Green, Kansas City . . . . Cornerback
Darrol Ray, New York Jets . . . . Safety
Bill Thompson, Denver . . . . Safety
Pat McInally, Cincinnati . . . . Punter

1981 ALL-NFC TEAM

Selected by United Press International.

OFFENSE

Alfred Jenkins, Atlanta	Wide Receiver
James Lofton, Green Bay	Wide Receiver
Joe Senser, Minnesota	Tight End
Keith Dorney, Detroit	Tackle
Mike Kenn, Atlanta	Tackle
Randy Cross, San Francisco	Guard
Herbert Scott, Dallas	Guard
Guy Morriss, Philadelphia	Center
Joe Montana, San Francisco	Quarterback
Tony Dorsett, Dallas	Running Back
George Rogers, New Orleans	Running Back
Rafael Septien, Dallas	Kicker

DEFENSE

Fred Dean, San Francisco	Defensive End
Ed Jones, Dallas	Defensive End
Charlie Johnson, Philadelphia	Defensive Tackle
Randy White, Dallas	Defensive Tackle
Harry Carson, New York Giants	Middle Linebacker
Jerry Robinson, Philadelphia	Outside Linebacker
Lawrence Taylor, New York Giants	Outside Linebacker
Ronnie Lott, San Francisco	Cornerback
Roynell Young, Philadelphia	Cornerback
Gary Fencik, Chicago	Safety
Dwight Hicks, San Francisco	Safety
Tom Skladany, Detroit	Punter

1981 ALL-ROOKIE TEAM
Selected by Professional Football Writers Association.

OFFENSE

Cris Collinsworth, Cincinnati. . . . . Wide Receiver
Ken Margerum, Chicago . . . . Wide Receiver
Greg LaFleur, St. Louis . . . . Tight End
Joe Jacoby, Washington . . . . Tackle
Keith Van Horne, Chicago . . . . Tackle
Billy Ard, New York Giants . . . . Guard
Curt Marsh, Oakland. . . . . Guard
John Scully, Atlanta . . . . Center
Neil Lomax, St. Louis. . . . . Quarterback
Joe Delaney, Kansas City. . . . . Running Back
George Rogers, New Orleans . . . . Running Back
Mick Luckhurst, Atlanta . . . . Kicker

DEFENSE

Curtis Green, Detroit . . . . Defensive End
Donnell Thompson, Baltimore . . . . Defensive End
Bill Neil, New York Giants . . . . Defensive Tackle
Johnny Robinson, Oakland . . . . Defensive Tackle
Mike Singletary, Chicago . . . . Middle Linebacker
Hugh Green, Tampa Bay . . . . Outside Linebacker
Lawrence Taylor, New York Giants . . . . Outside Linebacker
Ronnie Lott, San Francisco . . . . Cornerback
Everson Walls, Dallas. . . . . Cornerback
Ken Easley, Seattle . . . . Safety
Carlton Williamson, San Francisco. . . . . Safety
Tom Orosz, Miami . . . . Punter

PRO FOOTBALL HALL OF FAME

The Professional Football Hall of Fame is located in Canton, Ohio, site of the organizational meeting on September 17, 1920, from which the National Football League evolved. The NFL recognized Canton as the Hall of Fame site on April 27, 1961. Canton area individuals, foundations, and companies donated almost $400,000 in cash and services to provide funds for the construction of the original two-building complex, which was dedicated on September 7, 1963. The original Hall of Fame complex was almost doubled in size with the completion of a $620,000 expansion project that was dedicated on May 10, 1971. A second expansion project was completed on November 20, 1978. It features three exhibition areas and a theater twice the size of the original one.

The Hall represents the sport of pro football in many ways—through three large and colorful exhibition galleries, in the twin enshrinement halls, with numerous fan-participation electronic devices, a research library, and an NFL gift shop.

In recent years, the Pro Football Hall of Fame has become an extremely popular tourist attraction. At the end of 1981, a total of 3,169,300 fans had visited the Pro Football Hall of Fame.

New members of the Pro Football Hall of Fame are elected annually by a 29-member National Board of Selectors, made up of media representatives from every league city and the president of the Pro Football Writers Association. Between three and six new members are elected each year. An affirmative vote of approximately 80 percent is needed for election.

Any fan may nominate any eligible player or contributor simply by writing to the Pro Football Hall of Fame. Players must be retired five years to be eligible, while a coach need only to be retired with no time limit specified. Contributors (administrators, owners, *et al.*) may be elected while they are still active.

The charter class of 17 enshrinees was elected in 1963 and the honor roll now stands at 114 with the election of a four-man class in 1982. That class consists of Doug Atkins, Sam Huff, George Musso and Merlin Olsen.

Roster of Members

HERB ADDERLEY
Defensive back. 6-1, 200. Born in Philadelphia, Pennsylvania, June 8, 1939. Michigan State. Inducted 1980. 1961-69 Green Bay Packers, 1970-72 Dallas Cowboys.

LANCE ALWORTH
Wide receiver. 6-0, 184. Born in Houston, Texas, August 3, 1940. Arkansas. Inducted in 1978. 1962-1970 San Diego Chargers, 1971-72 Dallas Cowboys.

DOUG ATKINS
Defensive end, 6-8, 275. Born in Humboldt, Tennessee, May 8, 1930. Tennessee. Inducted in 1982. 1953-54 Cleveland Browns, 1955-1966 Chicago Bears, 1967-69 New Orleans Saints.

MORRIS (RED) BADGRO
End. 6-0, 190. Born in Orilla, Washington, December 1, 1902. USC. Inducted in 1981. 1927 New York Yankees, 1930-1935 New York Giants, 1936 Brooklyn Dodgers.

CLIFF BATTLES
Halfback. 6-1, 201. Born in Akron, Ohio, May 1, 1910. Died April 27, 1981. West Virginia Wesleyan. Inducted in 1968. 1932 Boston Braves, 1933-36 Boston Redskins, 1937 Washington Redskins.

SAMMY BAUGH

Quarterback. 6-2, 180. Born in Temple, Texas, March 17, 1914. Texas Christian. Inducted in 1963. 1937-1952 Washington Redskins.

CHUCK BEDNARIK

Center-linebacker. 6-3, 230. Born in Bethlehem, Pennsylvania, May 1, 1925. Pennsylvania. Inducted in 1967. 1949-1962 Philadelphia Eagles.

BERT BELL

Commissioner. Team owner. Born in Philadelphia, Pennsylvania, February 25, 1895. Died October 11, 1959. Pennsylvania. Inducted in 1963. 1933-1940 Philadelphia Eagles, 1941-42 Pittsburgh Steelers, 1943 Phil-Pitt, 1944-46 Pittsburgh Steelers.

RAYMOND BERRY

End. 6-2. 187. Born in Corpus Christi, Texas, February 27, 1933. Southern Methodist. Inducted in 1973. 1955-1967 Baltimore Colts.

CHARLES W. BIDWILL, SR.

Team owner. Born in Chicago, Illinois, September 16, 1895. Died April 19, 1947. Loyola of Chicago. Inducted in 1967. 1933-1943 Chicago Cardinals, 1944 Card-Pitt, 1945-47 Chicago Cardinals.

GEORGE BLANDA

Quarterback-kicker. 6-2, 215. Born in Youngwood, Pennsylvania, September 17, 1927. Kentucky. Inducted 1981. 1949-1958 Chicago Bears, 1960-66 Houston Oilers, 1967-1976 Oakland Raiders.

JIM BROWN

Fullback. 6-2, 232. Born in St. Simons, Georgia, February 17, 1936. Syracuse. Inducted in 1971. 1957-1965 Cleveland Browns.

PAUL BROWN

Coach. Born in Norwalk, Ohio, September 7, 1908. Miami, Ohio. Inducted in 1967. 1946-49 Cleveland Browns (AAFC), 1950-1962 Cleveland Browns, 1968-1975 Cincinnati Bengals.

ROOSEVELT BROWN

Offensive tackle. 6-3, 255. Born in Charlottesville, Virginia, October 20, 1932. Morgan State. Inducted in 1975. 1953-1965 New York Giants.

DICK BUTKUS

Linebacker. 6-3, 245. Born in Chicago, Illinois, December 9, 1942. Illinois. Inducted in 1979. 1965-1973 Chicago Bears.

TONY CANADEO

Halfback. 5-11, 195. Born in Chicago, Illinois, May 5, 1919. Gonzaga. Inducted in 1974. 1941-44 Green Bay Packers, 1946-1952 Green Bay Packers.

JOE CARR

NFL president. Born in Columbus, Ohio, October 22, 1880. Died May 20, 1939. Did not attend college. Inducted in 1963. President 1921-1939 National Football League.

GUY CHAMBERLIN

End. Coach. 6-2, 210. Born in Blue Springs, Nebraska, January 16, 1894. Died April 4, 1967. Nebraska. Inducted in 1965. 1920 Decatur Staleys, 1921 Chicago Staleys, 1922-23 Canton Bulldogs, 1924 Cleveland Bulldogs, 1925-26 Frankford Yellowjackets, 1927-28 Chicago Cardinals.

JACK CHRISTIANSEN

Defensive back. 6-1, 185. Born in Sublette, Kansas, December 20, 1928. Colorado State. Inducted in 1970. 1951-58 Detroit Lions.

EARL (DUTCH) CLARK

Quarterback. 6-0, 185. Born in Fowler, Colorado, October 11, 1906. Died August 5, 1978. Colorado College. Inducted in 1963. 1931-32 Portsmouth Spartans, 1934-38 Detroit Lions.

GEORGE CONNOR

Tackle-linebacker. 6-3, 240. Born in Chicago, Illinois, January 1, 1925. Holy Cross, Notre Dame. Inducted in 1975. 1948-1955 Chicago Bears.

JIMMY CONZELMAN

Quarterback. Coach. Team owner. 6-0, 180. Born in St. Louis, Missouri, March 6, 1898. Died July 31, 1970. Washington, Missouri. Inducted in 1964. 1920 Decatur Staleys, 1921-22 Rock Island, Ill., Independents, 1923-24 Milwaukee Badgers; owner-coach, 1925-26 Detroit Panthers, 1927-28, coach, 1929-1930 Providence Steamroller; coach, 1940-42 Chicago Cardinals, 1946-48 Chicago Cardinals.

WILLIE DAVIS

Defensive end. 6-3, 245. Born in Lisbon, Louisiana, July 24, 1934. Grambling. Inducted in 1981. 1958-1959 Cleveland Browns, 1960-1969 Green Bay Packers.

ART DONOVAN

Defensive tackle. 6-3, 265. Born in Bronx, New York, June 5, 1925. Boston College. Inducted in 1968. 1950 Baltimore Colts, 1951 New York Yanks, 1952 Dallas Texans, 1953-1961 Baltimore Colts.

JOHN (PADDY) DRISCOLL

Quarterback. 5-11, 160. Born in Evanston, Illinois, January 11, 1896. Died June 29, 1968. Northwestern. Inducted in 1965. 1920 Decatur Staleys, 1920-25 Chicago Cardinals, 1926-29 Chicago Bears. Head coach, 1956-57 Chicago Bears.

BILL DUDLEY

Halfback. 5-10, 176. Born in Bluefield, Viriginia, December 24, 1921. Virginia. Inducted in 1966. 1942 Pittsburgh Steelers, 1945-46 Pittsburgh Steelers, 1947-49 Detroit Lions, 1950-51, 1953 Washington Redskins.

GLEN (TURK) EDWARDS

Tackle. 6-2, 260. Born in Mold, Washington, September 28, 1907. Died January 10, 1973. Washington State. Inducted in 1969. 1932 Boston Braves, 1933-36 Boston Redskins, 1937-1940 Washington Redskins.

WEEB EWBANK

Coach. Born in Richmond, Indiana, May 6, 1907. Miami, Ohio. Inducted in 1978. 1954-1962 Baltimore Colts, 1963-1973 New York Jets.

TOM FEARS

End. 6-2, 215. Born in Los Angeles, California, December 3, 1923. Santa Clara, UCLA. Inducted in 1970. 1948-1956 Los Angeles Rams.

RAY FLAHERTY

Coach. Born in Spokane, Washington, September 1, 1904. Gonzaga. Inducted in 1976. 1926 Los Angeles Wildcats (AFL), 1927 New York Yankees, 1928-29, 1931-35 New York Giants. Coach, 1936 Boston Redskins, 1937-1942 Washington Redskins, 1946-1948 New York Yankees (AAFC), 1949 Chicago Hornets (AAFC).

LEN FORD

End. 6-5, 260. Born in Washington, D.C., February 18, 1926. Died March 14, 1972. Michigan. Inducted in 1976. 1948-49 Los Angeles Dons (AAFC), 1950-57 Cleveland Browns, 1958 Green Bay Packers.

DAN FORTMANN

Guard. 6-0, 207. Born in Pearl River, New York, April 11, 1916. Colgate. Inducted in 1965. 1936-1943 Chicago Bears.

BILL GEORGE

Linebacker. 6-2, 230. Born in Waynesburg, Pennsylvania, October 27, 1930. Wake Forest. Inducted in 1974. 1952-1965 Chicago Bears, 1966 Los Angeles Rams.

FRANK GIFFORD

Halfback. 6-1, 195. Born in Santa Monica, California, August 16, 1930. USC. Inducted in 1977. 1952-1960, 1962-64 New York Giants.

OTTO GRAHAM

Quarterback. 6-1, 195. Born in Waukegan, Illinois, December 6, 1921. Northwestern. Inducted in 1965. 1946-49 Cleveland Browns (AAFC), 1950-55 Cleveland Browns.

RED GRANGE

Halfback. 6-0, 185. Born in Forksville, Pennsylvania, June 13, 1903. Illinois. Inducted in 1963. 1925 Chicago Bears, 1926 New York Yankees (AFL), 1927 New York Yankees, 1929-1934 Chicago Bears.

FORREST GREGG

Tackle. 6-4, 250. Born in Sulphur Springs, Texas, October 18, 1933. Southern Methodist. Inducted in 1977. 1956, 1958-1970 Green Bay Packers, 1971 Dallas Cowboys.

LOU GROZA

Tackle-kicker. 6-3, 250. Born in Martin's Ferry, Ohio, January 25, 1924. Ohio State. Inducted in 1974. 1946-49 Cleveland Browns (AAFC), 1950-59 Cleveland Browns, 1961-67 Cleveland Browns.

JOE GUYON

Halfback. 6-1, 180. Born in Mahnomen, Minnesota, November 26, 1892. Died November 27, 1971. Carlisle, Georgia Tech. Inducted in 1966. 1920 Canton Bulldogs, 1921 Cleveland Indians, 1922-23 Oorang Indians, 1924 Rock Island, Ill., Independents, 1924-25 Kansas City Cowboys, 1927 New York Giants.

GEORGE HALAS

End. Coach. Team Owner. Born in Chicago, Illinois, February 2, 1895. Illinois. Inducted in 1963. 1920 Decatur Staleys, 1921 Chicago Staleys, 1922-29 Chicago Bears; coach, 1933-1942, 1946-1955, 1958-1967 Chicago Bears.

ED HEALEY

Tackle. 6-3, 220. Born in Indian Orchard, Massachusetts, December 28, 1894. Died December 9, 1978. Dartmouth. Inducted in 1964. 1920-22 Rock Island, Ill., Independents, 1922-27 Chicago Bears.

MEL HEIN

Center. 6-2, 225. Born in Redding, California, August 22, 1909. Washington State. Inducted in 1963. 1931-1945 New York Giants.

WILBUR (PETE) HENRY

Tackle. 6-0, 250. Born in Mansfield, Ohio, October 31, 1897. Died February 7, 1952. Washington & Jefferson. Inducted in 1963. 1920-23 Canton Bulldogs, 1925-26 Canton Bulldogs, 1927 New York Giants, 1927-28 Pottsville Maroons.

ARNIE HERBER

Quarterback. 6-1, 200. Born in Green Bay, Wisconsin, April 2, 1910. Died October 14, 1969. Wisconsin, Regis College. Inducted in 1966. 1930-1940 Green Bay Packers, 1944-45 New York Giants.

BILL HEWITT

End. 5-11, 191. Born in Bay City, Michigan, October 8, 1909. Died January 14, 1947. Michigan. Inducted in 1971. 1932-36 Chicago Bears, 1937-39 Philadelphia Eagles, 1943 Phil-Pitt.

CLARKE HINKLE

Fullback. 5-11, 201. Born in Toronto, Ohio, April 10, 1912. Bucknell. Inducted in 1964. 1932-1941 Green Bay Packers.

ELROY (CRAZYLEGS) HIRSCH

Halfback-end. 6-2, 190. Born in Wausau, Wisconsin, June 17, 1923. Wisconsin, Michigan. Inducted in 1968. 1946-48 Chicago Rockets (AAFC), 1949-1957 Los Angeles Rams.

CAL HUBBARD

Tackle. 6-5, 250. Born in Keytesville, Missouri, October 11, 1900. Died October 17, 1977. Centenary, Geneva. Inducted in 1963. 1927-28 New York Giants, 1929-1933 Green Bay Packers, 1935 Green Bay Packers, 1936 New York Giants, 1936 Pittsburgh Pirates.

SAM HUFF

Linebacker. 6-1, 230. Born in Morgantown, West Virginia, October 4, 1934. West Virginia. Inducted in 1982. 1956-63 New York Giants, 1964-68 Washington Redskins.

LAMAR HUNT

Team owner. Born in El Dorado, Arkansas, August 2, 1932. Southern Methodist. Inducted in 1972. 1960-62 Dallas Texans, 1963-1982 Kansas City Chiefs.

DON HUTSON

End. 6-1, 180. Born in Pine Bluff, Arkansas, January 31, 1913. Alabama. Inducted in 1963. 1935-1945 Green Bay Packers.

DAVID (DEACON) JONES

Defensive end. 6-5, 250. Born in Eatonville, Florida, December 9, 1938. South Carolina State. Inducted 1980. 1961-1971 Los Angeles Rams, 1972-73 San Diego Chargers, 1974 Washington Redskins.

WALT KIESLING

Guard. Coach. 6-2, 245. Born in St. Paul, Minnesota, March 27, 1903. Died March 2, 1962. St. Thomas (Minnesota). Inducted in 1966. 1926-27 Duluth Eskimos, 1928 Pottsville Maroons, 1929-1933 Chicago Cardinals, 1934 Chicago Bears, 1935-36 Green Bay Packers, 1937-38 Pittsburgh Pirates; coach, 1939-1942 Pittsburgh Steelers; co-coach, 1943 Phil-Pitt, 1944 Card-Pitt., 1954-56 Pittsburgh Steelers.

FRANK (BRUISER) KINARD

Tackle. 6-1, 210. Born in Pelahatchie, Mississippi, October 23, 1914. Mississippi. Inducted in 1971. 1938-1944 Brooklyn Dodgers-Tigers, 1946-47 New York Yankees (AAFC).

EARL (CURLY) LAMBEAU

Coach. Born in Green Bay, Wisconsin, April 9, 1898. Died June 1, 1965. Notre Dame. Inducted in 1963. 1919-1949 Green Bay Packers, 1950-51 Chicago Cardinals, 1952-53 Washington Redskins.

DICK (NIGHT TRAIN) LANE

Defensive back. 6-2, 210. Born in Austin, Texas, April 16, 1928. Scottsbluff Junior College. Inducted in 1974. 1952-53 Los Angeles Rams, 1954-59 Chicago Cardinals, 1960-65 Detroit Lions.

YALE LARY

Defensive back-punter. 5-11, 189. Born in Fort Worth, Texas, November 24, 1930. Texas A&M. Inducted in 1979. 1952-53, 1956-1964 Detroit Lions.

DANTE LAVELLI

End. 6-0, 199. Born in Hudson, Ohio, February 23, 1923. Ohio State. Inducted in 1975. 1946-49 Cleveland Browns (AAFC), 1950-56 Cleveland Browns.

BOBBY LAYNE

Quarterback. 6-2, 190. Born in Santa Anna, Texas, December 19, 1926. Texas. Inducted in 1967. 1948 Chicago Bears, 1949 New York Bulldogs, 1950-58 Detroit Lions, 1958-1962 Pittsburgh Steelers.

ALPHONSE (TUFFY) LEEMANS

Fullback. 6-0, 200. Born in Superior, Wisconsin, November 12, 1912. Died January 19, 1979. George Washington. Inducted in 1978. 1936-1943 New York Giants.

BOB LILLY

Defensive tackle. 6-5, 260. Born in Olney, Texas, July 24, 1939. Texas Christian. Inducted 1980. 1961-1974 Dallas Cowboys.

VINCE LOMBARDI

Coach. Born in Brooklyn, New York, June 11, 1913. Died September 3, 1970. Fordham. Inducted in 1971. 1959-1967 Green Bay Packers, 1969 Washington Redskins.

SID LUCKMAN

Quarterback. 6-0, 195. Born in Brooklyn, New York, November 21, 1916. Columbia. Inducted in 1965. 1939-1950 Chicago Bears.

ROY (LINK) LYMAN
Tackle. 6-2, 252. Born in Table Rock, Nebraska, November 30, 1898. Died December 28, 1972. Nebraska. Inducted in 1964. 1922-23 Canton Bulldogs, 1924 Cleveland Bulldogs, 1925 Canton Bulldogs, 1925 Frankford Yellowjackets, 1926-28, 1930-31, 1933-34 Chicago Bears.

TIM MARA
Owner. Born in New York, New York, July 29, 1887. Died February 17, 1959. Did not attend college. Inducted in 1963. 1925-1959 New York Giants.

GINO MARCHETTI
Defensive end. 6-4, 245. Born in Antioch, California, January 2, 1927. San Francisco. Inducted in 1972. 1952 Dallas Texans, 1953-1964 Baltimore Colts, 1966 Baltimore Colts.

GEORGE PRESTON MARSHALL
Team owner. Born in Grafton, West Virginia, October 11, 1897. Died August 9, 1969. Randolph-Macon. Inducted in 1963. 1932 Boston Braves, 1933-36 Boston Redskins, 1937-1969 Washington Redskins.

OLLIE MATSON
Halfback. 6-2, 220. Born in Trinity, Texas, May 1, 1930. San Francisco. Inducted in 1972. 1952 Chicago Cardinals, 1954-58 Chicago Cardinals, 1959-1962 Los Angeles Rams, 1963 Detroit Lions, 1964-66 Philadelphia Eagles.

GEORGE McAFEE
Halfback. 6-0, 177. Born in Ironton, Ohio, March 13, 1918. Duke. Inducted in 1966. 1940-41 Chicago Bears, 1945-1950 Chicago Bears.

HUGH McELHENNY
Halfback. 6-1, 198. Born in Los Angeles, California, December 31, 1928. Washington. Inducted in 1970. 1952-1960 San Francisco 49ers, 1961-62 Minnesota Vikings, 1963 New York Giants, 1964 Detroit Lions.

JOHNNY BLOOD (McNALLY)
Halfback. 6-0, 185. Born in New Richmond, Wisconsin, November 27, 1904. St. John's of Minnesota. Inducted in 1963. 1925-26 Milwaukee Badgers, 1926-27 Duluth Eskimos, 1928 Pottsville Maroons, 1929-1933 Green Bay Packers, 1934 Pittsburgh Pirates, 1935-36 Green Bay Packers. Player-coach, 1937-39 Pittsburgh Pirates.

MIKE MICHALSKE
Guard. 6-0, 209. Born in Cleveland, Ohio, April 24, 1903. Penn State. Inducted in 1964. 1926 New York Yankees (AFL), 1927-28 New York Yankees, 1929-1935 Green Bay Packers, 1937 Green Bay Packers.

WAYNE MILLNER
End. 6-0, 191. Born in Roxbury, Massachusetts, January 31, 1913. Died November 19, 1976. Notre Dame. Inducted in 1968. 1936 Boston Redskins, 1937-1941 Washington Redskins, 1945 Washington Redskins.

RON MIX
Tackle. 6-4, 250. Born in Los Angeles, California, March 10, 1938. USC. Inducted in 1979. 1960-69 San Diego Chargers, 1971 Oakland Raiders.

LENNY MOORE
Back. 6-1, 198. Born in Reading, Pennsylvania, November 25, 1933. Penn State. Inducted in 1975. 1956-1967 Baltimore Colts.

MARION MOTLEY
Fullback. 6-1, 238. Born in Leesburg, Georgia, June 5, 1920. South Carolina State, Nevada. Inducted in 1968. 1946-49 Cleveland Browns (AAFC), 1950-53 Cleveland Browns, 1955 Pittsburgh Steelers.

GEORGE MUSSO
Defensive and offensive guard. 6-2, 270. Born in Collinsville, Illinois. April 8, 1910. Milliken. Inducted in 1982. 1933-1944 Chicago Bears.

BRONKO NAGURSKI
Fullback. 6-2, 225. Born in Rainy River, Ontario, Canada, November 3, 1908. Minnesota. Inducted in 1963. 1930-37 Chicago Bears, 1943 Chicago Bears.

EARLE (GREASY) NEALE
Coach. Born in Parkersburg, West Virginia, November 5, 1891. Died November 2, 1973. West Virginia Wesleyan. Inducted in 1969. 1941-42 Philadelphia Eagles, co-coach Phil-Pitt 1943, 1944-1950 Philadelphia Eagles.

ERNIE NEVERS
Fullback. 6-1, 205. Born in Willow River, Minnesota, June 11, 1903. Died May 3, 1976. Stanford. Inducted in 1963. 1926-27 Duluth Eskimos, 1929-1931 Chicago Cardinals.

RAY NITSCHKE
Linebacker. 6-3, 235. Born in Elmwood Park, Illinois, December 29, 1936. Illinois. Inducted in 1978. 1958-1972 Green Bay Packers.

LEO NOMELLINI
Defensive tackle. 6-3, 264. Born in Lucca, Italy, June 19, 1924. Minnesota. Inducted in 1969. 1950-1963 San Francisco 49ers.

MERLIN OLSEN
Tackle. 6-5, 270. Born in Logan, Utah, September 14, 1940. Utah State. Inducted in 1982. 1962-1976 Los Angeles Rams.

JIM OTTO
Center. 6-2, 255. Born in Wausau, Wisconsin, January 5, 1938. Miami. Inducted 1980. 1960-1974 Oakland Raiders.

STEVE OWEN
Tackle. Coach. 6-0, 235. Born in Cleo Springs, Oklahoma, April 21, 1898. Died May 17, 1964. Phillips. Inducted in 1966. 1924-25 Kansas City Cowboys, 1926-1930 New York Giants; coach, 1931-1953 New York Giants.

CLARENCE (ACE) PARKER
Quarterback. 5-11, 168. Born in Portsmouth, Virginia, May 17, 1912. Duke. Inducted in 1972. 1937-1941 Brooklyn Dodgers, 1945 Boston Yanks, 1946 New York Yankees (AAFC).

JIM PARKER
Guard-tackle. 6-3, 273. Born in Macon, Georgia, April 3, 1934. Ohio State. Inducted in 1973. 1957-1967 Baltimore Colts.

JOE PERRY
Fullback. 6-0, 200. Born in Stevens, Arkansas, January 27, 1927. Compton Junior College. Inducted in 1969. 1948-49 San Francisco 49ers (AAFC), 1950-1960 San Francisco 49ers, 1961-62 Baltimore Colts, 1963 San Francisco 49ers.

PETE PIHOS
End. 6-1, 210. Born in Orlando, Florida, October 22, 1923. Indiana. Inducted in 1970. 1947-1955 Philadelphia Eagles.

HUGH (SHORTY) RAY
Supervisor of officials. Born in Highland Park, Illinois, September 21, 1884. Died September 16, 1956. Illinois. Inducted in 1966.

DAN REEVES
Team owner. Born in New York, New York, June 30, 1912. Died April 15, 1971. Georgetown. Inducted in 1967. 1941-45 Cleveland Rams, 1946-1971 Los Angeles Rams.

JIM RINGO
Center. 6-1, 235. Born in Orange, New Jersey, November 21, 1932. Syracuse. Inducted in 1981. 1953-1963 Green Bay Packers, 1964-1967 Philadelphia Eagles.

ANDY ROBUSTELLI
Defensive end. 6-0, 230. Born in Stamford, Connecticut, December 6, 1925. Arnold College. Inducted in 1971. 1951-55 Los Angeles Rams, 1956-1964 New York Giants.

ART ROONEY

Team owner. Born in Coulterville, Pennsylvania, January 27, 1901. Georgetown, Duquesne. Inducted in 1964. 1933-1940 Pittsburgh Pirates, 1941-42 Pittsburgh Steelers, 1943 Phil-Pitt; 1944 Card-Pitt, 1949-1982 Pittsburgh Steelers.

GALE SAYERS

Running back. 6-0, 200. Born in Wichita, Kansas, May 30, 1943. Kansas. Inducted in 1977. 1965-1971 Chicago Bears.

JOE SCHMIDT

Linebacker. 6-0, 222. Born in Pittsburgh, Pennsylvania, January 19, 1932. Pittsburgh. Inducted in 1973. 1953-1965 Detroit Lions.

BART STARR

Quarterback. 6-1, 200. Born in Montgomery, Alabama, January 9, 1934. Alabama. Inducted in 1977. 1956-1971 Green Bay Packers.

ERNIE STAUTNER

Defensive tackle. 6-2, 235. Born in Calm, Bavaria, Germany, April 20, 1925. Boston College. Inducted in 1969. 1950-1963 Pittsburgh Steelers.

KEN STRONG

Halfback. 5-11, 210. Born in New Haven, Connecticut, August 6, 1906. Died October 5, 1979. New York University. Inducted in 1967. 1929-1932 Staten Island Stapletons, 1933-35 New York Giants, 1936-37 New York Yanks (AFL), 1939 New York Giants, 1944-47 New York Giants.

JOE STYDAHAR

Tackle. 6-4, 230. Born in Kaylor, Pennsylvania, March 3, 1912. Died March 23, 1977. West Virginia. Inducted in 1967. 1936-1942 Chicago Bears, 1945-46 Chicago Bears.

JIM TAYLOR

Fullback. 6-0, 216. Born in Baton Rouge, Louisiana, September 20, 1935. Louisiana State. Inducted in 1976. 1958-1966 Green Bay Packers, 1967 New Orleans Saints.

JIM THORPE

Halfback. 6-1, 190. Born in Prague, Oklahoma, May 28, 1888. Died March 28, 1953. Carlisle. Inducted in 1963. 1920 Canton Bulldogs, 1921 Cleveland Indians, 1922-23 Oorang Indians, 1923 Toledo Maroons, 1924 Rock Island, Ill., Independents, 1925 New York Giants, 1926 Canton Bulldogs, 1928 Chicago Cardinals.

Y.A. TITTLE

Quarterback. 6-0, 200. Born in Marshall, Texas, October 24, 1926. Louisiana State. Inducted in 1971. 1948-49 Baltimore Colts (AAFC), 1950 Baltimore Colts, 1951-1960 San Francisco 49ers, 1961-64 New York Giants.

GEORGE TRAFTON

Center. 6-2, 235. Born in Chicago, Illinois, December 6, 1896. Died September 5, 1971. Notre Dame. Inducted in 1964. 1920 Decatur Staleys, 1921 Chicago Staleys, 1922-1932 Chicago Bears.

CHARLEY TRIPPI

Halfback. 6-0, 185. Born in Pittston, Pennsylvania, December 14, 1922. Georgia. Inducted in 1968. 1947-1955 Chicago Cardinals.

EMLEN TUNNELL

Safety. 6-1, 200. Born in Bryn Mawr, Pennsylvania, March 29, 1925. Died July 23, 1975. Toledo, Iowa. Inducted in 1967. 1948-1958 New York Giants, 1959-1961 Green Bay Packers.

CLYDE (BULLDOG) TURNER

Center. 6-2, 235. Born in Sweetwater, Texas, November 10, 1919. Hardin-Simmons. Inducted in 1966. 1940-1952 Chicago Bears.

JOHNNY UNITAS

Quarterback. 6-1, 195. Born in Pittsburgh, Pennsylvania, May 7, 1933. Louisville. Inducted in 1979. 1956-1972 Baltimore Colts, 1973 San Diego Chargers.

NORM VAN BROCKLIN

Quarterback. 6-1, 190. Born in Eagle Butte, South Dakota, March 15, 1926. Oregon. Inducted in 1971. 1949-1957 Los Angeles Rams, 1958-1960 Philadelphia Eagles.

STEVE VAN BUREN

Halfback. 6-1, 200. Born in La Ceiba, Honduras, December 28, 1920. Louisiana State. Inducted in 1965. 1944-1951 Philadelphia Eagles.

BOB WATERFIELD

Quarterback. 6-2, 200. Born in Elmira, New York, July 26, 1920. UCLA. Inducted in 1965. 1945 Cleveland Rams, 1946-1952 Los Angeles Rams.

BILL WILLIS

Guard. 6-2, 215. Born in Columbus, Ohio, October 5, 1921. Ohio State. Inducted in 1977. 1946-49 Cleveland Browns (AAFC), 1950-53 Cleveland Browns.

LARRY WILSON

Defensive back. 6-0, 190. Born in Rigby, Idaho, March 24, 1938. Utah. Inducted in 1978. 1960-1972 St. Louis Cardinals.

ALEX WOJCIECHOWICZ

Center. 6-0, 235. Born in South River, New Jersey, August 12, 1915. Fordham. Inducted in 1968. 1938-1946 Detroit Lions, 1946-1950 Philadelphia Eagles.

A CHRONOLOGY
OF PROFESSIONAL FOOTBALL

1892 Rutgers and Princeton had played a college soccer football game, the first ever, in 1869. Rugby had gained favor over soccer, however, and from it rugby football, then football, had evolved among American colleges. It was also played by athletic clubs. Intense competition existed between two Pittsburgh clubs, Allegheny Athletic Association and Pittsburgh Athletic Club. William (Pudge) Heffelfinger, former star at Yale, brought in by AAA, paid $500 to play in game against PAC, becoming first person known to have been paid openly to play football, Nov. 12. AAA won 4–0 when Heffelfinger picked up PAC fumble and ran for touchdown, which then counted four points.

1898 Morgan AC founded on Chicago's South Side, later became Chicago Normals, Racine (a Chicago street) Cardinals, Chicago Cardinals, and St. Louis Cardinals, oldest continuing operation in pro football.

1899 Duquesne Country and Athletic Club, or Pittsburgh Duquesnes, incurred large payroll signing players returning from Spanish-American War, sought help from Pittsburgh Sportsman William C. Temple. He bought football team from athletic club, became first known individual club owner.

1901 Temple and Barney Dreyfuss of baseball Pirates formed new team and urged cross-state rivalry with Philadelphia.

1902 Philadelphia Athletics, managed by Connie Mack, and Nationals or Phillies formed football teams. Athletics won first night football game, 39–0 over Kanaweola AC at Elmira, N.Y., Nov. 21.

Athletics claimed pro championship after winning two, losing one against Phillies and going 1–1–1 against Pittsburgh Pros. Pitcher Rube Waddell played for Athletics, pitcher Christy Mathewson was fullback for Pittsburgh in one game.

"World Series," actually four-team tournament, played among Athletics, New York Knickerbockers, Watertown, N.Y., Red and Blacks, and Syracuse AC was played in Madison Square Garden. Philadelphia and Syracuse played first indoor football game before 3,000, Dec. 28. Syracuse, with Pop Warner at guard, won game 6–0, went on to win tournament.

1903 Franklin (Pa.) AC won second and last "World Series" of pro football over Philadelphia, Watertown, and Orange, N.J. AC.

Pro football declined in Pittsburgh area. Some PAC players hired by Massillon, Ohio, Tigers, making Massillon first openly professional team in Ohio. Emphasis shifted there from Pennsylvania.

1904 Ohio had at least eight pro teams. Attempt failed to form league to end cutthroat bidding for players, write rules for all.

1905 Canton Bulldogs turned professional.

1906 Arch-rivals Massillon and Canton played twice, Massillon won both. Because of betting scandal, Canton manager Blondy Wallace left in disgrace, interest in pro football in two cities declined.

1913 Jim Thorpe, former football star for Carlisle Indian School and hero of 1912 Olympics, played season for Pine Village Pros in Indiana.

1915 Canton revived name "Bulldogs." and signed Thorpe for $250 a game.

1916 With Thorpe starring, Canton won 10 straight, most by lopsided scores, was acclaimed pro football champion of world.

1919 George Calhoun, Curly Lambeau organized Green Bay Packers. Indian Packing Company provided equipment, name "Packers." They had 10–1 record against other company teams.

1920 Pro football was in state of confusion, teams were loosely organized, players moved freely among teams, there was no system for recruiting players. A league in which all followed the same rules was needed. Meeting was held among interested teams in August, second meeting was held in Canton and American Professional Football Association, forerunner of National Football League, formed Sept. 17. Teams were from five states—Akron Pros, Canton Bulldogs, Cleveland Indians, Dayton Triangles, Massillon Tigers from Ohio; Hammond Pros, Muncie Flyers from Indiana; Racine Cardinals, Rock Island Independents, Decatur Staleys, represented by George Halas, from Illinois; Rochester, N.Y., Jeffersons; and "Wisconsin."

Capitalizing on his fame, Thorpe was chosen league president, Stan Cofall of Massillon vice-president. Membership fee of $100 arrived at to give aura of respectability. No team ever paid it. Massillon and Muncie did not field teams. Buffalo All-Americans, Chicago Tigers, Columbus, Ohio, Panhandles, and Detroit Tigers joined league later in year. League operated sporadically, teams played as many non-members as members, either no standings kept or have since been lost. Akron, Buffalo, Canton all claimed championship, hastily-arranged series of games, one of them between Buffalo and Canton at Polo Grounds, New York City, failed to settle issue of championship.

First recorded player deal sale of Bob Nash, tackle and end for Akron, to Buffalo for $300, five percent of gate receipts.

1921 APFA reorganized at Akron, Joe Carr of Panhandles named president, Apr. 30. Carl Storck of Dayton named secretary-treasurer. Carr established league headquarters at Columbus.

Chicago Tigers, beaten by Racine Cardinals in 1920 game for "rights" to Chicago, dropped out, so did Hammond.

J.E. Clair of Acme Packing Com-

pany granted franchise for Green Bay Packers, Aug. 27. Cincinnati Celts also joined league.

Thorpe moved from Canton to Cleveland Indians.

A.E. Staley turned Decatur Staleys over to George Halas, who moved them to Cubs Park in Chicago, promising to keep the name "Staleys" one more year.

Five teams that dropped out had records stricken from standings— Evansville, Hammond, Louisville, Minneapolis, and Muncie.

Chicago Staleys claimed league championship with 10–1–1 record. Buffalo, 9–1–2, claimed Chicago included nonleague games in record, but Carr ruled for Staleys.

1922 Packers disciplined for using college players under assumed names, Clair turned franchise back to league, Jan. 28. Curly Lambeau promised to obey rules, used $50 of own money to buy back franchise, June 24. Bad weather, low attendance plagued Packers, merchants raised $2,500, public non-profit corporation set up to operate team with Lambeau as manager, coach.

APFA changed name to National Football League, June 24. Staleys became Chicago Bears.

Thorpe, other Indian players formed Oorang Indians in Marion, Ohio, sponsored by Oorang dog kennels.

1923 Oorang folded with 1–10 record, Thorpe moved to Toledo Maroons. Player-coach Halas of Chicago recovered fumble by Thorpe in game against Oorang, ran 98 yards for touchdown.

1924 Frankford Yellowjackets of Philadelphia awarded franchise, that city entered league for first time. League champion Canton moved to Cleveland to play before larger crowds to meet rising payroll.

1925 Tim Mara and Billy Gibson awarded franchise for New York City for $500. Detroit Panthers, coached by Jimmy Conzelman, Pottsville, Pa., Maroons, Providence R.I., Steam Roller also entered league. New team in Canton took name "Bulldogs."

University of Illinois season ended and Red Grange signed contract to play for Chicago Bears immediately, Nov. 22. Crowd of 38,000 watched Grange and Bears in traditional Thanksgiving game against Cardinals. Barnstorming tour began in which Bears played seven games in 11 days in St. Louis, Philadelphia, New York, then cities in South and West. Crowd of 70,000 watched game against Giants at Polo Grounds, helping assure future of NFL franchise in New York.

Pottsville defeated Chicago Cardinals for what they thought was NFL championship, but week later played "Notre Dame All-Stars" in Philadelphia. Frankford protested, saying "territorial rights" had been impinged upon. Carr upheld protest, cancelled Pottsville franchise, ordered Cardinals to play two more games. They did, won both, were proclaimed NFL champions.

1926 Grange's manager, C. C. Pyle, asked Bears for five-figure salary for Grange, one-third ownership of team. Bears refused, lost Grange. Pyle leased Yankee Stadium in New York City, petitioned for NFL franchise, was refused, started first American Football League. It lasted one season, included Grange's New York Yankees, eight other teams. AFL champion Philadelphia Quakers played postseason game against NFL New York Giants, lost 31–0.

Halas pushed through rule prohibiting any team from signing player whose college class had not graduated, Feb. 6.

NFL membership swelled to 22, frustrating AFL growth. Paddy Driscoll of Cardinals moved to rival Bears. Ole Haugsrud, operator of Duluth, Minn., Eskimos, gained NFL franchise, signed Ernie Nevers of Stanford, giving NFL gate attraction to rival Grange. Thirteen-member Eskimos, "Iron Men of the North," played 28 exhibition or league games, 26 on road.

1927 AFL folded, NFL shrank to 12 teams. Akron, Canton, Columbus left NFL. New York Yankees and Grange joined NFL. Grange suffered knee injury. New York Giants won first NFL championship, scoring five consecutive shutouts at one point.

1928 Grange left football, appeared in movie and on vaudeville circuit. Duluth disbanded. Nevers quit pro football, played baseball, was assistant coach at Stanford.

1929 Chris O'Brien sold Chicago Cardinals to David Jones, July 27. NFL added fourth official, field judge, July 28. Cardinals became first pro team to go to out-of-town training camp, Coldwater, Mich., Aug. 21. Dayton played final season, last of original Ohio teams to leave league.

Grange, Nevers returned to NFL. Nevers scored 40 points for Cardinals against Bears, Nov. 28, six touchdowns rushing, four extra points. Grange returned to Bears.

Packers signed back Johnny Blood (McNally), tackle Cal Hubbard, guard Mike Michalske, and won first NFL championship.

1930 Portsmouth, Ohio, Spartans, joined NFL. Defunct Dayton franchise bought by John Dwyer, became Brooklyn Dodgers. Bears, Cardinals played exhibition for unemployment relief funds, indoors at Chicago Stadium, layer of dirt covering arena floor. New York Giants, "Notre Dame All-Stars" coached by Knute Rockne, played charity exhibition before 55,000 at Polo Grounds.

Halas retired as player, resigned as coach of Bears in favor of Ralph Jones.

Packers won second straight NFL championship.

1931 Pro football shrank to 10 teams. Carr fined Bears, Packers, Portsmouth $1,000 each for using players whose college classes had not graduated, July 11.

Playing career of Al Nesser, last of six brothers to play in NFL, ended when Cleveland Indians disbanded.

Green Bay won third straight NFL championship.

1932 George P. Marshall, Vincent Bendix, Jay O'Brien, M. Dorland Doyle awarded franchise for Boston, July 9. Named team "Braves" after baseball team using same park.

NFL membership dropped to eight, lowest in history. First playoff in NFL history arranged between Bears and Spartans. Moved indoors to Chicago Stadium because of blizzard conditions in city. Arena allowed only 80-yard field that came right to walls. For safety, goal posts moved from end to goal lines, inbounds lines or hashmarks drawn 10 yards from side lines for ball to be put in play. Bears won 9–0, Dec. 18, scoring touchdown disputed by Spartans who claimed Bronko Nagurski threw jump pass to Red Grange from point less than five yards behind line of scrimmage, violating existing passing rule.

1933 NFL made significant changes in rules of football first time. Innovations of 1932 indoor playoffs — inbounds lines or hashmarks 10 yards from sidelines, goal posts on goal lines — became rules, Feb. 25. Following resolution by George P. Marshall, NFL divided into two five-team divisions, winners to meet in annual championship playoff, July. 8.

Franchise was awarded to Art Rooney and A. McCool for Pittsburgh, July 8; team was named "Pirates." Inactive Frankford franchise declared forfeited, Philadelphia franchise awarded to Bert Bell, Lud Wray, July 9; named team "Eagles." Boston changed name to "Redskins." George Halas bought out Ed (Dutch) Sternaman, became sole owner of Chicago Bears, reinstated himself as head coach. David Jones sold Cardinals to Charles W. Bidwill. Cincinnati Reds joined league.

Eastern Division champion New York Giants met Western Division champion Bears at Wrigley Field in first NFL championship game, Dec. 17. Bears won 23–21.

1934 Bears played scoreless tie against collegians in first Chicago All-Star Game before 79,432 at Soldier Field, Aug. 31.

NFL legalized forward passes anywhere behind line of scrimmage.

G. A. (Dick) Richards purchased Portsmouth Spartans, moved them to Detroit, June 30; they took name "Lions." Cincinnati Reds franchise moved during season, became St. Louis Gunners.

Player waiver rule adopted, Dec. 10.

Grange retired from football.

1935 Bell of Philadelphia proposed, NFL adopted annual draft of college players, to begin in 1936, with team finishing last in standings having first choice each round of draft, May 19.

Cincinnati Reds-St. Louis Gunners franchise died.

Inbounds lines or hashmarks moved nearer center of field, 15 yards from sidelines.

1936 No franchise shifts for first time since formation of NFL and for first time all teams played same number of games.

Last-place previous year, Philadelphia Eagles made Jay Berwanger, University of Chicago back, first choice in first NFL draft, Feb. 8. Eagles later traded negotiation rights to him to Bears. He never played pro football.

Rival league was formed, became second to call itself American Football League. It included six teams, Boston Shamrocks won championship.

1937 Cleveland returned to NFL. Homer Marshman was granted a franchise, Feb. 12; he named new team "Rams." Marshall moved Redskins to Washington, Feb. 13.

Los Angeles Bulldogs had 8–0 record in American Football League; six-team league folded.

1938 Fifteen-yard penalty adopted for roughing passer.

Hugh (Shorty) Ray became technical advisor on rules and officiating to NFL. Marshall, Los Angeles newspaper officials established Pro Bowl game between NFL champion, team of all stars.

1939 New York Giants defeated Pro All-Stars 13–10 in first Pro Bowl game at Wrigley Field, Los Angeles, Jan. 15.

Carr, NFL president since 1921, died at Columbus, May 20. Carl Storck named successor, May 25.

National Broadcasting Company camera beamed Brooklyn Dodgers-

Philadelphia Eagles game from Ebbets Field back to studios of network, handful of sets then in New York City, first NFL game to be televised.

1940 Clipping penalty reduced from 25 to 15 yards, all distance penalties enforced from spot on field of play limited to half distance to goal, Apr. 12.

Pittsburgh changed nickname from Pirates to Steelers.

Rival league formed, became third to call itself American Football League. It included six teams, Columbus, Ohio, Bullies won championship.

Art Rooney sold Pittsburgh to Alexis Thompson, Dec. 9, and later purchased part-interest in Philadelphia.

Bears, playing T-formation with man-in-motion, defeated Washington 73–0 in NFL championship, Dec. 8. It was first championship carried on network radio, broadcast by Red Barber to 120 stations of Mutual Broadcasting System, which paid $2,500 for rights.

1941 Elmer Layden, head coach, athletic director at Notre Dame, named first commissioner of NFL, March 1. Moved league headquarters to Chicago. Carl Storck resigned as president-secretary, Apr. 5.

Co-owners Bell, Rooney of Eagles transferred them to Alexis Thompson in exchange for Pittsburgh franchise. Homer Marshman, associates sold Cleveland Rams to Daniel F. Reeves, Fred Levy, Jr., June 1.

Playoffs were provided for in case of ties in division races. Sudden death overtime provided for in case playoff was tied after four quarters.

Columbus won championship of five-team American Football League; it folded.

Bears defeated Green Bay 33–14 in first divisional playoff in NFL history, winning Western Division championship, Dec. 14.

1942 Players departing for service in World War II reduced rosters of NFL teams. Halas left Bears for armed forces, was replaced by co-coaches Hunk Anderson, Luke Johnsos.

1943 Cleveland Rams, with co-owners Lt. Daniel F. Reeves, Maj. Fred Levy, Jr. in service, granted permission to suspend operations for one season, Apr. 6. Levy transferred his stock in team to Reeves, Apr. 16.

NFL adopted free substitution, Apr. 7. Abbreviated wartime rosters, however, prevented its effects from taking place immediately.

Philadelphia, Pittsburgh granted permission to merge, became Phil-Pitt, June 19. They divided home games between two cities, Greasy Neale, Walt Kiesling were co-coaches. Merger automatically dissolved last day of season, Dec. 5.

Ted Collins granted franchise for Boston to become active in 1944.

1944 Collins, who had wanted franchise in Yankee Stadium in New York, named new team in Boston "Yanks." Cleveland resumed operations. Brooklyn Dodgers changed name to "Tigers."

Cardinals, Pittsburgh requested by league to merge for one year under name, Card-Pitt, Apr. 21. Merger automatically dissolved last day of season, Dec. 3.

Coaching from bench legalized, Apr. 20.

1945 Inbounds lines or hashmarks moved nearer center of field, 20 yards from sidelines. Players required to wear long stockings, Apr. 9.

Boston Yanks, Brooklyn Tigers merged as "Yanks," Apr. 10.

Halas rejoined Bears after service with U.S. Navy in Pacific. Returned to head coaching.

After Japanese surrender ending World War II count showed NFL service roster, limited to men who played in league games, totaled 638, 21 of whom had died.

1946 Layden resigned as commissioner, replaced by Bell, co-owner of Pittsburgh Steelers, Jan. 11. Bell moved league headquarters from Chicago to Philadelphia suburb of Bala Cynwyd.

Free substitution withdrawn, substitutions limited to no more than three men at time. Forward passes made automatically incomplete upon striking goal posts, Jan. 11.

NFL champion Cleveland given permission to transfer to Los Angeles, Jan. 12. NFL became coast-to-coast league first time.

Rival league, All-America Football Conference, formed. Four of its eight teams were in same population centers as NFL teams—Brooklyn Dodgers, New York Yankees, Chicago Rockets, Los Angeles Dons. Cleveland Browns won AAFC championship.

Backs Frank Filchock and Merle Hapes of the Giants questioned about attempt by New York man to fix championship game vs. Chicago; Commissioner Bell suspended Hapes, permitted Filchock to play. He played well but Chicago won 24–14. **1947** Bell's contract as commissioner was renewed for five years, Jan. 1; same day NFL Constitution amended imposing major penalty for anyone not reporting offer of bribe, attempt to fix game, or any other infraction of rules having to do with gambling.

NFL added fifth official, back judge. Sudden death readopted for championship games, Jan. 24.

"Bonus" draft choice made for first time; one team each year would get special bonus choice before first round began.

Halfback Fred Gehrke of Los Angeles Rams painted horns on Rams' helmets, first helmet emblems in pro football.

AAFC again had eight teams, Cleveland Browns won second championship.

1948 Plastic head protectors prohibited. Flexible artificial tee permitted at kickoff. Officials besides referee equipped with whistles, not horns, Jan. 14.

Fred Mandel sold Detroit to syndicate headed by D. Lyle Fife, Jan. 15.

Cleveland Browns won third straight championship of eight-team AAFC.

1949 Thompson sold NFL champion Philadelphia Eagles to syndicate headed by James P. Clark, Jan. 15.

Commissioner Bell, vice-president and treasurer Dennis Shea, given 10-year contracts, Jan. 20.

Free substitution adopted for one year, Jan. 20.

Boston Yanks became New York Bulldogs, shared Polo Grounds with Giants.

Cleveland won fourth straight championship of AAFC, reduced to seven teams. Bell announced merger agreement Dec. 9 in which three AAFC teams—Cleveland, San Francisco 49ers, Baltimore Colts—would enter NFL in 1950.

1950 Free substitution restored, way opened for two-platoon era, specialization in pro football, Jan. 23.

Name "National Football League" returned after about three months as "National-American Football League." American, National Conferences replaced Eastern, Western Divisions, Mar. 3.

New York Bulldogs became "Yanks," divided players of former AAFC Yankees with Giants. Special allocation draft held in which 13 teams drafted remaining AAFC players, with special consideration for Baltimore, 15 choices compared to 10 for other teams.

Los Angeles Rams became first NFL team to contract to have all its games televised. Arrangement covered both home and away games, sponsor agreed to make up difference in home game income if lower than year before (cost sponsor $307,000.). Washington also arranged to televise games, other teams made deals to put selected games on television.

For first time in history deadlocks occurred, playoffs were necessary in both conferences (divisions). Cleveland defeated Giants in American, Los Angeles defeated Bears in National. In one of most exciting championship games, Cleveland defeated Los Angeles 30–28, Dec. 24.

1951 Pro Bowl game, dormant since 1942, revived under new format matching all-stars of each conference at Los Angeles Memorial Coliseum. American Conference defeated National 28–27, Jan. 14.

Abraham Watner returned Baltimore Colts franchise to league, was voted $50,000 for Colts' players, Jan. 18.

Rule passed that no tackle, guard, or center eligible for forward pass, Jan. 18.

DuMont Network paid $75,000 for rights to championship game, televised coast-to-coast for first time. Los Angeles defeated Cleveland 24–17, Dec. 23.

1952 Ted Collins sold New York Yanks' franchise to NFL, Jan. 19. New franchise awarded to Dallas Texans, first NFL team in Texas, Jan. 24. Yanks had been, in order, Boston Yanks, New York Bulldogs, New York Yanks. Texans won 1, lost 11, folded, last NFL team to become extinct.

Pittsburgh Steelers abandoned single wing for T-formation, last pro team to do so.

Los Angeles reversed television policy, aired only road games.

1953 Baltimore re-entered NFL. League awarded holdings of defunct Dallas to group headed by Carroll Rosenbloom that formed team with name "Colts," same as former franchise, Jan. 23.

Names of American, National Conferences changed to Eastern, Western Conferences, Jan. 24.

Thorpe died, Mar. 28.

Arthur McBride sold Cleveland to syndicate headed by Dave R. Jones, June 10.

NFL policy of blacking out television of home games upheld by Judge Allan K. Grim of U.S. District Court in Philadelphia, Nov. 12.

1954 Bell given new 12-year contract.

1955 Sudden death overtime rule used for first time, on experimental basis in preseason game between Los Angeles, New York at Portland, Ore., Aug. 28. Los Angeles won 23–17 three minutes into overtime.

Runners could advance ball, even by crawling along ground, until stopped, sometimes leading to rough play. As result, rules changed so ball declared dead immediately if player touched ground with any part of body except hands or feet while in grasp of opponent.

Quarterback Otto Graham played last game for Cleveland, 38–14 victory over Los Angeles for NFL championship.

NBC replaced DuMont as network for title game, paying rights fee of $100,000.

1956 Halas retired as coach of Bears, replaced by Paddy Driscoll. Giants moved from Polo Grounds to Yankee Stadium.

Grabbing opponent's facemask made illegal, with exception of ball carrier's. "Loudspeaker coaching" from sideline prohibited. Brown ball with white stripes replaced white with black stripes for night games. Language of "dead ball rule" improved, stipulating ball dead when runner contacted by defensive player and touched ground with any part of body except hands or feet.

CBS became first to broadcast some NFL regular season games to selected television markets across nation.

Hugh (Shorty) Ray, former NFL rules advisor and rules author, died.

1957 Pete Rozelle named general manager of Los Angeles. Anthony J. Morabito, founder, co-owner of 49ers died of heart attack during game against Bears, Oct. 28. Then NFL record crowd, 102,368, saw 49ers-Rams game at Los Angeles Memorial Coliseum, Nov. 10. Detroit Lions came from 20 points down for playoff victory over 49ers 31–27, Dec. 22.

1958 "Bonus" draft choice eliminated, Jan. 29.

Halas reinstated himself as Bears coach for third time; others were in 1933, 1946.

Jim Brown of Cleveland gained NFL record 1,527 yards rushing.

Baltimore, coached by Weeb Ewbank, defeated New York 23–17 in first sudden death NFL championship game, Alan Ameche scoring for Colts after 8 minutes, 15 seconds of overtime, Dec. 28.

1959 Tim Mara, co-founder of Giants, died, Feb. 17.

Lamar Hunt announced intentions to form second pro football league. Hunt representing Dallas, others representing Denver, Houston, Los Angeles, Minneapolis-St. Paul, New York City held first meeting of league at Chicago, Aug. 14. Made plans to begin play in 1960. Eight days later at second meeting announced name of organization would be "American Football League." Buffalo became seventh AFL team, Oct. 28, Boston eighth, Nov. 22. First AFL draft held, Nov. 22. Joe Foss named AFL commissioner, Nov. 30. Second draft held, Dec. 2.

NFL commissioner Bell died of heart attack suffered at Franklin Field, Philadelphia, during last two minutes of game between Eagles, Pittsburgh, Oct. 11. Treasurer Austin Gunsel named President in office of Commissioner until January, 1960, annual meeting, Oct. 14.

1960 Pete Rozelle elected NFL commissioner on 23rd ballot, succeeding Bell, Jan. 26.

Hunt, founder of AFL, elected president for 1960, Jan. 26. Oakland became eighth AFL team, Jan. 30. Eastern, Western Divisions set up, Jan. 30. Five-year contract signed with American Broadcasting Company for network televising of selected games, June 9.

AFL adopted two-point option on points after touchdown, one point if successful kick, two for successful run or pass across goal line from 2 yard line, Jan. 28.

NFL awarded Dallas 1960 franchise, Minnesota 1961 franchise, expanding to 14 teams, Jan. 28. They took nicknames "Cowboys," "Vikings."

"No-tampering" verbal pact, relative to players' contracts, agreed to between NFL, AFL, Feb. 9.

Chicago Cardinals transferred to St. Louis, Mar. 13.

Boston Patriots defeated Bills 28–7 at Buffalo in first AFL preseason game before 16,000, July 30. Denver Broncos defeated Patriots 13–10 at Boston in first AFL regular season game before 21,597, Sept. 9.

1961 Houston Oilers defeated Los Angeles Chargers 24–16 for first AFL championship before 32,183 at Houston, Jan. 1.

Detroit defeated Cleveland 17–16 in first Playoff Bowl, or Bert Bell Benefit Bowl, between second-place teams in each conference in Miami, Jan. 7.

End Willard Dewveall of Bears played out his option, joined Houston of AFL, first player to deliberately move from one league to other, Jan. 14.

Ed McGah, Wayne Valley, Robert Osborne bought out their partners in ownership of Oakland Raiders, Jan. 17. Chargers transferred to San Diego, Feb. 10. Dave R. Jones sold Cleveland to group headed by Arthur B. Modell, Mar. 22. Howsam brothers sold Denver to group headed by Calvin Kunz, Gerry Phipps, May 26.

NBC awarded two-year contract for radio and television rights to NFL championship game for $615,000 annually, $300,000 of which was to go directly into NFL Player Benefit Plan, Apr. 5.

Canton, where league that became NFL had been formed in 1920, chosen site of Pro Football Hall of Fame, Apr. 27.

Bill legalizing single network television contracts by professional sports leagues introduced in Congress by Rep. Emanuel Celler passed House, Senate, signed into law by President John F. Kennedy, Sept. 30.

Green Bay won first NFL championship since 1944, defeating New York 37–0, Dec. 31.

1962 West defeated East 47–27 in first AFL All-Star Game before 20,973 in San Diego, Jan. 7.

NFL prohibited grabbing any player's facemask, Jan. 9.

Commissioners Rozelle of NFL Foss of AFL given new five-year contracts, Jan. 8, 9.

NFL entered into single network agreement with CBS for telecasting all regular season games for $4,650,000 annually, Jan. 10.

Judge Roszel Thompson of U.S. District Court, Baltimore, ruled against AFL in antitrust suit against NFL, May 21. AFL had charged monopoly, conspiracy in areas of expansion, television, player signings. Case lasted two and a half years, trial lasted two months.

McGah, Valley acquired controlling interest in Oakland, May 24. AFL assumed financial responsibility for New York Titans, Nov. 8. Dan Reeves purchased partners' stock in Los Angeles Rams, becoming majority owner, Dec. 27.

Dallas defeated Oilers 20–17 for AFL championship at Houston after 17 minutes, 54 seconds of sudden death overtime on 25-yard field goal by Tommy Brooker, Dec. 23. Game lasted record 77 minutes, 54 seconds.

Judge Edward Weinfeld of U.S. District Court, New York City, upheld legality of NFL's television blackout within 75-mile radius of home games, denied injunction sought by persons who had demanded championship between Giants, Green Bay be televised in New York City area, Dec. 28.

1963 AFL's guarantee for visiting teams during regular season increased from $20,000 to $30,000, Jan. 10.

Hunt's Dallas Texans transferred to Kansas City, becoming "Chiefs," Feb. 8. New York Titans sold to five-member syndicate headed by David (Sonny) Werblin, name changed to "Jets," Mar. 28.

Commissioner Rozelle suspended indefinitely Paul Hornung, Green Bay halfback, Alex Karras, Detroit defensive tackle, for placing bets on their own teams and on other NFL games; also fined five other Detroit players $2,000 each for betting on one game in which they did not participate, and the Detroit Lions Football Co. $2,000 on each of two counts for failure to report promptly information and for lack of sideline supervision.

AFL allowed New York, Oakland to select players from other franchises in hopes of giving league more competitive balance, May 11.

NBC awarded exclusive network broadcasting rights for 1963 AFL championship game for $926,000, May 23.

U.S. Fourth Circuit Court of Appeals reaffirmed lower court's finding for NFL in $10 million suit brought by AFL, ending three and a half years of litigation, Nov. 21.

Boston defeated Buffalo 26–8 in first divisional playoff in AFL history before 33,044 in Buffalo, Dec. 28.

Chicago defeated New York 14–10 for NFL championship, record sixth and last title for Halas in his thirty-sixth season as Bears' coach, Dec. 29.

1964 William Clay Ford, their president since 1961, purchased Detroit, Jan. 10. Group representing late James P. Clark sold Philadelphia to group headed by Jerry Wolman, Jan. 21. Carroll Rosenbloom, majority owner since 1953, acquired complete ownership of Baltimore, Jan. 23.

CBS submitted winning bid of $14.1 million per year for NFL regular season television rights for 1964, 1965, Jan. 24. CBS acquired rights to 1964, 1965 NFL championship games for $1.8 million per game, Apr. 17. AFL signed five-year, $36 million television contract with NBC to begin with 1965 season, assuring each team approximately $900,000 a year from television rights, Jan. 29.

Paul Hornung of Green Bay, Alex Karras of Detroit reinstated by Rozelle, Mar. 16.

Paul Brown departed Cleveland after 17 years as their head coach, Blanton Collier replaced him.

AFL Commissioner Foss given new three-year contract commencing in 1965, May 22.

New York defeated Denver 30–6 before then AFL record crowd of 45,665 in first game at Shea Stadium, Sept. 12.

Pete Gogolak of Cornell signed contract with Buffalo, becoming first soccer-style kicker in pro football.

1965 NFL teams pledged not to sign college seniors until completion of all their games, including bowl games, empowered commissioner to discipline club up to as much as loss of entire draft list for violation of pledge, Feb. 15.

NFL added sixth official, line judge, Feb. 19. Color of officials' penalty flags changed from white to bright gold, Apr. 5.

Atlanta awarded NFL franchise for 1966, with Rankin Smith as owner, June 30. Miami awarded AFL franchise for 1966, with Joe Robbie, Danny Thomas as owners, Aug. 16.

Green Bay defeated Baltimore 13–10 in sudden death Western Conference playoff game, Don Chandler kicking 25-yard field goal for Packers after 13 minutes, 39 seconds of overtime, Dec. 26.

CBS acquired rights to NFL regular season games in 1966, 1967, plus option for 1968, for $18.8 million per year, Dec. 29.

1966 AFL-NFL war reached its peak, leagues spent combined total of $7 million to sign 1966 draft choices. NFL signed 75 percent of its 232 draftees, AFL 46 percent of its 181. Of 111 common draft choices, 79 joined NFL, 28 joined AFL, four went unsigned.

Rights to NFL 1966, 1967 championship games sold to CBS for $2 million per game, Feb. 14.

Joe Foss resigned as AFL commissioner, Apr. 7. Al Davis, head coach, general manager of Oakland Raiders, named to replace him, Apr. 8.

Goal posts offset from goal line, colored bright gold, with uprights 20 feet above crossbar made standard in NFL, May 16.

Merger announced; NFL, AFL entered into agreement to form combined league of 24 teams, expanding to 26 in 1968, June 8. Rozelle named commissioner. Leagues agreed to play separate schedules until 1970 but would meet, starting in 1967, in world championship game (Super Bowl) and play each other in preseason games.

Davis rejoined Oakland Raiders, Milt Woodard named president of AFL, July 25.

Barron Hilton sold San Diego to group headed by Eugene Klein, Sam Schulman, Aug. 25.

Congress approved merger, passing special legislation exempting agreement itself from anti-trust action, Oct. 21.

New Orleans awarded NFL franchise to begin play in 1967, Nov. 1.

NFL realigned for 1967–69 seasons into Capitol, Century Divisions in Eastern Conference, Central, Coastal Divisions in Western Conference, Dec. 2. New Orleans, New York agreed to switch divisions in 1968, return to 1967 alignment in 1969.

Rights to Super Bowl for four years sold to CBS and NBC for $9.5 million, Dec. 13.

1967 Green Bay Packers of NFL defeated Kansas City of AFL 35–10 at Los Angeles in first Super Bowl, Jan. 15. Winning share for Packers was $15,000 each, losing share for Chiefs $7,500 each.

"Sling-shot" goal posts, six-foot-wide border around field made standard in NFL, Feb. 22.

Baltimore made Bubba Smith, Michigan State defensive lineman, first choice in first combined AFL-NFL draft, Mar. 14.

AFL awarded franchise to Cincinnati, to begin play in 1968, with Paul Brown as part-owner, general manager, head coach, May 24.

Arthur B. Modell, president of the Cleveland Browns, elected president of the NFL, May 28.

AFL team defeated NFL team for first time, Denver beat Detroit 13–7 in preseason game, Aug. 5.

Green Bay defeated Dallas 21–17 for NFL championship on last minute one-yard quarterback sneak by Bart Starr in 13-below temperature at Green Bay, Dec. 31.

George Halas retired fourth and last time as head coach of Chicago Bears at age 73.

1968 Green Bay defeated Oakland 33–14 in Super Bowl II at Miami, game had first $3 million gate in pro football history, Jan. 14.

Lombardi resigned as head coach of Packers, remained as general manager.

Sonny Werblin sold his shares in New York Jets to partners Don Lillis, Leon Hess, Townsend Martin, Phil Iselin; Lillis assumed presidency of Jets, May 21. Lillis died, July 23. Iselin appointed president, Aug. 6.

Ewbank became first coach to win

titles in both NFL, AFL, his Jets defeated Oakland 27–23 for AFL championship, Dec. 29.

1969 AFL established format of inter-divisional playoffs with winner in one division playing runner-up in other, for 1969 only, Jan. 11.

AFL team won Super Bowl for first time; Jets defeated Baltimore 16–7 at Miami, Jan. 12.

Lombardi became part-owner, executive vice-president, head coach of Washington Redskins.

NFL and AFL scrapped preseason experiment "Pressure Point" run or pass one-point conversion tried in 1969, Mar. 20.

Wolman sold Philadelphia Eagles to Leonard Tose, May 1.

Baltimore, Cleveland, Pittsburgh agreed to join AFL teams to form 13-team American Football Conference, remaining NFL teams to form National Football Conference in NFL in 1970, May 17. AFC teams voted to realign in Eastern, Central, Western Divisions.

Monday night football set for 1970; ABC acquired rights to televise 13 NFL regular season Monday night games in 1970, 1971, 1972.

George P. Marshall, president-emeritus of Redskins, died at 72, Aug. 9.

1970 Kansas City defeated Minnesota 23–7 in Super Bowl IV at New Orleans, Jan. 11. Gross receipts of approximately $3.8 million largest ever for one-day team sports event, television audience largest ever for one-day sports events.

NFC realigned into Eastern, Central, Western Divisions, Jan. 16.

CBS acquired rights to televise all NFC games, except Monday night games, in 1970–73, including divisional playoffs and NFC championship, also rights to Super Bowl in 1972, 1974, AFC-NFC Pro Bowl in 1971, 1973, Jan. 26.

NBC acquired rights to televise all AFC games, except Monday night games, in 1970–73, including divisional playoffs and AFC championship, also rights to Super Bowl in 1971, 1973, AFC-NFC Pro Bowl in 1972, 1974, Jan. 26.

Art Modell resigned as president of NFL, Mar. 12. Milt Woodard resigned as president of AFL, Mar. 13. Lamar Hunt elected president of AFC, George S. Halas, Sr. elected president of NFC, Mar. 19.

Merged league adopted rules changes putting names on backs of players' jerseys, making Wilson brand official football of league, making point after touchdown worth one point, making scoreboard clock official timing device of game, Mar. 18.

Players Negotiating Committee, NFL Players Association announced four-year agreement guaranteeing approximately $4,535,000 annually to player pension, insurance benefits, Aug. 3. Owners also agreed to contribute $250,000 annually to improve or implement such items as disability payments, widows' benefits, maternity benefits, dental benefits. Agreement also provided for increased preseason game per diem payments averaging approximately $2,600,000 annually.

Lombardi, executive vice-president, head coach of Redskins, died at 57, Sept. 3.

Tom Dempsey of New Orleans Saints kicked game-winning NFL record 63-yard field goal against Detroit Lions, Nov. 8.

1971 Baltimore defeated Dallas 16–13 on Jim O'Brien's 32-yard field goal with five seconds to go in Super Bowl V at Miami, Jan. 17. NBC telecast was viewed in estimated 23,980,000 homes, largest audience ever for one-day sports event.

NFC defeated AFC 27–6 in first AFC-NFC Pro Bowl at Los Angeles, Jan. 24.

Boston Patriots changed name to New England Patriots, Mar. 25.

Rules change adopted making sole criteria for determining intentional grounding whether passer was making deliberate attempt to prevent loss of yardage, Mar. 25.

Reeves, president, general manager of Rams, died at 58, Apr. 15.

Miami defeated Kansas City 27–24 in sudden death in AFC divisional playoff game, Garo Yepremian kicking 37-yard field goal for Dolphins after 22 minutes, 40 seconds of overtime, game lasting 82 minutes, 40 seconds in all, longest in history, Dec. 25.

1972 Dallas defeated Miami 24–3 in Super Bowl VI at Miami, Jan. 16. CBS telecast was viewed in estimated 27,450,000 homes, top-rated one-day telecast ever.

Inbounds lines or hashmarks moved nearer center of field, 23 yards, 1 foot, 9 inches from sidelines, Mar. 23. Exception made to the rule allowing team in possession on its own 15 yard line or within would put ball in play at spot 20 yards from nearest sideline so it could punt without direct conflict with goal post, May 24.

Method of determining won-lost percentage in standings changed, May 24. Tie games, previously not counted in standings, made equal to half-game won and half-game lost.

Hunt, Halas, reelected presidents of AFC, NFC, May 25.

Robert Irsay purchased Los Angeles, transferred ownership to Carroll Rosenbloom in exchange for Baltimore, July 13.

William V. Bidwill purchased stock of brother Charles (Stormy) Bidwill, became sole owner, president of St. Louis Cardinals, Sept. 2.

National District Attorneys Association endorsed position of professional leagues in opposing proposed legalization of gambling in professional team sports, Sept. 28.

1973 Rozelle announced all Super Bowl VII tickets sold, game would be telecast in Los Angeles, site of game, on experimental basis, Jan. 3.

Miami defeated Washington 14–7 in Super Bowl VII at Los Angeles, completing undefeated 17–0 record for 1972 season, Jan. 14. NBC telecast viewed by approximately 75,000,000 people. Although all 90,182 tickets had been sold and temperature reached 84 degrees on clear, sunny day, 8,476 ticket buyers did not attend game that was first ever televised locally.

AFC defeated NFC 33–28 in Pro

Bowl at Dallas, first time since 1951 game played outside Los Angeles, Jan. 21.

Jersey numbering system adopted, 1–19 for quarterbacks, specialists; 20–49, running, defensive backs; 50–59, centers, linebackers; 60–79, defensive linemen, interior offensive linemen except centers; 80–89, wide receivers, tight ends, Apr. 5. Players who had been in NFL in 1972 could continue to use old numbers.

Dan Rooney of Pittsburgh appointed chairman of Expansion Committee, Apr. 6.

NFL Charities non-profit organization created to derive income from monies generated by licensing of NFL trademarks and names, June 26; would support education, charitable activities, supply economic support to persons formerly associated with professional football no longer able to support themselves.

Congress adopted for three years experimental legislation requiring any NFL game that had been declared a sellout 72 hours prior to kickoff to be made available for local telecast, Sept. 14. Legislation provided for annual review to be made by Federal Communications Commission.

1974 Miami defeated Minnesota 24–7 in Super Bowl VIII at Houston, second straight Super Bowl championship for Miami, Jan. 13. CBS telecast viewed by approximately 75 million people.

Rival league formed; World Football League held organizational meeting, Jan. 14.

Rozelle given 10-year contract effective January 1, 1973, Feb. 27.

Tampa awarded franchise to begin play in 1976, Apr. 24. NFL announced one more franchise would be awarded to become operative in 1976.

Sweeping rules changes adopted as recommended by Competition Committee to add action, tempo to game: sudden death for preseason, regular season games, limited to one 15-minute overtime; goal posts moved from goal lines to end lines; kickoffs to be made from 35 not 40 yard line; after missed field goals ball to be returned to line of scrimmage or 20 yard line, whichever is farthest from goal line; restrictions placed on members of punting team to open up return possibilities; roll-blocking, cutting of wide receivers eliminated; extent of downfield contact defender can have with eligible receivers restricted; penalty for offensive holding, illegal use of hands, tripping reduced from 15 to 10 yards when occurs within three yards of line of scrimmage; wide receivers blocking back toward ball within three yards of line of scrimmage prevented from blocking below the waist, Apr. 25.

Toronto Northmen of World Football League signed Larry Csonka, Jim Kiick, Paul Warfield of Miami, Mar. 31.

Seattle awarded NFL franchise to begin play in 1976, June 4. Lloyd W. Nordstrom, president of Seattle Seahawks, Hugh F. Culverhouse, president of Tampa Bay Buccaneers, sign franchise agreement, Dec. 5.

Birmingham Americans defeated Florida Blazers 22–21 in WFL World Bowl, winning championship of the 12-team league, Dec. 5.

1975 Pittsburgh defeated Minnesota 16–6 in Super Bowl IX at New Orleans, Steelers' first championship since entering NFL in 1933. NBC telecast was viewed by approximately 78 million people.

Rules changed making incomplete pass into end zone on fourth down with line of scrimmage inside 20 returned to line of scrimmage instead of 20; double shift on or inside opponent's 20 permitted provided it has been shown three times in game instead of three times in quarter; penalty for ineligible receiver downfield reduced from 15 to 10 yards, Mar. 19.

Divisional winners with highest won-lost percentage made home teams for playoffs, surviving winners with highest percentage made home teams for championship games, June 26.

World Football League folded, Sept. 22.

1976 Pittsburgh defeated Dallas 21–17 in Super Bowl X in Miami;

Steelers joined Green Bay, Miami as two-time winners of Super Bowl. CBS telecast viewed by estimated 80 million people, largest television audience in history.

Lloyd Nordstrom, president of Seattle, died at 66, Jan. 20. His brother Elmer succeeded him as majority representative of the team.

Veteran player allocation held to stock Seattle, Tampa Bay franchises with 39 players each, Mar. 30–31. College draft held, with Seattle, Tampa Bay getting eight extra choices each, Apr. 8–9.

Steelers defeated College All-Stars 24–0 in storm-shortened final Chicago All-Star game, July 23. St. Louis defeated San Diego 20–10 in preseason game before 38,000 in Korakuen Stadium, Tokyo, in first NFL game outside North America Aug. 16.

1977 Oakland defeated Minnesota 32–14 before record crowd of 100,421 in Super Bowl XI at Pasadena, Jan. 9. Paid attendance was pro record 103,438. NBC telecast was viewed by 81.9 million people, largest ever to view sports event. Victory was fifth straight for AFC in Super Bowl.

Players Association, NFL Management Council ratified collective bargaining agreement extending until July 15, 1982, covering five football seasons while continuing pension plan—including years 1974, 1975, and 1976—with contributions totaling more than $55 million. Total cost of agreement estimated at $107 million. Agreement called for college draft at least through 1986, contained no-strike, no-suit clause, established 43-man active player limit, reducing pension vesting to four years, provided for increases in minimum salaries, preseason and postseason pay, improved insurance, medical, dental benefits, modified previous practices in player movement and control. Reaffirmed NFL commissioner's disciplinary authority. Additionally, agreement called for NFL member clubs to make payments totaling $16 million the next 10 years to settle various legal disputes, Feb. 25.

NFL regular season paid attendance was record 11,070,543.

San Francisco 49ers sold to Edward J. DeBartolo, Jr., Mar. 28.

Sixteen-game regular season, four-game preseason adopted to begin in 1978, Mar. 29. Second wild card team adopted for playoffs beginning in 1978, wild card teams to play each other with winners advancing to round of eight postseason series along with six division winners.

Defender permitted to contact eligible receiver either in three-yard zone at or beyond line of scrimmage or once beyond that zone, but not both, Mar. 31. Wide receivers prohibited from clipping anywhere, even in legal clipping zone. Penalty of loss of coin toss option in addition to 15-yard penalty provided if team does not arrive on field for warmup at least 15 minutes prior to scheduled kickoff.

Seattle Seahawks permanently aligned in AFC Western Division, Tampa Bay in NFC Central Division, Mar. 31.

NFL decided to experiment with seventh official in selected preseason games, Apr. 1.

Rules changes made it illegal to strike an opponent above shoulders (head slap) during initial charge of a defensive lineman; made it illegal for an offensive lineman to thrust his hands to an opponent's neck, face, or head; made it illegal for a back who lines up inside the tight end to break to the outside and then cut back inside to deliver a block below the waist of an opponent. Also, if a punting team commits a foul before its opponent takes possession and the receiving team subsequently commits a foul, the penalties offset each other and the down is replayed, June 14–15.

Commissioner Rozelle confirmed that agreements were negotiated with the three television networks—ABC, CBS, and NBC—to televise all NFL regular season and postseason games, plus selected preseason games, for four years beginning with the 1978 season. ABC was awarded rights to 16 Monday night, four prime

time (with possible expansion to six during the last three years of the contract), the AFC-NFC Pro Bowl, and the AFC-NFC Hall of Fame games. CBS received rights to all NFC regular season and postseason games (except those in the ABC package) and Super Bowls XIV (1980) and XVI (1982). NBC received rights to all AFC regular season and postseason games (except those in the ABC package) and Super Bowls XIII (1979) and XV (1981). Industry sources considered it the largest single television package ever negotiated, October.

Chicago's Walter Payton set a single game rushing record with 275 yards (40 carries) against Minnesota, Nov. 20.

Cincinnati defeated Kansas City 27–7 at Arrowhead Stadium in the NFL's 5,000th game in recorded history, Dec. 4.

1978 Dallas defeated Denver 27–10 in Super Bowl XII, held indoors for the first time, at the Louisiana Superdome in New Orleans, Jan. 15. CBS telecast viewed by 102,010,000 people, meaning the game was watched by more viewers than any other show of any kind in the history of television. Dallas's win was first NFC victory in last six Super Bowls.

According to Harris Sports Survey, 70 percent of the nation's sports fans say they follow football, compared to 54 percent who follow baseball. As far as fans' favorite sport, football increased its lead as the country's favorite sport to 26 to 16 percent over baseball, Jan. 19.

NFL regular season paid attendance was 11,018,632. In addition, during five years of TV blackout legislation, percent of capacity in NFL attendance has declined from record level of 95.5 percent in 1973 to 87.8 percent in 1977. NFL had over 1.5 million unsold seats in 1977, compared to fewer than one-half million in 1973.

Added seventh official, side judge, Mar. 14.

Study on the use of instant replay as an officiating aid to be made during seven nationally televised preseason games in 1978, Mar. 16.

Rules changes adopted permitting defender to maintain contact on receivers within a five-yard zone beyond scrimmage line, but restricted contact on receivers beyond that point; further clarified the pass blocking rule interpretation to permit extended arms and open hands, Mar. 17.

The NFL played for the first time in Mexico City with the Saints defeating the Eagles, 14–7, in a preseason game before a sellout crowd, Aug. 5.

1979 Pittsburgh defeated Dallas 35–31 in Super Bowl XIII to become the first team ever to win three Super Bowls, Jan. 21. Super Bowl XIII was the top ranked TV sporting event of all time, according to figures compiled by A. C. Nielsen Co. The NBC telecast was viewed in 35,090,000 homes, which bettered the previous record of Super Bowl XII with 34,410,000.

Bolstered by the expansion of the regular season schedule from 14 to 16 weeks, the NFL paid attendance exceeded 12 million (12,771,800) for the first time. The per-game average of 57,017 was the third highest in league history and best since 1973.

Rules changes emphasized additional player safety: prohibited players on the receiving team from blocking below the waist during kickoffs, punts, and field goal attempts; prohibited wearing of torn or altered equipment and exposed pads that may be hazardous; extended the zone in which there can be no crackback blocks from three yards on either side of the line of scrimmage to five yards in order to provide a greater measure of protection; permit free activation of three players from the injured reserve list after the final cutdown to 45 players, Mar. 16.

Commissioner Pete Rozelle announced that the 1980 AFC-NFC Pro Bowl Game will be played at Aloha Stadium in Honolulu, Hawaii. This will mark the first time in the 30-year history of the Pro Bowl that the game will be played in a non-NFL city.

Carroll D. Rosenbloom, president of the Rams, died at 72, April 2.

1980 Nielsen figures show that the CBS telecast of SB XIV between Pittsburgh and Los Angeles was the most watched sports event of all time. It was viewed in 35,330,000 homes.

Rule changes adopted placed greater restrictions on contact in the area of the head, neck, and face. Under the heading of "Personal Foul," players have been prohibited from directly striking, swinging, or clubbing on the head, neck, or face. Starting in 1980, a penalty may be called for such contact to the head, neck, or face whether or not the initial contact is made below the neck area.

The NFL entered into an agreement with the National Athletic Injury/Illness Reporting System (NAIRS) to proceed with developing a program to study injuries.

CBS, with a record bid of $12 million, won the national radio rights to 26 National Football League regular season games and all 10 postseason games for the 1980 through 1983 seasons.

NFL regular season attendance of nearly 13.4 million set a record for the second year in a row; 1979's total was 13.2 million. Average paid attendance for the 224-game 1980 regular season was 59,787, highest in the league's 61-year history. The previous high was 58,961 for 182 games in 1973. NFL games in 1980 were played before 92.4 percent of total stadium capacity.

Television ratings in 1980 were the second best in NFL history, trailing only the combined ratings of the 1976 season.

1981 The Oakland Raiders became the first Wild Card team to win the Super Bowl by defeating Philadelphia 27-10 at the Louisiana Superdome in New Orleans, Jan. 25. The Raiders finished second to San Diego in the AFC Western Division. In the playoffs they beat Houston at Oakland and Cleveland and San Diego on the road to advance to the Super Bowl.

The 1980 season concluded with a record Aloha Stadium crowd viewing the NFC's win over the AFC in the annual AFC-NFC Pro Bowl game in Honolulu, Feb. 1. It was the second straight sellout of the game in Honolulu.

Industrialist Edgar F. Kaiser, Jr. purchased the Denver Broncos from Gerald and Allan Phipps, Feb. 26.

1982 The 1981 NFL regular season paid attendance of 13,606,990 for an average of 60,745 was the highest in the league's 62-year history. It also was the first time the season average exceeded 60,000. NFL games in 1981 were played before 93.8 percent of total stadium capacity.

NFL signed a five-year contract with the three TV networks (ABC, CBS, NBC) to televise all NFL regular and postseason games starting with the 1982 season.

The San Francisco-Cincinnati Super Bowl game on January 24 achieved the highest rating of any televised sports event. The game was watched by a record 110,230,000 viewers in this country for a rating of 49.1.

PAST STANDINGS

1981

AMERICAN CONFERENCE
EASTERN DIVISION

	W	L	T	Pct.	Pts.	OP
Miami	11	4	1	.719	345	275
N.Y. Jets*	10	5	1	.656	355	287
Buffalo*	10	6	0	.625	311	276
Baltimore	2	14	0	.125	259	533
New England	2	14	0	.125	322	370

CENTRAL DIVISION

	W	L	T	Pct.	Pts.	OP
Cincinnati	12	4	0	.750	421	304
Pittsburgh	8	8	0	.500	356	297
Houston	7	9	0	.438	281	355
Cleveland	5	11	0	.313	276	375

WESTERN DIVISION

	W	L	T	Pct.	Pts.	OP
San Diego	10	6	0	.625	478	390
Denver	10	6	0	.625	321	289
Kansas City	9	7	0	.563	343	290
Oakland	7	9	0	.438	273	343
Seattle	6	10	0	.375	322	388

NATIONAL CONFERENCE
EASTERN DIVISION

	W	L	T	Pct.	Pts.	OP
Dallas	12	4	0	.750	367	277
Philadelphia*	10	6	0	.625	368	221
N.Y. Giants*	9	7	0	.563	295	257
Washington	8	8	0	.500	347	349
St. Louis	7	9	0	.438	315	408

CENTRAL DIVISION

	W	L	T	Pct.	Pts.	OP
Tampa Bay	9	7	0	.563	315	268
Detroit	8	8	0	.500	397	322
Green Bay	8	8	0	.500	324	361
Minnesota	7	9	0	.438	325	369
Chicago	6	10	0	.375	253	324

WESTERN DIVISION

	W	L	T	Pct.	Pts.	OP
San Francisco	13	3	0	.813	357	250
Atlanta	7	9	0	.438	426	355
Los Angeles	6	10	0	.375	303	351
New Orleans	4	12	0	.250	207	378

*Wild Card qualifier for playoffs

San Diego won AFC Western title over Denver on the basis of a better division record (6-2 to 5-3). Buffalo won a Wild Card playoff berth over Denver as the result of a 9-7 victory in head-to-head competition.

First round playoff: Buffalo 31, NEW YORK JETS 27
Divisional playoffs: San Diego 41, MIAMI 38 (OT, 13:52), CINCINNATI 28, Buffalo 21
AFC championship: CINCINNATI 27, San Diego 7
First round playoff: New York Giants 27, PHILADELPHIA 21
Divisional playoffs: DALLAS 38, Tampa Bay 0, SAN FRANCISCO 38, New York Giants 24
NFC championship: SAN FRANCISCO 28, Dallas 27
Super Bowl XVI: San Francisco (NFC) 26, Cincinnati (AFC) 21, Silverdome, Pontiac, Mich.

In the Past Standings section, home teams in playoff games are indicated by capital letters.

1980

AMERICAN CONFERENCE
EASTERN DIVISION

	W	L	T	Pct.	Pts.	OP
Buffalo	11	5	0	.688	320	260
New England	10	6	0	.625	441	325
Miami	8	8	0	.500	266	305
Baltimore	7	9	0	.438	355	387
N.Y. Jets	4	12	0	.250	302	395

CENTRAL DIVISION

	W	L	T	Pct.	Pts.	OP
Cleveland	11	5	0	.688	357	310
Houston*	11	5	0	.688	295	251
Pittsburgh	9	7	0	.563	352	313
Cincinnati	6	10	0	.375	244	312

WESTERN DIVISION

	W	L	T	Pct.	Pts.	OP
San Diego	11	5	0	.688	418	327
Oakland*	11	5	0	.688	364	306
Kansas City	8	8	0	.500	319	336
Denver	8	8	0	.500	310	323
Seattle	4	12	0	.250	291	408

NATIONAL CONFERENCE
EASTERN DIVISION

	W	L	T	Pct.	Pts.	OP
Philadelphia	12	4	0	.750	384	222
Dallas*	12	4	0	.750	454	311
Washington	6	10	0	.375	261	293
St. Louis	5	11	0	.313	299	350
N.Y. Giants	4	12	0	.250	249	425

CENTRAL DIVISION

	W	L	T	Pct.	Pts.	OP
Minnesota	9	7	0	.563	317	308
Detroit	9	7	0	.563	334	272
Chicago	7	9	0	.438	304	264
Tampa Bay	5	10	1	.344	271	341
Green Bay	5	10	1	.344	231	371

WESTERN DIVISION

	W	L	T	Pct.	Pts.	OP
Atlanta	12	4	0	.750	405	272
Los Angeles*	11	5	0	.688	424	289
San Francisco	6	10	0	.375	320	415
New Orleans	1	15	0	.063	291	487

*Wild Card qualifier for playoffs

Philadelphia won division title over Dallas on the basis of best net points in division games (plus 84 net points to plus 50). Minnesota won division title because of a better conference record than Detroit (8-4 to 9-5). Cleveland won division title because of a better conference record than Houston (8-4 to 7-5). San Diego won division title over Oakland on the basis of best net points in division games (plus 60 net points to plus 37).

First round playoff: OAKLAND 27, Houston 7
Divisional playoffs: SAN DIEGO 20, Buffalo 14; Oakland 14, CLEVELAND 12
AFC championship: Oakland 34, SAN DIEGO 27
First round playoff: DALLAS 34, Los Angeles 13
Divisional playoffs: PHILADELPHIA 31, Minnesota 16; Dallas 30, ATLANTA 27
NFC championship: PHILADELPHIA 20, Dallas 7
Super Bowl XV: Oakland (AFC) 27, Philadelphia (NFC) 10, Louisiana Superdome, New Orleans, La.

1979

AMERICAN CONFERENCE

EASTERN DIVISION

	W	L	T	Pct.	Pts.	OP
Miami	10	6	0	.625	341	257
New England	9	7	0	.563	411	326
N.Y. Jets	8	8	0	.500	337	383
Buffalo	7	9	0	.438	268	279
Baltimore	5	11	0	.313	271	351

CENTRAL DIVISION

	W	L	T	Pct.	Pts.	OP
Pittsburgh	12	4	0	.750	416	262
Houston*	11	5	0	.688	362	331
Cleveland	9	7	0	.563	359	352
Cincinnati	4	12	0	.250	337	421

WESTERN DIVISION

	W	L	T	Pct.	Pts.	OP
San Diego	12	4	0	.750	411	246
Denver*	10	6	0	.625	289	262
Seattle	9	7	0	.563	378	372
Oakland	9	7	0	.563	365	337
Kansas City	7	9	0	.438	238	262

NATIONAL CONFERENCE

EASTERN DIVISION

	W	L	T	Pct.	Pts.	OP
Dallas	11	5	0	.688	371	313
Philadelphia*	11	5	0	.688	339	282
Washington	10	6	0	.625	348	295
N.Y. Giants	6	10	0	.375	237	323
St. Louis	5	11	0	.313	307	358

CENTRAL DIVISION

	W	L	T	Pct.	Pts.	OP
Tampa Bay	10	6	0	.625	273	237
Chicago*	10	6	0	.625	306	249
Minnesota	7	9	0	.438	259	337
Green Bay	5	11	0	.313	246	316
Detroit	2	14	0	.125	219	365

WESTERN DIVISION

	W	L	T	Pct.	Pts.	OP
Los Angeles	9	7	0	.563	323	309
New Orleans	8	8	0	.500	370	360
Atlanta	6	10	0	.375	300	388
San Francisco	2	14	0	.125	308	416

Wild Card qualifier for playoffs

Dallas won division title because of a better conference record than Philadelphia (10-2 to 9-3). Tampa Bay won division title because of a better division record than Chicago (6-2 to 5-3). Chicago won a wild card berth over Washington on the basis of best net points in all games (plus 57 net points to plus 53).

First round playoff: HOUSTON 13; Denver 7
Divisional playoffs: Houston 17, SAN DIEGO 14; PITTSBURGH 34, Miami 14
AFC championship: PITTSBURGH 27, Houston 13
First round playoff: PHILADELPHIA 27, Chicago 17
Divisional playoffs: TAMPA BAY 24, Philadelphia 17; Los Angeles 21, DALLAS 19
NFC championship: Los Angeles 9, TAMPA BAY 0
Super Bowl XIV: Pittsburgh (AFC) 31, Los Angeles (NFC) 19, at Rose Bowl, Pasadena, Calif.

1978

AMERICAN CONFERENCE
EASTERN DIVISION

	W	L	T	Pct.	Pts.	OP
New England	11	5	0	.688	358	286
Miami*	11	5	0	.688	372	254
N.Y. Jets	8	8	0	.500	359	364
Buffalo	5	11	0	.313	302	354
Baltimore	5	11	0	.313	239	421

CENTRAL DIVISION

	W	L	T	Pct.	Pts.	OP
Pittsburgh	14	2	0	.875	356	195
Houston*	10	6	0	.625	283	298
Cleveland	8	8	0	.500	334	356
Cincinnati	4	12	0	.250	252	284

WESTERN DIVISION

	W	L	T	Pct.	Pts.	OP
Denver	10	6	0	.625	282	198
Oakland	9	7	0	.563	311	283
Seattle	9	7	0	.563	345	358
San Diego	9	7	0	.563	355	309
Kansas City	4	12	0	.250	243	327

NATIONAL CONFERENCE
EASTERN DIVISION

	W	L	T	Pct.	Pts.	OP
Dallas	12	4	0	.750	384	208
Philadelphia*	9	7	0	.563	270	250
Washington	8	8	0	.500	273	283
St. Louis	6	10	0	.375	248	296
N.Y. Giants	6	10	0	.375	264	298

CENTRAL DIVISION

	W	L	T	Pct.	Pts.	OP
Minnesota	8	7	1	.531	294	306
Green Bay	8	7	1	.531	249	269
Detroit	7	9	0	.438	290	300
Chicago	7	9	0	.438	253	274
Tampa Bay	5	11	0	.313	241	259

WESTERN DIVISION

	W	L	T	Pct.	Pts.	OP
Los Angeles	12	4	0	.750	316	245
Atlanta*	9	7	0	.563	240	290
New Orleans	7	9	0	.438	281	298
San Francisco	2	14	0	.125	219	350

Wild Card qualifier for playoffs

New England won division title on the basis of a better division record than Miami (6-2 to 5-3). Minnesota won division title because of a better head-to-head record against Green Bay (1-0-1).

First round playoff: Houston 17, MIAMI 9
Divisional playoffs: Houston 31, NEW ENGLAND 14; PITTSBURGH 33, Denver 10
AFC championship: PITTSBURGH 34, Houston 5
First round playoff: ATLANTA 14, Philadelphia 13
Divisional playoffs: DALLAS 27, Atlanta 20; LOS ANGELES 34, Minnesota 10
NFC championship: Dallas 28, LOS ANGELES 0
Super Bowl XIII: Pittsburgh (AFC) 35, Dallas (NFC) 31, at Orange Bowl, Miami, Fla.

1977

AMERICAN CONFERENCE
EASTERN DIVISION

	W	L	T	Pct.	Pts.	OP
Baltimore	10	4	0	.714	295	221
Miami	10	4	0	.714	313	197
New England	9	5	0	.643	278	217
N.Y. Jets	3	11	0	.214	191	300
Buffalo	3	11	0	.214	160	313

CENTRAL DIVISION

	W	L	T	Pct.	Pts.	OP
Pittsburgh	9	5	0	.643	283	243
Houston	8	6	0	.571	299	230
Cincinnati	8	6	0	.571	238	235
Cleveland	6	8	0	.429	269	267

WESTERN DIVISION

	W	L	T	Pct.	Pts.	OP
Denver	12	2	0	.857	274	148
Oakland*	11	3	0	.786	351	230
San Diego	7	7	0	.500	222	205
Seattle	5	9	0	.357	282	373
Kansas City	2	12	0	.143	225	349

NATIONAL CONFERENCE
EASTERN DIVISION

	W	L	T	Pct.	Pts.	OP
Dallas	12	2	0	.857	345	212
Washington	9	5	0	.643	196	189
St. Louis	7	7	0	.500	272	287
Philadelphia	5	9	0	.357	220	207
N.Y. Giants	5	9	0	.357	181	265

CENTRAL DIVISION

	W	L	T	Pct.	Pts.	OP
Minnesota	9	5	0	.643	231	227
Chicago*	9	5	0	.643	255	253
Detroit	6	8	0	.429	183	252
Green Bay	4	10	0	.286	134	219
Tampa Bay	2	12	0	.143	103	223

WESTERN DIVISION

	W	L	T	Pct.	Pts.	OP
Los Angeles	10	4	0	.714	302	146
Atlanta	7	7	0	.500	179	129
San Francisco	5	9	0	.357	220	260
New Orleans	3	11	0	.214	232	336

*Wild Card qualifier for playoffs

Baltimore won division title on the basis of a better conference record than Miami (9-3 to 8-4). Chicago won a wild card berth over Washington on the basis of best net points in conference games (plus 48 net points to plus 4).

Divisional playoffs: DENVER 34, Pittsburgh 21; Oakland 37, BALTIMORE 31, sudden death overtime

AFC championship: DENVER 20, Oakland 17

Divisional playoffs: DALLAS 37, Chicago 7; Minnesota 14, LOS ANGELES 7

NFC championship: DALLAS 23, Minnesota 6

Super Bowl XII: Dallas (NFC) 27, Denver (AFC) 10, at Louisiana Superdome, New Orleans, La.

1976

AMERICAN CONFERENCE
EASTERN DIVISION

	W	L	T	Pct.	Pts.	OP
Baltimore	11	3	0	.786	417	246
New England*	11	3	0	.786	376	236
Miami	6	8	0	.429	263	264
N.Y. Jets	3	11	0	.214	169	383
Buffalo	2	12	0	.143	245	363

CENTRAL DIVISION

	W	L	T	Pct.	Pts.	OP
Pittsburgh	10	4	0	.714	342	138
Cincinnati	10	4	0	.714	335	210
Cleveland	9	5	0	.643	267	287
Houston	5	9	0	.357	222	273

WESTERN DIVISION

	W	L	T	Pct.	Pts.	OP
Oakland	13	1	0	.929	350	237
Denver	9	5	0	.643	315	206
San Diego	6	8	0	.429	248	285
Kansas City	5	9	0	.357	290	376
Tampa Bay	0	14	0	.000	125	412

NATIONAL CONFERENCE
EASTERN DIVISION

	W	L	T	Pct.	Pts.	OP
Dallas	11	3	0	.786	296	194
Washington*	10	4	0	.714	291	217
St. Louis	10	4	0	.714	309	267
Philadelphia	4	10	0	.286	165	286
N.Y. Giants	3	11	0	.214	170	250

CENTRAL DIVISION

	W	L	T	Pct.	Pts.	OP
Minnesota	11	2	1	.821	305	176
Chicago	7	7	0	.500	253	216
Detroit	6	8	0	.429	262	220
Green Bay	5	9	0	.357	218	299

WESTERN DIVISION

	W	L	T	Pct.	Pts.	OP
Los Angeles	10	3	1	.750	351	190
San Francisco	8	6	0	.571	270	190
Atlanta	4	10	0	.286	172	312
New Orleans	4	10	0	.286	253	346
Seattle	2	12	0	.143	229	429

*Wild Card qualifier for playoffs

Baltimore won division title on the basis of a better division record than New England (7-1 to 6-2). Pittsburgh won division title because of a two-game sweep over Cincinnati. Washington won wild card berth over St. Louis because of a two-game sweep over Cardinals.

Divisional playoffs: OAKLAND 24, New England 21; Pittsburgh 40, BALTIMORE 14
AFC championship: OAKLAND 24, Pittsburgh 7
Divisional playoffs: MINNESOTA 35, Washington 20; Los Angeles 14, DALLAS 12
NFC championship: MINNESOTA 24, Los Angeles 13
Super Bowl XI: Oakland (AFC) 32, Minnesota (NFC) 14, at Rose Bowl, Pasadena, Calif.

1975

AMERICAN CONFERENCE
EASTERN DIVISION

	W	L	T	Pct.	Pts.	OP
Baltimore	10	4	0	.714	395	269
Miami	10	4	0	.714	357	222
Buffalo	8	6	0	.571	420	355
New England	3	11	0	.214	258	358
N.Y. Jets	3	11	0	.214	258	433

CENTRAL DIVISION

	W	L	T	Pct.	Pts.	OP
Pittsburgh	12	2	0	.857	373	162
Cincinnati*	11	3	0	.786	340	246
Houston	10	4	0	.714	293	226
Cleveland	3	11	0	.214	218	372

WESTERN DIVISION

	W	L	T	Pct.	Pts.	OP
Oakland	11	3	0	.786	375	255
Denver	6	8	0	.429	254	307
Kansas City	5	9	0	.357	282	341
San Diego	2	12	0	.143	189	345

NATIONAL CONFERENCE
EASTERN DIVISION

	W	L	T	Pct.	Pts.	OP
St. Louis	11	3	0	.786	356	276
Dallas*	10	4	0	.714	350	268
Washington	8	6	0	.571	325	276
N.Y. Giants	5	9	0	.357	216	306
Philadelphia	4	10	0	.286	225	302

CENTRAL DIVISION

	W	L	T	Pct.	Pts.	OP
Minnesota	12	2	0	.857	377	180
Detroit	7	7	0	.500	245	262
Chicago	4	10	0	.286	191	379
Green Bay	4	10	0	.286	226	285

WESTERN DIVISION

	W	L	T	Pct.	Pts.	OP
Los Angeles	12	2	0	.857	312	135
San Francisco	5	9	0	.357	255	286
Atlanta	4	10	0	.286	240	289
New Orleans	2	12	0	.143	165	360

*Wild Card qualifier for playoffs

Baltimore won division title on the basis of a two-game sweep over Miami.

Divisional playoffs: PITTSBURGH 28, Baltimore 10; OAKLAND 31, Cincinnati 28
AFC championship: PITTSBURGH 16, Oakland 10
Divisional playoffs: LOS ANGELES 35, St. Louis 23; Dallas 17, MINNESOTA 14
NFC championship: Dallas 37, LOS ANGELES 7
Super Bowl X: Pittsburgh (AFC) 21, Dallas (NFC) 17, at Orange Bowl, Miami, Fla.

1974

AMERICAN CONFERENCE
EASTERN DIVISION

	W	L	T	Pct.	Pts.	OP
Miami	11	3	0	.786	327	216
Buffalo*	9	5	0	.643	264	244
New England	7	7	0	.500	348	289
N.Y. Jets	7	7	0	.500	279	300
Baltimore	2	12	0	.143	190	329

CENTRAL DIVISION

	W	L	T	Pct.	Pts.	OP
Pittsburgh	10	3	1	.750	305	189
Cincinnati	7	7	0	.500	283	259
Houston	7	7	0	.500	236	282
Cleveland	4	10	0	.286	251	344

WESTERN DIVISION

	W	L	T	Pct.	Pts.	OP
Oakland	12	2	0	.857	355	228
Denver	7	6	1	.536	302	294
Kansas City	5	9	0	.357	233	293
San Diego	5	9	0	.357	212	285

NATIONAL CONFERENCE
EASTERN DIVISION

	W	L	T	Pct.	Pts.	OP
St. Louis	10	4	0	.714	285	218
Washington*	10	4	0	.714	320	196
Dallas	8	6	0	.571	297	235
Philadelphia	7	7	0	.500	242	217
N.Y. Giants	2	12	0	.143	195	299

CENTRAL DIVISION

	W	L	T	Pct.	Pts.	OP
Minnesota	10	4	0	.714	310	195
Detroit	7	7	0	.500	256	270
Green Bay	6	8	0	.429	210	206
Chicago	4	10	0	.286	152	279

WESTERN DIVISION

	W	L	T	Pct.	Pts.	OP
Los Angeles	10	4	0	.714	263	181
San Francisco	6	8	0	.429	226	236
New Orleans	5	9	0	.357	166	263
Atlanta	3	11	0	.214	111	271

*Wild Card qualifier for playoffs

St. Louis won division title because of a two-game sweep over Washington.
Divisional playoffs: OAKLAND 28, Miami 26; PITTSBURGH 32, Buffalo 14
AFC championship: Pittsburgh 24, OAKLAND 13
Divisional playoffs: MINNESOTA 30, St. Louis 14; LOS ANGELES 19, Washington 10
NFC championship: MINNESOTA 14, Los Angeles 10
Super Bowl IX: Pittsburgh (AFC) 16, Minnesota (NFC) 6, at Tulane Stadium, New Orleans, La.

1973

AMERICAN CONFERENCE
EASTERN DIVISION

	W	L	T	Pct.	Pts.	OP
Miami	12	2	0	.857	343	150
Buffalo	9	5	0	.643	259	230
New England	5	9	0	.357	258	300
Baltimore	4	10	0	.286	226	341
N.Y. Jets	4	10	0	.286	240	306

CENTRAL DIVISION

	W	L	T	Pct.	Pts.	OP
Cincinnati	10	4	0	.714	286	231
Pittsburgh*	10	4	0	.714	347	210
Cleveland	7	5	2	.571	234	255
Houston	1	13	0	.071	199	447

WESTERN DIVISION

	W	L	T	Pct.	Pts.	OP
Oakland	9	4	1	.679	292	175
Denver	7	5	2	.571	354	296
Kansas City	7	5	2	.571	231	192
San Diego	2	11	1	.179	188	386

NATIONAL CONFERENCE
EASTERN DIVISION

	W	L	T	Pct.	Pts.	OP
Dallas	10	4	0	.714	382	203
Washington*	10	4	0	.714	325	198
Philadelphia	5	8	1	.393	310	393
St. Louis	4	9	1	.321	286	365
N.Y. Giants	2	11	1	.179	226	362

CENTRAL DIVISION

	W	L	T	Pct.	Pts.	OP
Minnesota	12	2	0	.857	296	168
Detroit	6	7	1	.464	271	247
Green Bay	5	7	2	.429	202	259
Chicago	3	11	0	.214	195	334

WESTERN DIVISION

	W	L	T	Pct.	Pts.	OP
Los Angeles	12	2	0	.857	388	178
Atlanta	9	5	0	.643	318	224
New Orleans	5	9	0	.357	163	312
San Francisco	5	9	0	.357	262	319

*Wild Card qualifier for playoffs

Cincinnati won division title on the basis of a better conference record than Pittsburgh (8-3 to 7-4). Dallas won division title on the basis of a better point differential vs. Washington (net 13 points).
Divisional playoffs: OAKLAND 33, Pittsburgh 14; MIAMI 34, Cincinnati 16
AFC championship: MIAMI 27, Oakland 10
Divisional playoffs: MINNESOTA 27, Washington 20; DALLAS 27, Los Angeles 16
NFC championship: Minnesota 27, DALLAS 10
Super Bowl VIII: Miami (AFC) 24, Minnesota (NFC) 7, at Rice Stadium, Houston, Tex.

1972

AMERICAN CONFERENCE
EASTERN DIVISION

	W	L	T	Pct.	Pts.	OP
Miami	14	0	0	1.000	385	171
N.Y. Jets	7	7	0	.500	367	324
Baltimore	5	9	0	.357	235	252
Buffalo	4	9	1	.321	257	377
New England	3	11	0	.214	192	446

CENTRAL DIVISION

	W	L	T	Pct.	Pts.	OP
Pittsburgh	11	3	0	.786	343	175
Cleveland*	10	4	0	.714	268	249
Cincinnati	8	6	0	.571	299	229
Houston	1	13	0	.071	164	380

WESTERN DIVISION

	W	L	T	Pct.	Pts.	OP
Oakland	10	3	1	.750	365	248
Kansas City	8	6	0	.571	287	254
Denver	5	9	0	.357	325	350
San Diego	4	9	1	.321	264	344

NATIONAL CONFERENCE
EASTERN DIVISION

	W	L	T	Pct.	Pts.	OP
Washington	11	3	0	.786	336	218
Dallas*	10	4	0	.714	319	240
N.Y. Giants	8	6	0	.571	331	247
St. Louis	4	9	1	.321	193	303
Philadelphia	2	11	1	.179	145	352

CENTRAL DIVISION

	W	L	T	Pct.	Pts.	OP
Green Bay	10	4	0	.714	304	226
Detroit	8	5	1	.607	339	290
Minnesota	7	7	0	.500	301	252
Chicago	4	9	1	.321	225	275

WESTERN DIVISION

	W	L	T	Pct.	Pts.	OP
San Francisco	8	5	1	.607	353	249
Atlanta	7	7	0	.500	269	274
Los Angeles	6	7	1	.464	291	286
New Orleans	2	11	1	.179	215	361

*Wild Card qualifier for playoffs

Divisional playoffs: PITTSBURGH 13, Oakland 7; MIAMI 20, Cleveland 14

AFC championship: Miami 21, PITTSBURGH 17

Divisional playoffs: Dallas 30, SAN FRANCISCO 28; WASHINGTON 16, Green Bay 3

NFC championship: WASHINGTON 26, Dallas 3

Super Bowl VII: Miami (AFC) 14, Washington (NFC) 7, at Memorial Coliseum, Los Angeles, Calif.

1971

AMERICAN CONFERENCE
EASTERN DIVISION

	W	L	T	Pct.	Pts.	OP
Miami	10	3	1	.769	315	174
Baltimore*	10	4	0	.714	313	140
New England	6	8	0	.429	238	325
N.Y. Jets	6	8	0	.429	212	299
Buffalo	1	13	0	.071	184	394

CENTRAL DIVISION

	W	L	T	Pct.	Pts.	OP
Cleveland	9	5	0	.643	285	273
Pittsburgh	6	8	0	.429	246	292
Houston	4	9	1	.308	251	330
Cincinnati	4	10	0	.286	284	265

WESTERN DIVISION

	W	L	T	Pct.	Pts.	OP
Kansas City	10	3	1	.769	302	208
Oakland	8	4	2	.667	344	278
San Diego	6	8	0	.429	311	341
Denver	4	9	1	.308	203	275

NATIONAL CONFERENCE
EASTERN DIVISION

	W	L	T	Pct.	Pts.	OP
Dallas	11	3	0	.786	406	222
Washington*	9	4	1	.692	276	190
Philadelphia	6	7	1	.462	221	302
St. Louis	4	9	1	.308	231	279
N.Y. Giants	4	10	0	.286	228	362

CENTRAL DIVISION

	W	L	T	Pct.	Pts.	OP
Minnesota	11	3	0	.786	245	139
Detroit	7	6	1	.538	341	286
Chicago	6	8	0	.429	185	276
Green Bay	4	8	2	.333	274	298

WESTERN DIVISION

	W	L	T	Pct.	Pts.	OP
San Francisco	9	5	0	.643	300	216
Los Angeles	8	5	1	.615	313	260
Atlanta	7	6	1	.538	274	277
New Orleans	4	8	2	.333	266	347

*Wild Card qualifier for playoffs

Divisional playoffs: Miami 27, KANSAS CITY 24, sudden death overtime; Baltimore 20, CLEVELAND 3

AFC championship: MIAMI 21, Baltimore 0

Divisional playoffs: Dallas 20, MINNESOTA 12; SAN FRANCISCO 24, Washington 20

NFC championship: DALLAS 14, San Francisco 3

Super Bowl VI: Dallas (NFC) 24, Miami (AFC) 3, at Tulane Stadium, New Orleans, La.

1970

AMERICAN CONFERENCE
EASTERN DIVISION

	W	L	T	Pct.	Pts.	OP
Baltimore	11	2	1	.846	321	234
Miami*	10	4	0	.714	297	228
N.Y. Jets	4	10	0	.286	255	286
Buffalo	3	10	1	.231	204	337
Boston Patriots	2	12	0	.143	149	361

CENTRAL DIVISION

	W	L	T	Pct.	Pts.	OP
Cincinnati	8	6	0	.571	312	255
Cleveland	7	7	0	.500	286	265
Pittsburgh	5	9	0	.357	210	272
Houston	3	10	1	.231	217	352

WESTERN DIVISION

	W	L	T	Pct.	Pts.	OP
Oakland	8	4	2	.667	300	293
Kansas City	7	5	2	.583	272	244
San Diego	5	6	3	.455	282	278
Denver	5	8	1	.385	253	264

NATIONAL CONFERENCE
EASTERN DIVISION

	W	L	T	Pct.	Pts.	OP
Dallas	10	4	0	.714	299	221
N.Y. Giants	9	5	0	.643	301	270
St. Louis	8	5	1	.615	325	228
Washington	6	8	0	.429	297	314
Philadelphia	3	10	1	.231	241	332

CENTRAL DIVISION

	W	L	T	Pct.	Pts.	OP
Minnesota	12	2	0	.857	335	143
Detroit*	10	4	0	.714	347	202
Chicago	6	8	0	.429	256	261
Green Bay	6	8	0	.429	196	293

WESTERN DIVISION

	W	L	T	Pct.	Pts.	OP
San Francisco	10	3	1	.769	352	267
Los Angeles	9	4	1	.692	325	202
Atlanta	4	8	2	.333	206	261
New Orleans	2	11	1	.154	172	347

Wild Card qualifier for playoffs

Divisional playoffs: BALTIMORE 17, Cincinnati 0; OAKLAND 21, Miami 14
AFC championship: BALTIMORE 27, Oakland 17
Divisional playoffs: DALLAS 5, Detroit 0; San Francisco 17, MINNESOTA 14
NFC championship: Dallas 17, SAN FRANCISCO 10
Super Bowl V: Baltimore (AFC) 16, Dallas (NFC) 13, at Orange Bowl, Miami, Fla.

1969 NFL

EASTERN CONFERENCE
Capitol Division

	W	L	T	Pct.	Pts.	OP
Dallas	11	2	1	.846	369	223
Washington	7	5	2	.583	307	319
New Orleans	5	9	0	.357	311	393
Philadelphia	4	9	1	.308	279	377

Century Division

	W	L	T	Pct.	Pts.	OP
Cleveland	10	3	1	.769	351	300
N.Y. Giants	6	8	0	.429	264	298
St. Louis	4	9	1	.308	314	389
Pittsburgh	1	13	0	.071	218	404

WESTERN CONFERENCE
Coastal Division

	W	L	T	Pct.	Pts.	OP
Los Angeles	11	3	0	.786	320	243
Baltimore	8	5	1	.615	279	268
Atlanta	6	8	0	.429	276	268
San Francisco	4	8	2	.333	277	319

Central Division

	W	L	T	Pct.	Pts.	OP
Minnesota	12	2	0	.857	379	133
Detroit	9	4	1	.692	259	188
Green Bay	8	6	0	.571	269	221
Chicago	1	13	0	.071	210	339

Conference championships: Cleveland 38, DALLAS 14; MINNESOTA 23, Los Angeles 20
NFL championship: MINNESOTA 27, Cleveland 7
Super Bowl IV: Kansas City (AFL) 23, Minnesota (NFL) 7, at Tulane Stadium, New Orleans, La.

1969 AFL

EASTERN DIVISION

	W	L	T	Pct.	Pts.	OP
N.Y. Jets	10	4	0	.714	353	269
Houston	6	6	2	.500	278	279
Boston Patriots	4	10	0	.286	266	316
Buffalo	4	10	0	.286	230	359
Miami	3	10	1	.231	233	332

WESTERN DIVISION

	W	L	T	Pct.	Pts.	OP
Oakland	12	1	1	.923	377	242
Kansas City	11	3	0	.786	359	177
San Diego	8	6	0	.571	288	276
Denver	5	8	1	.385	297	344
Cincinnati	4	9	1	.308	280	367

Divisional Playoffs: Kansas City 13, N.Y. JETS 6; OAKLAND 56, Houston 7
AFL championship: Kansas City 17, OAKLAND 7

1968 NFL

EASTERN CONFERENCE
Capitol Division

	W	L	T	Pct.	Pts.	OP
Dallas	12	2	0	.857	431	186
N.Y. Giants	7	7	0	.500	294	325
Washington	5	9	0	.357	249	358
Philadelphia	2	12	0	.143	202	351

Century Division

	W	L	T	Pct.	Pts.	OP
Cleveland	10	4	0	.714	394	273
St. Louis	9	4	1	.692	325	289
New Orleans	4	9	1	.308	246	327
Pittsburgh	2	11	1	.154	244	397

WESTERN CONFERENCE
Coastal Division

	W	L	T	Pct.	Pts.	OP
Baltimore	13	1	0	.929	402	144
Los Angeles	10	3	1	.769	312	200
San Francisco	7	6	1	.538	303	310
Atlanta	2	12	0	.143	170	389

Central Division

	W	L	T	Pct.	Pts.	OP
Minnesota	8	6	0	.571	282	242
Chicago	7	7	0	.500	250	333
Green Bay	6	7	1	.462	281	227
Detroit	4	8	2	.333	207	241

Conference championships: CLEVELAND 31, Dallas 20; BALTIMORE 24, Minnesota 14
NFL championship: Baltimore 34, CLEVELAND 0
Super Bowl III: N.Y. Jets (AFL) 16, Baltimore (NFL) 7, at Orange Bowl, Miami, Fla.

1968 AFL

EASTERN DIVISION

	W	L	T	Pct.	Pts.	OP
N.Y. Jets	11	3	0	.786	419	280
Houston	7	7	0	.500	303	248
Miami	5	8	1	.385	276	355
Boston Patriots	4	10	0	.286	229	406
Buffalo	1	12	1	.077	199	367

WESTERN DIVISION

	W	L	T	Pct.	Pts.	OP
Oakland	12	2	0	.857	453	233
Kansas City	12	2	0	.857	371	170
San Diego	9	5	0	.643	382	310
Denver	5	9	0	.357	255	404
Cincinnati	3	11	0	.214	215	329

Western Division playoff: OAKLAND 41, Kansas City 6
AFL championship: N.Y. JETS 27, Oakland 23

1967 NFL

EASTERN CONFERENCE
Capitol Division

	W	L	T	Pct.	Pts.	OP
Dallas	9	5	0	.643	342	268
Philadelphia	6	7	1	.462	351	409
Washington	5	6	3	.455	347	353
New Orleans	3	11	0	.214	233	379

Century Division

	W	L	T	Pct.	Pts.	OP
Cleveland	9	5	0	.643	334	297
N.Y. Giants	7	7	0	.500	369	379
St. Louis	6	7	1	.462	333	356
Pittsburgh	4	9	1	.308	281	320

WESTERN CONFERENCE
Coastal Division

	W	L	T	Pct.	Pts.	OP
Los Angeles	11	1	2	.917	398	196
Baltimore	11	1	2	.917	394	198
San Francisco	7	7	0	.500	273	337
Atlanta	1	12	1	.077	175	422

Central Division

	W	L	T	Pct.	Pts.	OP
Green Bay	9	4	1	.692	332	209
Chicago	7	6	1	.538	239	218
Detroit	5	7	2	.417	260	259
Minnesota	3	8	3	.273	233	294

Conference championships: DALLAS 52, Cleveland 14; GREEN BAY 28, Los Angeles 7
NFL championship: GREEN BAY 21, Dallas 17
Super Bowl II: Green Bay (NFL) 33, Oakland (AFL) 14, at Orange Bowl, Miami, Fla.

1967 AFL

EASTERN DIVISION

	W	L	T	Pct.	Pts.	OP
Houston	9	4	1	.692	258	199
N.Y. Jets	8	5	1	.615	371	329
Buffalo	4	10	0	.286	237	285
Miami	4	10	0	.286	219	407
Boston Patriots	3	10	1	.231	280	389

WESTERN DIVISION

	W	L	T	Pct.	Pts.	OP
Oakland	13	1	0	.929	468	233
Kansas City	9	5	0	.643	408	254
San Diego	8	5	1	.615	360	352
Denver	3	11	0	.214	256	409

AFL championship: OAKLAND 40, Houston 7

1966 NFL

EASTERN CONFERENCE

	W	L	T	Pct.	Pts.	OP
Dallas	10	3	1	.769	445	239
Cleveland	9	5	0	.643	403	259
Philadelphia	9	5	0	.643	326	340
St. Louis	8	5	1	.615	264	265
Washington	7	7	0	.500	351	355
Pittsburgh	5	8	1	.385	316	347
Atlanta	3	11	0	.214	204	437
N.Y. Giants	1	12	1	.077	263	501

WESTERN CONFERENCE

	W	L	T	Pct.	Pts.	OP
Green Bay	12	2	0	.857	335	163
Baltimore	9	5	0	.643	314	226
Los Angeles	8	6	0	.571	289	212
San Francisco	6	6	2	.500	320	325
Chicago	5	7	2	.417	234	272
Detroit	4	9	1	.308	206	317
Minnesota	4	9	1	.308	292	304

NFL championship: Green Bay 34, DALLAS 27
Super Bowl I: Green Bay (NFL) 35, Kansas City (AFL) 10, at Memorial Coliseum, Los Angeles, Calif.

1966 AFL

EASTERN DIVISION

	W	L	T	Pct.	Pts.	OP
Buffalo	9	4	1	.692	358	255
Boston Patriots	8	4	2	.677	315	283
N.Y. Jets	6	6	2	.500	322	312
Houston	3	11	0	.214	355	396
Miami	3	11	0	.214	213	362

WESTERN DIVISION

	W	L	T	Pct.	Pts.	OP
Kansas City	11	2	1	.846	448	276
Oakland	8	5	1	.615	315	288
San Diego	7	6	1	.538	335	284
Denver	4	10	0	.286	196	381

AFL championship: Kansas City 31, BUFFALO 7

1965 NFL

EASTERN CONFERENCE

	W	L	T	Pct.	Pts.	OP
Cleveland	11	3	0	.786	363	325
Dallas	7	7	0	.500	325	280
N.Y. Giants	7	7	0	.500	270	338
Washington	6	8	0	.429	257	301
Philadelphia	5	9	0	.357	363	359
St. Louis	5	9	0	.357	296	309
Pittsburgh	2	12	0	.143	202	397

WESTERN CONFERENCE

	W	L	T	Pct.	Pts.	OP
Green Bay	10	3	1	.769	316	224
Baltimore	10	3	1	.769	389	284
Chicago	9	5	0	.643	409	275
San Francisco	7	6	1	.538	421	402
Minnesota	7	7	0	.500	383	403
Detroit	6	7	1	.462	257	295
Los Angeles	4	10	0	.286	269	328

Western Conference playoff: GREEN BAY 13, Baltimore 10, sudden death overtime
NFL championship: GREEN BAY 23, Cleveland 12

1965 AFL

EASTERN DIVISION

	W	L	T	Pct.	Pts.	OP
Buffalo	10	3	1	.769	313	226
N.Y. Jets	5	8	1	.385	285	303
Boston Patriots	4	8	2	.333	244	302
Houston	4	10	0	.286	298	429

WESTERN DIVISION

	W	L	T	Pct.	Pts.	OP
San Diego	9	2	3	.818	340	227
Oakland	8	5	1	.615	298	239
Kansas City	7	5	2	.583	322	285
Denver	4	10	0	.286	303	392

AFL championship: Buffalo 23, SAN DIEGO 0

1964 NFL

EASTERN CONFERENCE

	W	L	T	Pct.	Pts.	OP
Cleveland	10	3	1	.769	415	293
St. Louis	9	3	2	.750	357	331
Philadelphia	6	8	0	.429	312	313
Washington	6	8	0	.429	307	305
Dallas	5	8	1	.385	250	289
Pittsburgh	5	9	0	.357	253	315
N.Y. Giants	2	10	2	.167	241	399

WESTERN CONFERENCE

	W	L	T	Pct.	Pts.	OP
Baltimore	12	2	0	.857	428	225
Green Bay	8	5	1	.615	342	245
Minnesota	8	5	1	.615	355	296
Detroit	7	5	2	.583	280	260
Los Angeles	5	7	2	.417	283	339
Chicago	5	9	0	.357	260	379
San Francisco	4	10	0	.286	236	330

NFL championship: CLEVELAND 27, Baltimore 0

1964 AFL

EASTERN DIVISION

	W	L	T	Pct.	Pts.	OP
Buffalo	12	2	0	.857	400	242
Boston Patriots	10	3	1	.769	365	297
N.Y. Jets	5	8	1	.385	278	315
Houston	4	10	0	.286	310	355

WESTERN DIVISION

	W	L	T	Pct.	Pts.	OP
San Diego	8	5	1	.615	341	300
Kansas City	7	7	0	.500	366	306
Oakland	5	7	2	.417	303	350
Denver	2	11	1	.154	240	438

AFL championship: BUFFALO 20, San Diego 7

1963 NFL

EASTERN CONFERENCE

	W	L	T	Pct.	Pts.	OP
N.Y. Giants	11	3	0	.786	448	280
Cleveland	10	4	0	.714	343	262
St. Louis	9	5	0	.643	341	283
Pittsburgh	7	4	3	.636	321	295
Dallas	4	10	0	.286	305	378
Washington	3	11	0	.214	279	398
Philadelphia	2	10	2	.167	242	381

WESTERN CONFERENCE

	W	L	T	Pct.	Pts.	OP
Chicago	11	1	2	.917	301	144
Green Bay	11	2	1	.846	369	206
Baltimore	8	6	0	.571	316	285
Detroit	5	8	1	.385	326	265
Minnesota	5	8	1	.385	309	390
Los Angeles	5	9	0	.357	210	350
San Francisco	2	12	0	.143	198	391

NFL championship: CHICAGO 14, N.Y. Giants 10

1963 AFL

EASTERN DIVISION

	W	L	T	Pct.	Pts.	OP
Boston Patriots	7	6	1	.538	317	257
Buffalo	7	6	1	.538	304	291
Houston	6	8	0	.429	302	372
N.Y. Jets	5	8	1	.385	249	399

WESTERN DIVISION

	W	L	T	Pct.	Pts.	OP
San Diego	11	3	0	.786	399	255
Oakland	10	4	0	.714	363	282
Kansas City	5	7	2	.417	347	263
Denver	2	11	1	.154	301	473

Eastern Division playoff: Boston 26, BUFFALO 8
AFL championship: SAN DIEGO 51, Boston 10

1962 NFL

EASTERN CONFERENCE

	W	L	T	Pct.	Pts.	OP
N.Y. Giants	12	2	0	.857	398	283
Pittsburgh	9	5	0	.643	312	363
Cleveland	7	6	1	.538	291	257
Washington	5	7	2	.417	305	376
Dallas Cowboys	5	8	1	.385	398	402
St. Louis	4	9	1	.308	287	361
Philadelphia	3	10	1	.231	282	356

WESTERN CONFERENCE

	W	L	T	Pct.	Pts.	OP
Green Bay	13	1	0	.929	415	148
Detroit	11	3	0	.786	315	177
Chicago	9	5	0	.643	321	287
Baltimore	7	7	0	.500	293	288
San Francisco	6	8	0	.429	282	331
Minnesota	2	11	1	.154	254	410
Los Angeles	1	12	1	.077	220	334

NFL championship: Green Bay 16, N.Y. GIANTS 7

1962 AFL

EASTERN DIVISION

	W	L	T	Pct.	Pts.	OP
Houston	11	3	0	.786	387	270
Boston Patriots	9	4	1	.692	346	295
Buffalo	7	6	1	.538	309	272
N.Y. Titans	5	9	0	.357	278	423

WESTERN DIVISION

	W	L	T	Pct.	Pts.	OP
Dallas Texans	11	3	0	.786	389	233
Denver	7	7	0	.500	353	334
San Diego	4	10	0	.286	314	392
Oakland	1	13	0	.071	213	370

AFL championship: Dallas Texans 20, HOUSTON 17, sudden death overtime

1961 NFL

EASTERN CONFERENCE

	W	L	T	Pct.	Pts.	OP
N.Y. Giants	10	3	1	.769	368	220
Philadelphia	10	4	0	.714	361	297
Cleveland	8	5	1	.615	319	270
St. Louis	7	7	0	.500	279	267
Pittsburgh	6	8	0	.429	295	287
Dallas Cowboys	4	9	1	.308	236	380
Washington	1	12	1	.077	174	392

WESTERN CONFERENCE

	W	L	T	Pct.	Pts.	OP
Green Bay	11	3	0	.786	391	223
Detroit	8	5	1	.615	270	258
Baltimore	8	6	0	.571	302	307
Chi. Bears	8	6	0	.571	326	302
San Francisco	7	6	1	.538	346	272
Los Angeles	4	10	0	.286	263	333
Minnesota	3	11	0	.214	285	407

NFL championship: GREEN BAY 37, N.Y. Giants 0

1961 AFL

EASTERN DIVISION

	W	L	T	Pct.	Pts.	OP
Houston	10	3	1	.769	513	242
Boston Patriots	9	4	1	.692	413	313
N.Y. Titans	7	7	0	.500	301	390
Buffalo	6	8	0	.429	294	342

WESTERN DIVISION

	W	L	T	Pct.	Pts.	OP
San Diego	12	2	0	.857	396	219
Dallas Texans	6	8	0	.429	334	343
Denver	3	11	0	.214	251	432
Oakland	2	12	0	.143	237	458

AFL championship: Houston 10, SAN DIEGO 3

1960 NFL

EASTERN CONFERENCE

	W	L	T	Pct.	Pts.	OP
Philadelphia	10	2	0	.833	321	246
Cleveland	8	3	1	.727	362	217
N.Y. Giants	6	4	2	.600	271	261
St. Louis	6	5	1	.545	288	230
Pittsburgh	5	6	1	.455	240	275
Washington	1	9	2	.100	178	309

WESTERN CONFERENCE

	W	L	T	Pct.	Pts.	OP
Green Bay	8	4	0	.667	332	209
Detroit	7	5	0	.583	239	212
San Francisco	7	5	0	.583	208	205
Baltimore	6	6	0	.500	288	234
Chicago	5	6	1	.455	194	299
L.A. Rams	4	7	1	.364	265	297
Dallas Cowboys	0	11	1	.000	177	369

NFL championship: PHILADELPHIA 17, Green Bay 13

1960 AFL

EASTERN CONFERENCE

	W	L	T	Pct.	Pts.	OP
Houston	10	4	0	.714	379	285
N.Y. Titans	7	7	0	.500	382	399
Buffalo	5	8	1	.385	296	303
Boston Patriots	5	9	0	.357	286	349

WESTERN CONFERENCE

	W	L	T	Pct.	Pts.	OP
L.A. Chargers	10	4	0	.714	373	336
Dallas Texans	8	6	0	.571	362	253
Oakland	6	8	0	.429	319	388
Denver	4	9	1	.308	309	393

AFL championship: HOUSTON 24, L.A. Chargers 16

1959

EASTERN CONFERENCE

	W	L	T	Pct.	Pts.	OP
N.Y. Giants	10	2	0	.833	284	170
Cleveland	7	5	0	.583	270	214
Philadelphia	7	5	0	.583	268	278
Pittsburgh	6	5	1	.545	257	216
Washington	3	9	0	.250	185	350
Chi. Cardinals	2	10	0	.167	234	324

WESTERN CONFERENCE

	W	L	T	Pct.	Pts.	OP
Baltimore	9	3	0	.750	374	251
Chi. Bears	8	4	0	.667	252	196
Green Bay	7	5	0	.583	248	246
San Francisco	7	5	0	.583	255	237
Detroit	3	8	1	.273	203	275
Los Angeles	2	10	0	.167	242	315

NFL championship: BALTIMORE 31, N.Y. Giants 16

1958

EASTERN CONFERENCE						WESTERN CONFERENCE					
	W	L	T	Pct.	Pts.	OP		W	L	T	Pct.	Pts.	OP
N.Y. Giants	9	3	0	.750	246	183	Baltimore	9	3	0	.750	381	203
Cleveland	9	3	0	.750	302	217	Chi. Bears	8	4	0	.667	298	230
Pittsburgh	7	4	1	.636	261	230	Los Angeles	8	4	0	.667	344	278
Washington	4	7	1	.364	214	268	San Francisco	6	6	0	.500	257	324
Chi. Cardinals	2	9	1	.182	261	356	Detroit	4	7	1	.364	261	276
Philadelphia	2	9	1	.182	235	306	Green Bay	1	10	1	.091	193	382

Eastern Conference playoff: N.Y. GIANTS 10, Cleveland 0
NFL championship: Baltimore 23, N.Y. GIANTS 17, sudden death overtime

1957

EASTERN CONFERENCE						WESTERN CONFERENCE					
	W	L	T	Pct.	Pts.	OP		W	L	T	Pct.	Pts.	OP
Cleveland	9	2	1	.818	269	172	Detroit	8	4	0	.667	251	231
N.Y. Giants	7	5	0	.583	254	211	San Francisco	8	4	0	.667	260	264
Pittsburgh	6	6	0	.500	161	178	Baltimore	7	5	0	.583	303	235
Washington	5	6	1	.455	251	230	Los Angeles	6	6	0	.500	307	278
Philadelphia	4	8	0	.333	173	230	Chi. Bears	5	7	0	.417	203	211
Chi. Cardinals	3	9	0	.250	200	299	Green Bay	3	9	0	.250	218	311

Western Conference playoff: Detroit 31, SAN FRANCISCO 27
NFL championship: DETROIT 59, Cleveland 14

1956

EASTERN CONFERENCE						WESTERN CONFERENCE					
	W	L	T	Pct.	Pts.	OP		W	L	T	Pct.	Pts.	OP
N.Y. Giants	8	3	1	.727	264	197	Chi. Bears	9	2	1	.818	363	246
Chi. Cardinals	7	5	0	.583	240	182	Detroit	9	3	0	.750	300	188
Washington	6	6	0	.500	183	225	San Francisco	5	6	1	.455	233	284
Cleveland	5	7	0	.417	167	177	Baltimore	5	7	0	.417	270	322
Pittsburgh	5	7	0	.417	217	250	Green Bay	4	8	0	.333	264	342
Philadelphia	3	8	1	.273	143	215	Los Angeles	4	8	0	.333	291	307

NFL championship: N.Y. GIANTS 47, Chi. Bears 7

1955

EASTERN CONFERENCE						WESTERN CONFERENCE					
	W	L	T	Pct.	Pts.	OP		W	L	T	Pct.	Pts.	OP
Cleveland	9	2	1	.818	349	218	Los Angeles	8	3	1	.727	260	231
Washington	8	4	0	.667	246	222	Chi. Bears	8	4	0	.667	294	251
N.Y. Giants	6	5	1	.545	267	223	Green Bay	6	6	0	.500	258	276
Chi. Cardinals	4	7	1	.364	224	252	Baltimore	5	6	1	.455	214	239
Philadelphia	4	7	1	.364	248	231	San Francisco	4	8	0	.333	216	298
Pittsburgh	4	8	0	.333	195	285	Detroit	3	9	0	.250	230	275

NFL championship: Cleveland 38, LOS ANGELES 14

1954

EASTERN CONFERENCE						WESTERN CONFERENCE					
	W	L	T	Pct.	Pts.	OP		W	L	T	Pct.	Pts.	OP
Cleveland	9	3	0	.750	336	162	Detroit	9	2	1	.818	337	189
Philadelphia	7	4	1	.636	284	230	Chi. Bears	8	4	0	.667	301	279
N.Y. Giants	7	5	0	.583	293	184	San Francisco	7	4	1	.636	313	251
Pittsburgh	5	7	0	.417	219	263	Los Angeles	6	5	1	.545	314	285
Washington	3	9	0	.250	207	432	Green Bay	4	8	0	.333	234	251
Chi. Cardinals	2	10	0	.167	183	347	Baltimore	3	9	0	.250	131	279

NFL championship: CLEVELAND 56, Detroit 10

1953

EASTERN CONFERENCE

	W	L	T	Pct.	Pts.	OP
Cleveland	11	1	0	.917	348	162
Philadelphia	7	4	1	.636	352	215
Washington	6	5	1	.545	208	215
Pittsburgh	6	6	0	.500	211	263
N.Y. Giants	3	9	0	.250	179	277
Chi. Cardinals	1	10	1	.091	190	337

WESTERN CONFERENCE

	W	L	T	Pct.	Pts.	OP
Detroit	10	2	0	.833	271	205
San Francisco	9	3	0	.750	372	237
Los Angeles	8	3	1	.727	366	236
Chi. Bears	3	8	1	.273	218	262
Baltimore	3	9	0	.250	182	350
Green Bay	2	9	1	.182	200	338

NFL championship: DETROIT 17, Cleveland 16

1952

AMERICAN CONFERENCE

	W	L	T	Pct.	Pts.	OP
Cleveland	8	4	0	.667	310	213
N.Y. Giants	7	5	0	.583	234	231
Philadelphia	7	5	0	.583	252	271
Pittsburgh	5	7	0	.417	300	273
Chi. Cardinals	4	8	0	.333	172	221
Washington	4	8	0	.333	240	287

NATIONAL CONFERENCE

	W	L	T	Pct.	Pts.	OP
Detroit	9	3	0	.750	344	192
Los Angeles	9	3	0	.750	349	234
San Francisco	7	5	0	.583	285	221
Green Bay	6	6	0	.500	295	312
Chi. Bears	5	7	0	.417	245	326
Dallas Texans	1	11	0	.083	182	427

National Conference playoff: DETROIT 31, Los Angeles 21
NFL championship: Detroit 17, CLEVELAND 7

1951

AMERICAN CONFERENCE

	W	L	T	Pct.	Pts.	OP
Cleveland	11	1	0	.917	331	152
N.Y. Giants	9	2	1	.818	254	161
Washington	5	7	0	.417	183	296
Pittsburgh	4	7	1	.364	183	235
Philadelphia	4	8	0	.333	234	264
Chi. Cardinals	3	9	0	.250	210	287

NATIONAL CONFERENCE

	W	L	T	Pct.	Pts.	OP
Los Angeles	8	4	0	.667	392	261
Detroit	7	4	1	.636	336	259
San Francisco	7	4	1	.636	255	205
Chi. Bears	7	5	0	.583	286	282
Green Bay	3	9	0	.250	254	375
N.Y. Yanks	1	9	2	.100	241	382

NFL championship: LOS ANGELES 24, Cleveland 17

1950

AMERICAN CONFERENCE

	W	L	T	Pct.	Pts.	OP
Cleveland	10	2	0	.833	310	144
N.Y. Giants	10	2	0	.833	268	150
Philadelphia	6	6	0	.500	254	141
Pittsburgh	6	6	0	.500	180	195
Chi. Cardinals	5	7	0	.417	233	287
Washington	3	9	0	.250	232	326

NATIONAL CONFERENCE

	W	L	T	Pct.	Pts.	OP
Los Angeles	9	3	0	.750	466	309
Chi. Bears	9	3	0	.750	279	207
N.Y. Yanks	7	5	0	.583	366	367
Detroit	6	6	0	.500	321	285
Green Bay	3	9	0	.250	244	406
San Francisco	3	9	0	.250	213	300
Baltimore	1	11	0	.083	213	462

American Conference playoff: CLEVELAND 8, N.Y. Giants 3
National Conference playoff: LOS ANGELES 24, Chi. Bears 14
NFL championship: CLEVELAND 30, Los Angeles 28

1949

EASTERN DIVISION

	W	L	T	Pct.	Pts.	OP
Philadelphia	11	1	0	.917	364	134
Pittsburgh	6	5	1	.545	224	214
N.Y. Giants	6	6	0	.500	287	298
Washington	4	7	1	.364	268	339
N.Y. Bulldogs	1	10	1	.091	153	365

WESTERN DIVISION

	W	L	T	Pct.	Pts.	OP
Los Angeles	8	2	2	.800	360	239
Chi. Bears	9	3	0	.750	332	218
Chi. Cardinals	6	5	1	.545	360	301
Detroit	4	8	0	.333	237	259
Green Bay	2	10	0	.167	114	329

NFL championship: Philadelphia 14, LOS ANGELES 0

1948

EASTERN DIVISION	W	L	T	Pct.	Pts.	OP
Philadelphia	9	2	1	.818	376	156
Washington	7	5	0	.583	291	287
N.Y. Giants	4	8	0	.333	297	388
Pittsburgh	4	8	0	.333	200	243
Boston	3	9	0	.250	174	372

WESTERN DIVISION	W	L	T	Pct.	Pts.	OP
Chi. Cardinals	11	1	0	.917	395	226
Chi. Bears	10	2	0	.833	375	151
Los Angeles	6	5	1	.545	327	269
Green Bay	3	9	0	.250	154	290
Detroit	2	10	0	.167	200	407

NFL championship: PHILADELPHIA 7, Chi. Cardinals 0

1947

EASTERN DIVISION	W	L	T	Pct.	Pts.	OP
Philadelphia	8	4	0	.667	308	242
Pittsburgh	8	4	0	.667	240	259
Boston	4	7	1	.364	168	256
Washington	4	8	0	.333	295	367
N.Y. Giants	2	8	2	.200	190	309

WESTERN DIVISION	W	L	T	Pct.	Pts.	OP
Chi. Cardinals	9	3	0	.750	306	231
Chi. Bears	8	4	0	.667	363	241
Green Bay	6	5	1	.545	274	210
Los Angeles	6	6	0	.500	259	214
Detroit	3	9	0	.250	231	305

Eastern Division playoff: Philadelphia 21, PITTSBURGH 0
NFL championship: CHI. CARDINALS 28, Philadelphia 21

1946

EASTERN DIVISION	W	L	T	Pct.	Pts.	OP
N.Y. Giants	7	3	1	.700	236	162
Philadelphia	6	5	0	.545	231	220
Washington	5	5	1	.500	171	191
Pittsburgh	5	5	1	.500	136	117
Boston	2	8	1	.200	189	273

WESTERN DIVISION	W	L	T	Pct.	Pts.	OP
Chi. Bears	8	2	1	.800	289	193
Los Angeles	6	4	1	.600	277	257
Green Bay	6	5	0	.545	148	158
Chi. Cardinals	6	5	0	.545	260	198
Detroit	1	10	0	.091	142	310

NFL championship: Chi. Bears 24, N.Y. GIANTS 14

1945

EASTERN DIVISION	W	L	T	Pct.	Pts.	OP
Washington	8	2	0	.800	209	121
Philadelphia	7	3	0	.700	272	133
N.Y. Giants	3	6	1	.333	179	198
Boston	3	6	1	.333	123	211
Pittsburgh	2	8	0	.200	79	220

WESTERN DIVISION	W	L	T	Pct.	Pts.	OP
Cleveland	9	1	0	.900	244	136
Detroit	7	3	0	.700	195	194
Green Bay	6	4	0	.600	258	173
Chi. Bears	3	7	0	.300	192	235
Chi. Cardinals	1	9	0	.100	98	228

NFL championship: CLEVELAND 15, Washington 14

1944

EASTERN DIVISION	W	L	T	Pct.	Pts.	OP
N.Y. Giants	8	1	1	.889	206	75
Philadelphia	7	1	2	.875	267	131
Washington	6	3	1	.667	169	180
Boston	2	8	0	.200	82	233
Brooklyn	0	10	0	.000	69	166

WESTERN DIVISION	W	L	T	Pct.	Pts.	OP
Green Bay	8	2	0	.800	238	141
Chi. Bears	6	3	1	.667	258	172
Detroit	6	3	1	.667	216	151
Cleveland	4	6	0	.400	188	224
Card-Pitt	0	10	0	.000	108	328

NFL championship: Green Bay 14, N.Y. GIANTS 7

1943

EASTERN DIVISION	W	L	T	Pct.	Pts.	OP
Washington	6	3	1	.667	229	137
N.Y. Giants	6	3	1	.667	197	170
Phil-Pitt	5	4	1	.556	225	230
Brooklyn	2	8	0	.200	65	234

WESTERN DIVISION	W	L	T	Pct.	Pts.	OP
Chi. Bears	8	1	1	.889	303	157
Green Bay	7	2	1	.778	264	172
Detroit	3	6	1	.333	178	218
Chi. Cardinals	0	10	0	.000	95	238

Eastern Division playoff: Washington 28, N.Y. GIANTS 0
NFL championship: CHI. BEARS 41, Washington 21

1942

EASTERN DIVISION	W	L	T	Pct.	Pts.	OP
Washington	10	1	0	.909	227	102
Pittsburgh	7	4	0	.636	167	119
N.Y. Giants	5	5	1	.500	155	139
Brooklyn	3	8	0	.273	100	168
Philadelphia	2	9	0	.182	134	239

WESTERN DIVISION	W	L	T	Pct.	Pts.	OP
Chi. Bears	11	0	0	1.000	376	84
Green Bay	8	2	1	.800	300	215
Cleveland	5	6	0	.455	150	207
Chi. Cardinals	3	8	0	.273	98	209
Detroit	0	11	0	.000	38	263

NFL championship: WASHINGTON 14, Chi. Bears 6

1941

EASTERN DIVISION	W	L	T	Pct.	Pts.	OP
N.Y. Giants	8	3	0	.727	238	114
Brooklyn	7	4	0	.636	158	127
Washington	6	5	0	.545	176	174
Philadelphia	2	8	1	.200	119	218
Pittsburgh	1	9	1	.100	103	276

WESTERN DIVISION	W	L	T	Pct.	Pts.	OP
Chi. Bears	10	1	0	.909	396	147
Green Bay	10	1	0	.909	258	120
Detroit	4	6	1	.400	121	195
Chi. Cardinals	3	7	1	.300	127	197
Cleveland	2	9	0	.182	116	244

Western Division playoff: CHI. BEARS 33, Green Bay 14
NFL championship: CHI. BEARS 37, N.Y. Giants 9

1940

EASTERN DIVISION	W	L	T	Pct.	Pts.	OP
Washington	9	2	0	.818	245	142
Brooklyn	8	3	0	.727	186	120
N.Y. Giants	6	4	1	.600	131	133
Pittsburgh	2	7	2	.222	60	178
Philadelphia	1	10	0	.091	111	211

WESTERN DIVISION	W	L	T	Pct.	Pts.	OP
Chi. Bears	8	3	0	.727	238	152
Green Bay	6	4	1	.600	238	155
Detroit	5	5	1	.500	138	153
Cleveland	4	6	1	.400	171	191
Chi. Cardinals	2	7	2	.222	139	222

NFL championship: Chi. Bears 73, WASHINGTON 0

1939

EASTERN DIVISION	W	L	T	Pct.	Pts.	OP
N.Y. Giants	9	1	1	.900	168	85
Washington	8	2	1	.800	242	94
Brooklyn	4	6	1	.400	108	219
Philadelphia	1	9	1	.100	105	200
Pittsburgh	1	9	1	.100	114	216

WESTERN DIVISION	W	L	T	Pct.	Pts.	OP
Green Bay	9	2	0	.818	233	153
Chi. Bears	8	3	0	.727	298	157
Detroit	6	5	0	.545	145	150
Cleveland	5	5	1	.500	195	164
Chi. Cardinals	1	10	0	.091	84	254

NFL championship: GREEN BAY 27, N.Y. Giants 0

1938

EASTERN DIVISION	W	L	T	Pct.	Pts.	OP
N.Y. Giants	8	2	1	.800	194	79
Washington	6	3	2	.667	148	154
Brooklyn	4	4	3	.500	131	161
Philadelphia	5	6	0	.455	154	164
Pittsburgh	2	9	0	.182	79	169

WESTERN DIVISION	W	L	T	Pct.	Pts.	OP
Green Bay	8	3	0	.727	223	118
Detroit	7	4	0	.636	119	108
Chi. Bears	6	5	0	.545	194	148
Cleveland	4	7	0	.364	131	215
Chi. Cardinals	2	9	0	.182	111	168

NFL championship: N.Y. GIANTS 23, Green Bay 17

1937

EASTERN DIVISION	W	L	T	Pct.	Pts.	OP
Washington	8	3	0	.727	195	120
N.Y. Giants	6	3	2	.667	128	109
Pittsburgh	4	7	0	.364	122	145
Brooklyn	3	7	1	.300	82	174
Philadelphia	2	8	1	.200	86	177

WESTERN DIVISION	W	L	T	Pct.	Pts.	OP
Chi. Bears	9	1	1	.900	201	100
Green Bay	7	4	0	.636	220	122
Detroit	7	4	0	.636	180	105
Chi. Cardinals	5	5	1	.500	135	165
Cleveland	1	10	0	.091	75	207

NFL championship: Washington 28, CHI. BEARS 21

1936

EASTERN DIVISION	W	L	T	Pct.	Pts.	OP
Boston	7	5	0	.583	149	110
Pittsburgh	6	6	0	.500	98	187
N.Y. Giants	5	6	1	.455	115	163
Brooklyn	3	8	1	.273	92	161
Philadelphia	1	11	0	.083	51	206

WESTERN DIVISION	W	L	T	Pct.	Pts.	OP
Green Bay	10	1	1	.909	248	118
Chi. Bears	9	3	0	.750	222	94
Detroit	8	4	0	.667	235	102
Chi. Cardinals	3	8	1	.273	74	143

NFL championship: Green Bay 21, Boston 6, at Polo Grounds, N.Y.

1935

EASTERN DIVISION	W	L	T	Pct.	Pts.	OP
N.Y. Giants	9	3	0	.750	180	96
Brooklyn	5	6	1	.455	90	141
Pittsburgh	4	8	0	.333	100	209
Boston	2	8	1	.200	65	123
Philadelphia	2	9	0	.182	60	179

WESTERN DIVISION	W	L	T	Pct.	Pts.	OP
Detroit	7	3	2	.700	191	111
Green Bay	8	4	0	.667	181	96
Chi. Bears	6	4	2	.600	192	106
Chi. Cardinals	6	4	2	.600	99	97

NFL championship: DETROIT 26, N.Y. Giants 7
One game between Boston and Philadelphia was canceled.

1934

EASTERN DIVISION	W	L	T	Pct.	Pts.	OP
N.Y. Giants	8	5	0	.615	147	107
Boston	6	6	0	.500	107	94
Brooklyn	4	7	0	.364	61	153
Philadelphia	4	7	0	.364	127	85
Pittsburgh	2	10	0	.167	51	206

WESTERN DIVISION	W	L	T	Pct.	Pts.	OP
Chi. Bears	13	0	0	1.000	286	86
Detroit	10	3	0	.769	238	59
Green Bay	7	6	0	.538	156	112
Chi. Cardinals	5	6	0	.455	80	84
St. Louis	1	2	0	.333	27	61
Cincinnati	0	8	0	.000	10	243

NFL championship: N.Y. GIANTS 30, Chi. Bears 13

1933

EASTERN DIVISION	W	L	T	Pct.	Pts.	OP
N.Y. Giants	11	3	0	.786	244	101
Brooklyn	5	4	1	.556	93	54
Boston	5	5	2	.500	103	97
Philadelphia	3	5	1	.375	77	158
Pittsburgh	3	6	2	.333	67	208

WESTERN DIVISION	W	L	T	Pct.	Pts.	OP
Chi. Bears	10	2	1	.833	133	82
Portsmouth	6	5	0	.545	128	87
Green Bay	5	7	1	.417	170	107
Cincinnati	3	6	1	.333	38	110
Chi. Cardinals	1	9	1	.100	52	101

NFL championship: CHI. BEARS 23, N.Y. Giants 21

1932

	W	L	T	Pct.
Chicago Bears	7	1	6	.875
Green Bay Packers	10	3	1	.769
Portsmouth, O., Spartans	6	2	4	.750
Boston Braves	4	4	2	.500
New York Giants	4	6	2	.400
Brooklyn Dodgers	3	9	0	.250
Chicago Cardinals	2	6	2	.250
Stapleton Stapes	2	7	3	.222

1931

	W	L	T	Pct.
Green Bay Packers	12	2	0	.857
Portsmouth, O., Spartans	11	3	0	.786
Chicago Bears	8	5	0	.615
Chicago Cardinals	5	4	0	.556
N.Y. Giants	7	6	1	.538
Providence Steamroller	4	4	3	.500
Stapleton Stapes	4	6	1	.400
Cleveland Indians	2	8	0	.200
Brooklyn Dodgers	2	12	0	.143
Frankford Yellowjackets	1	6	1	.143

1930

	W	L	T	Pct.
Green Bay Packers	10	3	1	.769
New York Giants	13	4	0	.765
Chicago Bears	9	4	1	.692
Brooklyn Dodgers	7	4	1	.636
Providence Steamroller	6	4	1	.600
Stapleton Stapes	5	5	2	.500
Chicago Cardinals	5	6	2	.455
Portsmouth, O., Spartans	5	6	3	.455
Frankford Yellowjackets	4	14	1	.222
Minneapolis Red Jackets	1	7	1	.125
Newark Tornadoes	1	10	1	.091

1929

	W	L	T	Pct.
Green Bay Packers	12	0	1	1.000
New York Giants	13	1	1	.929
Frankford Yellowjackets	9	4	5	.692
Chicago Cardinals	6	6	1	.500
Boston Bulldogs	4	4	0	.500
Orange, N.J., Tornadoes	3	4	4	.429
Stapleton Stapes	3	4	3	.429
Providence Steamroller	4	6	2	.400
Chicago Bears	4	9	2	.308
Buffalo Bisons	1	7	1	.125
Minneapolis Red Jackets	1	9	0	.100
Dayton Triangles	0	6	0	.000

1928

	W	L	T	Pct.
Providence Steamroller	8	1	2	.889
Frankford Yellowjackets	11	3	2	.786
Detroit Wolverines	7	2	1	.778
Green Bay Packers	6	4	3	.600
Chicago Bears	7	5	1	.583
New York Giants	4	7	2	.364
New York Yankees	4	8	1	.333
Pottsville, Pa., Maroons	2	8	0	.200
Chicago Cardinals	1	5	0	.167
Dayton Triangles	0	7	0	.000

1927

	W	L	T	Pct.
New York Giants	11	1	1	.917
Green Bay Packers	7	2	1	.778
Chicago Bears	9	3	2	.750
Cleveland Bulldogs	8	4	1	.667
Providence Steamroller	8	5	1	.615
New York Yankees	7	8	1	.467
Frankford Yellowjackets	6	9	0	.400
Pottsville, Pa., Maroons	5	8	0	.385
Chicago Cardinals	3	7	1	.300
Dayton Triangles	1	6	1	.143
Duluth Eskimos	1	8	0	.111
Buffalo Bisons	0	5	0	.000

1926

	W	L	T	Pct.
Frankford Yellowjackets	14	1	1	.933
Chicago Bears	12	1	3	.923
Pottsville, Pa., Maroons	10	2	1	.833
Kansas City Cowboys	8	3	1	.727

	W	L	T	Pct.
Green Bay Packers	7	3	3	.700
Los Angeles Buccaneers	6	3	1	.667
New York Giants	8	4	1	.667
Duluth Eskimos	6	5	2	.545
Buffalo Rangers	4	4	2	.500
Chicago Cardinals	5	6	1	.455
Providence Steamroller	5	7	0	.417
Detroit Panthers	4	6	2	.400
Hartford Blues	3	7	0	.300
Brooklyn Lions	3	8	0	.273
Milwaukee Badgers	2	7	0	.222
Akron, Ohio, Indians	1	4	3	.200
Dayton Triangles	1	4	1	.200
Racine, Wis., Legion	1	4	0	.200
Columbus Tigers	1	6	0	.143
Canton, Ohio, Bulldogs	1	9	3	.100
Hammond, Ind., Pros	0	4	0	.000
Louisville Colonels	0	4	0	.000

1925

	W	L	T	Pct.
Chicago Cardinals	11	2	1	.846
Pottsville, Pa., Maroons	10	2	0	.833
Detroit Panthers	8	2	2	.800
New York Giants	8	4	0	.667
Akron, Ohio, Indians	4	2	2	.667
Frankford Yellowjackets	13	7	0	.650
Chicago Bears	9	5	3	.643
Rock Island Independents	5	3	3	.625
Green Bay Packers	8	5	0	.615
Providence Steamroller	6	5	1	.545
Canton, Ohio, Bulldogs	4	4	0	.500
Cleveland Bulldogs	5	8	1	.385
Kansas City Cowboys	2	5	1	.286
Hammond, Ind., Pros	1	3	0	.250
Buffalo Bisons	1	6	2	.143
Duluth Kelleys	0	3	0	.000
Rochester Jeffersons	0	6	1	.000
Milwaukee Badgers	0	6	0	.000
Dayton Triangles	0	7	1	.000
Columbus Tigers	0	9	0	.000

1924

	W	L	T	Pct.
Cleveland Bulldogs	7	1	1	.875
Chicago Bears	6	1	4	.857
Frankford Yellowjackets	11	2	1	.846
Duluth Kelleys	5	1	0	.833
Rock Island Independents	6	2	2	.750
Green Bay Packers	8	4	0	.667
Buffalo Bisons	6	4	0	.600
Racine, Wis., Legion	4	3	3	.571
Chicago Cardinals	5	4	1	.556
Columbus Tigers	4	4	0	.500
Hammond, Ind., Pros	2	2	1	.500
Milwaukee Badgers	5	8	0	.385
Dayton Triangles	2	7	0	.222
Kansas City Cowboys	2	7	0	.222
Akron, Ohio, Indians	1	6	0	.143
Kenosha, Wis., Maroons	0	5	1	.000
Minneapolis Marines	0	6	0	.000
Rochester Jeffersons	0	7	0	.000

1923

	W	L	T	Pct.
Canton, Ohio, Bulldogs	11	0	1	1.000
Chicago Bears	9	2	1	.818
Green Bay Packers	7	2	1	.778
Milwaukee Badgers	7	2	3	.778
Cleveland Indians	3	1	3	.750
Chicago Cardinals	8	4	0	.667
Duluth Kelleys	4	3	0	.571
Buffalo All-Americans	5	4	3	.556
Columbus Tigers	5	4	1	.556
Racine, Wis., Legion	4	4	2	.500
Toledo Maroons	2	3	2	.400
Rock Island Independents	2	3	3	.400
Minneapolis Marines	2	5	2	.286
St. Louis All-Stars	1	4	2	.200
Hammond, Ind., Pros	1	5	1	.167
Dayton Triangles	1	6	1	.143
Akron, Ohio, Indians	1	6	0	.143
Oorang Indians	1	10	0	.091
Rochester Jeffersons	0	2	0	.000
Louisville Brecks	0	3	0	.000

1922

	W	L	T	Pct.
Canton, Ohio, Bulldogs	10	0	2	1.000
Chicago Bears	9	3	0	.750
Chicago Cardinals	8	3	0	.727
Toledo Maroons	5	2	2	.714
Rock Island Independents	4	2	1	.667
Dayton Triangles	4	3	1	.571
Green Bay Packers	4	3	3	.571
Racine, Wis., Legion	5	4	1	.556
Akron, Ohio, Pros	3	4	2	.429
Buffalo All-Americans	3	4	1	.429
Milwaukee Badgers	2	4	3	.333
Oorang Indians	2	6	0	.250
Minneapolis Marines	1	3	0	.250
Evansville Crimson Giants	0	2	0	.000
Louisville Brecks	0	3	0	.000
Rochester Jeffersons	0	3	1	.000
Hammond, Ind., Pros	0	4	1	.000
Columbus Panhandles	0	7	0	.000

1921

	W	L	T	Pct.
Chicago Staleys	10	1	1	.909
Buffalo All-Americans	9	1	2	.900
Akron, Ohio, Pros	7	2	1	.778
Green Bay Packers	6	2	2	.750
Canton, Ohio, Bulldogs	4	3	3	.571
Dayton Triangles	4	3	1	.571
Rock Island Independents	5	4	1	.556
Chicago Cardinals	2	3	2	.400
Cleveland Indians	2	6	0	.250
Rochester Jeffersons	2	6	0	.250
Detroit Heralds	1	7	1	.125
Columbus Panhandles	0	6	0	.000
Cincinnati Celts	0	8	0	.000

ALL-TIME TEAM VS. TEAM RESULTS

ATLANTA vs. BALTIMORE
Colts lead series, 8-0
1966—Colts, 19-7 (A)
1967—Colts, 38-31 (B)
Colts, 49-7 (A)
1968—Colts, 28-20 (A)
Colts, 44-0 (B)
1969—Colts, 21-14 (A)
Colts, 13-6 (B)
1974—Colts, 17-7 (A)
(Points—Colts 229, Falcons 92)

ATLANTA vs. BUFFALO
Bills lead series, 2-1
1973—Bills, 17-6 (A)
1977—Bills, 3-0 (B)
1980—Falcons, 30-14 (B)
(Points—Falcons 36, Bills 34)

ATLANTA vs. CHICAGO
Falcons lead series, 8-4
1966—Bears, 23-6 (C)
1967—Bears, 23-14 (A)
1968—Falcons, 16-13 (C)
1969—Falcons, 48-31 (A)
1970—Bears, 23-14 (A)
1972—Falcons, 37-21 (C)
1973—Falcons, 46-6 (A)
1974—Falcons, 13-10 (A)
1976—Falcons, 10-0 (C)
1977—Falcons, 16-10 (C)
1978—Bears, 13-7 (C)
1980—Falcons, 28-17 (A)
(Points—Falcons 255, Bears 190)

ATLANTA vs. CINCINNATI
Bengals lead series, 3-1
1971—Falcons, 9-6 (C)
1975—Bengals, 21-14 (A)
1978—Bengals, 37-7 (C)
1981—Bengals, 30-28 (A)
(Points—Bengals 94, Falcons 58)

ATLANTA vs. CLEVELAND
Browns lead series, 5-1
1966—Browns, 49-17 (A)
1968—Browns, 30-7 (C)
1971—Falcons, 31-14 (C)
1976—Browns, 20-17 (A)
1978—Browns, 24-16 (A)
1981—Browns, 28-17 (C)
(Points—Browns 165, Falcons 105)

ATLANTA vs. DALLAS
Cowboys lead series, 7-1
1966—Cowboys, 47-14 (A)
1967—Cowboys, 37-7 (D)
1969—Cowboys, 24-17 (A)
1970—Cowboys, 13-0 (A)
1974—Cowboys, 24-0 (A)
1976—Falcons, 17-10 (A)
1978—*Cowboys, 27-20 (D)
1980—*Cowboys, 30-27 (A)
(Points—Cowboys 212, Falcons 102)

*NFC Divisional Playoff
ATLANTA vs. DENVER
Series tied, 2-2
1970—Broncos, 24-10 (D)
1972—Falcons, 23-20 (A)
1975—Falcons, 35-21 (A)
1979—Broncos, 20-17 (A) OT
(Points—Falcons 85, Broncos 85)

ATLANTA vs. DETROIT
Lions lead series, 10-3
1966—Lions, 28-10 (D)
1967—Lions, 24-3 (D)
1968—Lions, 24-7 (A)
1969—Lions, 27-21 (D)
1971—Lions, 41-38 (D)
1972—Lions, 26-23 (A)
1973—Falcons, 31-6 (D)
1975—Lions, 17-14 (A)
1976—Lions, 24-10 (D)
1977—Falcons, 17-6 (A)
1978—Falcons, 14-0 (A)
1979—Lions, 24-23 (D)
1980—Falcons, 43-28 (A)
(Points—Lions 300, Falcons 229)

ATLANTA vs. GREEN BAY
Packers lead series, 7-5
1966—Packers, 56-3 (Mil)
1967—Packers, 23-0 (Mil)
1968—Packers, 38-7 (A)
1969—Packers, 28-10 (A)
1970—Packers, 27-24 (GB)
1971—Falcons, 28-21 (A)
1972—Falcons, 10-9 (Mil)
1974—Falcons, 10-3 (A)
1975—Packers, 22-13 (GB)
1976—Packers, 24-20 (A)
1979—Falcons, 25-7 (A)
1981—Falcons, 31-17 (GB)
(Points—Packers 275, Falcons 181)

ATLANTA vs. HOUSTON
Falcons lead series, 3-1
1972—Falcons, 20-10 (A)
1976—Oilers, 20-14 (H)
1978—Falcons, 20-14 (A)
1981—Falcons, 31-27 (H)
(Points—Falcons 85, Oilers 71)

ATLANTA vs. KANSAS CITY
Chiefs lead series, 1-0
1972—Chiefs, 17-14 (A)

ATLANTA vs. LOS ANGELES
Rams lead series, 24-5-2
1966—Rams, 19-14 (A)
1967—Rams, 31-3 (A)
Rams, 20-3 (LA)
1968—Rams, 27-14 (LA)
Rams, 17-10 (A)
1969—Rams, 17-7 (LA)
Rams, 38-6 (A)
1970—Tie, 10-10 (LA)

155

All-Time Team vs. Team Results

Rams, 17-7 (A)
1971—Tie, 20-20 (LA)
Rams, 24-16 (A)
1972—Falcons, 31-3 (A)
Rams, 20-7 (LA)
1973—Rams, 31-0 (LA)
Falcons, 15-13 (A)
1974—Rams, 21-0 (LA)
Rams, 30-7 (A)
1975—Rams, 22-7 (LA)
Rams, 16-7 (A)
1976—Rams, 30-14 (A)
Rams, 59-0 (LA)
1977—Falcons, 17-6 (A)
Rams, 23-7 (LA)
1978—Rams, 10-0 (LA)
Falcons, 15-7 (A)
1979—Rams, 20-14 (LA)
Rams, 34-13 (A)
1980—Falcons, 13-10 (A)
Rams, 20-17 (LA) OT
1981—Rams, 37-35 (A)
Rams, 21-16 (LA)
(Points—Rams 673, Falcons 345)

ATLANTA vs. MIAMI
Dolphins lead series, 3-0
1970—Dolphins, 20-7 (A)
1974—Dolphins, 42-7 (M)
1980—Dolphins, 20-17 (A)
(Points—Dolphins 82, Falcons 31)

ATLANTA vs. MINNESOTA
Vikings lead series, 7-5
1966—Falcons, 20-13 (M)
1967—Falcons, 21-20 (A)
1968—Vikings, 47-7 (M)
1969—Falcons, 10-3 (A)
1970—Vikings, 37-7 (A)
1971—Vikings, 24-7 (M)
1973—Falcons, 20-14 (A)
1974—Vikings, 23-10 (M)
1975—Vikings, 38-0 (M)
1977—Vikings, 14-7 (A)
1980—Vikings, 24-23 (M)
1981—Falcons, 31-30 (A)
(Points—Vikings 287, Falcons 163)

ATLANTA vs. NEW ENGLAND
Patriots lead series, 2-1
1972—Patriots, 21-20 (NE)
1977—Patriots, 16-10 (A)
1980—Falcons, 37-21 (NE)
(Points—Falcons 67, Patriots 58)

ATLANTA vs. NEW ORLEANS
Falcons lead series, 19-7
1967—Saints, 27-24 (NO)
1969—Falcons, 45-17 (A)
1970—Falcons, 14-3 (NO)
Falcons, 32-14 (A)
1971—Falcons, 28-6 (A)
Falcons, 24-20 (NO)
1972—Falcons, 21-14 (NO)
Falcons, 36-20 (A)
1973—Falcons, 62-7 (NO)
Falcons, 14-10 (A)

1974—Saints, 14-13 (NO)
Saints, 13-3 (A)
1975—Falcons, 14-7 (A)
Saints, 23-7 (NO)
1976—Saints, 30-0 (NO)
Falcons, 23-20 (A)
1977—Saints, 21-20 (NO)
Falcons, 35-7 (A)
1978—Falcons, 20-17 (NO)
Falcons, 20-17 (A)
1979—Falcons, 40-34 (NO) OT
Saints, 37-6 (A)
1980—Falcons, 41-14 (NO)
Falcons, 31-13 (A)
1981—Falcons, 27-0 (A)
Falcons, 41-10 (NO)
(Points—Falcons 641, Saints 415)

ATLANTA vs. N.Y. GIANTS
Falcons lead series, 5-3
1966—Falcons, 27-16 (NY)
1968—Falcons, 24-21 (A)
1971—Giants, 21-17 (A)
1974—Falcons, 14-7 (New Haven)
1977—Falcons, 17-3 (A)
1978—Falcons, 23-20 (A)
1979—Giants, 24-3 (NY)
1981—Giants, 27-24 (A) OT
(Points—Falcons 149, Giants 139)

ATLANTA vs. N.Y. JETS
Series tied, 1-1
1973—Falcons, 28-20 (NY)
1980—Jets, 14-7 (A)
(Points—Falcons 35, Jets 34)

ATLANTA vs. OAKLAND
Raiders lead series, 2-1
1971—Falcons, 24-13 (A)
1975—Raiders, 37-34 (O) OT
1979—Raiders, 50-19 (O)
(Points—Raiders 100, Falcons 77)

ATLANTA vs. PHILADELPHIA
Falcons lead series, 5-4-1
1966—Eagles, 23-10 (P)
1967—Eagles, 38-7 (A)
1969—Falcons, 27-3 (P)
1970—Tie, 13-13 (P)
1973—Falcons, 44-27 (P)
1976—Eagles, 14-13 (A)
1978—*Falcons, 14-13 (A)
1979—Falcons, 14-10 (P)
1980—Falcons, 20-17 (P)
1981—Eagles, 16-13 (P)
(Points—Falcons 175, Eagles 174)
*NFC First Round Playoff

ATLANTA vs. PITTSBURGH
Steelers lead series, 5-1
1966—Steelers, 57-33 (A)
1968—Steelers, 41-21 (A)
1970—Falcons, 27-16 (A)
1974—Steelers, 24-17 (P)
1978—Steelers, 31-7 (P)
1981—Steelers, 34-20 (A)
(Points—Steelers 203, Falcons 125)

ATLANTA vs. ST. LOUIS

Cardinals lead series, 5-3
1966—Falcons, 16-10 (A)
1968—Cardinals, 17-12 (StL)
1971—Cardinals, 26-9 (A)
1973—Cardinals, 32-10 (A)
1975—Cardinals, 23-20 (StL)
1978—Cardinals, 42-21 (StL)
1980—Falcons, 33-27 (StL) OT
1981—Falcons, 41-20 (A)
(Points—Cardinals 197, Falcons 162)

ATLANTA vs. SAN DIEGO
Falcons lead series, 2-0
1973—Falcons, 41-0 (SD)
1979—Falcons, 28-26 (SD)
(Points—Falcons 69, Chargers 26)

ATLANTA vs. SAN FRANCISCO
49ers lead series, 16-15
1966—49ers, 44-7 (A)
1967—49ers, 38-7 (SF)
      49ers, 34-28 (A)
1968—49ers, 28-13 (SF)
      49ers, 14-12 (A)
1969—49ers, 24-12 (A)
      Falcons, 21-7 (SF)
1970—Falcons, 21-20 (A)
      49ers, 24-20 (SF)
1971—Falcons, 20-17 (A)
      49ers, 24-3 (SF)
1972—49ers, 49-14 (A)
      49ers, 20-0 (SF)
1973—49ers, 13-9 (A)
      Falcons, 17-3 (SF)
1974—49ers, 16-10 (A)
      49ers, 27-0 (SF)
1975—Falcons, 17-3 (SF)
      Falcons, 31-9 (A)
1976—49ers, 15-0 (SF)
      Falcons, 21-16 (A)
1977—Falcons, 7-0 (SF)
      49ers, 10-3 (A)
1978—Falcons, 20-17 (SF)
      Falcons, 21-10 (A)
1979—49ers, 20-15 (SF)
      Falcons, 31-21 (A)
1980—Falcons, 20-17 (SF)
      Falcons, 35-10 (A)
1981—Falcons, 34-17 (A)
      49ers, 17-14 (SF)
(Points—49ers 572, Falcons 495)

ATLANTA vs. SEATTLE
Seahawks lead series, 2-0
1976—Seahawks, 30-13 (S)
1979—Seahawks, 31-28 (A)
(Points—Seahawks 61, Falcons 41)

ATLANTA vs. TAMPA BAY
Series tied, 2-2
1977—Falcons, 17-0 (TB)
1978—Buccaneers, 14-9 (A)
1979—Falcons, 17-14 (A)
1981—Buccaneers, 24-23 (TB)
(Points—Falcons 66, Buccaneers 52)

ATLANTA vs. WASHINGTON
Redskins lead series, 6-2-1

1966—Redskins, 33-20 (W)
1967—Tie, 20-20 (A)
1969—Redskins, 27-20 (W)
1972—Redskins, 24-13 (W)
1975—Redskins, 30-27 (A)
1977—Redskins, 10-6 (W)
1978—Falcons, 20-17 (A)
1979—Redskins, 16-7 (A)
1980—Falcons, 10-6 (A)
(Points—Redskins 183, Falcons 143)

BALTIMORE vs. ATLANTA
Colts lead series, 8-0;
See Atlanta vs. Baltimore

BALTIMORE vs. BUFFALO
Colts lead series, 13-10-1
1970—Tie, 17-17 (Balt)
      Colts, 20-14 (Buff)
1971—Colts, 43-0 (Buff)
      Colts, 24-0 (Balt)
1972—Colts, 17-0 (Buff)
      Colts, 35-7 (Balt)
1973—Bills, 31-13 (Buff)
      Bills, 24-17 (Balt)
1974—Bills, 27-14 (Balt)
      Bills, 6-0 (Buff)
1975—Bills, 38-31 (Balt)
      Colts, 42-35 (Buff)
1976—Colts, 31-13 (Buff)
      Colts, 58-20 (Balt)
1977—Colts, 17-14 (Balt)
      Colts, 31-13 (Buff)
1978—Bills, 24-17 (Buff)
      Bills, 21-14 (Balt)
1979—Bills, 31-13 (Balt)
      Colts, 14-13 (Buff)
1980—Colts, 17-12 (Buff)
      Colts, 28-24 (Balt)
1981—Bills, 35-3 (Balt)
      Bills, 23-17 (Buff)
(Points—Colts 533, Bills 442)

BALTIMORE vs. CHICAGO
Colts lead series, 20-13
1953—Colts, 13-9 (B)
      Colts, 16-14 (C)
1954—Bears, 28-9 (C)
      Bears, 28-13 (B)
1955—Colts, 23-17 (B)
      Bears, 38-10 (C)
1956—Colts, 28-21 (B)
      Bears, 58-27 (C)
1957—Colts, 21-10 (B)
      Colts, 29-14 (C)
1958—Colts, 51-38 (B)
      Colts, 17-0 (C)
1959—Bears, 26-21 (B)
      Colts, 21-7 (C)
1960—Colts, 42-7 (B)
      Colts, 24-20 (C)
1961—Bears, 24-10 (C)
      Bears, 21-20 (B)
1962—Bears, 35-15 (C)
      Bears, 57-0 (B)

1963—Bears, 10-3 (C)
　　　Bears, 17-7 (B)
1964—Colts, 52-0 (B)
　　　Colts, 40-24 (C)
1965—Colts, 26-21 (C)
　　　Bears, 13-0 (B)
1966—Bears. 27-17 (C)
　　　Colts, 21-16 (B)
1967—Colts, 24-3 (C)
1968—Colts, 28-7 (B)
1969—Colts, 24-21 (C)
1970—Colts, 21-20 (B)
1975—Colts, 35-7 (C)
(Points—Colts 708, Bears 658)

BALTIMORE vs. CINCINNATI
Colts lead series, 4-3
1970—*Colts, 17-0 (B)
1972—Colts, 20-19 (C)
1974—Bengals, 24-14 (B)
1976—Colts, 28-27 (B)
1979—Colts, 38-28 (B)
1980—Bengals, 34-33 (C)
1981—Bengals, 41-19 (B)
(Points—Bengals 173, Colts 169)
*AFC Divisional Playoff

BALTIMORE vs. CLEVELAND
Browns lead series, 9-5
1956—Colts, 21-7 (C)
1959—Browns, 38-31 (B)
1962—Colts, 36-14 (C)
1964—*Browns, 27-0 (C)
1968—Browns, 30-20 (B)
　　　`Colts, 34-0 (C)
1971—Browns, 14-13 (B)
　　　**Colts, 20-3 (C)
1973—Browns, 24-14 (C)
1975—Colts, 21-7 (B)
1978—Browns, 45-24 (B)
1979—Browns, 13-10 (C)
1980—Browns, 28-27 (B)
1981—Browns, 42-28 (C)
(Points—Colts 299, Browns 292)
*NFL Championship
**AFC Divisional Playoff

BALTIMORE vs. DALLAS
Cowboys lead series, 5-3
1960—Colts, 45-7 (D)
1967—Colts, 23-17 (B)
1969—Cowboys, 27-10 (D)
1970—*Colts, 16-13 (Miami)
1972—Cowboys, 21-0 (B)
1976—Cowboys, 30-27 (D)
1978—Cowboys, 38-0 (D)
1981—Cowboys, 37-13 (B)
(Points—Cowboys 190, Colts 134)
*Super Bowl V

BALTIMORE vs. DENVER
Broncos lead series, 3-1
1974—Broncos, 17-6 (B)
1977—Broncos, 27-13 (D)
1978—Colts, 7-6 (B)
1981—Broncos, 28-10 (D)
(Points—Broncos 78, Colts 36)

BALTIMORE vs. DETROIT
Series tied, 16-16-2
1953—Lions, 27-17 (B)
　　　Lions, 17-7 (D)
1954—Lions, 35-0 (D)
　　　Lions, 27-3 (B)
1955—Colts, 28-13 (B)
　　　Lions, 24-14 (D)
1956—Lions, 31-14 (B)
　　　Lions, 27-3 (D)
1957—Colts, 34-14 (B)
　　　Lions, 31-27 (D)
1958—Colts, 28-15 (B)
　　　Colts, 40-14 (D)
1959—Colts, 21-9 (B)
　　　Colts, 31-24 (D)
1960—Lions, 30-17 (B)
　　　Lions, 20-15 (D)
1961—Lions, 16-15 (B)
　　　Colts, 17-14 (D)
1962—Lions, 29-20 (B)
　　　Lions, 21-14 (D)
1963—Colts, 25-21 (B)
　　　Colts, 24-21 (B)
1964—Colts, 34-0 (D)
　　　Lions, 31-14 (B)
1965—Colts, 31-7 (B)
　　　Tie, 24-24 (D)
1966—Colts, 45-14 (D)
　　　Lions, 20-14 (D)
1967—Colts, 41-7 (B)
1968—Colts, 27-10 (D)
1969—Tie, 17-17 (B)
1973—Colts, 29-27 (D)
1977—Lions, 13-10 (B)
1980—Colts, 10-9 (D)
(Points—Colts 710, Lions 659)

BALTIMORE vs. GREEN BAY
Packers lead series, 18-16
1953—Packers, 37-14 (GB)
　　　Packers, 35-24 (B)
1954—Packers, 7-6 (B)
　　　Packers, 24-13 (Mil)
1955—Colts, 24-20 (Mil)
　　　Colts, 14-10 (B)
1956—Packers, 38-33 (Mil)
　　　Colts, 28-21 (B)
1957—Colts, 45-17 (Mil)
　　　Packers, 24-21 (B)
1958—Colts, 24-17 (Mil)
　　　Colts, 56-0 (B)
1959—Colts, 38-21 (B)
　　　Colts, 28-24 (Mil)
1960—Packers, 35-21 (GB)
　　　Colts, 38-24 (B)
1961—Packers, 45-7 (GB)
　　　Colts, 45-21 (B)
1962—Packers, 17-6 (B)
　　　Packers, 17-13 (GB)
1963—Packers, 31-20 (GB)
　　　Packers, 34-20 (B)
1964—Colts, 21-20 (GB)
　　　Colts, 24-21 (B)

1965—Packers, 20-17 (Mil)
 Packers, 42-27 (B)
 *Packers, 13-10 (GB) OT
1966—Packers, 24-3 (Mil)
 Packers, 14-10 (B)
1967—Colts, 13-10 (B)
1968—Colts, 16-3 (GB)
1969—Colts, 14-6 (B)
1970—Colts, 13-10 (GB)
1974—Packers, 20-13 (B)
(Points—Packers 722, Colts 719)
*Conference Playoff

BALTIMORE vs. HOUSTON
Oilers lead series, 3-2
1970—Colts, 24-20 (H)
1973—Oilers, 31-27 (B)
1976—Colts, 38-14 (B)
1979—Colts, 28-16 (B)
1980—Oilers, 21-16 (H)
(Points—Colts 121, Oilers 114)

BALTIMORE vs. KANSAS CITY
Chiefs lead series, 5-3
1970—Chiefs, 44-24 (B)
1972—Chiefs, 24-10 (KC)
1975—Colts, 28-14 (B)
1977—Colts, 17-6 (KC)
1979—Chiefs, 14-0 (KC)
 Chiefs, 10-7 (B)
1980—Colts, 31-24 (KC)
 Chiefs, 38-28 (B)
(Points—Chiefs 174, Colts 145)

BALTIMORE vs. LOS ANGELES
Colts lead series, 20-14-2
1953—Rams, 21-13 (B)
 Rams, 45-2 (LA)
1954—Colts, 48-0 (B)
 Colts, 22-21 (LA)
1955—Tie, 17-17 (B)
 Rams, 20-14 (LA)
1956—Colts, 56-21 (B)
 Rams, 31-7 (LA)
1957—Colts, 31-14 (B)
 Rams, 37-21 (LA)
1958—Colts, 34-7 (B)
 Rams, 30-28 (LA)
1959—Colts, 35-21 (B)
 Colts, 45-26 (LA)
1960—Colts, 31-17 (B)
 Rams, 10-3 (LA)
1961—Colts, 27-24 (B)
 Rams, 34-17 (LA)
1962—Colts, 30-27 (B)
 Colts, 14-2 (LA)
1963—Rams, 17-16 (LA)
 Colts, 19-16 (B)
1964—Colts, 35-20 (B)
 Colts, 24-7 (LA)
1965—Colts, 35-20 (B)
 Colts, 20-17 (LA)
1966—Colts, 17-3 (LA)
 Rams, 23-7 (B)
1967—Tie, 24-24 (B)
 Rams, 34-10 (LA)

1968—Colts, 27-10 (B)
 Colts, 28-24 (LA)
1969—Rams, 27-20 (B)
 Colts, 13-7 (LA)
1971—Colts, 24-17 (B)
1975—Rams, 24-13 (LA)
(Points—Colts 779, Rams 763)

BALTIMORE vs. MIAMI
Dolphins lead series, 16-9
1970—Colts, 35-0 (B)
 Dolphins, 34-17 (M)
1971—Dolphins, 17-14 (M)
 Colts, 14-3 (B)
 *Dolphins, 21-0 (M)
1972—Dolphins, 23-0 (B)
 Dolphins, 16-0 (M)
1973—Dolphins, 44-0 (M)
 Colts, 16-3 (B)
1974—Dolphins, 17-7 (M)
 Dolphins, 17-16 (B)
1975—Colts, 33-17 (M)
 Colts, 10-7 (B) OT
1976—Colts, 28-14 (B)
 Colts, 17-16 (M)
1977—Colts, 45-28 (B)
 Dolphins, 17-6 (M)
1978—Dolphins, 42-0 (M)
 Dolphins, 26-8 (M)
1979—Dolphins, 19-0 (M)
 Dolphins, 28-24 (B)
1980—Colts, 30-17 (M)
 Dolphins, 24-14 (B)
1981—Dolphins, 31-28 (B)
 Dolphins, 27-10 (M)
(Points—Dolphins 508, Colts 372)
*AFC Championship

BALTIMORE vs. MINNESOTA
Colts lead series, 12-4-1
1961—Colts, 34-33 (B)
 Vikings, 28-20 (M)
1962—Colts, 34-7 (M)
 Colts, 42-17 (B)
1963—Colts, 37-34 (M)
 Colts, 41-10 (B)
1964—Vikings, 34-24 (M)
 Colts, 17-14 (B)
1965—Colts, 35-16 (B)
 Colts, 41-21 (M)
1966—Colts, 38-23 (M)
 Colts, 20-17 (B)
1967—Tie, 20-20 (M)
1968—Colts, 21-9 (B)
 *Colts, 24-14 (B)
1969—Vikings, 52-14 (M)
1971—Vikings, 10-3 (M)
(Points—Colts 465, Vikings 359)
*Conference Championship

BALTIMORE vs. *NEW ENGLAND
Colts lead series, 13-11
1970—Colts, 14-6 (Bos)
 Colts, 27-3 (Balt)
1971—Colts, 23-3 (NE)
 Patriots, 21-17 (Balt)

159

All-Time Team vs. Team Results

1972—Colts, 24-17 (NE)
      Colts, 31-0 (Balt)
1973—Patriots, 24-16 (NE)
      Colts, 18-13 (Balt)
1974—Patriots, 42-3 (NE)
      Patriots, 27-17 (Balt)
1975—Patriots, 21-10 (NE)
      Colts, 34-21 (Balt)
1976—Colts, 27-13 (NE)
      Patriots, 21-14 (Balt)
1977—Patriots, 17-3 (NE)
      Colts, 30-24 (Balt)
1978—Colts, 34-27 (NE)
      Patriots, 35-14 (Balt)
1979—Colts, 31-26 (Balt)
      Patriots, 50-21 (NE)
1980—Patriots, 37-21 (Balt)
      Patriots, 47-21 (NE)
1981—Colts, 29-28 (NE)
      Colts, 23-21 (Balt)
(Points—Patriots 544, Colts 502)
*Franchise in Boston prior to 1971

BALTIMORE vs. NEW ORLEANS
Colts lead series, 3-0
1967—Colts, 30-10 (B)
1969—Colts, 30-10 (NO)
1973—Colts, 14-10 (B)
(Points—Colts 74, Saints 30)

BALTIMORE vs. N.Y. GIANTS
Colts lead series, 7-3
1954—Colts, 20-14 (B)
1955—Giants, 17-7 (NY)
1958—Giants, 24-21 (NY)
      *Colts, 23-17 (NY) OT
1959—*Colts, 31-16 (B)
1963—Giants, 37-28 (NY)
1968—Colts, 26-0 (NY)
1971—Colts, 31-7 (NY)
1975—Colts, 21-0 (NY)
1979—Colts, 31-7 (NY)
(Points—Colts 239, Giants 139)
*NFL Championship

BALTIMORE vs. N.Y. JETS
Colts lead series, 14-11
1968—*Jets, 16-7 (Miami)
1970—Colts, 29-22 (NY)
      Colts, 35-20 (B)
1971—Colts, 22-0 (B)
      Colts, 14-13 (NY)
1972—Jets, 44-34 (B)
      Jets, 24-20 (NY)
1973—Colts, 34-10 (B)
      Jets, 20-17 (NY)
1974—Colts, 35-20 (NY)
      Jets, 45-38 (B)
1975—Colts, 45-28 (NY)
      Colts, 52-19 (B)
1976—Colts, 20-0 (NY)
      Colts, 33-16 (B)
1977—Colts, 20-12 (NY)
      Colts, 33-12 (B)
1978—Jets, 33-10 (B)
      Jets, 24-16 (NY)

1979—Colts, 10-8 (B)
      Jets, 30-17 (NY)
1980—Jets, 17-14 (NY)
      Colts, 35-21 (B)
1981—Jets, 41-14 (B)
      Jets, 25-0 (NY)
(Points—Colts 583, Jets 541)
*Super Bowl III

BALTIMORE vs. OAKLAND
Raiders lead series, 3-2
1970—*Colts, 27-17 (B)
1971—Colts, 37-14 (O)
1973—Raiders, 34-21 (B)
1975—Raiders, 31-20 (B)
1977—**Raiders, 37-31 (B) OT
(Points—Colts 136, Raiders 133)
*AFC Championship
**AFC Divisional Playoff

BALTIMORE vs. PHILADELPHIA
Series tied, 4-4
1953—Eagles, 45-14 (P)
1965—Colts, 34-24 (B)
1967—Colts, 38-6 (P)
1969—Colts, 24-20 (B)
1970—Colts, 29-10 (B)
1974—Eagles, 30-10 (P)
1978—Eagles, 17-14 (B)
1981—Eagles, 38-13 (P)
(Points—Eagles 190, Colts 176)

BALTIMORE vs. PITTSBURGH
Steelers lead series, 7-3
1957—Steelers, 19-13 (B)
1968—Colts, 41-7 (P)
1971—Colts, 34-21 (B)
1974—Steelers, 30-0 (B)
1975—*Steelers, 28-10 (P)
1976—*Steelers, 40-14 (B)
1977—Colts, 31-21 (B)
1978—Steelers, 35-13 (P)
1979—Steelers, 17-13 (P)
1980—Steelers, 20-17 (B)
(Points—Steelers 238, Colts 186)
*AFC Divisional Playoff

BALTIMORE vs. ST. LOUIS
Series tied, 4-4
1961—Colts, 16-0 (B)
1964—Colts, 47-27 (B)
1968—Colts, 27-0 (B)
1972—Cardinals, 10-3 (B)
1976—Cardinals, 24-17 (StL)
1978—Colts, 30-17 (StL)
1980—Cardinals, 17-10 (B)
1981—Cardinals, 35-24 (B)
(Points—Colts 174, Cardinals 130)

BALTIMORE vs. SAN DIEGO
Series tied, 2-2
1970—Colts, 16-14 (SD)
1972—Chargers, 23-20 (B)
1976—Colts, 37-21 (SD)
1981—Chargers, 43-14 (B)
(Points—Chargers 101, Colts 87)

BALTIMORE vs. SAN FRANCISCO
Colts lead series, 21-14

1953—49ers, 38-21 (B)
     49ers, 45-14 (SF)
1954—Colts, 17-13 (B)
     49ers, 10-7 (SF)
1955—Colts, 26-14 (B)
     49ers, 35-24 (SF)
1956—49ers, 20-17 (B)
     49ers, 30-17 (SF)
1957—Colts, 27-21 (B)
     49ers, 17-13 (SF)
1958—Colts, 35-27 (B)
     49ers, 21-12 (SF)
1959—Colts, 45-14 (B)
     Colts, 34-14 (SF)
1960—49ers, 30-22 (B)
     49ers, 34-10 (SF)
1961—Colts, 20-17 (B)
     Colts, 27-24 (SF)
1962—49ers, 21-13 (B)
     Colts, 22-3 (SF)
1963—Colts, 20-14 (SF)
     Colts, 20-3 (B)
1964—Colts, 37-7 (B)
     Colts, 14-3 (SF)
1965—Colts, 27-24 (B)
     Colts, 34-28 (SF)
1966—Colts, 36-14 (B)
     Colts, 30-14 (SF)
1967—Colts, 41-7 (B)
     Colts, 26-9 (SF)
1968—Colts, 27-10 (B)
     Colts, 42-14 (SF)
1969—49ers, 24-21 (B)
     49ers, 20-17 (SF)
1972—49ers, 24-21 (SF)
(Points—Colts 836, 49ers 663)

BALTIMORE vs. SEATTLE
Colts lead series, 2-0
1977—Colts, 29-14 (S)
1978—Colts, 17-14 (S)
(Points—Colts 46, Seahawks 28)

BALTIMORE vs. TAMPA BAY
Series tied, 1-1
1976—Colts, 42-17 (B)
1979—Buccaneers, 29-26 (B) OT
(Points—Colts 68, Buccaneers 46)

BALTIMORE vs. WASHINGTON
Colts lead series, 15-5
1953—Colts, 27-17 (B)
1954—Redskins, 24-21 (W)
1955—Redskins, 14-13 (B)
1956—Colts, 19-17 (B)
1957—Colts, 21-17 (W)
1958—Colts, 35-10 (B)
1959—Redskins, 27-24 (W)
1960—Colts, 20-0 (B)
1961—Colts, 27-6 (W)
1962—Colts, 34-21 (B)
1963—Colts, 36-20 (W)
1964—Colts, 45-17 (B)
1965—Colts, 38-7 (W)
1966—Colts, 37-10 (B)
1967—Colts, 17-13 (W)

1969—Colts, 41-17 (B)
1973—Redskins, 22-14 (W)
1977—Colts, 10-3 (B)
1978—Colts, 21-17 (B)
1981—Redskins, 38-14 (W)
(Points—Colts 514, Redskins 317)

BUFFALO vs. ATLANTA
Bills lead series, 2-1;
See Atlanta vs. Buffalo

BUFFALO vs. BALTIMORE
Colts lead series, 13-10-1
See Baltimore vs. Buffalo

BUFFALO vs. CHICAGO
Bears lead series, 2-1
1970—Bears, 31-13 (C)
1974—Bills, 16-6 (B)
1979—Bears, 7-0 (B)
(Points—Bears 44, Bills 29)

BUFFALO vs. CINCINNATI
Bengals lead series, 6-4
1968—Bengals, 34-23 (C)
1969—Bills, 16-13 (B)
1970—Bengals, 43-14 (B)
1973—Bengals, 16-13 (B)
1975—Bengals, 33-24 (C)
1978—Bills, 5-0 (B)
1979—Bengals, 51-24 (B)
1980—Bills, 14-0 (C)
1981—Bengals, 27-24 (C) OT
     *Bengals, 28-21 (C)
(Points—Bengals 218, Bills 205)
*AFC Divisional Playoff

BUFFALO vs. CLEVELAND
Browns lead series, 3-2
1972—Browns, 27-10 (C)
1974—Bills, 15-10 (C)
1977—Browns, 27-16 (C)
1978—Browns, 41-20 (C)
1981—Bills, 22-13 (B)
(Points—Browns 118, Bills 83)

BUFFALO vs. DALLAS
Cowboys lead series, 3-0
1971—Cowboys, 49-37 (B)
1976—Cowboys, 17-10 (D)
1981—Cowboys, 27-14 (D)
(Points—Cowboys 93, Bills 61)

BUFFALO vs. DENVER
Bills lead series, 13-8-1
1960—Broncos, 27-21 (B)
     Tie, 38-38 (D)
1961—Broncos, 22-10 (B)
     Bills, 23-10 (D)
1962—Broncos, 23-20 (B)
     Bills, 45-38 (D)
1963—Bills, 30-28 (D)
     Bills, 27-17 (B)
1964—Bills, 30-13 (B)
     Bills, 30-19 (D)
1965—Bills, 30-15 (D)
     Bills, 31-13 (B)
1966—Bills, 38-21 (B)
1967—Bills, 17-16 (D)

Broncos, 21-20 (B)
1968—Broncos, 34-32 (D)
1969—Bills, 41-28 (B)
1970—Broncos, 25-10 (B)
1975—Bills, 38-14 (B)
1977—Broncos, 26-6 (D)
1979—Broncos, 19-16 (B)
1981—Bills, 9-7 (B)
(Points—Bills 562, Broncos 474)

BUFFALO vs. DETROIT
Series tied, 1-1-1
1972—Tie, 21-21 (B)
1976—Lions, 27-14 (D)
1979—Bills, 20-17 (D)
(Points—Lions 65, Bills 55)

BUFFALO vs. GREEN BAY
Bills lead series, 2-0
1974—Bills, 27-7 (GB)
1979—Bills, 19-12 (B)
(Points—Bills 46, Packers 19)

BUFFALO vs. HOUSTON
Oilers lead series, 17-7
1960—Bills, 25-24 (B)
       Oilers, 31-23 (H)
1961—Bills, 22-12 (H)
       Oilers, 28-16 (B)
1962—Oilers, 28-23 (B)
       Oilers, 17-14 (H)
1963—Bills, 31-20 (B)
       Oilers, 28-14 (H)
1964—Bills, 48-17 (H)
       Bills, 24-10 (B)
1965—Oilers, 19-17 (B)
       Bills, 29-18 (H)
1966—Bills, 27-20 (B)
       Bills, 42-20 (H)
1967—Oilers, 20-3 (B)
       Oilers, 10-3 (H)
1968—Oilers, 30-7 (B)
       Oilers, 35-6 (H)
1969—Oilers, 17-3 (B)
       Oilers, 28-14 (H)
1971—Oilers, 20-14 (B)
1974—Oilers, 21-9 (B)
1976—Bills, 13-3 (B)
1978—Oilers, 17-10 (H)
(Points—Oilers 514, Bills 416)

BUFFALO vs. *KANSAS CITY
Bills lead series, 12-11-1
1960—Texans, 45-28 (B)
       Texans, 24-7 (D)
1961—Bills, 27-24 (B)
       Bills, 30-20 (D)
1962—Texans, 41-21 (D)
       Bills, 23-14 (B)
1963—Tie, 27-27 (B)
       Bills, 35-26 (KC)
1964—Bills, 34-17 (B)
       Bills, 35-22 (KC)
1965—Bills, 23-7 (KC)
       Bills, 34-25 (B)
1966—Chiefs, 42-20 (B)
       Bills, 29-14 (KC)

**Chiefs, 31-7 (B)
1967—Chiefs, 23-13 (KC)
1968—Chiefs, 18-7 (B)
1969—Chiefs, 29-7 (B)
       Chiefs, 22-19 (KC)
1971—Chiefs, 22-9 (KC)
1973—Bills, 23-14 (B)
1976—Bills, 50-17 (B)
1978—Bills, 28-13 (B)
       Chiefs, 14-10 (KC)
(Points—Chiefs 551, Bills 546)
*Franchise in Dallas prior to 1963 and known as Texans
**AFL Championship*

BUFFALO vs. LOS ANGELES
Rams lead series, 2-1
1970—Rams, 19-0 (B)
1974—Rams, 19-14 (LA)
1980—Bills, 10-7 (B) OT
(Points—Rams 45, Bills 24)

BUFFALO vs. MIAMI
Dolphins lead series, 25-6-1
1966—Bills, 58-24 (B)
       Bills, 29-0 (M)
1967—Bills, 35-13 (B)
       Dolphins, 17-14 (M)
1968—Tie, 14-14 (M)
       Dolphins, 21-17 (B)
1969—Dolphins, 24-6 (M)
       Bills, 28-3 (B)
1970—Dolphins, 33-14 (B)
       Dolphins, 45-7 (M)
1971—Dolphins, 29-14 (B)
       Dolphins, 34-0 (M)
1972—Dolphins, 24-23 (M)
       Dolphins, 30-16 (B)
1973—Dolphins, 27-6 (M)
       Dolphins, 17-0 (B)
1974—Dolphins, 24-16 (B)
       Dolphins, 35-28 (M)
1975—Dolphins, 35-30 (B)
       Dolphins, 31-21 (M)
1976—Dolphins, 30-21 (B)
       Dolphins, 45-27 (M)
1977—Dolphins, 13-0 (B)
       Dolphins, 31-14 (M)
1978—Dolphins, 31-24 (M)
       Dolphins, 25-24 (B)
1979—Dolphins, 9-7 (B)
       Dolphins, 17-7 (M)
1980—Bills, 17-7 (B)
       Dolphins, 17-14 (M)
1981—Bills, 31-21 (B)
       Dolphins, 16-6 (M)
(Points—Dolphins 742, Bills 568)

BUFFALO vs. MINNESOTA
Vikings lead series, 3-0
1971—Vikings, 19-0 (M)
1975—Vikings, 35-13 (B)
1979—Vikings, 10-3 (M)
(Points—Vikings 64, Bills 16)

BUFFALO vs. *NEW ENGLAND
Bills lead series, 23-21-1

1960—Bills, 13-0 (B)
　　　 Bills, 38-14 (Buff)
1961—Patriots, 23-21 (Buff)
　　　 Patriots, 52-21 (B)
1962—Tie, 28-28 (Buff)
　　　 Patriots, 21-10 (B)
1963—Bills, 28-21 (Buff)
　　　 Patriots, 17-7 (B)
　　　 **Patriots, 26-8 (Buff)
1964—Patriots, 36-28 (Buff)
　　　 Bills, 24-14 (B)
1965—Bills, 24-7 (Buff)
　　　 Bills, 23-7 (B)
1966—Patriots, 20-10 (Buff)
　　　 Patriots, 14-3 (B)
1967—Patriots, 23-0 (Buff)
　　　 Bills, 44-16 (B)
1968—Bills, 16-7 (Buff)
　　　 Patriots, 23-6 (B)
1969—Bills, 23-16 (Buff)
　　　 Patriots, 35-21 (B)
1970—Bills, 45-10 (B)
　　　 Patriots, 14-10 (Buff)
1971—Patriots, 38-33 (NE)
　　　 Bills, 27-20 (Buff)
1972—Bills, 38-14 (Buff)
　　　 Bills, 27-24 (NE)
1973—Bills, 31-13 (NE)
　　　 Bills, 37-13 (Buff)
1974—Bills, 30-28 (Buff)
　　　 Bills, 29-28 (NE)
1975—Bills, 45-31 (Buff)
　　　 Bills, 34-14 (NE)
1976—Patriots, 26-22 (Buff)
　　　 Patriots, 20-10 (NE)
1977—Bills, 24-14 (NE)
　　　 Patriots, 20-7 (Buff)
1978—Patriots, 14-10 (Buff)
　　　 Patriots, 26-24 (NE)
1979—Patriots, 26-6 (Buff)
　　　 Bills, 16-13 (NE) OT
1980—Bills, 31-13 (Buff)
　　　 Patriots, 24-2 (NE)
1981—Bills, 20-17 (Buff)
　　　 Bills, 19-10 (NE)
(Points—Bills 964, Patriots 899)
*Franchise in Boston prior to 1971
**Division Playoff
BUFFALO vs. NEW ORLEANS
Series tied, 1-1
1973—Saints, 13-0 (NO)
1980—Bills, 35-26 (NO)
(Points—Saints 39, Bills 35)
BUFFALO vs. N.Y. GIANTS
Giants lead series, 2-1
1970—Giants, 20-6 (NY)
1975—Giants, 17-14 (B)
1978—Bills, 41-17 (B)
(Points—Bills 61, Giants 54)
BUFFALO vs. *N.Y. JETS
Bills lead series, 25-20
1960—Titans, 27-3 (NY)
　　　 Titans, 17-13 (B)

1961—Bills, 41-31 (B)
　　　 Titans, 21-14 (NY)
1962—Titans, 17-6 (B)
　　　 Bills, 20-3 (NY)
1963—Bills, 45-14 (B)
　　　 Bills, 19-10 (NY)
1964—Bills, 34-24 (B)
　　　 Bills, 20-7 (NY)
1965—Bills, 33-21 (B)
　　　 Jets, 14-12 (NY)
1966—Bills, 33-23 (NY)
　　　 Bills, 14-3 (B)
1967—Bills, 20-17 (B)
　　　 Jets, 20-10 (NY)
1968—Bills, 37-35 (B)
　　　 Jets, 25-21 (NY)
1969—Jets, 33-19 (B)
　　　 Jets, 16-6 (NY)
1970—Bills, 34-31 (B)
　　　 Bills, 10-6 (NY)
1971—Jets, 28-17 (NY)
　　　 Jets, 20-7 (B)
1972—Jets, 41-24 (B)
　　　 Jets, 41-3 (NY)
1973—Bills, 9-7 (B)
　　　 Bills, 34-14 (NY)
1974—Bills, 16-12 (B)
　　　 Jets, 20-10 (NY)
1975—Bills, 42-14 (B)
　　　 Bills, 24-23 (NY)
1976—Jets, 17-14 (NY)
　　　 Jets, 19-14 (B)
1977—Jets, 24-19 (B)
　　　 Bills, 14-10 (NY)
1978—Jets, 21-20 (B)
　　　 Jets, 45-14 (NY)
1979—Bills, 46-31 (B)
　　　 Bills, 14-12 (NY)
1980—Bills, 20-10 (B)
　　　 Bills, 31-24 (NY)
1981—Bills, 31-0 (B)
　　　 Jets, 33-14 (NY)
　　　 **Bills, 31-27 (NY)
(Points—Bills 932, Jets 908)
*Jets known as Titans prior to 1963
**AFC First Round Playoff
BUFFALO vs. OAKLAND
Series tied, 11-11
1960—Bills, 38-9 (B)
　　　 Raiders, 20-7 (O)
1961—Raiders, 31-22 (B)
　　　 Bills, 26-21 (O)
1962—Bills, 14-6 (B)
　　　 Bills, 10-6 (O)
1963—Raiders, 35-17 (O)
　　　 Bills, 12-0 (B)
1964—Bills, 23-20 (B)
　　　 Raiders, 16-13 (O)
1965—Bills, 17-12 (B)
　　　 Bills, 17-14 (O)
1966—Bills, 31-10 (O)
1967—Raiders, 24-20 (B)
　　　 Raiders, 28-21 (O)

1968—Raiders, 48-6 (B)
  Raiders, 13-10 (O)
1969—Raiders, 50-21 (O)
1972—Raiders, 28-16 (O)
1974—Bills, 21-20 (B)
1977—Raiders, 34-13 (O)
1980—Bills, 24-7 (B)
(Points—Raiders 452, Bills 399)

BUFFALO vs. PHILADELPHIA
Series tied, 1-1
1973—Bills, 27-26 (B)
1981—Eagles, 20-14 (B)
(Points—Eagles 46, Bills 41)

BUFFALO vs. PITTSBURGH
Steelers lead series, 5-2
1970—Steelers, 23-10 (P)
1972—Steelers, 38-21 (B)
1974—*Steelers, 32-14 (P)
1975—Bills, 30-21 (P)
1978—Steelers, 28-17 (B)
1979—Steelers, 28-0 (P)
1980—Bills, 28-13 (B)
(Points—Steelers 183, Bills 120)
*AFC Divisional Playoff

BUFFALO vs. ST. LOUIS
Cardinals lead series, 2-1
1971—Cardinals, 28-23 (B)
1975—Bills, 32-14 (StL)
1981—Cardinals, 24-0 (StL)
(Points—Cardinals 66, Bills 55)

BUFFALO vs. *SAN DIEGO
Chargers lead series, 15-9-2
1960—Chargers, 24-10 (B)
  Bills, 32-3 (LA)
1961—Chargers, 19-11 (B)
  Chargers, 28-10 (SD)
1962—Bills, 35-10 (B)
  Bills, 40-20 (SD)
1963—Chargers, 14-10 (SD)
  Chargers, 23-13 (B)
1964—Bills, 30-3 (B)
  Bills, 27-24 (SD)
  **Bills, 20-7 (B)
1965—Chargers, 34-3 (B)
  Tie, 20-20 (SD)
  **Bills, 23-0 (SD)
1966—Chargers, 27-7 (SD)
  Tie, 17-17 (B)
1967—Chargers, 37-17 (B)
1968—Chargers, 21-6 (B)
1969—Chargers, 45-6 (SD)
1971—Chargers, 20-3 (SD)
1973—Chargers, 34-7 (SD)
1976—Chargers, 34-13 (B)
1979—Chargers, 27-19 (SD)
1980—Bills, 26-24 (SD)
  ***Chargers, 20-14 (SD)
1981—Bills, 28-27 (SD)
(Points—Chargers 562, Bills 447)
*Franchise in Los Angeles prior to 1961
**AFL Championship
***AFC Divisional Playoff

BUFFALO vs. SAN FRANCISCO

Bills lead series, 2-0
1972—Bills, 27-20 (B)
1980—Bills, 18-13 (SF)
(Points—Bills 45, 49ers 33)

BUFFALO vs. SEATTLE
Seahawks lead series, 1-0
1977—Seahawks, 56-17 (S)

BUFFALO vs. TAMPA BAY
Series tied, 1-1
1976—Bills, 14-9 (TB)
1978—Buccaneers, 31-10 (TB)
(Points—Buccaneers 40, Bills 24)

BUFFALO vs. WASHINGTON
Bills lead series, 2-1
1972—Bills, 24-17 (W)
1977—Redskins, 10-0 (B)
1981—Bills, 21-14 (B)
(Points—Bills 45, Redskins 41)

CHICAGO vs. ATLANTA
Falcons lead series, 8-4;
See Atlanta vs. Chicago

CHICAGO vs. BALTIMORE
Colts lead series, 20-13;
See Baltimore vs. Chicago

CHICAGO vs. BUFFALO
Bears lead series, 2-1;
See Buffalo vs. Chicago

CHICAGO vs. CINCINNATI
Bengals lead series, 2-0;
1972—Bengals, 13-3 (Chi)
1980—Bengals, 17-14 (Chi) OT
(Points—Bengals 30, Bears 17)

CHICAGO vs. CLEVELAND
Browns lead series, 6-2
1951—Browns, 42-21 (Cle)
1954—Browns, 39-10 (Chi)
1960—Browns, 42-0 (Cle)
1961—Bears, 17-14 (Chi)
1967—Browns, 24-0 (Cle)
1969—Browns, 28-24 (Chi)
1972—Bears, 17-0 (Cle)
1980—Browns, 27-21 (Cle)
(Points—Browns 216, Bears 110)

CHICAGO vs. DALLAS
Cowboys lead series, 7-3
1960—Bears, 17-7 (C)
1962—Bears, 34-33 (D)
1964—Cowboys, 24-10 (C)
1968—Cowboys, 34-3 (C)
1971—Bears, 23-19 (C)
1973—Cowboys, 20-17 (C)
1976—Cowboys, 31-21 (D)
1977—*Cowboys, 37-7 (D)
1979—Cowboys, 24-20 (D)
1981—Cowboys, 10-9 (D)
(Points—Cowboys 239, Bears 161)
*NFC Divisional Playoff

CHICAGO vs. DENVER
Broncos lead series, 3-2
1971—Broncos, 6-3 (D)
1973—Bears, 33-14 (D)
1976—Broncos, 28-14 (C)

1978—Broncos, 16-7 (D)
1981—Bears, 35-24 (C)
(Points—Bears 92, Broncos 88)
CHICAGO vs. *DETROIT
Bears lead series, 59-41-5
1930—Spartans, 7-6 (P)
     Bears, 14-6 (C)
1931—Bears, 9-6 (C)
     Spartans, 3-0 (P)
1932—Tie, 13-13 (C)
     Tie, 7-7 (P)
     **Bears, 9-0 (C)
1933—Bears, 17-14 (C)
     Bears, 17-7 (P)
1934—Bears, 19-16 (D)
     Bears, 10-7 (C)
1935—Tie, 20-20 (C)
     Lions, 14-2 (D)
1936—Bears, 12-10 (C)
     Lions, 13-7 (D)
1937—Bears, 28-20 (C)
     Bears, 13-0 (D)
1938—Lions, 13-7 (C)
     Lions, 14-7 (D)
1939—Lions, 10-0 (C)
     Bears, 23-13 (D)
1940—Bears, 7-0 (C)
     Lions, 17-14 (D)
1941—Bears, 49-0 (C)
     Bears, 24-7 (D)
1942—Bears, 16-0 (C)
     Bears, 42-0 (D)
1943—Bears, 27-21 (D)
     Bears, 35-14 (C)
1944—Tie, 21-21 (C)
     Lions, 41-21 (D)
1945—Lions, 16-10 (C)
     Lions, 35-28 (C)
1946—Bears, 42-6 (C)
     Bears, 45-24 (D)
1947—Bears, 33-24 (C)
     Bears, 34-14 (D)
1948—Bears, 28-0 (C)
     Bears, 42-14 (D)
1949—Bears, 27-24 (C)
     Bears, 28-7 (D)
1950—Bears, 35-21 (D)
     Bears, 6-3 (C)
1951—Bears, 28-23 (D)
     Lions, 41-28 (C)
1952—Bears, 24-23 (C)
     Lions, 45-21 (D)
1953—Lions, 20-16 (C)
     Lions, 13-7 (D)
1954—Lions, 48-23 (D)
     Bears, 28-24 (C)
1955—Bears, 24-14 (C)
     Bears, 21-20 (D)
1956—Lions, 42-10 (D)
     Bears, 38-21 (C)
1957—Bears, 27-7 (D)
     Lions, 21-13 (C)
1958—Bears, 20-7 (D)

Bears, 21-16 (C)
1959—Bears, 24-14 (D)
     Bears, 25-14 (C)
1960—Bears, 28-7 (C)
     Lions, 36-0 (D)
1961—Bears, 31-17 (D)
     Lions, 16-15 (C)
1962—Lions, 11-3 (D)
     Bears, 3-0 (C)
1963—Bears, 37-21 (D)
     Bears, 24-14 (C)
1964—Lions, 10-0 (C)
     Bears, 27-24 (D)
1965—Bears, 38-10 (C)
     Bears, 17-10 (D)
1966—Lions, 14-3 (D)
     Tie, 10-10 (C)
1967—Bears, 14-3 (C)
     Bears, 27-13 (D)
1968—Lions, 42-0 (D)
     Lions, 28-10 (C)
1969—Lions, 13-7 (D)
     Lions, 20-3 (C)
1970—Lions, 28-14 (D)
     Lions, 16-10 (C)
1971—Bears, 28-23 (D)
     Lions, 28-3 (C)
1972—Lions, 38-24 (C)
     Lions, 14-0 (D)
1973—Lions, 30-7 (C)
     Lions, 40-7 (D)
1974—Bears, 17-9 (C)
     Lions, 34-17 (D)
1975—Lions, 27-7 (D)
     Bears, 25-21 (C)
1976—Bears, 10-3 (C)
     Lions, 14-10 (D)
1977—Bears, 30-20 (C)
     Bears, 31-14 (D)
1978—Bears, 19-0 (D)
     Lions, 21-17 (C)
1979—Bears, 35-7 (C)
     Lions, 20-0 (D)
1980—Bears, 24-7 (C)
     Bears, 23-17 (D) OT
1981—Lions, 48-17 (D)
     Lions, 23-7 (C)
(Points—Bears 1,931, Lions 1,756)
*Franchise in Portsmouth prior to 1934
and known as the Spartans
**Championship
CHICAGO vs. GREEN BAY
Bears lead series, 66-53-6
1921—Staleys, 20-0 (C)
1923—Bears, 3-0 (GB)
1924—Bears, 3-0 (C)
1925—Packers, 14-10 (GB)
     Bears, 21-0 (C)
1926—Tie, 6-6 (GB)
     Bears, 19-13 (C)
     Tie, 3-3 (C)
1927—Bears, 7-6 (GB)
     Bears, 14-6 (C)

All-Time Team vs. Team Results

1928—Tie, 12-12 (GB)
Packers, 16-6 (C)
Packers, 6-0 (C)
1929—Packers, 23-0 (GB)
Packers, 14-0 (C)
Packers, 25-0 (C)
1930—Packers, 7-0 (GB)
Packers, 13-12 (C)
Bears, 21-0 (C)
1931—Packers, 7-0 (GB)
Packers, 6-2 (C)
Bears, 7-6 (C)
1932—Tie, 0-0 (GB)
Packers, 2-0 (C)
Bears, 9-0 (C)
1933—Bears, 14-7 (GB)
Bears, 10-7 (C)
Bears, 7-6 (C)
1934—Bears, 24-10 (GB)
Bears, 27-14 (C)
1935—Packers, 7-0 (GB)
Packers, 17-14 (C)
1936—Bears, 30-3 (GB)
Packers, 21-10 (C)
1937—Bears, 14-2 (GB)
Packers, 24-14 (C)
1938—Packers, 2-0 (GB)
Packers, 24-17 (C)
1939—Packers, 21-16 (GB)
Bears, 30-27 (C)
1940—Bears, 41-10 (GB)
Bears, 14-7 (C)
1941—Bears, 25-17 (GB)
Packers, 16-14 (C)
**Bears, 33-14 (C)
1942—Bears, 44-28 (GB)
Bears, 38-7 (C)
1943—Tie, 21-21 (GB)
Bears, 21-7 (C)
1944—Packers, 42-28 (GB)
Bears, 21-0 (C)
1945—Packers, 31-21 (GB)
Bears, 28-24 (C)
1946—Packers, 30-7 (GB)
Bears, 10-7 (C)
1947—Packers, 29-20 (GB)
Bears, 20-17 (C)
1948—Bears, 45-7 (GB)
Bears, 7-6 (C)
1949—Bears, 17-0 (GB)
Bears, 24-3 (C)
1950—Packers, 31-21 (GB)
Bears, 28-14 (C)
1951—Bears, 31-20 (GB)
Bears, 24-13 (C)
1952—Bears, 24-14 (GB)
Packers, 41-28 (C)
1953—Bears, 17-13 (GB)
Tie, 21-21 (C)
1954—Bears, 10-3 (GB)
Bears, 28-23 (C)
1955—Packers, 24-3 (GB)
Bears, 52-31 (C)

1956—Bears, 37-21 (GB)
Bears, 38-14 (C)
1957—Packers, 21-17 (GB)
Bears, 21-14 (C)
1958—Bears, 34-20 (GB)
Bears, 24-10 (C)
1959—Packers, 9-6 (GB)
Bears, 28-17 (C)
1960—Bears, 17-14 (GB)
Packers, 41-13 (C)
1961—Packers, 24-0 (GB)
Packers, 31-28 (C)
1962—Packers, 49-0 (GB)
Packers, 38-7 (C)
1963—Bears, 10-3 (GB)
Bears, 26-7 (C)
1964—Packers, 23-12 (GB)
Packers, 17-3 (C)
1965—Packers, 23-14 (GB)
Bears, 31-10 (C)
1966—Packers, 17-0 (C)
Packers, 13-6 (GB)
1967—Packers, 13-10 (GB)
Packers, 17-13 (C)
1968—Bears, 13-10 (GB)
Packers, 28-27 (C)
1969—Packers, 17-0 (GB)
Packers, 21-3 (C)
1970—Packers, 20-19 (GB)
Bears, 35-17 (C)
1971—Bears, 17-14 (C)
Packers, 31-10 (GB)
1972—Packers, 20-17 (GB)
Packers, 23-17 (C)
1973—Bears, 31-17 (GB)
Packers, 21-0 (C)
1974—Bears, 10-9 (C)
Packers, 20-3 (Mil)
1975—Bears, 27-14 (C)
Packers, 28-7 (GB)
1976—Bears, 24-13 (C)
Bears, 16-10 (GB)
1977—Bears, 26-0 (GB)
Bears, 21-10 (C)
1978—Packers, 24-14 (GB)
Bears, 14-0 (C)
1979—Bears, 6-3 (C)
Bears, 15-14 (GB)
1980—Packers, 12-6 (GB) OT
Bears, 61-7 (C)
1981—Packers, 16-9 (C)
Packers, 27-17 (GB)
(Points—Bears 2,070, Packers 1,832)
*Bears known as Staleys prior to 1922
**Division Playoff
CHICAGO vs. HOUSTON
Oilers lead series, 2-1
1973—Bears, 35-14 (C)
1977—Oilers, 47-0 (H)
1980—Oilers, 10-6 (C)
(Points—Oilers 71, Bears 41)
CHICAGO vs. KANSAS CITY
Bears lead series, 2-1

1973—Chiefs, 19-7 (KC)
1977—Bears, 28-27 (C)
1981—Bears, 16-13 (KC) OT
(Points—Chiefs 59, Bears 51)

CHICAGO vs. *LOS ANGELES
Bears lead series, 41-25-3
1937—Bears, 20-2 (Clev)
    Bears, 15-7 (C)
1938—Rams, 14-7 (C)
    Rams, 23-21 (Clev)
1939—Bears, 30-21 (Clev)
    Bears, 35-21 (C)
1940—Bears, 21-14 (Clev)
    Bears, 47-25 (C)
1941—Bears, 48-21 (Clev)
    Bears, 31-13 (C)
1942—Bears, 21-7 (Clev)
    Bears, 47-0 (C)
1944—Rams, 19-7 (Clev)
    Bears, 28-21 (C)
1945—Rams, 17-0 (Clev)
    Rams, 41-21 (C)
1946—Tie, 28-28 (C)
    Bears, 27-21 (LA)
1947—Bears, 41-21 (LA)
    Rams, 17-14 (C)
1948—Bears, 42-21 (C)
    Bears, 21-6 (LA)
1949—Rams, 31-16 (C)
    Rams, 27-24 (LA)
1950—Bears, 24-20 (LA)
    Bears, 24-14 (C)
    **Rams, 24-14 (LA)
1951—Rams, 42-17 (C)
1952—Rams, 31-7 (LA)
    Rams, 40-24 (C)
1953—Rams, 38-24 (LA)
    Bears, 24-21 (C)
1954—Rams, 42-38 (LA)
    Bears, 24-13 (C)
1955—Rams, 31-20 (LA)
    Bears, 24-3 (C)
1956—Bears, 35-24 (LA)
    Bears, 30-21 (C)
1957—Bears, 34-26 (C)
    Bears, 16-10 (LA)
1958—Bears, 31-10 (C)
    Rams, 41-35 (LA)
1959—Rams, 28-21 (C)
    Bears, 26-21 (LA)
1960—Bears, 34-27 (C)
    Tie, 24-24 (LA)
1961—Bears, 21-17 (LA)
    Bears, 28-24 (C)
1962—Bears, 27-23 (LA)
    Bears, 30-14 (C)
1963—Bears, 52-14 (LA)
    Bears, 6-0 (C)
1964—Bears, 38-17 (C)
    Bears, 34-24 (LA)
1965—Rams, 30-28 (LA)
    Bears, 31-6 (C)
1966—Rams, 31-17 (LA)

    Bears, 17-10 (C)
1967—Rams, 28-17 (C)
1968—Bears, 17-16 (LA)
1969—Rams, 9-7 (C)
1971—Rams, 17-3 (LA)
1972—Tie, 13-13 (C)
1973—Rams, 26-0 (C)
1975—Rams, 38-10 (LA)
1976—Rams, 20-12 (LA)
1977—Bears, 24-23 (C)
1979—Bears, 27-23 (C)
1981—Rams, 24-7 (C)
(Points—Bears 1,639, Rams 1,425)
*Franchise in Cleveland prior to 1946
**Conference Playoff

CHICAGO vs. MIAMI
Dolphins lead series, 3-0
1971—Dolphins, 34-3 (M)
1975—Dolphins, 46-13 (C)
1979—Dolphins, 31-16 (M)
(Points—Dolphins 111, Bears 32)

CHICAGO vs. MINNESOTA
Vikings lead series, 23-17-2
1961—Vikings, 37-13 (M)
    Bears, 52-35 (C)
1962—Bears, 13-0 (M)
    Bears, 31-30 (C)
1963—Bears, 28-7 (M)
    Tie, 17-17 (C)
1964—Bears, 34-28 (M)
    Vikings, 41-14 (C)
1965—Bears, 45-37 (M)
    Vikings, 24-17 (C)
1966—Bears, 13-10 (M)
    Bears, 41-28 (C)
1967—Bears, 17-7 (M)
    Tie, 10-10 (C)
1968—Bears, 27-17 (M)
    Bears, 26-24 (C)
1969—Vikings, 31-0 (C)
    Vikings, 31-14 (M)
1970—Vikings, 24-0 (C)
    Vikings, 16-13 (M)
1971—Bears, 20-17 (M)
    Vikings, 27-10 (C)
1972—Bears, 13-10 (C)
    Vikings, 23-10 (M)
1973—Vikings, 22-13 (C)
    Vikings, 31-13 (M)
1974—Vikings, 11-7 (M)
    Vikings, 17-0 (C)
1975—Vikings, 28-3 (M)
    Vikings, 13-9 (C)
1976—Vikings, 20-19 (M)
    Bears, 14-13 (C)
1977—Vikings, 22-16 (M) OT
    Bears, 10-7 (C)
1978—Vikings, 24-20 (C)
    Vikings, 17-14 (M)
1979—Bears, 26-7 (C)
    Vikings, 30-27 (M)
1980—Vikings, 34-14 (C)
    Vikings, 13-7 (M)

1981—Vikings, 24-21 (M)
   Bears, 10-9 (C)
(Points—Vikings 873, Bears 721)

CHICAGO vs. NEW ENGLAND
Patriots lead series, 2-0
1973—Patriots, 13-10 (C)
1979—Patriots, 27-7 (C)
(Points—Patriots 40, Bears 17)

CHICAGO vs. NEW ORLEANS
Bears lead series, 6-2
1968—Bears, 23-17 (NO)
1970—Bears, 24-3 (NO)
1971—Bears, 35-14 (C)
1973—Saints, 21-16 (NO)
1974—Bears, 24-10 (C)
1975—Bears, 42-17 (NO)
1977—Saints, 42-24 (C)
1980—Bears, 22-3 (C)
(Points—Bears 210, Saints 127)

CHICAGO vs. N.Y. GIANTS
Bears lead series, 26-16-2
1925—Bears, 19-7 (NY)
   Giants, 9-0 (C)
1926—Bears, 7-0 (C)
1927—Giants, 13-7 (NY)
1928—Bears, 13-0 (C)
1929—Giants, 26-14 (C)
   Giants, 34-0 (NY)
   Giants, 14-9 (NY)
1930—Giants, 12-0 (C)
   Bears, 12-0 (NY)
1931—Bears, 6-0 (C)
   Bears, 12-6 (NY)
   Giants, 25-6 (C)
1932—Bears, 28-8 (NY)
   Bears, 6-0 (C)
1933—Bears, 14-10 (C)
   Giants, 3-0 (NY)
   *Bears, 23-21 (C)
1934—Bears, 27-7 (C)
   Bears, 10-9 (NY)
   *Giants, 30-13 (NY)
1935—Bears, 20-3 (NY)
   Giants, 3-0 (C)
1936—Bears, 25-7 (NY)
1937—Tie, 3-3 (NY)
1939—Giants, 16-13 (NY)
1940—Bears, 37-21 (NY)
1941—*Bears, 37-9 (C)
1942—Bears, 26-7 (NY)
1943—Bears, 56-7 (NY)
1946—Giants, 14-0 (NY)
   *Bears, 24-14 (NY)
1948—Bears, 35-14 (C)
1949—Bears, 35-28 (NY)
1956—Tie, 17-17 (NY)
   *Giants, 47-7 (NY)
1962—Giants, 26-24 (C)
1963—*Bears, 14-10 (C)
1965—Bears, 35-14 (NY)
1967—Bears, 34-7 (C)
1969—Giants, 28-24 (NY)
1970—Bears, 24-16 (NY)

1974—Bears, 16-13 (C)
1977—Bears, 12-9 (NY) OT
(Points—Bears 737, Giants 574)
*NFL Championship

CHICAGO vs. N.Y. JETS
Series tied, 1-1
1974—Jets, 23-21 (C)
1979—Bears, 23-13 (C)
(Points—Bears 44, Jets 36)

CHICAGO vs. OAKLAND
Raiders lead series, 3-1
1972—Raiders, 28-21 (O)
1976—Raiders, 28-27 (C)
1978—Raiders, 25-19 (C) OT
1981—Bears, 23-6 (O)
(Points—Bears 90, Raiders 87)

CHICAGO vs. PHILADELPHIA
Bears lead series, 17-4-1
1933—Tie, 3-3 (P)
1935—Bears, 39-0 (P)
1936—Bears, 17-0 (P)
   Bears, 28-7 (P)
1938—Bears, 28-6 (P)
1939—Bears, 27-14 (C)
1941—Bears, 49-14 (P)
1942—Bears, 45-14 (C)
1944—Bears, 28-7 (P)
1946—Bears, 21-14 (C)
1947—Bears, 40-7 (C)
1948—Eagles, 12-7 (P)
1949—Bears, 38-21 (C)
1955—Bears, 17-10 (C)
1961—Eagles, 16-14 (P)
1963—Bears, 16-7 (C)
1968—Bears, 29-16 (P)
1970—Bears, 20-16 (C)
1972—Bears, 21-12 (P)
1975—Bears, 15-13 (C)
1979—*Eagles, 27-17 (P)
1980—Eagles, 17-14 (P)
(Points—Bears 533, Eagles 253)
*NFC First Round Playoff

CHICAGO vs. *PITTSBURGH
Bears lead series, 13-4-1
1934—Bears, 28-0 (P)
1935—Bears, 23-7 (P)
1936—Bears, 27-9 (P)
   Bears, 26-6 (C)
1937—Bears, 7-0 (P)
1939—Bears, 32-0 (P)
1941—Bears, 34-7 (C)
1945—Bears, 28-7 (P)
1947—Bears, 49-7 (C)
1949—Bears, 30-21 (C)
1958—Steelers, 24-10 (P)
1959—Bears, 27-21 (C)
1963—Tie, 17-17 (P)
1967—Steelers, 41-13 (P)
1969—Bears, 38-7 (C)
1971—Bears, 17-15 (C)
1975—Steelers, 34-3 (P)
1980—Steelers, 38-3 (P)
(Points—Bears 412, Steelers 261)

*CHICAGO vs. **ST. LOUIS
Bears lead series, 50-23-6
(NP denotes Normal Park;
Wr denotes Wrigley Field;
Co denotes Comiskey Park;
So denotes Soldier Field;
all Chicago)

1920—Cardinals, 7-6 (NP)
      Staleys, 10-0 (Wr)
1921—Tie, 0-0 (Wr)
1922—Cardinals, 6-0 (Co)
      Cardinals, 9-0 (Co)
1923—Bears, 3-0 (Wr)
1924—Bears, 6-0 (Wr)
      Bears, 21-0 (Co)
1925—Cardinals, 9-0 (Co)
      Tie, 0-0 (Wr)
1926—Bears, 16-0 (Wr)
      Bears, 10-0 (So)
      Tie, 0-0 (Wr)
1927—Bears, 9-0 (NP)
      Cardinals, 3-0 (Wr)
1928—Bears, 15-0 (NP)
      Bears, 34-0 (Wr)
1929—Tie, 0-0 (Wr)
      Cardinals, 40-6 (Co)
1930—Bears, 32-6 (Co)
      Bears, 6-0 (Wr)
1931—Bears, 26-13 (Wr)
      Bears, 18-7 (Wr)
1932—Tie, 0-0 (Wr)
      Bears, 34-0 (Wr)
1933—Bears, 12-9 (Wr)
      Bears, 22-6 (Wr)
1934—Bears, 20-0 (Wr)
      Bears, 17-6 (Wr)
1935—Tie, 7-7 (Wr)
      Bears, 13-0 (Wr)
1936—Bears, 7-3 (Wr)
      Cardinals, 14-7 (Wr)
1937—Bears, 16-7 (Wr)
      Bears, 42-28 (Wr)
1938—Bears, 16-13 (So)
      Bears, 34-28 (Wr)
1939—Bears, 44-7 (Wr)
      Bears, 48-7 (Co)
1940—Cardinals, 21-7 (Co)
      Bears, 31-23 (Wr)
1941—Bears, 53-7 (Wr)
      Bears, 34-24 (Co)
1942—Bears, 41-14 (Wr)
      Bears, 21-7 (Co)
1943—Bears, 20-0 (Wr)
      Bears, 35-24 (Co)
1945—Cardinals, 16-7 (Wr)
      Bears, 28-20 (Co)
1946—Bears, 34-17 (Co)
      Cardinals, 35-28 (Wr)
1947—Cardinals, 31-7 (Co)
      Cardinals, 30-21 (Wr)
1948—Bears, 28-17 (Co)
      Cardinals, 24-21 (Wr)

1949—Bears, 17-7 (Co)
      Bears, 52-21 (Wr)
1950—Bears, 27-6 (Wr)
      Cardinals, 20-10 (Co)
1951—Cardinals, 28-14 (Co)
      Cardinals, 24-14 (Wr)
1952—Cardinals, 21-10 (Co)
      Bears, 10-7 (Wr)
1953—Cardinals, 24-17 (Wr)
1954—Bears, 29-7 (Co)
1955—Cardinals, 53-14 (Co)
1956—Bears, 10-3 (Wr)
1957—Bears, 14-6 (Co)
1958—Bears, 30-14 (Wr)
1959—Bears, 31-7 (So)
1965—Bears, 34-13 (Wr)
1966—Cardinals, 24-17 (StL)
1967—Bears, 30-3 (Wr)
1969—Cardinals, 20-17 (StL)
1972—Bears, 27-10 (StL)
1975—Cardinals, 34-20 (So)
1977—Cardinals, 16-13 (StL)
1978—Bears, 17-10 (So)
1979—Bears, 42-6 (So)
(Points—Bears 1,489, Cardinals 929)
*Franchise in Decatur prior to 1921; Bears
known as Staleys prior to 1922
**Franchise in Chicago prior to 1960*

CHICAGO vs. SAN DIEGO
Chargers lead series, 3-1
1970—Chargers, 20-7 (C)
1974—Chargers, 28-21 (SD)
1978—Chargers, 40-7 (SD)
1981—Bears, 20-17 (C) OT
(Points—Chargers 105, Bears 55)

CHICAGO vs. SAN FRANCISCO
Series tied, 22-22-1
1950—Bears, 32-20 (SF)
      Bears, 17-0 (C)
1951—Bears, 13-7 (C)
1952—49ers, 40-16 (C)
      Bears, 20-17 (SF)
1953—49ers, 35-28 (C)
      49ers, 24-14 (SF)
1954—49ers, 31-24 (C)
      Bears, 31-27 (SF)
1955—49ers, 20-19 (C)
      Bears, 34-23 (SF)
1956—Bears, 31-7 (C)
      Bears, 38-21 (SF)
1957—49ers, 21-17 (C)
      49ers, 21-17 (SF)
1958—Bears, 28-6 (C)
      Bears, 27-14 (SF)
1959—49ers, 20-17 (SF)
      Bears, 14-3 (C)
1960—Bears, 27-10 (C)
      49ers, 25-7 (SF)
1961—Bears, 31-0 (C)
      49ers, 41-31 (SF)
1962—Bears, 30-14 (SF)
      49ers, 34-27 (C)
1963—49ers, 20-14 (SF)

All-Time Team vs. Team Results

Bears, 27-7 (C)
1964—49ers, 31-21 (SF)
Bears, 23-21 (C)
1965—49ers, 52-24 (SF)
Bears, 61-20 (C)
1966—Tie, 30-30 (C)
49ers, 41-14 (SF)
1967—Bears, 28-14 (SF)
1968—Bears, 27-19 (C)
1969—49ers, 42-21 (SF)
1970—49ers, 37-16 (C)
1971—49ers, 13-0 (SF)
1972—49ers, 34-21 (C)
1974—49ers, 34-0 (C)
1975—49ers, 31-3 (SF)
1976—Bears, 19-12 (SF)
1978—Bears, 16-13 (SF)
1979—Bears, 28-27 (SF)
1981—Bears, 28-17 (SF)
(Points—49ers 1,007, Bears 1,000)

CHICAGO vs. SEATTLE
Series tied, 1-1
1976—Bears, 34-7 (S)
1978—Seahawks, 31-29 (C)
(Points—Bears 63, Seahawks 38)

CHICAGO vs. TAMPA BAY
Bears lead series, 6-3
1977—Bears, 10-0 (TB)
1978—Buccaneers, 33-19 (TB)
Bears, 14-3 (C)
1979—Buccaneers, 17-13 (TB)
Bears, 14-0 (TB)
1980—Bears, 23-0 (C)
Bears, 14-13 (TB)
1981—Bears, 28-17 (C)
Buccaneers, 20-10 (TB)
(Points—Bears 145, Buccaneers 103)

CHICAGO vs. *WASHINGTON
Bears lead series, 18-11-1
1932—Tie, 7-7 (B)
1933—Bears, 7-0 (C)
Redskins, 10-0 (B)
1934—Bears, 21-0 (B)
1935—Bears, 30-14 (B)
1936—Bears, 26-0 (B)
1937—**Redskins, 28-21 (C)
1938—Bears, 31-7 (C)
1940—Redskins, 7-3 (W)
**Bears, 73-0 (W)
1941—Bears, 35-21 (C)
1942—**Redskins, 14-6 (W)
1943—Redskins, 21-7 (W)
**Bears, 41-21 (C)
1945—Redskins, 28-21 (W)
1946—Bears, 24-20 (C)
1947—Bears, 56-20 (W)
1948—Bears, 48-13 (C)
1949—Bears, 31-21 (W)
1951—Bears, 27-0 (W)
1953—Bears, 27-24 (W)
1957—Redskins, 14-3 (C)
1964—Redskins, 27-20 (W)
1968—Redskins, 38-28 (C)

1971—Bears, 16-15 (C)
1974—Redskins, 42-0 (W)
1976—Bears, 33-7 (C)
1978—Bears, 14-10 (W)
1980—Bears, 35-21 (C)
1981—Redskins, 24-7 (C)
(Points—Bears 698, Redskins 474)
*Franchise in Boston prior to 1937 and
known as Braves prior to 1933
**NFL Championship

CINCINNATI vs. ATLANTA
Bengals lead series, 3-1;
See Atlanta vs. Cincinnati
CINCINNATI vs. BALTIMORE
Colts lead series, 4-3;
See Baltimore vs. Cincinnati
CINCINNATI vs. BUFFALO
Bengals lead series, 6-4;
See Buffalo vs. Cincinnati
CINCINNATI vs. CHICAGO
Bengals lead series, 2-0;
See Chicago vs. Cincinnati
CINCINNATI vs. CLEVELAND
Browns lead series, 13-11
1970—Browns, 30-27 (Cle)
Bengals, 14-10 (Cin)
1971—Browns, 27-24 (Cin)
Browns, 31-27 (Cle)
1972—Browns, 27-6 (Cle)
Browns, 27-24 (Cin)
1973—Browns, 17-10 (Cle)
Bengals, 34-17 (Cin)
1974—Bengals, 33-7 (Cin)
Bengals, 34-24 (Cle)
1975—Bengals, 24-17 (Cin)
Browns, 35-23 (Cle)
1976—Bengals, 45-24 (Cle)
Bengals, 21-6 (Cin)
1977—Browns, 13-3 (Cin)
Bengals, 10-7 (Cle)
1978—Browns, 13-10 (Cle) OT
Bengals, 48-16 (Cin)
1979—Browns, 28-27 (Cle)
Bengals, 16-12 (Cin)
1980—Browns, 31-7 (Cle)
Browns, 27-24 (Cin)
1981—Browns, 20-17 (Cin)
Bengals, 41-21 (Cle)
(Points—Bengals 549, Browns 487)
CINCINNATI vs. DALLAS
Cowboys lead series, 2-0
1973—Cowboys, 38-10 (D)
1979—Cowboys, 38-13 (D)
(Points—Cowboys 76, Bengals 23)
CINCINNATI vs. DENVER
Series tied, 6-6
1968—Bengals, 24-10 (C)
Broncos, 10-7 (D)
1969—Broncos, 30-23 (C)
Broncos, 27-16 (D)
1971—Bengals, 24-10 (D)
1972—Bengals, 21-10 (C)

1973—Broncos, 28-10 (D)
1975—Bengals, 17-16 (D)
1976—Bengals, 17-7 (C)
1977—Broncos, 24-13 (C)
1979—Broncos, 10-0 (D)
1981—Bengals, 38-21 (C)
(Points—Bengals 210, Broncos 203)

CINCINNATI vs. DETROIT
Lions lead series, 2-0
1970—Lions, 38-3 (D)
1974—Lions, 23-19 (C)
(Points—Lions 61, Bengals 22)

CINCINNATI vs. GREEN BAY
Series tied, 2-2
1971—Packers, 20-17 (GB)
1976—Bengals, 28-7 (C)
1977—Bengals, 17-7 (Mil)
1980—Bengals, 14-9 (GB)
(Points—Bengals 71, Packers 48)

CINCINNATI vs. HOUSTON
Bengals lead series, 13-12-1
1968—Oilers, 27-17 (C)
1969—Tie, 31-31 (H)
1970—Oilers, 20-13 (C)
　　　Bengals, 30-20 (H)
1971—Oilers, 10-6 (H)
　　　Bengals, 28-13 (C)
1972—Bengals, 30-7 (C)
　　　Bengals, 61-17 (H)
1973—Bengals, 24-10 (C)
　　　Bengals, 27-24 (H)
1974—Oilers, 34-21 (C)
　　　Oilers, 20-3 (H)
1975—Bengals, 21-19 (H)
　　　Bengals, 23-19 (C)
1976—Bengals, 27-7 (H)
　　　Bengals, 31-27 (C)
1977—Bengals, 13-10 (C) OT
　　　Oilers, 21-16 (H)
1978—Bengals, 28-13 (C)
　　　Oilers, 17-10 (H)
1979—Oilers, 30-27 (C) OT
　　　Oilers, 42-21 (H)
1980—Oilers, 13-10 (C)
　　　Oilers, 23-3 (H)
1981—Oilers, 17-10 (H)
　　　Bengals, 34-21 (C)
(Points—Bengals 565, Oilers 512)

CINCINNATI vs. KANSAS CITY
Bengals lead series, 7-6
1968—Chiefs, 13-3 (KC)
　　　Chiefs, 16-9 (C)
1969—Bengals, 24-19 (C)
　　　Chiefs, 42-22 (KC)
1970—Chiefs, 27-19 (C)
1972—Bengals, 23-16 (KC)
1973—Bengals, 14-6 (C)
1974—Bengals, 33-6 (C)
1976—Bengals, 27-24 (KC)
1977—Bengals, 27-7 (KC)
1978—Chiefs, 24-23 (C)
1979—Chiefs, 10-7 (C)
1980—Bengals, 20-6 (KC)

(Points—Bengals 251, Chiefs 216)

CINCINNATI vs. LOS ANGELES
Bengals lead series, 3-1
1972—Rams, 15-12 (LA)
1976—Bengals, 20-12 (C)
1978—Bengals, 20-19 (LA)
1981—Bengals, 24-10 (C)
(Points—Bengals 76, Rams 56)

CINCINNATI vs. MIAMI
Dolphins lead series, 6-3
1968—Dolphins, 24-22 (C)
　　　Bengals, 38-21 (M)
1969—Bengals, 27-21 (C)
1971—Bengals, 23-13 (C)
1973—*Dolphins, 34-16 (M)
1974—Dolphins, 24-3 (M)
1977—Bengals, 23-17 (C)
1978—Dolphins, 21-0 (M)
1980—Dolphins, 17-16 (M)
(Points—Dolphins 202, Bengals 158)
*AFC Divisional Playoff

CINCINNATI vs. MINNESOTA
Bengals lead series, 2-1
1973—Bengals, 27-0 (C)
1977—Vikings, 42-10 (M)
1980—Bengals, 14-0 (C)
(Points—Bengals 51, Vikings 42)

CINCINNATI vs. *NEW ENGLAND
Patriots lead series, 4-3
1968—Patriots, 33-14 (B)
1969—Patriots, 25-14 (C)
1970—Bengals, 45-7 (C)
1972—Bengals, 31-7 (NE)
1975—Bengals, 27-10 (C)
1978—Patriots, 10-3 (C)
1979—Patriots, 20-14 (C)
(Points—Bengals 148, Patriots 112)
*Franchise in Boston prior to 1971

CINCINNATI vs. NEW ORLEANS
Series tied, 2-2
1970—Bengals, 26-6 (C)
1975—Bengals, 21-0 (NO)
1978—Saints, 20-18 (C)
1981—Saints, 17-7 (NO)
(Points—Bengals 72, Saints 43)

CINCINNATI vs. N. Y. GIANTS
Bengals lead series, 2-0
1972—Bengals, 13-10 (C)
1977—Bengals, 30-13 (C)
(Points—Bengals 43, Giants 23)

CINCINNATI vs. N. Y. JETS
Jets lead series, 4-3
1968—Jets, 27-14 (NY)
1969—Jets, 21-7 (C)
　　　Jets, 40-7 (NY)
1971—Jets, 35-21 (NY)
1973—Bengals, 20-14 (C)
1976—Bengals, 42-3 (NY)
1981—Jets, 31-30 (NY)
(Points—Jets 170, Bengals 142)

CINCINNATI vs. OAKLAND
Raiders lead series, 10-3
1968—Raiders, 31-10 (O)

All-Time Team vs. Team Results

Raiders, 34-0 (C)
1969—Bengals, 31-17 (C)
Raiders, 37-17 (O)
1970—Bengals, 31-21 (C)
1971—Raiders, 31-27 (O)
1972—Raiders, 20-14 (C)
1974—Raiders, 30-27 (O)
1975—Bengals, 14-10 (C)
*Raiders, 31-28 (O)
1976—Raiders, 35-20 (C)
1978—Raiders, 34-21 (C)
1980—Raiders, 28-17 (O)
(Points—Raiders 359, Bengals 257)
*AFC Divisional Playoff

CINCINNATI vs. PHILADELPHIA
Bengals lead series, 3-0
1971—Bengals, 37-14 (C)
1975—Bengals, 31-0 (C)
1979—Bengals, 37-13 (C)
(Points—Bengals 105, Eagles 27)

CINCINNATI vs. PITTSBURGH
Steelers lead series, 14-10
1970—Steelers, 21-10 (P)
Bengals, 34-7 (C)
1971—Steelers, 21-10 (P)
Steelers, 21-13 (C)
1972—Bengals, 15-10 (C)
Steelers, 40-17 (P)
1973—Bengals, 19-7 (C)
Steelers, 20-13 (P)
1974—Bengals, 17-10 (C)
Steelers, 27-3 (P)
1975—Steelers, 30-24 (C)
Steelers, 35-14 (P)
1976—Steelers, 23-6 (P)
Steelers, 7-3 (C)
1977—Steelers, 20-14 (P)
Bengals, 17-10 (C)
1978—Bengals, 28-3 (C)
Steelers, 7-6 (P)
1979—Bengals, 34-10 (C)
Steelers, 37-17 (P)
1980—Bengals, 30-28 (C)
Bengals, 17-16 (P)
1981—Bengals, 34-7 (C)
Bengals, 17-10 (P)
(Points—Steelers 452, Bengals 387)

CINCINNATI vs. ST. LOUIS
Bengals lead series, 2-0
1973—Bengals, 42-24 (C)
1979—Bengals, 34-28 (C)
(Points—Bengals 76, Cardinals 52)

CINCINNATI vs. SAN DIEGO
Chargers lead series, 8-7
1968—Chargers, 29-13 (SD)
Chargers, 31-10 (C)
1969—Bengals, 34-20 (C)
Chargers, 21-14 (SD)
1970—Bengals, 17-14 (SD)
1971—Bengals, 31-0 (C)
1973—Bengals, 20-13 (SD)
1974—Chargers, 20-17 (C)
1975—Bengals, 47-17 (C)

1977—Chargers, 24-3 (SD)
1978—Chargers, 22-13 (SD)
1979—Chargers, 26-24 (C)
1980—Chargers, 31-14 (C)
1981—Bengals, 40-17 (SD)
*Bengals, 27-7 (C)
(Points—Bengals 324, Chargers 292)
*AFC Championship

CINCINNATI vs. SAN FRANCISCO
49ers lead series, 3-1
1974—Bengals, 21-3 (SF)
1978—49ers, 28-12 (SF)
1981—49ers, 21-3 (C)
*49ers, 26-21 (Detroit)
(Points—49ers 78, Bengals 57)
*Super Bowl XVI

CINCINNATI vs. SEATTLE
Bengals lead series, 2-0
1977—Bengals, 42-20 (C)
1981—Bengals, 27-21 (C)
(Points—Bengals 69, Seahawks 41)

CINCINNATI vs. TAMPA BAY
Series tied, 1-1
1976—Bengals, 21-0 (C)
1980—Buccaneers, 17-12 (C)
(Points—Bengals 33, Buccaneers 17)

CINCINNATI vs. WASHINGTON
Redskins lead series, 2-1
1970—Redskins, 20-0 (W)
1974—Bengals, 28-17 (C)
1979—Redskins, 28-14 (W)
(Points—Redskins 65, Bengals 42)

CLEVELAND vs. ATLANTA
Browns lead series, 5-1;
See Atlanta vs. Cleveland

CLEVELAND vs. BALTIMORE
Browns lead series, 9-5;
See Baltimore vs. Cleveland

CLEVELAND vs. BUFFALO
Browns lead series, 3-2;
See Buffalo vs. Cleveland

CLEVELAND vs. CHICAGO
Browns lead series, 6-2;
See Chicago vs. Cleveland

CLEVELAND vs. CINCINNATI
Browns lead series, 13-11;
See Cincinnati vs. Cleveland

CLEVELAND vs. DALLAS
Browns lead series, 15-7
1960—Browns, 48-7 (D)
1961—Browns, 25-7 (C)
Browns, 38-17 (D)
1962—Browns, 19-10 (C)
Cowboys, 45-21 (D)
1963—Browns, 41-24 (D)
Browns, 27-17 (C)
1964—Browns, 27-6 (C)
Browns, 20-16 (D)
1965—Browns, 23-17 (C)
Browns, 24-17 (D)
1966—Browns, 30-21 (C)
Cowboys, 26-14 (D)

172

1967—Cowboys, 21-14 (C)
  *Cowboys, 52-14 (D)
1968—Cowboys, 28-7 (C)
  *Browns, 31-20 (C)
1969—Browns, 42-10 (C)
  *Browns, 38-14 (D)
1970—Cowboys, 6-2 (C)
1974—Cowboys, 41-17 (D)
1979—Browns, 26-7 (C)
(Points—Browns 548, Cowboys 429)
*Conference Championship

CLEVELAND vs. DENVER
Broncos lead series, 6-3
1970—Browns, 27-13 (D)
1971—Broncos, 27-0 (C)
1972—Browns, 27-20 (D)
1974—Browns, 23-21 (C)
1975—Broncos, 16-15 (D)
1976—Broncos, 44-13 (D)
1978—Broncos, 19-7 (C)
1980—Broncos, 19-16 (C)
1981—Broncos, 23-20 (D) OT
(Points—Broncos 202, Browns 148)

CLEVELAND vs. DETROIT
Lions lead series, 12-2
1952—Lions, 17-6 (D)
  *Lions, 17-7 (C)
1953—*Lions, 17-16 (D)
1954—Lions, 14-10 (C)
  *Browns, 56-10 (C)
1957—Lions, 20-7 (D)
  *Lions, 59-14 (D)
1958—Lions, 30-10 (C)
1963—Lions, 38-10 (D)
1964—Browns, 37-21 (C)
1967—Lions, 31-14 (D)
1969—Lions, 28-21 (D)
1970—Lions, 41-24 (C)
1975—Lions, 21-10 (D)
(Points—Lions 364, Browns 242)
*NFL Championship

CLEVELAND vs. GREEN BAY
Packers lead series, 6-5
1953—Browns, 27-0 (Mil)
1955—Browns, 41-10 (C)
1956—Browns, 24-7 (Mil)
1961—Packers, 49-17 (C)
1964—Packers, 28-21 (Mil)
1965—*Packers, 23-12 (GB)
1966—Packers, 21-20 (C)
1967—Packers, 55-7 (Mil)
1969—Browns, 20-7 (C)
1972—Packers, 26-10 (C)
1980—Browns, 26-21 (C)
(Points—Packers 247, Browns 225)
*NFL Championship

CLEVELAND vs. HOUSTON
Browns lead series, 14-10
1970—Browns, 28-14 (C)
  Browns, 21-10 (H)
1971—Browns, 31-0 (C)
  Browns, 37-24 (H)
1972—Browns, 23-17 (H)

  Browns, 20-0 (C)
1973—Browns, 42-13 (C)
  Browns, 23-13 (H)
1974—Browns, 20-7 (C)
  Oilers, 28-24 (H)
1975—Oilers, 40-10 (C)
  Oilers, 21-10 (H)
1976—Browns, 21-7 (H)
  Browns, 13-10 (C)
1977—Browns, 24-23 (H)
  Oilers, 19-15 (C)
1978—Oilers, 16-13 (C)
  Oilers, 14-10 (H)
1979—Oilers, 31-10 (H)
  Browns, 14-7 (C)
1980—Oilers, 16-7 (C)
  Browns, 17-14 (H)
1981—Oilers, 9-3 (C)
  Oilers, 17-13 (H)
(Points—Browns 449, Oilers 370)

CLEVELAND vs. KANSAS CITY
Series tied, 4-4-1
1971—Chiefs, 13-7 (KC)
1972—Chiefs, 31-7 (C)
1973—Tie, 20-20 (KC)
1975—Browns, 40-14 (C)
1976—Chiefs, 39-14 (KC)
1977—Browns, 44-7 (C)
1978—Chiefs, 17-3 (KC)
1979—Browns, 27-24 (KC)
1980—Browns, 20-13 (C)
(Points—Browns 182, Chiefs 178)

CLEVELAND vs. LOS ANGELES
Browns lead series, 8-6
1950—*Browns, 30-28 (C)
1951—Browns, 38-23 (LA)
  *Rams, 24-17 (LA)
1952—Browns, 37-7 (C)
1955—*Browns, 38-14 (LA)
1957—Browns, 45-31 (C)
1958—Browns, 30-27 (LA)
1963—Browns, 20-6 (C)
1965—Rams, 42-7 (LA)
1968—Rams, 24-6 (C)
1973—Rams, 30-17 (LA)
1977—Rams, 9-0 (C)
1978—Browns, 30-19 (C)
1981—Rams, 27-16 (LA)
(Points—Browns 331, Rams 311)
*NFL Championship

CLEVELAND vs. MIAMI
Browns lead series, 3-2
1970—Browns, 28-0 (M)
1972—*Dolphins, 20-14 (M)
1973—Dolphins, 17-9 (C)
1976—Browns, 17-13 (C)
1979—Browns, 30-24 (C) OT
(Points—Browns 98, Dolphins 74)
*AFC Divisional Playoff

CLEVELAND vs. MINNESOTA
Vikings lead series, 6-1
1965—Vikings, 27-17 (C)
1967—Browns, 14-10 (C)

1969—Vikings, 51-3 (M)
   *Vikings, 27-7 (M)
1973—Vikings, 26-3 (M)
1975—Vikings, 42-10 (C)
1980—Vikings, 28-23 (M)
(Points—Vikings 211, Browns 77)
*NFL Championship

CLEVELAND vs. NEW ENGLAND
Browns lead series, 3-1
1971—Browns, 27-7 (C)
1974—Browns, 21-14 (NE)
1977—Browns, 30-27 (C) OT
1980—Patriots, 34-17 (NE)
(Points—Browns 95, Patriots 82)

CLEVELAND vs. NEW ORLEANS
Browns lead series, 8-0
1967—Browns, 42-7 (NO)
1968—Browns, 24-10 (NO)
   Browns, 35-17 (C)
1969—Browns, 27-17 (NO)
1971—Browns, 21-17 (NO)
1975—Browns, 17-16 (C)
1978—Browns, 24-16 (NO)
1981—Browns, 20-17 (C)
(Points—Browns 210, Saints 117)

CLEVELAND vs. N. Y. GIANTS
Browns lead series, 25-16-2
1950—Giants, 6-0 (C)
   Giants, 17-13 (NY)
   *Browns, 8-3 (C)
1951—Browns, 14-13 (C)
   Browns, 10-0 (NY)
1952—Giants, 17-9 (C)
   Giants, 37-34 (NY)
1953—Browns, 7-0 (NY)
   Browns, 62-14 (C)
1954—Browns, 24-14 (C)
   Browns, 16-7 (NY)
1955—Browns, 24-14 (C)
   Tie, 35-35 (NY)
1956—Giants, 21-9 (C)
   Browns, 24-7 (NY)
1957—Browns, 6-3 (C)
   Browns, 34-28 (NY)
1958—Giants, 21-17 (C)
   Giants, 13-10 (NY)
   *Giants, 10-0 (NY)
1959—Giants, 10-6 (C)
   Giants, 48-7 (NY)
1960—Giants, 17-13 (C)
   Browns, 48-34 (NY)
1961—Giants, 37-21 (C)
   Tie, 7-7 (NY)
1962—Browns, 17-7 (C)
   Giants, 17-13 (NY)
1963—Browns, 35-24 (NY)
   Giants, 33-6 (C)
1964—Browns, 42-20 (C)
   Browns, 52-20 (NY)
1965—Browns, 38-14 (NY)
   Browns, 34-21 (C)
1966—Browns, 28-7 (NY)
   Browns, 49-40 (C)

1967—Giants, 38-34 (NY)
   Browns, 24-14 (C)
1968—Browns, 45-10 (C)
1969—Browns, 28-17 (C)
   Giants, 27-14 (NY)
1973—Browns, 12-10 (C)
1977—Browns, 21-7 (NY)
(Points—Browns 950, Giants 759)
*Conference Playoff

CLEVELAND vs. N. Y. JETS
Browns lead series, 6-1
1970—Browns, 31-21 (C)
1972—Browns, 26-10 (NY)
1976—Browns, 38-17 (C)
1978—Browns, 37-34 (C) OT
1979—Browns, 25-22 (NY) OT
1980—Browns, 17-14 (C)
1981—Jets, 14-13 (C)
(Points—Browns 187, Jets 132)

CLEVELAND vs. OAKLAND
Raiders lead series, 7-1
1970—Raiders, 23-20 (O)
1971—Raiders, 34-20 (C)
1973—Browns, 7-3 (O)
1974—Raiders, 40-24 (C)
1975—Raiders, 38-17 (O)
1977—Raiders, 26-10 (C)
1979—Raiders, 19-14 (O)
1980—*Raiders, 14-12 (C)
(Points—Raiders 197, Browns 124)
*AFC Divisional Playoff

CLEVELAND vs. PHILADELPHIA
Browns lead series, 29-10-1
1950—Browns, 35-10 (P)
   Browns, 13-7 (C)
1951—Browns, 20-17 (C)
   Browns, 24-9 (NY)
1952—Browns, 49-7 (P)
   Eagles, 28-20 (C)
1953—Browns, 37-13 (C)
   Eagles, 42-27 (P)
1954—Eagles, 28-10 (P)
   Browns, 6-0 (C)
1955—Browns, 21-17 (C)
   Eagles, 33-17 (P)
1956—Eagles, 16-0 (P)
   Browns, 17-14 (C)
1957—Browns, 24-7 (C)
   Eagles, 17-7 (P)
1958—Browns, 28-14 (C)
   Browns, 21-14 (P)
1959—Browns, 28-7 (C)
   Browns, 28-21 (P)
1960—Browns, 41-24 (P)
   Eagles, 31-29 (C)
1961—Eagles, 27-20 (P)
   Browns, 45-24 (C)
1962—Eagles, 35-7 (P)
   Tie, 14-14 (C)
1963—Browns, 37-7 (C)
   Browns, 23-17 (P)
1964—Browns, 28-20 (C)
   Browns, 38-24 (C)

1965—Browns, 35-17 (P)
    Browns, 38-34 (C)
1966—Browns, 27-7 (C)
    Eagles, 33-21 (P)
1967—Eagles, 28-24 (P)
1968—Browns, 47-13 (C)
1969—Browns, 27-20 (P)
1972—Browns, 27-17 (P)
1976—Browns, 24-3 (C)
1979—Browns, 24-19 (P)
(Points—Browns 1,024, Eagles 719)

CLEVELAND vs. PITTSBURGH
Browns lead series, 37-27
1950—Browns, 30-17 (P)
    Browns, 45-7 (C)
1951—Browns, 17-0 (C)
    Browns, 28-0 (P)
1952—Browns, 21-20 (P)
    Browns, 29-28 (C)
1953—Browns, 34-16 (C)
    Browns, 20-16 (P)
1954—Steelers, 55-27 (P)
    Browns, 42-7 (C)
1955—Browns, 41-14 (C)
    Browns, 30-7 (P)
1956—Browns, 14-10 (P)
    Steelers, 24-16 (C)
1957—Browns, 23-12 (P)
    Browns, 24-0 (C)
1958—Browns, 45-12 (P)
    Browns, 27-10 (C)
1959—Steelers, 17-7 (P)
    Steelers, 21-20 (C)
1960—Browns, 28-20 (C)
    Steelers, 14-10 (P)
1961—Browns, 30-28 (P)
    Steelers, 17-13 (C)
1962—Browns, 41-14 (P)
    Browns, 35-14 (C)
1963—Browns, 35-23 (C)
    Steelers, 9-7 (P)
1964—Steelers, 23-7 (C)
    Browns, 30-17 (P)
1965—Browns, 24-19 (C)
    Browns, 42-21 (P)
1966—Browns, 41-10 (C)
    Steelers, 16-6 (P)
1967—Browns, 21-10 (C)
    Browns, 34-14 (P)
1968—Browns, 31-24 (C)
    Browns, 45-24 (P)
1969—Browns, 42-31 (C)
    Browns, 24-3 (P)
1970—Browns, 15-7 (C)
    Steelers, 28-9 (P)
1971—Browns, 27-17 (C)
    Steelers, 26-9 (P)
1972—Browns, 26-24 (C)
    Steelers, 30-0 (P)
1973—Steelers, 33-6 (C)
    Browns, 21-16 (C)
1974—Steelers, 20-16 (P)
    Steelers, 26-16 (C)

1975—Steelers, 42-6 (C)
    Steelers, 31-17 (P)
1976—Steelers, 31-14 (P)
    Browns, 18-16 (C)
1977—Steelers, 28-14 (C)
    Steelers, 35-31 (P)
1978—Steelers, 15-9 (P) OT
    Steelers, 34-14 (C)
1979—Steelers, 51-35 (C)
    Steelers, 33-30 (P) OT
1980—Browns, 27-26 (C)
    Steelers, 16-13 (P)
1981—Steelers, 13-7 (P)
    Steelers, 32-10 (C)
(Points—Browns 1,476, Steelers 1,274)

CLEVELAND vs. *ST. LOUIS
Browns lead series, 30-9-3
1950—Browns, 34-24 (Cle)
    Browns, 10-7 (Chi)
1951—Browns, 34-17 (Chi)
    Browns, 49-28 (Cle)
1952—Browns, 28-13 (Cle)
    Browns, 10-0 (Chi)
1953—Browns, 27-7 (Chi)
    Browns, 27-16 (Cle)
1954—Browns, 31-7 (Cle)
    Browns, 35-3 (Chi)
1955—Browns, 26-20 (Chi)
    Browns, 35-24 (Cle)
1956—Cardinals, 9-7 (Chi)
    Cardinals, 24-7 (Cle)
1957—Browns, 17-7 (Chi)
    Browns, 31-0 (Cle)
1958—Browns, 35-28 (Cle)
    Browns, 38-24 (Chi)
1959—Browns, 34-7 (Cle)
    Browns, 17-7 (Cle)
1960—Browns, 28-27 (C)
    Tie, 17-17 (StL)
1961—Browns, 20-17 (C)
    Browns, 21-10 (StL)
1962—Browns, 34-7 (StL)
    Browns, 38-14 (C)
1963—Cardinals, 20-14 (C)
    Browns, 24-10 (StL)
1964—Tie, 33-33 (C)
    Cardinals, 28-19 (StL)
1965—Cardinals, 49-13 (C)
    Browns, 27-24 (StL)
1966—Cardinals, 34-28 (C)
    Browns, 38-10 (StL)
1967—Browns, 20-16 (C)
    Browns, 20-16 (StL)
1968—Cardinals, 27-21 (C)
    Cardinals, 27-16 (StL)
1969—Tie, 21-21 (C)
    Browns, 27-21 (StL)
1974—Cardinals, 29-7 (StL)
1979—Browns, 38-20 (StL)
(Points—Browns 1,056, Cardinals 749)
*Franchise in Chicago (Chi) prior to 1960

CLEVELAND vs. SAN DIEGO
Chargers lead series, 4-2-1

1970—Chargers, 27-10 (C)
1972—Browns, 21-17 (SD)
1973—Tie, 16-16 (C)
1974—Chargers, 36-35 (SD)
1976—Browns, 21-17 (C)
1977—Chargers, 37-14 (SD)
1981—Chargers, 44-14 (C)
(Points—Chargers 194, Browns 131)

CLEVELAND vs. SAN FRANCISCO
Browns lead series, 8-3
1950—Browns, 34-14 (C)
1951—49ers, 24-10 (SF)
1953—Browns, 23-21 (C)
1955—Browns, 38-3 (SF)
1959—49ers, 21-20 (C)
1962—Browns, 13-10 (SF)
1968—Browns, 33-21 (SF)
1970—49ers, 34-31 (SF)
1974—Browns, 7-0 (C)
1978—Browns, 24-7 (C)
1981—Browns, 15-12 (SF)
(Points—Browns 248, 49ers 167)

CLEVELAND vs. SEATTLE
Seahawks lead series, 4-1
1977—Seahawks, 20-19 (S)
1978—Seahawks, 47-24 (S)
1979—Seahawks, 29-24 (C)
1980—Browns, 27-3 (S)
1981—Seahawks, 42-21 (S)
(Points—Seahawks 141, Browns 115)

CLEVELAND vs. TAMPA BAY
Browns lead series, 2-0
1976—Browns, 24-7 (TB)
1980—Browns, 34-27 (TB)
(Points—Browns 58, Buccaneers 34)

CLEVELAND vs. WASHINGTON
Browns lead series, 31-7-1
1950—Browns, 20-14 (C)
      Browns, 45-21 (W)
1951—Browns, 45-0 (C)
1952—Browns, 19-15 (C)
      Browns, 48-24 (W)
1953—Browns, 30-14 (W)
      Browns, 27-3 (C)
1954—Browns, 62-3 (C)
      Browns, 34-14 (W)
1955—Redskins, 27-17 (C)
      Browns, 24-14 (W)
1956—Redskins, 20-9 (W)
      Redskins, 20-17 (C)
1957—Browns, 21-17 (C)
      Tie, 30-30 (W)
1958—Browns, 20-10 (W)
      Browns, 21-14 (C)
1959—Browns, 34-7 (C)
      Browns, 31-17 (W)
1960—Browns, 31-10 (W)
      Browns, 27-16 (C)
1961—Browns, 31-7 (C)
      Browns, 17-6 (W)
1962—Redskins, 17-16 (C)
      Redskins, 17-9 (W)
1963—Browns, 37-14 (C)

Browns, 27-20 (W)
1964—Browns, 27-13 (W)
      Browns, 34-24 (C)
1965—Browns, 17-7 (W)
      Browns, 24-16 (C)
1966—Browns, 38-14 (W)
      Browns, 14-3 (C)
1967—Browns, 42-37 (C)
1968—Browns, 24-21 (W)
1969—Browns, 27-23 (C)
1971—Browns, 20-13 (W)
1975—Redskins, 23-7 (C)
1979—Redskins, 13-9 (W)
(Points—Browns 1,032, Redskins 598)

DALLAS vs. ATLANTA
Cowboys lead series, 7-1;
See Atlanta vs. Dallas
DALLAS vs. BALTIMORE
Cowboys lead series, 5-3;
See Baltimore vs. Dallas
DALLAS vs. BUFFALO
Cowboys lead series, 3-0;
See Buffalo vs. Dallas
DALLAS vs. CHICAGO
Cowboys lead series, 7-3;
See Chicago vs. Dallas
DALLAS vs. CINCINNATI
Cowboys lead series, 2-0;
See Cincinnati vs. Dallas
DALLAS vs. CLEVELAND
Browns lead series, 15-7;
See Cleveland vs. Dallas
DALLAS vs. DENVER
Cowboys lead series, 3-1
1973—Cowboys, 22-10 (Den)
1977—Cowboys, 14-6 (Dal)
      *Cowboys, 27-10 (New Orleans)
1980—Broncos, 41-20 (Den)
(Points—Cowboys 83, Broncos 67)
*Super Bowl XII
DALLAS vs. DETROIT
Cowboys lead series, 6-2
1960—Lions, 23-14 (Det)
1963—Cowboys, 17-14 (Dal)
1968—Cowboys, 59-13 (Dal)
1970—*Cowboys, 5-0 (Dal)
1972—Cowboys, 28-24 (Dal)
1975—Cowboys, 36-10 (Det)
1977—Cowboys, 37-0 (Dal)
1981—Lions, 27-24 (Det)
(Points—Cowboys 220, Lions 111)
*NFC Divisional Playoff
DALLAS vs. GREEN BAY
Packers lead series, 8-3
1960—Packers, 41-7 (GB)
1964—Packers, 45-21 (D)
1965—Packers, 13-3 (Mil)
1966—*Packers, 34-27 (D)
1967—*Packers, 21-17 (GB)
1968—Packers, 28-17 (D)
1970—Cowboys, 16-3 (D)
1972—Packers, 16-13 (Mil)

1975—Packers, 19-17 (D)
1978—Cowboys, 42-14 (Mil)
1980—Cowboys, 28-7 (Mil)
(Points—Packers 241, Cowboys 208)
*NFL Championship

DALLAS vs. HOUSTON
Cowboys lead series, 2-1
1970—Cowboys, 52-10 (D)
1974—Cowboys, 10-0 (H)
1979—Oilers, 30-24 (D)
(Points—Cowboys 86, Oilers 40)

DALLAS vs. KANSAS CITY
Series tied, 1-1
1970—Cowboys, 27-16 (KC)
1975—Chiefs, 34-31 (D)
(Points—Cowboys 58, Chiefs 50)

DALLAS vs. LOS ANGELES
Cowboys lead series, 9-8
1960—Rams, 38-13 (D)
1962—Cowboys, 27-17 (LA)
1967—Rams, 35-13 (D)
1969—Rams, 24-23 (LA)
1971—Cowboys, 28-21 (D)
1973—Rams, 37-31 (LA)
        *Cowboys, 27-16 (D)
1975—Cowboys, 18-7 (D)
        **Cowboys, 37-7 (LA)
1976—*Rams, 14-12 (D)
1978—Rams, 27-14 (LA)
        **Cowboys, 28-0 (LA)
1979—Cowboys, 30-6 (D)
        *Rams, 21-19 (D)
1980—Rams, 38-14 (LA)
        ***Cowboys, 34-13 (D)
1981—Cowboys, 29-17 (D)
(Points—Cowboys 397, Rams 338)
*NFC Divisional Playoff
**NFC Championship
***NFC First Round Playoff

DALLAS vs. MIAMI
Series tied, 2-2
1971—*Cowboys, 24-3 (New Orleans)
1973—Dolphins, 14-7 (D)
1978—Dolphins, 23-16 (M)
1981—Cowboys, 28-27 (D)
(Points—Cowboys 75, Dolphins 67)
*Super Bowl VI

DALLAS vs. MINNESOTA
Cowboys lead series, 9-4
1961—Cowboys, 21-7 (D)
        Cowboys, 28-0 (M)
1966—Cowboys, 28-17 (D)
1968—Cowboys, 20-7 (M)
1970—Vikings, 54-13 (M)
1971—*Cowboys, 20-12 (M)
1973—**Vikings, 27-10 (D)
1974—Cowboys, 23-21 (D)
1975—*Cowboys, 17-14 (M)
1977—Cowboys, 16-10 (M) OT
        **Cowboys, 23-6 (D)
1978—Vikings, 21-10 (D)
1979—Cowboys, 36-20 (M)
(Points—Cowboys 263, Vikings 218)

*NFC Divisional Playoff
**NFC Championship
DALLAS vs. NEW ENGLAND
Cowboys lead series, 4-0
1971—Cowboys, 44-21 (D)
1975—Cowboys, 34-31 (NE)
1978—Cowboys, 17-10 (D)
1981—Cowboys, 35-21 (NE)
(Points—Cowboys 130, Patriots 83)

DALLAS vs. NEW ORLEANS
Cowboys lead series, 8-1
1967—Cowboys, 14-10 (D)
        Cowboys, 27-10 (NO)
1968—Cowboys, 17-3 (NO)
1969—Cowboys, 21-17 (NO)
        Cowboys, 33-17 (D)
1971—Saints, 24-14 (NO)
1973—Cowboys, 40-3 (D)
1976—Cowboys, 24-6 (NO)
1978—Cowboys, 27-7 (D)
(Points—Cowboys 217, Saints 97)

DALLAS vs. N.Y. GIANTS
Cowboys lead series, 28-11-2
1960—Tie, 31-31 (NY)
1961—Giants, 31-10 (D)
        Cowboys, 17-16 (NY)
1962—Giants, 41-10 (D)
        Giants, 41-31 (NY)
1963—Giants, 37-21 (NY)
        Giants, 34-27 (D)
1964—Tie, 13-13 (D)
        Cowboys, 31-21 (NY)
1965—Cowboys, 31-2 (D)
        Cowboys, 38-20 (NY)
1966—Cowboys, 52-7 (D)
        Cowboys, 17-7 (NY)
1967—Cowboys, 38-24 (D)
1968—Giants, 27-21 (D)
        Cowboys, 28-10 (NY)
1969—Cowboys, 25-3 (D)
1970—Cowboys, 28-10 (D)
        Giants, 23-20 (NY)
1971—Cowboys, 20-13 (D)
        Cowboys, 42-14 (NY)
1972—Cowboys, 23-14 (D)
        Giants, 23-3 (D)
1973—Cowboys, 45-28 (D)
        Cowboys, 23-10 (New Haven)
1974—Giants, 14-6 (D)
        Cowboys, 21-7 (New Haven)
1975—Cowboys, 13-7 (NY)
        Cowboys, 14-3 (D)
1976—Cowboys, 24-14 (NY)
        Cowboys, 9-3 (D)
1977—Cowboys, 41-21 (D)
        Cowboys, 24-10 (NY)
1978—Cowboys, 34-24 (NY)
        Cowboys, 24-3 (D)
1979—Cowboys, 16-14 (NY)
        Cowboys, 28-7 (D)
1980—Cowboys, 24-3 (D)
        Giants, 38-35 (NY)
1981—Cowboys, 18-10 (D)

Giants, 13-10 (NY) OT
(Points—Cowboys 986, Giants 691)

DALLAS vs. N.Y. JETS
Cowboys lead series, 3-0
1971—Cowboys, 52-10 (D)
1975—Cowboys, 31-21 (NY)
1978—Cowboys, 30-7 (NY)
(Points—Cowboys 113, Jets 38)

DALLAS vs. OAKLAND
Series tied, 1-1
1974—Raiders, 27-23 (O)
1980—Cowboys, 19-13 (O)
(Points—Cowboys 42, Raiders 40)

DALLAS vs. PHILADELPHIA
Cowboys lead series, 29-15
1960—Eagles, 27-25 (D)
1961—Eagles, 43-7 (D)
Eagles, 35-13 (P)
1962—Cowboys, 41-19 (D)
Eagles, 28-14 (P)
1963—Eagles, 24-21 (P)
Cowboys, 27-20 (D)
1964—Eagles, 17-14 (D)
Eagles, 24-14 (P)
1965—Eagles, 35-24 (D)
Cowboys, 21-19 (P)
1966—Cowboys, 56-7 (D)
Eagles, 24-23 (P)
1967—Eagles, 21-14 (P)
Cowboys, 38-17 (D)
1968—Cowboys, 45-13 (P)
Cowboys, 34-14 (D)
1969—Cowboys, 38-7 (P)
Cowboys, 49-14 (D)
1970—Cowboys, 17-7 (P)
Cowboys, 21-17 (D)
1971—Cowboys, 42-7 (P)
Cowboys, 20-7 (D)
1972—Cowboys, 28-6 (D)
Cowboys, 28-7 (P)
1973—Eagles, 30-16 (P)
Cowboys, 31-10 (D)
1974—Eagles, 13-10 (P)
Cowboys, 31-24 (D)
1975—Cowboys, 20-17 (P)
Cowboys, 27-17 (D)
1976—Cowboys, 27-7 (D)
Cowboys, 26-7 (P)
1977—Cowboys, 16-10 (P)
Cowboys, 24-14 (D)
1978—Cowboys, 14-7 (D)
Cowboys, 31-13 (P)
1979—Eagles, 31-21 (D)
Cowboys, 24-17 (P)
1980—Eagles, 17-10 (P)
Cowboys, 35-27 (D)
*Eagles, 20-7 (P)
1981—Cowboys, 17-14 (P)
Cowboys, 21-10 (D)
(Points—Cowboys 1,082, Eagles 764)
*NFC Championship

DALLAS vs. PITTSBURGH
Steelers lead series, 11-10

1960—Steelers, 35-28 (D)
1961—Cowboys, 27-24 (D)
Steelers, 37-7 (P)
1962—Steelers, 30-28 (D)
Cowboys, 42-27 (P)
1963—Steelers, 27-21 (P)
Steelers, 24-19 (D)
1964—Steelers, 23-17 (P)
Cowboys, 17-14 (D)
1965—Steelers, 22-13 (P)
Cowboys, 24-17 (D)
1966—Cowboys, 52-21 (D)
Cowboys, 20-7 (P)
1967—Cowboys, 24-21 (P)
1968—Cowboys, 28-7 (D)
1969—Cowboys, 10-7 (P)
1972—Cowboys, 17-13 (D)
1975—*Steelers, 21-17 (Miami)
1977—Steelers, 28-13 (P)
1978—**Steelers, 35-31 (Miami)
1979—Steelers, 14-3 (P)
(Points—Cowboys 458, Steelers 454)
*Super Bowl X
**Super Bowl XIII

DALLAS vs. ST. LOUIS
Cowboys lead series, 24-15-1
1960—Cardinals, 12-10 (StL)
1961—Cardinals, 31-17 (D)
Cardinals, 31-13 (StL)
1962—Cardinals, 28-24 (D)
Cardinals, 52-20 (StL)
1963—Cardinals, 34-7 (D)
Cowboys, 28-24 (StL)
1964—Cardinals, 16-6 (D)
Cowboys, 31-13 (StL)
1965—Cardinals, 20-13 (StL)
Cowboys, 27-13 (D)
1966—Tie, 10-10 (StL)
Cowboys, 31-17 (D)
1967—Cowboys, 46-21 (D)
1968—Cowboys, 27-10 (StL)
1969—Cowboys, 24-3 (D)
1970—Cardinals, 20-7 (StL)
Cardinals, 38-0 (D)
1971—Cowboys, 16-13 (StL)
Cowboys, 31-12 (D)
1972—Cowboys, 33-24 (D)
Cowboys, 27-6 (StL)
1973—Cowboys, 45-10 (D)
Cowboys, 30-3 (StL)
1974—Cardinals, 31-28 (StL)
Cowboys, 17-14 (D)
1975—Cowboys, 37-31 (D) OT
Cardinals, 31-17 (StL)
1976—Cardinals, 21-17 (StL)
Cowboys, 19-14 (D)
1977—Cowboys, 30-24 (StL)
Cardinals, 24-17 (D)
1978—Cowboys, 21-12 (D)
Cowboys, 24-21 (StL) OT
1979—Cowboys, 22-21 (StL)
Cowboys, 22-13 (D)
1980—Cowboys, 27-24 (StL)

Cowboys, 31-21 (D)
1981—Cowboys, 30-17 (D)
Cardinals, 20-17 (StL)
(Points—Cowboys 899, Cardinals 800)
DALLAS vs. SAN DIEGO
Cowboys lead series, 2-0
1972—Cowboys, 34-28 (SD)
1980—Cowboys, 42-31 (D)
(Points—Cowboys 76, Chargers 59)
DALLAS vs. SAN FRANCISCO
Cowboys lead series, 8-6-1
1960—49ers, 26-14 (D)
1963—49ers, 31-24 (SF)
1965—Cowboys, 39-31 (D)
1967—49ers, 24-16 (SF)
1969—Tie, 24-24 (D)
1970—*Cowboys, 17-10 (SF)
1971—*Cowboys, 14-3 (D)
1972—49ers, 31-10 (D)
**Cowboys, 30-28 (SF)
1974—Cowboys, 20-14 (D)
1977—Cowboys, 42-35 (SF)
1979—Cowboys, 21-13 (SF)
1980—Cowboys, 59-14 (D)
1981—49ers, 45-14 (SF)
*49ers, 28-27 (SF)
(Points—Cowboys 371, 49ers 357)
*NFC Championship
**NFC Divisional Playoff
DALLAS vs. SEATTLE
Cowboys lead series, 2-0
1976—Cowboys, 28-13 (S)
1980—Cowboys, 51-7 (D)
(Points—Cowboys 79, Seahawks 20)
DALLAS vs. TAMPA BAY
Cowboys lead series, 3-0
1977—Cowboys, 23-7 (D)
1980—Cowboys, 28-17 (D)
1981—*Cowboys, 38-0 (D)
(Points—Cowboys 89, Buccaneers 24)
*NFC Divisional Playoff
DALLAS vs. WASHINGTON
Cowboys lead series, 26-16-2
1960—Redskins, 26-14 (W)
1961—Tie, 28-28 (D)
Redskins, 34-24 (W)
1962—Tie, 35-35 (D)
Cowboys, 38-10 (W)
1963—Redskins, 21-17 (W)
Cowboys, 35-20 (D)
1964—Cowboys, 24-18 (D)
Redskins, 28-16 (W)
1965—Cowboys, 27-7 (D)
Redskins, 34-31 (W)
1966—Cowboys, 31-30 (W)
Redskins, 34-31 (D)
1967—Cowboys, 17-14 (W)
Redskins, 27-20 (D)
1968—Cowboys, 44-24 (W)
Cowboys, 29-20 (D)
1969—Cowboys, 41-28 (W)
Cowboys, 20-10 (D)
1970—Cowboys, 45-21 (W)

Cowboys, 34-0 (D)
1971—Redskins, 20-16 (D)
Cowboys, 13-0 (W)
1972—Redskins, 24-20 (W)
Cowboys, 34-24 (D)
*Redskins, 26-3 (W)
1973—Redskins, 14-7 (W)
Cowboys, 27-7 (D)
1974—Redskins, 28-21 (W)
Cowboys, 24-23 (W)
1975—Redskins, 30-24 (W) OT
Cowboys, 31-10 (D)
1976—Cowboys, 20-7 (W)
Redskins, 27-14 (D)
1977—Cowboys, 34-16 (D)
Cowboys, 14-7 (W)
1978—Redskins, 9-5 (W)
Cowboys, 37-10 (D)
1979—Redskins, 34-20 (W)
Cowboys, 35-34 (D)
1980—Cowboys, 17-3 (W)
Cowboys, 14-10 (D)
1981—Cowboys, 26-10 (W)
Cowboys, 24-10 (D)
(Points—Cowboys 1,081, Redskins 852)
*NFC Championship

DENVER vs. ATLANTA
Series lead, 2-2;
See Atlanta vs. Denver
DENVER vs. BALTIMORE
Broncos lead series, 3-1;
See Baltimore vs. Denver
DENVER vs. BUFFALO
Bills lead series, 13-8-1;
See Buffalo vs. Denver
DENVER vs. CHICAGO
Broncos lead series, 3-2;
See Chicago vs. Denver
DENVER vs. CINCINNATI
Series tied, 6-6;
See Cincinnati vs. Denver
DENVER vs. CLEVELAND
Broncos lead series, 6-3;
See Cleveland vs. Denver
DENVER vs. DALLAS
Cowboys lead series, 3-1;
See Dallas vs. Denver
DENVER vs. DETROIT
Series tied, 2-2
1971—Lions, 24-20 (Den)
1974—Broncos, 31-27 (Det)
1978—Lions, 17-14 (Det)
1981—Broncos, 27-21 (Den)
(Points—Broncos 92, Lions 89)
DENVER vs. GREEN BAY
Broncos lead series, 2-1
1971—Packers, 34-13 (Mil)
1975—Broncos, 23-13 (D)
1978—Broncos, 16-3 (D)
(Points—Broncos 52, Packers 50)
DENVER vs. HOUSTON
Oilers lead series, 18-8-1

All-Time Team vs. Team Results

1960—Oilers, 45-25 (D)
Oilers, 20-10 (H)
1961—Oilers, 55-14 (D)
Oilers, 45-14 (H)
1962—Broncos, 20-10 (D)
Oilers, 34-17 (H)
1963—Oilers, 20-14 (H)
Oilers, 33-24 (D)
1964—Oilers, 38-17 (D)
Oilers, 34-15 (H)
1965—Broncos, 28-17 (D)
Broncos, 31-21 (H)
1966—Oilers, 45-7 (H)
Broncos, 40-38 (D)
1967—Oilers, 10-6 (H)
Oilers, 20-18 (D)
1968—Oilers, 38-17 (H)
1969—Oilers, 24-21 (H)
Tie, 20-20 (D)
1970—Oilers, 31-21 (H)
1972—Broncos, 30-17 (D)
1973—Broncos, 48-20 (H)
1974—Broncos, 37-14 (D)
1976—Oilers, 17-3 (H)
1977—Broncos, 24-14 (H)
1979—*Oilers, 13-7 (H)
1980—Oilers, 20-16 (D)
(Points—Oilers 713, Broncos 544)
*AFC First Round Playoff
DENVER vs. *KANSAS CITY
Chiefs lead series, 30-14
1960—Texans, 17-14 (D)
Texans, 34-7 (Da)
1961—Texans, 19-12 (D)
Texans, 49-21 (Da)
1962—Texans, 24-3 (D)
Texans, 17-10 (Da)
1963—Chiefs, 59-7 (D)
Chiefs, 52-21 (KC)
1964—Broncos, 33-27 (D)
Chiefs, 49-39 (KC)
1965—Chiefs, 31-23 (D)
Chiefs, 45-35 (KC)
1966—Chiefs, 37-10 (KC)
Chiefs, 56-10 (D)
1967—Chiefs, 52-9 (KC)
Chiefs, 38-24 (D)
1968—Chiefs, 34-2 (KC)
Chiefs, 30-7 (D)
1969—Chiefs, 26-13 (D)
Chiefs, 31-17 (KC)
1970—Broncos, 26-13 (D)
Chiefs, 16-0 (KC)
1971—Chiefs, 16-3 (D)
Chiefs, 28-10 (KC)
1972—Chiefs, 45-24 (D)
Chiefs, 24-21 (KC)
1973—Chiefs, 16-14 (KC)
Broncos, 14-10 (D)
1974—Broncos, 17-14 (KC)
Chiefs, 42-34 (D)
1975—Broncos, 37-33 (D)
Chiefs, 26-13 (KC)
1976—Broncos, 35-26 (KC)

Broncos, 17-16 (D)
1977—Broncos, 23-7 (D)
Broncos, 14-7 (KC)
1978—Broncos, 23-17 (KC) OT
Broncos, 24-3 (D)
1979—Broncos, 24-10 (KC)
Broncos, 20-3 (D)
1980—Chiefs, 23-17 (D)
Chiefs, 31-14 (KC)
1981—Chiefs, 28-14 (KC)
Broncos, 16-13 (D)
(Points—Chiefs 1,194, Broncos 771)
*Franchise in Dallas prior to 1963 and
known as Texans
DENVER vs. LOS ANGELES
Rams lead series, 2-1
1972—Broncos, 16-10 (LA)
1974—Rams, 17-10 (D)
1979—Rams, 13-9 (D)
(Points—Rams 40, Broncos 35)
DENVER vs. MIAMI
Dolphins lead series, 4-2-1
1966—Dolphins, 24-7 (M)
Broncos, 17-7 (D)
1967—Dolphins, 35-21 (M)
1968—Broncos, 21-14 (D)
1969—Dolphins, 27-24 (M)
1971—Tie, 10-10 (D)
1975—Dolphins, 14-13 (M)
(Points—Dolphins 131, Broncos 113)
DENVER vs. MINNESOTA
Vikings lead series, 2-1
1972—Vikings, 23-20 (D)
1978—Vikings, 12-9 (M) OT
1981—Broncos, 19-17 (D)
(Points—Vikings 52, Broncos 48)
DENVER vs. *NEW ENGLAND
Patriots lead series, 12-10
1960—Broncos, 13-10 (B)
Broncos, 31-24 (D)
1961—Patriots, 45-17 (B)
Patriots, 28-24 (D)
1962—Patriots, 41-16 (B)
Patriots, 33-29 (D)
1963—Broncos, 14-10 (D)
Patriots, 40-21 (B)
1964—Patriots, 39-10 (D)
Patriots, 12-7 (B)
1965—Broncos, 27-10 (B)
Patriots, 28-20 (D)
1966—Patriots, 24-10 (D)
Broncos, 17-10 (B)
1967—Patriots, 26-21 (D)
1968—Patriots, 20-17 (D)
Broncos, 35-14 (B)
1969—Broncos, 35-7 (D)
1972—Broncos, 45-21 (D)
1976—Patriots, 38-14 (NE)
1979—Broncos, 45-10 (D)
1980—Patriots, 23-14 (NE)
(Points—Patriots 508, Broncos 487)
*Franchise in Boston prior to 1971
DENVER vs. NEW ORLEANS
Broncos lead series, 3-0

180

1970—Broncos, 31-6 (NO)
1974—Broncos, 33-17 (D)
1979—Broncos, 10-3 (D)
(Points—Broncos 74, Saints 26)
DENVER vs. N. Y. GIANTS
Broncos lead series, 2-1
1972—Giants, 29-17 (NY)
1976—Broncos, 14-13 (D)
1980—Broncos, 14-9 (NY)
(Points—Giants 51, Broncos 45)
DENVER vs. *N. Y. JETS
Series tied, 10-10-1
1960—Titans, 28-24 (NY)
       Titans, 30-27 (D)
1961—Titans, 35-28 (NY)
       Broncos, 27-10 (D)
1962—Broncos, 32-10 (NY)
       Titans, 46-45 (D)
1963—Tie, 35-35 (NY)
       Jets, 14-9 (D)
1964—Jets, 30-6 (NY)
       Broncos, 20-16 (D)
1965—Broncos, 16-13 (D)
       Jets, 45-10 (NY)
1966—Jets, 16-7 (D)
1967—Jets, 38-24 (D)
       Broncos, 33-24 (NY)
1968—Broncos, 21-13 (NY)
1969—Broncos, 21-19 (D)
1973—Broncos, 40-28 (NY)
1976—Broncos, 46-3 (D)
1978—Jets, 31-28 (D)
1980—Broncos, 31-24 (D)
(Points—Broncos 530, Jets 508)
*Jets known as Titans prior to 1963
DENVER vs. OAKLAND
Raiders lead series, 31-12-2
1960—Broncos, 31-14 (D)
       Raiders, 48-10 (O)
1961—Raiders, 33-19 (O)
       Broncos, 27-24 (D)
1962—Broncos, 44-7 (D)
       Broncos, 23-6 (O)
1963—Raiders, 26-10 (D)
       Raiders, 35-31 (O)
1964—Raiders, 40-7 (O)
       Tie, 20-20 (D)
1965—Raiders, 28-20 (D)
       Raiders, 24-13 (O)
1966—Raiders, 17-3 (D)
       Raiders, 28-10 (O)
1967—Raiders, 51-0 (O)
       Raiders, 21-17 (D)
1968—Raiders, 43-7 (D)
       Raiders, 33-27 (O)
1969—Raiders, 24-14 (O)
       Raiders, 41-10 (D)
1970—Raiders, 35-23 (O)
       Raiders, 24-19 (D)
1971—Raiders, 27-16 (O)
       Raiders, 21-13 (O)
1972—Broncos, 30-23 (O)
       Raiders, 37-20 (D)

1973—Tie, 23-23 (D)
       Raiders, 21-17 (O)
1974—Raiders, 28-17 (D)
       Broncos, 20-17 (O)
1975—Raiders, 42-17 (D)
       Raiders, 17-10 (O)
1976—Raiders, 17-10 (D)
       Raiders, 19-6 (O)
1977—Broncos, 30-7 (O)
       Raiders, 24-14 (D)
       *Broncos, 20-17 (D)
1978—Broncos, 14-6 (D)
       Broncos, 21-6 (O)
1979—Raiders, 27-3 (O)
       Raiders, 14-10 (D)
1980—Raiders, 9-3 (O)
       Raiders, 24-21 (D)
1981—Broncos, 9-7 (D)
       Broncos, 17-0 (O)
(Points—Raiders 1,055, Broncos 746)
*AFC Championship
DENVER vs. PHILADELPHIA
Eagles lead series, 2-1
1971—Eagles, 17-16 (P)
1975—Broncos, 25-10 (D)
1980—Eagles, 27-6 (P)
(Points—Eagles 54, Broncos 47)
DENVER vs. PITTSBURGH
Broncos lead series, 5-4-1
1970—Broncos, 16-13 (D)
1971—Broncos, 22-10 (P)
1973—Broncos, 23-13 (P)
1974—Tie, 35-35 (D) OT
1975—Steelers, 20-9 (P)
1977—Broncos, 21-7 (D)
       *Broncos, 34-21 (D)
1978—Steelers, 21-17 (D)
       *Steelers, 33-10 (P)
1979—Steelers, 42-7 (P)
(Points—Steelers 215, Broncos 194)
*AFC Divisional Playoff
DENVER vs. ST. LOUIS
Broncos lead series, 1-0-1
1973—Tie, 17-17 (StL)
1977—Broncos, 7-0 (D)
(Points—Broncos 24, Cardinals 17)
DENVER vs. *SAN DIEGO
Chargers lead series, 23-20-1
1960—Chargers, 23-19 (D)
       Chargers, 41-33 (LA)
1961—Chargers, 37-0 (SD)
       Chargers, 19-16 (D)
1962—Broncos, 30-21 (D)
       Broncos, 23-20 (SD)
1963—Broncos, 50-34 (D)
       Chargers, 58-20 (SD)
1964—Chargers, 42-14 (SD)
       Chargers, 31-20 (D)
1965—Chargers, 34-31 (SD)
       Chargers, 33-21 (D)
1966—Chargers, 24-17 (SD)
       Broncos, 20-17 (D)

1967—Chargers, 38-21 (D)
Chargers, 24-20 (SD)
1968—Chargers, 55-24 (SD)
Chargers, 47-23 (D)
1969—Broncos, 13-0 (D)
Chargers, 45-24 (SD)
1970—Chargers, 24-21 (SD)
Tie, 17-17 (D)
1971—Broncos, 20-16 (D)
Chargers, 45-17 (SD)
1972—Chargers, 37-14 (SD)
Broncos, 38-13 (D)
1973—Broncos, 30-19 (D)
Broncos, 42-28 (SD)
1974—Broncos, 27-7 (D)
Chargers, 17-0 (SD)
1975—Broncos, 27-17 (SD)
Broncos, 13-10 (D) OT
1976—Broncos, 26-0 (D)
Broncos, 17-0 (SD)
1977—Broncos, 17-14 (D)
Broncos, 17-9 (SD)
1978—Broncos, 27-14 (D)
Chargers, 23-0 (SD)
1979—Broncos, 7-0 (D)
Chargers, 17-7 (SD)
1980—Chargers, 30-13 (D)
Broncos, 20-13 (SD)
1981—Broncos, 42-24 (D)
Chargers, 34-17 (SD)
(Points—Chargers 1,071, Broncos 915)
Franchise in Los Angeles prior to 1961

DENVER vs. SAN FRANCISCO
49ers lead series, 2-1
1970—49ers, 19-14 (SF)
1973—49ers, 36-34 (D)
1979—Broncos, 38-28 (SF)
(Points—Broncos 86, 49ers 83)

DENVER vs. SEATTLE
Broncos lead series, 7-2
1977—Broncos, 24-13 (S)
1978—Broncos, 28-7 (D)
Broncos, 20-17 (S) OT
1979—Broncos, 37-34 (D)
Seahawks, 28-23 (S)
1980—Broncos, 36-20 (D)
Broncos, 25-17 (S)
1981—Seahawks, 13-10 (S)
Broncos, 23-13 (D)
(Points—Broncos 226, Seahawks 162)

DENVER vs. TAMPA BAY
Broncos lead series, 2-0
1976—Broncos, 48-13 (D)
1981—Broncos, 24-7 (TB)
(Points—Broncos 72, Buccaneers 20)

DENVER vs. WASHINGTON
Redskins lead series, 2-1
1970—Redskins, 19-3 (D)
1974—Redskins, 30-3 (W)
1980—Broncos, 20-17 (D)
(Points—Redskins 66, Broncos 26)

DETROIT vs. ATLANTA

Lions lead series, 10-3;
See Atlanta vs. Detroit
DETROIT vs. BALTIMORE
Series tied, 16-16-2;
See Baltimore vs. Detroit
DETROIT vs. BUFFALO
Series tied, 1-1-1;
See Buffalo vs. Detroit
DETROIT vs. CHICAGO
Bears lead series, 59-41-5;
See Chicago vs. Detroit
DETROIT vs. CINCINNATI
Lions lead series, 2-0;
See Cincinnati vs. Detroit
DETROIT vs. CLEVELAND
Lions lead series, 12-2;
See Cleveland vs. Detroit
DETROIT vs. DALLAS
Cowboys lead series, 6-2;
See Dallas vs. Detroit
DETROIT vs. DENVER
Series tied, 2-2;
See Denver vs. Detroit
*DETROIT vs. GREEN BAY
Packers lead series, 54-42-7
1930—Packers, 47-13 (GB)
Tie, 6-6 (P)
1932—Packers, 15-10 (GB)
Spartans, 19-0 (P)
1933—Packers, 17-0 (GB)
Spartans, 7-0 (P)
1934—Lions, 3-0 (GB)
Packers, 3-0 (D)
1935—Packers, 13-9 (GB)
Packers, 31-7 (GB)
Lions, 20-10 (D)
1936—Packers, 20-18 (GB)
Packers, 26-17 (D)
1937—Packers, 26-6 (GB)
Packers, 14-13 (D)
1938—Lions, 17-7 (GB)
Packers, 28-7 (D)
1939—Packers, 26-7 (D)
Packers, 12-7 (D)
1940—Lions, 23-14 (GB)
Packers, 50-7 (D)
1941—Packers, 23-0 (GB)
Packers, 24-7 (D)
1942—Packers, 38-7 (Mil)
Packers, 28-7 (D)
1943—Packers, 35-14 (GB)
Packers, 27-6 (D)
1944—Packers, 27-6 (GB)
Packers, 14-0 (D)
1945—Packers, 57-21 (Mil)
Lions, 14-3 (D)
1946—Packers, 10-7 (Mil)
Packers, 9-0 (D)
1947—Packers, 34-17 (GB)
Packers, 35-14 (D)
1948—Packers, 33-21 (GB)
Lions, 24-20 (D)
1949—Packers, 16-14 (GB)

Lions, 21-7 (D)
1950—Lions, 45-7 (GB)
    Lions, 24-21 (D)
1951—Lions, 24-17 (GB)
    Lions, 52-35 (D)
1952—Lions, 52-17 (GB)
    Lions, 48-24 (D)
1953—Lions, 14-7 (GB)
    Lions, 34-15 (D)
1954—Lions, 21-17 (GB)
    Lions, 28-24 (D)
1955—Packers, 20-17 (GB)
    Lions, 24-10 (D)
1956—Lions, 20-16 (GB)
    Packers, 24-20 (D)
1957—Lions, 24-14 (GB)
    Lions, 18-6 (D)
1958—Tie, 13-13 (GB)
    Lions, 24-14 (D)
1959—Packers, 28-10 (GB)
    Packers, 24-17 (D)
1960—Packers, 28-9 (GB)
    Lions, 23-10 (D)
1961—Lions, 17-13 (Mil)
    Packers, 17-9 (D)
1962—Packers, 9-7 (GB)
    Lions, 26-14 (D)
1963—Packers, 31-10 (Mil)
    Tie, 13-13 (D)
1964—Packers, 14-10 (D)
    Packers, 30-7 (GB)
1965—Packers, 31-21 (GB)
    Lions, 12-7 (GB)
1966—Packers, 23-14 (GB)
    Packers, 31-7 (D)
1967—Tie, 17-17 (GB)
    Packers, 27-17 (D)
1968—Lions, 23-17 (GB)
    Tie, 14-14 (D)
1969—Packers, 28-17 (D)
    Lions, 16-10 (GB)
1970—Lions, 40-0 (GB)
    Lions, 20-0 (D)
1971—Lions, 31-28 (D)
    Tie, 14-14 (Mil)
1972—Packers, 24-23 (D)
    Packers, 33-7 (GB)
1973—Tie, 13-13 (GB)
    Lions, 34-0 (D)
1974—Packers, 21-19 (Mil)
    Lions, 19-17 (D)
1975—Packers, 30-16 (Mil)
    Lions, 13-10 (D)
1976—Packers, 24-14 (GB)
    Lions, 27-6 (D)
1977—Lions, 10-6 (D)
    Packers, 10-9 (GB)
1978—Lions, 13-7 (D)
    Packers, 35-14 (Mil)
1979—Packers, 24-16 (Mil)
    Packers, 18-13 (D)
1980—Lions, 29-7 (Mil)
    Lions, 24-3 (D)

1981—Lions, 31-27 (D)
    Packers, 31-17 (GB)
(Points—Packers 1,922, Lions 1,708)
*Franchise in Portsmouth prior to 1934
and known as the Spartans
DETROIT vs. HOUSTON
Series tied, 1-1
1971—Lions, 31-7 (H)
1975—Oilers, 24-8 (H)
(Points—Lions 39, Oilers 31)
DETROIT vs. KANSAS CITY
Series tied, 2-2
1971—Lions, 32-21 (D)
1975—Chiefs, 24-21 (KC) OT
1980—Chiefs, 20-17 (KC)
1981—Lions, 27-10 (D)
(Points—Lions 97, Chiefs 75)
DETROIT vs. *LOS ANGELES
Rams lead series, 35-33-1
1937—Lions, 28-0 (C)
    Lions, 27-7 (D)
1938—Rams, 21-17 (C)
    Lions, 6-0 (D)
1939—Lions, 15-7 (D)
    Rams, 14-3 (C)
1940—Lions, 6-0 (D)
    Rams, 24-0 (C)
1941—Rams, 17-7 (D)
    Lions, 14-0 (C)
1942—Rams, 14-0 (D)
    Rams, 27-7 (C)
1944—Rams, 20-17 (D)
    Lions, 26-14 (C)
1945—Rams, 28-21 (D)
1946—Rams, 35-14 (LA)
    Rams, 41-20 (D)
1947—Rams, 27-13 (D)
    Rams, 28-17 (LA)
1948—Rams, 44-7 (LA)
    Rams, 34-27 (D)
1949—Rams, 27-24 (LA)
    Rams, 21-10 (D)
1950—Rams, 30-28 (D)
    Rams, 65-24 (LA)
1951—Rams, 27-21 (D)
    Lions, 24-22 (LA)
1952—Lions, 17-14 (LA)
    Lions, 24-16 (D)
    **Lions, 31-21 (D)
1953—Rams, 31-19 (D)
    Rams, 37-24 (LA)
1954—Lions, 21-3 (D)
    Lions, 27-24 (LA)
1955—Rams, 17-10 (D)
    Rams, 24-13 (LA)
1956—Lions, 24-21 (D)
    Lions, 16-7 (LA)
1957—Lions, 10-7 (D)
    Rams, 35-17 (LA)
1958—Rams, 42-28 (D)
    Lions, 41-24 (LA)
1959—Lions, 17-7 (LA)
    Lions, 23-17 (D)

All-Time Team vs. Team Results

1960—Rams, 48-35 (LA)
    Lions, 12-10 (D)
1961—Lions, 14-13 (D)
    Lions, 28-10 (LA)
1962—Lions, 13-10 (D)
    Lions, 12-3 (LA)
1963—Lions, 23-2 (LA)
    Rams, 28-21 (D)
1964—Tie, 17-17 (LA)
    Lions, 37-17 (D)
1965—Lions, 20-0 (D)
    Lions, 31-7 (LA)
1966—Rams, 14-7 (D)
    Rams, 23-3 (LA)
1967—Rams, 31-7 (D)
1968—Rams, 10-7 (LA)
1969—Lions, 28-0 (D)
1970—Lions, 28-23 (LA)
1971—Rams, 21-13 (D)
1972—Lions, 34-17 (LA)
1974—Rams, 16-13 (LA)
1975—Rams, 20-0 (D)
1976—Rams, 20-17 (D)
1980—Lions, 41-20 (LA)
1981—Rams, 20-13 (LA)
(Points—Rams 1,331, Lions 1,269)
*Franchise in Cleveland prior to 1946
**Conference Playoff

DETROIT vs. MIAMI
Dolphins lead series, 2-0
1973—Dolphins, 34-7 (M)
1979—Dolphins, 28-10 (D)
(Points—Dolphins 62, Lions 17)

DETROIT vs. MINNESOTA
Vikings lead series, 26-14-2
1961—Lions, 37-10 (M)
    Lions, 13-7 (D)
1962—Lions, 17-6 (M)
    Lions, 37-23 (D)
1963—Lions, 28-10 (D)
    Vikings, 34-31 (M)
1964—Lions, 24-20 (M)
    Tie, 23-23 (D)
1965—Lions, 31-29 (M)
    Vikings, 29-7 (D)
1966—Lions, 32-31 (M)
    Vikings, 28-16 (D)
1967—Tie, 10-10 (M)
    Lions, 14-3 (D)
1968—Vikings, 24-10 (M)
    Vikings, 13-6 (D)
1969—Vikings, 24-10 (M)
    Vikings, 27-0 (D)
1970—Vikings, 30-17 (D)
    Vikings, 24-20 (M)
1971—Vikings, 16-13 (D)
    Vikings, 29-10 (M)
1972—Vikings, 34-10 (M)
    Vikings, 16-14 (M)
1973—Vikings, 23-9 (D)
    Vikings, 28-7 (M)
1974—Vikings, 7-6 (D)
    Lions, 20-16 (M)

1975—Vikings, 25-19 (M)
    Lions, 17-10 (D)
1976—Vikings, 10-9 (D)
    Vikings, 31-23 (M)
1977—Vikings, 14-7 (M)
    Vikings, 30-21 (D)
1978—Vikings, 17-7 (M)
    Lions, 45-14 (D)
1979—Vikings, 13-10 (D)
    Vikings, 14-7 (M)
1980—Lions, 27-7 (D)
    Vikings, 34-0 (M)
1981—Vikings, 26-24 (M)
    Lions, 45-7 (D)
(Points—Vikings 826, Lions 733)

DETROIT vs. NEW ENGLAND
Lions lead series, 2-1
1971—Lions, 34-7 (NE)
1976—Lions, 30-10 (D)
1979—Patriots, 24-17 (NE)
(Points—Lions 81, Patriots 41)

DETROIT vs. NEW ORLEANS
Series tied, 4-4-1
1968—Tie, 20-20 (D)
1970—Saints, 19-17 (NO)
1972—Lions, 27-14 (D)
1973—Saints, 20-13 (NO)
1974—Lions, 19-14 (D)
1976—Saints, 17-16 (NO)
1977—Lions, 23-19 (D)
1979—Saints, 17-7 (NO)
1980—Lions, 24-13 (D)
(Points—Lions 166, Saints 153)

*DETROIT vs. N. Y. GIANTS
Lions lead series, 17-10-1
1930—Giants, 19-6 (P)
1931—Spartans, 14-6 (P)
    Giants, 14-0 (NY)
1932—Spartans, 7-0 (P)
    Spartans, 6-0 (NY)
1933—Spartans, 17-7 (P)
    Giants, 13-10 (NY)
1934—Lions, 9-0 (D)
1935—**Lions, 26-7 (D)
1936—Giants, 14-7 (NY)
    Lions, 38-0 (D)
1937—Lions, 17-0 (NY)
1939—Lions, 18-14 (D)
1941—Giants, 20-13 (NY)
1943—Tie, 0-0 (D)
1945—Lions, 35-14 (NY)
1947—Lions, 35-7 (D)
1949—Lions, 45-21 (NY)
1953—Lions, 27-16 (NY)
1955—Giants, 24-19 (D)
1958—Giants, 19-17 (D)
1962—Lions, 17-14 (NY)
1964—Lions, 26-3 (D)
1967—Lions, 30-7 (NY)
1969—Lions, 24-0 (D)
1972—Lions, 30-16 (D)
1974—Lions, 20-19 (D)
1976—Giants, 24-10 (NY)

(Points—Lions 499, Giants 322)
*Franchise in Portsmouth prior to 1934 and
known as the Spartans
**NFL Championship

DETROIT vs. N. Y. JETS
Series tied, 1-1
1972—Lions, 37-20 (D)
1979—Jets, 31-10 (NY)
(Points—Jets 51, Lions 47)

DETROIT vs. OAKLAND
Series tied, 2-2
1970—Lions, 28-14 (D)
1974—Raiders, 35-13 (O)
1978—Raiders, 29-17 (O)
1981—Lions, 16-0 (D)
(Points—Raiders 78, Lions 74)

*DETROIT vs. PHILADELPHIA
Lions lead series, 11-9-1
1933—Spartans, 25-0 (P)
1934—Lions, 10-0 (P)
1935—Lions, 35-0 (D)
1936—Lions, 23-0 (P)
1938—Eagles, 21-7 (D)
1940—Lions, 21-0 (P)
1941—Lions, 21-17 (D)
1945—Lions, 28-24 (D)
1948—Eagles, 45-21 (P)
1949—Eagles, 22-14 (D)
1951—Lions, 28-10 (P)
1954—Tie, 13-13 (D)
1957—Lions, 27-16 (P)
1960—Eagles, 28-10 (P)
1961—Eagles, 27-24 (D)
1965—Lions, 35-28 (P)
1968—Eagles, 12-0 (D)
1971—Eagles, 23-20 (D)
1974—Eagles, 28-17 (P)
1977—Lions, 17-13 (D)
1979—Eagles, 44-7 (P)
(Points—Lions 403, Eagles 371)
*Franchise in Portsmouth prior to 1934 and
known as the Spartans

DETROIT vs. *PITTSBURGH
Lions lead series, 12-8-1
1934—Lions, 40-7 (D)
1936—Lions, 28-3 (D)
1937—Lions, 7-3 (D)
1938—Lions, 16-7 (D)
1940—Pirates, 10-7 (D)
1942—Steelers, 35-7 (D)
1946—Lions, 17-7 (D)
1947—Steelers, 17-10 (P)
1948—Lions, 17-14 (D)
1949—Steelers, 14-7 (P)
1950—Lions, 10-7 (D)
1952—Lions, 31-6 (P)
1953—Lions, 38-21 (D)
1955—Lions, 31-28 (D)
1956—Lions, 45-7 (D)
1959—Tie, 10-10 (P)
1962—Lions, 45-7 (D)
1966—Steelers, 17-3 (P)
1967—Steelers, 24-14 (D)

1969—Steelers, 16-13 (P)
1973—Steelers, 24-10 (P)
(Points—Lions 406, Steelers 284)
*Steelers known as Pirates prior to 1941

*DETROIT vs. **ST. LOUIS
Lions lead series, 25-15-5
1930—Tie, 0-0 (C)
       Cardinals, 23-0 (C)
1931—Cardinals, 20-19 (C)
1932—Tie, 7-7 (P)
1933—Spartans, 7-6 (P)
1934—Lions, 6-0 (D)
       Lions, 17-13 (C)
1935—Tie, 10-10 (D)
       Lions, 7-6 (C)
1936—Lions, 39-0 (D)
       Lions, 14-7 (C)
1937—Lions, 16-7 (C)
       Lions, 16-7 (D)
1938—Lions, 10-0 (D)
       Lions, 7-3 (C)
1939—Lions, 21-3 (D)
       Lions, 17-3 (C)
1940—Tie, 0-0 (Buffalo)
       Lions, 43-14 (C)
1941—Tie, 14-14 (C)
       Lions, 21-3 (D)
1942—Cardinals, 13-0 (C)
       Cardinals, 7-0 (D)
1943—Lions, 35-17 (D)
       Lions, 7-0 (C)
1945—Lions, 10-0 (C)
       Lions, 26-0 (D)
1946—Cardinals, 34-14 (C)
       Cardinals, 36-14 (D)
1947—Cardinals, 45-21 (C)
       Cardinals, 17-7 (D)
1948—Cardinals, 56-20 (C)
       Cardinals, 28-14 (D)
1949—Lions, 24-7 (C)
       Cardinals, 42-19 (D)
1959—Lions, 45-21 (D)
1961—Lions, 45-14 (StL)
1967—Cardinals, 38-28 (StL)
1969—Lions, 20-0 (D)
1970—Lions, 16-3 (D)
1973—Lions, 20-16 (StL)
1975—Cardinals, 24-13 (D)
1978—Cardinals, 21-14 (StL)
1980—Lions, 20-7 (D)
       Cardinals, 24-23 (StL)
(Points—Lions 746, Cardinals 626)
*Franchise in Portsmouth prior to 1934 and
known as the Spartans
**Franchise in Chicago prior to 1960

DETROIT vs. SAN DIEGO
Lions lead series, 3-1
1972—Lions, 34-20 (D)
1977—Lions, 20-0 (D)
1978—Lions, 31-14 (D)
1981—Chargers, 28-23 (SD)
(Points—Lions 108, Chargers 62)

DETROIT vs. SAN FRANCISCO

185

Lions lead series, 25-21-1
1950—Lions, 24-7 (D)
      49ers, 28-27 (SF)
1951—49ers, 20-10 (D)
      49ers, 21-17 (SF)
1952—49ers, 17-3 (SF)
      49ers, 28-0 (D)
1953—Lions, 24-21 (D)
      Lions, 14-10 (SF)
1954—49ers, 37-31 (SF)
      Lions, 48-7 (D)
1955—49ers, 27-24 (D)
      49ers, 38-21 (SF)
1956—Lions, 20-17 (D)
      Lions, 17-13 (SF)
1957—49ers, 35-31 (SF)
      Lions, 31-10 (D)
      *Lions, 31-27 (SF)
1958—49ers, 24-21 (SF)
      Lions, 35-21 (D)
1959—49ers, 34-13 (D)
      49ers, 33-7 (SF)
1960—49ers, 14-10 (D)
      Lions, 24-0 (SF)
1961—49ers, 49-0 (D)
      Tie, 20-20 (SF)
1962—Lions, 45-24 (D)
      Lions, 38-24 (SF)
1963—Lions, 26-3 (D)
      Lions, 45-7 (SF)
1964—Lions, 26-17 (SF)
      Lions, 24-7 (D)
1965—49ers, 27-21 (D)
      49ers, 17-14 (SF)
1966—49ers, 27-24 (SF)
      49ers, 41-14 (D)
1967—Lions, 45-3 (SF)
1968—49ers, 14-7 (D)
1969—Lions, 26-14 (SF)
1970—Lions, 28-7 (D)
1971—49ers, 31-27 (SF)
1973—Lions, 30-20 (D)
1974—Lions, 17-13 (D)
1975—Lions, 28-17 (SF)
1977—49ers, 28-7 (SF)
1978—Lions, 33-14 (D)
1980—Lions, 17-13 (D)
1981—Lions, 24-17 (D)
(Points—Lions 1,069, 49ers 943)
*Conference Playoff
DETROIT vs. SEATTLE
Series tied, 1-1
1976—Lions, 41-14 (S)
1978—Seahawks, 28-16 (S)
(Points—Lions 57, Seahawks 42)
DETROIT vs. TAMPA BAY
Lions lead series, 5-4
1977—Lions, 16-7 (D)
1978—Lions, 15-7 (TB)
      Lions, 34-23 (D)
1979—Buccaneers, 31-16 (TB)
      Buccaneers, 16-14 (D)
1980—Lions, 24-10 (TB)

Lions, 27-14 (D)
1981—Buccaneers, 28-10 (TB)
      Buccaneers, 20-17 (D)
(Points—Lions 173, Buccaneers 156)
*DETROIT vs. **WASHINGTON
Redskins lead series, 15-8
1932—Spartans, 10-0 (P)
1933—Spartans, 13-0 (B)
1934—Lions, 24-0 (D)
1935—Lions, 17-7 (B)
      Lions, 14-0 (D)
1938—Redskins, 7-5 (D)
1939—Redskins, 31-7 (W)
1940—Redskins, 20-14 (D)
1942—Redskins, 15-3 (D)
1943—Redskins, 42-20 (W)
1946—Redskins, 17-16 (W)
1947—Lions, 38-21 (D)
1948—Redskins, 46-21 (W)
1951—Lions, 35-17 (D)
*956—Redskins, 18-17 (W)
1965—Lions, 14-10 (D)
1968—Redskins, 14-3 (W)
1970—Redskins, 31-10 (W)
1973—Redskins, 20-0 (D)
1976—Redskins, 20-7 (W)
1978—Redskins, 21-19 (D)
1979—Redskins, 27-24 (D)
1981—Redskins, 33-31 (W)
(Points—Redskins 417, Lions 362)
*Franchise in Portsmouth prior to 1934
and known as the Spartans.
**Franchise in Boston prior to 1937

GREEN BAY vs. ATLANTA
Packers lead series, 7-5;
See Atlanta vs. Green Bay
GREEN BAY vs. BALTIMORE
Packers lead series, 18-16;
See Baltimore vs. Green Bay
GREEN BAY vs. BUFFALO
Bills lead series, 2-0;
See Buffalo vs. Green Bay
GREEN BAY vs. CHICAGO
Bears lead series, 66-53-6;
See Chicago vs. Green Bay
GREEN BAY vs. CINCINNATI
Series tied, 2-2;
See Cincinnati vs. Green Bay
GREEN BAY vs. CLEVELAND
Packers lead series, 6-5;
See Cleveland vs. Green Bay
GREEN BAY vs. DALLAS
Packers lead series, 8-3;
See Dallas vs. Green Bay
GREEN BAY vs. DENVER
Broncos lead series, 2-1;
See Denver vs. Green Bay
GREEN BAY vs. DETROIT
Packers lead series, 54-42-7;
See Detroit vs. Green Bay
GREEN BAY vs. HOUSTON
Oilers lead series, 2-1

1972—Packers, 23-10 (H)
1977—Oilers, 16-10 (GB)
1980—Oilers, 22-3 (GB)
(Points—Oilers 48, Packers 36)
GREEN BAY vs. KANSAS CITY
Series tied, 1-1-1
1966—*Packers, 35-10 (Los Angeles)
1973—Tie, 10-10 (Mil)
1977—Chiefs, 20-10 (KC)
(Points—Packers 55, Chiefs 40)
*Super Bowl I
GREEN BAY vs. *LOS ANGELES
Rams lead series, 38-31-2
1937—Packers, 35-10 (C)
       Packers, 35-7 (GB)
1938—Packers, 26-17 (GB)
       Packers, 28-7 (C)
1939—Rams, 27-24 (GB)
       Packers, 7-6 (C)
1940—Packers, 31-14 (GB)
       Tie, 13-13 (C)
1941—Packers, 24-7 (Mil)
       Packers, 17-14 (C)
1942—Packers, 45-28 (GB)
       Packers, 30-12 (C)
1944—Packers, 30-21 (GB)
       Packers, 42-7 (C)
1945—Rams, 27-14 (GB)
       Rams, 20-7 (C)
1946—Packers, 21-17 (Mil)
       Rams, 38-17 (LA)
1947—Packers, 17-14 (Mil)
       Packers, 30-10 (LA)
1948—Packers, 16-0 (GB)
       Rams, 24-10 (LA)
1949—Packers, 48-7 (GB)
       Rams, 35-7 (LA)
1950—Rams, 45-14 (Mil)
       Rams, 51-14 (LA)
1951—Rams, 28-0 (Mil)
       Rams, 42-14 (LA)
1952—Rams, 30-28 (Mil)
       Rams, 45-27 (LA)
1953—Rams, 38-20 (Mil)
       Rams, 33-17 (LA)
1954—Packers, 35-17 (Mil)
       Rams, 35-27 (LA)
1955—Packers, 30-28 (Mil)
       Rams, 31-17 (LA)
1956—Packers, 42-17 (Mil)
       Rams, 49-21 (LA)
1957—Rams, 31-27 (Mil)
       Rams, 42-17 (LA)
1958—Packers, 20-7 (GB)
       Rams, 34-20 (LA)
1959—Rams, 45-6 (Mil)
       Packers, 38-20 (LA)
1960—Rams, 33-31 (Mil)
       Packers, 35-2 (LA)
1961—Packers, 35-17 (GB)
       Packers, 24-17 (LA)
1962—Packers, 41-10 (Mil)
       Packers, 20-17 (LA)

1963—Packers, 42-10 (GB)
       Packers, 31-14 (LA)
1964—Rams, 27-17 (Mil)
       Tie, 24-24 (LA)
1965—Packers, 6-3 (Mil)
       Rams, 21-10 (LA)
1966—Packers, 24-13 (GB)
       Packers, 27-23 (LA)
1967—Rams, 27-24 (LA)
       **Packers, 28-7 (Mil)
1968—Rams, 16-14 (Mil)
1969—Rams, 34-21 (LA)
1970—Rams, 31-21 (GB)
1971—Rams, 30-13 (LA)
1973—Rams, 24-7 (LA)
1974—Packers, 17-6 (Mil)
1975—Rams, 22-5 (LA)
1977—Rams, 24-6 (LA)
1978—Rams, 31-14 (LA)
1980—Rams, 51-21 (LA)
1981—Rams, 35-23 (LA)
(Points—Rams 1,696, Packers 1,531)
*Franchise in Cleveland prior to 1946
**Conference Championship
GREEN BAY vs. MIAMI
Dolphins lead series, 3-0
1971—Dolphins, 27-6 (Mia)
1975—Dolphins, 31-7 (GB)
1979—Dolphins, 27-7 (Mia)
(Points—Dolphins 85, Packers 20)
GREEN BAY vs. MINNESOTA
Vikings lead series, 23-18-1
1961—Packers, 33-7 (Minn)
       Packers, 28-10 (Mil)
1962—Packers, 34-7 (GB)
       Packers, 48-21 (Minn)
1963—Packers, 37-28 (Minn)
       Packers, 28-7 (GB)
1964—Vikings, 24-23 (GB)
       Packers, 42-13 (Minn)
1965—Packers, 38-13 (Min)
       Packers, 24-19 (GB)
1966—Vikings, 20-17 (GB)
       Packers, 28-16 (Minn)
1967—Vikings, 10-7 (Mil)
       Packers, 30-27 (Minn)
1968—Vikings, 26-13 (Mil)
       Vikings, 14-10 (Minn)
1969—Vikings, 19-7 (Minn)
       Vikings, 9-7 (Mil)
1970—Packers, 13-10 (Mil)
       Vikings, 10-3 (Minn)
1971—Vikings, 24-13 (GB)
       Vikings, 3-0 (Minn)
1972—Vikings, 27-13 (GB)
       Packers, 23-7 (Minn)
1973—Vikings, 11-3 (Min)
       Vikings, 31-7 (GB)
1974—Vikings, 32-17 (GB)
       Packers, 19-7 (Minn)
1975—Vikings, 28-17 (GB)
       Vikings, 24-3 (Minn)
1976—Vikings, 17-10 (Mil)

Vikings, 20-9 (Minn)
1977—Vikings, 19-7 (Minn)
Vikings, 13-6 (GB)
1978—Vikings, 21-7 (Minn)
Tie, 10-10 (GB) OT
1979—Vikings, 27-21 (Minn) OT
Packers, 19-7 (Mil)
1980—Packers, 16-3 (GB)
Packers, 25-13 (Minn)
1981—Vikings, 30-13 (Mil)
Packers, 35-23 (Minn)
(Points—Packers 763, Vikings 707)

GREEN BAY vs. NEW ENGLAND
Series tied, 1-1
1973—Patriots, 33-24 (NE)
1979—Packers, 27-14 (GB)
(Points—Packers 51, Patriots 47)

GREEN BAY vs. NEW ORLEANS
Packers lead series, 8-2
1968—Packers, 29-7 (Mil)
1971—Saints, 29-21 (Mil)
1972—Packers, 30-20 (NO)
1973—Packers, 30-10 (Mil)
1975—Saints, 20-19 (NO)
1976—Packers, 32-27 (Mil)
1977—Packers, 24-20 (NO)
1978—Packers, 28-17 (Mil)
1979—Packers, 28-19 (Mil)
1981—Packers, 35-7 (NO)
(Points—Packers 276, Saints 176)

GREEN BAY vs. N.Y. GIANTS
Packers lead series, 23-17-2
1928—Giants, 6-0 (GB)
Packers, 7-0 (NY)
1929—Packers, 20-6 (NY)
1930—Packers, 14-7 (NY)
Giants, 13-6 (NY)
1931—Packers, 27-7 (GB)
Packers, 14-10 (NY)
1932—Packers, 13-0 (GB)
Giants, 6-0 (NY)
1933—Giants, 10-7 (Mil)
Giants, 17-6 (NY)
1934—Packers, 20-6 (Mil)
Giants, 17-3 (NY)
1935—Packers, 16-7 (GB)
1936—Packers, 26-14 (NY)
1937—Giants, 10-0 (NY)
1938—Giants, 15-3 (NY)
*Giants, 23-17 (NY)
1939—*Packers, 27-0 (Mil)
1940—Packers, 7-3 (NY)
1942—Tie, 21-21 (NY)
1943—Packers, 35-21 (NY)
1944—Giants, 24-0 (NY)
*Packers, 14-7 (NY)
1945—Packers, 23-14 (NY)
1947—Tie, 24-24 (NY)
1948—Giants, 49-3 (Mil)
1949—Giants, 30-10 (NY)
1952—Packers, 17-3 (NY)
1957—Giants, 31-17 (GB)
1959—Giants, 20-3 (NY)

1961—Packers, 20-17 (Mil)
*Packers, 37-0 (GB)
1962—*Packers, 16-7 (NY)
1967—Packers, 48-21 (NY)
1969—Packers, 20-10 (Mil)
1971—Giants, 42-40 (GB)
1973—Packers, 16-14 (New Haven)
1975—Packers, 40-14 (NY)
1980—Giants, 27-21 (NY)
1981—Packers, 27-14 (NY)
Packers, 26-24 (Mil)
(Points—Packers 707, Giants 615)
*NFL Championship

GREEN BAY vs. N.Y. JETS
Jets lead series, 2-1
1973—Packers, 23-7 (Mil)
1979—Jets, 27-22 (GB)
1981—Jets, 28-3 (NY)
(Points—Jets 62, Packers 48)

GREEN BAY vs. OAKLAND
Raiders lead series, 3-1
1967—*Packers, 33-14 (Miami)
1972—Raiders, 20-14 (GB)
1976—Raiders, 18-14 (O)
1978—Raiders, 28-3 (GB)
(Points—Raiders 80, Packers 64)
*Super Bowl II

GREEN BAY vs. PHILADELPHIA
Packers lead series, 17-5
1933—Packers, 35-9 (GB)
Packers, 10-0 (P)
1934—Packers, 19-6 (GB)
1935—Packers, 13-6 (P)
1937—Packers, 37-7 (Mil)
1939—Packers, 23-16 (P)
1940—Packers, 27-20 (GB)
1942—Packers, 7-0 (P)
1946—Packers, 19-7 (P)
1947—Eagles, 28-14 (P)
1951—Packers, 37-24 (GB)
1952—Packers, 12-10 (Mil)
1954—Packers, 37-14 (P)
1958—Packers, 38-35 (GB)
1960—*Eagles, 17-13 (P)
1962—Packers, 49-0 (P)
1968—Packers, 30-13 (GB)
1970—Packers, 30-17 (Mil)
1974—Eagles, 36-14 (P)
1976—Packers, 28-13 (GB)
1978—Eagles, 10-3 (P)
1979—Eagles, 21-10 (GB)
(Points—Packers 505, Eagles 309)
*NFL Championship

GREEN BAY vs. *PITTSBURGH
Packers lead series, 16-9
1933—Packers, 47-0 (GB)
1935—Packers, 27-0 (GB)
Packers, 34-14 (P)
1936—Packers, 42-10 (Mil)
1938—Packers, 20-0 (GB)
1940—Packers, 24-3 (Mil)
1941—Packers, 54-7 (P)
1942—Packers, 24-21 (Mil)

1946—Packers, 17-7 (GB)
1947—Steelers, 18-17 (Mil)
1948—Steelers, 38-7 (P)
1949—Steelers, 30-7 (Mil)
1951—Packers, 35-33 (Mil)
       Steelers, 28-7 (P)
1953—Steelers, 31-14 (P)
1954—Steelers, 21-20 (GB)
1957—Packers, 27-10 (P)
1960—Packers, 19-13 (P)
1963—Packers, 33-14 (Mil)
1965—Packers, 41-9 (P)
1967—Steelers, 24-17 (GB)
1969—Packers, 38-34 (P)
1970—Packers, 20-12 (P)
1975—Steelers, 16-13 (Mil)
1980—Steelers, 22-20 (P)
(Points—Packers 624, Steelers 415)
*Steelers known as Pirates prior to 1941

GREEN BAY vs. *ST. LOUIS
Packers lead series, 36-20-4
1921—Tie, 3-3 (C)
1922—Cardinals, 16-3 (C)
1924—Cardinals, 3-0 (C)
1925—Cardinals, 9-6 (C)
1926—Cardinals, 13-7 (GB)
       Packers, 3-0 (C)
1927—Packers, 13-0 (GB)
       Tie, 6-6 (C)
1928—Packers, 20-0 (GB)
1929—Packers, 9-2 (GB)
       Packers, 7-6 (C)
       Packers, 12-0 (C)
1930—Packers, 14-0 (GB)
       Cardinals, 13-6 (C)
1931—Packers, 26-7 (GB)
       Cardinals, 21-13 (C)
1932—Packers, 15-7 (GB)
       Packers, 19-9 (C)
1933—Packers, 14-6 (C)
1934—Packers, 15-0 (GB)
       Cardinals, 9-0 (Mil)
       Cardinals, 6-0 (C)
1935—Cardinals, 7-6 (GB)
       Cardinals, 3-0 (Mil)
       Cardinals, 9-7 (C)
1936—Packers, 10-7 (GB)
       Packers, 24-0 (Mil)
       Tie, 0-0 (C)
1937—Cardinals, 14-7 (GB)
       Packers, 34-13 (Mil)
1938—Packers, 28-7 (Mil)
       Packers, 24-22 (Buffalo)
1939—Packers, 14-10 (GB)
       Packers, 27-20 (Mil)
1940—Packers, 31-6 (Mil)
       Packers, 28-7 (C)
1941—Packers, 14-13 (Mil)
       Packers, 17-9 (GB)
1942—Packers, 17-13 (C)
       Packers, 55-24 (Mil)
1943—Packers, 28-7 (C)
       Packers, 35-14 (Mil)

1945—Packers, 33-14 (GB)
1946—Packers, 19-7 (C)
       Cardinals, 24-6 (GB)
1947—Cardinals, 14-10 (GB)
       Cardinals, 21-20 (C)
1948—Cardinals, 17-7 (Mil)
       Cardinals, 42-7 (C)
1949—Cardinals, 39-17 (Mil)
       Cardinals, 41-21 (C)
1955—Packers, 31-14 (GB)
1956—Packers, 24-21 (C)
1962—Packers, 17-0 (Mil)
1963—Packers, 30-7 (StL)
1967—Packers, 31-23 (StL)
1969—Packers, 45-28 (GB)
1971—Tie, 16-16 (StL)
1973—Packers, 25-21 (GB)
1976—Cardinals, 29-0 (StL)
(Points—Packers 976, Cardinals 719)
*Franchise in Chicago prior to 1960

GREEN BAY vs. SAN DIEGO
Packers lead series, 3-0
1970—Packers, 22-20 (SD)
1974—Packers, 34-0 (GB)
1978—Packers, 24-3 (SD)
(Points—Packers 80, Chargers 23)

GREEN BAY vs. SAN FRANCISCO
49ers lead series, 22-20-1
1950—Packers, 25-21 (GB)
       49ers, 30-14 (SF)
1951—49ers, 31-19 (SF)
1952—49ers, 24-14 (SF)
1953—49ers, 37-7 (Mil)
       49ers, 48-14 (SF)
1954—49ers, 23-17 (Mil)
       49ers, 35-0 (SF)
1955—Packers, 27-21 (Mil)
       Packers, 28-7 (SF)
1956—49ers, 17-16 (GB)
       49ers, 38-20 (SF)
1957—49ers, 24-14 (Mil)
       49ers, 27-20 (SF)
1958—49ers, 33-12 (Mil)
       49ers, 48-21 (SF)
1959—Packers, 21-20 (GB)
       Packers, 36-14 (SF)
1960—Packers, 41-14 (Mil)
       Packers, 13-0 (SF)
1961—Packers, 30-10 (GB)
       49ers, 22-21 (SF)
1962—Packers, 31-13 (Mil)
       Packers, 31-21 (SF)
1963—Packers, 28-10 (Mil)
       Packers 21-17 (SF)
1964—Packers, 24-14 (Mil)
       49ers, 24-14 (SF)
1965—Packers, 27-10 (GB)
       Tie, 24-24 (SF)
1966—49ers, 21-20 (SF)
       Packers, 20-7 (Mil)
1967—Packers, 13-0 (GB)
1968—49ers, 27-20 (SF)
1969—Packers, 14-7 (Mil)

All-Time Team vs. Team Results

1970—49ers, 26-10 (SF)
1972—Packers, 34-24 (Mil)
1973—49ers, 20-6 (SF)
1974—49ers, 7-6 (SF)
1976—49ers, 26-14 (GB)
1977—Packers, 16-14 (Mil)
1980—Packers, 23-16 (Mil)
1981—49ers, 13-3 (Mil)
(Points—49ers 885, Packers 829)

GREEN BAY vs. SEATTLE
Packers lead series, 3-0
1976—Packers, 27-20 (Mil)
1978—Packers, 45-28 (Mil)
1981—Packers, 34-24 (GB)
(Points—Packers 106, Seahawks 72)

GREEN BAY vs. TAMPA BAY
Buccaneers lead series, 5-3-1
1977—Packers, 13-0 (TB)
1978—Packers, 9-7 (GB)
　　　Packers, 17-7 (TB)
1979—Buccaneers, 21-10 (GB)
　　　Buccaneers, 21-3 (TB)
1980—Tie, 14-14 (TB) OT
　　　Buccaneers, 20-17 (Mil)
1981—Buccaneers, 21-10 (GB)
　　　Buccaneers, 37-3 (TB)
(Points—Buccaneers 148, Packers 96)

GREEN BAY vs. *WASHINGTON
Packers lead series, 13-11-1
1932—Packers, 21-0 (B)
1933—Tie, 7-7 (GB)
　　　Redskins, 20-7 (B)
1934—Packers, 10-0 (B)
1936—Packers, 31-2 (GB)
　　　Packers, 7-3 (B)
　　　**Packers, 21-6 (New York)
1937—Redskins, 14-6 (W)
1939—Packers, 24-14 (Mil)
1941—Packers, 22-17 (W)
1943—Redskins, 33-7 (Mil)
1946—Packers, 20-7 (W)
1947—Packers, 27-10 (Mil)
1948—Packers, 23-7 (Mil)
1949—Redskins, 30-0 (W)
1950—Packers, 35-21 (Mil)
1952—Packers, 35-20 (Mil)
1958—Redskins, 37-21 (W)
1959—Packers, 21-0 (GB)
1968—Packers, 27-7 (W)
1972—Redskins, 21-16 (W)
　　　***Redskins, 16-3 (W)
1974—Redskins, 17-6 (GB)
1977—Redskins, 10-9 (W)
1979—Redskins, 38-21 (W)
(Points—Packers 411, Redskins 373)
*Franchise in Boston prior to 1937 and
known as Braves prior to 1933
**NFL Championship
***NFC Divisional Playoff

HOUSTON vs. ATLANTA
Falcons lead series, 3-1;
See Atlanta vs. Houston

HOUSTON vs. BALTIMORE
Oilers lead series, 3-2;
See Baltimore vs. Houston

HOUSTON vs. BUFFALO
Oilers lead series, 17-7;
See Buffalo vs. Houston

HOUSTON vs. CHICAGO
Oilers lead series, 2-1;
See Chicago vs. Houston

HOUSTON vs. CINCINNATI
Bengals lead series, 13-12-1;
See Cincinnati vs. Houston

HOUSTON vs. CLEVELAND
Browns lead series, 14-10;
See Cleveland vs. Houston

HOUSTON vs. DALLAS
Cowboys lead series, 2-1;
See Dallas vs. Houston

HOUSTON vs. DENVER
Oilers lead series, 18-8-1;
See Denver vs. Houston

HOUSTON vs. DETROIT
Series tied, 1-1;
See Detroit vs. Houston

HOUSTON vs. GREEN BAY
Oilers lead series, 2-1;
See Green Bay vs. Houston

HOUSTON vs. *KANSAS CITY
Chiefs lead series, 19-10
1960—Oilers, 20-10 (H)
　　　Texans, 24-0 (D)
1961—Texans, 26-21 (D)
　　　Oilers, 38-7 (H)
1962—Texans, 31-7 (H)
　　　Oilers, 14-6 (D)
　　　**Texans, 20-17 (H) OT
1963—Chiefs, 28-7 (KC)
　　　Oilers, 28-7 (H)
1964—Chiefs, 28-7 (KC)
　　　Chiefs, 28-19 (H)
1965—Chiefs, 52-21 (KC)
　　　Oilers, 38-36 (H)
1966—Chiefs, 48-23 (KC)
1967—Chiefs, 25-20 (H)
　　　Oilers, 24-19 (KC)
1968—Chiefs, 26-21 (H)
　　　Chiefs, 24-10 (KC)
1969—Chiefs, 24-0 (KC)
1970—Chiefs, 24-9 (KC)
1971—Chiefs, 20-16 (H)
1973—Chiefs, 38-14 (KC)
1974—Chiefs, 17-7 (H)
1975—Oilers, 17-13 (KC)
1977—Oilers, 34-20 (H)
1978—Oilers, 20-17 (KC)
1979—Oilers, 20-6 (H)
1980—Chiefs, 21-20 (KC)
1981—Chiefs, 23-10 (KC)
(Points—Chiefs 668, Oilers 502)
*Franchise in Dallas prior to 1963 and
known as Texans
**AFL Championship

HOUSTON vs. LOS ANGELES

Rams lead series, 2-1
1973—Rams, 31-26 (H)
1978—Rams, 10-6 (H)
1981—Oilers, 27-20 (LA)
(Points—Rams 61, Oilers 59)
HOUSTON vs. MIAMI
Oilers lead series, 9-7
1966—Dolphins, 20-13 (H)
        Dolphins, 29-28 (M)
1967—Oilers, 17-14 (H)
        Oilers, 41-10 (M)
1968—Oilers, 24-10 (M)
        Dolphins, 24-7 (H)
1969—Oilers, 22-10 (H)
        Oilers, 32-7 (M)
1970—Dolphins, 20-10 (H)
1972—Dolphins, 34-13 (M)
1975—Oilers, 20-19 (H)
1977—Dolphins, 27-7 (M)
1978—Oilers, 35-30 (H)
        *Oilers, 17-9 (M)
1979—Oilers, 9-6 (M)
1981—Dolphins, 16-10 (H)
(Points—Oilers 305, Dolphins 285)
*AFC First Round Playoff
HOUSTON vs. MINNESOTA
Series tied, 1-1
1974—Vikings, 51-10 (M)
1980—Oilers, 20-16 (H)
(Points—Vikings 67, Oilers 30)
HOUSTON vs. *NEW ENGLAND
Series tied, 13-13-1
1960—Oilers, 24-10 (B)
        Oilers, 37-21 (H)
1961—Tie, 31-31 (B)
        Oilers, 27-15 (H)
1962—Patriots, 34-21 (B)
        Oilers, 21-17 (H)
1963—Patriots, 45-3 (B)
        Patriots, 46-28 (H)
1964—Patriots, 25-24 (B)
        Patriots, 34-17 (H)
1965—Oilers, 31-10 (H)
        Patriots, 42-14 (B)
1966—Patriots, 27-21 (B)
        Patriots, 38-14 (H)
1967—Patriots, 18-7 (B)
        Oilers, 27-6 (H)
1968—Oilers, 16-0 (B)
        Oilers, 45-17 (H)
1969—Patriots, 24-0 (B)
        Oilers, 27-23 (H)
1971—Patriots, 28-20 (NE)
1973—Oilers, 32-0 (H)
1975—Oilers, 7-0 (NE)
1978—Oilers, 26-23 (NE)
        **Oilers, 31-14 (NE)
1980—Oilers, 38-34 (H)
1981—Patriots, 38-10 (NE)
(Points—Patriots 652, Oilers 567)
*Franchise in Boston prior to 1971
**AFC Divisional Playoff
HOUSTON vs. NEW ORLEANS

Oilers lead series, 2-1-1
1971—Tie, 13-13 (H)
1976—Oilers, 31-26 (NO)
1978—Oilers, 17-12 (NO)
1981—Saints, 27-24 (H)
(Points—Oilers 85, Saints 78)
HOUSTON vs. N.Y. GIANTS
Giants lead series, 1-0
1973—Giants, 34-14 (NY)
HOUSTON vs. *N.Y. JETS
Oilers lead series, 14-10-1
1960—Oilers, 27-21 (H)
        Oilers, 42-28 (NY)
1961—Oilers, 49-13 (H)
        Oilers, 48-21 (NY)
1962—Oilers, 56-17 (H)
        Oilers, 44-10 (NY)
1963—Jets, 24-17 (NY)
        Oilers, 31-27 (H)
1964—Jets, 24-21(NY)
        Oilers, 33-17 (H)
1965—Oilers, 27-21 (H)
        Jets, 41-14 (NY)
1966—Jets, 52-13 (NY)
        Oilers, 24-0 (H)
1967—Tie, 28-28 (NY)
1968—Jets, 20-14 (H)
        Jets, 26-7 (NY)
1969—Jets, 26-17 (NY)
        Jets, 34-26 (H)
1972—Oilers, 26-20 (H)
1974—Oilers, 27-22 (NY)
1977—Oilers, 20-0 (H)
1979—Oilers, 27-24 (H) OT
1980—Jets, 31-28 (NY) OT
1981—Jets, 33-17 (NY)
(Points—Oilers 683, Jets 580)
*Jets known as Titans prior to 1963
HOUSTON vs. OAKLAND
Raiders lead series, 19-10
1960—Oilers, 37-22 (O)
        Raiders, 14-13 (H)
1961—Oilers, 55-0 (H)
        Oilers, 47-16 (O)
1962—Oilers, 28-20 (O)
        Oilers, 32-17 (H)
1963—Raiders, 24-13 (H)
        Raiders, 52-49 (O)
1964—Oilers, 42-28 (H)
        Raiders, 20-10 (O)
1965—Oilers, 21-17 (O)
        Raiders, 33-21 (H)
1966—Oilers, 31-0 (H)
        Raiders, 38-23 (O)
1967—Raiders, 19-7 (H)
        *Raiders, 40-7 (O)
1968—Raiders, 24-15 (H)
1969—Raiders, 21-17 (O)
        **Raiders, 56-7 (O)
1971—Raiders, 41-21 (O)
1972—Raiders, 34-0 (H)
1973—Raiders, 17-6 (H)
1975—Oilers, 27-26 (O)

All-Time Team vs. Team Results

1976—Raiders, 14-13 (H)
1977—Raiders, 34-29 (O)
1978—Raiders, 21-17 (O)
1979—Oilers, 31-17 (H)
1980— ***Raiders, 27-7 (O)
1981—Oilers, 17-16 (H)
(Points—Raiders 712, Oilers 639)
*AFL Championship
**Inter-Divisional Playoff
***AFC First Round Playoff
HOUSTON vs. PHILADELPHIA
Eagles lead series, 2-0
1972—Eagles, 18-17 (H)
1979—Eagles, 26-20 (H)
(Points—Eagles 44, Oilers 37)
HOUSTON vs. PITTSBURGH
Steelers lead series, 18-8
1970—Oilers, 19-7 (P)
　　　Steelers, 7-3 (H)
1971—Steelers, 23-16 (P)
　　　Oilers, 29-3 (H)
1972—Steelers, 24-7 (P)
　　　Steelers, 9-3 (H)
1973—Steelers, 36-7 (H)
　　　Steelers, 33-7 (P)
1974—Steelers, 13-7 (H)
　　　Oilers, 13-10 (P)
1975—Steelers, 24-17 (P)
　　　Steelers, 32-9 (H)
1976—Steelers, 32-16 (P)
　　　Steelers, 21-0 (H)
1977—Oilers, 27-10 (H)
　　　Steelers, 27-10 (P)
1978—Oilers, 24-17 (P)
　　　Steelers, 13-3 (H)
　　　*Steelers, 34-5 (P)
1979—Steelers, 38-7 (H)
　　　Oilers, 20-17 (H)
　　　*Steelers, 27-13 (P)
1980—Steelers, 31-17 (P)
　　　Oilers, 6-0 (H)
1981—Steelers, 26-13 (P)
　　　Oilers, 21-20 (H)
(Points—Steelers 534, Oilers 319)
*AFC Championship
HOUSTON vs. ST. LOUIS
Cardinals lead series, 3-0
1970—Cardinals, 44-0 (StL)
1974—Cardinals, 31-27 (H)
1979—Cardinals, 24-17 (H)
(Points—Cardinals 99, Oilers 44)
HOUSTON vs. *SAN DIEGO
Chargers lead series, 15-11-1
1960—Oilers, 38-28 (H)
　　　Chargers, 24-21 (LA)
　　　**Oilers, 24-16 (H)
1961—Chargers, 34-24 (SD)
　　　Oilers, 33-13 (H)
　　　**Oilers, 10-3 (SD)
1962—Oilers, 42-17 (SD)
　　　Oilers, 33-27 (H)
1963—Chargers, 27-0 (SD)
　　　Chargers 20-14 (H)

1964—Chargers, 27-21 (SD)
　　　Chargers, 20-17 (H)
1965—Chargers, 31-14 (SD)
　　　Chargers, 37-26 (H)
1966—Chargers, 28-22 (H)
1967—Chargers, 13-3 (SD)
　　　Oilers, 24-17 (H)
1968—Chargers, 30-14 (SD)
1969—Chargers, 21-17 (H)
1970—Tie, 31-31 (SD)
1971—Oilers, 49-33 (H)
1972—Chargers, 34-20 (SD)
1974—Oilers, 21-14 (H)
1975—Oilers, 33-17 (H)
1976—Chargers, 30-27 (SD)
1978—Chargers, 45-24 (H)
1979—***Oilers, 17-14 (SD)
(Points—Chargers 651, Oilers 619)
*Franchise in Los Angeles prior to 1961
**AFL Championship
***AFC Divisional Playoff
HOUSTON vs. SAN FRANCISCO
Series tied, 2-2
1970—49ers, 30-20 (H)
1975—Oilers, 27-13 (SF)
1978—Oilers, 20-19 (H)
1981—49ers, 28-6 (SF)
(Points—49ers 90, Oilers 73)
HOUSTON vs. SEATTLE
Series tied, 2-2
1977—Oilers, 22-10 (S)
1979—Seahawks, 34-14 (S)
1980—Seahawks, 26-7 (H)
1981—Oilers, 35-17 (H)
(Points—Seahawks 87, Oilers 78)
HOUSTON vs. TAMPA BAY
Oilers lead series, 2-0
1976—Oilers, 20-0 (H)
1980—Oilers, 20-14 (H)
(Points—Oilers 40, Buccaneers 14)
HOUSTON vs. WASHINGTON
Oilers lead series, 2-1
1971—Redskins, 22-13 (W)
1975—Oilers, 13-10 (H)
1979—Oilers, 29-27 (W)
(Points—Redskins 59, Oilers 55)

KANSAS CITY vs. ATLANTA
Chiefs lead series, 1-0;
See Atlanta vs. Kansas City
KANSAS CITY vs. BALTIMORE
Chiefs lead series, 5-3;
See Baltimore vs. Kansas City
KANSAS CITY vs. BUFFALO
Bills lead series, 12-11-1;
See Buffalo vs. Kansas City
KANSAS CITY vs. CHICAGO
Bears lead series, 2-1;
See Chicago vs. Kansas City
KANSAS CITY vs. CINCINNATI
Bengals lead series, 7-6;
See Cincinnati vs. Kansas City
KANSAS CITY vs. CLEVELAND

192

Series tied, 4-4-1;
See Cleveland vs. Kansas City
KANSAS CITY vs. DALLAS
Series tied, 1-1;
See Dallas vs. Kansas City
KANSAS CITY vs. DENVER
Chiefs lead series, 30-14;
See Denver vs. Kansas City
KANSAS CITY vs. DETROIT
Series tied, 2-2;
See Detroit vs. Kansas City
KANSAS CITY vs. GREEN BAY
Series tied, 1-1-1;
See Green Bay vs. Kansas City
KANSAS CITY vs. HOUSTON
Chiefs lead series, 19-10;
See Houston vs. Kansas City
KANSAS CITY vs. LOS ANGELES
Rams lead series, 1-0
1973—Rams, 23-13 (KC)
KANSAS CITY vs. MIAMI
Chiefs lead series, 7-4
1966—Chiefs, 34-16 (KC)
      Chiefs, 19-18 (M)
1967—Chiefs, 24-0 (M)
      Chiefs, 41-0 (KC)
1968—Chiefs, 48-3 (M)
1969—Chiefs, 17-10 (KC)
1971—*Dolphins, 27-24 (KC) OT
1972—Dolphins, 20-10 (KC)
1974—Dolphins, 9-3 (M)
1976—Chiefs, 20-17 (M) OT
1981—Dolphins, 17-7 (KC)
(Points—Chiefs 247, Dolphins 137)
*AFC Divisional Playoff
KANSAS CITY vs. MINNESOTA
Series tied, 2-2
1969—*Chiefs, 23-7 (New Orleans)
1970—Vikings, 27-10 (M)
1974—Vikings, 35-15 (KC)
1981—Chiefs, 10-6 (M)
(Points—Vikings 75, Chiefs 58)
*Super Bowl IV
*KANSAS CITY vs. **NEW ENGLAND
Chiefs lead series, 11-7-3
1960—Patriots, 42-14 (B)
      Texans, 34-0 (D)
1961—Patriots, 18-17 (D)
      Patriots, 28-21 (B)
1962—Texans, 42-28 (D)
      Texans, 27-7 (B)
1963—Tie, 24-24 (B)
      Chiefs, 35-3 (KC)
1964—Patriots, 24-7 (B)
      Patriots, 31-24 (KC)
1965—Chiefs, 27-17 (KC)
      Tie, 10-10 (B)
1966—Chiefs, 43-24 (B)
      Tie, 27-27 (KC)
1967—Chiefs, 33-10 (B)
1968—Chiefs, 31-17 (KC)
1969—Chiefs, 31-0 (B)
1970—Chiefs, 23-10 (KC)

1973—Chiefs, 10-7 (NE)
1977—Patriots, 21-17 (NE)
1981—Patriots, 33-17 (NE)
(Points—Chiefs 514, Patriots 381)
*Franchise located in Dallas prior to 1963
and known as Texans
**Franchise in Boston prior to 1971
KANSAS CITY vs. NEW ORLEANS
Series tied, 1-1
1972—Chiefs, 20-17 (NO)
1976—Saints, 27-17 (KC)
(Points—Saints 44, Chiefs 37)
KANSAS CITY vs. N. Y. GIANTS
Giants lead series, 3-0
1974—Giants, 33-27 (KC)
1978—Giants, 26-10 (NY)
1979—Giants, 21-17 (KC)
(Points—Giants 80, Chiefs 54)
*KANSAS CITY vs. **N. Y. JETS
Chiefs lead series, 12-9
1960—Titans, 37-35 (D)
      Titans, 41-35 (NY)
1961—Titans, 28-7 (NY)
      Texans, 35-24 (D)
1962—Texans, 20-17 (D)
      Texans, 52-31 (NY)
1963—Jets, 17-0 (NY)
      Chiefs, 48-0 (KC)
1964—Jets, 27-14 (NY)
      Chiefs, 24-7 (KC)
1965—Chiefs, 14-10 (KC)
      Jets, 13-10 (KC)
1966—Chiefs, 32-24 (NY)
1967—Chiefs, 42-18 (KC)
      Chiefs, 21-7 (NY)
1968—Jets, 20-19 (KC)
1969—Chiefs, 34-16 (NY)
      ***Chiefs, 13-6 (NY)
1971—Jets, 13-10 (NY)
1974—Chiefs, 24-16 (NY)
1975—Jets, 30-24 (KC)
(Points—Chiefs 513, Jets 402)
*Franchise in Dallas prior to 1963 and
known as Texans
**Jets known as Titans prior to 1963
***Inter-Divisional Playoff
*KANSAS CITY vs. OAKLAND
Raiders lead series, 24-20-2
1960—Texans, 34-16 (O)
      Raiders, 20-19 (D)
1961—Texans, 42-35 (O)
      Texans, 43-11 (D)
1962—Texans, 26-16 (O)
      Texans, 35-7 (D)
1963—Raiders, 10-7 (O)
      Raiders, 22-7 (KC)
1964—Chiefs, 21-9 (O)
      Chiefs, 42-7 (KC)
1965—Raiders, 37-10 (O)
      Chiefs, 14-7 (KC)
1966—Chiefs, 32-10 (KC)
      Raiders, 34-13 (KC)
1967—Raiders, 23-21 (O)

Raiders, 44-22 (KC)
1968—Chiefs, 24-10 (KC)
Raiders, 38-21 (O)
**Raiders, 41-6 (O)
1969—Chiefs, 27-24 (KC)
Raiders, 10-6 (O)
***Chiefs, 17-7 (O)
1970—Tie, 17-17 (KC)
Raiders, 20-6 (O)
1971—Tie, 20-20 (O)
Chiefs, 16-14 (KC)
1972—Chiefs, 27-14 (KC)
Raiders, 26-3 (O)
1973—Chiefs, 16-3 (KC)
Raiders, 37-7 (O)
1974—Raiders, 27-7 (O)
Raiders, 7-6 (KC)
1975—Chiefs, 42-10 (KC)
Raiders, 28-20 (O)
1976—Raiders, 24-21 (KC)
Raiders, 21-10 (O)
1977—Raiders, 37-28 (KC)
Raiders, 21-20 (O)
1978—Raiders, 28-6 (O)
Raiders, 20-10 (KC)
1979—Chiefs, 35-7 (KC)
Chiefs, 24-21 (O)
1980—Raiders, 27-14 (KC)
Chiefs, 31-17 (O)
1981—Chiefs, 27-0 (KC)
Chiefs, 28-17 (O)
(Points—Chiefs 927, Raiders 904)
*Franchise in Dallas prior to 1963 and
known as Texans*
**Division Playoff*
***AFL Championship*
KANSAS CITY vs. PHILADELPHIA
Eagles lead series, 1-0
1972—Eagles, 21-20 (KC)
KANSAS CITY vs. PITTSBURGH
Steelers lead series, 7-3
1970—Chiefs, 31-14 (P)
1971—Chiefs, 38-16 (KC)
1972—Steelers, 16-7 (P)
1974—Steelers, 34-24 (KC)
1975—Steelers, 28-3 (P)
1976—Steelers, 45-0 (KC)
1978—Steelers, 27-24 (P)
1979—Steelers, 30-3 (KC)
1980—Steelers, 21-16 (P)
1981—Chiefs, 37-33 (P)
(Points—Steelers 264, Chiefs 183)
KANSAS CITY vs. ST. LOUIS
Chiefs lead series, 2-0-1
1970—Tie, 6-6 (KC)
1974—Chiefs, 17-13 (StL)
1980—Chiefs, 21-13 (StL)
(Points—Chiefs 44, Cardinals 32)
***KANSAS CITY vs. **SAN DIEGO**
Chargers lead series, 23-20-1
1960—Chargers, 21-20 (LA)
Texans, 17-0 (D)
1961—Chargers, 26-10 (D)

Chargers, 24-14 (SD)
1962—Chargers, 32-28 (SD)
Texans, 26-17 (D)
1963—Chargers, 24-10 (SD)
Chargers, 38-17 (KC)
1964—Chargers, 28-14 (KC)
Chiefs, 49-6 (SD)
1965—Tie, 10-10 (SD)
Chiefs, 31-7 (KC)
1966—Chiefs, 24-14 (KC)
Chiefs, 27-17 (SD)
1967—Chargers, 45-31 (SD)
Chargers, 17-16 (KC)
1968—Chiefs, 27-20 (SD)
Chiefs, 40-3 (SD)
1969—Chiefs, 27-9 (SD)
Chiefs, 27-3 (KC)
1970—Chiefs, 26-14 (KC)
Chargers, 31-13 (SD)
1971—Chargers, 21-14 (SD)
Chiefs, 31-10 (KC)
1972—Chiefs, 26-14 (SD)
Chargers, 27-17 (KC)
1973—Chiefs, 19-0 (KC)
Chiefs, 33-6 (KC)
1974—Chiefs, 24-14 (SD)
Chargers, 14-7 (KC)
1975—Chiefs, 12-10 (SD)
Chargers, 28-20 (KC)
1976—Chargers, 30-16 (KC)
Chiefs, 23-20 (SD)
1977—Chargers, 23-7 (KC)
Chiefs, 21-16 (SD)
1978—Chargers, 29-23 (SD) OT
Chiefs, 23-0 (KC)
1979—Chargers, 20-14 (KC)
Chargers, 28-7 (SD)
1980—Chargers, 24-7 (KC)
Chargers, 20-7 (SD)
1981—Chargers, 42-31 (KC)
Chargers, 22-20 (SD)
(Points—Chiefs 906, Chargers 824)
*Franchise in Dallas prior to 1963 and
known as Texans*
**Franchise in Los Angeles prior to 1961*
KANSAS CITY vs. SAN FRANCISCO
Series tied, 1-1
1971—Chiefs, 26-17 (SF)
1975—49ers, 20-3 (KC)
(Points—49ers 37, Chiefs 29)
KANSAS CITY vs. SEATTLE
Chiefs lead series, 5-4
1977—Seahawks, 34-31 (KC)
1978—Seahawks, 13-10 (KC)
Seahawks, 23-19 (S)
1979—Chiefs, 24-6 (S)
Chiefs, 37-21 (KC)
1980—Seahawks, 17-16 (KC)
Chiefs, 31-30 (S)
1981—Chiefs, 20-14 (S)
Chiefs, 40-13 (KC)
(Points—Chiefs 228, Seahawks 171)
KANSAS CITY vs. TAMPA BAY

Series tied, 2-2
1976—Chiefs, 28-19 (TB)
1978—Buccaneers, 30-13 (KC)
1979—Buccaneers, 3-0 (TB)
1981—Chiefs, 19-10 (KC)
(Points—Buccaneers 62, Chiefs 60)

KANSAS CITY vs. WASHINGTON
Chiefs lead series, 2-0
1971—Chiefs, 27-20 (KC)
1976—Chiefs, 33-30 (W)
(Points—Chiefs 60, Redskins 50)

LOS ANGELES vs. ATLANTA
Rams lead series, 24-5-2;
See Atlanta vs. Los Angeles

LOS ANGELES vs. BALTIMORE
Colts lead series, 20-14-2;
See Baltimore vs. Los Angeles

LOS ANGELES vs. BUFFALO
Rams lead series, 2-1;
See Buffalo vs. Los Angeles

LOS ANGELES vs. CHICAGO
Bears lead series, 41-25-3;
See Chicago vs. Los Angeles

LOS ANGELES vs. CINCINNATI
Bengals lead series, 3-1;
See Cincinnati vs. Los Angeles

LOS ANGELES vs. CLEVELAND
Browns lead series, 8-6;
See Cleveland vs. Los Angeles

LOS ANGELES vs. DALLAS
Cowboys lead series, 9-8;
See Dallas vs. Los Angeles

LOS ANGELES vs. DENVER
Rams lead series, 2-1;
See Denver vs. Los Angeles

LOS ANGELES vs. DETROIT
Rams lead series, 35-33-1;
See Detroit vs. Los Angeles

LOS ANGELES vs. GREEN BAY
Rams lead series, 38-31-2;
See Green Bay vs. Los Angeles

LOS ANGELES vs. HOUSTON
Rams lead series, 2-1;
See Houston vs. Los Angeles

LOS ANGELES vs. KANSAS CITY
Rams lead series, 1-0;
See Kansas City vs. Los Angeles

LOS ANGELES vs. MIAMI
Dolphins lead series, 2-1
1971—Dolphins, 20-14 (LA)
1976—Rams, 31-28 (M)
1980—Dolphins, 35-14 (LA)
(Points—Dolphins 83, Rams 59)

LOS ANGELES vs. MINNESOTA
Vikings lead series, 15-11-2
1961—Rams, 31-17 (LA)
        Vikings, 42-21 (M)
1962—Vikings, 38-14 (LA)
        Tie, 24-24 (M)
1963—Rams, 27-24 (LA)
        Vikings, 21-13 (M)
1964—Rams, 22-13 (LA)

Vikings, 34-13 (M)
1965—Vikings, 38-35 (LA)
        Vikings, 24-13 (M)
1966—Vikings, 35-7 (M)
        Rams, 21-6 (LA)
1967—Rams, 39-3 (LA)
1968—Rams, 31-3 (M)
1969—Vikings, 20-13 (LA)
        *Vikings, 23-20 (M)
1970—Vikings, 13-3 (M)
1972—Vikings, 45-41 (LA)
1973—Vikings, 10-9 (M)
1974—Rams, 20-17 (LA)
        **Vikings, 14-10 (M)
1976—Tie, 10-10 (M) OT
        **Vikings, 24-13 (M)
1977—Rams, 35-3 (LA)
        ***Vikings, 14-7 (LA)
1978—Rams, 34-17 (M)
        ***Rams, 34-10 (LA)
1979—Rams, 27-21 (LA) OT
(Points—Rams 587, Vikings 563)
*Conference Championship
**NFC Championship
***NFC Divisional Playoff

LOS ANGELES vs. NEW ENGLAND
Series tied, 1-1
1974—Patriots, 20-14 (NE)
1980—Rams, 17-14 (NE)
(Points—Patriots 34, Rams 31)

LOS ANGELES vs. NEW ORLEANS
Rams lead series, 18-8
1967—Rams 27-13 (NO)
1969—Rams, 36-17 (LA)
1970—Rams; 30-17 (NO)
        Rams, 34-16 (LA)
1971—Saints, 24-20 (NO)
        Rams, 45-28 (LA)
1972—Rams, 34-14 (LA)
        Saints, 19-16 (NO)
1973—Rams, 29-7 (NO)
        Rams, 24-13 (NO)
1974—Rams, 24-0 (LA)
        Saints, 20-7 (NO)
1975—Rams, 38-14 (LA)
        Rams, 14-7 (NO)
1976—Rams, 16-10 (NO)
        Rams, 33-14 (LA)
1977—Rams, 14-7 (LA)
        Saints, 27-26 (NO)
1978—Rams, 26-20 (NO)
        Saints, 10-3 (LA)
1979—Rams, 35-17 (NO)
        Saints, 29-14 (LA)
1980—Rams, 45-31 (LA)
        Rams, 27-7 (NO)
1981—Saints, 23-17 (NO)
        Saints, 21-13 (LA)
(Points—Rams 647, Saints 425)

*LOS ANGELES vs. N.Y. GIANTS
Rams lead series, 14-6
1938—Giants, 28-0 (NY)
1940—Rams, 13-0 (NY)

All-Time Team vs. Team Results

1941—Giants, 49-14 (NY)
1945—Rams, 21-17 (NY)
1946—Rams, 31-21 (NY)
1947—Rams, 34-10 (LA)
1948—Rams, 52-37 (NY)
1953—Rams, 21-7 (LA)
1954—Rams, 17-16 (NY)
1959—Giants, 23-21 (LA)
1961—Giants, 24-14 (NY)
1966—Rams, 55-14 (LA)
1968—Rams, 24-21 (LA)
1970—Rams, 31-3 (NY)
1973—Rams, 40-6 (LA)
1976—Rams, 24-10 (LA)
1978—Rams, 20-17 (NY)
1979—Giants, 20-14 (LA)
1980—Rams, 28-7 (NY)
1981—Rams, 10-7 (NY)
(Points—Rams 481, Giants 340)
*Franchise in Cleveland prior to 1946

LOS ANGELES vs. N.Y. JETS
Rams lead series, 2-1
1970—Jets, 31-20 (LA)
1974—Rams, 20-13 (NY)
1980—Rams, 38-13 (LA)
(Points—Rams 78, Jets 57)

LOS ANGELES vs. OAKLAND
Raiders lead series, 2-1
1972—Raiders, 45-17 (O)
1977—Rams, 20-14 (LA)
1979—Raiders, 24-17 (LA)
(Points—Raiders 83, Rams 54)

*LOS ANGELES vs. PHILADELPHIA
Rams lead series, 14-8-1
1937—Rams, 21-3 (P)
1939—Rams, 35-13 (Colorado Springs)
1940—Rams, 21-13 (C)
1942—Rams, 24-14 (Akron)
1944—Eagles, 26-13 (P)
1945—Eagles, 28-14 (P)
1946—Eagles, 25-14 (LA)
1947—Eagles, 14-7 (P)
1948—Tie, 28-28 (LA)
1949—Eagles, 38-14 (P)
　　　**Eagles, 14-0 (LA)
1950—Eagles, 56-20 (P)
1955—Rams, 23-21 (P)
1956—Rams, 27-7 (LA)
1957—Rams, 17-13 (LA)
1959—Eagles, 23-20 (P)
1964—Rams, 20-10 (LA)
1967—Rams, 33-17 (LA)
1969—Rams, 23-17 (P)
1972—Rams, 34-3 (P)
1975—Rams, 42-3 (P)
1977—Rams, 20-0 (LA)
1978—Rams, 16-14 (P)
(Points—Rams 486, Eagles 400)
*Franchise in Cleveland prior to 1946
**NFL Championship

*LOS ANGELES vs. **PITTSBURGH
Rams lead series, 12-3-2
1938—Rams, 13-7 (New Orleans)

1939—Tie, 14-14 (C)
1941—Rams, 17-14 (Akron)
1947—Rams, 48-7 (P)
1948—Rams, 31-14 (LA)
1949—Tie, 7-7 (P)
1952—Rams, 28-14 (LA)
1955—Rams, 27-26 (LA)
1956—Steelers, 30-13 (P)
1961—Rams, 24-14 (LA)
1964—Rams, 26-14 (P)
1968—Rams, 45-10 (LA)
1971—Rams, 23-14 (P)
1975—Rams, 10-3 (LA)
1978—Rams, 10-7 (LA)
1979—***Steelers, 31-19 (Pasadena)
1981—Steelers, 24-0 (P)
(Points—Rams 355, Steelers 250)
*Franchise in Cleveland prior to 1946
**Steelers known as Pirates prior to 1941
***Super Bowl XIV

*LOS ANGELES vs. **ST. LOUIS
Rams lead series, 18-15-2
1937—Cardinals, 6-0 (Clev)
　　　Cardinals, 13-7 (Chi)
1938—Cardinals, 7-6 (Clev)
　　　Cardinals, 31-17 (Chi)
1939—Rams, 24-0 (Chi)
　　　Rams, 14-0 (Clev)
1940—Rams, 26-14 (Clev)
　　　Cardinals, 17-7 (Chi)
1941—Rams, 10-6 (Clev)
　　　Cardinals, 7-0 (Chi)
1942—Cardinals, 7-0 (Chi)
　　　Rams, 7-3 (Clev)
1945—Rams, 21-0 (Clev)
　　　Rams, 35-21 (Chi)
1946—Cardinals, 34-10 (Chi)
　　　Rams, 17-14 (LA)
1947—Rams, 27-7 (LA)
　　　Cardinals, 17-10 (Chi)
1948—Cardinals, 27-22 (LA)
　　　Cardinals, 27-24 (Chi)
1949—Tie, 28-28 (Chi)
　　　Cardinals, 31-27 (LA)
1951—Rams, 45-21 (LA)
1953—Tie, 24-24 (Chi)
1954—Rams, 28-17 (LA)
1958—Rams, 20-14 (Chi)
1960—Cardinals, 43-21 (LA)
1965—Rams, 27-3 (StL)
1968—Rams, 24-13 (StL)
1970—Rams, 34-13 (LA)
1972—Cardinals, 24-14 (StL)
1975—***Rams, 35-23 (LA)
1976—Cardinals, 30-28 (LA)
1979—Rams, 21-0 (LA)
1980—Rams, 21-13 (StL)
(Points—Rams 681, Cardinals 555)
*Franchise in Cleveland prior to 1946
**Franchise in Chicago prior to 1960
***NFC Divisional Playoff

LOS ANGELES vs. SAN DIEGO
Rams lead series, 2-1

1970—Rams, 37-10 (LA)
1975—Rams, 13-10 (SD) OT
1979—Chargers, 40-16 (LA)
(Points—Rams 66, Chargers 60)
LOS ANGELES vs. SAN FRANCISCO
Rams lead series, 41-21-2
1950—Rams, 35-14 (SF)
     Rams, 28-21 (LA)
1951—49ers, 44-17 (SF)
     Rams, 23-16 (LA)
1952—Rams, 35-9 (LA)
     Rams, 34-21 (SF)
1953—49ers, 31-30 (SF)
     49ers, 31-27 (LA)
1954—Tie, 24-24 (LA)
     Rams, 42-34 (SF)
1955—Rams, 23-14 (SF)
     Rams, 27-14 (LA)
1956—49ers, 33-30 (SF)
     Rams, 30-6 (LA)
1957—49ers, 23-20 (SF)
     Rams, 37-24 (LA)
1958—Rams, 33-3 (SF)
     Rams, 56-7 (LA)
1959—49ers, 34-0 (SF)
     49ers, 24-16 (LA)
1960—49ers, 13-9 (SF)
     49ers, 23-7 (LA)
1961—49ers, 35-0 (SF)
     Rams, 17-7 (LA)
1962—Rams, 28-14 (SF)
     49ers, 24-17 (LA)
1963—Rams, 28-21 (LA)
     Rams, 21-17 (SF)
1964—Rams, 42-14 (LA)
     49ers, 28-7 (SF)
1965—49ers, 45-21 (LA)
     49ers, 30-27 (SF)
1966—Rams, 34-3 (LA)
     49ers, 21-13 (SF)
1967—49ers, 27-24 (LA)
     Rams, 17-7 (SF)
1968—Rams, 24-10 (LA)
     Tie, 20-20 (SF)
1969—Rams, 27-21 (SF)
     Rams, 41-30 (LA)
1970—49ers, 20-6 (LA)
     Rams, 30-13 (SF)
1971—Rams, 20-13 (LA)
     Rams, 17-6 (LA)
1972—Rams, 31-7 (LA)
     Rams, 26-16 (SF)
1973—Rams, 40-20 (LA)
     Rams, 31-13 (LA)
1974—Rams, 37-14 (LA)
     Rams, 15-13 (SF)
1975—Rams, 23-14 (SF)
     49ers, 24-23 (LA)
1976—49ers, 16-0 (LA)
     Rams, 23-3 (SF)
1977—Rams, 34-14 (LA)
     Rams, 23-10 (SF)
1978—Rams, 27-10 (LA)

Rams, 31-28 (SF)
1979—Rams, 27-24 (LA)
     Rams, 26-20 (SF)
1980—Rams, 48-26 (LA)
     Rams, 31-17 (SF)
1981—49ers, 20-17 (SF)
     49ers, 33-31 (LA)
(Points—Rams 1,608, 49ers 1,231)
LOS ANGELES vs. SEATTLE
Rams lead series, 2-0
1976—Rams, 45-6 (LA)
1979—Rams, 24-0 (S)
(Points—Rams 69, Seahawks 6)
LOS ANGELES vs. TAMPA BAY
Rams lead series, 3-2
1977—Rams, 31-0 (LA)
1978—Rams, 26-23 (LA)
1979—Buccaneers, 21-6 (TB)
     *Rams, 9-0 (TB)
1980—Buccaneers, 10-9 (TB)
(Points—Rams 81, Buccaneers 54)
*NFC Championship
***LOS ANGELES vs. WASHINGTON**
Redskins lead series, 12-5-1
1937—Redskins, 16-7 (C)
1938—Redskins, 37-13 (W)
1941—Redskins, 17-13 (W)
1942—Redskins, 33-14 (W)
1944—Redskins, 14-10 (W)
1945—**Rams, 15-14 (C)
1948—Rams, 41-13 (W)
1949—Rams, 53-27 (LA)
1951—Redskins, 31-21 (W)
1962—Redskins, 20-14 (W)
1963—Redskins, 37-14 (LA)
1967—Tie, 28-28 (LA)
1969—Rams, 24-13 (W)
1971—Redskins, 38-24 (LA)
1974—Redskins, 23-17 (LA)
     ***Rams, 19-10 (LA)
1977—Redskins, 17-14 (W)
1981—Redskins, 30-7 (LA)
(Points—Redskins 418, Rams 348)
*Franchise in Cleveland prior to 1946
**NFL Championship
***NFC Championship
_____

MIAMI vs. ATLANTA
Dolphins lead series, 3-0;
See Atlanta vs. Miami
MIAMI vs. BALTIMORE
Dolphins lead series, 16-9;
See Baltimore vs. Miami
MIAMI vs. BUFFALO
Dolphins lead series, 25-6-1;
See Buffalo vs. Miami
MIAMI vs. CHICAGO
Dolphins lead series, 3-0;
See Chicago vs. Miami
MIAMI vs. CINCINNATI
Dolphins lead series, 6-3;
See Cincinnati vs. Miami
MIAMI vs. CLEVELAND

All-Time Team vs. Team Results

Browns lead series, 3-2;
See Cleveland vs. Miami

MIAMI vs. DALLAS
Series tied, 2-2;
See Dallas vs. Miami

MIAMI vs. DENVER
Dolphins lead series, 4-2-1;
See Denver vs. Miami

MIAMI vs. DETROIT
Dolphins lead series, 2-0;
See Detroit vs. Miami

MIAMI vs. GREEN BAY
Dolphins lead series, 3-0;
See Green Bay vs. Miami

MIAMI vs. HOUSTON
Oilers lead series, 9-7;
See Houston vs. Miami

MIAMI vs. KANSAS CITY
Chiefs lead series, 7-4;
See Kansas City vs. Miami

MIAMI vs. LOS ANGELES
Dolphins lead series, 2-1;
See Los Angeles vs. Miami

MIAMI vs. MINNESOTA
Dolphins lead series, 3-1
1972—Dolphins, 16-14 (Minn)
1973—*Dolphins, 24-7 (Houston)
1976—Vikings, 29-7 (Mia)
1979—Dolphins, 27-12 (Minn)
(Points—Dolphins 74, Vikings 62)
*Super Bowl VIII

MIAMI vs. *NEW ENGLAND
Dolphins lead series, 20-11
1966—Patriots, 20-14 (M)
1967—Patriots, 41-10 (B)
        Dolphins, 41-32 (M)
1968—Dolphins, 34-10 (B)
        Dolphins, 38-7 (M)
1969—Dolphins, 17-16 (B)
        Patriots, 38-23 (Tampa)
1970—Patriots, 27-14 (B)
        Dolphins, 37-20 (M)
1971—Dolphins, 41-3 (M)
        Patriots, 34-13 (NE)
1972—Dolphins, 52-0 (M)
        Dolphins, 37-21 (NE)
1973—Dolphins, 44-23 (M)
        Dolphins, 30-14 (NE)
1974—Patriots, 34-24 (NE)
        Dolphins, 34-27 (M)
1975—Dolphins, 22-14 (NE)
        Dolphins, 20-7 (M)
1976—Patriots, 30-14 (NE)
        Dolphins, 10-3 (M)
1977—Dolphins, 17-5 (M)
        Patriots, 14-10 (NE)
1978—Patriots, 33-24 (NE)
        Dolphins, 23-3 (M)
1979—Patriots, 28-13 (NE)
        Dolphins, 39-24 (M)
1980—Patriots, 34-0 (NE)
        Dolphins, 16-13 (M) OT
1981—Dolphins, 30-27 (NE) OT

Dolphins, 24-14 (M)
(Points—Dolphins 765, Patriots 616)
*Franchise in Boston prior to 1971

MIAMI vs. NEW ORLEANS
Dolphins lead series, 3-0
1970—Dolphins, 21-10 (M)
1974—Dolphins, 21-0 (NO)
1980—Dolphins, 21-16 (M)
(Points—Dolphins 63, Saints 26)

MIAMI vs. N.Y. GIANTS
Dolphins lead series, 1-0
1972—Dolphins, 23-13 (NY)

MIAMI vs. N.Y. JETS
Jets lead series, 17-14-1
1966—Jets, 19-14 (M)
        Jets, 30-13 (NY)
1967—Jets, 29-7 (NY)
        Jets, 33-14 (M)
1968—Jets, 35-17 (M)
        Jets, 31-7 (M)
1969—Jets, 34-31 (NY)
        Jets, 27-9 (M)
1970—Dolphins, 20-6 (NY)
        Dolphins, 16-10 (M)
1971—Jets, 14-10 (M)
        Dolphins, 30-14 (NY)
1972—Dolphins, 27-17 (NY)
        Dolphins, 28-24 (M)
1973—Dolphins, 31-3 (M)
        Dolphins, 24-14 (NY)
1974—Dolphins, 21-17 (M)
        Jets, 17-14 (NY)
1975—Dolphins, 43-0 (NY)
        Dolphins, 27-7 (M)
1976—Dolphins, 16-0 (M)
        Dolphins, 27-7 (NY)
1977—Dolphins, 21-17 (M)
        Dolphins, 14-10 (NY)
1978—Jets, 33-20 (NY)
        Jets, 24-13 (M)
1979—Jets, 33-27 (NY)
        Jets, 27-24 (M)
1980—Jets, 17-14 (NY)
        Jets, 24-17 (M)
1981—Tie, 28-28 (M) OT
        Jets, 16-15 (NY)
(Points—Dolphins 639, Jets 617)

MIAMI vs. OAKLAND
Raiders lead series, 12-3-1
1966—Raiders, 23-14 (M)
        Raiders, 21-10 (O)
1967—Raiders, 31-17 (M)
1968—Raiders, 47-21 (M)
1969—Raiders, 20-17 (O)
        Tie, 20-20 (M)
1970—Dolphins, 20-13 (M)
        *Raiders, 21-14 (O)
1973—Raiders, 12-7 (O)
        **Dolphins, 27-10 (M)
1974—*Raiders, 28-26 (O)
1975—Raiders, 31-21 (M)
1978—Dolphins, 23-6 (M)
1979—Raiders, 13-3 (O)

1980—Raiders, 16-10 (O)
1981—Raiders, 33-17 (M)
(Points—Raiders 345, Dolphins 267)
*AFC Divisional Playoff
**AFC Championship
MIAMI vs. PHILADELPHIA
Series tied, 2-2
1970—Eagles, 24-17 (P)
1975—Dolphins, 24-16 (M)
1978—Eagles, 17-3 (P)
1981—Dolphins, 13-10 (M)
(Points—Eagles 67, Dolphins 57)
MIAMI vs. PITTSBURGH
Dolphins lead series, 4-3
1971—Dolphins, 24-21 (M)
1972—*Dolphins, 21-17 (P)
1973—Dolphins, 30-26 (M)
1976—Steelers, 14-3 (P)
1979—**Steelers, 34-14 (P)
1980—Steelers, 23-10 (P)
1981—Dolphins, 30-10 (M)
(Points—Steelers 145, Dolphins 132)
*AFC Championship
**AFC Divisional Playoff
MIAMI vs. ST. LOUIS
Dolphins lead series, 4-0
1972—Dolphins, 31-10 (M)
1977—Dolphins, 55-14 (StL)
1978—Dolphins, 24-10 (M)
1981—Dolphins, 20-7 (StL)
(Points—Dolphins 130, Cardinals 41)
MIAMI vs. SAN DIEGO
Chargers lead series, 7-4
1966—Chargers, 44-10 (SD)
1967—Chargers, 24-0 (SD)
       Dolphins, 41-24 (M)
1968—Chargers, 34-28 (SD)
1969—Chargers, 21-14 (M)
1972—Dolphins, 24-10 (M)
1974—Chargers, 28-21 (SD)
1977—Chargers, 14-13 (M)
1978—Dolphins, 28-21 (SD)
1980—Chargers, 27-24 (M) OT
1981—*Chargers, 41-38 (M) OT
(Points—Chargers 281, Dolphins 248)
*AFC Divisional Playoff
MIAMI vs. SAN FRANCISCO
Dolphins lead series, 3-0
1973—Dolphins, 21-13 (M)
1977—Dolphins, 19-15 (SF)
1980—Dolphins, 17-13 (M)
(Points—Dolphins 57, 49ers 41)
MIAMI vs. SEATTLE
Dolphins lead series, 2-0
1977—Dolphins, 31-13 (M)
1979—Dolphins, 19-10 (M)
(Points—Dolphins 50, Seahawks 23)
MIAMI vs. TAMPA BAY
Dolphins lead series, 1-0
1976—Dolphins, 23-20 (TB)
MIAMI vs. WASHINGTON
Dolphins lead series, 3-1
1972—*Dolphins, 14-7 (Los Angeles)

1974—Redskins, 20-17 (W)
1978—Dolphins, 16-0 (W)
1981—Dolphins, 13-10 (M)
(Points—Dolphins 60, Redskins 37)
*Super Bowl VII
———————————————————

MINNESOTA vs. ATLANTA
Vikings lead series, 7-5;
See Atlanta vs. Minnesota
MINNESOTA vs. BALTIMORE
Colts lead series, 12-4-1;
See Baltimore vs. Minnesota
MINNESOTA vs. BUFFALO
Vikings lead series, 3-0;
See Buffalo vs. Minnesota
MINNESOTA vs. CHICAGO
Vikings lead series, 23-17-2;
See Chicago vs. Minnesota
MINNESOTA vs. CINCINNATI
Bengals lead series, 2-1;
See Cincinnati vs. Minnesota
MINNESOTA vs. CLEVELAND
Vikings lead series, 6-1;
See Cleveland vs. Minnesota
MINNESOTA vs. DALLAS
Cowboys lead series, 9-4;
See Dallas vs. Minnesota
MINNESOTA vs. DENVER
Vikings lead series, 2-1;
See Denver vs. Minnesota
MINNESOTA vs. DETROIT
Vikings lead series, 26-14-2;
See Detroit vs. Minnesota
MINNESOTA vs. GREEN BAY
Vikings lead series, 23-18-1
See Green Bay vs. Minnesota
MINNESOTA vs. HOUSTON
Series tied, 1-1;
See Houston vs. Minnesota
MINNESOTA vs. KANSAS CITY
Series tied, 2-2;
See Kansas City vs. Minnesota
MINNESOTA vs. LOS ANGELES
Vikings lead series, 15-11-2;
See Los Angeles vs. Minnesota
MINNESOTA vs. MIAMI
Dolphins lead series, 3-1;
See Miami vs. Minnesota
MINNESOTA vs. *NEW ENGLAND
Patriots lead series, 2-1
1970—Vikings, 35-14 (B)
1974—Patriots, 17-14 (M)
1979—Patriots, 27-23 (NE)
(Points—Vikings 72, Patriots 58)
*Franchise in Boston prior to 1971
MINNESOTA vs. NEW ORLEANS
Vikings lead series, 8-2
1968—Saints, 20-17 (NO)
1970—Vikings, 26-0 (M)
1971—Vikings, 23-10 (NO)
1972—Vikings, 37-6 (M)
1974—Vikings, 29-9 (M)
1975—Vikings, 20-7 (NO)

1976—Vikings, 40-9 (NO)
1978—Saints, 31-24 (NO)
1980—Vikings, 23-20 (NO)
1981—Vikings, 20-10 (M)
(Points—Vikings 259, Saints 122)

MINNESOTA vs. N. Y. GIANTS
Vikings lead series, 6-1
1964—Vikings, 30-21 (NY)
1965—Vikings, 40-14 (M)
1967—Vikings, 27-24 (M)
1969—Giants, 24-23 (NY)
1971—Vikings, 17-10 (NY)
1973—Vikings, 31-7 (New Haven)
1976—Vikings, 24-7 (M)
(Points—Vikings 192, Giants 107)

MINNESOTA vs. N. Y. JETS
Jets lead series, 2-1
1970—Jets, 20-10 (NY)
1975—Vikings, 29-21 (M)
1979—Jets, 14-7 (NY)
(Points—Jets 55, Vikings 46)

MINNESOTA vs. OAKLAND
Raiders lead series, 4-1
1973—Vikings, 24-16 (M)
1976—*Raiders, 32-14 (Pasadena)
1977—Raiders, 35-13 (O)
1978—Raiders, 27-20 (O)
1981—Raiders, 36-10 (M)
(Points—Raiders 146, Vikings 81)
Super Bowl XI

MINNESOTA vs. PHILADELPHIA
Vikings lead series, 8-2
1962—Vikings, 31-21 (M)
1963—Vikings, 34-13 (P)
1968—Vikings, 24-17 (P)
1971—Vikings, 13-0 (P)
1973—Vikings, 28-21 (M)
1976—Vikings, 31-12 (P)
1978—Vikings, 28-27 (M)
1980—Eagles, 42-7 (M)
        *Eagles, 31-16 (P)
1981—Vikings, 35-23 (M)
(Points—Vikings 247, Eagles 207)
NFC Divisional Playoff

MINNESOTA vs. PITTSBURGH
Series tied, 4-4
1962—Steelers, 39-31 (P)
1964—Vikings, 30-10 (M)
1967—Vikings, 41-27 (P)
1969—Vikings, 52-14 (M)
1972—Steelers, 23-10 (P)
1974—*Steelers, 16-6 (New Orleans)
1976—Vikings, 17-6 (M)
1980—Steelers, 23-17 (M)
(Points—Vikings 204, Steelers 158)
Super Bowl IX

MINNESOTA vs. ST. LOUIS
Cardinals lead series, 6-3
1963—Cardinals, 56-14 (M)
1967—Cardinals, 34-24 (M)
1969—Vikings, 27-10 (StL)
1972—Cardinals, 19-17 (M)
1974—Vikings, 28-24 (StL)

      *Vikings, 30-14 (M)
1977—Cardinals, 27-7 (M)
1979—Cardinals, 37-7 (StL)
1981—Cardinals, 30-17 (StL)
(Points—Cardinals 251, Vikings 171)
NFC Divisional Playoff

MINNESOTA vs. SAN DIEGO
Series tied, 2-2
1971—Chargers, 30-14 (SD)
1975—Vikings, 28-13 (M)
1978—Chargers, 13-7 (M)
1981—Vikings, 33-31 (SD)
(Points—Chargers 87, Vikings 82)

MINNESOTA vs. SAN FRANCISCO
Vikings lead series, 12-10-1
1961—49ers, 38-24 (M)
        49ers, 38-28 (SF)
1962—49ers, 21-7 (SF)
        49ers, 35-12 (M)
1963—Vikings, 24-20 (SF)
        Vikings, 45-14 (M)
1964—Vikings, 27-22 (SF)
        Vikings, 24-7 (M)
1965—Vikings, 42-41 (SF)
        49ers, 45-24 (M)
1966—Tie, 20-20 (SF)
        Vikings, 28-3 (M)
1967—49ers, 27-21 (M)
1968—Vikings, 30-20 (SF)
1969—Vikings, 10-7 (M)
1970—*49ers, 17-14 (M)
1971—49ers, 13-9 (M)
1972—Vikings, 20-17 (SF)
1973—Vikings, 17-13 (SF)
1975—Vikings, 27-17 (M)
1976—49ers, 20-16 (SF)
1977—Vikings, 28-27 (M)
1979—Vikings, 28-22 (M)
(Points—Vikings 522, 49ers 507)
NFC Divisional Playoff

MINNESOTA vs. SEATTLE
Series tied, 1-1
1976—Vikings, 27-21 (M)
1978—Seahawks, 29-28 (S)
(Points—Vikings 55, Seahawks 50)

MINNESOTA vs. TAMPA BAY
Vikings lead series, 6-3
1977—Vikings, 9-3 (TB)
1978—Buccaneers, 16-10 (M)
        Vikings, 24-7 (TB)
1979—Buccaneers, 12-10 (M)
        Vikings, 23-22 (TB)
1980—Vikings, 38-30 (M)
        Vikings, 21-10 (TB)
1981—Buccaneers, 21-13 (TB)
        Vikings, 25-10 (M)
(Points—Vikings 173, Buccaneers 131)

MINNESOTA vs. WASHINGTON
Vikings lead series, 5-2
1968—Vikings, 27-14 (M)
1970—Vikings, 19-10 (W)
1972—Redskins, 24-21 (M)
1973—*Vikings, 27-20 (M)

1975—Redskins, 31-30 (W)
1976— *Vikings 35-20 (M)
1980—Vikings, 39-14 (W)
(Points—Vikings 198, Redskins 133)
*NFC Divisional Playoff

NEW ENGLAND vs. ATLANTA
Patriots lead series, 2-1;
See Atlanta vs. New England
NEW ENGLAND vs. BALTIMORE
Colts lead series, 13-11;
See Baltimore vs. New England
NEW ENGLAND vs. BUFFALO
Bills lead series, 23-21-1;
See Buffalo vs. New England
NEW ENGLAND vs. CHICAGO
Patriots lead series, 2-0;
See Chicago vs. New England
NEW ENGLAND vs. CINCINNATI
Patriots lead series, 4-3;
See Cincinnati vs. New England
NEW ENGLAND vs. CLEVELAND
Browns lead series, 3-1;
See Cleveland vs. New England
NEW ENGLAND vs. DALLAS
Cowboys lead series, 4-0;
See Dallas vs. New England
NEW ENGLAND vs. DENVER
Patriots lead series, 12-10;
See Denver vs. New England
NEW ENGLAND vs. DETROIT
Lions lead series, 2-1;
See Detroit vs. New England
NEW ENGLAND vs. GREEN BAY
Series tied, 1-1;
See Green Bay vs. New England
NEW ENGLAND vs. HOUSTON
Series tied, 13-13-1;
See Houston vs. New England
NEW ENGLAND vs. KANSAS CITY
Chiefs lead series, 11-7-3;
See Kansas City vs. New England
NEW ENGLAND vs. LOS ANGELES
Series tied, 1-1;
See Los Angeles vs. New England
NEW ENGLAND vs. MIAMI
Dolphins lead series, 20-11;
See Miami vs. New England
NEW ENGLAND vs. MINNESOTA
Patriots lead series, 2-1;
See Minnesota vs. New England
NEW ENGLAND vs. NEW ORLEANS
Patriots lead series, 3-0
1972—Patriots, 17-10 (NO)
1976—Patriots, 27-6 (NE)
1980—Patriots, 38-27 (NO)
(Points—Patriots 82, Saints 43)
***NEW ENGLAND vs. N. Y. GIANTS**
Series tied, 1-1
1970—Giants, 16-0 (B)
1974—Patriots, 28-20 (New Haven)
(Points—Giants 36, Patriots 28)
*Franchise in Boston prior to 1971

***NEW ENGLAND vs. **N. Y. JETS**
Jets lead series, 26-17-1
1960—Patriots, 28-24 (NY)
       Patriots, 38-21 (B)
1961—Titans, 21-20 (B)
       Titans, 37-30 (NY)
1962—Patriots, 43-14 (NY)
       Patriots, 24-17 (B)
1963—Patriots, 38-14 (B)
       Jets, 31-24 (NY)
1964—Patriots, 26-10 (B)
       Jets, 35-14 (NY)
1965—Jets, 30-20 (B)
       Patriots, 27-23 (NY)
1966—Tie, 24-24 (B)
       Jets, 38-28 (NY)
1967—Jets, 30-23 (NY)
       Jets, 29-24 (B)
1968—Jets, 47-31 (Birmingham)
       Jets, 48-14 (NY)
1969—Jets, 23-14 (B)
       Jets, 23-17 (NY)
1970—Jets, 31-21 (B)
       Jets, 17-3 (NY)
1971—Patriots, 20-0 (NE)
       Jets, 13-6 (NY)
1972—Jets, 41-13 (NE)
       Jets, 34-10 (NY)
1973—Jets, 9-7 (NE)
       Jets, 33-13 (NY)
1974—Jets, 24-0 (NY)
       Jets, 21-16 (NE)
1975—Jets, 36-7 (NY)
       Jets, 30-28 (NE)
1976—Patriots, 41-7 (NE)
       Patriots, 38-24 (NY)
1977—Jets, 30-27 (NY)
       Patriots, 24-13 (NE)
1978—Patriots, 55-21 (NE)
       Patriots, 19-17 (NY)
1979—Patriots, 56-3 (NE)
       Jets, 27-26 (NY)
1980—Patriots, 21-11 (NY)
       Patriots, 34-21 (NE)
1981—Jets, 28-24 (NY)
       Jets, 17-6 (NE)
(Points—Patriots 1,046, Jets 1,023)
*Franchise in Boston prior to 1971
**Jets known as Titans prior to 1963
***NEW ENGLAND vs. OAKLAND**
Series tied, 11-11-1
1960—Raiders, 27-14 (O)
       Patriots, 34-28 (B)
1961—Patriots, 20-17 (B)
       Patriots, 35-21 (O)
1962—Patriots, 26-16 (B)
       Raiders, 20-0 (O)
1963—Patriots, 20-14 (O)
       Patriots, 20-14 (B)
1964—Patriots, 17-14 (O)
       Tie, 43-43 (B)
1965—Raiders, 24-10 (B)
       Raiders, 30-21 (O)

201

All-Time Team vs. Team Results

1966—Patriots, 24-21 (B)
1967—Raiders, 35-7 (O)
    Raiders, 48-14 (B)
1968—Raiders, 41-10 (O)
1969—Raiders, 38-23 (B)
1971—Patriots, 20-6 (NE)
1974—Raiders, 41-26 (O)
1976—Patriots, 48-17 (NE)
    **Raiders, 24-21 (O)
1978—Raiders, 21-14 (O)
1981—Raiders, 27-17 (O)
(Points—Raiders 580, Patriots 491)
*Franchise in Boston prior to 1971
**AFC Divisional Playoff
NEW ENGLAND vs. PHILADELPHIA
Series tied, 2-2
1973—Eagles, 24-23 (P)
1977—Patriots, 14-6 (NE)
1978—Patriots, 24-14 (NE)
1981—Eagles, 13-3 (P)
(Points—Patriots 64, Eagles 57)
NEW ENGLAND vs. PITTSBURGH
Steelers lead series, 4-1
1972—Steelers, 33-3 (P)
1974—Steelers, 21-17 (NE)
1976—Patriots, 30-27 (P)
1979—Steelers, 16-13 (NE) OT
1981—Steelers, 27-21 (P) OT
(Points—Steelers 124, Patriots 84)
*NEW ENGLAND vs. ST. LOUIS
Cardinals lead series, 3-1
1970—Cardinals, 31-0 (StL)
1975—Cardinals, 24-17 (StL)
1978—Patriots, 16-6 (StL)
1981—Cardinals, 27-20 (NE)
(Points—Cardinals 88, Patriots 53)
*Franchise in Boston prior to 1971
*NEW ENGLAND vs. **SAN DIEGO
Series tied, 12-12-2
1960—Patriots, 35-0 (LA)
    Chargers, 45-16 (B)
1961—Chargers, 38-27 (B)
    Patriots, 41-0 (SD)
1962—Patriots, 24-20 (B)
    Patriots, 20-14 (SD)
1963—Chargers, 17-13 (SD)
    Chargers, 7-6 (B)
    ***Chargers, 51-10 (SD)
1964—Chargers, 33-28 (SD)
    Chargers, 26-17 (B)
1965—Tie, 10-10 (B)
    Patriots, 22-6 (SD)
1966—Chargers, 24-0 (SD)
    Patriots, 35-17 (B)
1967—Chargers, 28-14 (SD)
    Tie, 31-31 (SD)
1968—Chargers, 27-17 (B)
1969—Chargers, 13-10 (B)
    Chargers, 28-18 (SD)
1970—Chargers, 16-14 (SD)
1973—Patriots, 30-14 (NE)
1975—Patriots, 33-19 (SD)
1977—Patriots, 24-20 (SD)

1978—Patriots, 28-23 (NE)
1979—Patriots, 27-21 (NE)
(Points—Patriots 555, Chargers 543)
*Franchise in Boston prior to 1971
**Franchise in Los Angeles prior to 1961
***AFL Championship
NEW ENGLAND vs. SAN FRANCISCO
49ers lead series, 2-1
1971—49ers, 27-10 (SF)
1975—Patriots, 24-16 (NE)
1980—49ers, 21-17 (SF)
(Points—49ers 64, Patriots 51)
NEW ENGLAND vs. SEATTLE
Patriots lead series, 2-0
1977—Patriots, 31-0 (NE)
1980—Patriots, 37-31 (S)
(Points—Patriots 68, Seahawks 31)
NEW ENGLAND vs. TAMPA BAY
Patriots lead series, 1-0
1976—Patriots, 31-14 (TB)
NEW ENGLAND vs. WASHINGTON
Redskins lead series, 2-1
1972—Patriots, 24-23 (NE)
1978—Redskins, 16-14 (NE)
1981—Redskins, 24-22 (W)
(Points—Redskins 63, Patriots 60)

NEW ORLEANS vs. ATLANTA
Falcons lead series, 19-7;
See Atlanta vs. New Orleans
NEW ORLEANS vs. BALTIMORE
Colts lead series, 3-0;
See Baltimore vs. New Orleans
NEW ORLEANS vs. BUFFALO
Series tied, 1-1;
See Buffalo vs. New Orleans
NEW ORLEANS vs. CHICAGO
Bears lead series, 6-2;
See Chicago vs. New Orleans
NEW ORLEANS vs. CINCINNATI
Series tied, 2-2;
See Cincinnati vs. New Orleans
NEW ORLEANS vs. CLEVELAND
Browns lead series, 8-0;
See Cleveland vs. New Orleans
NEW ORLEANS vs. DALLAS
Cowboys lead series, 8-1;
See Dallas vs. New Orleans
NEW ORLEANS vs. DENVER
Broncos lead series, 3-0;
See Denver vs. New Orleans
NEW ORLEANS vs. DETROIT
Series tied, 4-4-1;
See Detroit vs. New Orleans
NEW ORLEANS vs. GREEN BAY
Packers lead series, 8-2;
See Green Bay vs. New Orleans
NEW ORLEANS vs. HOUSTON
Oilers lead series, 2-1-1;
See Houston vs. New Orleans
NEW ORLEANS vs. KANSAS CITY
Series tied, 1-1;
See Kansas City vs. New Orleans

NEW ORLEANS vs. LOS ANGELES
Rams lead series, 18-8;
See Los Angeles vs. New Orleans
NEW ORLEANS vs. MIAMI
Dolphins lead series, 3-0;
See Miami vs. New Orleans
NEW ORLEANS vs. MINNESOTA
Vikings lead series, 8-2;
See Minnesota vs. New Orleans
NEW ORLEANS vs. NEW ENGLAND
Patriots lead series, 3-0;
See New England vs. New Orleans
NEW ORLEANS vs. N. Y. GIANTS
Giants lead series, 5-4
1967—Giants, 27-21 (NY)
1968—Giants, 38-21 (NY)
1969—Saints, 25-24 (NY)
1970—Saints, 14-10 (NO)
1972—Giants, 45-21 (NY)
1975—Giants, 28-14 (NY)
1978—Saints, 28-17 (NO)
1979—Saints, 24-14 (NO)
1981—Giants, 20-7 (NY)
(Points—Giants 223, Saints 175)
NEW ORLEANS vs. N. Y. JETS
Jets lead series, 2-1
1972—Jets, 18-17 (NY)
1977—Jets, 16-13 (NO)
1980—Saints, 21-20 (NY)
(Points—Jets 54, Saints 51)
NEW ORLEANS vs. OAKLAND
Raiders lead series, 2-0-1
1971—Tie, 21-21 (NO)
1975—Raiders, 48-10 (O)
1979—Raiders, 42-35 (NO)
(Points—Raiders 111, Saints 66)
NEW ORLEANS vs. PHILADELPHIA
Eagles lead series, 8-4
1967—Saints, 31-24 (NO)
       Eagles, 48-21 (P)
1968—Eagles, 29-17 (P)
1969—Eagles, 13-10 (P)
       Saints, 26-17 (NO)
1972—Saints, 21-3 (NO)
1974—Saints, 14-10 (NO)
1977—Eagles, 28-7 (P)
1978—Eagles, 24-17 (NO)
1979—Eagles, 26-14 (NO)
1980—Eagles, 34-21 (NO)
1981—Eagles, 31-14 (NO)
(Points—Eagles 287, Saints 213)
NEW ORLEANS vs. PITTSBURGH
Steelers lead series, 4-3
1967—Steelers, 14-10 (NO)
1968—Saints, 16-12 (P)
       Saints, 24-14 (NO)
1969—Saints, 27-24 (NO)
1974—Steelers, 28-7 (NO)
1978—Steelers, 20-14 (P)
1981—Saints, 20-6 (NO)
(Points—Steelers 132, Saints 104)
NEW ORLEANS vs. ST. LOUIS
Cardinals lead series, 7-2

1967—Cardinals, 31-20 (StL)
1968—Cardinals, 21-20 (NO)
       Cardinals, 31-17 (StL)
1969—Saints, 51-42 (StL)
1970—Cardinals, 24-17 (StL)
1974—Saints, 14-0 (NO)
1977—Cardinals, 49-31 (StL)
1980—Cardinals, 40-7 (NO)
1981—Cardinals, 30-3 (StL)
(Points—Cardinals 268, Saints 180)
NEW ORLEANS vs. SAN DIEGO
Chargers lead series, 3-0
1973—Chargers, 17-14 (SD)
1977—Chargers, 14-0 (NO)
1979—Chargers, 35-0 (NO)
(Points—Chargers 66, Saints 14)
NEW ORLEANS vs. SAN FRANCISCO
49ers lead series, 17-7-2
1967—49ers, 27-13 (SF)
1969—Saints, 43-38 (NO)
1970—Tie, 20-20 (SF)
       49ers, 38-27 (NO)
1971—49ers, 38-20 (NO)
       Saints, 26-20 (SF)
1972—49ers, 37-2 (NO)
       Tie, 20-20 (SF)
1973—49ers, 40-0 (SF)
       Saints, 16-10 (NO)
1974—49ers, 17-13 (NO)
       49ers, 35-21 (SF)
1975—49ers, 35-21 (SF)
       49ers, 16-6 (NO)
1976—49ers, 33-3 (SF)
       49ers, 27-7 (NO)
1977—49ers, 10-7 (NO) OT
       49ers, 20-17 (SF)
1978—Saints, 14-7 (SF)
       Saints, 24-13 (NO)
1979—Saints, 30-21 (SF)
       Saints, 31-20 (NO)
1980—49ers, 26-23 (NO)
       49ers, 38-35 (SF) OT
1981—49ers, 21-14 (SF)
       49ers, 21-17 (NO)
(Points—49ers 648, Saints 470)
NEW ORLEANS vs. SEATTLE
Series tied, 1-1
1976—Saints, 51-27 (S)
1979—Seahawks, 38-24 (S)
(Points—Saints 75, Seahawks 65)
NEW ORLEANS vs. TAMPA BAY
Series tied, 2-2
1977—Buccaneers, 33-14 (NO)
1978—Saints, 17-10 (TB)
1979—Saints, 42-14 (TB)
1981—Buccaneers, 31-14 (NO)
(Points—Buccaneers 88, Saints 87)
NEW ORLEANS vs. WASHINGTON
Redskins lead series, 6-4
1967—Redskins, 30-10 (NO)
       Saints, 30-14 (W)
1968—Saints, 37-17 (NO)
1969—Redskins, 26-20 (NO)

Redskins, 17-14 (W)
1971—Redskins, 24-14 (W)
1973—Saints, 19-3 (NO)
1975—Redskins, 41-3 (W)
1979—Saints, 14-10 (W)
1980—Redskins, 22-14 (W)
(Points—Redskins 204, Saints 175)

N.Y. GIANTS vs. ATLANTA
Falcons lead series, 5-3;
See Atlanta vs. N.Y. Giants
N.Y. GIANTS vs. BALTIMORE
Colts lead series, 7-3;
See Baltimore vs. N.Y. Giants
N.Y. GIANTS vs. BUFFALO
Giants lead series, 2-1;
See Buffalo vs. N.Y. Giants
N.Y. GIANTS vs. CHICAGO
Bears lead series, 26-16-2;
See Chicago vs. N.Y. Giants
N.Y. GIANTS vs. CINCINNATI
Bengals lead series, 2-0;
See Cincinnati vs. N.Y. Giants
N.Y. GIANTS vs. CLEVELAND
Browns lead series, 25-16-2;
See Cleveland vs. N.Y. Giants
N.Y. GIANTS vs. DALLAS
Cowboys lead series, 28-11-2;
See Dallas vs. N.Y. Giants
N.Y. GIANTS vs. DENVER
Broncos lead series, 2-1;
See Denver vs. N.Y. Giants
N.Y. GIANTS VS. DETROIT
Lions lead series, 17-10-1;
See Detroit vs. N.Y. Giants
N.Y. GIANTS vs. GREEN BAY
Packers lead series, 23-17-2;
See Green Bay vs. N.Y. Giants
N.Y. GIANTS vs. HOUSTON
Giants lead series, 1-0;
See Houston vs. N.Y. Giants
N.Y. GIANTS vs. KANSAS CITY
Giants lead series, 3-0;
See Kansas City vs. N.Y. Giants
N.Y. GIANTS vs. LOS ANGELES
Rams lead series, 14-6;
See Los Angeles vs. N.Y. Giants
N.Y. GIANTS vs. MIAMI
Dolphins lead series, 1-0;
See Miami vs. N.Y. Giants
N.Y. GIANTS vs. MINNESOTA
Vikings lead series, 6-1;
See Minnesota vs. N.Y. Giants
N.Y. GIANTS vs. NEW ENGLAND
Series tied, 1-1;
See New England vs. N.Y. Giants
N.Y. GIANTS vs. NEW ORLEANS
Giants lead series, 5-4;
See New Orleans vs. N.Y. Giants
N.Y. GIANTS vs. N.Y. JETS
Jets lead series, 2-1
1970—Giants, 22-10 (NYJ)
1974—Jets, 26-20 (New Haven) OT
1981—Jets, 26-7 (NYG)

(Points—Jets 62, Giants 49)
N.Y. GIANTS vs. OAKLAND
Raiders lead series, 2-0
1973—Raiders, 42-0 (O)
1980—Raiders, 33-17 (NY)
(Points—Raiders 75, Giants 17)
N.Y. GIANTS vs. PHILADELPHIA
Giants lead series, 50-43-2
1933—Giants, 56-0 (NY)
    Giants, 20-14 (P)
1934—Giants, 17-0 (NY)
    Eagles, 6-0 (P)
1935—Giants, 10-0 (NY)
    Giants, 21-14 (P)
1936—Eagles, 10-7 (P)
    Giants, 21-17 (NY)
1937—Giants, 16-7 (P)
    Giants, 21-0 (NY)
1938—Eagles, 14-10 (P)
    Giants, 17-7 (NY)
1939—Giants, 13-3 (P)
    Giants, 27-10 (NY)
1940—Giants, 20-14 (P)
    Giants, 17-7 (NY)
1941—Giants, 24-0 (P)
    Giants, 16-0 (NY)
1942—Giants, 35-17 (NY)
    Giants, 14-0 (NY)
1944—Eagles, 24-17 (NY)
    Tie, 21-21 (P)
1945—Eagles, 38-17 (P)
    Giants, 28-21 (NY)
1946—Eagles, 24-14 (P)
    Giants, 45-17 (NY)
1947—Eagles, 23-0 (P)
    Eagles, 41-24 (NY)
1948—Eagles, 45-0 (P)
    Eagles, 35-14 (NY)
1949—Eagles, 24-3 (NY)
    Eagles, 17-3 (P)
1950—Giants, 7-3 (NY)
    Giants, 9-7 (P)
1951—Giants, 26-24 (NY)
    Giants, 23-7 (P)
1952—Giants, 31-7 (P)
    Eagles, 14-10 (NY)
1953—Eagles, 30-7 (P)
    Giants, 37-28 (NY)
1954—Giants, 27-14 (NY)
    Eagles, 29-14 (P)
1955—Eagles, 27-17 (P)
    Giants, 31-7 (NY)
1956—Giants, 20-3 (NY)
    Giants, 21-7 (P)
1957—Giants, 24-20 (P)
    Giants, 13-0 (NY)
1958—Eagles, 27-24 (P)
    Giants, 24-10 (NY)
1959—Eagles, 49-21 (P)
    Giants, 24-7 (NY)
1960—Eagles, 17-10 (NY)
    Eagles, 31-23 (P)
1961—Giants, 38-21 (NY)

Giants, 28-24 (P)
1962—Giants, 29-13 (P)
Giants, 19-14 (NY)
1963—Giants, 37-14 (P)
Giants, 42-14 (NY)
1964—Eagles, 38-7 (P)
Eagles, 23-17 (NY)
1965—Giants, 16-14 (P)
Giants, 35-27 (NY)
1966—Eagles, 35-17 (P)
Eagles, 31-3 (NY)
1967—Giants, 44-7 (NY)
1968—Giants, 34-25 (P)
Giants, 7-6 (NY)
1969—Eagles, 23-20 (NY)
1970—Giants, 30-23 (NY)
Eagles, 23-20 (P)
1971—Eagles, 23-7 (P)
Eagles, 41-28 (NY)
1972—Giants, 27-12 (P)
Giants, 62-10 (NY)
1973—Tie, 23-23 (NY)
Eagles, 20-16 (P)
1974—Eagles, 35-7 (P)
Eagles, 20-7 (New Haven)
1975—Giants, 23-14 (P)
Eagles, 13-10 (NY)
1976—Eagles, 20-7 (P)
Eagles, 10-0 (NY)
1977—Eagles, 28-10 (NY)
Eagles, 17-14 (P)
1978—Eagles, 19-17 (NY)
Eagles, 20-3 (P)
1979—Eagles, 23-17 (P)
Eagles, 17-13 (NY)
1980—Eagles, 35-3 (P)
Eagles, 31-16 (NY)
1981—Eagles, 24-10 (NY)
Giants, 20-10 (P)
*Giants, 27-21 (P)
(Points—Giants 1,821, Eagles 1,699)
*NFC First Round Playoff
N.Y. GIANTS vs. *PITTSBURGH
Giants lead series, 40-26-3
1933—Giants, 23-2 (P)
Giants, 27-3 (NY)
1934—Giants, 14-12 (P)
Giants, 17-7 (NY)
1935—Giants, 42-7 (P)
Giants, 13-0 (NY)
1936—Pirates, 10-7 (P)
1937—Giants, 10-7 (P)
Giants, 17-0 (NY)
1938—Giants, 27-14 (P)
Pirates, 13-10 (NY)
1939—Giants, 14-7 (P)
Giants, 23-7 (NY)
1940—Tie, 10-10 (P)
Giants, 12-0 (NY)
1941—Giants, 37-10 (P)
Giants, 28-7 (NY)
1942—Steelers, 13-10 (P)
Steelers, 17-9 (NY)

1945—Giants, 34-6 (P)
Steelers, 21-7 (NY)
1946—Giants, 17-14 (P)
Giants, 7-0 (NY)
1947—Steelers, 38-21 (NY)
Steelers, 24-7 (P)
1948—Giants, 34-27 (NY)
Steelers, 38-28 (P)
1949—Steelers, 28-7 (P)
Steelers, 21-17 (NY)
1950—Giants, 18-7 (P)
Steelers, 17-6 (NY)
1951—Tie, 13-13 (P)
Giants, 14-0 (NY)
1952—Steelers, 63-7 (P)
1953—Steelers, 24-14 (P)
Steelers, 14-10 (NY)
1954—Giants, 30-6 (P)
Giants, 24-3 (NY)
1955—Steelers, 30-23 (P)
Steelers, 19-17 (NY)
1956—Giants, 38-10 (NY)
Giants, 17-14 (P)
1957—Giants, 35-0 (NY)
Steelers, 21-10 (P)
1958—Giants, 17-6 (NY)
Steelers, 31-10 (P)
1959—Giants, 21-16 (P)
Steelers, 14-9 (NY)
1960—Giants, 19-17 (P)
Giants, 27-24 (NY)
1961—Giants, 17-14 (P)
Giants, 42-21 (NY)
1962—Giants, 31-27 (P)
Steelers, 20-17 (NY)
1963—Steelers, 31-0 (P)
Giants, 33-17 (NY)
1964—Steelers, 27-24 (P)
Steelers, 44-17 (NY)
1965—Giants, 23-13 (P)
Giants, 35-10 (NY)
1966—Tie, 34-34 (P)
Steelers, 47-28 (NY)
1967—Giants, 27-24 (P)
Giants, 28-20 (NY)
1968—Giants, 34-20 (P)
1969—Giants, 10-7 (NY)
Giants, 21-17 (P)
1971—Steelers, 17-13 (P)
1976—Steelers, 27-0 (NY)
(Points—Giants 1,342, Steelers 1,149)
*Steelers known as Pirates prior to 1941
N.Y. GIANTS vs. *ST. LOUIS
Giants lead series, 50-28-1
1926—Giants, 20-0 (NY)
1927—Giants, 28-7 (NY)
1929—Giants, 24-21 (NY)
1930—Giants, 25-12 (NY)
Giants, 13-7 (C)
1935—Cardinals, 14-13 (NY)
1936—Giants, 14-6 (NY)
1938—Giants, 6-0 (NY)
1939—Giants, 17-7 (NY)

205

All-Time Team vs. Team Results

1941—Cardinals, 10-7 (NY)
1942—Giants, 21-7 (NY)
1943—Giants, 24-13 (NY)
1946—Giants, 28-24 (NY)
1947—Giants, 35-31 (NY)
1948—Cardinals, 63-35 (NY)
1949—Giants, 41-38 (C)
1950—Cardinals, 17-3 (C)
      Giants, 51-21 (NY)
1951—Cardinals, 28-17 (NY)
      Giants, 10-0 (C)
1952—Cardinals, 24-23 (NY)
      Giants, 28-6 (C)
1953—Giants, 21-7 (NY)
      Giants, 23-20 (C)
1954—Giants, 41-10 (C)
      Giants, 31-17 (NY)
1955—Cardinals, 28-17 (C)
      Giants, 10-0 (NY)
1956—Cardinals, 35-27 (C)
      Giants, 23-10 (NY)
1957—Giants, 27-14 (NY)
      Giants, 28-21 (C)
1958—Giants, 37-7 (Buffalo)
      Cardinals, 23-6 (NY)
1959—Giants, 9-3 (NY)
      Giants, 30-20 (Minn)
1960—Giants, 35-14 (StL)
      Cardinals, 20-13 (NY)
1961—Giants, 21-10 (NY)
      Giants, 24-9 (StL)
1962—Giants, 31-14 (StL)
      Giants, 31-28 (NY)
1963—Giants, 38-21 (StL)
      Cardinals, 24-17 (NY)
1964—Giants, 34-17 (NY)
      Tie, 10-10 (StL)
1965—Giants, 14-10 (NY)
      Giants, 28-15 (StL)
1966—Cardinals, 24-19 (StL)
      Cardinals, 20-17 (NY)
1967—Giants, 37-20 (StL)
      Giants, 37-14 (NY)
1968—Cardinals, 28-21 (NY)
1969—Cardinals, 42-17 (StL)
      Giants, 49-6 (NY)
1970—Giants, 35-17 (NY)
      Giants, 34-17 (StL)
1971—Giants, 21-20 (StL)
      Cardinals, 24-7 (NY)
1972—Giants, 27-21 (NY)
      Giants, 13-7 (StL)
1973—Cardinals, 35-27 (StL)
      Giants, 24-13 (New Haven)
1974—Cardinals, 23-21 (New Haven)
      Cardinals, 26-14 (StL)
1975—Cardinals, 26-14 (StL)
      Cardinals, 20-13 (NY)
1976—Cardinals, 27-21 (StL)
      Cardinals, 17-14 (NY)
1977—Cardinals, 28-0 (StL)
      Giants, 27-7 (NY)
1978—Cardinals, 20-10 (StL)

      Giants, 17-0 (NY)
1979—Cardinals, 27-14 (NY)
      Cardinals, 29-20 (StL)
1980—Cardinals, 41-35 (StL)
      Cardinals, 23-7 (NY)
1981—Giants, 34-14 (NY)
      Giants, 20-10 (StL)
(Points—Giants 1,781, Cardinals 1,403)
Franchise in Chicago prior to 1960

N. Y. GIANTS vs. SAN DIEGO
Giants lead series, 2-1
1971—Giants, 35-17 (NY)
1975—Giants, 35-24 (NY)
1980—Chargers, 44-7 (SD)
(Points—Chargers 85, Giants 77)

N. Y. GIANTS vs. SAN FRANCISCO
Giants lead series, 9-5
1952—Giants, 23-14 (NY)
1956—Giants, 38-21 (SF)
1957—49ers, 27-17 (NY)
1960—Giants, 21-19 (SF)
1963—Giants, 48-14 (NY)
1968—49ers, 26-10 (NY)
1972—Giants, 23-17 (SF)
1975—Giants, 26-23 (SF)
1977—Giants, 20-17 (NY)
1978—Giants, 27-10 (NY)
1979—Giants, 32-16 (NY)
1980—49ers, 12-0 (SF)
1981—49ers, 17-10 (SF)
      *49ers, 38-24 (SF)
(Points—Giants 319, 49ers 271)
NFC Divisional Playoff

N. Y. GIANTS vs. SEATTLE
Giants lead series, 3-0
1976—Giants, 28-16 (NY)
1980—Giants, 27-21 (S)
1981—Giants, 32-0 (S)
(Points—Giants 87, Seahawks 37)

N. Y. GIANTS vs. TAMPA BAY
Giants lead series, 4-2
1977—Giants, 10-0 (TB)
1978—Giants, 19-13 (TB)
      Giants, 17-14 (NY)
1979—Giants, 17-14 (NY)
      Buccaneers, 31-3 (TB)
1980—Buccaneers, 30-13 (TB)
(Points—Buccaneers 102, Giants 79)

N. Y. GIANTS vs. *WASHINGTON
Giants lead series, 56-40-3
1932—Braves, 14-6 (B)
      Tie, 0-0 (NY)
1933—Redskins, 21-20 (B)
      Giants, 7-0 (NY)
1934—Giants, 16-13 (B)
      Giants, 3-0 (NY)
1935—Giants, 20-12 (B)
      Giants, 17-6 (NY)
1936—Giants, 7-0 (B)
      Redskins, 14-0 (NY)
1937—Redskins, 13-3 (W)
      Redskins, 49-14 (NY)
1938—Giants, 10-7 (W)

Giants, 36-0 (NY)
1939 — Tie, 0-0 (W)
Giants, 9-7 (NY)
1940 — Redskins, 21-7 (W)
Giants, 21-7 (NY)
1941 — Giants, 17-10 (W)
Giants, 20-13 (NY)
1942 — Giants, 14-7 (W)
Redskins, 14-7 (NY)
1943 — Giants, 14-10 (W)
Giants, 31-7 (W)
**Redskins, 28-0 (NY)
1944 — Giants, 16-13 (W)
Giants, 31-0 (W)
1945 — Redskins, 24-14 (NY)
Redskins, 17-0 (W)
1946 — Redskins, 24-14 (W)
Giants, 31-0 (NY)
1947 — Redskins, 28-20 (W)
Giants, 35-10 (NY)
1948 — Redskins, 41-10 (W)
Redskins, 28-21 (NY)
1949 — Giants, 45-35 (W)
Giants, 23-7 (NY)
1950 — Giants, 21-17 (W)
Giants, 24-21 (NY)
1951 — Giants, 35-14 (W)
Giants, 28-14 (NY)
1952 — Giants, 14-10 (W)
Redskins, 27-17 (NY)
1953 — Redskins, 13-9 (W)
Redskins, 24-21 (NY)
1954 — Giants, 51-21 (W)
Giants, 24-7 (NY)
1955 — Giants, 35-7 (NY)
Giants, 27-20 (W)
1956 — Redskins, 33-7 (W)
Giants, 28-14 (NY)
1957 — Giants, 24-20 (W)
Redskins, 31-14 (NY)
1958 — Giants, 21-14 (W)
Giants, 30-0 (NY)
1959 — Giants, 45-14 (W)
Giants, 24-10 (NY)
1960 — Tie, 24-24 (NY)
Giants, 17-3 (W)
1961 — Giants, 24-21 (NY)
Giants, 53-0 (W)
1962 — Giants, 49-34 (NY)
Giants, 42-24 (W)
1963 — Giants, 24-14 (W)
Giants, 44-14 (NY)
1964 — Giants, 13-10 (NY)
Redskins, 36-21 (W)
1965 — Redskins, 23-7 (NY)
Giants, 27-10 (W)
1966 — Giants, 13-10 (NY)
Redskins, 72-41 (W)
1967 — Redskins, 38-34 (W)
1968 — Giants, 48-21 (NY)
Giants, 13-10 (W)
1969 — Redskins, 20-14 (W)
1970 — Giants, 35-33 (NY)

Giants, 27-24 (W)
1971 — Redskins, 30-3 (NY)
Redskins, 23-7 (W)
1972 — Redskins, 23-16 (NY)
Redskins, 27-13 (W)
1973 — Redskins, 21-3 (New Haven)
Redskins, 27-24 (W)
1974 — Redskins, 13-10 (New Haven)
Redskins, 24-3 (W)
1975 — Redskins, 49-13 (W)
Redskins, 21-13 (NY)
1976 — Redskins, 19-17 (W)
Giants, 12-9 (NY)
1977 — Giants, 20-17 (NY)
Giants, 17-6 (W)
1978 — Giants, 17-6 (NY)
Redskins, 16-13 (W) OT
1979 — Redskins, 27-0 (W)
Giants, 14-6 (NY)
1980 — Redskins, 23-21 (NY)
Redskins, 16-13 (W)
1981 — Giants, 17-7 (W)
Redskins, 30-27 (NY) OT
(Points — Giants 1,921, Redskins 1,712)
*Franchise in Boston prior to 1937 and
known as Braves prior to 1933
**Division Playoff

N. Y. JETS vs. ATLANTA
Series tied, 1-1;
See Atlanta vs. N. Y. Jets
N. Y. JETS vs. BALTIMORE
Colts lead series, 14-11;
See Baltimore vs. N. Y. Jets
N. Y. JETS vs. BUFFALO
Bills lead series, 25-20;
See Buffalo vs. N. Y. Jets
N. Y. JETS vs. CHICAGO
Series tied, 1-1;
See Chicago vs. N. Y. Jets
N. Y. JETS vs. CINCINNATI
Jets lead series, 4-3;
See Cincinnati vs. N. Y. Jets
N. Y. JETS vs. CLEVELAND
Browns lead series, 6-1;
See Cleveland vs. N. Y. Jets
N. Y. JETS vs. DALLAS
Cowboys lead series, 3-0;
See Dallas vs. N. Y. Jets
N. Y. JETS vs. DENVER
Series tied, 10-10-1;
See Denver vs. N. Y. Jets
N. Y. JETS vs. DETROIT
Series tied, 1-1;
See Detroit vs. N. Y. Jets
N. Y. JETS vs. GREEN BAY
Jets lead series, 2-1;
See Green Bay vs. N. Y. Jets
N. Y. JETS vs. HOUSTON
Oilers lead series, 14-10-1;
See Houston vs. N. Y. Jets
N. Y. JETS vs. KANSAS CITY
Chiefs lead series, 12-9;

See Kansas City vs. N. Y. Jets
N. Y. JETS vs. LOS ANGELES
Rams lead series, 2-1;
See Los Angeles vs. N. Y. Jets
N. Y. JETS vs. MIAMI
Jets lead series, 17-14-1;
See Miami vs. N. Y. Jets
N. Y. JETS vs. MINNESOTA
Jets lead series, 2-1;
See Minnesota vs. N. Y. Jets
N. Y. JETS vs. NEW ENGLAND
Jets lead series, 26-17-1;
See New England vs. N. Y. Jets
N. Y. JETS vs. NEW ORLEANS
Jets lead series, 2-1;
See New Orleans vs. N. Y. Jets
N. Y. JETS vs. N. Y. GIANTS
Jets lead series, 2-1;
See N. Y. Giants vs. N. Y. Jets
*N. Y. JETS vs. OAKLAND
Raiders lead series, 11-10-2
1960—Raiders, 28-27 (NY)
   Titans, 31-28 (O)
1961—Titans, 14-6 (O)
   Titans, 23-12 (NY)
1962—Titans, 28-17 (O)
   Titans, 31-21 (NY)
1963—Jets, 10-7 (NY)
   Raiders, 49-26 (O)
1964—Jets, 35-13 (NY)
   Raiders, 35-26 (O)
1965—Tie, 24-24 (NY)
   Raiders, 24-14 (O)
1966—Raiders, 24-21 (NY)
   Tie, 28-28 (O)
1967—Jets, 27-14 (NY)
   Raiders, 38-29 (O)
1968—Raiders, 43-32 (O)
   **Jets, 27-23 (NY)
1969—Raiders, 27-14 (NY)
1970—Raiders, 14-13 (NY)
1972—Raiders, 24-16 (O)
1977—Raiders, 28-27 (NY)
1979—Jets, 28-19 (NY)
(Points—Jets 551, Raiders 546)
*Jets known as Titans prior to 1963
**AFL Championship
N. Y. JETS vs. PHILADELPHIA
Eagles lead series, 3-0
1973—Eagles, 24-23 (P)
1977—Eagles, 27-0 (P)
1978—Eagles, 17-9 (P)
(Points—Eagles 68, Jets 32)
N. Y. JETS vs. PITTSBURGH
Steelers lead series, 6-0
1970—Steelers, 21-17 (P)
1973—Steelers, 26-14 (P)
1975—Steelers, 20-7 (NY)
1977—Steelers, 23-20 (NY)
1978—Steelers, 28-17 (NY)
1981—Steelers, 38-10 (P)
(Points—Steelers 156, Jets 85)
N. Y. JETS vs. ST. LOUIS

Cardinals lead series, 2-1
1971—Cardinals, 17-10 (StL)
1975—Cardinals, 37-6 (NY)
1978—Jets, 23-10 (NY)
(Points—Cardinals 64, Jets 39)
*N. Y. JETS vs. **SAN DIEGO
Chargers lead series, 14-6-1
1960—Chargers, 21-7 (NY)
   Chargers, 50-43 (LA)
1961—Chargers, 25-10 (NY)
   Chargers, 48-13 (SD)
1962—Chargers, 40-14 (SD)
   Titans, 23-3 (NY)
1963—Chargers, 24-20 (SD)
   Chargers, 53-7 (NY)
1964—Tie, 17-17 (NY)
   Chargers, 38-3 (SD)
1965—Chargers, 34-9 (NY)
   Chargers, 38-7 (SD)
1966—Jets, 17-16 (NY)
   Chargers, 42-27 (SD)
1967—Jets, 42-31 (SD)
1968—Jets, 23-20 (NY)
   Jets, 37-15 (SD)
1969—Chargers, 34-27 (SD)
1971—Chargers, 49-21 (SD)
1974—Jets, 27-14 (NY)
1975—Chargers, 24-16 (SD)
(Points—Chargers 636, Jets 410)
*Jets known as Titans prior to 1963
**Franchise in Los Angeles prior to 1961
N. Y. JETS vs. SAN FRANCISCO
49ers lead series, 3-0
1971—49ers, 24-21 (NY)
1976—49ers, 17-6 (SF)
1980—49ers, 37-27 (NY)
(Points—49ers 78, Jets 54)
N. Y. JETS vs. SEATTLE
Seahawks lead series, 6-0
1977—Seahawks, 17-0 (NY)
1978—Seahawks, 24-17 (NY)
1979—Seahawks, 30-7 (S)
1980—Seahawks, 27-17 (NY)
1981—Seahawks, 19-3 (NY)
   Seahawks, 27-23 (S)
(Points—Seahawks 144, Jets 67)
N. Y. JETS vs. TAMPA BAY
Jets lead series, 1-0
1976—Jets, 34-0 (NY)
N. Y. JETS vs. WASHINGTON
Redskins lead series, 3-0
1972—Redskins, 35-17 (NY)
1976—Redskins, 37-16 (NY)
1978—Redskins, 23-3 (W)
(Points—Redskins 95, Jets 36)

OAKLAND vs. ATLANTA
Raiders lead series, 2-1;
See Atlanta vs. Oakland
OAKLAND vs. BALTIMORE
Raiders lead series, 3-2;
See Baltimore vs. Oakland
OAKLAND vs. BUFFALO

Series tied, 11-11;
See Buffalo vs. Oakland
OAKLAND vs. CHICAGO
Raiders lead series, 3-1;.
See Chicago vs. Oakland
OAKLAND vs. CINCINNATI
Raiders lead series, 10-3;
See Cincinnati vs. Oakland
OAKLAND vs. CLEVELAND
Raiders lead series, 7-1;
See Cleveland vs. Oakland
OAKLAND vs. DALLAS
Series tied, 1-1;
See Dallas vs. Oakland
OAKLAND vs. DENVER
Raiders lead series, 31-12-2;
See Denver vs. Oakland
OAKLAND vs. DETROIT
Series tied, 2-2;
See Detroit vs. Oakland
OAKLAND vs. GREEN BAY
Raiders lead series, 3-1;
See Green Bay vs. Oakland
OAKLAND vs. HOUSTON
Raiders lead series, 19-10;
See Houston vs. Oakland
OAKLAND vs. KANSAS CITY
Raiders lead series, 24-20-2;
See Kansas City vs. Oakland
OAKLAND vs. LOS ANGELES
Raiders lead series, 2-1;
See Los Angeles vs. Oakland
OAKLAND vs. MIAMI
Raiders lead series, 12-3-1;
See Miami vs. Oakland
OAKLAND vs. MINNESOTA
Raiders lead series, 4-1;
See Minnesota vs. Oakland
OAKLAND vs. NEW ENGLAND
Series tied, 11-11-1;
See New England vs. Oakland
OAKLAND vs. NEW ORLEANS
Raiders lead series, 2-0-1;
See New Orleans vs. Oakland
OAKLAND vs. N.Y. GIANTS
Raiders lead series, 2-0;
See N.Y. Giants vs. Oakland
OAKLAND vs. N.Y. JETS
Raiders lead series, 11-10-2;
See N.Y. Jets vs. Oakland
OAKLAND vs. PHILADELPHIA
Raiders lead series, 3-1
1971—Raiders, 34-10 (O)
1976—Raiders, 26-7 (P)
1980—Eagles, 10-7 (P)
        *Raiders, 27-10 (New Orleans)
(Points—Raiders 94, Eagles 37)
*Super Bowl XV
OAKLAND vs. PITTSBURGH
Raiders lead series, 8-5
1970—Raiders, 31-14 (O)
1972—Steelers, 34-28 (P)
        *Steelers, 13-7 (P)

1973—Steelers, 17-9 (O)
        *Raiders, 33-14 (O)
1974—Raiders, 17-0 (P)
        **Steelers, 24-13 (O)
1975—**Steelers, 16-10 (P)
1976—Raiders, 31-28 (O)
        **Raiders, 24-7 (O)
1977—Raiders, 16-7 (P)
1980—Raiders, 45-34 (P)
1981—Raiders, 30-27 (O)
(Points—Raiders 294, Steelers 235)
*AFC Divisional Playoff
**AFC Championship
OAKLAND vs. ST. LOUIS
Raiders lead series, 1-0
1973—Raiders, 17-10 (StL)
OAKLAND vs. *SAN DIEGO
Raiders lead series, 26-17-2
1960—Chargers, 52-28 (LA)
        Chargers, 41-17 (O)
1961—Chargers, 44-0 (O)
        Chargers, 41-10 (O)
1962—Chargers, 42-33 (O)
        Chargers, 31-21 (SD)
1963—Raiders, 34-33 (SD)
        Raiders, 41-27 (O)
1964—Chargers, 31-17 (O)
        Raiders, 21-20 (SD)
1965—Chargers, 17-6 (O)
        Chargers, 24-14 (SD)
1966—Chargers, 29-20 (O)
        Raiders, 41-19 (SD)
1967—Raiders, 51-10 (O)
        Raiders, 41-21 (SD)
1968—Chargers, 23-14 (O)
        Raiders, 34-27 (SD)
1969—Raiders, 24-12 (SD)
        Raiders, 21-16 (O)
1970—Tie, 27-27 (SD)
        Raiders, 20-17 (O)
1971—Raiders, 34-0 (SD)
        Raiders, 34-33 (O)
1972—Tie, 17-17 (O)
        Raiders, 21-19 (SD)
1973—Raiders, 27-17 (O)
        Raiders, 31-3 (O)
1974—Raiders, 14-10 (SD)
        Raiders, 17-10 (O)
1975—Raiders, 6-0 (O)
        Raiders, 25-0 (O)
1976—Raiders, 27-17 (SD)
        Raiders, 24-0 (O)
1977—Raiders, 24-0 (O)
        Chargers, 12-7 (SD)
1978—Raiders, 21-20 (SD)
        Chargers, 27-23 (O)
1979—Chargers, 30-10 (SD)
        Raiders, 45-22 (O)
1980—Chargers, 30-24 (SD) OT
        Raiders, 38-24 (O)
        **Raiders, 34-27 (SD)
1981—Chargers, 55-21 (O)
        Chargers, 23-10 (SD)

All-Time Team vs. Team Results

(Points—Raiders 1,069, Chargers 1,000)
*Franchise in Los Angeles prior to 1961
**AFC Championship

OAKLAND vs. SAN FRANCISCO
Raiders lead series, 2-1
1970—49ers, 38-7 (O)
1974—Raiders, 35-24 (SF)
1979—Raiders, 23-10 (O)
(Points—49ers 72, Raiders 65)

OAKLAND vs. SEATTLE
Raiders lead series, 5-4
1977—Raiders, 44-7 (O)
1978—Seahawks, 27-7 (S)
        Seahawks, 17-16 (O)
1979—Seahawks, 27-10 (S)
        Seahawks, 29-24 (O)
1980—Raiders, 33-14 (O)
        Raiders, 19-17 (S)
1981—Raiders, 20-10 (O)
        Raiders, 32-31 (S)
(Points—Raiders 205, Seahawks 179)

OAKLAND vs. TAMPA BAY
Raiders lead series, 2-0
1976—Raiders, 49-16 (O)
1981—Raiders, 18-16 (O)
(Points—Raiders 67, Buccaneers 32)

OAKLAND vs. WASHINGTON
Raiders lead series, 3-0
1970—Raiders, 34-20 (O)
1975—Raiders, 26-23 (W) OT
1980—Raiders, 24-21 (O)
(Points—Raiders 84, Redskins 64)

PHILADELPHIA vs. ATLANTA
Falcons lead series, 5-4-1;
See Atlanta vs. Philadelphia
PHILADELPHIA vs. BALTIMORE
Series tied, 4-4;
See Baltimore vs. Philadelphia
PHILADELPHIA vs. BUFFALO
Series tied, 1-1;
See Buffalo vs. Philadelphia
PHILADELPHIA vs. CHICAGO
Bears lead series, 17-4-1;
See Chicago vs. Philadelphia
PHILADELPHIA vs. CINCINNATI
Bengals lead series, 3-0;
See Cincinnati vs. Philadelphia
PHILADELPHIA vs. CLEVELAND
Browns lead series, 29-10-1;
See Cleveland vs. Philadelphia
PHILADELPHIA vs. DALLAS
Cowboys lead series, 29-15;
See Dallas vs. Philadelphia
PHILADELPHIA vs. DENVER
Eagles lead series, 2-1;
See Denver vs. Philadelphia
PHILADELPHIA vs. DETROIT
Lions lead series, 12-9-1;
See Detroit vs. Philadelphia
PHILADELPHIA vs. GREEN BAY
Packers lead series, 17-5;
See Green Bay vs. Philadelphia
PHILADELPHIA vs. HOUSTON

Eagles lead series, 2-0;
See Houston vs. Philadelphia
PHILADELPHIA vs. KANSAS CITY
Eagles lead series, 1-0;
See Kansas City vs. Philadelphia
PHILADELPHIA vs. LOS ANGELES
Rams lead series, 14-8-1;
See Los Angeles vs. Philadelphia
PHILADELPHIA vs. MIAMI
Series tied, 2-2;
See Miami vs. Philadelphia
PHILADELPHIA vs. MINNESOTA
Vikings lead series, 8-2;
See Minnesota vs. Philadelphia
PHILADELPHIA vs. NEW ENGLAND
Series tied, 2-2;
See New England vs. Philadelphia
PHILADELPHIA vs. NEW ORLEANS
Eagles lead series, 8-4;
See New Orleans vs. Philadelphia
PHILADELPHIA vs. N.Y. GIANTS
Giants lead series, 50-43-2;
See N.Y. Giants vs. Philadelphia
PHILADELPHIA vs. N.Y. JETS
Eagles lead series, 2-0;
See N.Y. Jets vs. Philadelphia
PHILADELPHIA vs. OAKLAND
Raiders lead series, 3-1;
See Oakland vs. Philadelphia
PHILADELPHIA vs. *PITTSBURGH
Eagles lead series, 42-25-3
1933—Eagles, 25-6 (Phila)
1934—Eagles, 17-0 (Pitt)
        Pirates, 9-7 (Phila)
1935—Pirates, 17-7 (Phila)
        Eagles, 17-6 (Pitt)
1936—Pirates, 17-0 (Pitt)
        Pirates, 6-0 (Johnstown, Pa.)
1937—Pirates, 27-14 (Pitt)
        Pirates, 16-7 (Pitt)
1938—Eagles, 27-7 (Buffalo)
        Eagles, 14-7 (Charleston, W. Va)
1939—Eagles, 17-14 (Phila)
        Pirates, 24-12 (Pitt)
1940—Pirates, 7-3 (Pitt)
        Eagles, 7-0 (Phila)
1941—Eagles, 10-7 (Pitt)
        Tie, 7-7 (Phila)
1942—Eagles, 24-14 (Pitt)
        Steelers, 14-0 (Phila)
1945—Eagles, 45-3 (Pitt)
        Eagles, 30-6 (Phila)
1946—Steelers, 10-7 (Pitt)
        Eagles, 10-7 (Phila)
1947—Steelers, 35-24 (Pitt)
        Eagles, 21-0 (Phila)
        **Eagles, 21-0 (Pitt)
1948—Eagles, 34-7 (Pitt)
        Eagles, 17-0 (Phila)
1949—Eagles, 38-7 (Pitt)
        Eagles, 34-17 (Phila)
1950—Eagles, 17-10 (Pitt)
        Steelers, 9-7 (Phila)

1951—Eagles, 34-13 (Pitt)
      Steelers, 17-13 (Phila)
1952—Eagles, 31-25 (Pitt)
      Eagles, 26-21 (Phila)
1953—Eagles, 23-17 (Phila)
      Eagles, 35-7 (Pitt)
1954—Eagles, 24-22 (Phila)
      Steelers, 17-7 (Pitt)
1955—Steelers, 13-7 (Pitt)
      Eagles, 24-0 (Phila)
1956—Eagles, 35-21 (Pitt)
      Eagles, 14-7 (Phila)
1957—Steelers, 6-0 (Pitt)
      Eagles, 7-6 (Phila)
1958—Steelers, 24-3 (Pitt)
      Steelers, 31-24 (Phila)
1959—Eagles, 28-24 (Phila)
      Steelers, 31-0 (Pitt)
1960—Eagles, 34-7 (Phila)
      Steelers, 27-21 (Pitt)
1961—Eagles, 21-16 (Phila)
      Eagles, 35-24 (Pitt)
1962—Steelers, 13-7 (Pitt)
      Steelers, 26-17 (Phila)
1963—Tie, 21-21 (Phila)
      Tie, 20-20 (Pitt)
1964—Eagles, 21-7 (Phila)
      Eagles, 34-10 (Pitt)
1965—Steelers, 20-14 (Phila)
      Eagles, 47-13 (Pitt)
1966—Eagles, 31-14 (Pitt)
      Eagles, 27-23 (Phila)
1967—Eagles, 34-24 (Phila)
1968—Steelers, 6-3 (Pitt)
1969—Eagles, 41-27 (Phila)
1970—Eagles, 30-20 (Phila)
1974—Steelers, 27-0 (Pitt)
1979—Eagles, 17-14 (Phila)
(Points—Eagles 1,330, Steelers 967)
*Steelers known as Pirates prior to 1941
**Division Playoff
PHILADELPHIA vs. *ST. LOUIS
Cardinals lead series, 35-32-4
1935—Cardinals, 12-3 (C)
1936—Cardinals, 13-0 (C)
1937—Tie, 6-6 (P)
1938—Eagles, 7-0 (Erie, Pa.)
1941—Eagles, 21-14 (P)
1945—Eagles, 21-6 (P)
1947—Cardinals, 45-21 (P)
      **Cardinals, 28-21 (C)
1948—Cardinals, 21-14 (C)
      **Eagles, 7-0 (P)
1949—Eagles, 28-3 (P)
1950—Eagles, 45-7 (C)
      Cardinals, 14-10 (P)
1951—Eagles, 17-14 (C)
1952—Eagles, 10-7 (P)
      Cardinals, 28-22 (C)
1953—Eagles, 56-17 (C)
      Eagles, 38-0 (P)
1954—Eagles, 35-16 (C)
      Eagles, 30-14 (P)

1955—Tie, 24-24 (C)
      Eagles, 27-3 (P)
1956—Cardinals, 20-6 (P)
      Cardinals, 28-17 (C)
1957—Eagles, 38-21 (C)
      Cardinals, 31-27 (P)
1958—Tie, 21-21 (C)
      Eagles, 49-21 (P)
1959—Eagles, 28-24 (Minn)
      Eagles, 27-17 (P)
1960—Eagles, 31-27 (P)
      Eagles, 20-6 (StL)
1961—Cardinals, 30-27 (P)
      Eagles, 20-7 (StL)
1962—Cardinals, 27-21 (P)
      Cardinals, 45-35 (StL)
1963—Cardinals, 28-24 (P)
      Cardinals, 38-14 (StL)
1964—Cardinals, 38-13 (P)
      Cardinals, 36-34 (StL)
1965—Eagles, 34-27 (P)
      Eagles, 28-24 (StL)
1966—Cardinals, 16-13 (StL)
      Cardinals, 41-10 (P)
1967—Cardinals, 48-14 (StL)
1968—Cardinals, 45-17 (P)
1969—Eagles, 34-30 (StL)
1970—Cardinals, 35-20 (P)
      Cardinals, 23-14 (StL)
1971—Eagles, 37-20 (StL)
      Eagles, 19-7 (P)
1972—Tie, 6-6 (P)
      Cardinals, 24-23 (StL)
1973—Cardinals, 34-23 (P)
      Eagles, 27-24 (StL)
1974—Cardinals, 7-3 (StL)
      Cardinals, 13-3 (P)
1975—Cardinals, 31-20 (StL)
      Cardinals, 24-23 (P)
1976—Cardinals, 33-14 (StL)
      Cardinals, 17-14 (P)
1977—Cardinals, 21-17 (P)
      Cardinals, 21-16 (StL)
1978—Cardinals, 16-10 (P)
      Eagles, 14-10 (StL)
1979—Eagles, 24-20 (StL)
      Eagles, 16-13 (P)
1980—Cardinals, 24-14 (StL)
      Eagles, 17-3 (P)
1981—Eagles, 52-10 (StL)
      Eagles, 38-0 (P)
(Points—Eagles 1,529, Cardinals 1,424)
*Franchise in Chicago prior to 1960
**NFL Championship
PHILADELPHIA vs. SAN DIEGO
Series tied, 1-1
1974—Eagles, 13-7 (SD)
1980—Chargers, 22-21 (SD)
(Points—Eagles 34, Chargers 29)
PHILADELPHIA vs. SAN FRANCISCO
49ers lead series, 8-3-1
1951—Eagles, 21-14 (P)
1953—49ers, 31-21 (SF)

All-Time Team vs. Team Results

1956—Tie, 10-10 (P)
1958—49ers, 30-24 (P)
1959—49ers, 24-14 (SF)
1964—49ers, 28-24 (P)
1966—Eagles, 35-34 (SF)
1967—49ers, 28-27 (P)
1969—49ers, 14-13 (SF)
1971—49ers, 31-3 (P)
1973—49ers, 38-28 (SF)
1975—Eagles, 27-17 (P)
(Points—49ers 299, Eagles 247)

PHILADELPHIA vs. SEATTLE
Eagles lead series, 2-0
1976—Eagles, 27-10 (P)
1980—Eagles, 27-20 (S)
(Points—Eagles 54, Seahawks 30)

PHILADELPHIA vs. TAMPA BAY
Eagles lead series, 2-1
1977—Eagles, 13-3 (P)
1979—*Buccaneers, 24-17 (TB)
1981—Eagles, 20-10 (P)
(Points—Eagles 50, Buccaneers 37)
*NFC Divisional Playoff

**PHILADELPHIA vs.
*WASHINGTON**
Redskins lead series, 51-37-5
1934—Redskins, 6-0 (B)
        Redskins, 14-7 (P)
1935—Eagles, 7-6 (B)
1963—Redskins, 26-3 (P)
        Redskins, 17-7 (B)
1937—Eagles, 14-0 (W)
        Redskins, 10-7 (P)
1938—Redskins, 26-23 (P)
        Redskins, 20-14 (W)
1939—Redskins, 7-0 (P)
        Redskins, 7-6 (W)
1940—Redskins, 34-17 (P)
        Redskins, 13-6 (W)
1941—Redskins, 21-17 (P)
        Redskins, 20-14 (W)
1942—Redskins, 14-10 (P)
        Redskins, 30-27 (W)
1944—Tie, 31-31 (P)
        Eagles, 37-7 (W)
1945—Redskins, 24-14 (W)
        Eagles, 16-0 (P)
1946—Eagles, 28-24 (W)
        Redskins, 27-10 (P)
1947—Eagles, 45-42 (P)
        Eagles, 38-14 (W)
1948—Eagles, 45-0 (W)
        Eagles, 42-21 (P)
1949—Eagles, 49-14 (P)
        Eagles, 44-21 (W)
1950—Eagles, 35-3 (P)
        Eagles, 33-0 (W)
1951—Eagles, 27-23 (P)
        Eagles, 35-21 (W)
1952—Eagles, 38-20 (P)
        Redskins, 27-21 (W)
1953—Tie, 21-21 (P)
        Redskins, 10-0 (W)

1954—Eagles, 49-21 (W)
        Eagles, 41-33 (P)
1955—Redskins, 31-30 (P)
        Redskins, 34-21 (W)
1956—Eagles, 13-9 (P)
        Redskins, 19-17 (W)
1957—Eagles, 21-12 (P)
        Redskins, 42-7 (W)
1958—Redskins, 24-14 (P)
        Redskins, 20-0 (W)
1959—Eagles, 30-23 (P)
        Eagles, 34-14 (W)
1960—Eagles, 19-13 (P)
        Eagles, 38-28 (W)
1961—Eagles, 14-7 (P)
        Eagles, 27-24 (W)
1962—Redskins, 27-21 (P)
        Eagles, 37-14 (W)
1963—Eagles, 37-24 (W)
        Redskins, 13-10 (P)
1964—Redskins, 35-20 (W)
        Redskins, 21-10 (P)
1965—Redskins, 23-21 (W)
        Eagles, 21-14 (P)
1966—Redskins, 27-13 (P)
        Eagles, 37-28 (W)
1967—Eagles, 35-24 (P)
        Tie, 35-35 (W)
1968—Redskins, 17-14 (W)
        Redskins, 16-10 (P)
1969—Tie, 28-28 (W)
        Redskins, 34-29 (P)
1970—Redskins, 33-21 (P)
        Redskins, 24-6 (W)
1971—Tie, 7-7 (W)
        Redskins, 20-13 (P)
1972—Redskins, 14-0 (W)
        Redskins, 23-7 (P)
1973—Redskins, 28-7 (P)
        Redskins, 38-20 (W)
1974—Redskins, 27-20 (P)
        Redskins, 26-7 (W)
1975—Eagles, 26-10 (P)
        Eagles, 26-3 (W)
1976—Redskins, 20-17 (P) OT
        Redskins, 24-0 (W)
1977—Redskins, 23-17 (W)
        Redskins, 17-14 (P)
1978—Redskins, 35-30 (W)
        Eagles, 17-10 (P)
1979—Eagles, 28-17 (P)
        Redskins, 17-7 (W)
1980—Eagles, 24-14 (P)
        Eagles, 24-0 (W)
1981—Eagles, 36-13 (P)
        Redskins, 15-13 (W)
(Points—Eagles 1,924, Redskins 1,817)
*Franchise in Boston prior to 1937

PITTSBURGH vs. ATLANTA
Steelers lead series, 5-1;
See Atlanta vs. Pittsburgh
PITTSBURGH vs. BALTIMORE

Steelers lead series, 7-3;
See Baltimore vs. Pittsburgh
PITTSBURGH vs. BUFFALO
Steelers lead series, 5-2;
See Buffalo vs. Pittsburgh
PITTSBURGH vs. CHICAGO
Bears lead series, 13-4-1;
See Chicago vs. Pittsburgh
PITTSBURGH vs. CINCINNATI
Steelers lead series, 14-10;
See Cincinnati vs. Pittsburgh
PITTSBURGH vs. CLEVELAND
Browns lead series, 37-27;
See Cleveland vs. Pittsburgh
PITTSBURGH vs. DALLAS
Steelers lead series, 11-10;
See Dallas vs. Pittsburgh
PITTSBURGH vs. DENVER
Broncos lead series, 5-4-1;
See Denver vs. Pittsburgh
PITTSBURGH vs. DETROIT
Lions lead series, 12-8-1;
See Detroit vs. Pittsburgh
PITTSBURGH vs. GREEN BAY
Packers lead series, 16-9;
See Green Bay vs. Pittsburgh
PITTSBURGH vs. HOUSTON
Steelers lead series, 18-8;
See Houston vs. Pittsburgh
PITTSBURGH vs. KANSAS CITY
Steelers lead series, 7-3;
See Kansas City vs. Pittsburgh
PITTSBURGH vs. LOS ANGELES
Rams lead series, 12-3-2;
See Los Angeles vs. Pittsburgh
PITTSBURGH vs. MIAMI
Dolphins lead series, 4-3;
See Miami vs. Pittsburgh
PITTSBURGH vs. MINNESOTA
Series tied, 4-4;
See Minnesota vs. Pittsburgh
PITTSBURGH vs. NEW ENGLAND
Steelers lead series, 4-1;
See New England vs. Pittsburgh
PITTSBURGH vs. NEW ORLEANS
Steelers lead series, 4-3;
See New Orleans vs. Pittsburgh
PITTSBURGH vs. N.Y. GIANTS
Giants lead series, 40-26-3;
See N.Y. Giants vs. Pittsburgh
PITTSBURGH vs. N.Y. JETS
Steelers lead series, 6-0;
See N.Y. Jets vs. Pittsburgh
PITTSBURGH vs. OAKLAND
Raiders lead series, 8-5;
See Oakland vs. Pittsburgh
PITTSBURGH vs. PHILADELPHIA
Eagles lead series, 42-25-3;
See Philadelphia vs. Pittsburgh
*PITTSBURGH vs. **ST. LOUIS
Steelers lead series, 28-20-3
1933—Pirates, 14-13 (C)
1935—Pirates, 17-13 (P)

1936—Cardinals, 14-6 (C)
1937—Cardinals, 13-7 (P)
1939—Cardinals, 10-0 (P)
1940—Tie, 7-7 (P)
1942—Steelers, 19-3 (P)
1945—Steelers, 23-0 (P)
1946—Steelers, 14-7 (P)
1948—Cardinals 24-7 (P)
1950—Steelers, 28-17 (C)
          Steelers, 28-7 (P)
1951—Steelers, 28-14 (C)
1952—Steelers, 34-28 (C)
          Steelers, 17-14 (P)
1953—Steelers, 31-28 (P)
          Steelers, 21-17 (C)
1954—Cardinals 17-14 (C)
          Steelers, 20-17 (P)
1955—Steelers, 14-7 (P)
          Cardinals 27-13 (C)
1956—Steelers, 14-7 (P)
          Cardinals, 38-27 (C)
1957—Steelers, 29-20 (C)
          Steelers, 27-2 (C)
1958—Steelers, 27-20 (C)
          Steelers, 38-21 (P)
1959—Cardinals, 45-24 (C)
          Steelers, 35-20 (P)
1960—Steelers, 27-14 (P)
          Cardinals, 38-7 (StL)
1961—Steelers, 30-27 (P)
          Cardinals, 20-0 (StL)
1962—Steelers, 26-17 (StL)
          Steelers, 19-7 (P)
1963—Steelers, 23-10 (P)
          Cardinals, 24-23 (StL)
1964—Cardinals, 34-30 (StL)
          Cardinals, 21-20 (P)
1965—Cardinals, 20-7 (P)
          Cardinals, 21-17 (StL)
1966—Steelers, 30-9 (P)
          Cardinals, 6-3 (StL)
1967—Cardinals, 28-14 (P)
          Tie, 14-14 (StL)
1968—Tie, 28-28 (StL)
          Cardinals, 20-10 (P)
1969—Cardinals, 27-14 (P)
          Cardinals, 47-10 (StL)
1972—Steelers, 25-19 (StL)
1979—Steelers, 24-21 (StL)
(Points — Steelers 984, Cardinals 942)
*Steelers known as Pirates prior to 1941
**Franchise in Chicago prior to 1960
PITTSBURGH vs. SAN DIEGO
Steelers lead series, 6-2
1971—Steelers, 21-17 (P)
1972—Steelers, 24-2 (SD)
1973—Steelers, 38-21 (P)
1975—Steelers, 37-0 (SD)
1976—Steelers, 23-0 (P)
1977—Steelers, 10-9 (SD)
1979—Chargers, 35-7 (SD)
1980—Chargers, 26-17 (SD)
(Points—Steelers 177, Chargers 110)

All-Time Team vs. Team Results

PITTSBURGH vs. SAN FRANCISCO
49ers lead series, 6-5
1951—49ers, 28-24 (P)
1952—49ers, 24-7 (SF)
1954—49ers, 31-3 (SF)
1958—49ers, 23-20 (SF)
1961—49ers, 20-10 (SF)
1965—49ers, 27-17 (SF)
1968—49ers, 45-28 (P)
1973—Steelers, 37-14 (SF)
1977—Steelers, 27-0 (P)
1978—Steelers, 24-7 (SF)
1981—49ers, 17-14 (P)
(Points—Steelers 238, 49ers 209)

PITTSBURGH vs. SEATTLE
Steelers lead series, 2-1
1977—Steelers, 30-20 (P)
1978—Steelers, 21-10 (P)
1981—Seahawks, 24-21 (S)
(Points—Steelers 72, Seahawks 54)

PITTSBURGH vs. TAMPA BAY
Steelers lead series, 2-0
1976—Steelers, 42-0 (P)
1980—Steelers, 24-21 (TB)
(Points—Steelers 66, Buccaneers 21)

*PITTSBURGH vs. **WASHINGTON
Redskins lead series, 39-27-3
1933—Redskins, 21-6 (P)
        Pirates, 16-14 (B)
1934—Redskins, 7-0 (P)
        Redskins, 39-0 (B)
1935—Pirates, 6-0 (P)
        Redskins, 13-3 (B)
1936—Pirates, 10-0 (P)
        Redskins, 30-0 (B)
1937—Redskins, 34-20 (W)
        Pirates, 21-13 (P)
1938—Redskins, 7-0 (P)
        Redskins, 15-0 (W)
1939—Redskins, 44-14 (W)
        Redskins, 21-14 (P)
1940—Redskins, 40-10 (P)
        Redskins, 37-10 (W)
1941—Redskins, 24-20 (P)
        Redskins, 23-3 (W)
1942—Redskins, 28-14 (W)
        Redskins, 14-0 (P)
1945—Redskins, 14-0 (P)
        Redskins, 24-0 (W)
1946—Tie, 14-14 (W)
        Steelers, 14-7 (P)
1947—Redskins, 27-26 (W)
        Steelers, 21-14 (P)
1948—Redskins, 17-14 (W)
        Steelers, 10-7 (P)
1949—Redskins, 27-14 (P)
        Redskins, 27-14 (W)
1950—Redskins, 26-7 (W)
        Steelers, 24-7 (P)
1951—Redskins, 22-7 (P)
        Steelers, 20-10 (W)
1952—Redskins, 28-24 (P)
        Steelers, 24-23 (W)

1953—Redskins, 17-9 (P)
        Steelers, 14-13 (W)
1954—Steelers, 37-7 (P)
        Redskins, 17-14 (W)
1955—Redskins, 23-14 (P)
        Redskins, 28-17 (W)
1956—Steelers, 30-13 (P)
        Steelers, 23-0 (W)
1957—Steelers, 28-7 (P)
        Redskins, 10-3 (W)
1958—Steelers, 24-16 (P)
        Tie, 14-14 (W)
1959—Redskins, 23-17 (P)
        Steelers, 27-6 (W)
1960—Tie, 27-27 (W)
        Steelers, 22-10 (P)
1961—Steelers, 20-0 (P)
        Steelers, 30-14 (W)
1962—Steelers, 23-21 (P)
        Steelers, 27-24 (W)
1963—Steelers, 38-27 (P)
        Steelers, 34-28 (W)
1964—Redskins, 30-0 (P)
        Steelers, 14-7 (W)
1965—Redskins, 31-3 (P)
        Redskins, 35-14 (W)
1966—Redskins, 33-27 (P)
        Redskins, 24-10 (W)
1967—Redskins, 15-10 (P)
1968—Redskins, 16-13 (W)
1969—Redskins, 14-7 (P)
1973—Steelers, 21-16 (P)
1979—Steelers, 38-7 (P)
(Points—Redskins 1,289, Steelers 1,051)
*Steelers known as Pirates prior to 1941
**Franchise in Boston prior to 1937

ST. LOUIS vs. ATLANTA
Cardinals lead series, 5-3;
See Atlanta vs. St. Louis

ST. LOUIS vs. BALTIMORE
Series tied, 4-4;
See Baltimore vs. St. Louis

ST. LOUIS vs BUFFALO
Cardinals lead series, 2-1;
See Buffalo vs. St. Louis

ST. LOUIS vs. CHICAGO
Bears lead series, 50-23-6;
See Chicago vs. St. Louis

ST. LOUIS vs. CINCINNATI
Bengals lead series, 2-0;
See Cincinnati vs. St. Louis

ST. LOUIS vs. CLEVELAND
Browns lead series, 30-9-3;
See Cleveland vs. St. Louis

ST. LOUIS vs. DALLAS
Cowboys lead series, 24-15-1;
See Dallas vs. St. Louis

ST. LOUIS vs. DENVER
Broncos lead series, 1-0-1;
See Denver vs. St. Louis

ST. LOUIS vs. DETROIT
Lions lead series, 25-15-5;

See Detroit vs. St. Louis
ST. LOUIS vs. GREEN BAY
Packers lead series 36-20-4;
See Green Bay vs. St. Louis
ST. LOUIS vs. HOUSTON
Cardinals lead series, 3-0;
See Houston vs. St. Louis
ST. LOUIS vs. KANSAS CITY
Chiefs lead series, 2-0-1;
See Kansas City vs. St. Louis
ST. LOUIS vs. LOS ANGELES
Rams lead series, 18-15-2;
See Los Angeles vs. St. Louis
ST. LOUIS vs. MIAMI
Dolphins lead series, 4-0;
See Miami vs. St. Louis
ST. LOUIS vs. MINNESOTA
Cardinals lead series, 6-3;
See Minnesota vs. St. Louis
ST. LOUIS vs. NEW ENGLAND
Cardinals lead series, 3-1;
See New England vs. St. Louis
ST. LOUIS vs. NEW ORLEANS
Cardinals lead series, 7-2;
See New Orleans vs. St. Louis
ST. LOUIS vs. N.Y. GIANTS
Giants lead series, 50-28-1;
See N.Y. Giants vs. St. Louis
ST. LOUIS vs. N.Y. JETS
Cardinals lead series, 2-1;
See N.Y. Jets vs. St. Louis
ST. LOUIS vs. OAKLAND
Raiders lead series, 1-0;
See Oakland vs. St. Louis
ST. LOUIS vs. PHILADELPHIA
Cardinals lead series, 35-32-4;
See Philadelphia vs. St. Louis
ST. LOUIS vs. PITTSBURGH
Steelers lead series, 28-20-3;
See Pittsburgh vs. St. Louis
ST. LOUIS vs. SAN DIEGO
Chargers lead series, 2-0;
1971—Chargers, 20-17 (SD)
1976—Chargers, 43-24 (SD)
(Points—Chargers 63, Cardinals 41)
*ST. LOUIS vs. SAN FRANCISCO
Cardinals lead series, 7-4
1951—Cardinals, 27-21 (SF)
1957—Cardinals, 20-10 (SF)
1962—49ers, 24-17 (StL)
1964—Cardinals, 23-13 (SF)
1968—49ers, 35-17 (SF)
1971—49ers, 26-14 (StL)
1974—Cardinals, 34-9 (SF)
1976—Cardinals, 23-20 (StL) OT
1978—Cardinals, 16-10 (SF)
1979—Cardinals, 13-10 (StL)
1980—49ers, 24-21 (SF) OT
(Points—Cardinals 225, 49ers 202)
*Team in Chicago prior to 1960
ST. LOUIS vs. SEATTLE
Cardinals lead series, 1-0
1976—Cardinals, 30-24 (S)

ST. LOUIS vs. TAMPA BAY
Buccaneers lead series, 2-0
1977—Buccaneers, 17-7 (TB)
1981—Buccaneers, 20-10 (TB)
(Points—Buccaneers 37, Cardinals 17)
*ST. LOUIS vs. **WASHINGTON
Redskins lead series, 42-31-2
1932—Cardinals, 9-0 (B)
      Braves, 8-6 (C)
1933—Redskins, 10-0 (C)
      Tie, 0-0 (B)
1934—Redskins, 9-0 (B)
1935—Cardinals, 6-0 (B)
1936—Redskins, 13-10 (B)
1937—Cardinals, 21-14 (W)
1939—Redskins, 28-7 (W)
1940—Redskins, 28-21 (W)
1942—Redskins, 28-0 (W)
1943—Redskins, 13-7 (W)
1945—Redskins, 24-21 (W)
1947—Redskins, 45-21 (W)
1949—Cardinals, 38-7 (C)
1950—Cardinals, 38-28 (W)
1951—Redskins, 7-3 (C)
      Redskins, 20-17 (W)
1952—Redskins, 23-7 (C)
      Cardinals, 17-6 (W)
1953—Cardinals, 24-13 (C)
      Redskins, 28-17 (W)
1954—Cardinals, 38-16 (C)
      Redskins, 37-20 (W)
1955—Cardinals, 24-10 (W)
      Redskins, 31-0 (C)
1956—Cardinals, 31-3 (W)
      Redskins, 17-14 (C)
1957—Redskins, 37-14 (C)
      Cardinals, 44-14 (W)
1958—Cardinals, 37-10 (C)
      Redskins, 45-31 (W)
1959—Cardinals, 49-21 (C)
      Redskins, 23-14 (W)
1960—Cardinals, 44-7 (StL)
      Cardinals, 26-14 (W)
1961—Cardinals, 24-0 (W)
      Cardinals, 38-24 (StL)
1962—Redskins, 24-14 (W)
      Tie, 17-17 (StL)
1963—Cardinals, 21-7 (W)
      Cardinals, 24-20 (StL)
1964—Cardinals, 23-17 (W)
      Cardinals, 38-24 (StL)
1965—Cardinals, 37-16 (W)
      Redskins, 24-20 (StL)
1966—Cardinals, 23-7 (StL)
      Redskins, 26-20 (W)
1967—Cardinals, 27-21 (W)
1968—Cardinals, 41-14 (StL)
1969—Redskins, 33-17 (W)
1970—Cardinals, 27-17 (StL)
      Redskins, 28-27 (W)
1971—Cardinals, 24-17 (StL)
      Redskins, 20-0 (W)
1972—Redskins, 24-10 (W)

215

Redskins, 33-3 (StL)
1973—Cardinals, 34-27 (StL)
Redskins, 31-13 (W)
1974—Cardinals, 17-10 (W)
Cardinals, 23-20 (StL)
1975—Redskins, 27-17 (W)
Cardinals, 20-17 (StL) OT
1976—Redskins, 20-10 (W)
Redskins, 16-10 (StL)
1977—Redskins, 24-14 (W)
Redskins, 26-20 (StL)
1978—Redskins, 28-10 (StL)
Cardinals, 27-17 (W)
1979—Redskins, 17-7 (StL)
Redskins, 30-28 (W)
1980—Redskins, 23-0 (W)
Redskins, 31-7 (StL)
1981—Cardinals, 40-30 (StL)
Redskins, 42-21 (W)
(Points—Redskins 1,504, Cardinals 1,451)
*Team in Chicago prior to 1960
**Team in Boston prior to 1937 and known as Braves prior to 1933

SAN DIEGO vs. ATLANTA
Falcons lead series, 2-0;
See Atlanta vs. San Diego
SAN DIEGO vs. BALTIMORE
Series tied, 2-2;
See Baltimore vs. San Diego
SAN DIEGO vs. BUFFALO
Chargers lead series, 15-9-2;
See Buffalo vs. San Diego
SAN DIEGO vs. CHICAGO
Chargers lead series, 3-1;
See Chicago vs. San Diego
SAN DIEGO vs. CINCINNATI
Chargers lead series, 8-7;
See Cincinnati vs. San Diego
SAN DIEGO vs. CLEVELAND
Chargers lead series, 4-2-1;
See Cleveland vs. San Diego
SAN DIEGO vs. DALLAS
Cowboys lead series, 2-0;
See Dallas vs. San Diego
SAN DIEGO vs. DENVER
Chargers lead series, 23-20-1;
See Denver vs. San Diego
SAN DIEGO vs. DETROIT
Lions lead series, 3-1;
See Detroit vs. San Diego
SAN DIEGO vs. GREEN BAY
Packers lead series, 3-0;
See Green Bay vs. San Diego
SAN DIEGO vs. HOUSTON
Chargers lead series, 15-11-1;
See Houston vs. San Diego
SAN DIEGO vs. KANSAS CITY
Chargers lead series, 23-20-1;
See Kansas City vs. San Diego
SAN DIEGO vs. LOS ANGELES
Rams lead series, 2-1;
See Los Angeles vs. San Diego

SAN DIEGO vs. MIAMI
Chargers lead series, 7-4;
See Miami vs. San Diego
SAN DIEGO vs. MINNESOTA
Series tied, 2-2;
See Minnesota vs. San Diego
SAN DIEGO vs. NEW ENGLAND
Series tied, 12-12-2;
See New England vs. San Diego
SAN DIEGO vs. NEW ORLEANS
Chargers lead series, 3-0;
See New Orleans vs. San Diego
SAN DIEGO vs. N.Y. GIANTS
Giants lead series, 2-1;
See N.Y. Giants vs. San Diego
SAN DIEGO vs. N.Y. JETS
Chargers lead series, 14-6-1;
See N.Y. Jets vs. San Diego
SAN DIEGO vs. OAKLAND
Raiders lead series, 26-17-2;
See Oakland vs. San Diego
SAN DIEGO vs. PHILADELPHIA
Series tied, 1-1;
See Philadelphia vs. San Diego
SAN DIEGO vs. PITTSBURGH
Steelers lead series, 6-2;
See Pittsburgh vs. San Diego
SAN DIEGO vs. ST. LOUIS
Chargers lead series, 2-0;
See St. Louis vs. San Diego
SAN DIEGO vs. SAN FRANCISCO
Chargers lead series, 2-1
1972—49ers, 34-3 (SF)
1976—Chargers, 13-7 (SD) OT
1979—Chargers, 31-9 (SD)
(Points—49ers 50, Chargers 47)
SAN DIEGO vs. SEATTLE
Chargers lead series, 8-1
1977—Chargers, 30-28 (S)
1978—Chargers, 24-20 (S)
Chargers, 37-10 (SD)
1979—Chargers, 33-16 (S)
Chargers, 20-10 (SD)
1980—Chargers, 34-13 (S)
Chargers, 21-14 (SD)
1981—Chargers, 24-10 (SD)
Seahawks, 44-23 (S)
(Points—Chargers 246, Seahawks 165)
SAN DIEGO vs. TAMPA BAY
Chargers lead series, 2-0
1976—Chargers, 23-0 (TB)
1981—Chargers, 24-23 (TB)
(Points—Chargers 47, Buccaneers 23)
SAN DIEGO vs. WASHINGTON
Redskins lead series, 2-0
1973—Redskins, 38-0 (W)
1980—Redskins, 40-17 (W)
(Points—Redskins 78, Chargers 17)

SAN FRANCISCO vs. ATLANTA
49ers lead series, 16-15;
See Atlanta vs. San Francisco
SAN FRANCISCO vs. BALTIMORE

Colts lead series, 21-14;
See Baltimore vs. San Francisco
SAN FRANCISCO vs. BUFFALO
Bills lead series, 2-0;
See Buffalo vs. San Francisco
SAN FRANCISCO vs. CHICAGO
Series tied, 22-22-1;
See Chicago vs. San Francisco
SAN FRANCISCO vs. CINCINNATI
49ers lead series, 3-1;
See Cincinnati vs. San Francisco
SAN FRANCISCO vs. CLEVELAND
Browns lead series, 8-3;
See Cleveland vs. San Francisco
SAN FRANCISCO vs. DALLAS
Cowboys lead series, 8-6-1;
See Dallas vs. San Francisco
SAN FRANCISCO vs. DENVER
49ers lead series, 2-1;
See Denver vs. San Francisco
SAN FRANCISCO vs. DETROIT
Lions lead series, 25-21-1;
See Detroit vs. San Francisco
SAN FRANCISCO vs. GREEN BAY
49ers lead series, 22-20-1;
See Green Bay vs. San Francisco
SAN FRANCISCO vs. HOUSTON
Series tied, 2-2;
See Houston vs. San Francisco
SAN FRANCISCO vs. KANSAS CITY
Series tied, 1-1;
See Kansas City vs. San Francisco
SAN FRANCISCO vs. LOS ANGELES
Rams lead series, 41-21-2;
See Los Angeles vs. San Francisco
SAN FRANCISCO vs. MIAMI
Dolphins lead series, 3-0;
See Miami vs. San Francisco
SAN FRANCISCO vs. MINNESOTA
Vikings lead series, 12-10-1;
See Minnesota vs. San Francisco
SAN FRANCISCO vs. NEW ENGLAND
49ers lead series, 2-1;
See New England vs. San Francisco
SAN FRANCISCO vs. NEW ORLEANS
49ers lead series, 17-7-2;
See New Orleans vs. San Francisco
SAN FRANCISCO vs. N.Y. GIANTS
Giants lead series, 9-5;
See N.Y. Giants vs. San Francisco
SAN FRANCISCO vs. N.Y. JETS
49ers lead series, 3-0;
See N.Y. Jets vs. San Francisco
SAN FRANCISCO vs. OAKLAND
Raiders lead series, 2-1;
See Oakland vs. San Francisco
SAN FRANCISCO vs. PHILADELPHIA
49ers lead series, 8-3-1;
See Philadelphia vs. San Francisco
SAN FRANCISCO vs. PITTSBURGH
49ers lead series, 6-5;
See Pittsburgh vs. San Francisco
SAN FRANCISCO vs. ST. LOUIS

Cardinals lead series, 7-4;
See St. Louis vs. San Francisco
SAN FRANCISCO vs. SAN DIEGO
Chargers lead series, 2-1;
See San Diego vs. San Francisco
SAN FRANCISCO vs. SEATTLE
Series tied, 1-1
1976— 49ers, 37-21 (S)
1979—Seahawks, 35-24 (SF)
(Points—49ers 61, Seahawks 56)
SAN FRANCISCO vs. TAMPA BAY
49ers lead series, 3-1
1977—49ers, 20-10 (SF)
1978—49ers, 6-3 (SF)
1979—49ers, 23-7 (SF)
1980—Buccaneers, 24-23 (SF)
(Points—49ers 72, Buccaneers 44)
SAN FRANCISCO vs. WASHINGTON
49ers lead series, 6-5-1
1952—49ers, 23-17 (W)
1954—49ers, 41-7 (SF)
1955—Redskins, 7-0 (W)
1961—49ers, 35-3 (SF)
1967—Redskins, 31-28 (W)
1969—Tie, 17-17 (SF)
1970—49ers, 26-17 (SF)
1971—*49ers, 24-20 (SF)
1973—Redskins, 33-9 (W)
1976—Redskins, 24-21 (SF)
1978—Redskins, 38-20 (W)
1981—49ers, 30-17 (W)
(Points—49ers 274, Redskins 231)
*NFC Divisional Playoff

SEATTLE vs. ATLANTA
Seahawks lead series, 2-0;
See Atlanta vs. Seattle
SEATTLE vs. BALTIMORE
Colts lead series, 2-0;
See Baltimore vs. Seattle
SEATTLE vs. BUFFALO
Seahawks lead series, 1-0;
See Buffalo vs. Seattle
SEATTLE vs. CHICAGO
Series tied, 1-1;
See Chicago vs. Seattle
SEATTLE vs. CINCINNATI
Bengals lead series, 2-0;
See Cincinnati vs. Seattle
SEATTLE vs. CLEVELAND
Seahawks lead series, 4-1;
See Cleveland vs. Seattle
SEATTLE vs. DALLAS
Cowboys lead series, 2-0;
See Dallas vs. Seattle
SEATTLE vs. DENVER
Broncos lead series, 7-2;
See Denver vs. Seattle
SEATTLE vs. DETROIT
Series tied, 1-1;
See Detroit vs. Seattle
SEATTLE vs. GREEN BAY
Packers lead series, 3-0;

All-Time Team vs. Team Results

See Green Bay vs. Seattle
SEATTLE vs. HOUSTON
Series tied, 2-2;
See Houston vs. Seattle
SEATTLE vs. KANSAS CITY
Chiefs lead series, 5-4;
See Kansas City vs. Seattle
SEATTLE vs. LOS ANGELES
Rams lead series, 2-0;
See Los Angeles vs. Seattle
SEATTLE vs. MIAMI
Dolphins lead series, 2-0;
See Miami vs. Seattle
SEATTLE vs. MINNESOTA
Series tied, 1-1;
See Minnesota vs. Seattle
SEATTLE vs. NEW ENGLAND
Patriots lead series, 2-0;
See New England vs. Seattle
SEATTLE vs. NEW ORLEANS
Series tied, 1-1;
See New Orleans vs. Seattle
SEATTLE vs. N.Y. GIANTS
Giants lead series, 3-0;
See N.Y. Giants vs. Seattle
SEATTLE vs. N.Y. JETS
Seahawks lead series, 6-0;
See N.Y. Jets vs. Seattle
SEATTLE vs. OAKLAND
Raiders lead series, 5-4;
See Oakland vs. Seattle
SEATTLE vs. PHILADELPHIA
Eagles lead series, 2-0;
See Philadelphia vs. Seattle
SEATTLE vs. PITTSBURGH
Steelers lead series, 2-1;
See Pittsburgh vs. Seattle
SEATTLE vs. ST. LOUIS
Cardinals lead series, 1-0;
See St. Louis vs. Seattle
SEATTLE vs. SAN DIEGO
Chargers lead series, 8-1;
See San Diego vs. Seattle
SEATTLE vs. SAN FRANCISCO
Series tied, 1-1;
See San Francisco vs. Seattle
SEATTLE vs. TAMPA BAY
Seahawks lead series, 2-0
1976—Seahawks, 13-10 (TB)
1977—Seahawks, 30-23 (S)
(Points—Seahawks 43, Buccaneers 33)
SEATTLE vs. WASHINGTON
Series tied, 1-1
1976—Redskins, 31-7 (W)
1980—Seahawks, 14-0 (W)
(Points—Redskins 31, Seahawks 21)

TAMPA BAY vs. ATLANTA
Series tied, 2-2;
See Atlanta vs. Tampa Bay
TAMPA BAY vs. BALTIMORE
Series tied, 1-1;
See Baltimore vs. Tampa Bay

TAMPA BAY vs. BUFFALO
Series tied, 1-1;
See Buffalo vs. Tampa Bay
TAMPA BAY vs. CHICAGO
Bears lead series, 6-3;
See Chicago vs. Tampa Bay
TAMPA BAY vs. CINCINNATI
Series tied, 1-1;
See Cincinnati vs. Tampa Bay
TAMPA BAY vs. CLEVELAND
Browns lead series, 2-0;
See Cleveland vs. Tampa Bay
TAMPA BAY vs. DALLAS
Cowboys lead series, 3-0;
See Dallas vs. Tampa Bay
TAMPA BAY vs. DENVER
Broncos lead series, 2-0;
See Denver vs. Tampa Bay
TAMPA BAY vs. DETROIT
Lions lead series, 5-4;
See Detroit vs. Tampa Bay
TAMPA BAY vs. GREEN BAY
Buccaneers lead series, 5-3-1;
See Green Bay vs. Tampa Bay
TAMPA BAY vs. HOUSTON
Oilers lead series, 2-0;
See Houston vs. Tampa Bay
TAMPA BAY vs. KANSAS CITY
Series tied, 2-2;
See Kansas City vs. Tampa Bay
TAMPA BAY vs. LOS ANGELES
Rams lead series, 3-2;
See Los Angeles vs. Tampa Bay
TAMPA BAY vs. MIAMI
Dolphins lead series, 1-0;
See Miami vs. Tampa Bay
TAMPA BAY vs. MINNESOTA
Vikings lead series, 6-3;
See Minnesota vs. Tampa Bay
TAMPA BAY vs. NEW ENGLAND
Patriots lead series, 1-0;
See New England vs. Tampa Bay
TAMPA BAY vs. NEW ORLEANS
Series tied, 2-2;
See New Orleans vs. Tampa Bay
TAMPA BAY vs. N.Y. GIANTS
Giants lead series, 4-2;
See N.Y. Giants vs. Tampa Bay
TAMPA BAY vs. N.Y. JETS
Jets lead series, 1-0;
See N.Y. Jets vs. Tampa Bay
TAMPA BAY vs. OAKLAND
Raiders lead series, 2-0;
See Oakland vs. Tampa Bay
TAMPA BAY vs. PHILADELPHIA
Eagles lead series, 2-1;
See Philadelphia vs. Tampa Bay
TAMPA BAY vs. PITTSBURGH
Steelers lead series, 2-0;
See Pittsburgh vs. Tampa Bay
TAMPA BAY vs. ST. LOUIS
Buccaneers lead series, 2-0;
See St. Louis vs. Tampa Bay

TAMPA BAY vs. SAN DIEGO
Chargers lead series, 2-0;
See San Diego vs. Tampa Bay
TAMPA BAY vs. SAN FRANCISCO
49ers lead series, 3-1;
See San Francisco vs. Tampa Bay
TAMPA BAY vs. SEATTLE
Seahawks lead series, 2-0;
See Seattle vs. Tampa Bay
TAMPA BAY vs. WASHINGTON
Redskins lead series, 1-0
1977—Redskins, 10-0 (TB)

WASHINGTON vs. ATLANTA
Redskins lead series, 6-2-1;
See Atlanta vs. Washington
WASHINGTON vs. BALTIMORE
Colts lead series, 15-5;
See Baltimore vs. Washington
WASHINGTON vs. BUFFALO
Bills lead series, 2-1;
See Buffalo vs. Washington
WASHINGTON vs. CHICAGO
Bears lead series, 18-11-1;
See Chicago vs. Washington
WASHINGTON vs. CINCINNATI
Redskins lead series, 2-1;
See Cincinnati vs. Washington
WASHINGTON vs. CLEVELAND
Browns lead series, 31-7-1;
See Cleveland vs. Washington
WASHINGTON vs. DALLAS
Cowboys lead series, 26-16-2;
See Dallas vs. Washington
WASHINGTON vs. DENVER
Redskins lead series, 2-1;
See Denver vs. Washington
WASHINGTON vs. DETROIT
Redskins lead series, 15-8;
See Detroit vs. Washington
WASHINGTON vs. GREEN BAY
Packers lead series, 13-11-1;
See Green Bay vs. Washington
WASHINGTON vs. HOUSTON
Oilers lead series, 2-1;
See Houston vs. Washington

WASHINGTON vs. KANSAS CITY
Chiefs lead series, 2-0;
See Kansas City vs. Washington
WASHINGTON vs. LOS ANGELES
Redskins lead series, 12-5-1;
See Los Angeles vs. Washington
WASHINGTON vs. MIAMI
Dolphins lead series, 3-1;
See Miami vs. Washington
WASHINGTON vs. MINNESOTA
Vikings lead series, 5-2;
See Minnesota vs. Washington
WASHINGTON vs. NEW ENGLAND
Redskins lead series, 2-1;
See New England vs. Washington
WASHINGTON vs. NEW ORLEANS
Redskins lead series, 6-4;
See New Orleans vs. Washington
WASHINGTON vs. N.Y. GIANTS
Giants lead series, 56-40-3;
See N.Y. Giants vs. Washington
WASHINGTON vs. N.Y. JETS
Redskins lead series, 3-0;
See N.Y. Jets vs. Washington
WASHINGTON vs. OAKLAND
Raiders lead series, 3-0;
See Oakland vs. Washington
WASHINGTON vs. PHILADELPHIA
Redskins lead series, 51-37-5;
See Philadelphia vs. Washington
WASHINGTON vs. PITTSBURGH
Redskins lead series, 39-27-3;
See Pittsburgh vs. Washington
WASHINGTON vs. ST. LOUIS
Redskins lead series, 42-31-2;
See St. Louis vs. Washington
WASHINGTON vs. SAN DIEGO
Redskins lead series, 2-0;
See San Diego vs. Washington
WASHINGTON vs. SAN FRANCISCO
49ers lead series, 6-5-1;
See San Francisco vs. Washington
WASHINGTON vs. SEATTLE
Series tied, 1-1;
See Seattle vs. Washington
WASHINGTON vs. TAMPA BAY
Redskins lead series, 1-0;
See Tampa Bay vs. Washington

NUMBER ONE DRAFT CHOICES

Season	Team	Player	Position	College
1982	New England	Ken Sims	DT	Texas
1981	New Orleans	George Rogers	RB	South Carolina
1980	Detroit	Billy Sims	RB	Oklahoma
1979	Buffalo	Tom Cousineau	LB	Ohio State
1978	Houston	Earl Campbell	RB	Texas
1977	Tampa Bay	Ricky Bell	RB	So. California
1976	Tampa Bay	Lee Roy Selmon	DE	Oklahoma
1975	Atlanta	Steve Bartkowski	QB	California
1974	Dallas	Ed Jones	DE	Tennessee State
1973	Houston	John Matuszak	DE	Tampa
1972	Buffalo	Walt Patulski	DE	Notre Dame
1971	New England	Jim Plunkett	QB	Stanford
1970	Pittsburgh	Terry Bradshaw	QB	Louisiana Tech
1969	Buffalo (AFL)	O. J. Simpson	RB	So. California
1968	Minnesota	Ron Yary	T	So. California
1967	Baltimore	Bubba Smith	DT	Michigan State
1966	Atlanta	Tommy Nobis	LB	Texas
	Miami (AFL)	Jim Grabowski	RB	Illinois
1965	N.Y. Giants	Tucker Frederickson	RB	Auburn
	Houston (AFL)	Lawrence Elkins	E	Baylor
1964	San Francisco	Dave Parks	E	Texas Tech
	Boston (AFL)	Jack Concannon	QB	Boston College
1963	Los Angeles	Terry Baker	QB	Oregon State
	Kansas City (AFL)	Buck Buchanan	DT	Grambling
1962	Washington	Ernie Davis	RB	Syracuse
	Oakland (AFL)	Roman Gabriel	QB	N. Carolina State
1961	Minnesota	Tommy Mason	RB	Tulane
	Buffalo (AFL)	Ken Rice	G	Auburn
1960	Los Angeles	Billy Cannon	RB	LSU
	(AFL had no formal first pick)			
1959	Green Bay	Randy Duncan	QB	Iowa
1958	Chi. Cardinals	King Hill	QB	Rice
1957	Green Bay	Paul Hornung	HB	Notre Dame
1956	Pittsburgh	Gary Glick	DB	Colorado A&M
1955	Baltimore	George Shaw	QB	Oregon
1954	Cleveland	Bobby Garrett	QB	Stanford
1953	San Francisco	Harry Babcock	E	Georgia
1952	Los Angeles	Bill Wade	QB	Vanderbilt
1951	N.Y. Giants	Kyle Rote	HB	SMU
1950	Detroit	Leon Hart	E	Notre Dame
1949	Philadelphia	Chuck Bednarik	C	Pennsylvania
1948	Washington	Harry Gilmer	QB	Alabama
1947	Chi. Bears	Bob Fenimore	HB	Oklahoma A&M
1946	Boston	Frank Dancewicz	QB	Notre Dame
1945	Chi. Cardinals	Charley Trippi	HB	Georgia
1944	Boston	Angelo Bertelli	QB	Notre Dame
1943	Detroit	Frank Sinkwich	HB	Georgia
1942	Pittsburgh	Bill Dudley	HB	Virginia
1941	Chi. Bears	Tom Harmon	HB	Michigan
1940	Chi. Cardinals	George Cafego	HB	Tennessee
1939	Chi. Cardinals	Ki Aldrich	C	TCU
1938	Cleveland	Corbett Davis	FB	Indiana
1937	Philadelphia	Sam Francis	FB	Nebraska
1936	Philadelphia	Jay Berwanger	HB	Chicago

DRAFT LIST FOR 1982

ATLANTA FALCONS

1. Riggs, Gerald—9, RB, Arizona State
2. Rogers, Doug—36, DE, Stanford
3. Bailey, Stacey—63, WR, San Jose State
4. Brown, Reggie—95, RB, Oregon
5. Mansfield, Von—122, DB, Wisconsin
6. Kelley, Mike—149, QB, Georgia Tech
7. Toloumu, David—176, RB, Hawaii
8. Eberhardt, Ricky—203, DB, Morris Brown
9. Horan, Mike—235, P, Cal State-Long Beach
10. Stowers, Curtis—262, LB, Mississippi State
11. Keller, Jeff—288, WR, Washington State
12. Levenick, Dave—315, LB, Wisconsin

BALTIMORE COLTS

1. Cooks, Johnie—2, LB, Mississippi State
   Schlichter, Art—4, QB, Ohio State, from Los Angeles
2. Wisniewski, Leo—28, DT, Penn State
   Stark, Rohn—34, P, Florida State, from Los Angeles
3. Burroughs, Jim—57, DB, Michigan State
4. Pagel, Mike—84, QB, Arizona State
5. Crouch, Terry—113, G, Oklahoma
6. Beach, Pat—140, TE, Washington State
7. Jenkins, Fletcher—169, DT, Washington
8. Loia, Tony—196, G, Arizona State
9. Berryhill, Tony—225, C, Clemson
10. Deery, Tom—252, DB, Widener
11. Meacham, Lamont—280, DB, Western Kentucky
12. Wright, Johnnie—307, RB, South Carolina

BUFFALO BILLS

1. Tuttle, Perry—19, WR, Clemson, from Denver
   Choice to Denver
2. Kofler, Matt—48, QB, San Diego State
3. Marve, Eugene—59, LB, Saginaw Valley, from Cleveland
   Choice to Seattle
4. Williams, Van—93, RB, Carson-Newman, from St. Louis
   Choice to Denver
5. Choice to Washington
6. Chivers, DeWayne—160, TE, South Carolina
7. Anderson, Gary—171, K, Syracuse, from Cleveland
   Choice to Detroit through Los Angeles
8. Tousignant, Luc—218, QB, Fairmont State
9. Edwards, Dennis—245, DT, Southern California
10. James, Vic—272, DB, Colorado
11. Kalil, Frank—298, G, Arizona
12. Suber, Tony—329, DT, Gardner-Webb

CHICAGO BEARS

1. McMahon, Jim—5, QB, Brigham Young
2. Choice to Tampa Bay
3. Wrightman, Tim—62, TE, UCLA
4. Gentry, Dennis—89, RB, Baylor
5. Hartnett, Perry—116, G, Southern Methodist
   Tabron, Dennis—134, DB, Duke, from San Diego
6. Becker, Kurt—146, G, Michigan
7. Waechter, Henry—173, DT, Nebraska
8. Doerger, Jerry—200, T, Wisconsin
9. Hatchett, Mike—230, DB, Texas
10. Turner, Joe—257, DB, Southern California
11. Boliaux, Guy—283, LB, Wisconsin
12. Young, Ricky—313, LB, Oklahoma State

CINCINNATI BENGALS

1. Collins, Glen—26, DE, Mississippi State
2. Weaver, Emanuel—54, DT, South Carolina
3. Holman, Rodney—82, TE, Tulane
4. Tate, Rodney—110, RB, Texas
5. Sorensen, Paul—138, DB, Washington State
6. King, Arthur—166, DT, Grambling
7. Needham, Ben—194, LB, Michigan
8. Yli-Renko, Kari—222, T, Cincinnati
9. Bennett, James—250, WR, N.W. Louisiana
10. Hogue, Larry—278, DB, Utah State
11. Davis, Russell—350, RB, Idaho
12. Feraday, Dan—333, QB, Toronto

CLEVELAND BROWNS

1. Banks, Chip—3, LB, Southern California
2. Baldwin, Keith—31, DE, Texas A&M
3. Choice to Buffalo
4. Walker, Dwight—87, WR, Nicholls State
5. Babb, Mike—115, C, Texas
6. Choice to Dallas
   Whitwell, Mike—162, WR, Texas A&M, from Denver
7. Choice to Buffalo
8. Kafentzis, Mark—199, DB, Hawaii
   Heflin, Van—204, TE, Vanderbilt, from Oakland
   Jackson, Bill—211, DB, North Carolina, from Washington
9. Baker, Milton—227, TE, West Texas State
10. Floyd, Ricky—255, RB, Southern Mississippi
11. Michuta, Steve—282, QB, Grand Valley State
12. Nicolas, Scott—310, LB, Miami

DALLAS COWBOYS

1. Hill, Rod—25, DB, Kentucky State
2. Rohrer, Jeff—53, LB, Yale
3. Eliopulos, Jim—81, LB, Wyoming
4. Carpenter, Brian—101, DB, Michigan, from Tampa Bay
5. Hunter, Monty—109, DB, Salem, W. Va.
   Pozderac, Phil—137, T, Notre Dame
6. Hammond, Ken—143, G, Vanderbilt, from Cleveland
   Daum, Charles—165, DT, Cal Poly-San Luis Obispo
7. Purifoy, Bill—193, DE, Tulsa
8. Peoples, George—216, RB, Auburn, from Denver through Buffalo
   Sullivan, Dwight—221, RB, North Carolina State
9. Gary, Joe—249, DT, UCLA
10. Eckerson, Todd—277, T, North Carolina State
11. Thompson, George—295, WR, Albany State, Ga., from Tampa Bay
    Whiting, Mike—304, RB, Florida State
12. Burtness, Rich—332, G, Montana

DENVER BRONCOS

1. Choice to Buffalo
   Willhite, Gerald—21, RB, San Jose State, from Buffalo
2. McDaniel, Orlando—50, WR, Louisiana State
3. Choice to Houston through Los Angeles
4. Choice to Kansas City
   Plater, Dan—106, WR, Brigham Young, from Buffalo
5. Winder, Sammy—131, RB, Southern Mississippi
6. Choice to Cleveland
7. Ruben, Alvin—189, DE, Houston
8. Choice to Dallas through Buffalo
9. Uecker, Keith—243, T, Auburn
10. Woodward, Ken—274, LB, Tuskegee
11. Yatsko, Stuart—300, G, Oregon
12. Clark, Brian—327, G, Clemson

DETROIT LIONS

1. Williams, Jimmy—15, LB, Nebraska
2. Watkins, Bobby—42, DB, S.W. Texas State
3. Doig, Steve—69, LB, New Hampshire
4. McNorton, Bruce—96, DB, Georgetown, Ky.
5. Graham, William—127, DB, Texas
6. Machurek, Mike—154, QB, Idaho State
7. Bates, Phil—175, RB, Nebraska, from Houston
   Choice to Los Angeles
   Simmons, Victor—187, WR, Oregon State, from Buffalo through Los Angeles
8. Moss, Martin—208, DE, UCLA
9. Wagoner, Danny—231, DB, Kansas, from Oakland through Los Angeles Choice to Miami
10. Barnes, Roosevelt—266, LB, Purdue
11. Lee, Edward—292, WR, South Carolina State
12. Porter, Ricky—319, RB, Slippery Rock State, Pa.
    Rubick, Rob—326, TE, Grand Valley State, from San Diego

GREEN BAY PACKERS

1. Choice to New Orleans through San Diego
   Hallstrom, Ron—22, G, Iowa, from San Diego
2. Choice to New England through San Diego
3. Rodgers, Del—71, RB, Utah
4. Brown, Robert—98, LB, Virginia Tech
5. Meade, Mike—126, RB, Penn State
6. Parlavecchio, Chet—152, LB, Penn State
7. Whitley, Joey—183, DB, Texas-El Paso
8. Boyd, Thomas—210, LB, Alabama
9. Riggins, Charles—237, DE, Bethune-Cookman
10. Garcia, Eddie—264, K, Southern Methodist
11. Macaulay, John—294, C, Stanford
12. Epps, Phillip—321, WR, Texas Christian

HOUSTON OILERS

1. Munchak, Mike—8, G, Penn State
2. Choice to Oakland
   Luck, Oliver—44, QB, West Virginia, from Tampa Bay through Miami and Los Angeles
3. Choice to Los Angeles
   Edwards, Stan—72, RB, Michigan, from New York Giants
   Abraham, Robert—77, LB, North Carolina State, from Denver through Los Angeles
4. Bryant, Steve—94, WR, Purdue
5. Taylor, Malcolm—121, DE, Tennessee State
6. Allen, Gary—148, RB, Hawaii
7. Choice to Detroit
8. Choice to Los Angeles
9. Bradley, Matt—234, DB, Penn State
10. Reeves, Ron—261, QB, Texas Tech
11. Campbell, Jim—287, TE, Kentucky
12. Craft, Donnie—314, RB, Louisville

KANSAS CITY CHIEFS

1. Hancock, Anthony—11, WR, Tennessee, from St. Louis
   Choice to St. Louis
2. Daniels, Calvin—46, LB, North Carolina
3. Choice to St. Louis
4. Haynes, Louis—100, LB, North Texas State
   Anderson, Stuart—104, LB, Virginia, from Denver
5. Thompson, Delbert—130, RB, Texas-El Paso
6. Roquemore, Durwood—157, DB, Texas A&I
7. Smith, Greg—184, DT, Kansas
8. DeBruijn, Case—214, P-K, Idaho State
9. Byford, Lyndle—241, T, Oklahoma
10. Brodsky, Larry—268, WR, Miami
11. Carter, Bob—297, WR, Arizona
12. Miller, Mike—324, DB, S.W. Texas State

LOS ANGELES RAMS

1. Choice to Baltimore
   Redden, Barry—14, RB, Richmond,
   from Washington
2. Choice to Baltimore
3. Choice to Washington
   Bechtold, Bill—67, C, Oklahoma,
   from Houston
4. Gaylord, Jeff—88, LB, Missouri
5. Kersten, Wally—117, T, Minnesota,
   from Seattle
   Barnett, Doug, 118, DE, Azusa Pacific
6. Locklin, Kerry—145, TE, New Mexico
   State
7. Choice to Pittsburgh through
   Washington
   Shearin, Joe—181, G, Texas,
   from Detroit
8. Jones, A. J.—202, RB, Texas
   Reilly, Mike—207, DE, Oklahoma,
   from Houston
9. Speight, Bob—229, T, Boston University
10. McPherson, Miles—256, DB, New
    Haven College
11. Coffman, Ricky—285, WR, UCLA
12. Coley, Raymond—312, DT, Alabama
    A&M

MIAMI DOLPHINS

1. Foster, Roy—24, G, Southern California
2. Duper, Mark—52, WR, N.W. Louisiana
3. Lankford, Paul—80, DB, Penn State
4. Bowser, Charles—108, LB, Duke
5. Nelson, Bob—120, DT, Miami,
   from Minnesota
   Diana, Richard—136, RB, Yale
6. Tutson, Tom—161, DB, South Carolina
   State, from San Diego
   Hester, Ron—164, LB, Florida State
7. Johnson, Dan—170, TE, Iowa State,
   from New Orleans
   Cowan, Larry—192, RB, Jackson State
8. Randle, Tate—220, DB, Texas Tech
9. Clark, Steve—239, DE, Utah,
   from Detroit
   Boatner, Mack—248, RB, S.E. Louisiana
10. Fisher, Robin—271, LB, Florida,
    from Philadelphia
    Jones, Wayne—276, T, Utah
11. Crum, Gary—303, T, Wyoming
12. Rodrique, Mike—331, WR, Miami

MINNESOTA VIKINGS

1. Nelson, Darrin—7, RB, Stanford
2. Tausch, Terry—39, T, Texas
3. Choice to New Orleans
4. Fahnhorst, Jim—92, LB, Minnesota
5. Choice to Miami
6. Storr, Greg—147, LB, Boston College
7. Jordan, Steve—179, TE, Brown
8. Harmon, Kirk—206, LB, Pacific
9. Howard, Bryan—233, DB, Tennessee
   State
10. Lucear, Gerald—260, WR, Temple
11. Rouse, Curtis—286, G, Tennessee-
    Chattanooga
12. Milner, Hobson—318, RB, Cincinnati

NEW ENGLAND PATRIOTS

1. Sims, Ken—1, DE, Texas
   Williams, Lester—27, DT, Miami,
   from San Francisco
2. Choice to San Francisco
   Weathers, Robert—40, RB, Arizona State,
   from Green Bay through
   San Diego
   Tippett, Andre—41, LB, Iowa, from
   Washington through San Francisco
   Haley, Darryl—55, T, Utah,
   from San Francisco
3. Jones, Cedric—56, WR, Duke
   Weishuhn, Clayton—60, LB, Angelo
   State, from Seattle
4. Crump, George—85, DE, East Carolina
   Ingram, Brian—111, LB, Tennessee,
   from San Francisco
5. Marion, Fred—112, DB, Miami
6. Smith, Ricky—141, DB, Alabama State
7. Roberts, Jeff—168, LB, Tulane
8. Collins, Ken—197, LB, Washington State
9. Murdock, Kelvin—224, WR, Troy State
10. Clark, Brian—253, K, Florida
11. Choice exercised in Supplemental Draft
12. Sandon, Steve—296, QB, Northern
    Iowa, from New York Giants
    Taylor, Greg—308, KR, Virginia

NEW ORLEANS SAINTS

1. Choice exercised in Supplemental Draft
   Scott, Lindsay — 13, WR, Georgia,
   from Green Bay through San Diego
2. Edelman, Brad — 30, C, Missouri
3. Lewis, Rodney — 58, DB, Nebraska
   Goodlow, Eugene — 66, WR, Kansas
   State, from Minnesota
   Duckett, Ken — 68, WR, Wake Forest,
   from Washington
   Krimm, John — 76, DB, Notre Dame,
   from San Diego
4. Andersen, Morten — 86, K, Michigan
   State
5. Elliott, Tony — 114, DE, North Texas State
6. Lewis, Marvin — 142, RB, Tulane
7. Choice to Miami
8. Slaughter, Chuck — 198, T, South
   Carolina
9. Choice to Washington
10. Choice to Washington
11. Choice to Washington
12. Choice to Washington

NEW YORK GIANTS

1. Woolfolk, Butch — 18, RB, Michigan
2. Morris, Joe — 45, RB, Syracuse
3. Choice to Houston
4. Raymond, Gerry — 102, G, Boston
   College
5. Umphrey, Rich — 129, C, Colorado
6. Nicholson, Darrell — 156, LB, North
   Carolina
7. Wiska, Jeff — 186, G, Michigan State
8. Hubble, Robert — 213, TE, Rice
9. Higgins, John — 240, DB, Nevada-Las
   Vegas
10. Baldinger, Rich — 270, T, Wake Forest
11. Choice to New England
12. Seale, Mark — 323, DT, Richmond

NEW YORK JETS

1. Crable, Bob — 23, LB, Notre Dame
2. McElroy, Reggie — 51, T, West Texas State
3. Crutchfield, Dwayne — 79, RB, Iowa State
4. Floyd, George — 107, DB, Eastern
   Kentucky
5. Jerue, Mark — 135, LB, Washington
6. Phea, Lonell — 163, WR, Houston
7. Coombs, Tom — 191, TE, Idaho
8. Texada, Lawrence — 219, RB,
   Henderson, Ark.
9. Klever, Rocky — 247, RB, Montana
10. Hemphill, Darryl — 275, DB, West Texas
    State
11. Parmelee, Perry — 302, WR, Santa Clara
12. Carlstrom, Tom — 330, G, Nebraska

OAKLAND RAIDERS

1. Allen, Marcus — 10, RB, Southern
   California
2. Squirek, Jack — 35, LB, Illinois,
   from Houston
   Romano, Jim — 37, C, Penn State
3. McElroy, Vann — 64, DB, Baylor
4. Muransky, Ed — 91, T, Michigan
5. Jackson, Ed — 123, LB, Louisiana Tech
6. Choice to San Francisco
7. Jackson, Jeff — 177, DE, Toledo
8. Choice to Cleveland
9. Choice to Detroit through Los Angeles
10. D'Amico, Rich — 263, LB, Penn State
11. Turner, Willie — 289, WR, Louisiana State
12. Smith, Randy — 316, WR, East Texas
    State

PHILADELPHIA EAGLES

1. Quick, Mike—20, WR, North Carolina State
2. Sampleton, Lawrence—47, TE, Texas
3. Kab, Vyto—78, TE, Penn State
4. Griggs, Anthony—105, LB, Ohio State
5. DeVaughn, Dennis—132, DB, Bishop
6. Grieve, Curt—159, WR, Yale
7. Armstrong, Harvey—190, DT, Southern Methodist
8. Fritzsche, Jim—217, T, Purdue
9. Woodruff, Tony—244, WR, Fresno State
10. Choice to Miami
11. Ingram, Ron—301, WR, Oklahoma State
12. Taylor, Rob—328, T, Northwestern

PITTSBURGH STEELERS

1. Abercrombie, Walter—12, RB, Baylor
2. Meyer, John—43, T, Arizona State
3. Merriweather, Mike—70, LB, Pacific
4. Woods, Rick—97, DB, Boise State
5. Dallafior, Ken—124, T, Minnesota
6. Perko, Mike—155, DT, Utah State
   Bingham, Craig—167, LB, Syracuse, from San Francisco through New Orleans
7. Nelson, Edmund—172, DT, Auburn, from Los Angeles
   Boures, Emil—182, C, Pittsburgh
8. Goodson, John—209, P, Texas
9. Hirn, Mike—236, TE, Central Michigan
10. Sunseri, Sal—267, LB, Pittsburgh
11. Sorboor, Mikal Abdul—293, G, Morgan State
12. Hughes, Al—320, DE, Western Michigan

ST. LOUIS CARDINALS

1. Choice to Kansas City
   Sharpe, Luis—16, T, UCLA, from Kansas City
2. Galloway, David—38, DT, Florida
3. Perrin, Benny—65, DB, Alabama
   Guilbeau, Rusty—73, DE, McNeese State, from Kansas City
4. Robbins, Tootie—90, T, East Carolina, from Seattle
5. Bedford, Vance—119, DB, Texas
   Ferrell, Earl—125, RB, East Tennessee State, from Washington
6. Shaffer, Craig—150, LB, Indiana State
7. Sebro, Bob—178, C, Colorado
8. Lindstrom, Chris—205, DT, Boston University
9. Dailey, Darnell—232, LB, Maryland
10. McGill, Eddie—259, TE, Western Carolina
11. Williams, James—290, DE, North Carolina A&T
12 Atha, Bob—317, K, Ohio State

SAN DIEGO CHARGERS

1. Choice to Green Bay
2. Choice to Washington through Los Angeles
3. Choice to New Orleans
4. Choice to Tampa Bay
5. Choice to Chicago
6. Choice to Miami
7. Hall, Hollis—188, DB, Clemson
8. Buford, Maury—215, P, Texas Tech
9. Lyles, Warren—246, DT, Alabama
10. Young, Andre—273, DB, Louisiana Tech
11. Watson, Anthony—299, DB, New Mexico State
12. Choice to Detroit

SAN FRANCISCO 49ERS

1. Choice to New England
2. Paris, Bubba—29, T, Michigan, from New England
3. Choice to Tampa Bay through San Diego
4. Choice to New England
5. Williams, Newton—139, RB, Arizona State
6. Choice to Pittsburgh through New Orleans
   Williams, Vince—151, RB, Oregon, from Oakland
7. Ferrari, Ron—195, LB, Illinois
8. Choice to Washington through New Orleans
9. Clark, Bryan—251, QB, Michigan State
10. McLemore, Dana—269, KR, Hawaii, from Tampa Bay
    Barbian, Tim—279, DT, Western Illinois
11. Gibson, Gary—306, LB, Arizona
12. Washington, Tim—334, DB, Fresno State

SEATTLE SEAHAWKS

1. Bryant, Jeff—6, DE, Clemson
2. Scholtz, Bruce—33, LB, Texas
3. Choice to New England
   Metzelaars, Pete—75, TE, Wabash, from Buffalo
4. Choice to St. Louis
5. Choice to Los Angeles
6. Campbell, Jack—144, T, Utah
7. Williams, Eugene—174, LB, Tulsa
8. Cooper, Chester—201, WR, Minnesota
9. Jefferson, David—228, LB, Miami
10. Austin, Craig—258, LB, South Dakota
11. Clancy, Sam—284, DE-DT, Pittsburgh
12. Naylor, Frank—311, C, Rutgers

TAMPA BAY BUCCANEERS

1. Farrell, Sean—17, G, Penn State
2. Choice to Houston through Miami and Los Angeles
   Reese, Booker—32, DE, Bethune-Cookman, from Chicago
3. Bell, Jerry—74, TE, Arizona State
   Cannon, John—83, DE, William & Mary, from San Francisco through San Diego
4. Choice to Dallas
   Barrett, Dave—103, RB, Houston, from San Diego
5. Davis, Jeff—128, LB, Clemson
6. Tyler, Andre—158, WR, Stanford
7. Morris, Tom—185, DB, Michigan State
8. Atkins, Kelvin—212, LB, Illinois
9. Lane, Bob—242, QB, N.E. Louisiana
10. Choice to San Francisco
11. Choice to Dallas
12. Morton, Michael—325, KR, Nevada-Las Vegas

WASHINGTON REDSKINS

1. Choice to Baltimore through Los Angeles
2. Choice to New England through San Francisco
   Dean, Vernon—49, DB, San Diego State, from San Diego through Los Angeles
3. Powell, Carl—61, WR, Jackson State, from Los Angeles
   Choice to New Orleans
4. Liebenstein, Todd—99, DE, Nevada-Las Vegas
5. Choice to St. Louis
   Williams, Michael—133, TE, Alabama A&M, from Buffalo
6. Jeffers, Lamont—153, LB, Tennessee
7. Schachtner, John—180, LB, Northern Arizona
8. Choice to Cleveland
   Warthen, Ralph—223, DT, Gardner-Webb, from San Francisco through New Orleans
9. Coffey, Ken—226, DB, S.W. Texas State, from New Orleans
   Trautman, Randy—238, DT, Boise State
10. Smith, Harold—254, DE, Kentucky State, from New Orleans
    Daniels, Terry—265, DB, Tennessee
11. Miller, Dan—281, K, Miami, from New Orleans
    Holly, Bob—291, QB, Princeton
12. Laster, Don—309, T, Tennessee State, from New Orleans
    Goff, Jeff—322, LB, Arkansas

ALL-TIME RECORDS

Compiled by Elias Sports Bureau

The following records reflect all available official information on the National Football League from its formation in 1920 to date. Also included are all applicable records from the American Football League, 1960-69.

INDIVIDUAL RECORDS

SERVICE

Most Seasons
- 26 George Blanda, Chi. Bears, 1949, 1950-58; Baltimore, 1950; Houston, 1960-66; Oakland, 1967-75
- 21 Earl Morrall, San Francisco, 1956; Pittsburgh, 1957-58; Detroit, 1958-64; N.Y. Giants, 1965-67; Baltimore, 1968-71; Miami, 1972-76
- 20 Jim Marshall, Cleveland, 1960; Minnesota, 1961-79

Most Seasons, One Club
- 19 Jim Marshall, Minnesota, 1961-79
- 17 Lou Groza, Cleveland, 1950-59, 1961-67
  - Johnny Unitas, Baltimore, 1956-72
  - John Brodie, San Francisco, 1957-73
  - Jim Bakken, St. Louis, 1962-78
  - Mick Tingelhoff, Minnesota, 1962-78
- 16 Sammy Baugh, Washington, 1937-52
  - Bart Starr, Green Bay, 1956-71
  - Jimmy Johnson, San Francisco, 1961-76
  - Jim Hart, St. Louis, 1966-81

Most Games Played, Career
- 340 George Blanda, Chi. Bears, 1949, 1950-58; Baltimore, 1950; Houston, 1960-66; Oakland, 1967-75
- 282 Jim Marshall, Cleveland, 1960; Minnesota, 1961-79
- 255 Earl Morrall, San Francisco, 1958; Pittsburgh, 1957-58; Detroit, 1958-64; N.Y. Giants, 1965-67; Baltimore, 1968-71; Miami, 1972-76

Most Consecutive Games Played, Career
- 282 Jim Marshall, Cleveland, 1960; Minnesota, 1961-79
- 240 Mick Tingelhoff, Minnesota, 1962-78
- 234 Jim Bakken, St. Louis, 1962-78

Most Seasons, Coach
- 40 George Halas, Chi. Bears, 1920-29, 1933-42, 1946-55, 1958-67
- 33 Earl (Curly) Lambeau, Green Bay, 1921-49; Chi. Cardinals, 1950-51; Washington, 1952-53
- 23 Steve Owen, N.Y. Giants, 1931-53

SCORING

Most Seasons Leading League
- 5 Don Hutson, Green Bay, 1940-44
  - Gino Cappelletti, Boston, 1961, 1963-66
- 3 Earl (Dutch) Clark, Portsmouth, 1932; Detroit, 1935-36
  - Pat Harder, Chi. Cardinals, 1947-49
  - Paul Hornung, Green Bay, 1959-61
- 2 Jack Manders, Chi. Bears, 1934, 1937
  - Gordy Soltau, San Francisco, 1952-53
  - Doak Walker, Detroit, 1950, 1955
  - Gene Mingo, Denver, 1960, 1962
  - Jim Turner, N.Y. Jets, 1968-69
  - Fred Cox, Minnesota, 1969-70
  - Chester Marcol, Green Bay, 1972, 1974
  - John Smith, New England, 1979-80

Most Consecutive Seasons Leading League
- 5 Don Hutson, Green Bay, 1940-44
- 4 Gino Cappelletti, Boston, 1963-66

3 Pat Harder, Chi. Cardinals, 1947-49
Paul Hornung, Green Bay, 1959-61

POINTS
Most Points, Career
2,002 George Blanda, Chi. Bears, 1949, 1950-58; Baltimore, 1950; Houston, 1960-66; Oakland, 1967-75 (9-td, 943-pat, 335-fg)
1,439 Jim Turner, N.Y. Jets, 1964-70; Denver, 1971-79 (1-td, 521-pat, 304-fg)
1,380 Jim Bakken, St. Louis, 1962-78 (534-pat, 282-fg)
Most Points, Season
176 Paul Hornung, Green Bay, 1960 (15-td, 41-pat, 15-fg)
155 Gino Cappelletti, Boston, 1964 (7-td, 38-pat, 25-fg)
147 Gino Cappelletti, Boston, 1961 (8-td, 48-pat, 17-fg)
Most Seasons, 100 or More Points
6 Gino Cappelletti, Boston, 1961-66
George Blanda, Houston, 1960-61; Oakland, 1967-69, 1973
Bruce Gossett, Los Angeles, 1966-67, 1969; San Francisco, 1970-71, 1973
Jan Stenerud, Kansas City, 1967-71; Green Bay, 1981
5 Lou Michaels, Pittsburgh, 1962; Baltimore, 1964-65, 1967-68
4 Fred Cox, Minnesota, 1964-65, 1969-70
Most Points, Rookie, Season
132 Gale Sayers, Chicago, 1965 (22-td)
128 Doak Walker, Detroit, 1950 (11-td, 38-pat, 8-fg)
Cookie Gilchrist, Buffalo, 1962 (15-td, 14-pat, 8-fg)
Chester Marcol, Green Bay, 1972 (29-pat, 33-fg)
123 Gene Mingo, Denver, 1960 (6-td, 33-pat, 18-fg)
Most Points, Game
40 Ernie Nevers, Chi. Cardinals vs. Chi. Bears, Nov. 28, 1929 (6-td, 4-pat)
36 Dub Jones, Cleveland vs. Chi. Bears, Nov. 25, 1951 (6-td)
Gale Sayers, Chicago vs. San Francisco, Dec. 12, 1965 (6-td)
33 Paul Hornung, Green Bay vs. Baltimore, Oct. 8, 1961 (4-td, 6-pat, 1-fg)
Most Consecutive Games Scoring
151. Fred Cox, Minnesota, 1963-73
133 Garo Yepremian, Miami, 1970-78; New Orleans, 1979
118 Jim Turner, N.Y. Jets, 1966-70; Denver, 1971-74

TOUCHDOWNS
Most Seasons Leading League
8 Don Hutson, Green Bay, 1935-38, 1941-44
3 Jim Brown, Cleveland, 1958-59, 1963
Lance Alworth, San Diego, 1964-66
2 By many players
Most Consecutive Seasons Leading League
4 Don Hutson, Green Bay, 1935-38, 1941-44
3 Lance Alworth, San Diego, 1964-66
2 By many players
Most Touchdowns, Career
126 Jim Brown, Cleveland, 1957-65 (106-r, 20-p)
113 Lenny Moore, Baltimore, 1956-67 (63-r, 48-p, 2-ret)
105 Don Hutson, Green Bay, 1935-45 (3-r, 99-p, 3-ret)
Most Touchdowns, Season
23 O.J. Simpson, Buffalo, 1975 (16-r, 7-p)
22 Gale Sayers, Chicago, 1965 (14-r, 6-p, 2-ret)
Chuck Foreman, Minnesota, 1975 (13-r, 9-p)
21 Jim Brown, Cleveland, 1965 (17-r, 4-p)
Most Touchdowns, Rookie, Season
22 Gale Sayers, Chicago, 1965 (14-r, 6-p, 2-ret)
16 Billy Sims, Detroit, 1980 (13-r, 3-p)
15 Cookie Gilchrist, Buffalo, 1962 (13-r, 2-p)
Most Touchdowns, Game
6 Ernie Nevers, Chi. Cardinals vs. Chi. Bears, Nov. 28, 1929 (6-r)
Dub Jones, Cleveland vs. Chi. Bears, Nov. 25, 1951 (4-r, 2-p)
Gale Sayers, Chicago vs. San Francisco, Dec. 12, 1965 (4-r, 1-p, 1-ret)

5   Bob Shaw, Chi. Cardinals vs. Baltimore, Oct. 2, 1950 (5-p)
Jim Brown, Cleveland vs. Baltimore, Nov. 1, 1959 (5-r)
Abner Haynes, Dall. Texans vs. Oakland, Nov. 26, 1961 (4-r, 1-p)
Billy Cannon, Houston vs. N.Y. Titans, Dec. 10, 1961 (3-r, 2-p)
Cookie Gilchrist, Buffalo vs. N.Y. Jets, Dec. 8, 1963 (5-r)
Paul Hornung, Green Bay vs. Baltimore, Dec. 12, 1965 (3-r, 2-p)
Kellen Winslow, San Diego vs. Oakland, Nov. 22, 1981 (5-p)
4   By many players

Most Consecutive Games Scoring Touchdowns
18   Lenny Moore, Baltimore, 1963-65
14   O.J. Simpson, Buffalo, 1975
11   Elroy (Crazylegs) Hirsch, Los Angeles, 1950-51
Buddy Dial, Pittsburgh, 1959-60

POINTS AFTER TOUCHDOWN
Most Seasons Leading League
8   George Blanda, Chi. Bears, 1956; Houston, 1961-62; Oakland, 1967-69, 1972, 1974
4   Bob Waterfield, Cleveland, 1945; Los Angeles, 1946, 1950, 1952
3   Earl (Dutch) Clark, Portsmouth, 1932; Detroit, 1935-36
Jack Manders, Chi. Bears, 1933-35
Don Hutson, Green Bay, 1941-42, 1945

Most Points After Touchdown Attempted, Career
959   George Blanda, Chi. Bears, 1949, 1950-58; Baltimore, 1950; Houston, 1960-66; Oakland, 1967-75
657   Lou Groza, Cleveland, 1950-59, 1961-67
553   Jim Bakken, St. Louis, 1962-78

Most Points After Touchdown Attempted, Season
65   George Blanda, Houston, 1961
61   Rolf Benirschke, San Diego, 1981
60   Rafael Septien, Dallas, 1980

Most Points After Touchdown Attempted, Game
10   Charlie Gogolak, Washington vs. N.Y. Giants, Nov. 27, 1966
9   Pat Harder, Chi. Cardinals vs. N.Y. Giants, Oct. 17, 1948; vs. N.Y. Bulldogs, Nov. 13, 1949
Bob Waterfield, Los Angeles vs. Baltimore, Oct. 22, 1950
Bob Thomas, Chicago vs. Green Bay, Dec. 7, 1980
8   By many players

Most Points After Touchdown, Career
943   George Blanda, Chi. Bears, 1949, 1950-58; Baltimore, 1950; Houston, 1960-66; Oakland, 1967-75
641   Lou Groza, Cleveland, 1950-59, 1961-67
534   Jim Bakken, St. Louis, 1962-78

Most Points After Touchdown, Season
64   George Blanda, Houston, 1961
59   Rafael Septien, Dallas, 1980
56   Danny Villanueva, Dallas, 1966
George Blanda, Oakland, 1967

Most Points After Touchdown, Game
9   Pat Harder, Chi. Cardinals vs. N.Y. Giants, Oct. 17, 1948
Bob Waterfield, Los Angeles vs. Baltimore, Oct. 22, 1950
Charlie Gogolak, Washington vs. N.Y. Giants, Nov. 27, 1966
8   By many players

Most Consecutive Points After Touchdown
234   Tommy Davis, San Francisco, 1959-65
221   Jim Turner, N.Y. Jets, 1967-70; Denver, 1971-74
201   George Blanda, Oakland, 1967-71

Highest Points After Touchdown Percentage, Career (200 points after touchdown)
99.43   Tommy Davis, San Francisco, 1959-69 (350-348)
98.33   George Blanda, Chi. Bears, 1949, 1950-58; Baltimore, 1950; Houston, 1960-66; Oakland, 1967-75 (959-943)
97.93   Danny Villanueva, L.A. Rams, 1960-64; Dallas, 1965-67 (241-236)

Most Points After Touchdown, No Misses, Season
56   Danny Villanueva, Dallas, 1966

- 54   Mike Clark, Dallas, 1968
  - George Blanda, Oakland, 1968
- 53   Pat Harder, Chi. Cardinals, 1948

Most Points After Touchdown, No Misses, Game
- 9   Pat Harder, Chi. Cardinals vs. N.Y. Giants, Oct. 17, 1948
  - Bob Waterfield, Los Angeles vs. Baltimore, Oct. 22, 1950
- 8   By many players

FIELD GOALS

Most Seasons Leading League
- 5   Lou Groza, Cleveland, 1950, 1952-54, 1957
- 4   Jack Manders, Chi. Bears, 1933-34, 1936-37
  - Ward Cuff, N.Y. Giants, 1938-39, 1943; Green Bay, 1947
- 3   Bob Waterfield, Los Angeles, 1947, 1949, 1951
  - Gino Cappelletti, Boston, 1961, 1963-64
  - Fred Cox, Minnesota, 1965, 1969-70
  - Jan Stenerud, Kansas City, 1967, 1970, 1975
  - Mark Moseley, Washington, 1976-77, 1979

Most Consecutive Seasons Leading League
- 3   Lou Groza, Cleveland, 1952-54
- 2   By many players

Most Field Goals Attempted, Career
- 638   George Blanda, Chi. Bears, 1949, 1950-58; Baltimore, 1950; Houston, 1960-66; Oakland, 1967-75
- 488   Jim Turner, N.Y. Jets, 1964-70; Denver, 1971-79
- 465   Jan Stenerud, Kansas City, 1967-79; Green Bay, 1980-81

Most Field Goals Attempted, Season
- 49   Bruce Gossett, Los Angeles, 1966
  - Curt Knight, Washington, 1971
- 48   Chester Marcol, Green Bay, 1972
- 47   Jim Turner, N.Y. Jets, 1969
  - David Ray, Los Angeles, 1973

Most Field Goals Attempted, Game
- 9   Jim Bakken, St. Louis vs. Pittsburgh, Sept. 24, 1967
- 8   Lou Michaels, Pittsburgh vs. St. Louis, Dec. 2, 1962
  - Garo Yepremian, Detroit vs. Minnesota, Nov. 13, 1966
  - Jim Turner, N.Y. Jets vs. Buffalo, Nov. 3, 1968
- 7   By many players

Most Field Goals, Career
- 335   George Blanda, Chi. Bears, 1949, 1950-58; Baltimore, 1950; Houston, 1960-66; Oakland, 1967-75
- 304   Jim Turner, N.Y. Jets, 1964-70; Denver, 1971-79
  - Jan Stenerud, Kansas City, 1967-79; Green Bay, 1980-81
- 282   Fred Cox, Minnesota, 1963-77
  - Jim Bakken, St. Louis, 1962-78

Most Field Goals, Season
- 34   Jim Turner, N.Y. Jets, 1968
- 33   Chester Marcol, Green Bay, 1972
- 32   Jim Turner, N.Y. Jets, 1969

Most Field Goals, Rookie, Season
- 33   Chester Marcol, Green Bay, 1972
- 29   Frank Corral, Los Angeles, 1978
- 27   Ed Murray, Detroit, 1980

Most Field Goals, Game
- 7   Jim Bakken, St. Louis vs. Pittsburgh, Sept. 24, 1967
- 6   Gino Cappelletti, Boston vs. Denver, Oct. 4, 1964
  - Garo Yepremian, Detroit vs. Minnesota, Nov. 13, 1966
  - Jim Turner, N.Y. Jets vs. Buffalo, Nov. 3, 1968
  - Tom Dempsey, Philadelphia vs. Houston, Nov. 12, 1972
  - Bobby Howfield, N.Y. Jets vs. New Orleans, Dec. 3, 1972
  - Jim Bakken, St. Louis vs. Atlanta, Dec. 9, 1973
  - Joe Danelo, N.Y. Giants vs. Seattle, Oct. 18, 1981
- 5   By many players

All-Time Records

Most Field Goals, One Quarter
4	Garo Yepremian, Detroit vs. Minnesota, Nov. 13, 1966 (second quarter)
	Curt Knight, Washington vs. N.Y. Giants, Nov. 15, 1970 (second quarter)
3	By many players

Most Consecutive Games Scoring Field Goals
31	Fred Cox, Minnesota, 1968-70
28	Jim Turner, N.Y. Jets, 1970; Denver, 1971-72
21	Bruce Gossett, San Francisco, 1970-72

Most Consecutive Field Goals
20	Garo Yepremian, Miami, 1978; New Orleans, 1979
16	Jan Stenerud, Kansas City, 1969
	Don Cockroft, Cleveland, 1974-75
	Rolf Benirschke, San Diego, 1978-80
14	Toni Fritsch, Houston, 1979-80

Longest Field Goal
63	Tom Dempsey, New Orleans vs. Detroit, Nov. 8, 1970
59	Tony Franklin, Philadelphia vs. Dallas, Nov. 12, 1979
57	Don Cockroft, Cleveland vs. Denver, Oct. 29, 1972
	Nick Lowery, Kansas City vs. Seattle, Sept. 14, 1980
	Fred Steinfort, Denver vs. Washington, Oct. 13, 1980

Highest Field Goal Percentage, Career (100 field goals)
68.79	Efren Herrera, Dallas, 1974, 1976-77; Seattle, 1978-81 (157-108)
68.30	Toni Fritsch, Dallas, 1971-73, 1975; San Diego, 1976; Houston, 1977-81 (224-153)
67.80	John Smith, New England, 1974-81 (177-120)

Highest Field Goal Percentage, Season (14 attempts)
91.67	Jan Stenerud, Green Bay, 1981 (24-22)
88.46	Lou Groza, Cleveland, 1953 (26-23)
87.50	Don Cockroft, Cleveland, 1974 (16-14)

Most Field Goals, No Misses, Game
6	Gino Cappelletti, Boston vs. Denver, Oct. 4, 1964
	Joe Danelo, N.Y. Giants vs. Seattle, Oct. 18, 1981
5	Roger LeClerc, Chicago vs. Detroit, Dec. 3, 1961
	Lou Michaels, Baltimore vs. San Francisco, Sept. 25, 1966
	Mac Percival, Chicago vs. Philadelphia, Oct. 20, 1968
	Roy Gerela, Houston vs. Miami, Sept. 28, 1969
	Jan Stenerud, Kansas City vs. Buffalo, Nov. 2, 1969; vs. Buffalo, Dec. 7, 1969
	Horst Muhlmann, Cincinnati vs. Buffalo, Nov. 8, 1970; vs. Pittsburgh, Sept. 24, 1972
	Bruce Gossett, San Francisco vs. Denver, Sept. 23, 1973
	Nick Mike-Mayer, Atlanta vs. Los Angeles, Nov. 4, 1973
	Curt Knight, Washington vs. Baltimore, Nov. 18, 1973
	Tim Mazzetti, Atlanta vs. Los Angeles, Oct. 30, 1978
	Ed Murray, Detroit vs. Green Bay, Sept. 14, 1980

SAFETIES
Most Safeties, Career
4	Ted Hendricks, Baltimore, 1969-73; Green Bay, 1974; Oakland, 1975-81
3	Bill McPeak, Pittsburgh, 1949-57
	Charlie Krueger, San Francisco, 1959-73
	Ernie Stautner, Pittsburgh, 1950-63
	Jim Katcavage, N.Y. Giants, 1956-68
	Roger Brown, Detroit, 1960-66; Los Angeles, 1967-69
	Bruce Maher, Detroit, 1960-67; N.Y. Giants, 1968-69
	Ron McDole, St. Louis, 1961; Houston, 1962; Buffalo, 1963-70; Washington, 1971-78
	Alan Page, Minnesota, 1967-78; Chicago, 1979-81
2	By many players

Most Safeties, Season
2	Tom Nash, Green Bay, 1932
	Roger Brown, Detroit, 1962
	Ron McDole, Buffalo, 1964
	Alan Page, Minnesota, 1971
	Fred Dryer, Los Angeles, 1973

Benny Barnes, Dallas, 1973
James Young, Houston, 1977
Tom Hannon, Minnesota, 1981

Most Safeties, Game
2   Fred Dryer, Los Angeles vs. Green Bay, Oct. 21, 1973

RUSHING

Most Seasons Leading League
8   Jim Brown, Cleveland, 1957-61, 1963-65
4   Steve Van Buren, Philadelphia, 1945, 1947-49
    O.J. Simpson, Buffalo, 1972-73, 1975-76
3   Earl Campbell, Houston, 1978-80

Most Consecutive Seasons Leading League
5   Jim Brown, Cleveland, 1957-61
3   Steve Van Buren, Philadelphia, 1947-49
    Jim Brown, Cleveland, 1963-65
    Earl Campbell, Houston, 1978-80
2   Bill Paschal, N.Y. Giants, 1943-44
    Joe Perry, San Francisco, 1953-54
    Jim Nance, Boston, 1966-67
    Leroy Kelly, Cleveland, 1967-68
    O.J. Simpson, Buffalo, 1972-73; 1975-76

ATTEMPTS
Most Seasons Leading League
6   Jim Brown, Cleveland, 1958-59, 1961, 1963-65
4   Steve Van Buren, Philadelphia, 1947-50
    Walter Payton, Chicago, 1976-79
3   Cookie Gilchrist, Buffalo, 1963-64; Denver, 1965
    Jim Nance, Boston, 1966-67, 1969
    O. J. Simpson, Buffalo, 1973-75

Most Consecutive Seasons Leading League
4   Steve Van Buren, Philadelphia, 1947-50
    Walter Payton, Chicago, 1976-79
3   Jim Brown, Cleveland, 1963-65
    Cookie Gilchrist, Buffalo, 1963-64; Denver, 1965
    O. J. Simpson, Buffalo, 1973-75
2   By many players

Most Attempts, Career
2,462   Franco Harris, Pittsburgh, 1972-81
2,404   O.J. Simpson, Buffalo, 1969-77; San Francisco, 1978-79
2,359   Jim Brown, Cleveland, 1957-65

Most Attempts, Season
378   George Rogers, New Orleans, 1981
373   Earl Campbell, Houston, 1980
369   Walter Payton, Chicago, 1979

Most Attempts, Rookie, Season
378   George Rogers, New Orleans, 1981
331   Ottis Anderson, St. Louis, 1979
306   Joe Cribbs, Buffalo, 1980

Most Attempts, Game
41   Franco Harris, Pittsburgh vs. Cincinnati, Oct. 17, 1976
40   Lydell Mitchell, Baltimore vs. N.Y. Jets, Oct. 20, 1974
     Walter Payton, Chicago vs. Minnesota, Nov. 20, 1977
39   O.J. Simpson, Buffalo vs. Kansas City, Oct. 29, 1973
     Terdell Middleton, Green Bay vs. Minnesota, Nov. 26, 1978 (OT)
     Walter Payton, Chicago vs. Buffalo, Oct. 7, 1979
     Ricky Bell, Tampa Bay vs. Kansas City, Dec. 16, 1979
     Earl Campbell, Houston vs. Seattle, Oct. 11, 1981

YARDS GAINED

Most Yards Gained, Career

12,312	Jim Brown, Cleveland, 1957-65
11,236	O.J. Simpson, Buffalo, 1969-77; San Francisco, 1978-79
10,339	Franco Harris, Pittsburgh, 1972-81

Most Seasons, 1,000 or More Yards Rushing

7	Jim Brown, Cleveland, 1958-61, 1963-65
	Franco Harris, Pittsburgh, 1972, 1974-79
6	Walter Payton, Chicago, 1976-81
5	Jim Taylor, Green Bay, 1960-64
	O.J. Simpson, Buffalo, 1972-76
	Tony Dorsett, Dallas, 1977-81

Most Yards Gained, Season

2,003	O.J. Simpson, Buffalo, 1973
1,934	Earl Campbell, Houston, 1980
1,863	Jim Brown, Cleveland, 1963

Most Yards Gained, Rookie, Season

1,674	George Rogers, New Orleans, 1981
1,605	Ottis Anderson, St. Louis, 1979
1,450	Earl Campbell, Houston, 1978

Most Yards Gained, Game

275	Walter Payton, Chicago vs. Minnesota, Nov. 20, 1977
273	O.J. Simpson, Buffalo vs. Detroit, Nov. 25, 1976
250	O.J. Simpson, Buffalo vs. New England, Sept. 16, 1973

Most Games, 200 or More Yards Rushing

6	O.J. Simpson, Buffalo, 1969-77; San Francisco, 1978-79
4	Jim Brown, Cleveland, 1957-65
	Earl Campbell, Houston, 1978-81
2	Walter Payton, Chicago, 1975-81

Most Games, 200 or More Yards Rushing, Season

4	Earl Campbell, Houston, 1980
3	O.J. Simpson, Buffalo, 1973
2	Jim Brown, Cleveland, 1963
	O.J. Simpson, Buffalo, 1976
	Walter Payton, Chicago, 1977

Most Consecutive Games, 200 or More Yards Rushing

2	O.J. Simpson, Buffalo, 1973, 1976
	Earl Campbell, Houston, 1980

Most Games, 100 or More Yards Rushing, Career

58	Jim Brown, Cleveland, 1957-65
46	Walter Payton, Chicago, 1975-81
42	O.J. Simpson, Buffalo, 1969-77; San Francisco, 1978-79

Most Games, 100 or More Yards Rushing, Season

11	O.J. Simpson, Buffalo, 1973
	Earl Campbell, Houston, 1979
10	Walter Payton, Chicago, 1977
	Earl Campbell, Houston, 1980
9	Jim Brown, Cleveland, 1958, 1963
	Ottis Anderson, St. Louis, 1979
	Tony Dorsett, Dallas, 1981
	George Rogers, New Orleans, 1981

Most Consecutive Games, 100 or More Yards Rushing

7	O.J. Simpson, Buffalo, 1972-73
	Earl Campbell, Houston, 1979
6	Jim Brown, Cleveland, 1958
	Franco Harris, Pittsburgh, 1972
	Earl Campbell, Houston, 1980
5	Rob Goode, Washington, 1951
	Jim Brown, Cleveland, 1961
	Jim Nance, Boston, 1966
	O.J. Simpson, Buffalo, 1973, 1975
	Walter Payton, Chicago, 1977

Longest Run From Scrimmage

 97 Andy Uram, Green Bay vs. Chi. Cardinals, Oct. 8, 1939 (TD)
    Bob Gage, Pittsburgh vs. Chi. Bears, Dec. 4, 1949 (TD)
 96 Jim Spavital, Baltimore vs. Green Bay, Nov. 5, 1950 (TD)
    Bob Hoernschemeyer, Detroit vs. N.Y. Yanks, Nov. 23, 1950 (TD)
 94 O.J. Simpson, Buffalo vs. Pittsburgh, Oct. 29, 1972 (TD)

AVERAGE GAIN

Highest Average Gain, Career (700 attempts)

 5.22 Jim Brown, Cleveland, 1957-65 (2,359-12,312)
 5.14 Eugene (Mercury) Morris, Miami, 1969-75; San Diego, 1976 (804-4,133)
 5.00 Gale Sayers, Chicago, 1965-71 (991-4,956)

Highest Average Gain, Season (Qualifiers)

 9.94 Beattie Feathers, Chi. Bears, 1934 (101-1,004)
 6.87 Bobby Douglass, Chicago, 1972 (141-968)
 6.78 Dan Towler, Los Angeles, 1951 (126-854)

Highest Average Gain, Game (10 attempts)

 17.09 Marion Motley, Cleveland vs. Pittsburgh, Oct. 29, 1950 (11-188)
 16.70 Bill Grimes, Green Bay vs. N.Y. Yanks, Oct. 8, 1950 (10-167)
 16.57 Bobby Mitchell, Cleveland vs. Washington, Nov. 15, 1959 (14-232)

TOUCHDOWNS

Most Seasons Leading League

 5 Jim Brown, Cleveland, 1957-59, 1963, 1965
 4 Steve Van Buren, Philadelphia, 1945, 1947-49
 3 Abner Haynes, Dall. Texans, 1960-62
   Cookie Gilchrist, Buffalo, 1962-64
   Paul Lowe, L.A. Chargers, 1960; San Diego, 1961, 1965
   Leroy Kelly, Cleveland, 1966-68

Most Consecutive Seasons Leading League

 3 Steve Van Buren, Philadelphia, 1947-49
   Jim Brown, Cleveland, 1957-59
   Abner Haynes, Dall. Texans, 1960-62
   Cookie Gilchrist, Buffalo, 1962-64
   Leroy Kelly, Cleveland, 1966-68

Most Touchdowns, Career

 106 Jim Brown, Cleveland, 1957-65
  84 Franco Harris, Pittsburgh, 1972-81
  83 Jim Taylor, Green Bay, 1958-66; New Orleans, 1967

Most Touchdowns, Season

 19 Jim Taylor, Green Bay, 1962
   Earl Campbell, Houston, 1979
   Chuck Muncie, San Diego, 1981
 17 Jim Brown, Cleveland, 1958, 1965
 16 Lenny Moore, Baltimore, 1964
   Leroy Kelly, Cleveland, 1968
   Pete Banaszak, Oakland, 1975
   O.J. Simpson, Buffalo, 1975

Most Touchdowns, Rookie, Season

 14 Gale Sayers, Chicago, 1965
 13 Cookie Gilchrist, Buffalo, 1962
   Earl Campbell, Houston, 1978
   Billy Sims, Detroit, 1980
   George Rogers, New Orleans, 1981
 12 Tony Dorsett, Dallas, 1977

Most Touchdowns, Game

 6 Ernie Nevers, Chi. Cardinals vs. Chi. Bears, Nov. 28, 1929
 5 Jim Brown, Cleveland vs. Baltimore, Nov. 1, 1959
   Cookie Gilchrist, Buffalo vs. N.Y. Jets, Dec. 8, 1963
 4 By many players

Most Consecutive Games Rushing for Touchdowns

 11 Lenny Moore, Baltimore, 1963-64
  9 Leroy Kelly, Cleveland, 1968
  8 Steve Van Buren, Philadelphia, 1947

PASSING

Most Seasons Leading League

  6 Sammy Baugh, Washington, 1937, 1940, 1943, 1945, 1947, 1949

  4 Len Dawson, Dall. Texans; 1962; Kansas City, 1964, 1966, 1968

      Roger Staubach, Dallas, 1971, 1973, 1978-79

  3 Arnie Herber, Green Bay, 1932, 1934, 1936

      Norm Van Brocklin, Los Angeles, 1950, 1952, 1954

      Bart Starr, Green Bay, 1962, 1964, 1966

      Ken Anderson, Cincinnati, 1974-75, 1981

Most Consecutive Seasons Leading League

  2 Cecil Isbell, Green Bay, 1941-42

      Milt Plum, Cleveland, 1960-61

      Ken Anderson, Cincinnati, 1974-75

      Roger Staubach, Dallas, 1978-79

ATTEMPTS

Most Seasons Leading League

  4 Sammy Baugh, Washington, 1937, 1943, 1947-48

      Johnny Unitas, Baltimore, 1957, 1959-61

      George Blanda, Chi. Bears, 1953; Houston, 1963-65

  3 Arnie Herber, Green Bay, 1932, 1934, 1936

      Sonny Jurgensen, Washington, 1966-67, 1969

  2 By many players

Most Consecutive Seasons Leading League

  3 Johnny Unitas, Baltimore, 1959-61

      George Blanda, Houston, 1963-65

  2 By many players

Most Passes Attempted, Career

6,467 Fran Tarkenton, Minnesota, 1961-66, 1972-78; N.Y. Giants, 1967-71

5,186 Johnny Unitas, Baltimore, 1956-72; San Diego, 1973

4,945 Jim Hart, St. Louis, 1966-81

Most Passes Attempted, Season

  609 Dan Fouts, San Diego, 1981

  593 Tommy Kramer, Minnesota, 1981

  589 Dan Fouts, San Diego, 1980

Most Passes Attempted, Rookie, Season

  439 Jim Zorn, Seattle, 1976

  392 Butch Songin, Boston, 1960

  375 Norm Snead, Washington, 1961

Most Passes Attempted, Game

  68 George Blanda, Houston vs. Buffalo, Nov. 1, 1964

  62 Joe Namath, N.Y. Jets vs. Baltimore, Oct. 18, 1970

     Steve Dils, Minnesota vs. Tampa Bay, Sept. 5, 1981

  61 Tommy Kramer, Minnesota vs. Buffalo, Dec. 16, 1979

COMPLETIONS

Most Seasons Leading League

  5 Sammy Baugh, Washington, 1937, 1943, 1945, 1947-48

  4 George Blanda, Chi. Bears, 1953; Houston, 1963-65

      Sonny Jurgensen, Philadephia, 1961; Washington, 1966-67, 1969

  3 Arnie Herber, Green Bay, 1932, 1934, 1936

      Johnny Unitas, Baltimore, 1959-60, 1963

      John Brodie, San Francisco, 1965, 1968, 1970

      Fran Tarkenton, Minnesota, 1975-76, 1978

Most Consecutive Seasons Leading League

  3 George Blanda, Houston, 1963-65

  2 By many players

Most Passes Completed, Career

3,686 Fran Tarkenton, Minnesota, 1961-66, 1972-78; N.Y. Giants, 1967-71

2,830 Johnny Unitas, Baltimore, 1956-72; San Diego, 1973

2,521 Jim Hart, St. Louis, 1966-81

Most Passes Completed, Season

  360 Dan Fouts, San Diego, 1981

348   Dan Fouts, San Diego, 1980
347   Steve DeBerg, San Francisco, 1979

Most Passes Completed, Rookie, Season

208   Jim Zorn, Seattle, 1976
187   Butch Songin, Boston, 1960
183   Jeff Komlo, Detroit, 1979

Most Passes Completed, Game

42   Richard Todd, N.Y. Jets vs. San Francisco, Sept. 21, 1980
38   Tommy Kramer, Minnesota vs. Cleveland, Dec. 14, 1980
      Tommy Kramer, Minnesota vs. Green Bay, Nov. 29, 1981
37   George Blanda, Houston vs. Buffalo, Nov. 1, 1964
      Steve Dils, Minnesota vs. Tampa Bay, Sept. 5, 1981

Most Consecutive Passes Completed

17   Bert Jones, Baltimore vs. N.Y. Jets, Dec. 15, 1974
16   Ken Anderson, Cincinnati vs. Baltimore (8), Nov. 3; vs. Pittsburgh (8),
         Nov. 10, 1974
      Craig Morton, Denver vs. Kansas City, Dec. 10, 1978
      Tommy Kramer, Minnesota vs. Green Bay, Nov. 11, 1979
15   Len Dawson, Kansas City vs. Houston, Sept. 9, 1967
      Joe Namath, N.Y. Jets vs. Miami (12), Oct. 22; vs. Boston (3), Oct. 29, 1967
      Archie Manning, New Orleans vs. Tampa Bay (8), Oct. 14; vs. Detroit (7),
         Oct. 21, 1979
      Lynn Dickey, Green Bay vs. San Francisco, Nov. 9, 1980
      Dan Fouts, San Diego vs. Cleveland, Sept. 7, 1981

COMPLETION PERCENTAGE

Most Seasons Leading League

8   Len Dawson, Dall. Texans, 1962; Kansas City, 1964-69, 1975
7   Sammy Baugh, Washington, 1940, 1942-43, 1945, 1947-49
4   Bart Starr, Green Bay, 1962, 1966, 1968-69

Most Consecutive Seasons Leading League

6   Len Dawson, Kansas City, 1964-69
3   Sammy Baugh, Washington, 1947-49
    Otto Graham, Cleveland, 1953-55
    Milt Plum, Cleveland, 1959-61
2   By many players

Highest Completion Percentage, Career (1,500 attempts)

60.32   Ken Stabler, Oakland, 1970-79; Houston, 1980-81 (3,223-1,944)
57.73   Dan Fouts, San Diego, 1973-81 (3,203-1,849)
57.53   Ken Anderson, Cincinnati, 1971-81 (3,539-2,036)

Highest Completion Percentage, Season (Qualifiers)

70.33   Sammy Baugh, Washington, 1945 (182-128)
66.67   Ken Stabler, Oakland, 1976 (291-194)
66.43   Len Dawson, Kansas City, 1975 (140-93)

Highest Completion Percentage, Rookie, Season (Qualifiers)

56.07   Fran Tarkenton, Minnesota, 1961 (280-157)
55.56   Johnny Unitas, Baltimore, 1956 (198-110)
55.45   Dennis Shaw, Buffalo, 1970 (321-178)

Highest Completion Percentage, Game (20 attempts)

90.91   Ken Anderson, Cincinnati vs. Pittsburgh, Nov. 10, 1974 (22-20)
90.48   Lynn Dickey, Green Bay vs. New Orleans, Dec. 13, 1981 (21-19)
86.36   Craig Morton, Denver vs. Kansas City, Dec. 10, 1978 (22-19)

YARDS GAINED

Most Seasons Leading League

5   Sonny Jurgensen, Philadelphia, 1961-62; Washington, 1966-67, 1969
4   Sammy Baugh, Washington, 1937, 1940, 1947-48
    Johnny Unitas, Baltimore, 1957, 1959-60, 1963
3   Arnie Herber, Green Bay, 1932, 1934, 1936
    Sid Luckman, Chi. Bears, 1943, 1945-46
    John Brodie, San Francisco, 1965, 1968, 1970
    John Hadl, San Diego, 1965, 1968, 1971
    Joe Namath, N.Y. Jets, 1966-67, 1972

Dan Fouts, San Diego, 1979-81

Most Consecutive Seasons Leading League
- 3 Dan Fouts, San Diego, 1979-81
- 2 By many players

Most Yards Gained, Career
- 47,003 Fran Tarkenton, Minnesota, 1961-66, 1972-78; N.Y. Giants, 1967-71
- 40,239 Johnny Unitas, Baltimore, 1956-72; San Diego, 1973
- 33,848 Jim Hart, St. Louis, 1966-81

Most Seasons, 3,000 or More Yards Passing
- 5 Sonny Jurgensen, Philadelphia, 1961-62; Washington, 1966-67, 1969
- 3 Johnny Unitas, Baltimore, 1960, 1963, 1967
  - George Blanda, Houston, 1961, 1963-64
  - Joe Namath, N.Y. Jets, 1966-68
  - Daryle Lamonica, Oakland, 1967-69
  - John Hadl, San Diego, 1967-68, 1971
  - Bert Jones, Baltimore, 1976, 1980-81
  - Archie Manning, New Orleans, 1978-80
  - Jim Zorn, Seattle, 1978-80
  - Dan Fouts, San Diego, 1979-81
  - Tommy Kramer, Minnesota, 1979-81
  - Brian Sipe, Cleveland, 1979-81
- 2 By many players

Most Yards Gained, Season
- 4,802 Dan Fouts, San Diego, 1981
- 4,715 Dan Fouts, San Diego, 1980
- 4,132 Brian Sipe, Cleveland, 1980

Most Yards Gained, Rookie, Season
- 2,571 Jim Zorn, Seattle, 1976
- 2,507 Dennis Shaw, Buffalo, 1970
- 2,476 Butch Songin, Boston, 1960

Most Yards Gained, Game
- 554 Norm Van Brocklin, Los Angeles vs. N.Y. Yanks, Sept. 28, 1951
- 505 Y.A. Tittle, N.Y. Giants vs. Washington, Oct. 28, 1962
- 496 Joe Namath, N.Y. Jets vs. Baltimore, Sept. 24, 1972

Most Games, 300 or More Yards Passing, Career
- 26 Johnny Unitas, Baltimore, 1956-72; San Diego, 1973
- 25 Sonny Jurgensen, Philadephia, 1957-63; Washington, 1964-74
  - Dan Fouts, San Diego, 1973-81
- 21 Joe Namath, N.Y. Jets, 1965-76; Los Angeles, 1977

Most Games, 300 or More Yards Passing, Season
- 8 Dan Fouts, San Diego, 1980
- 7 Dan Fouts, San Diego, 1981
- 6 Joe Namath, N.Y. Jets, 1967
  - Dan Fouts, San Diego, 1979
  - Archie Manning, New Orleans, 1980
  - Brian Sipe, Cleveland, 1980

Most Consecutive Games, 300 or More Yards, Passing, Season
- 4 Dan Fouts, San Diego, 1979
- 3 Frank Tripucka, Denver, 1960
  - Johnny Unitas, Baltimore, 1963
  - George Blanda, Houston, 1964
  - Cotton Davidson, Oakland, 1964
  - John Hadl, San Diego, 1967
  - Sonny Jurgensen, Washington, 1967
  - Dan Fouts, San Diego, 1980
- 2 By many players

Longest Pass Completion (All TDs except as noted)
- 99 Frank Filchock (to Farkas), Washington vs. Pittsburgh, Oct. 15, 1939
  - George Izo (to Mitchell), Washington vs. Cleveland, Sept. 15, 1963
  - Karl Sweetan (to Studstill), Detroit vs. Baltimore, Oct. 16, 1966
  - Sonny Jurgensen (to Allen), Washington vs. Chicago, Sept. 15, 1968
- 98 Doug Russell (to Tinsley), Chi. Cardinals vs. Cleveland, Nov. 27, 1938
  - Ogden Compton (to Lane), Chi. Cardinals vs. Green Bay, Nov. 13, 1955

Bill Wade (to Farrington), Chicago Bears vs. Detroit, Oct. 8, 1961
Jacky Lee (to Dewveall), Houston vs. San Diego, Nov. 25, 1962
Earl Morrall (to Jones), N.Y. Giants vs. Pittsburgh, Sept. 11, 1966
Jim Hart (to Moore), St. Louis vs. Los Angeles, Dec. 10, 1972 (no TD)
97 Pat Coffee (to Tinsley), Chi. Cardinals vs. Chi. Bears, Dec. 5, 1937
Bobby Layne (to Box), Detroit vs. Green Bay, Nov. 26, 1953
George Shaw (to Tarr), Denver vs. Boston, Sept. 21, 1962

AVERAGE GAIN
Most Seasons Leading League
7 Sid Luckman, Chi. Bears, 1939-43, 1946-47
3 Arnie Herber, Green Bay, 1932, 1934, 1936
Norm Van Brocklin, Los Angeles, 1950, 1952, 1954
Len Dawson, Dall. Texans. 1962; Kansas City, 1966, 1968
Bart Starr, Green Bay, 1966-68

Most Consecutive Seasons Leading League
5 Sid Luckman, Chi. Bears, 1939-43
3 Bart Starr, Green Bay, 1966-68
2 Bernie Masterson, Chi. Bears, 1937-38
Sid Luckman, Chi. Bears, 1946-47
Johnny Unitas, Baltimore, 1964-65
Terry Bradshaw, Pittsburgh, 1977-78
Steve Grogan, New England, 1980-81

Highest Average Gain, Career (1,500 attempts)
8.63 Otto Graham, Cleveland, 1950-55 (1,565-13,499)
8.42 Sid Luckman, Chi: Bears, 1939-50 (1,744-14,686)
8.16 Norm Van Brocklin, Los Angeles, 1949-57; Philadelphia, 1958-60 (2,895-23,611)

Highest Average Gain, Season (Qualifiers)
11.17 Tommy O'Connell, Cleveland, 1957 (110-1,229)
10.86 Sid Luckman, Chi. Bears, 1943 (202-2,194)
10.55 Otto Graham, Cleveland, 1953 (258-2,722)

Highest Average Gain, Rookie, Season (Qualifiers)
9.411 Greg Cook Cincinnati, 1969 (197-1,854)
9.409 Bob Waterfield, Cleveland, 1945 (171-1,609)
8.36 Zeke Bratkowski, Chi. Bears, 1954 (130-1,087)

Highest Average Gain, Game (20 attempts)
18.58 Sammy Baugh, Washington vs. Boston, Oct. 31, 1948 (24-446)
18.50 Johnny Unitas, Baltimore vs. Atlanta, Nov. 12, 1967 (20-370)
17.71 Joe Namath, N.Y. Jets vs. Baltimore, Sept. 24, 1972 (28-496)

TOUCHDOWNS
Most Seasons Leading League
4 Johnny Unitas, Baltimore, 1957-60
Len Dawson, Dall. Texans, 1962; Kansas City, 1963, 1965-66
3 Arnie Herber, Green Bay, 1932, 1934, 1936
Sid Luckman, Chi. Bears, 1943, 1945-46
Y.A. Tittle, San Francisco, 1955; N.Y. Giants, 1962-63
2 By many players

Most Consecutive Seasons Leading League
4 Johnny Unitas, Baltimore, 1957-60
2 By many players

Most Touchdown Passes, Career
342 Fran Tarkenton, Minnesota, 1961-66, 1972-78; N.Y. Giants, 1967-71
290 Johnny Unitas, Baltimore, 1956-72; San Diego, 1973
255 Sonny Jurgensen, Philadelphia, 1957-63; Washington, 1964-74

Most Touchdown Passes, Season
36 George Blanda, Houston, 1961
Y.A. Tittle, N.Y. Giants, 1963
34 Daryle Lamonica, Oakland, 1969
33 Y.A. Tittle, N.Y. Giants, 1962
Dan Fouts, San Diego, 1981

All-Time Records

Most Touchdown Passes, Rookie, Season
- 22 Charlie Conerly, N.Y. Giants, 1948
     Butch Songin, Boston, 1960
- 19 Jim Plunkett, New England, 1971
- 18 Fran Tarkenton, Minnesota, 1961
     Joe Namath, N.Y. Jets, 1965

Most Touchdown Passes, Game
- 7 Sid Luckman, Chi. Bears vs. N.Y. Giants, Nov. 14, 1943
    Adrian Burk, Philadelphia vs. Washington, Oct. 17, 1954
    George Blanda, Houston vs. N.Y. Titans, Nov. 19, 1961
    Y.A. Tittle, N.Y. Giants vs. Washington, Oct. 28, 1962
    Joe Kapp, Minnesota vs. Baltimore, Sept. 28, 1969
- 6 By many players. Last time: Dan Fouts, San Diego vs. Oakland, Nov. 22, 1981

Most Consecutive Games, Touchdown Passes
- 47 Johnny Unitas, Baltimore, 1956-60
- 25 Daryle Lamonica, Oakland, 1968-70
- 23 Frank Ryan, Cleveland, 1965-67
     Sonny Jurgensen, Washington, 1966-68

HAD INTERCEPTED
Fewest Passes Had Intercepted, Season (Qualifiers)
- 1 Joe Ferguson, Buffalo, 1976
- 3 Gary Wood, N.Y. Giants, 1964
    Bart Starr, Green Bay, 1966
- 4 Sammy Baugh, Washington, 1945
    Harry Gilmer, Detroit, 1955
    Charlie Conerly, N.Y. Giants, 1959
    Bart Starr, Green Bay, 1964
    Roger Staubach, Dallas, 1971
    Len Dawson, Kansas City, 1975

Most Consecutive Passes Attempted, None Intercepted
- 294 Bart Starr, Green Bay, 1964-65
- 208 Milt Plum, Cleveland, 1959-60
- 206 Roman Gabriel, Los Angeles, 1968-69

Most Passes Had Intercepted, Career
- 277 George Blanda, Chi. Bears, 1949, 1950-58; Baltimore, 1950; Houston, 1960-66; Oakland, 1967-75
- 268 John Hadl, San Diego, 1962-72; Los Angeles, 1973-74; Green Bay, 1974-75; Houston, 1976-77
- 266 Fran Tarkenton, Minnesota, 1961-66, 1972-78; N.Y. Giants, 1967-71

Most Passes Had Intercepted, Season
- 42 George Blanda, Houston, 1962
- 34 Frank Tripucka, Denver, 1960
- 32 John Hadl, San Diego, 1968
     Fran Tarkenton, Minnesota, 1978

Most Passes Had Intercepted, Game
- 8 Jim Hardy, Chi. Cardinals vs. Philadelphia, Sept. 24, 1950
- 7 Parker Hall, Cleveland vs. Green Bay, Nov. 8, 1942
    Frank Sinkwich, Detroit vs. Green Bay, Oct. 24, 1943
    Bob Waterfield, Los Angeles vs. Green Bay, Oct. 17, 1948
    Zeke Bratkowski, Chicago vs. Baltimore, Oct. 2, 1960
    Tommy Wade, Pittsburgh vs. Philadelphia, Dec. 12, 1965
    Ken Stabler, Oakland vs. Denver, Oct. 16, 1977
- 6 By many players

LOWEST PERCENTAGE, PASSES HAD INTERCEPTED
Most Seasons Leading League, Lowest Percentage, Passes Had Intercepted
- 5 Sammy Baugh, Washington, 1940, 1942, 1944-45, 1947
- 3 Charlie Conerly, N.Y. Giants, 1950, 1956, 1959
    Bart Starr, Green Bay, 1962, 1964, 1966
    Roger Staubach, Dallas, 1971, 1977, 1979
- 2 By many players

Lowest Percentage, Passes Had Intercepted, Career (1,500 attempts)
- 3.31 Roman Gabriel, Los Angeles, 1962-72; Philadelphia, 1973-77 (4,498-149)
- 3.50 Ken Anderson, Cincinnati, 1971-81 (3,539-124)
- 3.68 Roger Staubach, Dallas, 1969-79 (2,958-109)

Lowest Percentage, Passes Had Intercepted, Season (Qualifiers)
- 0.66 Joe Ferguson, Buffalo, 1976 (151-1)
- 1.20 Bart Starr, Green Bay, 1966 (251-3)
- 1.47 Bart Starr, Green Bay, 1964 (272-4)

Lowest Percentage, Passes Had Intercepted, Rookie, Season (Qualifiers)
- 2.10 Gary Wood, N.Y. Giants, 1964 (143-3)
- 3.83 Butch Songin, Boston, 1960 (392-15)
- 4.12 Doug Williams, Tampa Bay, 1978 (194-8)

PASS RECEIVING

Most Seasons Leading League
- 8 Don Hutson, Green Bay, 1936-37, 1939, 1941-45
- 5 Lionel Taylor, Denver, 1960-63, 1965
- 3 Tom Fears, Los Angeles, 1948-50
  Pete Pihos, Philadelphia, 1953-55
  Billy Wilson, San Francisco, 1954, 1956-57
  Raymond Berry, Baltimore, 1958-60
  Lance Alworth, San Diego, 1966, 1968-69

Most Consecutive Seasons Leading League
- 5 Don Hutson, Green Bay, 1941-45
- 4 Lionel Taylor, Denver, 1960-63
- 3 Tom Fears, Los Angeles, 1948-50
  Pete Pihos, Philadelphia, 1953-55
  Raymond Berry, Baltimore, 1958-60

Most Pass Receptions, Career
- 649 Charley Taylor, Washington, 1964-75, 1977
- 633 Don Maynard, N.Y. Giants, 1958; N.Y. Jets, 1960-72; St. Louis, 1973
- 631 Raymond Berry, Baltimore, 1955-67

Most Seasons, 50 or More Pass Receptions
- 7 Raymond Berry, Baltimore, 1958-62, 1965-66
  Art Powell, N.Y. Titans, 1960-62; Oakland, 1963-66
  Lance Alworth, San Diego, 1963-69
  Charley Taylor, Washington, 1964, 1966-67, 1969, 1973-75
- 6 Lionel Taylor, Denver, 1960-65
  Bobby Mitchell, Washington, 1962-67
  Ahmad Rashad, Minnesota, 1976-81
- 5 Billy Wilson, San Francisco, 1953-57
  Pete Retzlaff, Philadelphia, 1958, 1961, 1963-65
  Bernie Casey, San Francisco, 1962, 1964-66; Los Angeles, 1967
  Don Maynard, N.Y. Jets, 1960, 1962, 1965, 1967-68
  Lydell Mitchell, Baltimore, 1974-77; San Diego, 1978
  Harold Carmichael, Philadelphia, 1973-74, 1978-79, 1981
  Steve Largent, Seattle, 1976, 1978-81

Most Pass Receptions, Season
- 101 Charley Hennigan, Houston, 1964
- 100 Lionel Taylor, Denver, 1961
- 93 Johnny Morris, Chicago, 1964

Most Pass Receptions, Rookie, Season
- 83 Earl Cooper, San Francisco, 1980
- 72 Bill Groman, Houston, 1960
- 67 Jack Clancy, Miami, 1967
  Cris Collinsworth, Cincinnati, 1981

Most Pass Receptions, Game
- 18 Tom Fears, Los Angeles vs. Green Bay, Dec. 3, 1950
- 17 Clark Gaines, N.Y. Jets vs. San Francisco, Sept. 21, 1980
- 16 Sonny Randle, St. Louis vs. N.Y. Giants, Nov. 4, 1962

Most Consecutive Games, Pass Receptions
- 127 Harold Carmichael, Philadelphia, 1972-80
- 117 Mel Gray, St. Louis, 1973-81 (current)

105 Dan Abramowicz, New Orleans, 1967-73; San Francisco, 1973-74

YARDS GAINED
Most Seasons Leading League
7 Don Hutson, Green Bay, 1936, 1938-39, 1941-44
3 Raymond Berry, Baltimore, 1957, 1959-60
Lance Alworth, San Diego, 1965-66, 1968
2 By many players
Most Consecutive Seasons Leading League
4 Don Hutson, Green Bay, 1941-44
2 By many players
Most Yards Gained, Career
11,834 Don Maynard, N.Y. Giants, 1958; N.Y. Jets, 1960-72; St. Louis, 1973
10,266 Lance Alworth, San Diego, 1962-70; Dallas, 1971-72
10,246 Harold Jackson, Los Angeles, 1968, 1973-77; Philadelphia, 1969-72;
New England, 1978-81
Most Seasons, 1,000 or More Yards, Pass Receiving
7 Lance Alworth, San Diego, 1963-69
5 Art Powell, N.Y. Titans, 1960, 1962; Oakland, 1963-64, 1966
Don Maynard, N.Y. Jets, 1960, 1962, 1965, 1967-68
4 Del Shofner, Los Angeles, 1958; N.Y. Giants, 1961-63
Lionel Taylor, Denver, 1960-61, 1963, 1965
Charlie Joiner, San Diego, 1976, 1979-81
Steve Largent, Seattle, 1978-81
Most Yards Gained, Season
1,746 Charley Hennigan, Houston, 1961
1,602 Lance Alworth, San Diego, 1965
1,546 Charley Hennigan, Houston, 1964
Most Yards Gained, Rookie, Season
1,473 Bill Groman, Houston, 1960
1,231 Bill Howton, Green Bay, 1952
1,124 Harlon Hill, Chi. Bears, 1954
Most Yards Gained, Game
303 Jim Benton, Cleveland vs. Detroit, Nov. 22, 1945
302 Cloyce Box, Detroit vs. Baltimore, Dec. 3, 1950
272 Charley Hennigan, Houston vs. Boston, Oct. 13, 1961
Most Games, 100 or More Yards Pass Receiving, Career
50 Don Maynard, N.Y. Giants, 1958; N.Y. Jets, 1960-72; St. Louis, 1973
41 Lance Alworth, San Diego, 1962-70; Dallas, 1971-72
31 Art Powell, Philadelphia, 1959; N.Y. Titans, 1960-62; Oakland, 1963-66;
Buffalo, 1967; Minnesota, 1968
Most Games, 100 or More Yards Pass Receiving, Season
10 Charley Hennigan, Houston, 1961
9 Elroy (Crazylegs) Hirsch, Los Angeles, 1951
Bill Groman, Houston, 1960
Lance Alworth, San Diego, 1965
Don Maynard, N.Y. Jets, 1967
8 Charley Hennigan, Houston, 1964
Lance Alworth, San Diego, 1967
Most Consecutive Games, 100 or More Yards Pass Receiving
7 Charley Hennigan, Houston, 1961
Bill Groman, Houston, 1961
6 Raymond Berry, Baltimore, 1960
Pat Studstill, Detroit, 1966
5 Elroy (Crazylegs) Hirsch, Los Angeles, 1951
Bob Boyd, Los Angeles, 1954
Terry Barr, Detroit, 1963
Lance Alworth, San Diego, 1966
Longest Pass Reception (All TDs except as noted)
99 Andy Farkas (from Filchock), Washington vs. Pittsburgh, Oct. 15, 1939
Bobby Mitchell (from Izo), Washington vs. Cleveland, Sept. 15, 1963
Pat Studstill (from Sweetan), Detroit vs. Baltimore, Oct. 16, 1966
Gerry Allen (from Jurgensen), Washington vs. Chicago, Sept. 15, 1968

98 Gaynell Tinsley (from Russell), Chi. Cardinals vs. Cleveland, Nov. 17, 1938
Dick (Night Train) Lane (from Compton), Chi. Cardinals vs. Green Bay,
   Nov. 13, 1955
John Farrington (from Wade), Chicago vs. Detroit, Oct. 8, 1961
Willard Dewveall (from Lee), Houston vs. San Diego, Nov. 25, 1962
Homer Jones (from Morrall), N.Y. Giants vs. Pittsburgh, Sept. 11, 1966
Bobby Moore (from Hart), St. Louis vs. Los Angeles, Dec. 10, 1972 (no TD)
97 Gaynell Tinsley (from Coffee), Chi. Cardinals vs. Chi. Bears, Dec. 5, 1937
Cloyce Box (from Layne), Detroit vs. Green Bay, Nov. 26, 1953
Jerry Tarr (from Shaw), Denver vs. Boston, Sept. 21, 1962

TOUCHDOWNS
Most Seasons Leading League
9 Don Hutson, Green Bay, 1935-38, 1940-44
3 Lance Alworth, San Diego, 1964-66
2 By many players
Most Consecutive Seasons Leading League
5 Don Hutson, Green Bay, 1940-44
4 Don Hutson, Green Bay, 1935-38
3 Lance Alworth, San Diego, 1964-66
Most Touchdowns, Career
99 Don Hutson, Green Bay, 1935-45
88 Don Maynard, N.Y. Giants, 1958; N.Y. Jets, 1960-72; St. Louis, 1973
85 Lance Alworth, San Diego, 1962-70; Dallas, 1971-72
Paul Warfield, Cleveland, 1964-69; 1976-77; Miami, 1970-74
Most Touchdowns, Season
17 Don Hutson, Green Bay, 1942
Elroy (Crazylegs) Hirsch, Los Angeles, 1951
Bill Groman, Houston, 1961
16 Art Powell, Oakland, 1963
15 Cloyce Box, Detroit, 1952
Sonny Randle, St. Louis, 1960
Most Touchdowns, Rookie, Season
13 Bill Howton, Green Bay, 1952
John Jefferson, San Diego, 1979
12 Harlon Hill, Chi. Bears, 1954
Bill Groman, Houston, 1960
Mike Ditka, Chicago, 1961
Bob Hayes, Dallas, 1965
10 Bill Swiacki, N.Y. Giants, 1948
Bucky Pope, Los Angeles, 1964
Sammy White, Minnesota, 1976
Most Touchdowns, Game
5 Bob Shaw, Chi. Cardinals vs. Baltimore, Oct. 2, 1950
Kellen Winslow, San Diego vs. Oakland, Nov. 22, 1981
4 By many players
Most Consecutive Games, Touchdowns
11 Elroy (Crazylegs) Hirsch, Los Angeles, 1950-51
Buddy Dial, Pittsburgh, 1959-60
9 Lance Alworth, San Diego, 1963
8 Bill Groman, Houston, 1961
Dave Parks, San Francisco, 1965

INTERCEPTIONS BY
Most Seasons Leading League
2 Dick (Night Train) Lane, Los Angeles, 1952; Chi. Cardinals, 1954
Jack Christiansen, Detroit, 1953, 1957
Milt Davis, Baltimore, 1957, 1959
Dick Lynch, N.Y. Giants, 1961, 1963
Johnny Robinson, Kansas City, 1966, 1970
Bill Bradley, Philadelphia, 1971-72
Emmitt Thomas, Kansas City, 1969, 1974

All-Time Records

Most Interceptions By, Career
81   Paul Krause, Washington, 1964-67; Minnesota, 1968-79
79   Emlen Tunnell, N.Y. Giants, 1948-58; Green Bay, 1959-61
68   Dick (Night Train) Lane, Los Angeles, 1952-53; Chi. Cardinals, 1954-59; Detroit, 1960-65

Most Interceptions By, Season
14   Dick (Night Train) Lane, Los Angeles, 1952
13   Dan Sandifer, Washington, 1948
      Orban (Spec) Sanders, N.Y. Yanks, 1950
      Lester Hayes, Oakland, 1980
12   By nine players

Most Interceptions By, Rookie, Season
14   Dick (Night Train) Lane, Los Angeles, 1952
13   Dan Sandifer, Washington, 1948
12   Woodley Lewis, Los Angeles, 1950
      Paul Krause, Washington, 1964

Most Interceptions By, Game
4   Sammy Baugh, Washington vs. Detroit, Nov. 14, 1943
   Dan Sandifer, Washington vs. Boston, Oct. 31, 1948
   Don Doll, Detroit vs. Chi. Cardinals, Oct. 23, 1949
   Bob Nussbaumer, Chi. Cardinals vs. N.Y. Bulldogs, Nov. 13, 1949
   Russ Craft, Philadelphia vs. Chi. Cardinals, Sept. 24, 1950
   Bobby Dillon, Green Bay vs. Detroit, Nov. 26, 1953
   Jack Butler, Pittsburgh vs. Washington, Dec. 13, 1953
   Austin (Goose) Gonsoulin, Denver vs. Buffalo, Sept. 18, 1960
   Jerry Norton, St. Louis vs. Washington, Nov. 20, 1960; vs. Pittsburgh, Nov. 26, 1961
   Dave Baker, San Francisco vs. L.A. Rams, Dec. 4, 1960
   Bobby Ply, Dall. Texans vs. San Diego, Dec. 16, 1962
   Bobby Hunt, Kansas City vs. Houston, Oct. 4, 1964
   Willie Brown, Denver vs. N.Y. Jets, Nov. 15, 1964
   Dick Anderson, Miami vs. Pittsburgh, Dec. 3, 1973
   Willie Buchanon, Green Bay vs. San Diego, Sept. 24, 1978

Most Consecutive Games, Passes Intercepted By
8   Tom Morrow, Oakland, 1962-63
7   Paul Krause, Washington, 1964
   Larry Wilson, St. Louis, 1966
   Ben Davis, Cleveland, 1968
6   Dick (Night Train) Lane, Chi. Cardinals, 1954-55
   Will Sherman, Los Angeles, 1954-55
   Jim Shofner, Cleveland, 1960
   Paul Krause, Minnesota, 1968
   Willie Williams, N.Y. Giants, 1968
   Kermit Alexander, San Francisco, 1968-69
   Eric Harris, Kansas City, 1980
   Lester Hayes, Oakland, 1980

YARDS GAINED

Most Seasons Leading League
2   Dick (Night Train) Lane, Los Angeles, 1952; Chi. Cardinals, 1954
   Herb Adderley, Green Bay, 1965, 1969
   Dick Anderson, Miami, 1968, 1970

Most Yards Gained, Career
1,282   Emlen Tunnell, N.Y. Giants, 1948-58; Green Bay, 1959-61
1,207   Dick (Night Train) Lane, Los Angeles, 1952-53; Chi. Cardinals, 1954-59; Detroit, 1960-65
1,185   Paul Krause, Washington, 1964-67; Minnesota, 1968-79

Most Yards Gained, Season
349   Charley McNeil, San Diego, 1961
301   Don Doll, Detroit, 1949
298   Dick (Night Train) Lane, Los Angeles, 1952

Most Yards Gained, Rookie, Season
301   Don Doll, Detroit, 1949

        298   Dick (Night Train) Lane, Los Angeles, 1952
        275   Woodley Lewis, Los Angeles, 1950
Most Yards Gained, Game
        177   Charley McNeil, San Diego vs. Houston, Sept. 24, 1961
        167   Dick Jauron, Detroit vs. Chicago, Nov. 18, 1973
        151   Tom Myers, New Orleans vs. Minnesota, Sept. 3, 1978
Longest Return (All TDs)
        102   Bob Smith, Detroit vs. Chi. Bears, Nov. 24, 1949
              Erich Barnes, N.Y. Giants vs. Dall. Cowboys, Oct. 22, 1961
              Gary Barbaro, Kansas City vs. Seattle, Dec. 11, 1977
              Louis Breeden, Cincinnati vs. San Diego, Nov. 8, 1981
        101   Richie Petitbon, Chicago vs Los Angeles, Dec. 9, 1962
              Henry Carr, N.Y. Giants vs. Los Angeles, Nov. 13, 1966
              Tony Greene, Buffalo vs. Kansas City, Oct. 3, 1976
              Tom Pridemore, Atlanta vs. San Francisco, Sept. 20, 1981
        100   Vern Huffman, Detroit vs. Brooklyn, Oct. 17, 1937
              Mike Gaechter, Dall. Cowboys vs. Philadelphia, Oct. 14, 1962
              Les (Speedy) Duncan, San Diego vs. Kansas City, Oct. 15, 1967
              Tom Janik, Buffalo vs. N.Y. Jets, Sept. 29, 1968
              Tim Collier, Kansas City vs. Oakland, Dec. 18, 1977

TOUCHDOWNS
Most Touchdowns, Career
        9   Ken Houston, Houston, 1967-72; Washington, 1973-80
        7   Herb Adderley, Green Bay, 1961-69; Dallas, 1970-72
            Erich Barnes, Chi. Bears, 1958-60; N.Y. Giants, 1961-64; Cleveland, 1965-70
            Lem Barney, Detroit, 1967-77
        6   Tom Janik, Denver, 1963-64; Buffalo, 1965-68; Boston, 1969-70;
                 New England, 1971
            Miller Farr, Denver, 1965; San Diego, 1965-66; Houston, 1967-69;
                 St. Louis, 1970-72; Detroit, 1973
            Bobby Bell, Kansas City, 1963-74
Most Touchdowns, Season
        4   Ken Houston, Houston, 1971
            Jim Kearney, Kansas City, 1972
        3   Dick Harris, San Diego, 1961
            Dick Lynch, N.Y. Giants, 1963
            Herb Adderley, Green Bay, 1965
            Lem Barney, Detroit, 1967
            Miller Farr, Houston, 1967
            Monte Jackson, Los Angeles, 1976
            Rod Perry, Los Angeles, 1978
            Ronnie Lott, San Francisco, 1981
        2   By many players
Most Touchdowns, Rookie, Season
        3   Lem Barney, Detroit, 1967
            Ronnie Lott, San Francisco, 1981
        2   By many players
Most Touchdowns, Game
        2   Bill Blackburn, Chi. Cardinals vs. Boston, Oct. 24, 1948
            Dan Sandifer, Washington vs. Boston, Oct. 31, 1948
            Bob Franklin, Cleveland vs. Chicago, Dec. 11, 1960
            Bill Stacy, St. Louis vs. Dall. Cowboys, Nov. 5, 1961
            Jerry Norton, St. Louis vs. Pittsburgh, Nov. 26, 1961
            Miller Farr, Houston vs. Buffalo, Dec. 7, 1968
            Ken Houston, Houston vs. San Diego, Dec. 19, 1971
            Jim Kearney, Kansas City vs. Denver, Oct. 1, 1972
            Lemar Parrish, Cincinnati vs. Houston, Dec. 17, 1972
            Dick Anderson, Miami vs. Pittsburgh, Dec. 3, 1973
            Prentice McCray, New England vs. N.Y. Jets, Nov. 21, 1976

PUNTING

Most Seasons Leading League
4	Sammy Baugh, Washington, 1940-43
	Jerrel Wilson, Kansas City, 1965, 1968, 1972-73
3	Yale Lary, Detroit, 1959, 1961, 1963
	Jim Fraser, Denver, 1962-64
	Ray Guy, Oakland, 1974-75, 1977
2	By many players

Most Consecutive Seasons Leading League
4	Sammy Baugh, Washington, 1940-43
3	Jim Fraser, Denver, 1962-64
2	By many players

PUNTS
Most Punts, Career
1,072	Jerrel Wilson, Kansas City, 1963-77; New England, 1978
978	Mike Bragg, Washington, 1968-79; Baltimore, 1980
974	Bobby Walden, Minnesota, 1964-67; Pittsburgh, 1968-76

Most Punts, Season
114	Bob Parsons, Chicago, 1981
109	John James, Atlanta, 1978
106	David Beverly, Green Bay, 1978

Most Punts, Rookie, Season
96	Mike Connell, San Francisco, 1978
93	Wilbur Summers, Detroit, 1977
	Ken Clark, Los Angeles, 1979
90	Bucky Dilts, Denver, 1977

Most Punts, Game
14	Dick Nesbitt, Chi. Cardinals vs. Chi. Bears, Nov. 30, 1933
	Keith Molesworth, Chi. Bears vs. Green Bay, Dec. 10, 1933
	Sammy Baugh, Washington vs. Philadelphia, Nov. 5, 1939
	Carl Kinscherf, N.Y. Giants vs. Detroit, Nov. 7, 1943
	George Taliaferro, N.Y. Yanks vs. Los Angeles, Sept. 28, 1951
12	Parker Hall, Cleveland vs. Green Bay, Nov. 26, 1939
	Beryl Clark, Chi. Cardinals vs. Detroit, Sept. 15, 1940
	Len Barnum, Philadelphia vs. Washington, Oct. 4, 1942
	Horace Gillom, Cleveland vs. Philadelphia, Dec. 3, 1950
	Adrian Burk, Philadelphia vs. Green Bay, Nov. 2, 1952; vs. N.Y. Giants, Dec. 12, 1954
	Bob Scarpitto, Denver vs. Oakland, Sept. 10, 1967
	Bill Van Heusen, Denver vs. Cincinnati, Oct. 6, 1968
	Tom Blanchard, New Orleans vs. Minnesota, Nov. 16, 1975
	Rusty Jackson, Los Angeles vs. San Francisco, Nov. 21, 1976
	Wilbur Summers, Detroit vs. San Francisco, Oct. 23, 1977
	John James, Atlanta vs. Washington, Dec. 10, 1978
	Luke Prestridge, Denver vs. Buffalo, Oct. 25, 1981
11	By many players

Longest Punt
98	Steve O'Neal, N.Y. Jets vs. Denver, Sept. 21, 1969
94	Joe Lintzenich, Chi. Bears vs. N.Y. Giants, Nov. 16, 1931
90	Don Chandler, Green Bay vs. San Francisco, Oct. 10, 1965

AVERAGE YARDAGE
Highest Average, Punting, Career (300 punts)
45.10	Sammy Baugh, Washington, 1937-52
44.68	Tommy Davis, San Francisco, 1959-69
44.29	Yale Lary, Detroit, 1952-53, 1956-64

Highest Average, Punting, Season (Qualifiers)
51.40	Sammy Baugh, Washington, 1940
48.94	Yale Lary, Detroit, 1963
48.73	Sammy Baugh, Washington, 1941

Highest Average, Punting, Rookie, Season (Qualifiers)
    46.40   Bobby Walden, Minnesota, 1964
    46.22   Dave Lewis, Cincinnati, 1970
    45.92   Frank Sinkwich, Detroit, 1943
Highest Average, Punting, Game (4 punts)
    61.75   Bob Cifers, Detroit vs. Chi. Bears, Nov. 24, 1946
    61.60   Roy McKay, Green Bay vs. Chi. Cardinals, Oct. 28, 1945
    59.40   Sammy Baugh, Washington vs. Detroit, Oct. 27, 1940

PUNT RETURNS

Most Seasons Leading League
    3   Les (Speedy) Duncan, San Diego, 1965-66; Washington, 1971
    2   Dick Christy, N.Y. Titans, 1961-62
        Claude Gibson, Oakland, 1963-64
        Billy Johnson, Houston, 1975, 1977
        Rick Upchurch, Denver, 1976, 1978

PUNT RETURNS
Most Punt Returns, Career
    258   Emlen Tunnell, N.Y. Giants, 1948-58; Green Bay, 1959-61
    253   Alvin Haymond, Baltimore, 1964-67; Philadelphia, 1968; Los Angeles, 1969-71; Washington, 1972; Houston, 1973
    235   Ron Smith, Chicago, 1965, 1970-72; Atlanta, 1966-67; Los Angeles, 1968-69; San Diego, 1973; Oakland, 1974
          Mike Fuller, San Diego, 1975-80; Cincinnati, 1981
Most Punt Returns, Season
    70   Danny Reece, Tampa Bay, 1979
    58   J. T. Smith, Kansas City, 1979
    57   Eddie Brown, Washington, 1977
         Danny Reece, Tampa Bay, 1980
Most Punt Returns, Rookie, Season
    54   James Jones, Dallas, 1980
    52   Leon Bright, N.Y. Giants, 1981
         Robbie Martin, Detroit, 1981
    48   Neal Colzie, Oakland, 1975
         Kevin Miller, Minnesota, 1978
         Mike Nelms, Washington, 1980
Most Punt Returns, Game
    11   Eddie Brown, Washington vs. Tampa Bay, Oct. 9, 1977
    10   Theo Bell, Pittsburgh vs. Buffalo, Dec. 16, 1979
    9   Rodger Bird, Oakland vs. Denver, Sept. 10, 1967
        Ralph McGill, San Francisco vs. Atlanta, Oct. 29, 1972
        Ed Podolak, Kansas City vs. San Diego, Nov. 10, 1974
        Anthony Leonard, San Francisco vs. New Orleans, Oct. 17, 1976
        Butch Johnson, Dallas vs. Buffalo, Nov. 15, 1976
        Larry Marshall, Philadelphia vs. Tampa Bay, Sept. 18, 1977
        Nesby Glasgow, Baltimore vs. Kansas City, Sept. 2, 1979
        Mike Nelms, Washington vs. St. Louis, Dec. 21, 1980

FAIR CATCHES
Most Fair Catches, Season
    24   Ken Graham, San Diego, 1969
    22   Lem Barney, Detroit, 1976
    21   Ed Podolak, Kansas City, 1970
         Steve Schubert, Chicago, 1978
         Stanley Morgan, New England, 1979
Most Fair Catches, Game
    7   Lem Barney, Detroit vs. Chicago, Nov. 21, 1976
    6   Jake Scott, Miami vs. Buffalo, Dec. 20, 1970
    5   By many players

YARDS GAINED
Most Seasons Leading League
3	Alvin Haymond, Baltimore, 1965-66; Los Angeles, 1969
2	Bill Dudley, Pittsburgh, 1942, 1946
	Emlen Tunnell, N.Y. Giants, 1951-52
	Dick Christy, N.Y. Titans, 1961-62
	Claude Gibson, Oakland, 1963-64
	Rodger Bird, Oakland, 1966-67
	J. T. Smith, Kansas City, 1979-80

Most Yards Gained, Career
2,714	Rick Upchurch, Denver, 1975-81
2,565	Mike Fuller, San Diego, 1975-80; Cincinnati, 1981
2,209	Emlen Tunnell, N.Y. Giants, 1948-58; Green Bay, 1959-61

Most Yards Gained, Season
655	Neal Colzie, Oakland, 1975
653	Rick Upchurch, Denver, 1977
646	Eddie Brown, Washington, 1976

Most Yards Gained, Rookie, Season
655	Neal Colzie, Oakland, 1975
608	Mike Haynes, New England, 1976
577	Lynn Swann, Pittsburgh, 1974

Most Yards Gained, Game
207	Leroy Irvin, Los Angeles vs. Atlanta, Oct. 11, 1981
205	George Atkinson, Oakland vs. Buffalo, Sept. 15, 1968
184	Tom Watkins, Detroit vs. San Francisco, Oct. 6, 1963

Longest Punt Return (All TDs)
98	Gil LeFebvre, Cincinnati vs. Brooklyn, Dec. 3, 1933
	Charlie West, Minnesota vs. Washington, Nov. 3, 1968
	Dennis Morgan, Dallas vs. St. Louis, Oct. 13, 1974
96	Bill Dudley, Washington vs. Pittsburgh, Dec. 3, 1950
95	Frank Bernardi, Chi. Cardinals vs. Washington, Oct. 14, 1956
	Les (Speedy) Duncan, San Diego vs. N.Y. Jets, Nov. 24, 1968
	Steve Odom, Green Bay vs. Chicago, Nov. 10, 1974

AVERAGE YARDAGE
Highest Average, Career (75 returns)
13.16	Billy Johnson, Houston, 1974-80
12.78	George McAfee, Chi. Bears, 1940-41, 1945-50
12.75	Jack Christiansen, Detroit, 1951-58

Highest Average, Season (Qualifiers)
23.00	Herb Rich, Baltimore, 1950
21.47	Jack Christiansen, Detroit, 1952
21.28	Dick Christy, N.Y. Titans, 1961

Highest Average, Rookie, Season (Qualifiers)
23.00	Herb Rich, Baltimore, 1950
20.88	Jerry Davis, Chi. Cardinals, 1948
20.73	Frank Sinkwich, Detroit, 1943

Highest Average, Game (3 returns)
47.67	Chuck Latourette, St. Louis vs. New Orleans, Sept. 29, 1968
47.33	Johnny Roland, St. Louis vs. Philadelphia, Oct. 2, 1966
45.67	Dick Christy, N.Y. Titans vs. Denver, Sept. 24, 1961

TOUCHDOWNS
Most Touchdowns, Career
8	Jack Christiansen, Detroit, 1951-58
6	Rick Upchurch, Denver, 1975-81
5	Emlen Tunnell, N.Y. Giants, 1948-58; Green Bay, 1959-61
	Billy Johnson, Houston, 1974-80

Most Touchdowns, Season
4	Jack Christiansen, Detroit, 1951
	Rick Upchurch, Denver, 1976
3	Emlen Tunnell, N.Y. Giants, 1951
	Billy Johnson, Houston, 1975

Leroy Irvin, Los Angeles, 1981
2 By many players
Most Touchdowns, Rookie, Season
4 Jack Christiansen, Detroit, 1951
2 By five players
Most Touchdowns, Game
2 Jack Christiansen, Detroit vs. Los Angeles, Oct. 14, 1951; vs. Green Bay,
Nov. 22, 1951
Dick Christy, N.Y. Titans vs. Denver, Sept. 24, 1961
Rick Upchurch, Denver vs. Cleveland, Sept. 26, 1976
Leroy Irvin, Los Angeles vs. Atlanta, Oct. 11, 1981

KICKOFF RETURNS

Most Seasons Leading League
3 Abe Woodson, San Francisco, 1959, 1962-63
2 Lynn Chandnois, Pittsburgh, 1951-52
Bobby Jancik, Houston, 1962-63
Travis Williams, Green Bay, 1967; Los Angeles, 1971

KICKOFF RETURNS
Most Kickoff Returns, Career
275 Ron Smith, Chicago, 1965, 1970-72; Atlanta, 1966-67; Los Angeles, 1968-69;
San Diego, 1973; Oakland, 1974
224 Bruce Harper, N.Y. Jets, 1977-81
193 Abe Woodson, San Francisco, 1958-64; St. Louis, 1965-66
Most Kickoff Returns, Season
60 Drew Hill, Los Angeles, 1981
55 Bruce Harper, N.Y. Jets, 1978, 1979
David Turner, Cincinnati, 1979
Stump Mitchell, St. Louis, 1981
53 Eddie Payton, Minnesota, 1980
Most Kickoff Returns, Rookie, Season
55 Stump Mitchell, St. Louis, 1981
50 Nesby Glasgow, Baltimore, 1979
Dino Hall, Cleveland, 1979
47 Odell Barry, Denver, 1964
Most Kickoff Returns, Game
9 Noland Smith, Kansas City vs. Oakland, Nov. 23, 1967
Dino Hall, Cleveland vs. Pittsburgh, Oct. 7, 1979
8 George Taliaferro, N.Y. Yanks vs. N.Y. Giants, Dec. 3, 1950
Bobby Jancik, Houston vs. Boston, Dec. 8, 1963; vs. Oakland, Dec. 22, 1963
Mel Renfro, Dallas vs. Green Bay, Nov. 29, 1964
Willie Porter, Boston vs. N.Y. Jets, Sept. 22, 1968
Keith Moody, Buffalo vs. Seattle, Oct. 30, 1977
Brian Baschnagel, Chicago vs. Houston, Nov. 6, 1977
Bruce Harper, N.Y. Jets vs. New England, Oct. 29, 1978; vs. New England,
Sept. 9, 1979
Terry Metcalf, Washington vs. St. Louis, Sept. 20, 1981
7 By many players

YARDS GAINED
Most Seasons Leading League
3 Bruce Harper, N.Y. Jets, 1977-79
2 Marshall Goldberg, Chi. Cardinals, 1941-42
Woodley Lewis, Los Angeles, 1953-54
Al Carmichael, Green Bay, 1956-57
Timmy Brown, Philadelphia, 1961, 1963
Bobby Jancik, Houston, 1963, 1966
Ron Smith, Atlanta, 1966-67
Most Yards Gained, Career
6,922 Ron Smith, Chicago, 1965, 1970-72; Atlanta, 1966-67; Los Angeles, 1968-69;
San Diego, 1973; Oakland, 1974
5,538 Abe Woodson, San Francisco, 1958-64; St. Louis, 1965-66

All-Time Records

5,023   Bruce Harper, N.Y. Jets, 1977-81

Most Yards Gained, Season

1,317   Bobby Jancik, Houston, 1963
1,314   Dave Hampton, Green Bay, 1971
1,292   Stump Mitchell, St. Louis, 1981

Most Yards Gained, Rookie, Season

1,292   Stump Mitchell, St. Louis, 1981
1,245   Odell Barry, Denver, 1964
1,148   Noland Smith, Kansas City, 1967

Most Yards Gained, Game

294   Wally Triplett, Detroit vs. Los Angeles, Oct. 29, 1950
247   Timmy Brown, Philadelphia vs. Dallas, Nov. 6, 1966
244   Noland Smith, Kansas City vs. San Diego, Oct. 15, 1967

Longest Kickoff Return (All TDs)

106   Al Carmichael, Green Bay vs. Chi. Bears, Oct. 7, 1956
        Noland Smith, Kansas City vs. Denver, Dec. 17, 1967
        Roy Green, St. Louis vs. Dallas, Oct. 21, 1979
105   Frank Seno, Chi. Cardinals vs. N.Y. Giants, Oct. 20, 1946
        Ollie Matson, Chi. Cardinals vs. Washington, Oct. 14, 1956
        Abe Woodson, San Francisco vs. Los Angeles, Nov. 8, 1959
        Timmy Brown, Philadelphia vs. Cleveland, Sept. 17, 1961
        Jon Arnett, Los Angeles vs. Detroit, Oct. 29, 1961
        Eugene (Mercury) Morris, Miami vs. Cincinnati, Sept. 14, 1969
        Travis Williams, Los Angeles vs. New Orleans, Dec. 5, 1971
104   By many players

AVERAGE YARDAGE

Highest Average, Career (75 returns)

30.56   Gale Sayers, Chicago, 1965-71
29.57   Lynn Chandnois, Pittsburgh, 1950-56
28.69   Abe Woodson, San Francisco, 1958-64; St. Louis, 1965-66

Highest Average, Season (Qualifiers)

41.06   Travis Williams, Green Bay, 1967
37.69   Gale Sayers, Chicago, 1967
35.50   Ollie Matson, Chi. Cardinals, 1958

Highest Average, Rookie, Season (Qualifiers)

41.06   Travis Williams, Green Bay, 1967
33.08   Tom Moore, Green Bay, 1960
32.88   Duriel Harris, Miami, 1976

Highest Average, Game (3 returns)

73.50   Wally Triplett, Detroit vs. Los Angeles, Oct. 29, 1950
67.33   Lenny Lyles, San Francisco vs. Baltimore, Dec. 18, 1960
65.33   Ken Hall, Houston vs. N.Y. Titans, Oct. 23, 1960

TOUCHDOWNS

Most Touchdowns, Career

6   Ollie Matson, Chi. Cardinals, 1952, 1954-58; L.A. Rams, 1959-62; Detroit, 1963; Philadelphia, 1964
      Gale Sayers, Chicago, 1965-71
      Travis Williams, Green Bay, 1967-70; Los Angeles, 1971
5   Bobby Mitchell, Cleveland, 1958-61; Washington, 1962-68
      Abe Woodson, San Francisco, 1958-64; St. Louis, 1965-66
      Timmy Brown, Green Bay, 1959; Philadelphia, 1960-67; Baltimore, 1968
4   Cecil Turner, Chicago, 1968-73

Most Touchdowns, Season

4   Travis Williams, Green Bay, 1967
      Cecil Turner, Chicago, 1970
3   Verda (Vitamin T) Smith, Los Angeles, 1950
      Abe Woodson, San Francisco, 1963
      Gale Sayers, Chicago, 1967
      Raymond Clayborn, New England, 1977
2   By many players

Most Touchdowns, Rookie, Season
- 4 Travis Williams, Green Bay, 1967
- 3 Raymond Clayborn, New England, 1977
- 2 By six players

Most Touchdowns, Game
- 2 Timmy Brown, Philadelphia vs. Dallas, Nov. 6, 1966
  Travis Williams, Green Bay vs. Cleveland, Nov. 12, 1967

COMBINED KICK RETURNS

Most Combined Kick Returns, Career
- 510 Ron Smith, Chicago, 1965, 1970-72; Atlanta, 1966-67; Los Angeles, 1968-69; San Diego, 1973; Oakland, 1974 (p-235, k-275)
- 423 Alvin Haymond, Baltimore, 1964-67; Philadelphia, 1968; Los Angeles, 1969-71; Washington, 1972; Houston, 1973 (p-253, k-170)
- 384 Bruce Harper, N.Y. Jets, 1977-81 (p-160, k-224)

Most Combined Kick Returns, Season
- 100 Larry Jones, Washington, 1975 (p-53, k-47)
- 97 Stump Mitchell, St. Louis, 1981 (p-42, k-55)
- 94 Nesby Glasgow, Baltimore, 1979 (k-50, p-44)

Most Combined Kick Returns, Game
- 13 Stump Mitchell, St. Louis vs. Atlanta, Oct. 18, 1981 (p-6, k-7)
- 12 Mel Renfro, Dallas vs. Green Bay, Nov. 29, 1964 (p-4, k-8)
  Larry Jones, Washington vs. Dallas, Dec. 13, 1975 (p-6, k-6)
  Eddie Brown, Washington vs. Tampa Bay, Oct. 9, 1977 (p-11, k-1)
  Nesby Glasgow, Baltimore vs. Denver, Sept. 2, 1979 (p-9, k-3)
- 11 Noland Smith, Kansas City vs. Oakland, Nov. 23, 1967 (p-2, k-9)
  Larry Jones, Washington vs. Oakland, Nov. 23, 1975 (p-6, k-5)
  Rolland Lawrence, Atlanta vs. New Orleans, Oct. 10, 1976 (p-6, k-5)
  Butch Johnson, Dallas vs. Buffalo, Nov. 15, 1976 (p-9, k-2)
  Larry Marshall, Philadelphia vs. Tampa Bay, Sept. 18, 1977 (p-9, k-2)
  Dino Hall, Cleveland vs. Pittsburgh, Oct. 7, 1979 (k-9, p-2)

YARDS GAINED

Most Yards Returned, Career
- 8,710 Ron Smith, Chicago, 1965, 1970-72; Atlanta, 1966-67; Los Angeles, 1968-69; San Diego, 1973; Oakland, 1974 (p-1,788, k-6,922)
- 6,740 Les (Speedy) Duncan, San Diego, 1964-70; Washington, 1971-74 (p-2,201, k-4,539)
- 6,623 Bruce Harper, N.Y. Jets, 1977-81 (p-1,600, k-5,023)

Most Yards Returned, Season
- 1,737 Stump Mitchell, St. Louis, 1981 (p-445, k-1,292)
- 1,658 Bruce Harper, N.Y. Jets, 1978 (p-378, k-1,280)
- 1,591 Mike Nelms, Washington, 1981 (p-492, k-1,099)

Most Yards Returned, Game
- 294 Wally Triplett, Detroit vs. Los Angeles, Oct. 29, 1950 (k-294)
  Woodley Lewis, Los Angeles vs. Detroit, Oct. 18, 1953 (p-120, k-174)
- 289 Eddie Payton, Detroit vs. Minnesota, Dec. 17, 1977 (p-105, k-184)
- 282 Les (Speedy) Duncan, San Diego vs. N.Y. Jets, Nov. 24, 1968 (p-102, k-180)

TOUCHDOWNS

Most Touchdowns, Career
- 9 Ollie Matson, Chi. Cardinals, 1952, 1954-58; Los Angeles, 1959-62; Detroit, 1963; Philadelphia, 1964-66 (p-3, k-6)
- 8 Jack Christiansen, Detroit, 1951-58 (p-8)
  Bobby Mitchell, Cleveland, 1958-61; Washington, 1962-68 (p-3, k-5)
  Gale Sayers, Chicago, 1965-71 (p-2, k-6)
- 7 Abe Woodson, San Francisco, 1958-64; St. Louis, 1965-66 (p-2, k-5)
  Billy Johnson, Houston, 1974-80 (p-5, k-2)

Most Touchdowns, Season
- 4 Jack Christiansen, Detroit, 1951 (p-4)
  Emlen Tunnell, N.Y. Giants, 1951 (p-3, k-1)
  Gale Sayers, Chicago, 1967 (p-1, k-3)
  Travis Williams, Green Bay, 1967 (k-4)

       Cecil Turner, Chicago, 1970 (k-4)
       Billy Johnson, Houston, 1975 (p-3, k-1)
       Rick Upchurch, Denver, 1976 (p-4)
  3 Verda (Vitamin T) Smith, Los Angeles, 1950 (k-3)
       Abe Woodson, San Francisco, 1963 (k-3)
       Raymond Clayborn, New England, 1977 (k-3)
       Billy Johnson, Houston, 1977 (p-2, k-1)
       Leroy Irvin, Los Angeles, 1981 (p-3)
  2 By many players

Most Touchdowns, Game

  2 Jack Christiansen, Detroit vs. Los Angeles, Oct. 14, 1951 (p-2); vs. Green Bay, Nov. 22, 1951 (p-2)
       Jim Patton, N.Y. Giants vs. Washington, Oct. 30, 1955 (p-1, k-1)
       Bobby Mitchell, Cleveland vs. Philadelphia, Nov. 23, 1958 (p-1, k-1)
       Dick Christy, N.Y. Titans vs. Denver, Sept. 24, 1961 (p-2)
       Al Frazier, Denver vs. Boston, Dec. 3, 1961 (p-1, k-1)
       Timmy Brown, Philadelphia vs. Dallas, Nov. 6, 1966 (k-2)
       Travis Williams, Green Bay vs. Cleveland, Nov. 12, 1967 (k-2); vs. Pittsburgh, Nov. 2, 1969 (p-1, k-1)
       Gale Sayers, Chicago vs. San Francisco, Dec. 3, 1967 (p-1, k-1)
       Rick Upchurch, Denver vs. Cleveland, Sept. 26, 1976 (p-2)
       Eddie Payton, Detroit vs. Minnesota, Dec. 17, 1977 (p-1, k-1)
       Leroy Irvin, Los Angeles vs. Atlanta, Oct. 11, 1981 (p-2)

FUMBLES

Most Fumbles, Career

 105 Roman Gabriel, Los Angeles, 1962-72; Philadelphia, 1973-77
  95 Johnny Unitas, Baltimore, 1956-72; San Diego, 1973
  84 Len Dawson, Pittsburgh, 1957-59; Cleveland, 1960-61; Dall. Texans, 1962; Kansas City, 1963-75
       Fran Tarkenton, Minnesota, 1961-66, 1972-78; N.Y. Giants, 1967-71

Most Fumbles, Season

  17 Dan Pastorini, Houston, 1973
  16 Don Meredith, Dallas, 1964
       Joe Cribbs, Buffalo, 1980
       Steve Fuller, Kansas City, 1980
  15 Paul Christman, Chi. Cardinals, 1946
       Sammy Baugh, Washington, 1947
       Sam Etcheverry, St. Louis, 1961
       Len Dawson, Kansas City, 1964
       Terry Metcalf, St. Louis, 1976

Most Fumbles, Game

  7 Len Dawson, Kansas City vs. San Diego, Nov. 15, 1964
  6 Sam Etcheverry, St. Louis vs. N.Y. Giants, Sept. 17, 1961
  5 Paul Christman, Chi. Cardinals vs. Green Bay, Nov. 10, 1946
       Charlie Conerly, N.Y. Giants vs San Francisco, Dec. 1, 1957
       Jack Kemp, Buffalo vs. Houston, Oct. 29, 1967
       Roman Gabriel, Philadelphia vs. Oakland, Nov. 21, 1976

FUMBLES RECOVERED

Most Fumbles Recovered, Career, Own and Opponents'

  43 Fran Tarkenton, Minnesota, 1961-66, 1972-78; N.Y. Giants, 1967-71 (43 own)
  38 Jack Kemp, Pittsburgh, 1957; L.A. Chargers, 1960; San Diego, 1961-62; Buffalo, 1962-67, 1969 (38 own)
  37 Roman Gabriel, Los Angeles, 1962-72; Philadelphia, 1973-77 (37 own)

Most Fumbles Recovered, Season, Own and Opponents'

  9 Don Hultz, Minnesota, 1963 (9 opp)
  8 Paul Christman, Chi. Cardinals, 1945 (8 own)
       Joe Schmidt, Detroit, 1955 (8 own)
       Bill Butler, Minnesota, 1963 (8 own)
       Kermit Alexander, San Francisco, 1965 (4 own, 4 opp)
       Jack Lambert, Pittsburgh, 1976 (1 own, 7 opp)
       Danny White, Dallas, 1981 (8 own)

      7 By many players

Most Fumbles Recovered, Game, Own and Opponents'
- 4 Otto Graham, Cleveland vs. N.Y. Giants, Oct. 25, 1953 (4 own)
-    Sam Etcheverry, St. Louis vs. N.Y. Giants, Sept. 17, 1961 (4 own)
-    Roman Gabriel, Los Angeles vs. San Francisco, Oct. 12, 1969 (4 own)
-    Joe Ferguson, Buffalo vs. Miami, Sept. 18, 1977 (4 own)
- 3 By many players

OWN FUMBLES RECOVERED
Most Own Fumbles Recovered, Career
- 43 Fran Tarkenton, Minnesota, 1961-66, 1972-78; N.Y. Giants, 1967-71
- 38 Jack Kemp, Pittsburgh, 1957; L.A. Chargers, 1960; San Diego, 1961-62; Buffalo, 1962-67, 1969
- 37 Roman Gabriel, Los Angeles, 1962-72; Philadelphia, 1973-77

Most Own Fumbles Recovered, Season
- 8 Paul Christman, Chi. Cardinals, 1945
-    Bill Butler, Minnesota, 1963
-    Danny White, Dallas, 1981
- 7 Sammy Baugh, Washington, 1947
-    Tommy Thompson, Philadelphia, 1947
-    John Roach, St. Louis, 1960
-    Jack Larscheid, Oakland, 1960
-    Gary Huff, Chicago, 1974
-    Terry Metcalf, St. Louis, 1974
-    Joe Ferguson, Buffalo, 1977
-    Fran Tarkenton, Minnesota, 1978
- 6 By many players

Most Own Fumbles Recovered, Game
- 4 Otto Graham, Cleveland vs. N.Y. Giants, Oct. 25, 1953
-    Sam Etcheverry, St. Louis vs. N.Y. Giants, Sept. 17, 1961
-    Roman Gabriel, Los Angeles vs. San Francisco, Oct. 12, 1969
-    Joe Ferguson, Buffalo vs. Miami, Sept. 18, 1977
- 3 By many players

OPPONENTS' FUMBLES RECOVERED
Most Opponents' Fumbles Recovered, Career
- 29 Jim Marshall, Cleveland, 1960; Minnesota, 1961-79
- 25 Dick Butkus, Chicago, 1965-73
- 23 Carl Eller, Minnesota, 1964-78; Seattle, 1979

Most Opponents' Fumbles Recovered, Season
- 9 Don Hultz, Minnesota, 1963
- 8 Joe Schmidt, Detroit, 1955
- 7 Alan Page, Minnesota, 1970
-    Jack Lambert, Pittsburgh, 1976

Most Opponents' Fumbles Recovered, Game
- 3 Corwin Clatt, Chi. Cardinals vs. Detroit, Nov. 6, 1949
-    Vic Sears, Philadelphia vs. Green Bay, Nov. 2, 1952
-    Ed Beatty, San Francisco vs. Los Angeles, Oct. 7, 1956
-    Ron Carroll, Houston vs. Cincinnati, Oct. 27, 1974
-    Maurice Spencer, New Orleans vs. Atlanta, Oct. 10, 1976
-    Steve Nelson, New England vs. Philadelphia, Oct. 8, 1978
-    Charles Jackson, Kansas City vs. Pittsburgh, Sept. 6, 1981
-    Willie Buchanon, San Diego vs. Denver, Sept. 27, 1981
- 2 By many players

YARDS RETURNING FUMBLES
Longest Fumble Run (All TDs)
- 104 Jack Tatum, Oakland vs. Green Bay, Sept. 24, 1972 (opp)
- 98 George Halas, Chi. Bears vs. Oorang Indians, Marion, Ohio, Nov. 4, 1923 (opp)
- 97 Chuck Howley, Dallas vs. Atlanta, Oct. 2, 1966 (opp)

TOUCHDOWNS
Most Touchdowns, Career (Total)
- 4   Bill Thompson, Denver, 1969-81
- 3   Ralph Heywood, Detroit, 1947-48; Boston, 1948; N.Y. Bulldogs, 1949
      Leo Sugar, Chi. Cardinals, 1954-59; St. Louis, 1960; Philadelphia, 1961; Detroit, 1962
      Bud McFadin, Los Angeles, 1952-56; Denver, 1960-63; Houston, 1964-65
      Doug Cline, Houston, 1960-66; San Diego, 1966
      Bob Lilly, Dall. Cowboys, 1961-74
      Chris Hanburger, Washington, 1965-78
      Lemar Parrish, Cincinnati, 1970-77; Washington, 1978-81
      Paul Krause, Washington, 1964-67; Minnesota, 1968-79
      Brad Dusek, Washington, 1974-81
- 2   By many players

Most Touchdowns, Season (Total)
- 2   Harold McPhail, Boston, 1934
      Harry Ebding, Detroit, 1937
      John Morelli, Boston, 1944
      Frank Maznicki, Boston, 1947
      Fred (Dippy) Evans, Chi. Bears, 1948
      Ralph Heywood, Boston, 1948
      Art Tait, N.Y. Yanks, 1951
      John Dwyer, Los Angeles, 1952
      Leo Sugar, Chi. Cardinals, 1957
      Doug Cline, Houston, 1961
      Jim Bradshaw, Pittsburgh, 1964
      Royce Berry, Cincinnati, 1970
      Ahmad Rashad, Buffalo, 1974
      Tim Gray, Kansas City, 1977
      Charles Phillips, Oakland, 1978
      Kenny Johnson, Atlanta, 1981
      George Martin, N.Y. Giants, 1981

Most Touchdowns, Career (Own recovered)
- 2   Ken Kavanaugh, Chi. Bears, 1940-41, 1945-50
      Mike Ditka, Chicago, 1961-66; Philadelphia, 1967-68; Dallas, 1969-72
      Gail Cogdill, Detroit, 1960-68; Baltimore, 1968; Atlanta, 1969-70
      Ahmad Rashad, St. Louis, 1972-73; Buffalo, 1974; Minnesota, 1976-81
      Jim Mitchell, Atlanta, 1969-79
      Drew Pearson, Dallas, 1973-81

Most Touchdowns, Season (Own recovered)
- 2   Ahmad Rashad, Buffalo, 1974
- 1   By many players

Most Touchdowns, Career (Opponents' recovered)
- 3   Leo Sugar, Chi. Cardinals, 1954-59; St. Louis, 1960; Philadelphia, 1961; Detroit, 1962
      Doug Cline, Houston, 1960-66; San Diego, 1966
      Bud McFadin, Los Angeles, 1952-56; Denver, 1960-63; Houston, 1964-65
      Bob Lilly, Dall. Cowboys, 1961-74
      Chris Hanburger, Washington, 1965-78
      Paul Krause, Washington, 1964-67; Minnesota, 1968-79
      Lemar Parrish, Cincinnati, 1970-77; Washington, 1978-81
      Bill Thompson, Denver, 1969-81
      Brad Dusek, Washington, 1974-81
- 2   By many players

Most Touchdowns, Season (Opponents' recovered)
- 2   Harold McPhail, Boston, 1934
      Harry Ebding, Detroit, 1937
      John Morelli, Boston, 1944
      Frank Maznicki, Boston, 1947
      Fred Evans, Chi. Bears, 1948
      Ralph Heywood, Boston, 1948
      Art Tait, N.Y. Yanks, 1951
      John Dwyer, Los Angeles, 1952

Leo Sugar, Chi. Cardinals, 1957
Doug Cline, Houston, 1961
Jim Bradshaw, Pittsburgh, 1964
Royce Berry, Cincinnati, 1970
Tim Gray, Kansas City, 1977
Charles Phillips, Oakland, 1978
Kenny Johnson, Atlanta, 1981
George Martin, N.Y. Giants, 1981

Most Touchdowns, Game (Opponents' recovered)
2   Fred (Dippy) Evans, Chi. Bears vs. Washington, Nov. 28, 1948

COMBINED NET YARDS GAINED

Rushing, receiving, interception returns, punt returns, kickoff returns, and fumble returns

Most Seasons Leading League
5   Jim Brown, Cleveland, 1958-61, 1964
3   Cliff Battles, Boston, 1932-33; Washington, 1937
    Gale Sayers, Chicago, 1965-67
2   By many players

Most Consecutive Seasons Leading League
4   Jim Brown, Cleveland, 1958-61
3   Gale Sayers, Chicago, 1965-67
2   Cliff Battles, Boston, 1932-33
    Charley Trippi, Chi. Cardinals, 1948-49
    Timmy Brown, Philadelphia, 1962-63
    Floyd Little, Denver, 1967-68

ATTEMPTS

Most Attempts, Career
2,728   Franco Harris, Pittsburgh, 1972-81
2,658   Jim Brown, Cleveland, 1957-65
2,648   O.J. Simpson, Buffalo, 1969-77; San Francisco, 1978-79

Most Attempts, Season
402   Walter Payton, Chicago, 1979
399   Earl Campbell, Houston, 1981
395   George Rogers, New Orleans, 1981

Most Attempts, Rookie, Season
395   George Rogers, New Orleans, 1981
390   Joe Cribbs, Buffalo, 1980
373   Ottis Anderson, St. Louis, 1979

Most Attempts, Game
43   Lydell Mitchell, Baltimore vs. N.Y. Jets, Oct. 20, 1974
42   Walter Payton, Chicago vs. Minnesota, Nov. 20, 1977
    Earl Campbell, Houston vs. Seattle, Oct. 11, 1981
41   Ron Johnson, N.Y. Giants vs. Philadelphia, Oct. 2, 1972
    Franco Harris, Pittsburgh vs. Cincinnati, Oct. 17, 1976
    Terdell Middleton, Green Bay vs. Minnesota, Nov. 26, 1978 (OT)
    Walter Payton, Chicago vs. Buffalo, Oct. 7, 1979
    Franco Harris, Pittsburgh vs. Cleveland, Nov. 25, 1979 (OT)

YARDS GAINED

Most Yards Gained, Career
15,459   Jim Brown, Cleveland, 1957-65
14,368   O.J. Simpson, Buffalo, 1969-77; San Francisco, 1978-79
14,078   Bobby Mitchell, Cleveland, 1958-61; Washington, 1962-68

Most Yards Gained, Season
2,462   Terry Metcalf, St. Louis, 1975
2,444   Mack Herron, New England, 1974
2,440   Gale Sayers, Chicago, 1966

Most Yards Gained, Rookie, Season
2,272   Gale Sayers, Chicago, 1965
2,100   Abner Haynes, Dall. Texans, 1960
2,093   James Brooks, San Diego, 1981

Most Yards Gained, Game

  373 Billy Cannon, Houston vs. N.Y. Titans, Dec. 10, 1961
  341 Timmy Brown, Philadelphia vs. St. Louis, Dec. 16, 1962
  339 Gale Sayers, Chicago vs. Minnesota, Dec. 18, 1966

MISCELLANEOUS

Longest Return of Missed Field Goal (All TDs)

  101 Al Nelson, Philadelphia vs. Dallas, Sept. 26, 1971
  100 Al Nelson, Philadelphia vs. Cleveland, Dec. 11, 1966
       Ken Ellis, Green Bay vs. N.Y. Giants, Sept. 19, 1971
   99 Jerry Williams, Los Angeles vs. Green Bay, Dec. 16, 1951
       Carl Taseff, Baltimore vs. Los Angeles, Dec. 12, 1959
       Timmy Brown, Philadelphia vs. St. Louis, Sept. 16, 1962

TEAM RECORDS

CHAMPIONSHIPS

Most Seasons League Champion

  11 Green Bay, 1929-31, 1936, 1939, 1944, 1961-62, 1965-67
   8 Chi. Bears, 1921, 1932-33, 1940-41, 1943, 1946, 1963
   4 N.Y. Giants, 1927, 1934, 1938, 1956
      Detroit, 1935, 1952-53, 1957
      Clev. Browns, 1950, 1954-55, 1964
      Baltimore, 1958-59, 1968, 1970
      Pittsburgh, 1974-75, 1978-79

Most Consecutive Seasons League Champion

   3 Green Bay, 1929-31, 1965-67
   2 Canton, 1922-23
      Chi. Bears, 1932-33, 1940-41
      Philadelphia, 1948-49
      Detroit, 1952-53
      Cleveland, 1954-55
      Baltimore, 1958-59
      Houston, 1960-61
      Green Bay, 1961-62
      Buffalo, 1964-65
      Miami, 1972-73
      Pittsburgh, 1974-75, 1978-79

Most Times Finishing First, Regular Season (Since 1933)

  14 N.Y. Giants, 1933-35, 1938-39, 1941, 1944, 1946, 1956, 1958-59, 1961-63
      Clev./L.A. Rams, 1945, 1949-51, 1955, 1967, 1969, 1973-79
      Clev. Browns, 1950-55, 1957, 1964-65, 1967-69, 1971, 1980
  12 Dallas, 1966-71, 1973, 1976-79, 1981
  11 Green Bay, 1936, 1938-39, 1944, 1960-62, 1965-67, 1972
      Minnesota, 1968-71, 1973-78, 1980

Most Consecutive Times Finishing First, Regular Season (Since 1933)

   7 Los Angeles, 1973-79
   6 Cleveland, 1950-55
      Dallas, 1966-71
      Minnesota, 1973-78
      Pittsburgh, 1974-79
   5 Oakland, 1972-76

GAMES WON

Most Consecutive Games Won (Incl. postseason games)

  18 Chi. Bears, 1933-34, 1941-42
      Miami, 1972-73
  17 Oakland, 1976-77
  14 Washington, 1942-43

Most Consecutive Games Won (Regular season)

  17 Chi. Bears, 1933-34
  16 Chi. Bears, 1941-42
      Miami, 1971-73

15 L.A. Chargers/San Diego, 1960-61

Most Consecutive Games Without Defeat (Incl. postseason games)
24 Canton, 1922-23 (won 21, tied 3)
23 Green Bay, 1928-30 (won 21, tied 2)
18 Chi. Bears, 1933-34 (won 18); 1941-42 (won 18)
    Miami, 1972-73 (won 18)

Most Consecutive Games Without Defeat (Regular season)
24 Canton, 1922-23 (won 21, tied 3)
    Chi. Bears, 1941-43 (won 23, tied 1)
23 Green Bay, 1928-30 (won 21, tied 2)
17 Chi. Bears, 1933-34 (won 17)

Most Games Won, One Season (Incl. postseason games)
17 Miami, 1972
    Pittsburgh, 1978
16 Oakland, 1976
    San Francisco, 1981
15 Miami, 1973
    Baltimore, 1968
    Pittsburgh, 1975, 1979
    Dallas, 1977
    Oakland, 1980

Most Games Won, Season (Since 1932)
14 Miami, 1972
    Pittsburgh, 1978
13 Chi. Bears, 1934
    Green Bay, 1962
    Oakland, 1967, 1976
    Baltimore, 1968
    San Francisco, 1981
12 By many teams

Most Consecutive Games Won, One Season (Incl. postseason games)
17 Miami, 1972
13 Chi. Bears, 1934
    Oakland, 1976
12 Minnesota, 1969

Most Consecutive Games Won, One Season
14 Miami, 1972
13 Chi. Bears, 1934
12 Minnesota, 1969

Most Consecutive Games Won, Start of Season
14 Miami, 1972, entire season
13 Chi. Bears, 1934, entire season
11 Chi. Bears, 1942, entire season
    Cleveland, 1953
    San Diego, 1961
    Los Angeles, 1969

Most Consecutive Games Won, End of Season
14 Miami, 1972, entire season
13 Chi. Bears, 1934, entire season
11 Chi. Bears, 1942, entire season
    Cleveland, 1951

Most Consecutive Games Without Defeat, One Season (Incl. postseason games)
17 Miami, 1972
13 Chi. Bears, 1926, 1934
    Green Bay, 1929
    Baltimore, 1967
    Oakland, 1976
12 Canton, 1922, 1923
    Minnesota, 1969

Most Consecutive Games Without Defeat, One Season
14 Miami, 1972
13 Chi. Bears, 1926; 1934
    Green Bay, 1929

         Baltimore, 1967
    12   Canton, 1922, 1923
         Minnesota, 1969

Most Consecutive Games Without Defeat, Start of Season
    14   Miami, 1972, entire season
    13   Chi. Bears, 1926; 1934, entire season
         Green Bay, 1929, entire season
         Baltimore, 1967
    12   Canton, 1922, 1923, entire seasons

Most Consecutive Games Without Defeat, End of Season
    14   Miami, 1972, entire season
    13   Green Bay, 1929, entire season
         Chi. Bears, 1934, entire season
    12   Canton, 1922, 1923, entire seasons

Most Consecutive Home Games Won
    27   Miami, 1971-74
    20   Green Bay, 1929-32
    18   Oakland, 1968-70
         Dallas, 1979-81 (current)

Most Consecutive Home Games Without Defeat
    30   Green Bay, 1928-33 (won 27, tied 3)
    26   Miami, 1971-74 (won 26)
    18   Chi. Bears, 1932-35 (won 17, tied 1); 1941-44 (won 17, tied 1)
         Oakland, 1968-70 (won 18)
         Dallas, 1979-81 (won 18) (current)

Most Consecutive Road Games Won
    11   L.A. Chargers/San Diego, 1960-61
    10   Chi. Bears, 1941-42
         Dallas, 1968-69
     9   Chi. Bears, 1933-34
         Kansas City, 1966-67
         Oakland, 1967-68, 1974-75, 1976-77
         Pittsburgh, 1974-75

Most Consecutive Road Games Without Defeat
    13   Chi. Bears, 1941-43 (won 12, tied 1)
    12   Green Bay, 1928-30 (won 10, tied 2)
    11   L.A. Chargers/San Diego, 1960-61 (won 11)
         Los Angeles, 1966-68 (won 10, tied 1)

Most Shutout Games Won or Tied, Season (Since 1932)
     7   Chi. Bears, 1932 (won 4, tied 3)
         Green Bay, 1932 (won 6, tied 1)
         Detroit, 1934 (won 7)
     5   Chi. Cardinals, 1934 (won 5)
         N.Y. Giants, 1944 (won 5)
         Pittsburgh, 1976 (won 5)
     4   By many teams

Most Consecutive Shutout Games Won or Tied (Since 1932)
     7   Detroit, 1934 (won 7)
     3   Chi. Bears, 1932 (tied 3)
         Green Bay, 1932 (won 3)
         New York, 1935 (won 3)
         St. Louis, 1970 (won 3)
         Pittsburgh, 1976 (won 3)
     2   By many teams

GAMES LOST

Most Consecutive Games Lost
    26   Tampa Bay, 1976-77
    19   Chi. Cardinals, 1942-43, 1945
         Oakland, 1961-62
    18   Houston, 1972-73

Most Consecutive Games Without Victory
    26   Tampa Bay, 1976-77 (lost 26)

23 Washington, 1960-61 (lost 20, tied 3)

Most Games Lost, Season (Since 1932)
15 New Orleans, 1980
14 Tampa Bay, 1976
   San Francisco, 1978, 1979
   Detroit, 1979
   Baltimore, 1981
   New England, 1981
13 Oakland, 1962
   Chicago, 1969
   Pittsburgh, 1969
   Buffalo, 1971
   Houston, 1972, 1973

Most Consecutive Games Lost, One Season
14 Tampa Bay, 1976
   New Orleans, 1980
   Baltimore, 1981
13 Oakland, 1962
12 Tampa Bay, 1977

Most Consecutive Games Lost, Start of Season
14 Tampa Bay, 1976, entire season
   New Orleans, 1980
13 Oakland, 1962
12 Tampa Bay, 1977

Most Consecutive Games Lost, End of Season
14 Tampa Bay, 1976, entire season
13 Pittsburgh, 1969
11 Philadelphia, 1936
   Detroit, 1942, entire season
   Houston, 1972

Most Consecutive Games Without Victory, One Season
14 Tampa Bay, 1976, entire season
   New Orleans, 1980
   Baltimore, 1981
13 Washington, 1961
   Oakland, 1962
12 Dall. Cowboys, 1960, entire season
   Tampa Bay, 1977

Most Consecutive Games Without Victory, Start of Season
14 Tampa Bay, 1976, entire season
   New Orleans, 1980
13 Washington, 1961
   Oakland, 1962
12 Dall. Cowboys, 1960, entire season
   Tampa Bay, 1977

Most Consecutive Games Without Victory, End of Season
14 Tampa Bay, 1976, entire season
13 Pittsburgh, 1969
12 Dall. Cowboys, 1960, entire season

Most Consecutive Home Games Lost
13 Houston, 1972-73
   Tampa Bay, 1976-77
11 Oakland, 1961-62
   Los Angeles, 1961-63
10 Pittsburgh, 1937-39, 1943-45
   Washington, 1960-61
   N.Y. Giants, 1973-75
   New Orleans, 1979-80

Most Consecutive Home Games Without Victory
13 Houston, 1972-73 (lost 13)
   Tampa Bay, 1976-77 (lost 13)
12 Philadelphia, 1936-38 (lost 11, tied 1)
11 Washington, 1960-61 (lost 10, tied 1)

      Oakland, 1961-62 (lost 11)
      Los Angeles, 1961-63 (lost 11)

Most Consecutive Road Games Lost

  18 San Francisco, 1977-79
  16 Chicago, 1973-75
  14 Brooklyn, 1942-44
      Chi. Cardinals, 1942-45
      New Orleans, 1972-74

Most Consecutive Road Games Without Victory

  18 Washington, 1959-62 (lost 15, tied 3)
      New Orleans, 1971-74 (lost 17, tied 1)
      San Francisco, 1977-79 (lost 18)
  17 Denver, 1962-65 (lost 16, tied 1)
  16 Chicago, 1973-75 (lost 16)

Most Shutout Games Lost or Tied, Season (Since 1932)

  6 Cincinnati, 1934 (lost 6)
    Pittsburgh, 1934 (lost 6)
    Philadelphia, 1936 (lost 6)
    Tampa Bay, 1977 (lost 6)
  5 Boston, 1932 (lost 4, tied 1), 1933 (lost 4, tied 1)
    N.Y. Giants, 1932 (lost 4, tied 1)
    Cincinnati, 1933 (lost 4, tied 1)
    Brooklyn, 1934 (lost 5), 1942 (lost 5)
    Detroit, 1942 (lost 5)
    Tampa Bay, 1976 (lost 5)
  4 By many teams

Most Consecutive Shutout Games Lost or Tied (Since 1932)

  6 Brooklyn, 1942-43 (lost 6)
  4 Chi. Bears, 1932 (lost 1, tied 3)
    Philadelphia, 1936 (lost 4)
  3 Chi. Cardinals, 1934 (lost 3), 1938 (lost 3)
    Brooklyn, 1935 (lost 3), 1937 (lost 3)
    Oakland, 1981 (lost 3)

TIE GAMES

Most Tie Games, Season

  6 Chi. Bears, 1932
  5 Frankford, 1929
  4 Chi. Bears, 1924
    Orange, 1929
    Portsmouth, 1929

Most Consecutive Tie Games

  3 Chi. Bears, 1932
  2 By many teams

SCORING

Most Seasons Leading League

  9 Chi. Bears, 1934-35, 1939, 1941-43, 1946-47, 1956
  6 Green Bay, 1932, 1936-38, 1961-62
    L.A. Rams, 1950-52, 1957, 1967, 1973
  5 Oakland, 1967-69, 1974, 1977
    Dall. Cowboys, 1966, 1968, 1971, 1978, 1980

Most Consecutive Seasons Leading League

  3 Green Bay, 1936-38
    Chi. Bears, 1941-43
    Los Angeles, 1950-52
    Oakland, 1967-69

POINTS

Most Points, Season

  513 Houston, 1961
  478 San Diego, 1981
  468 Oakland, 1967

Fewest Points, Season (Since 1932)
- 37 Cincinnati/St. Louis, 1934
- 38 Cincinnati, 1933
- Detroit, 1942
- 51 Pittsburgh, 1934
- Philadelphia, 1936

Most Points, Game
- 72 Washington vs. N.Y. Giants, Nov. 27, 1966
- 70 Los Angeles vs. Baltimore, Oct. 22, 1950
- 65 Chi. Cardinals vs. N.Y. Bulldogs, Nov. 13, 1949
- Los Angeles vs. Detroit, Oct. 29, 1950

Most Points, Both Teams, Game
- 113 Washington (72) vs. N.Y. Giants (41), Nov. 27, 1966
- 101 Oakland (52) vs. Houston (49), Dec. 22, 1963
- 98 Chi. Cardinals (63) vs. N.Y. Giants (35), Oct. 17, 1948

Fewest Points, Both Teams, Game
- 0 In many games. Last time: N.Y. Giants vs. Detroit, Nov. 7, 1943

Most Points, Shutout Victory, Game
- 64 Philadelphia vs. Cincinnati, Nov. 6, 1934
- 59 Los Angeles vs. Atlanta, Dec. 4, 1976
- 57 Chicago vs. Baltimore, Nov. 25, 1962

Fewest Points, Shutout Victory, Game
- 2 Green Bay vs. Chi. Bears, Oct. 16, 1932
- Chi. Bears vs. Green Bay, Sept. 18, 1938

Most Points Overcome to Win Game
- 28 San Francisco vs. New Orleans, Dec. 7, 1980 (OT) (trailed 7-35, won 38-35)
- 24 Philadelphia vs. Washington, Oct. 27, 1946 (trailed 0-24, won 28-24)
- Denver vs. Boston, Oct. 23, 1960 (trailed 0-24, won 31-24)
- Miami vs. New England, Dec. 15, 1974 (trailed 0-24, won 34-27)
- Minnesota vs. San Francisco, Dec. 4, 1977 (trailed 0-24, won 28-27)
- Denver vs. Seattle, Sept. 23, 1979 (trailed 10-34, won 37-34)

Most Points Overcome to Tie Game
- 31* Denver vs. Buffalo, Nov. 27, 1960 (trailed 7-38, tied 38-38)
- 28 Los Angeles vs. Philadelphia, Oct. 3, 1948 (trailed 0-28, tied 28-28)

Most Points, Each Half
- 1st: 45 Green Bay vs. Cleveland, Nov. 12, 1967
- 2nd: 48 Chi. Cardinals vs. Baltimore, Oct. 2, 1950
- N.Y. Giants vs. Baltimore, Nov. 19, 1950

Most Points, Both Teams, Each Half
- 1st: 70 Houston (35) vs. Oakland (35), Dec. 22, 1963
- 2nd: 65 Washington (38) vs. N.Y. Giants (27), Nov. 27, 1966

Most Points, One Quarter
- 41 Green Bay vs. Detroit, Oct. 7, 1945 (second quarter)
- Los Angeles vs. Detroit, Oct. 29, 1950 (third quarter)
- 37 Los Angeles vs. Green Bay, Sept. 21, 1980 (second quarter)
- 35 Chi. Cardinals vs. Boston, Oct. 24, 1948 (third quarter)
- Green Bay vs. Cleveland, Nov. 12, 1967 (first quarter)

Most Points, Both Teams, One Quarter
- 49 Oakland (28) vs. Houston (21), Dec. 22, 1963 (second quarter)
- 48 Green Bay (41) vs. Detroit (7), Oct. 7, 1945 (second quarter)
- Los Angeles (41) vs. Detroit (7), Oct. 29, 1950 (third quarter)
- 47 St. Louis (27) vs. Philadelphia (20), Dec. 13, 1964 (second quarter)

Most Points, Each Quarter
- 1st: 35 Green Bay vs. Cleveland, Nov. 12, 1967
- 2nd: 41 Green Bay vs. Detroit, Oct. 7, 1945
- 3rd: 41 Los Angeles vs. Detroit, Oct. 29, 1950
- 4th: 31 Oakland vs. Denver, Dec. 17, 1960; vs. San Diego, Dec. 8, 1963
- Atlanta vs. Green Bay, Sept. 13, 1981

Most Points, Both Teams, Each Quarter
- 1st: 42 Green Bay (35) vs. Cleveland (7), Nov. 12, 1967
- 2nd: 49 Oakland (28) vs. Houston (21), Dec. 22, 1963
- 3rd: 48 Los Angeles (41) vs. Detroit (7), Oct. 29, 1950
- 4th: 42 Chi. Cardinals (28) vs. Philadelphia (14), Dec. 7, 1947

Green Bay (28) vs. Chi. Bears (14), Nov. 6, 1955
N.Y. Jets (28) vs. Boston (14), Oct. 27, 1968
Pittsburgh (21) vs. Cleveland (21), Oct. 18, 1969

GAMES
Most Consecutive Games Scoring
274 Cleveland, 1950-71
217 Oakland, 1966-81
179 Kansas City, 1963-76

TOUCHDOWNS
Most Seasons Leading League, Touchdowns
13 Chi. Bears, 1932, 1934-35, 1939, 1941-44, 1946-48, 1956, 1965
7 Dall. Cowboys, 1966, 1968, 1971, 1973, 1977-78, 1980
6 Oakland, 1967-69, 1972, 1974, 1977
Most Consecutive Seasons Leading League, Touchdowns
4 Chi. Bears, 1941-44
 Los Angeles, 1949-52
3 Chi. Bears, 1946-48
 Baltimore, 1957-59
 Oakland, 1967-69
Most Touchdowns, Season
66 Houston, 1961
64 Los Angeles, 1950
61 San Diego, 1981
Fewest Touchdowns, Season (Since 1932)
3 Cincinnati, 1933
4 Cincinnati/St. Louis, 1934
5 Detroit, 1942
Most Touchdowns, Game
10 Philadelphia vs. Cincinnati, Nov. 6, 1934
 Los Angeles vs. Baltimore, Oct. 22, 1950
 Washington vs. N.Y. Giants, Nov. 27, 1966
9 Chi. Cardinals vs. Rochester, Oct. 7, 1923; vs. N.Y. Giants, Oct. 17, 1948; vs.
 N.Y. Bulldogs, Nov. 13, 1949
 Los Angeles vs. Detroit, Oct. 29, 1950
 Pittsburgh vs. N.Y. Giants, Nov. 30, 1952
 Chicago vs. San Francisco, Dec. 12, 1965; vs. Green Bay, Dec. 7, 1980
8 By many teams.
Most Touchdowns, Both Teams, Game
16 Washington (10) vs. N.Y. Giants (6), Nov. 27, 1966
14 Chi. Cardinals (9) vs. N.Y. Giants (5), Oct. 17, 1948
 Los Angeles (10) vs. Baltimore (4), Oct. 22, 1950
 Houston (7) vs. Oakland (7), Dec. 22, 1963
13 New Orleans (7) vs. St. Louis (6), Nov. 2, 1969
Most Consecutive Games Scoring Touchdowns
166 Cleveland, 1957-69
97 Oakland, 1966-73
96 Kansas City, 1963-70

POINTS AFTER TOUCHDOWN
Most Points After Touchdown, Season
65 Houston, 1961
59 Los Angeles, 1950
 Dallas, 1980
56 Dallas, 1966
 Oakland, 1967
Fewest Points After Touchdown, Season
2 Chi. Cardinals, 1933
3 Cincinnati, 1933
 Pittsburgh, 1934
4 Cincinnati/St. Louis, 1934

Most Points After Touchdown, Game

  10 Los Angeles vs. Baltimore, Oct. 22, 1950
   9 Chi. Cardinals vs. N.Y. Giants, Oct. 17, 1948
        Pittsburgh vs. N.Y. Giants, Nov. 30, 1952
        Washington vs. N.Y. Giants, Nov. 27, 1966
   8 By many teams

Most Points After Touchdown, Both Teams, Game

  14 Chi. Cardinals (9) vs. N.Y. Giants (5), Oct. 17, 1948
        Houston (7) vs. Oakland (7), Dec. 22, 1963
        Washington (9) vs. N.Y. Giants (5), Nov. 27, 1966
  13 Los Angeles (10) vs. Baltimore (3), Oct. 22, 1950
  12 In many games

FIELD GOALS

Most Seasons Leading League, Field Goals

  11 Green Bay, 1935-36, 1940-43, 1946-47, 1955, 1972, 1974
   6 N.Y. Giants, 1933, 1937, 1939, 1941, 1944, 1959
        Washington, 1945, 1956, 1971, 1976-77, 1979
   5 Clev. Browns, 1950, 1952-54, 1957
        L.A. Rams, 1949, 1951, 1958, 1966, 1973
        Portsmouth/Detroit, 1932-33, 1937-38, 1980

Most Consecutive Seasons Leading League, Field Goals

   4 Green Bay, 1940-43
   3 Cleveland, 1952-54
   2 By many teams

Most Field Goals Attempted, Season

  49 Los Angeles, 1966
        Washington, 1971
  48 Green Bay, 1972
  47 N.Y. Jets, 1969
        Los Angeles, 1973

Fewest Field Goals Attempted, Season (Since 1938)

   0 Chi. Bears, 1944
   2 Cleveland, 1939
        Card-Pitt, 1944
        Boston, 1946
        Chi. Bears, 1947
   3 Chi. Bears, 1945
        Cleveland, 1945

Most Field Goals Attempted, Game

   9 St. Louis vs. Pittsburgh, Sept. 24, 1967
   8 Pittsburgh vs. St. Louis, Dec. 2, 1962
        Detroit vs. Minnesota, Nov. 13, 1966
        N.Y. Jets vs. Buffalo, Nov. 3, 1968
   7 By many teams

Most Field Goals Attempted, Both Teams, Game

  11 St. Louis (6) vs. Pittsburgh (5), Nov. 13, 1966
        Washington (6) vs. Chicago (5), Nov. 14, 1971
        Green Bay (6) vs. Detroit (5), Sept. 29, 1974
        Washington (6) vs. N.Y. Giants (5), Nov. 14, 1976
  10 Denver (5) vs. Boston (5), Nov. 11, 1962
        Boston (7) vs. San Diego (3), Sept. 20, 1964
        Buffalo (7) vs. Houston (3), Dec. 5, 1965
        St. Louis (7) vs. Atlanta (3), Dec. 11, 1966
        Boston (7) vs. Buffalo (3), Sept. 24, 1967
        Detroit (7) vs. Minnesota (3), Sept. 20, 1971
        Washington (7) vs. Houston (3), Oct. 10, 1971
        Green Bay (5) vs. St. Louis (5), Dec. 5, 1971
        Kansas City (7) vs. Buffalo (3), Dec. 5, 1971
        Kansas City (5) vs. San Diego (5), Oct. 29, 1972
        Minnesota (6) vs. Chicago (4), Sept. 23, 1973
        Cleveland (7) vs. Denver (3), Oct. 19, 1975
        Cleveland (5) vs. Denver (5), Oct. 5, 1980
   9 In many games

All-Time Records

Most Field Goals, Season
    34 N.Y. Jets, 1968
    33 Green Bay, 1972
    32 N.Y. Jets, 1969

Fewest Field Goats, Season (Since 1932)
     0 Boston, 1932, 1935
        Chi. Cardinals, 1932, 1945
        Green Bay, 1932, 1944
        New York, 1932
        Brooklyn, 1944
        Card-Pitt, 1944
        Chi. Bears, 1944, 1947
        Boston, 1946
        Baltimore, 1950
        Dallas, 1952

Most Field Goals, Game
     7 St. Louis vs. Pittsburgh, Sept. 24, 1967
     6 Boston vs. Denver, Oct. 4, 1964
        Detroit vs. Minnesota, Nov. 13, 1966
        N.Y. Jets vs. Buffalo, Nov. 3, 1968; vs. New Orleans, Dec. 3, 1972
        Philadelphia vs. Houston, Nov. 12, 1972
        St. Louis vs. Atlanta, Dec. 9, 1973
        N.Y. Giants vs. Seattle, Oct. 18, 1981
     5 By many teams

Most Field Goals, Both Teams, Game
     8 Cleveland (4) vs. St. Louis (4), Sept. 20, 1964
        Chicago (5) vs. Philadelphia (3), Oct. 20, 1968
        Washington (5) vs. Chicago (3), Nov. 14, 1971
        Kansas City (5) vs. Buffalo (3), Dec. 19, 1971
        Detroit (4) vs. Green Bay (4), Sept. 29, 1974
        Cleveland (5) vs. Denver (3), Oct. 19, 1975
        New England (4) vs. San Diego (4), Nov. 9, 1975
     7 In many games

Most Consecutive Games Scoring Field Goals
    31 Minnesota, 1968-70
    21 San Francisco, 1970-72
    20 Los Angeles, 1970-71
        Miami, 1970-72

SAFETIES

Most Safeties, Season
     4 Detroit, 1962
     3 Green Bay, 1932, 1975
        Pittsburgh, 1947
        N.Y. Yanks, 1950
        Detroit, 1960
        St. Louis, 1960
        Buffalo, 1964
        Minnesota, 1965, 1981
        Cleveland, 1970
        Los Angeles, 1973
        Houston, 1977
        Dallas, 1981
        Oakland, 1981
     2 By many teams

Most Safeties, Game
     2 Cincinnati vs. Chi. Cardinals, Nov. 19, 1933
        Detroit vs. Brooklyn, Dec. 1, 1935
        N.Y. Giants vs. Pittsburgh, Sept. 17, 1950; vs. Washington, Nov. 5, 1961
        Chicago vs. Pittsburgh, Nov. 9, 1969
        Dallas vs. Philadelphia, Nov. 19, 1972
        Los Angeles vs. Green Bay, Oct. 21, 1973
        Oakland vs. San Diego, Oct. 26, 1975

Most Safeties, Both Teams, Game

  2 Chi. Bears (1) vs. San Francisco (1), Oct. 19, 1952
    Cincinnati (1) vs. Los Angeles (1), Oct. 22, 1972
    Atlanta (1) vs. Detroit (1), Oct. 5, 1980
    (Also see previous record)

FIRST DOWNS

Most Seasons Leading League

  9 Chi. Bears, 1935, 1939, 1941, 1943, 1945, 1947-49, 1955
  6 L.A. Rams, 1946, 1950-51, 1954, 1957, 1973
  5 Green Bay, 1940, 1942, 1944, 1960, 1962

Most Consecutive Seasons Leading League

  3 Chi. Bears, 1947-49
  2 By many teams

Most First Downs, Season

 379 San Diego, 1981
 372 San Diego, 1980
 364 Cleveland, 1981

Fewest First Downs, Season

  51 Cincinnati, 1933
  64 Pittsburgh, 1935
  67 Philadelphia, 1937

Most First Downs, Game

  38 Los Angeles vs. N.Y. Giants, Nov. 13, 1966
  37 Green Bay vs. Philadelphia, Nov. 11, 1962
  36 Pittsburgh vs. Cleveland, Nov. 25, 1979 (OT)

Fewest First Downs, Game

  0 N.Y. Giants vs. Green Bay, Oct. 1, 1933; vs. Washington, Sept. 27, 1942
    Pittsburgh vs. Boston, Oct. 29, 1933
    Philadelphia vs. Detroit, Sept. 20, 1935
    Denver vs. Houston, Sept. 3, 1966

Most First Downs, Both Teams, Game

  58 Los Angeles (30) vs. Chi. Bears (28), Oct. 24, 1954
    Denver (34) vs. Kansas City (24), Nov. 18, 1974
    Atlanta (35) vs. New Orleans (23), Sept. 2, 1979 (OT)
    Pittsburgh (36) vs. Cleveland (22), Nov. 25, 1979 (OT)
  57 Los Angeles (32) vs. N.Y. Yanks (25), Nov. 19, 1950
    Baltimore (33) vs. N.Y. Jets (24), Dec. 15, 1974
  56 Buffalo (28) vs. Cincinnati (28), Oct. 29, 1978

Fewest First Downs, Both Teams, Game

  5 N.Y. Giants (0) vs. Green Bay (5), Oct. 1, 1933

Most First Downs, Rushing, Season

 181 New England, 1978
 177 Los Angeles, 1973
 170 Miami, 1972

Fewest First Downs, Rushing, Season

  36 Cleveland, 1942
    Boston, 1944
  39 Brooklyn, 1943
  40 Philadelphia, 1940
    Detroit, 1945

Most First Downs, Rushing, Game

  25 Philadelphia vs. Washington, Dec. 2, 1951
  21 Cleveland vs. Philadelphia, Dec. 13, 1959
    Los Angeles vs. New Orleans, Nov. 25, 1973
    Pittsburgh vs. Kansas City, Nov. 7, 1976
    New England vs. Denver, Nov. 28, 1976
    Oakland vs. Green Bay, Sept. 17, 1978
  20 By eight teams

Fewest First Downs, Rushing, Game

  0 By many teams

Most First Downs, Passing, Season

 244 San Diego, 1980

224 San Diego, 1981
217 Minnesota, 1981

Fewest First Downs, Passing, Season

18 Pittsburgh, 1941
23 Brooklyn, 1942
    N.Y. Giants, 1944
24 N.Y. Giants, 1943

Most First Downs, Passing, Game

25 Denver vs. Kansas City, Nov. 18, 1974
    N.Y Jets vs. San Francisco, Sept. 21, 1980
24 Houston vs. Buffalo, Nov. 1, 1964
    Minnesota vs. Baltimore, Sept. 28, 1969
23 Dallas vs. San Francisco, Nov. 10, 1963
    Denver vs. Houston, Dec. 20, 1964
    San Diego vs. N.Y. Giants, Oct. 19, 1980

Fewest First Downs, Passing, Game

0 By many teams

Most First Downs, Penalty, Season

39 Seattle, 1978
37 Cleveland, 1981
36 Baltimore, 1979
    Cleveland, 1979

Fewest First Downs, Penalty, Season

2 Brooklyn, 1940
4 Chi. Cardinals, 1940
   N.Y. Giants, 1942, 1944
   Washington, 1944
   Cleveland, 1952
   Kansas City, 1969
5 Brooklyn, 1939
   Chi. Bears, 1939
   Detroit, 1953
   Los Angeles, 1953

Most First Downs, Penalty, Game

9 Chi. Bears vs. Cleveland, Nov. 25, 1951
   Baltimore vs. Pittsburgh, Oct. 30. 1977
8 Philadelphia vs. Detroit, Dec. 2, 1979
7 Boston vs. Houston, Sept. 19, 1965
   Baltimore vs. Detroit, Nov. 19, 1967; vs. Buffalo, Dec. 17, 1978;
       vs. Pittsburgh, Sept. 14, 1980
   Oakland vs. Boston, Oct. 6, 1968
   Cleveland vs. Buffalo, Oct. 23, 1977; vs. Pittsburgh, Sept. 24, 1978;
       vs. Atlanta, Sept. 27, 1981
   Buffalo vs. Cleveland, Oct. 29, 1978
   Cincinnati vs. Oakland, Nov. 9, 1980

Fewest First Downs, Penalty, Game

0 By many teams

NET YARDS GAINED RUSHING AND PASSING

Most Seasons Leading League

12 Chi. Bears, 1932, 1934-35, 1939, 1941-44, 1947, 1949, 1955-56
6 L.A. Rams, 1946, 1950-51, 1954, 1957, 1973
   Baltimore, 1958-60, 1964, 1967, 1976
   Dall. Cowboys, 1966, 1968-69, 1971, 1974, 1977
4 San Diego, 1963, 1965, 1980-81

Most Consecutive Seasons Leading League

4 Chi. Bears, 1941-44
3 Baltimore, 1958-60
   Houston, 1960-62
   Oakland, 1968-70
2 By many teams

Most Yards Gained, Season

6,744 San Diego, 1981

        6,410   San Diego, 1980
        6,288   Houston, 1961

Fewest Yards Gained, Season
        1,150   Cincinnati, 1933
        1,443   Chi. Cardinals, 1934
        1,486   Chi. Cardinals, 1933

Most Yards Gained, Game
        735   Los Angeles vs. N.Y. Yanks, Sept. 28, 1951
        683   Pittsburgh vs. Chi. Cardinals, Dec. 13, 1958
        682   Chi. Bears vs. N.Y. Giants, Nov. 14, 1943

Fewest Yards Gained, Game
        −7   Seattle vs. Los Angeles, Nov. 4, 1979
        −5   Denver vs. Oakland, Sept. 10, 1967
        14   Chi. Cardinals vs. Detroit, Sept. 15, 1940

Most Yards Gained, Both Teams, Game
        1,133   Los Angeles (636) vs. N.Y. Yanks (497), Nov. 19, 1950
        1,087   St. Louis (589) vs. Philadelphia (498), Dec. 16, 1962
        1,064   Atlanta (552) vs. New Orleans (512), Sept. 2, 1979 (OT)

Fewest Yards Gained, Both Teams, Game
        30   Chi. Cardinals (14) vs. Detroit (16), Sept. 15, 1940

Most Consecutive Games, 400 or More Yards Gained
        6   Houston, 1961-62
              San Diego, 1981
        5   Chi. Bears, 1947, 1955
              Los Angeles, 1950
              Philadelphia, 1953
              Oakland, 1968
              New England, 1981
        4   Chi. Cardinals, 1948
              Los Angeles, 1954
              Houston, 1961
              Oakland, 1967, 1975
              Dallas, 1976
              Kansas City, 1976
              Baltimore, 1976
              Cleveland, 1980

Most Consecutive Games, 300 or More Yards Gained
        29   Los Angeles, 1949-51
        20   Chi. Bears, 1948-50
        19   Cleveland, 1978-79

RUSHING

Most Seasons Leading League
        11   Chi. Bears, 1932, 1934-35, 1939-42, 1951, 1955-56, 1968, 1977
        6   Clev. Browns, 1958-59, 1963, 1965-67
        4   Green Bay, 1946, 1961-62, 1964
              Dall. Texans/Kansas City, 1961, 1966, 1968-69
              Buffalo, 1962, 1964, 1973, 1975
              Detroit, 1936-38, 1981

Most Consecutive Seasons Leading League
        4   Chi. Bears, 1939-42
        3   Detroit, 1936-38
              San Francisco, 1952-54
              Cleveland, 1965-67
        2   By many teams

Most Rushing Attempts, Season
        681   Oakland, 1977
        671   New England, 1978
        659   Los Angeles, 1973

Fewest Rushing Attempts, Season
        274   Detroit, 1946
        285   Philadelphia, 1937
        294   Detroit, 1943

Most Rushing Attempts, Game
72 Chi. Bears vs. Brooklyn, Oct. 20, 1935
70 Chi. Cardinals vs. Green Bay, Nov. 25, 1951
69 Chi. Cardinals vs. Green Bay, Dec. 6, 1936
     Kansas City vs. Cincinnati, Sept. 3, 1978

Fewest Rushing Attempts, Game
6 Chi. Cardinals vs. Boston, Oct. 29, 1933
7 Oakland vs. Buffalo, Oct. 15, 1963
8 Denver vs. Oakland, Dec. 17, 1960

Most Rushing Attempts, Both Teams, Game
108 Chi. Cardinals (70) vs. Green Bay (38), Dec. 5, 1948
105 Oakland (62) vs. Atlanta (43), Nov. 30, 1975 (OT)
103 Kansas City (53) vs. San Diego (50), Nov. 12, 1978 (OT)

Fewest Rushing Attempts, Both Teams, Game
36 Cincinnati (16) vs. Chi. Bears (20), Sept. 30, 1934
38 N.Y. Jets (13) vs. Buffalo (25), Nov. 8, 1964
39 Denver (16) vs. N.Y. Titans (23), Sept. 24, 1961
     Denver (14) vs. Boston (25), Sept. 21, 1962
     Denver (14) vs. Houston (25), Dec. 2, 1962

YARDS GAINED
Most Yards Gained Rushing, Season
3,165 New England, 1978
3,088 Buffalo, 1973
2,986 Kansas City, 1978

Fewest Yards Gained Rushing, Season
298 Philadelphia, 1940
467 Detroit, 1946
471 Boston, 1944

Most Yards Gained Rushing, Game
426 Detroit vs. Pittsburgh, Nov. 4, 1934
423 N.Y. Giants vs. Baltimore, Nov. 19, 1950
420 Boston vs. N.Y. Giants, Oct. 8, 1933

Fewest Yards Gained Rushing, Game
−53 Detroit vs. Chi. Cardinals, Oct. 17, 1943
−36 Philadelphia vs. Chi. Bears, Nov. 19, 1939
−33 Phil-Pitt vs. Brooklyn, Oct. 2, 1943

Most Yards Gained Rushing, Both Teams, Game
595 Los Angeles (371) vs. N.Y. Yanks (224), Nov. 18, 1951
574 Chi. Bears (396) vs. Pittsburgh (178), Oct. 10, 1934
557 Chi. Bears (406) vs. Green Bay (151), Nov. 6, 1955

Fewest Yards Gained Rushing, Both Teams, Game
−15 Detroit (−53) vs. Chi. Cardinals (38), Oct. 17, 1943
4 Detroit (−10) vs. Chi. Cardinals (14), Sept. 15, 1940
63 Chi. Cardinals (−1) vs. N.Y. Giants (64), Oct. 18, 1953

AVERAGE GAIN
Highest Average Gain, Rushing, Season
5.74 Cleveland, 1963
5.65 San Francisco, 1954
5.56 San Diego, 1963

Lowest Average Gain, Rushing, Season
0.94 Philadelphia, 1940
1.45 Boston, 1944
1.55 Pittsburgh, 1935

TOUCHDOWNS
Most Touchdowns, Rushing, Season
36 Green Bay, 1962
33 Pittsburgh, 1976
30 Chi. Bears, 1941
     New England, 1978

Fewest Touchdowns, Rushing, Season

    1 Brooklyn, 1934
    2 Chi. Cardinals, 1933
        Cincinnati, 1933
        Pittsburgh, 1934, 1940
        Philadelphia, 1935, 1936, 1937, 1938, 1972
    3 By eight teams

Most Touchdowns, Rushing, Game

    7 Los Angeles vs. Atlanta, Dec. 4, 1976
    6 By many teams

Most Touchdowns, Rushing, Both Teams, Game

    8 Los Angeles (6) vs. N.Y. Yanks (2), Nov. 18, 1951
        Cleveland (6) vs. Los Angeles (2), Nov. 24, 1957
    7 In many games

PASSING

Most Seasons Leading League

   10 Washington, 1937, 1939-40, 1942-45, 1947, 1967, 1974
    9 N.Y. Giants, 1932, 1934-35, 1938, 1948, 1959, 1962-63, 1972
    6 L.A. Rams, 1946, 1949-51, 1954, 1973

ATTEMPTS

Most Passes Attempted, Season

  709 Minnesota, 1981
  629 San Diego, 1981
  624 Cleveland, 1981

Fewest Passes Attempted, Season

  102 Cincinnati, 1933
  106 Boston, 1933
  120 Detroit, 1937

Most Passes Attempted, Game

   68 Houston vs. Buffalo, Nov 1, 1964
   63 Minnesota vs. Tampa Bay, Sept. 5, 1981
   62 N.Y. Jets vs. Denver, Dec. 3, 1967; vs Baltimore, Oct. 18, 1970

Fewest Passes Attempted, Game

    0 Green Bay vs. Portsmouth, Oct. 8, 1933; vs. Chi. Bears, Sept. 25, 1949
        Detroit vs. Cleveland, Sept. 10, 1937
        Pittsburgh vs. Brooklyn, Nov. 16, 1941; vs. Los Angeles, Nov. 13, 1949
        Cleveland vs. Philadelphia, Dec. 3, 1950

Most Passes Attempted, Both Teams, Game

   98 Minnesota (56) vs. Baltimore (42), Sept. 28, 1969
   97 Denver (53) vs. Houston (44), Dec. 2, 1962
   96 Tampa Bay (56) vs. Minnesota (40), Nov. 16, 1980

Fewest Passes Attempted, Both Teams, Game

    4 Chi. Cardinals (1) vs. Detroit (3), Nov. 3, 1935
        Detroit (0) vs. Cleveland (4), Sept. 10, 1937
    6 Chi. Cardinals (2) vs. Detroit (4), Sept 15, 1940
    8 Brooklyn (2) vs. Philadelphia (6), Oct. 1, 1939

COMPLETIONS

Most Passes Completed, Season

  382 Minnesota, 1981
  368 San Diego, 1981
  363 San Francisco, 1980

Fewest Passes Completed, Season

   25 Cincinnati, 1933
   33 Boston, 1933
   34 Chi. Cardinals, 1934
        Detroit, 1934

Most Passes Completed, Game

   42 N.Y. Jets vs. San Francisco, Sept. 21, 1980
   38 Minnesota vs. Cleveland, Dec. 14, 1980; vs. Green Bay, Nov. 29, 1981
   37 Houston vs. Buffalo, Nov. 1, 1964

Minnesota vs. Tampa Bay, Sept. 5, 1981

Most Passes Completed, Both Teams, Game

63	N.Y. Jets (42) vs. San Francisco (21), Sept. 21, 1980
58	Minnesota (38) vs. Cleveland (20), Dec. 14, 1980
56	Minnesota (36) vs. Baltimore (20), Sept. 28, 1969
	Minnesota (38) vs. Green Bay (18), Nov. 29, 1981

Fewest Passes Completed, Both Teams, Game

1	Chi. Cardinals (0) vs. Philadelphia (1), Nov. 8, 1936
	Detroit (0) vs. Cleveland (1), Sept. 10, 1937
	Chi. Cardinals (0) vs. Detroit (1), Sept. 15, 1940
	Brooklyn (0) vs. Pittsburgh (1), Nov. 29, 1942
2	Chi. Cardinals (0) vs. Detroit (2), Nov. 3, 1935
	Buffalo (0) vs. N.Y. Jets (2), Sept. 29, 1974
3	Brooklyn (1) vs. Philadelphia (2), Oct. 1, 1939

YARDS GAINED

Most Seasons Leading League, Passing Yardage

8	Chi. Bears, 1932, 1939, 1941, 1943, 1945, 1949, 1954, 1964
7	Washington, 1938, 1940, 1944, 1947-48, 1967, 1974
	San Diego, 1965, 1968, 1971, 1978-81
5	Green Bay, 1934-37, 1942
	Philadelphia, 1953, 1955, 1961-62, 1973
	Baltimore, 1957, 1959-60, 1963, 1976

Most Consecutive Seasons Leading League, Passing Yardage

4	Green Bay, 1934-37
	San Diego, 1978-81
2	By many teams

Most Yards Gained, Passing, Season

4,739	San Diego, 1981
4,531	San Diego, 1980
4,392	Houston, 1961

Fewest Yards Gained, Passing, Season

302	Chi. Cardinals, 1934
357	Cincinnati, 1933
459	Boston, 1934

Most Yards Gained, Passing, Game

554	Los Angeles vs. N.Y. Yanks, Sept. 28, 1951
530	Minnesota vs. Baltimore, Sept. 28, 1969
505	N.Y. Giants vs. Washington, Oct. 28, 1962

Fewest Yards Gained, Passing, Game

−53	Denver vs. Oakland, Sept. 10, 1967
−52	Cincinnati vs. Houston, Oct. 31, 1971
−39	Atlanta vs. San Francisco, Oct. 23, 1976

Most Yards Gained, Passing, Both Teams, Game

834	Philadelphia (419) vs. St. Louis (415), Dec. 16, 1962
822	N.Y. Jets (490) vs. Baltimore (332), Sept. 24, 1972
821	N.Y. Giants (505) vs. Washington (316), Oct. 28, 1962

Fewest Yards Gained, Passing, Both Teams, Game

−11	Green Bay (−10) vs. Dallas (−1), Oct. 24, 1965
1	Chi. Cardinals (0) vs. Philadelphia (1), Nov. 8, 1936
7	Brooklyn (0) vs. Pittsburgh (7), Nov. 29, 1942

TACKLED ATTEMPTING PASSES

Most Times Tackled, Attempting Passes, Season

70	Atlanta, 1968
68	Dallas, 1964
67	Detroit, 1976

Fewest Times Tackled, Attempting Passes, Season

8	San Francisco, 1970
	St. Louis, 1975
9	N.Y. Jets, 1966
10	N.Y. Giants, 1972

Most Times Tackled, Attempting Passes, Game

- 12   Pittsburgh vs. Dallas, Nov. 20, 1966
       Baltimore vs. St. Louis, Oct. 26, 1980
- 11   St. Louis vs. N.Y. Giants, Nov. 1, 1964
       Los Angeles vs. Baltimore, Nov. 22, 1964
       Denver vs. Buffalo, Dec. 13, 1964; vs. Oakland, Nov. 5, 1967
       Green Bay vs. Detroit, Nov. 7, 1965
       Buffalo vs. Oakland, Oct. 15, 1967
       Atlanta vs. St. Louis, Nov. 24, 1968
       Detroit vs. Dallas, Oct. 6, 1975
- 10   By many teams. Last time: N.Y. Giants vs. San Francisco, Nov. 23, 1980

Most Times Tackled, Attempting Passes, Both Teams, Game

- 18   Green Bay (10) vs. San Diego (8), Sept. 24, 1978
- 17   Buffalo (10) vs. N.Y. Titans (7), Nov. 23, 1961
       Pittsburgh (12) vs. Dallas (5), Nov. 20, 1966
- 16   Los Angeles (11) vs. Baltimore (5), Nov. 22, 1964
       Buffalo (11) vs. Oakland (5), Oct. 15, 1967

COMPLETION PERCENTAGE

Most Seasons Leading League, Completion Percentage

- 11   Washington, 1937, 1939-40, 1942-45, 1947-48, 1969-70
- 7   Green Bay, 1936, 1941, 1961-62, 1964, 1966, 1968
- 6   Clev. Browns, 1951, 1953-55, 1959-60
       Dall. Texans/Kansas City, 1962, 1964, 1966-69

Most Consecutive Seasons Leading League, Completion Percentage

- 4   Washington, 1942-45
       Kansas City, 1966-69
- 3   Cleveland, 1953-55
- 2   By many teams

Highest Completion Percentage, Season

- 64.3   Oakland, 1976
- 64.0   Washington, 1945
- 63.9   Houston, 1980

Lowest Completion Percentage, Season

- 22.9   Philadelphia, 1936
- 24.5   Cincinnati, 1933
- 25.0   Pittsburgh, 1941

TOUCHDOWNS

Most Touchdowns, Passing, Season

- 48   Houston, 1961
- 39   N.Y. Giants, 1963
- 36   Oakland, 1969

Fewest Touchdowns, Passing, Season

- 0   Cincinnati, 1933
       Pittsburgh, 1945
- 1   Boston, 1932, 1933
       Chi. Cardinals, 1934
       Cincinnati/St. Louis, 1934
       Detroit, 1942
- 2   Chi. Cardinals, 1932, 1935
       Stapleton, 1932
       Brooklyn, 1936
       Pittsburgh, 1942

Most Touchdowns, Passing, Game

- 7   Chi. Bears vs. N.Y. Giants, Nov. 14, 1943
       Philadelphia vs. Washington, Oct. 17, 1954
       Houston vs. N.Y. Titans, Nov. 19, 1961; vs. N.Y. Titans, Oct. 14, 1962
       N.Y. Giants vs. Washington, Oct. 28, 1962
       Minnesota vs. Baltimore, Sept. 28, 1969
       San Diego vs. Oakland, Nov. 22, 1981
- 6   By many teams.

Most Touchdowns, Passing, Both Teams, Game

- 12 New Orleans (6) vs. St. Louis (6), Nov. 2, 1969
- 11 N.Y. Giants (7) vs. Washington (4), Oct. 28, 1962
  - Oakland (6) vs. Houston (5), Dec. 22, 1963
- 9 In many games

PASSES HAD INTERCEPTED
Most Passes Had Intercepted, Season

- 48 Houston, 1962
- 45 Denver, 1961
- 41 Card-Pitt, 1944

Fewest Passes Had Intercepted, Season

- 5 Cleveland, 1960
  - Green Bay, 1966
- 6 Green Bay, 1964
- 7 Los Angeles, 1969

Most Passes Had Intercepted, Game

- 9 Detroit vs. Green Bay, Oct. 24, 1943
  - Pittsburgh vs. Philadelphia, Dec. 12, 1965
- 8 Green Bay vs. N.Y. Giants, Nov. 21, 1948
  - Chi. Cardinals vs. Philadelphia, Sept. 24, 1950
  - N.Y. Yanks vs. N.Y. Giants, Dec. 16, 1951
  - Denver vs. Houston, Dec. 2, 1962
  - Chi. Bears vs. Detroit, Sept. 22, 1968
  - Baltimore vs. N.Y. Jets, Sept. 23, 1973
- 7 By many teams

Most Passes Had Intercepted, Both Teams, Game

- 13 Denver (8) vs. Houston (5), Dec. 2, 1962
- 11 Philadelphia (7) vs. Boston (4), Nov. 3, 1935
  - Boston (6) vs. Pittsburgh (5), Dec. 1, 1935
  - Cleveland (7) vs. Green Bay (4), Oct. 30, 1938
  - Green Bay (7) vs. Detroit (4), Oct. 20, 1940
  - Detroit (7) vs. Chi. Bears (4), Nov. 22, 1942
  - Detroit (7) vs. Cleveland (4), Nov. 26, 1944
  - Chi. Cardinals (8) vs. Philadelphia (3), Sept. 24, 1950
  - Washington (7) vs. N.Y. Giants (4), Dec. 8, 1963
  - Pittsburgh (9) vs. Philadelphia (2), Dec 12, 1965
- 10 In many games

PUNTING
Most Seasons Leading League (Average distance)

- 6 Washington, 1940-43, 1945, 1958
- 5 Denver, 1962-64, 1966-67
  - Kansas City, 1968, 1971-73, 1979
- 4 L.A. Rams, 1946, 1949, 1955-56

Most Consecutive Seasons Leading League (Average Distance)

- 4 Washington, 1940-43
- 3 Cleveland, 1950-52
  - Denver, 1962-64
  - Kansas City, 1971-73

Most Punts, Season

- 114 Chicago, 1981
- 113 Boston, 1934
  - Brooklyn, 1934
- 112 Boston, 1935

Fewest Punts, Season

- 32 Chi. Bears, 1941
- 33 Washington, 1945
- 38 Chi. Bears, 1947

Most Punts, Game

- 17 Chi. Bears vs. Green Bay, Oct. 22, 1933
  - Cincinnati vs. Pittsburgh, Oct. 22, 1933
- 16 Cincinnati vs. Portsmouth, Sept. 17, 1933

Chi. Cardinals vs. Chi. Bears, Nov. 30, 1933; vs. Detroit, Sept. 15, 1940

Fewest Punts, Game

   0 By many teams. Last time: Tampa Bay vs. Green Bay, Nov. 22, 1981

Most Punts, Both Teams, Game

  31 Chi. Bears (17) vs. Green Bay (14), Oct. 22, 1933
      Cincinnati (17), vs. Pittsburgh (14), Oct. 22, 1933
  29 Chi. Cardinals (15) vs. Cincinnati (14), Nov. 12, 1933
      Chi. Cardinals (16) vs. Chi. Bears (13), Nov. 30, 1933
      Chi. Cardinals (16) vs. Detroit (13), Sept. 15, 1940

Fewest Punts, Both Teams, Game

   1 Dall. Cowboys (0) vs. Cleveland (1), Dec. 3, 1961
      Chicago (0) vs. Detroit (1), Oct. 1, 1972
      San Francisco (0) vs. N.Y. Giants (1), Oct. 15, 1972
   2 Philadelphia (0) vs. Cleveland (2), Sept. 25, 1960
      Philadelphia (0) vs. Dall. Cowboys (2), Oct. 22, 1961
      Detroit (0) vs. Kansas City (2), Nov. 25, 1971
      N.Y. Giants (1) vs. Philadelphia (1), Nov. 25, 1973
      Buffalo (0) vs. New England (2), Nov. 3, 1974
      San Diego (0) vs. Cleveland (2), Dec. 4, 1977
      Miami (0) vs. Chicago (2), Sept. 23, 1979
      Oakland (0) vs. Seattle (2), Dec. 16, 1979
      Kansas City (1) vs. New England (1), Oct. 4, 1981
   3 In many games

AVERAGE YARDAGE

Highest Average Distance, Punting, Season

  47.6 Detroit, 1961
  47.0 Pittsburgh, 1961
  46.9 Pittsburgh, 1953

Lowest Average Distance, Punting, Season

  32.7 Card-Pitt, 1944
  33.9 Detroit, 1969
  34.4 Phil-Pitt, 1943

PUNT RETURNS

Most Seasons Leading League (Average return)

   8 Detroit, 1943-45, 1951-52, 1962, 1966, 1969
   5 Chi. Cardinals, 1948-49, 1955-56, 1959
      Clev. Browns, 1958, 1960, 1964-65, 1967
      Green Bay, 1950, 1953-54, 1971, 1972
      Dall. Texans/Kansas City, 1960, 1968, 1970, 1979-80
   3 Denver, 1963, 1967, 1969
      San Diego, 1965-66, 1973
      Washington, 1957, 1963, 1976
      N.Y. Jets, 1961-62, 1978

Most Consecutive Seasons Leading League (Average Return)

   3 Detroit, 1943-45
   2 By many teams

Most Punt Returns, Season

  71 Pittsburgh, 1976
      Tampa Bay, 1979
  67 Pittsburgh, 1974
      Los Angeles, 1978
  65 San Francisco, 1976

Fewest Punt Returns, Season

  12 Baltimore, 1981
  14 Los Angeles, 1961
      Philadelphia, 1962
  15 Houston, 1960
      Washington, 1960
      Oakland, 1961
      N.Y. Giants, 1969
      Philadelphia, 1973

Most Punt Returns, Game

12	Philadelphia vs. Cleveland, Dec. 3, 1950
11	Chi. Bears vs. Chi. Cardinals, Oct. 8, 1950
	Washington vs. Tampa Bay, Oct. 9, 1977
10	Philadelphia vs. N.Y. Giants, Nov. 26, 1950
	Philadelphia vs. Tampa Bay, Sept. 18, 1977
	Pittsburgh vs. Buffalo, Dec. 16, 1979

Most Punt Returns, Both Teams, Game

17	Philadelphia (12) vs. Cleveland (5), Dec. 3, 1950
16	N.Y. Giants (9) vs. Philadelphia (7), Dec. 12, 1954
	Washington (11) vs. Tampa Bay (5), Oct. 9, 1977
15	Detroit (8) vs. Cleveland (7), Sept. 27, 1942
	Los Angeles (8) vs. Baltimore (7), Nov. 27, 1966
	Pittsburgh (8) vs. Houston (7), Dec. 1, 1974
	Philadelphia (10) vs. Tampa Bay (5), Sept. 18, 1977
	Baltimore (9) vs. Kansas City (6), Sept. 2, 1979

FAIR CATCHES
Most Fair Catches, Season

34	Baltimore, 1971
32	San Diego, 1969
30	St. Louis, 1967
	Minnesota, 1971

Fewest Fair Catches, Season

0	San Diego, 1975
	New England, 1976
	Tampa Bay, 1976
	Pittsburgh, 1977
1	Cleveland, 1974
	San Francisco, 1975
	Kansas City, 1976
	St. Louis, 1976
	San Diego, 1976
2	By many teams

Most Fair Catches, Game

7	Minnesota vs. Dallas, Sept. 25, 1966
	Detroit vs. Chicago, Nov. 21, 1976
6	Minnesota vs. Baltimore, Nov. 17, 1963; vs. Atlanta, Nov. 28, 1971
	Chicago vs. St. Louis, Oct. 31, 1966; vs. Minnesota, Dec. 10, 1967
	Cleveland vs. St. Louis, Dec. 17, 1966
	San Francisco vs. Baltimore, Oct. 13, 1968
	Miami vs. Buffalo, Dec. 20, 1970
	Cincinnati vs. Pittsburgh, Sept. 26, 1971
	N.Y. Giants vs. Minnesota, Oct. 31, 1971
	Baltimore vs. N.Y. Jets, Nov. 14, 1971
	Green Bay vs. Chicago, Dec. 16, 1973
	San Diego vs. Chicago, Dec. 4, 1978
5	By many teams

YARDS GAINED
Most Yards, Punt Returns, Season

781	Chi. Bears, 1948
774	Pittsburgh, 1974
729	Green Bay, 1950

Fewest Yards, Punt Returns, Season

27	St. Louis, 1965
35	N.Y. Giants, 1965
37	New England, 1972

Most Yards, Punt Returns, Game

231	Detroit vs. San Francisco, Oct. 6, 1963
225	Oakland vs. Buffalo, Sept. 15, 1968
219	Los Angeles vs. Atlanta, Oct. 11, 1981

Most Yards, Punt Returns, Both Teams, Game
- 282 Los Angeles (219) vs. Atlanta (63), Oct. 11, 1981
- 245 Detroit (231) vs. San Francisco (14), Oct. 6, 1963
- 244 Oakland (225) vs. Buffalo (19), Sept. 15, 1968

AVERAGE YARDS RETURNING PUNTS
Highest Average, Punt Returns, Season
- 20.2 Chi. Bears, 1941
- 19.1 Chi. Cardinals, 1948
- 18.2 Chi. Cardinals, 1949

Lowest Average, Punt Returns, Season
- 1.2 St. Louis, 1965
- 1.5 N.Y. Giants, 1965
- 1.7 Washington, 1970

TOUCHDOWNS RETURNING PUNTS
Most Touchdowns, Punt Returns, Season
- 5 Chi. Cardinals, 1959
- 4 Chi. Cardinals, 1948
  Detroit, 1951
  N.Y. Giants, 1951
  Denver, 1976
- 3 Washington, 1941
  Detroit, 1952
  Pittsburgh, 1952
  Houston, 1975
  Los Angeles, 1981

Most Touchdowns, Punt Returns, Game
- 2 Detroit vs. Los Angeles, Oct. 14, 1951; vs. Green Bay, Nov. 22, 1951
  Chi. Cardinals vs. Pittsburgh, Nov. 1, 1959; vs. N.Y. Giants, Nov. 22, 1959
  N.Y. Titans vs. Denver, Sept. 24, 1961
  Denver vs. Cleveland, Sept. 26, 1976
  Los Angeles vs. Atlanta, Oct. 11, 1981

Most Touchdowns, Punt Returns, Both Teams, Game
- 2 Philadelphia (1) vs. Washington (1), Nov. 9, 1952
  Kansas City (1) vs. Buffalo (1), Sept. 11, 1966
  Baltimore (1) vs. New England (1), Nov. 18, 1979
  (Also see previous record)

KICKOFF RETURNS
Most Seasons Leading League (Average return)
- 7 Washington, 1942, 1947, 1962-63, 1973-74, 1981
- 5 N.Y. Giants, 1944, 1946, 1949, 1951, 1953
  Chi. Bears, 1943, 1948, 1958, 1966, 1972
- 4 Houston, 1960, 1962-63, 1968

Most Consecutive Seasons Leading League (Average return)
- 3 Denver, 1965-67
- 2 By many teams

Most Kickoff Returns, Season
- 88 New Orleans, 1980
- 84 Balitmore, 1981
- 82 Atlanta, 1966

Fewest Kickoff Returns, Season
- 17 N.Y. Giants, 1944
- 20 N.Y. Giants, 1941
  Chi. Bears, 1942
  N.Y. Giants, 1943
- 23 Washington, 1942

Most Kickoff Returns, Game
- 12 N.Y. Giants vs. Washington, Nov. 27, 1966
- 10 By many teams

Most Kickoff Returns, Both Teams, Game
- 19 N.Y. Giants (12) vs. Washington (7), Nov. 27, 1966

18 Houston (10) vs. Oakland (8), Dec. 22, 1963
16 N.Y. Giants (10) vs. Chi. Cardinals (6), Oct. 17, 1948
N.Y. Titans (10) vs. L.A. Chargers (6), Dec. 18, 1960
Cleveland (8) vs. St. Louis (8), Sept. 20, 1964
Cleveland (8) vs. N.Y. Giants (8), Dec. 4, 1966

YARDS GAINED
Most Yards, Kickoff Returns, Season
1,973 New Orleans, 1980
1,824 Houston, 1963
1,801 Denver, 1963
Fewest Yards, Kickoff Returns, Season
282 N.Y. Giants, 1940
381 Green Bay, 1940
424 Chicago, 1963
Most Yards, Kickoff Returns, Game
362 Detroit vs. Los Angeles, Oct. 29, 1950
304 Chi. Bears vs. Green Bay, Nov. 9, 1952
295 Denver vs. Boston, Oct. 4, 1964
Most Yards, Kickoff Returns, Both Teams, Game
560 Detroit (362) vs. Los Angeles (198), Oct. 29, 1950
453 Washington (236) vs. Philadelphia (217), Sept. 28, 1947
447 N.Y. Giants (236) vs. Cleveland (211), Dec. 4, 1966

AVERAGE YARDAGE
Highest Average, Kickoff Returns, Season
29.4 Chicago, 1972
28.9 Pittsburgh, 1952
28.2 Washington, 1962
Lowest Average, Kickoff Returns, Season
16.3 Chicago, 1963
16.5 San Diego, 1961
16.7 Chi. Cardinals, 1947

TOUCHDOWNS
Most Touchdowns, Kickoff Returns, Season
4 Green Bay, 1967
Chicago, 1970
3 Los Angeles, 1950
Chi. Cardinals, 1954
San Francisco, 1963
Denver, 1966
Chicago, 1967
New England, 1977
2 By many teams
Most Touchdowns, Kickoff Returns, Game
2 Chi. Bears vs. Green Bay, Sept. 22, 1940; vs. Green Bay, Nov. 9, 1952
Philadelphia vs. Dallas, Nov. 6, 1966
Green Bay vs. Cleveland, Nov. 12, 1967
Most Touchdowns, Kickoff Returns, Both Teams, Game
2 Washington (1) vs. Philadelphia (1), Nov. 1, 1942
Washington (1) vs. Philadelphia (1), Sept. 28, 1947
Los Angeles (1) vs. Detroit (1), Oct. 29, 1950
N.Y. Yanks (1) vs. N.Y. Giants (1), Nov. 4, 1951 (consecutive)
Baltimore (1) vs. Chi. Bears (1), Oct. 4, 1958
Buffalo (1) vs. Boston (1), Nov. 3, 1962
Pittsburgh (1) vs. Dallas (1), Oct. 30, 1966
St. Louis (1) vs. Washington (1), Sept. 23, 1973 (consecutive)
(Also see previous record)

FUMBLES

Most Fumbles, Season
56 Chi. Bears, 1938

San Francisco, 1978
54 Philadelphia, 1946
51 New England, 1973

Fewest Fumbles, Season
8 Cleveland, 1959
11 Green Bay, 1944
12 Brooklyn, 1934
Detroit, 1943

Most Fumbles, Game
10 Phil-Pitt vs. New York, Oct. 9, 1943
Detroit vs. Minnesota, Nov. 12, 1967
Kansas City vs. Houston, Oct. 12, 1969
San Francisco vs. Detroit, Dec. 17, 1978
9 Philadelphia vs. Green Bay, Oct. 13, 1946
Kansas City vs. San Diego, Nov. 15, 1964
N.Y. Giants vs. Buffalo, Oct. 20, 1975
St. Louis vs. Washington, Oct. 25, 1976
San Diego vs. Green Bay, Sept. 24, 1978
Pittsburgh vs. Cincinnati, Oct. 14, 1979
Cleveland vs. Seattle, Dec. 20, 1981
8 By many teams

Most Fumbles, Both Teams, Game
14 Chi. Bears (7) vs. Cleveland (7), Nov. 24, 1940
St. Louis (8) vs. N.Y. Giants (6), Sept. 17, 1961
Kansas City (10) vs. Houston (4), Oct. 12, 1969
13 Washington (8) vs. Pittsburgh (5), Nov. 14, 1937
Philadelphia (7) vs. Boston (6), Dec. 8, 1946
N.Y. Giants (7) vs. Washington (6), Nov. 5, 1950
Kansas City (9) vs. San Diego (4), Nov. 15, 1964
Buffalo (7) vs. Denver (6), Dec. 13, 1964
N.Y. Jets (7) vs. Houston (6), Sept. 12, 1965
Houston (8) vs. Pittsburgh (5), Dec. 9, 1973
St. Louis (9) vs. Washington (4), Oct. 25, 1976
Cleveland (9) vs. Seattle (4), Dec. 20, 1981
12 In many games

FUMBLES LOST

Most Fumbles Lost, Season
36 Chi. Cardinals, 1959
29 Chi. Cardinals, 1946
28 Pittsburgh, 1977

Fewest Fumbles Lost, Season
3 Philadelphia, 1938
Minnesota, 1980
4 San Francisco, 1960
5 Chi. Cardinals, 1943
Detroit, 1943
N.Y. Giants, 1943
Cleveland, 1959

Most Fumbles Lost, Game
8 St. Louis vs. Washington, Oct. 25, 1976
7 Cincinnati vs. Buffalo, Oct. 25, 1976
Cleveland vs. Seattle, Dec. 20, 1981
6 By many teams

FUMBLES RECOVERED

Most Fumbles Recovered, Season, Own and Opponents'
58 Minnesota, 1963 (27 own, 31 opp)
51 Chi. Bears, 1938 (37 own, 14 opp)
San Francisco, 1978 (24 own, 27 opp)
47 Atlanta, 1978 (22 own, 25 opp)

Fewest Fumbles Recovered, Season, Own and Opponents'
13 Baltimore, 1967 (5 own, 8 opp)

N.Y. Jets, 1967 (7 own, 6 opp)
Philadelphia, 1968 (6 own, 7 opp)
Miami, 1973 (5 own, 8 opp)

14 Cleveland, 1956 (6 own, 8 opp)
Kansas City, 1966 (5 own, 9 opp)

15 Chi. Bears, 1943 (9 own, 6 opp)
San Francisco, 1951 (6 own, 9 opp)
Cleveland, 1959 (3 own, 12 opp)
Kansas City, 1971 (9 own, 6 opp)

Most Fumbles Recovered, Game, Own and Opponents'

10 Denver vs. Buffalo, Dec. 13, 1964 (5 own, 5 opp)
Pittsburgh vs. Houston, Dec. 9, 1973 (5 own, 5 opp)
Washington vs. St. Louis, Oct. 25, 1976 (2 own, 8 opp)

9 St. Louis vs. N.Y. Giants, Sept. 17, 1961 (6 own, 3 opp)
Houston vs. Cincinnati, Oct. 27, 1974 (4 own, 5 opp)
Kansas City vs. Dallas, Nov. 10, 1975 (4 own, 5 opp)

8 By many teams

Most Own Fumbles Recovered, Season

37 Chi. Bears, 1938
27 Philadelphia, 1946
Minnesota, 1963
26 Washington, 1940
Pittsburgh, 1948

Fewest Own Fumbles Recovered, Season

2 Washington, 1958
3 Detroit, 1956
Cleveland, 1959
4 By many teams

Most Opponents' Fumbles Recovered, Season

31 Minnesota, 1963
29 Cleveland, 1951
28 Green Bay, 1946
Houston, 1977

Fewest Opponents' Fumbles Recovered, Season

3 Los Angeles, 1974
4 Philadelphia, 1944
6 Brooklyn, 1939
Chi. Bears, 1943, 1945
Washington, 1945
N.Y. Jets, 1967
San Diego, 1969
Kansas City, 1971
Oakland, 1975

Most Opponents' Fumbles Recovered, Game

8 Washington vs. St. Louis, Oct. 25, 1976
7 Buffalo vs. Cincinnati, Nov. 30, 1969
Seattle vs. Cleveland, Dec. 20, 1981
6 By many teams

TOUCHDOWNS

Most Touchdowns, Fumbles Recovered, Season, Own and Opponents'

5 Chi. Bears, 1942 (1 own, 4 opp)
Los Angeles, 1952 (1 own, 4 opp)
San Francisco, 1965 (1 own, 4 opp)
Oakland, 1978 (2 own, 3 opp)

4 Chi. Bears, 1948 (1 own, 3 opp)
Boston, 1948 (4 opp)
Denver, 1979 (1 own, 3 opp)
Atlanta, 1981 (1 own, 3 opp)

3 By many teams

Most Touchdowns, Own Fumbles Recovered, Season

2 Chi. Bears, 1953
New England, 1973
Buffalo, 1974

Denver, 1975
Oakland, 1978

Most Touchdowns, Opponents' Fumbles Recovered, Season
4 Detroit, 1937
 Chi. Bears, 1942
 Boston, 1948
 Los Angeles, 1952
 San Francisco, 1965
3 By many teams

Most Touchdowns, Fumbles Recovered, Game, Own and Opponents'
2 Detroit vs. Cleveland, Nov. 7, 1937 (2 opp); vs. Los Angeles, Sept. 17, 1950
 (1 own, 1 opp); vs. Chi. Cardinals, Dec. 6, 1959 (1 own, 1 opp);
 vs. Minnesota, Dec. 9, 1962 (1 own, 1 opp)
 Philadelphia vs. New York, Sept. 25, 1938 (2 opp) vs. St. Lou   Nov. 21, 1971
 (1 own, 1 opp)
 Chi. Bears vs. Washington, Nov. 28, 1948 (2 opp)
 N.Y. Giants vs. Pittsburgh, Sept. 17, 1950 (2 opp); vs. Green Bay, Sept. 19,
 1971 (2 opp)
 Cleveland vs. Dall. Cowboys, Dec. 3, 1961 (2 opp); vs. N.Y. Giants, Oct. 25,
 1964 (2 opp)
 Green Bay vs. Dallas, Nov. 26, 1964 (2 opp)
 San Francisco vs. Detroit, Nov. 14, 1965 (2 opp)
 Oakland vs. Buffalo, Dec. 24, 1967 (2 opp)
 Washington vs. San Diego, Sept. 16, 1973 (2 opp)
 New Orleans vs. San Francisco, Oct 19, 1975 (2 opp)
 Cincinnati vs. Pittsburgh, Oct. 14, 1979 (2 opp)
 Atlanta vs. Detroit, Oct. 5, 1980 (2 opp)
 Kansas City vs. Oakland, Oct. 5, 1980 (2 opp)
 New England vs. Baltimore, Nov. 23, 1980 (2 opp)

Most Touchdowns, Own Fumbles Recovered, Game
1 By many teams

Most Touchdowns, Opponents' Fumbles Recovered, Game
2 Detroit vs. Cleveland, Nov. 7, 1937
 Philadelphia vs. N.Y. Giants, Sept. 25, 1938
 Chi. Bears vs. Washington, Nov. 28, 1948
 N.Y. Giants vs. Pittsburgh, Sept. 17, 1950; vs. Green Bay, Sept. 19, 1971
 Cleveland vs. Dall. Cowboys, Dec. 3, 1961; vs. N.Y. Giants, Oct. 25, 1964
 Green Bay vs. Dallas, Nov. 26, 1964
 San Francisco vs. Detroit, Nov. 14, 1965
 Oakland vs. Buffalo, Dec. 24, 1967
 Washington vs. San Diego, Sept. 16, 1973
 New Orleans vs. San Francisco, Oct. 19, 1975
 Cincinnati vs. Pittsburgh, Oct. 14, 1979
 Atlanta vs. Detroit, Oct. 5, 1980
 Kansas City vs. Oakland, Oct. 5, 1980
 New England vs. Baltimore, Nov. 23, 1980

TURNOVERS

(Number of times losing the ball on interceptions and fumbles.)

Most Turnovers, Season
63 San Francisco, 1978
58 Chi. Bears, 1947
 Pittsburgh, 1950
57 Green Bay, 1950
 Houston, 1962, 1963
 Pittsburgh, 1965

Fewest Turnovers, Season
14 N.Y. Giants, 1943
 Cleveland, 1959
16 San Francisco, 1960
17 N.Y. Giants, 1939
 St. Louis, 1974

Most Turnovers, Game

12	Detroit vs. Chi. Bears, Nov. 22, 1942
	Chi. Cardinals vs. Philadelphia, Sept. 24, 1950
	Pittsburgh vs. Philadelphia, Dec. 12, 1965
11	San Diego vs. Green Bay, Sept. 24, 1978
10	Washington vs. N.Y. Giants, Dec. 4, 1938; vs. N.Y. Giants, Dec. 8, 1963
	Pittsburgh vs. Green Bay, Nov. 23, 1941
	Detroit vs. Green Bay, Oct. 24, 1943
	Chi. Cardinals vs. Green Bay, Nov. 10, 1946; vs. N.Y. Giants, Nov. 2, 1952
	Minnesota vs. Detroit, Dec. 9, 1962
	Houston vs. Oakland, Sept. 7, 1963
	Chicago vs. Detroit, Sept. 22, 1968
	St. Louis vs. Washington, Oct. 25, 1976
	N.Y. Jets vs. New England, Nov. 21, 1976
	San Francisco vs. Dallas, Oct. 12, 1980
	Cleveland vs. Seattle, Dec. 20, 1981

Most Turnovers, Both Teams, Game

17	Detroit (12) vs. Chi. Bears (5), Nov. 22, 1942
	Boston (9) vs. Philadelphia (8), Dec. 8, 1946
16	Chi. Cardinals (12) vs. Philadelphia (4), Sept. 24, 1950
	Chi. Cardinals (8) vs. Chi. Bears (8), Dec. 7, 1958
	Minnesota (10) vs. Detroit (6), Dec. 9, 1962
	Houston (9) vs. Kansas City (7), Oct. 12, 1969
15	Philadelphia (8) vs. Chi. Cardinals (7), Oct. 3, 1954
	Denver (9) vs. Houston (6), Dec. 2, 1962
	Washington (10) vs. N.Y. Giants (5), Dec. 8, 1963

PENALTIES

Most Seasons Leading League, Fewest Penalties

9	Pittsburgh, 1946-47, 1950-52, 1954, 1963, 1965, 1968
7	Miami, 1968, 1976-81
5	Green Bay, 1955-56, 1966-67, 1974

Most Consecutive Seasons Leading League, Fewest Penalties

6	Miami, 1976-81
3	Pittsburgh, 1950-52
2	By many teams

Most Seasons Leading League, Most Penalties

16	Chi. Bears, 1941-44, 1946-49, 1951, 1959-61, 1963, 1965, 1968, 1976
6	L.A. Rams, 1950, 1952, 1962, 1969, 1978, 1980
5	Oakland, 1963, 1966, 1968-69, 1975

Most Consecutive Seasons Leading League, Most Penalties

4	Chi. Bears, 1941-44, 1946-49
3	Chi. Cardinals, 1954-56
	Chi. Bears, 1959-61

Fewest Penalties, Season

19	Detroit, 1937
21	Boston, 1935
24	Philadelphia, 1936

Most Penalties, Season

137	Baltimore, 1979
133	Los Angeles, 1978
132	Denver, 1978

Fewest Penalties, Game

0	By many teams. Last time: Dallas vs. Washington, Nov. 23, 1980

Most Penalties, Game

22	Brooklyn vs. Green Bay, Sept. 17, 1944
	Chi. Bears vs. Philadelphia, Nov. 26, 1944
21	Cleveland vs. Chi. Bears, Nov. 25, 1951
20	Tampa Bay vs. Seattle, Oct. 17, 1976

Fewest Penalties, Both Teams, Game

0	Brooklyn vs. Pittsburgh, Oct. 28, 1934
	Brooklyn vs. Boston, Sept. 28, 1936
	Cleveland vs. Chi. Bears, Oct. 9, 1938

Pittsburgh vs. Philadelphia, Nov. 10, 1940

Most Penalties, Both Teams, Game
- 37 Cleveland (21) vs. Chi. Bears (16), Nov. 25, 1951
- 35 Tampa Bay (20) vs. Seattle (15), Oct. 17, 1976
- 33 Brooklyn (22) vs. Green Bay (11), Sept. 17, 1944

YARDS PENALIZED

Most Seasons Leading League, Fewest Yards Penalized
- 8 Miami, 1967-68, 1973, 1977-81
- 7 Pittsburgh, 1946-47, 1950, 1952, 1962, 1965, 1968
   Boston/Washington, 1935, 1953-54, 1956-58, 1970
- 4 Philadelphia, 1936, 1940, 1951, 1964
   Boston, 1962, 1964-66

Most Consecutive Seasons Leading League, Fewest Yards Penalized
- 5 Miami, 1977-81
- 3 Washington, 1956-58
   Boston, 1964-66
- 2 By many teams

Most Seasons Leading League, Most Yards Penalized
- 15 Chi. Bears, 1935, 1937, 1939-44, 1946-47, 1949, 1951, 1961-62, 1968
- 5 Oakland, 1963-64, 1968-69, 1975
   Cleveland, 1965, 1976-78, 1980
   Buffalo, 1962, 1967, 1970, 1972, 1981
- 4 Baltimore, 1957, 1959, 1963, 1979

Most Consecutive Seasons Leading League, Most Yards Penalized
- 6 Chi. Bears, 1939-44
- 3 Cleveland, 1976-78
- 2 By many teams

Fewest Yards Penalized, Season
- 139 Detroit, 1937
- 146 Philadelphia, 1937
- 159 Philadelphia, 1936

Most Yards Penalized, Season
- 1,274 Oakland, 1969
- 1,239 Baltimore, 1979
- 1,194 Chicago, 1968

Fewest Yards Penalized, Game
- 0 By many teams. Last time: Dallas vs. Washington, Nov. 23, 1980

Most Yards Penalized, Game
- 209 Cleveland vs. Chi. Bears, Nov. 25, 1951
- 190 Tampa Bay vs. Seattle, Oct. 17, 1976
- 189 Houston vs. Buffalo, Oct. 31, 1965

Fewest Yards Penalized, Both Teams, Game
- 0 Brooklyn vs. Pittsburgh, Oct. 28, 1934
   Brooklyn vs. Boston, Sept. 28, 1936
   Cleveland vs. Chi. Bears, Oct. 9, 1938
   Pittsburgh vs. Philadelphia, Nov. 10, 1940

Most Yards Penalized, Both Teams, Game
- 374 Cleveland (209) vs. Chi. Bears (165), Nov. 25, 1951
- 310 Tampa Bay (190) vs. Seattle (120), Oct. 17, 1976
- 309 Green Bay (184) vs. Boston (125), Oct. 21, 1945

DEFENSE

SCORING

Most Seasons Leading League, Fewest Points Allowed
- 8 N.Y. Giants, 1935, 1938-39, 1941, 1944, 1958-59, 1961
- 6 Cleveland, 1951, 1953-57
   Chi. Bears, 1932, 1936-37, 1942, 1948, 1963
- 5 Green Bay, 1935, 1947, 1962, 1965-66

Most Consecutive Seasons Leading League, Fewest Points Allowed
- 5 Cleveland, 1953-57
- 3 Buffalo, 1964-66
   Minnesota, 1969-71

2 By many teams

Fewest Points Allowed, Season (Since 1932)

44 Chi. Bears, 1932
54 Brooklyn, 1933
59 Detroit, 1934

Most Points Allowed, Season

533 Baltimore, 1981
501 N.Y. Giants, 1966
487 New Orleans, 1980

Fewest Touchdowns Allowed, Season (Since 1932)

6 Chi. Bears, 1932
Brooklyn, 1933
7 Detroit, 1934
8 Green Bay, 1932

Most Touchdowns Allowed, Season

68 Baltimore, 1981
66 N.Y. Giants, 1966
63 Baltimore, 1950

FIRST DOWNS

Fewest First Downs Allowed Season

77 Detroit, 1935
79 Boston, 1935
82 Washington, 1937

Most First Downs Allowed, Season

406 Baltimore, 1981
371 Seattle, 1981
365 San Diego, 1981

Fewest First Downs Allowed, Rushing, Season

35 Chi. Bears, 1942
40 Green Bay, 1939
41 Brooklyn, 1944

Most First Downs Allowed, Rushing, Season

178 New Orleans, 1980
175 Seattle, 1981
171 Buffalo, 1978

Fewest First Downs Allowed, Passing, Season

33 Chi. Bears, 1943
34 Pittsburgh, 1941
Washington, 1943
35 Detroit, 1940
Philadelphia, 1940, 1944

Most First Downs Allowed, Passing, Season

216 San Diego, 1981
214 Baltimore, 1981
198 N.Y. Jets, 1979, 1980

Fewest First Downs Allowed, Penalty, Season

1 Boston, 1944
3 Philadelphia, 1940
Pittsburgh, 1945
Washington, 1957
4 Cleveland, 1940
Green Bay, 1943
N.Y. Giants, 1943

Most First Downs Allowed, Penalty, Season

41 Detroit, 1979
40 Pittsburgh, 1978
38 Cleveland, 1978, 1980

NET YARDS ALLOWED RUSHING AND PASSING

Most Seasons Leading League, Fewest Yards Allowed

6 N.Y. Giants, 1938, 1940-41, 1951, 1956, 1959
5 Boston/Washington, 1935-37, 1939, 1946

Chi. Bears, 1942-43, 1948, 1958, 1963
Philadelphia, 1944-45, 1949, 1953, 1981
4 Cleveland, 1950, 1952, 1954-55

Most Consecutive Seasons Leading League, Fewest Yards Allowed
3 Boston/Washington, 1935-37
2 By many teams

Fewest Yards Allowed, Season
1,539 Chi. Cardinals, 1934
1,703 Chi. Bears, 1942
1,789 Brooklyn, 1933

Most Yards Allowed, Season
6,793 Baltimore, 1981
6,218 New Orleans, 1980
6,136 San Diego, 1981

RUSHING

Most Seasons Leading League, Fewest Yards Allowed
7 Detroit, 1938, 1950, 1952, 1962, 1970, 1980-81
6 Chi. Bears, 1937, 1939, 1942, 1946, 1949, 1963
Dallas, 1966-69, 1972, 1978
5 Philadelphia, 1944-45, 1947-48, 1953

Most Consecutive Seasons Leading League, Fewest Yards Allowed
4 Dallas, 1966-69
2 By many teams

Fewest Yards Allowed, Rushing, Season
519 Chi. Bears, 1942
558 Philadelphia, 1944
793 Phil-Pitt, 1943

Most Yards Allowed, Rushing, Season
3,228 Buffalo, 1978
3,106 New Orleans, 1980
3,010 Baltimore, 1978

Fewest Touchdowns Allowed, Rushing, Season
2 Detroit, 1934
Dallas, 1968
Minnesota, 1971
3 By many teams

Most Touchdowns Allowed, Rushing, Season
36 Oakland, 1961
31 N.Y. Giants, 1980
30 Baltimore, 1981

PASSING

Most Seasons Leading League, Fewest Yards Allowed
8 Green Bay, 1947-48, 1962, 1964-68
6 Chi. Bears, 1938, 1943-44, 1958, 1960, 1963
Washington, 1939, 1942, 1945, 1952-53, 1980
5 Pittsburgh, 1941, 1946, 1951, 1955, 1974
Minnesota, 1969-70, 1972, 1975-76
Philadelphia, 1934, 1936, 1940, 1949, 1981

Most Consecutive Seasons Leading League, Fewest Yards Allowed
5 Green Bay, 1964-68
2 By many teams

Fewest Yards Allowed, Passing, Season
545 Philadelphia, 1934
558 Portsmouth, 1933
585 Chi. Cardinals, 1934

Most Yards Allowed, Passing, Season
4,311 San Diego, 1981
4,128 Baltimore, 1981
4,115 N.Y. Jets, 1979

Most Opponents Tackled Attempting Passes, Season
67 Oakland, 1967

    66   N.Y. Jets, 1981
    61   San Francisco, 1976

Fewest Opponents Tackled Attempting Passes, Season
    13   Baltimore, 1981
    15   New England, 1972
    16   Miami, 1966
           Cincinnati, 1969
           N.Y. Jets, 1976

Most Opponents Tackled Attempting Passes, Game
    12   Dallas vs. Pittsburgh, Nov. 20, 1966
           St. Louis vs. Baltimore, Oct. 26, 1980
    11   N.Y. Giants vs. St. Louis, Nov. 1, 1964
           Baltimore vs. Los Angeles, Nov. 22, 1964
           Buffalo vs. Denver, Dec. 13, 1964
           Detroit vs. Green Bay, Nov. 7, 1965
           Oakland vs. Buffalo, Oct. 15, 1967; vs. Denver, Nov. 5, 1967
           St. Louis vs. Atlanta, Nov. 24, 1968
           Dallas vs. Detroit, Oct. 6, 1975
    10   By many teams. Last time: San Francisco vs. N.Y. Giants, Nov. 23, 1980

Most Opponents Yards Lost Attempting to Pass, Season
   666   Oakland, 1967
   573   San Francisco, 1976
   526   Boston, 1963

Fewest Opponents Yards Lost Attempting to Pass, Season
    75   Green Bay, 1956
    77   N.Y. Bulldogs, 1949
    78   Green Bay, 1958

Fewest Touchdowns Allowed, Passing, Season
     1   Portsmouth, 1932
          Philadelphia, 1934
     2   Brooklyn, 1933
          Chi. Bears, 1934
     3   Chi. Bears, 1932, 1934
          Green Bay, 1932, 1934
          N.Y. Giants, 1939, 1944

Most Touchdowns Allowed, Passing, Season
    40   Denver, 1963
    38   St. Louis, 1969
    37   Washington, 1961
           Baltimore, 1981

INTERCEPTIONS BY

Most Seasons Leading League
     9   N.Y. Giants, 1933, 1937-39, 1944, 1948, 1951, 1954, 1961
     8   Green Bay, 1940, 1942-43, 1947, 1955, 1957, 1962, 1965
     6   Chi. Bears, 1935-36, 1941-42, 1946, 1963
          Kansas City, 1966-70, 1974

Most Consecutive Seasons Leading League
     5   Kansas City, 1966-70
     3   N.Y. Giants, 1937-39
     2   By many teams

Most Passes Intercepted By, Season
    49   San Diego, 1961
    42   Green Bay, 1943
    41   N.Y. Giants, 1951

Fewest Passes Intercepted By, Season
     6   Houston, 1972
     7   Los Angeles, 1959
     8   Pittsbugh, 1940
          Boston, 1970
          San Francisco, 1977

Most Passes Intercepted By, Game
     9   Green Bay vs. Detroit, Oct. 24, 1943

Philadelphia vs. Pittsburgh, Dec. 12, 1965
8 N.Y. Giants vs. Green Bay, Nov. 21, 1948; vs. N.Y. Yanks, Dec. 16, 1951
Philadelphia vs. Chi. Cardinals, Sept. 24, 1950
Houston vs. Denver, Dec. 2, 1962
Detroit vs. Chicago, Sept. 22, 1968
N.Y. Jets vs. Baltimore, Sept. 23, 1973
7 By many teams

Most Consecutive Games, One or More Interceptions By
46 L.A. Chargers/San Diego, 1960-63
37 Detroit, 1960-63
36 Boston, 1944-47
Washington, 1962-65

Most Yards Returning Interceptions, Season
929 San Diego, 1961
712 Los Angeles, 1952
676 Houston, 1967

Fewest Yards Returning Interceptions, Season
5 Los Angeles, 1959
51 Philadelphia, 1968
62 Pittsburgh, 1940
N.Y. Giants, 1976

Most Yards Returning Interceptions, Game
314 Los Angeles vs. San Francisco, Oct. 18, 1964
245 Houston vs. N.Y. Jets, Oct. 15, 1967
235 Buffalo vs. N.Y. Jets, Sept. 29, 1968

Most Touchdowns, Returning Interceptions, Season
9 San Diego, 1961
6 Cleveland, 1960
Green Bay, 1966
Detroit, 1967
Houston, 1967
5 By 10 teams

Most Touchdowns Returning Interceptions, Game
3 Baltimore vs. Green Bay, Nov. 5, 1950
Cleveland vs. Chicago, Dec. 11, 1960
Philadelphia vs. Pittsburgh, Dec. 12, 1965
Baltimore vs. Pittsburgh, Sept. 29, 1968
Buffalo vs. N.Y. Jets, Sept. 29, 1968
Houston vs. San Diego, Dec. 19, 1971
Cincinnati vs. Houston, Dec. 17, 1972
Tampa Bay vs. New Orleans, Dec. 11, 1977
2 By many teams

Most Touchdowns Returning Interceptions, Both Teams, Game
4 Philadelphia (3) vs. Pittsburgh (1), Dec. 12, 1965
3 Los Angeles (2) vs. Detroit (1), Nov. 1, 1953
Cleveland (2) vs. N.Y. Giants (1), Dec. 18, 1960
(Also see previous record)

PUNT RETURNS

Fewest Opponents Punt Returns, Season
7 Washington, 1962
11 Boston, 1962
13 Boston, 1961
Green Bay, 1967

Most Opponents Punt Returns, Season
71 Tampa Bay, 1976, 1977
69 N.Y. Giants, 1953
68 Cleveland, 1974

Fewest Yards Allowed, Punt Returns, Season
22 Green Bay, 1967
34 Washington, 1962
39 Cleveland, 1959
Washington, 1972

Most Yards Allowed, Punt Returns, Season

932	Green Bay, 1949
913	Boston, 1947
906	New Orleans, 1974

Lowest Average Allowed, Punt Returns, Season

1.20	Chi. Cardinals, 1954
1.22	Cleveland, 1959
1.50	Chi. Cardinals, 1953

Highest Average Allowed, Punt Returns, Season

18.6	Green Bay, 1949
18.0	Cleveland, 1977
17.9	Boston, 1960

Most Touchdowns Allowed, Punt Returns, Season

4	New York, 1959
3	Green Bay, 1949
	Chi. Cardinals, 1951
	Los Angeles, 1951
	Washington, 1952
	Dallas, 1952
	Pittsburgh, 1959
	N.Y. Jets, 1968
	Cleveland, 1977

KICKOFF RETURNS

Fewest Opponents Kickoff Returns, Season

10	Brooklyn, 1943
15	Detroit, 1942
	Brooklyn, 1944
18	Cleveland, 1941
	Boston, 1944

Most Opponents Kickoff Returns, Season

89	New England, 1980
88	San Diego, 1981
84	Kansas City, 1966

Fewest Yards Allowed, Kickoff Returns, Season

225	Brooklyn, 1943
293	Brooklyn, 1944
368	Chi. Cardinals, 1945

Most Yards Allowed, Kickoff Returns, Season

2,045	Kansas City, 1966
1,816	N.Y. Giants, 1963
1,785	N.Y. Titans, 1960

Lowest Average Allowed, Kickoff Returns, Season

14.3	Cleveland, 1980
15.8	Oakland, 1977
16.0	Chi. Bears, 1946

Highest Average Allowed, Kickoff Returns, Season

29.5	N.Y. Jets, 1972
29.4	Los Angeles, 1950
29.1	New England, 1971

Most Touchdowns Allowed, Kickoff Returns, Season

3	Minnesota, 1963, 1970
	Dallas, 1966
	Detroit, 1980
2	By many teams

FUMBLES

Fewest Opponents Fumbles, Season

11	Cleveland, 1956
13	Los Angeles, 1956
	Chicago, 1960
	Cleveland, 1963, 1965
	Detroit, 1967

San Diego, 1969
14 Baltimore, 1970
Oakland, 1975
Most Opponents Fumbles, Season
50 Minnesota, 1963
San Francisco, 1978
48 N.Y. Giants, 1980
47 N.Y. Giants, 1977

TURNOVERS

(Number of times losing the ball on interceptions and fumbles.)

Fewest Opponents Turnovers, Season
18 San Francisco, 1977
19 Brooklyn, 1944
Chicago, 1960
Cincinnati, 1968
20 Philadelphia, 1968
Cincinnati, 1974

Most Opponents Turnovers, Season
68 Denver, 1961
66 San Diego, 1961
57 Detroit, 1952

Most Opponents Turnovers, Game
12 Chi. Bears vs. Detroit, Nov. 22, 1942
Philadelphia vs. Chi. Cardinals, Sept. 24, 1950; vs. Pittsburgh, Dec. 12, 1965
11 Green Bay vs. San Diego, Sept. 24, 1978
10 N.Y. Giants vs. Washington, Dec. 4, 1938; vs. Chi. Cardinals, Nov. 2, 1952;
      vs. Washington, Dec. 8, 1963
Green Bay vs. Pittsburgh, Nov. 23, 1941; vs. Detroit, Oct. 24, 1943;
      vs. Chi. Cardinals, Nov. 10, 1946
Detroit vs. Minnesota, Dec. 9, 1962; vs. Chicago, Sept. 22, 1968
Oakland vs. Houston, Sept. 7, 1963
Washington vs. St. Louis, Oct. 25, 1976
New England vs. N.Y. Jets, Nov. 21, 1976
Dallas vs. San Francisco, Oct. 12, 1980
Seattle vs. Cleveland, Dec. 20, 1981

OUTSTANDING PERFORMERS

1,000 YARDS RUSHING IN A SEASON

Year	Player, Team	Att.	Yards	Avg.	Long	TD
1981	*George Rogers, New Orleans	378	1,674	4.4	79	13
	Tony Dorsett, Dallas[5]	342	1,646	4.8	75	4
	Billy Sims, Detroit[2]	296	1,437	4.9	51	13
	Wilbert Montgomery, Philadelphia[3]	286	1,402	4.9	41	8
	Ottis Anderson, St. Louis[3]	328	1,376	4.2	28	9
	Earl Campbell, Houston[4]	361	1,376	3.8	43	10
	William Andrews, Atlanta[3]	289	1,301	4.5	29	10
	Walter Payton, Chicago[6]	339	1,222	3.6	39	6
	Chuck Muncie, San Diego[2]	251	1,144	4.6	73	19
	*Joe Delaney, Kansas City	234	1,121	4.8	82	3
	Mike Pruitt, Cleveland[3]	247	1,103	4.5	21	7
	Joe Cribbs, Buffalo[2]	257	1,097	4.3	35	3
	Pete Johnson, Cincinnati	274	1,077	3.9	39	12
	Wendell Tyler, Los Angeles[2]	260	1,074	4.1	69	12
	Ted Brown, Minnesota	274	1,063	3.9	34	6
1980	Earl Campbell, Houston[3]	373	1,934	5.2	55	13
	Walter Payton, Chicago[5]	317	1,460	4.6	69	6
	Ottis Anderson, St. Louis[2]	301	1,352	4.5	52	9
	William Andrews, Atlanta[2]	265	1,308	4.9	33	4
	*Billy Sims, Detroit	313	1,303	4.2	52	13
	Tony Dorsett, Dallas[4]	278	1,185	4.3	56	11
	*Joe Cribbs, Buffalo	306	1,185	3.9	48	11
	Mike Pruitt, Cleveland[2]	249	1,034	4.2	56	6
1979	Earl Campbell, Houston[2]	368	1,697	4.6	61	19
	Walter Payton, Chicago[4]	369	1,610	4.4	43	14
	*Ottis Anderson, St. Louis	331	1,605	4.8	76	8
	Wilbert Montgomery, Philadelphia[2]	338	1,512	4.5	62	9
	Mike Pruitt, Cleveland	264	1,294	4.9	77	9
	Ricky Bell, Tampa Bay	283	1,263	4.5	49	7
	Chuck Muncie, New Orleans	238	1,198	5.0	69	11
	Franco Harris, Pittsburgh[7]	267	1,186	4.4	71	11
	John Riggins, Washington[3]	260	1,153	4.4	66	9
	Wendell Tyler, Los Angeles	218	1,109	5.1	63	9
	Tony Dorsett, Dallas[3]	250	1,107	4.4	41	6
	*William Andrews, Atlanta	239	1,023	4.3	23	3
1978	*Earl Campbell, Houston	302	1,450	4.8	81	13
	Walter Payton, Chicago[3]	333	1,395	4.2	76	11
	Tony Dorsett, Dallas[2]	290	1,325	4.6	63	7
	Delvin Williams, Miami[2]	272	1,258	4.6	58	8
	Wilbert Montgomery, Philadelphia	259	1,220	4.7	47	9
	Terdell Middleton, Green Bay	284	1,116	3.9	76	11
	Franco Harris, Pittsburgh[6]	310	1,082	3.5	37	8
	Mark van Eeghen, Oakland[3]	270	1,080	4.0	34	9
	*Terry Miller, Buffalo	238	1,060	4.5	60	7
	Tony Reed, Kansas City	206	1,053	5.1	62	5
	John Riggins, Washington[2]	248	1,014	4.1	31	5
1977	Walter Payton, Chicago[2]	339	1,852	5.5	73	14
	Mark van Eeghen, Oakland[2]	324	1,273	3.9	27	7
	Lawrence McCutcheon, Los Angeles[4]	294	1,238	4.2	48	7
	Franco Harris, Pittsburgh[5]	300	1,162	3.9	61	11
	Lydell Mitchell, Baltimore[3]	301	1,159	3.9	64	3
	Chuck Foreman, Minnesota[3]	270	1,112	4.1	51	6
	Greg Pruitt, Cleveland[3]	236	1,086	4.6	78	3
	Sam Cunningham, New England	270	1,015	3.8	31	4
	*Tony Dorsett, Dallas	208	1,007	4.8	84	12
1976	O. J. Simpson, Buffalo[5]	290	1,503	5.2	75	8
	Walter Payton, Chicago	311	1,390	4.5	60	13

Year	Player	Att	Yards	Avg	Long	TD
	Delvin Williams, San Francisco	248	1,203	4.9	80	7
	Lydell Mitchell, Baltimore[2]	289	1,200	4.2	43	5
	Lawrence McCutcheon, Los Angeles[3]	291	1,168	4.0	40	9
	Chuck Foreman, Minnesota[2]	278	1,155	4.2	46	13
	Franco Harris, Pittsburgh[4]	289	1,128	3.9	30	14
	Mike Thomas, Washington	254	1,101	4.3	28	5
	Rocky Bleier, Pittsburgh	220	1,036	4.7	28	5
	Mark van Eeghen, Oakland	233	1,012	4.3	21	3
	Otis Armstrong, Denver[2]	247	1,008	4.1	31	5
	Greg Pruitt, Cleveland[2]	209	1,000	4.8	64	4
1975	O.J. Simpson, Buffalo[4]	329	1,817	5.5	88	16
	Franco Harris, Pittsburgh[3]	262	1,246	4.8	36	10
	Lydell Mitchell, Baltimore	289	1,193	4.1	70	11
	Jim Otis, St. Louis	269	1,076	4.0	30	5
	Chuck Foreman, Minnesota	280	1,070	3.8	31	13
	Greg Pruitt, Cleveland	217	1,067	4.9	50	8
	John Riggins, N.Y. Jets	238	1,005	4.2	42	8
	Dave Hampton, Atlanta	250	1,002	4.0	22	5
1974	Otis Armstrong, Denver	263	1,407	5.3	43	9
	*Don Woods, San Diego	227	1,162	5.1	56	7
	O.J. Simpson, Buffalo[3]	270	1,125	4.2	41	3
	Lawrence McCutcheon, Los Angeles[2]	236	1,109	4.7	23	3
	Franco Harris, Pittsburgh[2]	208	1,006	4.8	54	5
1973	O.J. Simpson, Buffalo[2]	332	2,003	6.0	80	12
	John Brockington, Green Bay[3]	265	1,144	4.3	53	3
	Calvin Hill, Dallas[2]	273	1,142	4.2	21	6
	*Lawrence McCutcheon, Los Angeles	210	1,097	5.2	37	2
	Larry Csonka, Miami[3]	219	1,003	4.6	25	5
1972	O.J. Simpson, Buffalo	292	1,251	4.3	94	6
	Larry Brown, Washington[2]	285	1,216	4.3	38	8
	Ron Johnson, N.Y. Giants[2]	298	1,182	4.0	35	9
	Larry Csonka, Miami[2]	213	1,117	5.2	45	6
	Marv Hubbard, Oakland	219	1,100	5.0	39	4
	*Franco Harris, Pittsburgh	188	1,055	5.6	75	10
	Calvin Hill, Dallas	245	1,036	4.2	26	6
	Mike Garrett, San Diego[2]	272	1,031	3.8	41	6
	John Brockington, Green Bay[2]	274	1,027	3.7	30	8
	Eugene (Mercury) Morris, Miami	190	1,000	5.3	33	12
1971	Floyd Little, Denver	284	1,133	4.0	40	6
	*John Brockington, Green Bay	216	1,105	5.1	52	4
	Larry Csonka, Miami	195	1,051	5.4	28	7
	Steve Owens, Detroit	246	1,035	4.2	23	8
	Willie Ellison, Los Angeles	211	1,000	4.7	80	4
1970	Larry Brown, Washington	237	1,125	4.7	75	5
	Ron Johnson, N.Y. Giants	263	1,027	3.9	68	8
1969	Gale Sayers, Chicago[2]	236	1,032	4.4	28	8
1968	Leroy Kelly, Cleveland[3]	248	1,239	5.0	65	16
	*Paul Robinson, Cincinnati	238	1,023	4.3	87	8
1967	Jim Nance, Boston[2]	269	1,216	4.5	53	7
	Leroy Kelly, Cleveland[2]	235	1,205	5.1	42	11
	Hoyle Granger, Houston	236	1,194	5.1	67	6
	Mike Garrett, Kansas City	236	1,087	4.6	58	9
1966	Jim Nance, Boston	299	1,458	4.9	65	11
	Gale Sayers, Chicago	229	1,231	5.4	58	8
	Leroy Kelly, Cleveland	209	1,141	5.5	70	15
	Dick Bass, Los Angeles[2]	248	1,090	4.4	50	8
1965	Jim Brown, Cleveland[7]	289	1,544	5.3	67	17
	Paul Lowe, San Diego[2]	222	1,121	5.0	59	7
1964	Jim Brown, Cleveland[6]	280	1,446	5.2	71	7
	Jim Taylor, Green Bay[5]	235	1,169	5.0	84	12
	John Henry Johnson, Pittsburgh[2]	235	1,048	4.5	45	7
1963	Jim Brown, Cleveland[5]	291	1,863	6.4	80	12
	Clem Daniels, Oakland	215	1,099	5.1	74	3

		Att	Yards	Avg	Long	TD
	Jim Taylor, Green Bay[4]	248	1,018	4.1	40	9
	Paul Lowe, San Diego	177	1,010	5.7	66	8
1962	Jim Taylor, Green Bay[3]	272	1,474	5.4	51	19
	John Henry Johnson, Pittsburgh	251	1,141	4.5	40	7
	*Cookie Gilchrist, Buffalo	214	1,096	5.1	44	13
	Abner Haynes, Dall. Texans	221	1,049	4.7	71	13
	Dick Bass, Los Angeles	196	1,033	5.3	57	6
	Charlie Tolar, Houston	244	1,012	4.1	25	7
1961	Jim Brown, Cleveland[4]	305	1,408	4.6	38	8
	Jim Taylor, Green Bay[2]	243	1,307	5.4	53	15
1960	Jim Brown, Cleveland[3]	215	1,257	5.8	71	9
	Jim Taylor, Green Bay	230	1,101	4.8	32	11
	John David Crow, St. Louis	183	1,071	5.9	57	6
1959	Jim Brown, Cleveland[2]	290	1,329	4.6	70	14
	J. D. Smith, San Francisco	207	1,036	5.0	73	10
1958	Jim Brown, Cleveland	257	1,527	5.9	65	17
1956	Rick Casares, Chi. Bears	234	1,126	4.8	68	12
1954	Joe Perry, San Francisco[2]	173	1,049	6.1	58	8
1953	Joe Perry, San Francisco	192	1,018	5.3	51	10
1949	Steve Van Buren, Philadelphia[2]	263	1,146	4.4	41	11
	Tony Canadeo, Green Bay	208	1,052	5.1	54	4
1947	Steve Van Buren, Philadelphia	217	1,008	4.6	45	13
1934	*Beattie Feathers, Chi. Bears	101	1,004	9.9	82	8

*First year in the league.

200 YARDS RUSHING IN A GAME

Date	Player, Team, Opponent	Att.	Yards	TD
Dec. 21, 1980	Earl Campbell, Houston vs. Minnesota	29	203	1
Nov. 16, 1980	Earl Campbell, Houston vs. Chicago	31	206	0
Oct. 26, 1980	Earl Campbell, Houston vs. Cincinnati	27	202	2
Oct. 19, 1980	Earl Campbell, Houston vs. Tampa Bay	33	203	0
Nov. 26, 1978	*Terry Miller, Buffalo vs.N.Y. Giants	21	208	2
Dec. 4, 1977	*Tony Dorsett, Dallas vs. Philadelphia	23	206	2
Nov. 20, 1977	Walter Payton, Chicago vs. Minnesota	40	275	1
Oct. 30, 1977	Walter Payton, Chicago vs. Green Bay	23	205	2
Dec. 5, 1976	O. J. Simpson, Buffalo vs. Miami	24	203	1
Nov. 25, 1976	O. J. Simpson, Buffalo vs. Detroit	29	273	2
Oct. 24, 1976	Chuck Foreman, Minnesota vs. Philadelphia	28	200	2
Dec. 14, 1975	Greg Pruitt, Cleveland vs. Kansas City	26	214	3
Sept. 28, 1975	O. J. Simpson, Buffalo vs. Pittsburgh	28	227	1
Dec. 16, 1973	O. J. Simpson, Buffalo vs. N.Y. Jets	34	200	1
Dec. 9, 1973	O. J. Simpson, Buffalo vs. New England	22	219	1
Sept. 16, 1973	O. J. Simpson, Buffalo vs. New England	29	250	2
Dec. 5, 1971	Willie Ellison, Los Angeles vs. New Orleans	26	247	1
Dec. 20, 1970	John (Frenchy) Fuqua, Pittsburgh vs. Philadelphia	20	218	2
Nov. 3, 1968	Gale Sayers, Chicago vs. Green Bay	24	205	0
Oct. 30, 1966	Jim Nance, Boston vs. Oakland	38	208	2
Oct. 10, 1964	John Henry Johnson, Pittsburgh vs. Cleveland	30	200	3
Dec. 8, 1963	Cookie Gilchrist, Buffalo vs. N.Y. Jets	36	243	5
Nov. 3, 1963	Jim Brown, Cleveland vs. Philadelphia	28	223	1
Oct. 20, 1963	Clem Daniels, Oakland vs. N.Y. Jets	27	200	2
Sept. 22, 1963	Jim Brown, Cleveland vs. Dallas	20	232	2
Dec. 10, 1961	Billy Cannon, Houston vs. N.Y. Titans	25	216	3
Nov. 19, 1961	Jim Brown, Cleveland vs. Philadelphia	34	237	4
Dec. 18, 1960	John David Crow, St. Louis vs. Pittsburgh	24	203	0
Nov. 15, 1959	Bobby Mitchell, Cleveland vs. Washington	14	232	3
Nov. 24, 1957	*Jim Brown, Cleveland vs. Los Angeles	31	237	4
Dec. 16, 1956	*Tom Wilson, Los Angeles vs. Green Bay	23	223	0
Nov. 22, 1953	Dan Towler, Los Angeles vs. Baltimore	14	205	1
Nov. 12, 1950	Gene Roberts, N.Y. Giants vs. Chi. Cardinals	26	218	2
Nov. 27, 1949	Steve Van Buren, Philadelphia vs. Pittsburgh	27	205	0
Oct. 8, 1933	Cliff Battles, Boston vs. N.Y. Giants	16	215	1

*First year in the league.

400 YARDS PASSING IN A GAME

Date	Player, Team, Opponent	Att.	Comp.	Yards	TD
Nov. 15, 1981	Steve Bartkowski, Atlanta vs. Pittsburgh	50	33	416	2
Oct. 25, 1981	Brian Sipe, Cleveland vs. Baltimore	41	30	444	4
Oct. 25, 1981	David Woodley, Miami vs. Dallas	37	21	408	3
Oct. 11, 1981	Tommy Kramer, Minnesota vs. San Diego	43	27	444	4
Dec. 14, 1980	Tommy Kramer, Minnesota vs. Cleveland	49	38	456	4
Nov. 16, 1980	Doug Williams, Tampa Bay vs. Minnesota	55	30	486	4
Oct. 19, 1980	Dan Fouts, San Diego vs. N. Y. Giants	41	26	444	3
Oct. 12, 1980	Lynn Dickey, Green Bay vs. Tampa Bay	51	35	418	1
Sept. 21, 1980	Richard Todd, N. Y. Jets vs. San Francisco	60	42	447	3
Oct. 3, 1976	James Harris, Los Angeles vs. Miami	29	17	436	2
Nov. 17, 1975	Ken Anderson, Cincinnati vs. Buffalo	46	30	447	2
Nov. 18, 1974	Charley Johnson, Denver vs. Kansas City	42	28	445	2
Dec. 11, 1972	Joe Namath, N.Y. Jets vs. Oakland	46	25	403	1
Sept. 24, 1972	Joe Namath, N.Y. Jets vs. Baltimore	28	15	496	6
Dec. 21, 1969	Don Horn, Green Bay vs. St. Louis	31	22	410	5
Sept. 28, 1969	Joe Kapp, Minnesota vs. Baltimore	43	28	449	7
Sept. 9, 1968	Pete Beathard, Houston vs. Kansas City	48	23	413	2
Nov. 26, 1967	Sonny Jurgensen, Washington vs. Cleveland	50	32	418	3
Oct. 1, 1967	Joe Namath, N.Y. Jets vs. Miami	39	23	415	3
Sept. 17, 1967	Johnny Unitas, Baltimore vs. Atlanta	32	22	401	2
Nov. 13, 1966	Don Meredith, Dallas vs. Washington	29	21	406	2
Nov. 28, 1965	Sonny Jurgensen, Washington vs. Dallas	43	26	411	3
Oct. 24, 1965	Fran Tarkenton, Minnesota vs. San Francisco	35	21	407	3
Nov. 1, 1964	Len Dawson, Kansas City vs. Denver	38	23	435	6
Oct. 25, 1964	Cotton Davidson, Oakland vs. Denver	36	23	427	5
Oct. 16, 1964	Babe Parilli, Boston vs. Oakland	47	25	422	4
Dec. 22, 1963	Tom Flores, Oakland vs. Houston	29	17	407	6
Nov. 17, 1963	Norm Snead, Washington vs. Pittsburgh	40	23	424	2
Nov. 10, 1963	Don Meredith, Dallas vs. San Francisco	48	30	460	3
Oct. 13, 1963	Charley Johnson, St. Louis vs. Pittsburgh	41	20	428	2
Dec. 16, 1962	Sonny Jurgensen, Philadelphia vs. St. Louis	34	15	419	5
Nov. 18, 1962	Bill Wade, Chicago vs. Dall. Cowboys	46	28	466	2
Oct. 28, 1962	Y.A. Tittle, N.Y. Giants vs. Washington	39	27	505	7
Sept. 15, 1962	Frank Tripucka, Denver vs. Buffalo	56	29	447	2
Dec. 17, 1961	Sonny Jurgensen, Philadelphia vs. Detroit	42	27	403	3
Nov. 19, 1961	George Blanda, Houston vs. N.Y. Titans	32	20	418	7
Oct. 29, 1961	Sonny Jurgensen, Philadelphia vs. Washington	41	27	436	3
Oct. 29, 1961	George Blanda, Houston vs. Buffalo	32	18	464	4
Oct. 13, 1961	Jacky Lee, Houston vs. Boston	41	27	457	2
Dec. 13, 1958	Bobby Layne, Pittsburgh vs. Chi. Cardinals	49	23	409	2
Nov. 8, 1953	Bobby Thomason, Philadelphia vs. N.Y. Giants	44	22	437	4
Oct. 4, 1952	Otto Graham, Cleveland vs. Pittsburgh	49	21	401	3
Sept. 28, 1951	Norm Van Brocklin, Los Angeles vs. N.Y. Yanks	41	27	554	5
Dec. 11, 1949	Johnny Lujack, Chi. Bears vs. Chi. Cardinals	39	24	468	6
Oct. 31, 1948	Jim Hardy, Los Angeles vs. Chi. Cardinals	53	28	406	3
Oct. 31, 1948	Sammy Baugh, Washington vs. Boston	24	17	446	4
Nov. 14, 1943	Sid Luckman, Chi. Bears vs. N.Y. Giants	32	21	433	7

1,000 YARDS PASS RECEIVING IN A SEASON

Year	Player, Team	No.	Yards	Avg.	Long	TD
1981	Alfred Jenkins, Atlanta[2]	70	1,358	19.4	67	13
	James Lofton, Green Bay[2]	71	1,294	18.2	75	8
	Frank Lewis, Buffalo[2]	70	1,244	17.8	33	4
	Steve Watson, Denver	60	1,244	20.7	95	13
	Steve Largent, Seattle[4]	75	1,224	16.3	57	9
	Charlie Joiner, San Diego[4]	70	1,188	17.0	57	7
	Kevin House, Tampa Bay	56	1,176	21.0	84	9
	Wes Chandler, N.O.-San Diego[2]	69	1,142	16.6	51	6
	Dwight Clark, San Francisco	85	1,105	13.0	78	4
	John Stallworth, Pittsburgh[2]	63	1,098	17.4	55	5

Year	Player	No.	Yards	Avg	Long	TD
	Kellen Winslow, San Diego[2]	88	1,075	12.2	67	10
	Pat Tilley, St. Louis	66	1,040	15.8	75	3
	Stanley Morgan, New England[2]	44	1,029	23.4	76	6
	Harold Carmichael, Philadelphia[3]	61	1,028	16.9	85	6
	Freddie Scott, Detroit	53	1,022	19.3	48	5
	*Cris Collinsworth, Cincinnati	67	1,009	15.1	74	8
	Joe Senser, Minnesota	79	1,004	12.7	53	8
	Ozzie Newsome, Cleveland	69	1,002	14.5	62	6
	Sammy White, Minnesota	66	1,001	15.2	53	3
1980	John Jefferson, San Diego[2]	82	1,340	16.3	58	13
	Kellen Winslow, San Diego	89	1,290	14.5	65	9
	James Lofton, Green Bay	71	1,226	17.3	47	4
	Charlie Joiner, San Diego[3]	71	1,132	15.9	51	4
	Ahmad Rashad, Minnesota[2]	69	1,095	15.9	76	5
	Steve Largent, Seattle[3]	66	1,064	16.1	67	6
	Tony Hill, Dallas[2]	60	1,055	17.6	58	8
	Alfred Jenkins, Atlanta	57	1,026	18.0	57	6
1979	Steve Largent, Seattle[2]	66	1,237	18.7	55	9
	John Stallworth, Pittsburgh	70	1,183	16.9	65	8
	Ahmad Rashad, Minnesota	80	1,156	14.5	52	9
	John Jefferson, San Diego[2]	61	1,090	17.9	65	10
	Frank Lewis, Buffalo	54	1,082	20.0	55	2
	Wes Chandler, New Orleans	65	1,069	16.4	85	6
	Tony Hill, Dallas	60	1,062	17.7	75	10
	Drew Pearson, Dallas[2]	55	1,026	18.7	56	8
	Wallace Francis, Atlanta	74	1,013	13.7	42	8
	Harold Jackson, New England[3]	45	1,013	22.5	59	7
	Charlie Joiner, San Diego[2]	72	1,008	14.0	39	4
	Stanley Morgan, New England	44	1,002	22.8	63	12
1978	Wesley Walker, N.Y. Jets	48	1,169	24.4	77	8
	Steve Largent, Seattle	71	1,168	16.5	57	8
	Harold Carmichael, Philadelphia[2]	55	1,072	19.5	56	8
	*John Jefferson, San Diego	56	1,001	17.9	46	13
1976	Roger Carr, Baltimore	43	1,112	25.9	79	11
	Cliff Branch, Oakland[2]	46	1,111	24.2	88	12
	Charlie Joiner, San Diego	50	1,056	21.1	81	7
1975	Ken Burrough, Houston	53	1,063	20.1	77	8
1974	Cliff Branch, Oakland	60	1,092	18.2	67	13
	Drew Pearson, Dallas	62	1,087	17.5	50	2
1973	Harold Carmichael, Philadelphia	67	1,116	16.7	73	9
1972	Harold Jackson, Philadelphia[2]	62	1,048	16.9	77	4
	John Gilliam, Minnesota	47	1,035	22.0	66	7
1971	Otis Taylor, Kansas City[2]	57	1,110	19.5	82	7
1970	Gene Washington, San Francisco	53	1,100	20.8	79	12
	Marlin Briscoe, Buffalo	57	1,036	18.2	48	8
	Dick Gordon, Chicago	71	1,026	14.5	69	13
	Gary Garrison, San Diego[2]	44	1,006	22.9	67	12
1969	Warren Wells, Oakland[2]	47	1,260	26.8	80	14
	Harold Jackson, Philadelphia	65	1,116	17.2	65	9
	Roy Jefferson, Pittsburgh[2]	67	1,079	16.1	63	9
	Dan Abramowicz, New Orleans	73	1,015	13.9	49	7
	Lance Alworth, San Diego[7]	64	1,003	15.7	76	4
1968	Lance Alworth, San Diego[6]	68	1,312	19.3	80	10
	Don Maynard, N.Y. Jets[5]	57	1,297	22.8	87	10
	George Sauer, N.Y. Jets[3]	66	1,141	17.3	43	3
	Warren Wells, Oakland	53	1,137	21.5	94	11
	Gary Garrison, San Diego	52	1,103	21.2	84	10
	Roy Jefferson, Pittsburgh	58	1,074	18.5	62	11
	Paul Warfield, Cleveland	50	1,067	21.3	65	12
	Homer Jones, N.Y. Giants[3]	45	1,057	23.5	84	7
	Fred Biletnikoff, Oakland	61	1,037	17.0	82	6
	Lance Rentzel, Dallas	54	1,009	18.7	65	6
1967	Don Maynard, N.Y. Jets[4]	71	1,434	20.2	75	10

Year	Player	No.	Yards	Avg.	Long	TD
	Ben Hawkins, Philadelphia	59	1,265	21.4	87	10
	Homer Jones, N.Y. Giants[2]	49	1,209	24.7	70	13
	Jackie Smith, St. Louis	56	1,205	21.5	76	9
	George Sauer, N.Y. Jets[2]	75	1,189	15.9	61	6
	Lance Alworth, San Diego[5]	52	1,010	19.4	71	9
1966	Lance Alworth, San Diego[4]	73	1,383	18.9	78	13
	Otis Taylor, Kansas City	58	1,297	22.4	89	8
	Pat Studstill, Detroit	67	1,266	18.9	99	5
	Bob Hayes, Dallas[2]	64	1,232	19.3	95	13
	Charlie Frazier, Houston	57	1,129	19.8	79	12
	Charley Taylor, Washington	72	1,119	15.5	86	12
	George Sauer, N.Y. Jets	63	1,081	17.2	77	5
	Homer Jones, N.Y. Giants	48	1,044	21.8	98	8
	Art Powell, Oakland[5]	53	1,026	19.4	46	11
1965	Lance Alworth, San Diego[3]	69	1,602	23.2	85	14
	Dave Parks, San Francisco	80	1,344	16.8	53	12
	Don Maynard, N.Y. Jets[3]	68	1,218	17.9	56	14
	Pete Retzlaff, Philadelphia	66	1,190	18.0	78	10
	Lionel Taylor, Denver[4]	85	1,131	13.3	63	6
	Tommy McDonald, Los Angeles[3]	67	1,036	15.5	51	9
	*Bob Hayes, Dallas	46	1,003	21.8	82	12
1964	Charley Hennigan, Houston[3]	101	1,546	15.3	53	8
	Art Powell, Oakland[4]	76	1,361	17.9	77	11
	Lance Alworth, San Diego[2]	61	1,235	20.2	82	13
	Johnny Morris, Chicago	93	1,200	12.9	63	10
	Elbert Dubenion, Buffalo	42	1,139	27.1	72	10
	Terry Barr, Detroit[2]	57	1,030	18.1	58	9
1963	Bobby Mitchell, Washington[2]	69	1,436	20.8	99	7
	Art Powell, Oakland[3]	73	1,304	17.9	85	16
	Buddy Dial, Pittsburgh[2]	60	1,295	21.6	83	9
	Lance Alworth, San Diego	61	1,205	19.8	85	11
	Del Shofner, N.Y. Giants[4]	64	1,181	18.5	70	9
	Lionel Taylor, Denver[3]	78	1,101	14.1	72	10
	Terry Barr, Detroit	66	1,086	16.5	75	13
	Charley Hennigan, Houston[2]	61	1,051	17.2	83	10
	Sonny Randle, St. Louis[2]	51	1,014	19.9	68	12
	Bake Turner, N.Y. Jets	71	1,009	14.2	53	6
1962	Bobby Mitchell, Washington	72	1,384	19.2	81	11
	Sonny Randle, St. Louis	63	1,158	18.4	86	7
	Tommy McDonald, Philadelphia[2]	58	1,146	19.8	60	10
	Del Shofner, N.Y. Giants[3]	53	1,133	21.4	69	12
	Art Powell, N.Y. Titans[2]	64	1,130	17.7	80	8
	Frank Clarke, Dall. Cowboys[2]	47	1,043	22.2	66	14
	Don Maynard, N.Y. Titans[2]	56	1,041	18.6	86	8
1961	Charley Hennigan, Houston	82	1,746	21.3	80	12
	Lionel Taylor, Denver[2]	100	1,176	11.8	52	4
	Bill Groman, Houston[2]	50	1,175	23.5	80	17
	Tommy McDonald, Philadelphia	64	1,144	17.9	66	13
	Del Shofner, N.Y. Giants[2]	68	1,125	16.5	46	11
	Jim Phillips, Los Angeles	78	1,092	14.0	69	5
	*Mike Ditka, Chicago	56	1,076	19.2	76	12
	Dave Kocourek, San Diego	55	1,055	19.2	76	4
	Buddy Dial, Pittsburgh	53	1,047	19.8	88	6
	R.C. Owens, San Francisco	55	1,032	18.8	54	5
1960	*Bill Groman, Houston	72	1,473	20.5	92	12
	Raymond Berry, Baltimore	74	1,298	17.5	70	10
	Don Maynard, N.Y. Titans	72	1,265	17.6	65	6
	Lionel Taylor, Denver	92	1,235	13.4	80	12
	Art Powell, N.Y. Titans	69	1,167	16.9	76	14
1958	Del Shofner, Los Angeles	51	1,097	21.5	92	8
1956	Bill Howton, Green Bay[2]	55	1,188	21.6	66	12
	Harlon Hill, Chi. Bears[2]	47	1,128	24.0	79	11
1954	Bob Boyd, Los Angeles	53	1,212	22.9	80	6

	*Harlon Hill, Chi. Bears	45	1,124	25.0	76	12
1953	Pete Pihos, Philadelphia	63	1,049	16.7	59	10
1952	*Bill Howton, Green Bay	53	1,231	23.2	90	13
1951	Elroy (Crazylegs) Hirsch, Los Angeles	66	1,495	22.7	91	17
1950	Tom Fears, Los Angeles[2]	84	1,116	13.3	53	7
	Cloyce Box, Detroit	50	1,009	20.2	82	11
1949	Bob Mann, Detroit	66	1,014	15.4	64	4
	Tom Fears, Los Angeles	77	1,013	13.2	51	9
1945	Jim Benton, Cleveland	45	1,067	23.7	84	8
1942	Don Hutson, Green Bay	74	1,211	16.4	73	17

*First year in the league.

250 YARDS PASS RECEIVING IN A GAME

Date	Player, Team, Opponent	No.	Yards	TD
Sept. 23, 1979	*Jerry Butler, Buffalo vs. N.Y. Jets	10	255	4
Nov. 4, 1962	Sonny Randle, St. Louis vs. N.Y. Giants	16	256	1
Oct. 28, 1962	Del Shofner, N.Y. Giants vs. Washington . . .	11	269	1
Oct. 13, 1961	Charley Hennigan, Houston vs. Boston	13	272	1
Oct. 21, 1956	Billy Howton, Green Bay vs. Los Angeles . .	7	257	2
Dec. 3, 1950	Cloyce Box, Detroit vs. Baltimore	12	302	4
Nov. 22, 1945	Jim Benton, Cleveland vs. Detroit	10	303	1

*First year in the league.

2,000 COMBINED NET YARDS GAINED IN A SEASON

Year, Player, Team	Rushing Att.-Yds	Pass Rec.	Punt Ret.	Kickoff Ret.	Fum. Runs	Total Yds.
1981 *James Brooks, San Diego .	109-525	46-329	22-290	40-949	2-0	219-2,093
William Andrews, Atlanta . .	289-1,301	81-735	0-0	0-0	0-0	370-2,036
1980 Bruce Harper, N.Y. Jets . . .	45-126	50-634	28-242	49-1,070	3-0	175-2,072
1979 Wilbert Montgomery, Phil. .	338-1,512	41-494	0-0	1-6	2-0	382-2,012
1978 Bruce Harper, N.Y. Jets	58-303	13-196	30-378	55-1,280	1-0	157-2,157
1977 Walter Payton, Chicago . . .	339-1,852	27-269	0-0	2-95	5-0	373-2,216
Terry Metcalf, St. Louis	149-739	34-403	14-108	32-772	1-0	230-2,022
1975 Terry Metcalf, St. Louis	165-816	43-378	23-285	35-960	2-23	268-2,462
O.J. Simpson, Buffalo	329-1,817	28-426	0-0	0-0	1-0	358-2,243
1974 Mack Herron, New England	231-824	38-474	35-517	28-629	3-0	335-2,444
Otis Armstrong, Denver . . .	263-1,407	38-405	0-0	16-386	1-0	318-2,198
Terry Metcalf, St. Louis	152-718	50-377	26-340	20-623	7-0	255-2,058
1973 O.J. Simpson, Buffalo	332-2,003	6-70	0-0	0-0		338-2,073
1966 Gale Sayers, Chicago	229-1,231	34-447	6-44	23-718	3-0	295-2,440
Leroy Kelly, Cleveland	209-1,141	32-366	13-104	19-403	0-0	273-2,014
1965 *Gale Sayers, Chicago	166-867	29-507	16-238	21-660	4-0	236-2,272
1963 Timmy Brown, Philadelphia	192-841	36-487	16-152	33-945	2-3	279-2,428
Jim Brown, Cleveland	291-1,863	24-268	0-0	0-0	0-0	315-2,131
1962 Timmy Brown, Philadelphia	137-545	52-849	6-81	30-831	4-0	229-2,306
Dick Christy, N.Y. Titans . . .	114-535	62-538	15-250	38-824	2-0	231-2,147
1961 Billy Cannon, Houston	200-948	43-586	9-70	18-439	2-0	272-2,043
1960 *Abner Haynes, Dall. Texans	156-875	55-576	14-215	19-434	4-0	248-2,100

*First year in the league.

300 COMBINED NET YARDS GAINED IN A GAME

Date	Player, Team, Opponent	No.	Yards	TD
Dec. 21, 1975	Walter Payton, Chicago vs. New Orleans	32	300	1
Nov. 23, 1975	Greg Pruitt, Cleveland vs. Cincinnati	28	304	2
Nov. 1, 1970	Eugene (Mercury) Morris, Miami vs. Baltimore . .	17	302	0
Oct. 4, 1970	O. J. Simpson, Buffalo vs. N.Y. Jets	26	303	2
Dec. 6, 1969	Jerry LeVias, Houston vs. N.Y. Jets	18	329	1
Nov. 2, 1969	Travis Williams, Green Bay vs. Pittsburgh	11	314	3
Dec. 18, 1966	Gale Sayers, Chicago vs. Minnesota	20	339	2
Dec. 12, 1965	Gale Sayers, Chicago vs. San Francisco	17	336	6

Nov. 17, 1963	Gary Ballman, Pittsburgh vs. Washington	12	320	2
Dec. 16, 1962	Timmy Brown, Philadelphia vs. St. Louis	19	341	2
Dec. 10, 1961	Billy Cannon, Houston vs. N.Y. Titans	32	373	5
Nov 19, 1961	Jim Brown, Cleveland vs. Philadelphia	38	313	4
Dec. 3, 1950	Cloyce Box, Detroit vs. Baltimore	13	302	4
Oct. 29, 1950	Wally Triplett, Detroit vs. Los Angeles	11	331	1
Nov. 22, 1945	Jim Benton, Cleveland vs. Detroit	10	303	1

TOP 10 SCORERS

Player	Years	TD	FG	PAT	TP
George Blanda	26	9	335	943	2,002
Jim Turner.	16	1	304	521	1,439
Jim Bakken.	17	0	282	534	1,380
Fred Cox	15	0	282	519	1,365
Lou Groza.	17	1	234	641	1,349
Jan Stenerud	15	0	304	432	1,344
Gino Cappelletti	11	42	176	350	1,130
Don Cockroft	13	0	216	432	1,080
Garo Yepremian.	14	0	210	444	1,074
Bruce Gossett	11	0	219	374	1,031

Cappelletti's total includes four two-point conversions.

TOP 10 TOUCHDOWN SCORERS

Player	Years	Rush	Pass Rec.	Returns	Total TD
Jim Brown.	9	106	20	0	126
Lenny Moore	12	63	48	2	113
Don Hutson	11	3	99	3	105
Jim Taylor	10	83	10	0	93
Franco Harris	10	84	7	0	91
Bobby Mitchell.	11	18	65	8	91
Leroy Kelly	10	74	13	3	90
Charley Taylor	13	11	79	0	90
Don Maynard	15	0	88	0	88
Lance Alworth	11	2	85	0	87

TOP 10 RUSHERS

Player	Years	Att.	Yards	Avg.	Long	TD
Jim Brown.	9	2,359	12,312	5.2	80	106
O. J. Simpson.	11	2,404	11,236	4.7	94	61
Franco Harris	10	2,462	10,339	4.2	75	84
Walter Payton	7	2,204	9,608	4.4	76	71
Jim Taylor	10	1,941	8,597	4.4	84	83
Joe Perry	14	1,737	8,378	4.8	78	53
Larry Csonka	11	1,891	8,081	4.3	54	64
John Riggins	10	1,861	7,536	4.0	66	55
Leroy Kelly	10	1,727	7,274	4.2	70	74
John Henry Johnson.	13	1,571	6,803	4.3	87	48

TOP 10 PASSERS

Player	Years	Att.	Comp.	Pct. Comp.	Yards	TD	Pct. TD	Int.	Pct. Int.	Avg. Gain	Rating
Roger Staubach	11	2,958	1,685	57.0	22,700	153	5.2	109	3.7	7.67	83.5
Sonny Jurgensen	18	4,262	2,433	57.1	32,224	255	6.0	189	4.4	7.56	82.8
Len Dawson	19	3,741	2,136	57.1	28,711	239	6.4	183	4.9	7.67	82.6
Ken Anderson	11	3,539	2,036	57.5	25,562	160	4.5	124	3.5	7.22	80.5
Fran Tarkenton	18	6,467	3,686	57.0	47,003	342	5.3	266	4.1	7.27	80.5
Bart Starr	16	3,149	1,808	57.4	24,718	152	4.8	138	4.4	7.85	80.3
Bert Jones	9	2,464	1,382	56.1	17,663	122	5.0	97	3.9	7.17	79.1
Dan Fouts	9	3,203	1,849	57.7	24,256	145	4.5	142	4.4	7.57	78.4
Johnny Unitas	18	5,186	2,830	54.6	40,239	290	5.6	253	4.9	7.76	78.2
Otto Graham	6	1,565	872	55.7	13,499	88	5.6	94	6.0	8.63	78.1

1,500 or more attempts. The passing ratings are based on performance standards established for completion percentage, interception percentage, touchdown percentage, and average gain. Passers are allocated points according to how their marks compare with those standards.

TOP 10 PASS RECEIVERS

Player	Years	No.	Yards	Avg.	Long	TD
Charley Taylor	13	649	9,110	14.0	88	79
Don Maynard	15	633	11,834	18.7	87	88
Raymond Berry	13	631	9,275	14.7	70	68
Fred Biletnikoff	14	589	8,974	15.2	82	76
Harold Jackson	14	571	10,246	17.9	79	75
Lionel Taylor	10	567	7,195	12.7	80	45
Lance Alworth	11	542	10,266	18.9	85	85
Bobby Mitchell	11	521	7,954	15.3	99	65
Harold Carmichael	11	516	7,923	15.4	85	72
Billy Howton	12	503	8,459	16.8	90	61

TOP 10 INTERCEPTORS

Player	Years	No.	Yards	Avg.	Long	TD
Paul Krause	16	81	1,185	14.6	81	3
Emlen Tunnell	14	79	1,282	16.2	55	4
Dick (Night Train) Lane	14	68	1,207	17.8	80	5
Dick LeBeau	13	62	762	12.3	70	3
Emmitt Thomas	13	58	937	16.2	73	5
Bobby Boyd	9	57	994	17.4	74	4
Johnny Robinson	12	57	741	13.0	57	1
Lem Barney	11	56	1,077	19.2	71	7
Pat Fischer	17	56	941	16.8	69	4
Willie Brown	16	54	472	8.7	45	2

TOP 10 PUNTERS

Player	Years	No.	Yards	Avg.	Long	Blk.
Sammy Baugh	16	338	15,245	45.1	85	9
Tommy Davis	11	511	22,833	44.7	82	2
Yale Lary	11	503	22,279	44.3	74	4
Horace Gillom	7	385	16,872	43.8	80	5
Jerry Norton	11	358	15,671	43.8	78	2
Don Chandler	12	660	28,678	43.5	90	4
Ray Guy	9	654	28,262	43.2	74	3
Jerrel Wilson	16	1,072	46,139	43.0	72	12
Norm Van Brocklin	12	523	22,413	42.9	72	3
Danny Villanueva	8	488	20,862	42.8	68	2

300 or more punts.

TOP 10 PUNT RETURNERS

Player	Years	No.	Yards	Avg.	Long	TD
Billy Johnson	7	155	2,040	13.2	87	5
George McAfee	8	112	1,431	12.8	74	2
Jack Christiansen	8	85	1,084	12.8	89	8
Claude Gibson	5	110	1,381	12.6	85	3
Bill Dudley	9	124	1,515	12.2	96	3
Rick Upchurch	7	229	2,714	11.9	92	6
Mack Herron	3	84	982	11.7	66	0
Bill Thompson	13	157	1,814	11.6	60	0
J. T. Smith	4	152	1,754	11.5	88	4
Rodger Bird	3	94	1,063	11.3	78	0

75 or more returns.

TOP 10 KICKOFF RETURNERS

Player	Years	No.	Yards	Avg.	Long	TD
Gale Sayers	7	91	2,781	30.6	103	6
Lynn Chandnois	7	92	2,720	29.6	93	3
Abe Woodson	9	193	5,538	28.7	105	5
Claude (Buddy) Young	6	90	2,514	27.9	104	2
Travis Williams	5	102	2,801	27.5	105	6
Joe Arenas	7	139	3,798	27.3	96	1
Clarence Davis	8	79	2,140	27.1	76	0
Steve Van Buren	8	76	2,030	26.7	98	3
Lenny Lyles	12	81	2,161	26.7	103	3
Eugene (Mercury) Morris	8	111	2,947	26.5	105	3

75 or more returns.

YEARLY STATISTICAL LEADERS

ANNUAL SCORING LEADERS

Year	Player, Team	TD	FG	PAT	TP
1981	Ed Murray, Detroit, NFC.	0	25	46	121
	Rafael Septien, Dallas, NFC.	0	27	40	121
	Jim Breech, Cincinnati, AFC	0	22	49	115
	Nick Lowery, Kansas City, AFC	0	26	37	115
1980	John Smith, New England, AFC.	0	26	51	129
	*Ed Murray, Detroit, NFC.	0	27	35	116
1979	John Smith, New England, AFC.	0	23	46	115
	Mark Moseley, Washington, NFC.	0	25	39	114
1978	*Frank Corral, Los Angeles, NFC.	0	29	31	118
	Pat Leahy, N.Y. Jets, AFC.	0	22	41	107
1977	Errol Mann, Oakland, AFC.	0	20	39	99
	Walter Payton, Chicago, NFC.	16	0	0	96
1976	Toni Linhart, Baltimore, AFC.	0	20	49	109
	Mark Moseley, Washington, NFC.	0	22	31	97
1975	O.J. Simpson, Buffalo, AFC.	23	0	0	138
	Chuck Foreman, Minnesota, NFC	22	0	0	132
1974	Chester Marcol, Green Bay, NFC.	0	25	19	94
	Roy Gerela, Pittsburgh, AFC	0	20	33	93
1973	David Ray, Los Angeles, NFC	0	30	40	130
	Roy Gerela, Pittsburgh, AFC	0	29	36	123
1972	*Chester Marcol, Green Bay, NFC	0	33	29	128
	Bobby Howfield, N.Y. Jets, AFC.	0	27	40	121
1971	Garo Yepremian, Miami, AFC.	0	28	33	117
	Curt Knight, Washington, NFC.	0	29	27	114
1970	Fred Cox, Minnesota, NFC.	0	30	35	125
	Jan Stenerud, Kansas City, AFC	0	30	26	116
1969	Jim Turner, N.Y. Jets, AFL.	0	32	33	129
	Fred Cox, Minnesota, NFL.	0	26	43	121
1968	Jim Turner, N.Y. Jets, AFL.	0	34	43	145
	Leroy Kelly, Cleveland, NFL.	20	0	0	120
1967	Jim Bakken St. Louis, NFL.	0	27	36	117
	George Blanda, Oakland, AFL.	0	20	56	116
1966	Gino Cappelletti, Boston, AFL.	6	16	35	119
	Bruce Gossett, Los Angeles, NFL.	0	28	29	113
1965	*Gale Sayers, Chicago, NFL.	22	0	0	132
	Gino Cappelletti, Boston, AFL.	9	17	27	132
1964	Gino Cappelletti, Boston, AFL.	7	25	36	155
	Lenny Moore, Baltimore, NFL.	20	0	0	120
1963	Gino Cappelletti, Boston, AFL.	2	22	35	113
	Don Chandler, N.Y. Giants, NFL.	0	18	52	106
1962	Gene Mingo, Denver, AFL.	4	27	32	137
	Jim Taylor, Green Bay, NFL.	19	0	0	114
1961	Gino Cappelletti, Boston, AFL.	8	17	48	147
	Paul Hornung, Green Bay, NFL.	10	15	41	146
1960	Paul Hornung, Green Bay, NFL.	15	15	41	176
	*Gene Mingo, Denver, AFL.	6	18	33	123
1959	Paul Hornung, Green Bay.	7	7	31	94
1958	Jim Brown, Cleveland.	18	0	0	108
1957	Sam Baker, Washington	1	14	29	77
	Lou Groza, Cleveland.	0	15	32	77
1956	Bobby Layne, Detroit.	5	12	33	99
1955	Doak Walker, Detroit.	7	9	27	96
1954	Bobby Walston, Philadelphia.	11	4	36	114
1953	Gordy Soltau, San Francisco.	6	10	48	114
1952	Gordy Soltau, San Francisco.	7	6	34	94
1951	Elroy (Crazylegs) Hirsch, Los Angeles.	17	0	0	102
1950	*Doak Walker, Detroit.	11	8	38	128

1949	Pat Harder, Chi. Cardinals	8	3	45	102
	Gene Roberts, N.Y. Giants	17	0	0	102
1948	Pat Harder, Chi. Cardinals	6	7	53	110
1947	Pat Harder, Chi. Cardinals	7	7	39	102
1946	Ted Fritsch, Green Bay	10	9	13	100
1945	Steve Van Buren, Philadelphia	18	0	2	110
1944	Don Hutson, Green Bay	9	0	31	85
1943	Don Hutson, Green Bay	12	3	36	117
1942	Don Hutson, Green Bay	17	1	33	138
1941	Don Hutson, Green Bay	12	1	20	95
1940	Don Hutson, Green Bay	7	0	15	57
1939	Andy Farkas, Washington	11	0	2	68
1938	Clarke Hinkle, Green Bay	7	3	7	58
1937	Jack Manders, Chi. Bears	5	8	15	69
1936	Earl (Dutch) Clark, Detroit	7	4	19	73
1935	Earl (Dutch) Clark, Detroit	6	1	16	55
1934	Jack Manders, Chi. Bears	3	10	28	76
1933	Ken Strong, N.Y. Giants	6	5	13	64
	Glenn Presnell, Portsmouth	6	6	10	64
1932	Earl (Dutch) Clark, Portsmouth	6	3	10	55

First year in the league.

ANNUAL LEADERS—MOST FIELD GOALS MADE

Year	Player, Team	Att.	Made	Pct.
1981	Rafael Septien, Dallas, NFC	35	27	77.1
	Nick Lowery, Kansas City, AFC	36	26	72.2
1980	*Ed Murray, Detroit, NFC	42	27	64.3
	John Smith, New England, AFC	34	26	76.5
	Fred Steinfort, Denver, AFC	34	26	76.5
1979	Mark Moseley, Washington, NFC	33	25	75.8
	John Smith, New England, AFC	33	23	69.7
1978	*Frank Corral, Los Angeles, NFC	43	29	67.4
	Pat Leahy, N.Y. Jets, AFC	30	22	73.3
1977	Mark Moseley, Washington, NFC	37	21	56.8
	Errol Mann, Oakland, AFC	28	20	71.4
1976	Mark Moseley, Washington, NFC	34	22	64.7
	Jan Stenerud, Kansas City, AFC	38	21	55.3
1975	Jan Stenerud, Kansas City, AFC	32	22	68.8
	Toni Fritsch, Dallas, NFC	35	22	62.9
1974	Chester Marcol, Green Bay, NFC	39	25	64.1
	Roy Gerela, Pittsburgh, AFC	29	20	69.0
1973	David Ray, Los Angeles, NFC	47	30	63.8
	Roy Gerela, Pittsburgh, AFC	43	29	67.4
1972	*Chester Marcol, Green Bay, NFC	48	33	68.8
	Roy Gerela, Pittsburgh, AFC	41	28	68.3
1971	Curt Knight, Washington, NFC	49	29	59.2
	Garo Yepremian, Miami, AFC	40	28	70.0
1970	Fred Cox, Minnesota, NFC	46	30	65.2
	Jan Stenerud, Kansas City, AFC	42	30	71.4
1969	Jim Turner, N.Y. Jets, AFL	47	32	68.1
	Fred Cox, Minnesota, NFL	37	26	70.3
1968	Jim Turner, N.Y. Jets, AFL	46	34	73.9
	Mac Percival, Chicago, NFL	36	25	69.4
1967	Jim Bakken, St. Louis, NFL	39	27	69.2
	Jan Stenerud, Kansas City, AFL	36	21	58.3
1966	Bruce Gossett, Los Angeles, NFL	49	28	57.1
	Mike Mercer, Oakland-Kansas City, AFL	30	21	70.0
1965	Pete Gogolak, Buffalo, AFL	46	28	60.9
	Fred Cox, Minnesota, NFL	35	23	65.7
1964	Jim Bakken, St. Louis, NFL	38	25	65.8
	Gino Cappelletti, Boston, AFL	39	25	64.1
1963	Jim Martin, Baltimore, NFL	39	24	61.5
	Gino Cappelletti, Boston, AFL	38	22	57.9

1962	Gene Mingo, Denver, AFL	39	27	69.2
	Lou Michaels, Pittsburgh, NFL	42	26	61.9
1961	Steve Myhra, Baltimore, NFL	39	21	53.8
	Gino Cappelletti, Boston, AFL	32	17	53.1
1960	Tommy Davis, San Francisco, NFL	32	19	59.4
	*Gene Mingo, Denver, AFL	28	18	64.3
1959	Pat Summerall, New York Giants	29	20	69.0
1958	Paige Cothren, Los Angeles	25	14	56.0
	*Tom Miner, Pittsburgh	28	14	50.0
1957	Lou Groza, Cleveland	22	15	68.2
1956	Sam Baker, Washington	25	17	68.0
1955	Fred Cone, Green Bay	24	16	66.7
1954	Lou Groza, Cleveland	24	16	66.7
1953	Lou Groza, Cleveland	26	23	88.5
1952	Lou Groza, Cleveland	33	19	57.6
1951	Bob Waterfield, Los Angeles	23	13	56.5
1950	*Lou Groza, Cleveland	19	13	68.4
1949	Cliff Patton, Philadelphia	18	9	50.0
	Bob Waterfield, Los Angeles	16	9	56.3
1948	Cliff Patton, Philadelphia	12	8	66.7
1947	Ward Cuff, Green Bay	16	7	43.8
	Pat Harder, Chi. Cardinals	10	7	70.0
	Bob Waterfield, Los Angeles	16	7	43.8
1946	Ted Fritsch, Green Bay	17	9	52.9
1945	Joe Aguirre, Washington	13	7	53.8
1944	Ken Strong, N.Y. Giants	12	6	50.0
1943	Ward Cuff, N.Y. Giants	9	3	33.3
	Don Hutson, Green Bay	5	3	60.0
1942	Bill Daddio, Chi. Cardinals	10	5	50.0
1941	Clarke Hinkle, Green Bay	14	6	42.9
1940	Clarke Hinkle, Green Bay	14	9	64.3
1939	Ward Cuff, N.Y. Giants	16	7	43.8
1938	Ward Cuff, N.Y. Giants	9	5	55.6
	Ralph Kercheval, Brooklyn	13	5	38.5
1937	Jack Manders, Chi. Bears		8	
1936	Jack Manders, Chi. Bears		7	
	Armand Niccolai, Pittsburgh		7	
1935	Armand Niccolai, Pittsburgh		6	
	Bill Smith, Chi. Cardinals		6	
1934	Jack Manders, Chi. Bears		10	
1933	*Jack Manders, Chi. Bears		6	
	Glenn Presnell, Portsmouth		6	
1932	Earl (Dutch) Clark, Portsmouth		3	

*First year in the league.

ANNUAL RUSHING LEADERS

Year	Player, Team	Att.	Yards	Avg.	TD
1981	*George Rogers, New Orleans, NFC	378	1,674	4.4	13
	Earl Campbell, Houston, AFC	361	1,376	3.8	10
1980	Earl Campbell, Houston, AFC	373	1,934	5.2	13
	Walter Payton, Chicago, NFC	317	1,460	4.6	6
1979	Earl Campbell, Houston, AFC	368	1,697	4.6	19
	Walter Payton, Chicago, NFC	369	1,610	4.4	14
1978	*Earl Campbell, Houston, AFC	302	1,450	4.8	13
	Walter Payton, Chicago, NFC	333	1,395	4.2	11
1977	Walter Payton, Chicago, NFC	339	1,852	5.5	14
	Mark van Eeghen, Oakland, AFC	324	1,273	3.9	7
1976	O.J. Simpson, Buffalo, AFC	290	1,503	5.2	8
	Walter Payton, Chicago, NFC	311	1,390	4.5	13
1975	O.J. Simpson, Buffalo, AFC	329	1,817	5.5	16
	Jim Otis, St. Louis, NFC	269	1,076	4.0	5
1974	Otis Armstrong, Denver, AFC	263	1,407	5.3	9
	Lawrence McCutcheon, Los Angeles, NFC	236	1,109	4.7	3

Year	Player, Team	Att	Yards	Avg	TD
1973	O.J. Simpson, Buffalo, AFC	332	2,003	6.0	12
	John Brockington, Green Bay, NFC	265	1,144	4.3	3
1972	O.J. Simpson, Buffalo, AFC	292	1,251	4.3	6
	Larry Brown, Washington, NFC	285	1,216	4.3	8
1971	Floyd Little, Denver, AFC	284	1,133	4.0	6
	*John Brockington, Green Bay, NFC	216	1,105	5.1	4
1970	Larry Brown, Washington, NFC	237	1,125	4.7	5
	Floyd Little, Denver, AFC	209	901	4.3	3
1969	Gale Sayers, Chicago, NFL	236	1,032	4.4	8
	Dickie Post, San Diego, AFL	182	873	4.8	6
1968	Leroy Kelly, Cleveland, NFL	248	1,239	5.0	16
	*Paul Robinson, Cincinnati, AFL	238	1,023	4.3	8
1967	Jim Nance, Boston, AFL	269	1,216	4.5	7
	Leroy Kelly, Cleveland, NFL	235	1,205	5.1	11
1966	Jim Nance, Boston, AFL	299	1,458	4.9	11
	Gale Sayers, Chicago, NFL	229	1,231	5.4	8
1965	Jim Brown, Cleveland, NFL	289	1,544	5.3	17
	Paul Lowe, San Diego, AFL	222	1,121	5.0	7
1964	Jim Brown, Cleveland, NFL	280	1,446	5.2	7
	Cookie Gilchrist, Buffalo, AFL	230	981	4.3	6
1963	Jim Brown, Cleveland, NFL	291	1,863	6.4	12
	Clem Daniels, Oakland, AFL	215	1,099	5.1	3
1962	Jim Taylor, Green Bay, NFL	272	1,474	5.4	19
	*Cookie Gilchrist, Buffalo, AFL	214	1,096	5.1	13
1961	Jim Brown, Cleveland, NFL	305	1,408	4.6	8
	Billy Cannon, Houston, AFL	200	948	4.7	6
1960	Jim Brown, Cleveland, NFL	215	1,257	5.8	9
	*Abner Haynes, Dall. Texans, AFL	156	875	5.6	9
1959	Jim Brown, Cleveland	290	1,329	4.6	14
1958	Jim Brown, Cleveland	257	1,527	5.9	17
1957	*Jim Brown, Cleveland	202	942	4.7	9
1956	Rick Casares, Chi. Bears	234	1,126	4.8	12
1955	*Alan Ameche, Baltimore	213	961	4.5	9
1954	Joe Perry, San Francisco	173	1,049	6.1	8
1953	Joe Perry, San Francisco	192	1,018	5.3	10
1952	Dan Towler, Los Angeles	156	894	5.7	10
1951	Eddie Price, N.Y. Giants	271	971	3.6	7
1950	*Marion Motley, Cleveland	140	810	5.8	3
1949	Steve Van Buren, Philadelphia	263	1,146	4.4	11
1948	Steve Van Buren, Philadelphia	201	945	4.7	10
1947	Steve Van Buren, Philadelphia	217	1,008	4.6	13
1946	Bill Dudley, Pittsburgh	146	604	4.1	3
1945	Steve Van Buren, Philadelphia	143	832	5.8	15
1944	Bill Paschal, N.Y. Giants	196	737	3.8	9
1943	*Bill Paschal, N.Y. Giants	147	572	3.9	10
1942	*Bill Dudley, Pittsburgh	162	696	4.3	5
1941	Clarence (Pug) Manders, Brooklyn	111	486	4.4	5
1940	Byron (Whizzer) White, Detroit	146	514	3.5	5
1939	*Bill Osmanski, Chicago	121	699	5.8	7
1938	*Byron (Whizzer) White, Pittsburgh	152	567	3.7	4
1937	Cliff Battles, Washington	216	874	4.0	5
1936	*Alphonse (Tuffy) Leemans, N.Y. Giants	206	830	4.0	2
1935	Doug Russell, Chi. Cardinals	140	499	3.6	0
1934	*Beattie Feathers, Chi. Bears	101	1,004	9.9	8
1933	Jim Musick, Boston	173	809	4.7	5
1932	*Cliff Battles, Boston	148	576	3.9	3

*First year in the league.

ANNUAL PASSING LEADERS

Year	Player, Team	Att.	Comp.	Yards	TD	Int.
1981	Ken Anderson, Cincinnati, AFC	479	300	3,754	29	10
	Joe Montana, San Francisco, NFC	488	311	3,565	19	12
1980	Brian Sipe, Cleveland, AFC	554	337	4,132	30	14

Year	Player	Att	Comp	Yards	TD	Int
	Ron Jaworski, Philadelphia, NFC	451	257	3,529	27	12
1979	Roger Staubach, Dallas, NFC	461	267	3,586	27	11
	Dan Fouts, San Diego, AFC	530	332	4,082	24	24
1978	Roger Staubach, Dallas, NFC	413	231	3,190	25	16
	Terry Bradshaw, Pittsburgh, AFC	368	207	2,915	28	20
1977	Bob Griese, Miami, AFC	307	180	2,252	22	13
	Roger Staubach, Dallas, NFC	361	210	2,620	18	9
1976	Ken Stabler, Oakland, AFC	291	194	2,737	27	17
	James Harris, Los Angeles, NFC	158	91	1,460	8	6
1975	Ken Anderson, Cincinnati, AFC	377	228	3,169	21	11
	Fran Tarkenton, Minnesota, NFC	425	273	2,994	25	13
1974	Ken Anderson, Cincinnati, AFC	328	213	2,667	18	10
	Sonny Jurgensen, Washington, NFC	167	107	1,185	11	5
1973	Roger Staubach, Dallas, NFC	286	179	2,428	23	15
	Ken Stabler, Oakland, AFC	260	163	1,997	14	10
1972	Norm Snead, N.Y. Giants, NFC	325	196	2,307	17	12
	Earl Morrall, Miami, AFC	150	83	1,360	11	7
1971	Roger Staubach, Dallas, NFC	211	126	1,882	15	4
	Bob Griese, Miami, AFC	263	145	2,089	19	9
1970	John Brodie, San Francisco, NFC	378	223	2,941	24	10
	Daryle Lamonica, Oakland, AFC	356	179	2,516	22	15
1969	Sonny Jurgensen, Washington, NFL	442	274	3,102	22	15
	*Greg Cook, Cincinnati, AFL	197	106	1,854	15	11
1968	Len Dawson, Kansas City, AFL	224	131	2,109	17	9
	Earl Morrall, Baltimore, NFL	317	182	2,909	26	17
1967	Sonny Jurgensen, Washington, NFL	508	288	3,747	31	16
	Daryle Lamonica, Oakland, AFL	425	220	3,228	30	20
1966	Bart Starr, Green Bay, NFL	251	156	2,257	14	3
	Len Dawson, Kansas City, AFL	284	159	2,527	26	10
1965	Rudy Bukich, Chicago, NFL	312	176	2,641	20	9
	John Hadl, San Diego, AFL	348	174	2,798	20	21
1964	Len Dawson, Kansas City, AFL	354	199	2,879	30	18
	Bart Starr, Green Bay, NFL	272	163	2,144	15	4
1963	Y.A. Tittle, N.Y. Giants, NFL	367	221	3,145	36	14
	Tobin Rote, San Diego, AFL	286	170	2,510	20	17
1962	Len Dawson, Dall. Texans, AFL	310	189	2,759	29	17
	Bart Starr, Green Bay, NFL	285	178	2,438	12	9
1961	George Blanda, Houston, AFL	362	187	3,330	36	22
	Milt Plum, Cleveland, NFL	302	177	2,416	18	10
1960	Milt Plum, Cleveland, NFL	250	151	2,297	21	5
	Jack Kemp, L.A. Chargers, AFL	406	211	3,018	20	25
1959	Charlie Conerly, N.Y. Giants	194	113	1,706	14	4
1958	Eddie LeBaron, Washington	145	79	1,365	11	10
1957	Tommy O'Connell, Cleveland	110	63	1,229	9	8
1956	Ed Brown, Chi. Bears	168	96	1,667	11	12
1955	Otto Graham, Cleveland	185	98	1,721	15	8
1954	Norm Van Brocklin, Los Angeles	260	139	2,637	13	21
1953	Otto Graham, Cleveland	258	167	2,722	11	9
1952	Norm Van Brocklin, Los Angeles	205	113	1,736	14	17
1951	Bob Waterfield, Los Angeles	176	88	1,566	13	10
1950	Norm Van Brocklin, Los Angeles	233	127	2,061	18	14
1949	Sammy Baugh, Washington	255	145	1,903	18	14
1948	Tommy Thompson, Philadelphia	246	141	1,965	25	11
1947	Sammy Baugh, Washington	354	210	2,938	25	15
1946	Bob Waterfield, Los Angeles	251	127	1,747	18	17
1945	Sammy Baugh, Washington	182	128	1,669	11	4
	Sid Luckman, Chi. Bears	217	117	1,725	14	10
1944	Frank Filchock, Washington	147	84	1,139	13	9
1943	Sammy Baugh, Washington	239	133	1,754	23	19
1942	Cecil Isbell, Green Bay	268	146	2,021	24	14
1941	Cecil Isbell, Green Bay	206	117	1,479	15	11
1940	Sammy Baugh, Washington	177	111	1,367	12	10
1939	*Parker Hall, Cleveland	208	106	1,227	9	13

		No.	Yards		
1938	Ed Danowski, N.Y. Giants	129	70	848	7	8
1937	*Sammy Baugh, Washington	171	81	1,127	8	14
1936	Arnie Herber, Green Bay	173	77	1,239	11	13
1935	Ed Danowski, N.Y. Giants	113	57	794	10	9
1934	Arnie Herber, Green Bay	115	42	799	8	12
1933	*Harry Newman, N.Y. Giants	136	53	973	11	17
1932	Arnie Herber, Green Bay	101	37	639	9	9

*First year in the league.

ANNUAL PASS RECEIVING LEADERS

Year	Player, Team	No.	Yards	Avg.	TD
1981	Kellen Winslow, San Diego, AFC	88	1,075	12.2	10
	Dwight Clark, San Francisco, NFC	85	1,105	13.0	4
1980	Kellen Winslow, San Diego, AFC	89	1,290	14.5	9
	*Earl Cooper, San Francisco, NFC	83	567	6.8	4
1979	Joe Washington, Baltimore, AFC	82	750	9.1	3
	Ahmad Rashad, Minnesota, NFC	80	1,156	14.5	9
1978	Rickey Young, Minnesota, NFC	88	704	8.0	5
	Steve Largent, Seattle, AFC	71	1,168	16.5	8
1977	Lydell Mitchell, Baltimore, AFC	71	620	8.7	4
	Ahmad Rashad, Minnesota, NFC	51	681	13.4	2
1976	MacArthur Lane, Kansas City, AFC	66	686	10.4	1
	Drew Pearson, Dallas, NFC	58	806	13.9	6
1975	Chuck Foreman, Minnesota, NFC	73	691	9.5	9
	Reggie Rucker, Cleveland, AFC	60	770	12.8	3
	Lydell Mitchell, Baltimore, AFC	60	544	9.1	4
1974	Lydell Mitchell, Baltimore, AFC	72	544	7.6	2
	Charles Young, Philadelphia, NFC	63	696	11.0	3
1973	Harold Carmichael, Philadelphia, NFC	67	1,116	16.7	9
	Fred Willis, Houston, AFC	57	371	6.5	1
1972	Harold Jackson, Philadelphia, NFC	62	1,048	16.9	4
	Fred Biletnikoff, Oakland, AFC	58	802	13.8	7
1971	Fred Biletnikoff, Oakland, AFC	61	929	15.2	9
	Bob Tucker, N.Y. Giants, NFC	59	791	13.4	4
1970	Dick Gordon, Chicago, NFC	71	1,026	14.5	13
	Marlin Briscoe, Buffalo, AFC	57	1,036	18.2	8
1969	Dan Abramowicz, New Orleans, NFL	73	1,015	13.9	7
	Lance Alworth, San Diego, AFL	64	1,003	15.7	4
1968	Clifton McNeil, San Francisco, NFL	71	994	14.0	7
	Lance Alworth, San Diego, AFL	68	1,312	19.3	10
1967	George Sauer, N.Y. Jets, AFL	75	1,189	15.9	6
	Charley Taylor, Washington, NFL	70	990	14.1	9
1966	Lance Alworth, San Diego, AFL	73	1,383	18.9	13
	Charley Taylor, Washington, NFL	72	1,119	15.5	12
1965	Lionel Taylor, Denver, AFL	85	1,131	13.3	6
	Dave Parks, San Francisco, NFL	80	1,344	16.8	12
1964	Charley Hennigan, Houston, AFL	101	1,546	15.3	8
	Johnny Morris, Chicago, NFL	93	1,200	12.9	10
1963	Lionel Taylor, Denver, AFL	78	1,101	14.1	10
	Bobby Joe Conrad, St. Louis, NFL	73	967	13.2	10
1962	Lionel Taylor, Denver, AFL	77	908	11.8	4
	Bobby Mitchell, Washington, NFL	72	1,384	19.2	11
1961	Lionel Taylor, Denver, AFL	100	1,176	11.8	4
	Jim (Red) Phillips, Los Angeles, NFL	78	1,092	14.0	5
1960	Lionel Taylor, Denver, AFL	92	1,235	13.4	12
	Raymond Berry, Baltimore, NFL	74	1,298	17.5	10
1959	Raymond Berry, Baltimore	66	959	14.5	14
1958	Raymond Berry, Baltimore	56	794	14.2	9
	Pete Retzlaff, Philadelphia	56	766	13.7	2
1957	Billy Wilson, San Francisco	52	757	14.6	6
1956	Billy Wilson, San Francisco	60	889	14.8	5
1955	Pete Pihos, Philadelphia	62	864	13.9	7
1954	Pete Pihos, Philadelphia	60	872	14.5	10

	Billy Wilson, San Francisco	60	830	13.8	5
1953	Pete Pihos, Philadelphia	63	1,049	16.7	10
1952	Mac Speedie, Cleveland	62	911	14.7	5
1951	Elroy (Crazylegs) Hirsch, Los Angeles...	66	1,495	22.7	17
1950	Tom Fears, Los Angeles	84	1,116	13.3	7
1949	Tom Fears, Los Angeles	77	1,013	13.2	9
1948	*Tom Fears, Los Angeles	51	698	13.7	4
1947	Jim Keane, Chi. Bears	64	910	14.2	10
1946	Jim Benton, Los Angeles	63	981	15.6	6
1945	Don Hutson, Green Bay	47	834	17.7	9
1944	Don Hutson, Green Bay	58	866	14.9	9
1943	Don Hutson, Green Bay	47	776	16.5	11
1942	Don Hutson, Green Bay	74	1,211	16.4	17
1941	Don Hutson, Green Bay	58	738	12.7	10
1940	*Don Looney, Philadelphia	58	707	12.2	4
1939	Don Hutson, Green Bay	34	846	24.9	6
1938	Gaynell Tinsley, Chi. Cardinals	41	516	12.6	1
1937	Don Hutson, Green Bay	41	552	13.5	7
1936	Don Hutson, Green Bay	34	536	15.8	8
1935	*Tod Goodwin, N.Y. Giants	26	432	16.6	4
1934	Joe Carter, Philadelphia	16	238	14.9	4
	Morris (Red) Badgro, N.Y. Giants	16	206	12.9	1
1933	John (Shipwreck) Kelly, Brooklyn	22	246	11.2	3
1932	Ray Flaherty, N.Y. Giants	21	350	16.7	3

*First year in the league.

ANNUAL INTERCEPTION LEADERS

Year	Player, Team	No.	Yards	TD
1981	*Everson Walls, Dallas, NFC	11	133	0
	John Harris, Seattle, AFC	10	155	2
1980	Lester Hayes, Oakland, AFC	13	273	1
	Nolan Cromwell, Los Angeles, NFC	8	140	1
1979	Mike Reinfeldt, Houston, AFC	12	205	0
	Lemar Parrish, Washington, NFC	9	65	0
1978	Thom Darden, Cleveland, AFC	10	200	0
	Ken Stone, St. Louis, NFC	9	139	0
	Willie Buchanon, Green Bay, NFC	9	93	1
1977	Lyle Blackwood, Baltimore, AFC	10	163	0
	Rolland Lawrence, Atlanta, NFC	7	138	0
1976	Monte Jackson, Los Angeles, NFC	10	173	3
	Ken Riley, Cincinnati, AFC	9	141	1
1975	Mel Blount, Pittsburgh, AFC	11	121	0
	Paul Krause, Minnesota, NFC	10	201	0
1974	Emmitt Thomas, Kansas City, AFC	12	214	2
	Ray Brown, Atlanta, NFC	8	164	1
1973	Dick Anderson, Miami, AFC	8	163	2
	Mike Wagner, Pittsburgh, AFC	8	134	0
	Bobby Bryant, Minnesota, NFC	7	105	1
1972	Bill Bradley, Philadelphia, NFC	9	73	0
	Mike Sensibaugh, Kansas City, AFC	8	65	0
1971	Bill Bradley, Philadelphia, NFC	11	248	0
	Ken Houston, Houston, AFC	9	220	4
1970	Johnny Robinson, Kansas City, AFC	10	155	0
	Dick LeBeau, Detroit, NFC	9	96	0
1969	Mel Renfro, Dallas, NFL	10	118	0
	Emmitt Thomas, Kansas City, AFL	9	146	1
1968	Dave Grayson, Oakland, AFL	10	195	1
	Willie Williams, N.Y. Giants, NFL	10	103	0
1967	Miller Farr, Houston, AFL	10	264	3
	*Lem Barney, Detroit, NFL	10	232	3
	Tom Janik, Buffalo AFL	10	222	2
	Dave Whitsell, New Orleans, NFL	10	178	2
	Dick Westmoreland, Miami, AFL	10	127	1

1966	Larry Wilson, St. Louis. NFL	10	180	2
	Johnny Robinson, Kansas City, AFL	10	136	1
	Bobby Hunt, Kansas City, AFL	10	113	0
1965	W.K. Hicks, Houston, AFL	9	156	0
	Bobby Boyd, Baltimore, NFL	9	78	1
1964	Dainard Paulson, N.Y. Jets, AFL	12	157	1
	*Paul Krause, Washington, NFL	12	140	1
1963	Fred Glick, Houston, AFL	12	180	1
	Dick Lynch, N.Y. Giants, NFL	9	251	3
	Roosevelt Taylor, Chicago, NFL	9	172	1
1962	Lee Riley, N.Y. Titans, AFL	11	122	0
	Willie Wood, Green Bay, NFL	9	132	0
1961	Billy Atkins, Buffalo, AFL	10	158	0
	Dick Lynch, N.Y. Giants, NFL	9	60	0
1960	*Austin (Goose) Gonsoulin, Denver, AFL	11	98	0
	Dave Baker, San Francisco, NFL	10	96	0
	Jerry Norton, St. Louis, NFL	10	96	0
1959	Dean Derby, Pittsburgh	7	127	0
	Milt Davis, Baltimore	7	119	1
	Don Shinnick, Baltimore	7	70	0
1958	Jim Patton, N.Y. Giants	11	183	0
1957	*Milt Davis, Baltimore	10	219	2
	Jack Christiansen, Detroit	10	137	1
	Jack Butler, Pittsburgh	10	85	0
1956	Lindon Crow, Chi. Cardinals	11	170	0
1955	Will Sherman, Los Angeles	11	101	1
1954	Dick (Night Train) Lane, Chi. Cardinals	10	181	0
1953	Jack Christiansen, Detroit	12	238	1
1952	*Dick (Night Train) Lane, Los Angeles	14	298	2
1951	Otto Schnellbacher, N.Y. Giants	11	194	2
1950	*Orban (Spec) Sanders, N.Y. Yanks	12	199	0
1949	Bob Nussbaumer, Chi. Cardinals	12	157	0
1948	*Dan Sandifer, Washington	13	258	2
1947	Frank Reagan, N.Y. Giants	10	203	0
	Frank Seno, Boston	10	100	0
1946	Bill Dudley, Pittsburgh	10	242	1
1945	Roy Zimmerman, Philadelphia	7	90	0
1944	*Howard Livingston, N.Y. Giants	9	172	1
1943	Sammy Baugh, Washington	11	112	0
1942	*Clyde (Bulldog) Turner, Chi. Bears	8	96	1
1941	Marshall Goldberg, Chi. Cardinals	7	54	0
	*Art Jones, Pittsburgh	7	35	0
1940	Clarence (Ace) Parker, Brooklyn	6	146	1
	Kent Ryan, Detroit	6	65	0
	Don Hutson, Green Bay	6	24	0

*First year in the league.

ANNUAL PUNTING LEADERS

Year	Player, Team	No.	Avg.	Long
1981	Pat McInally, Cincinnati, AFC	72	45.4	62
	Tom Skladany, Detroit, NFC	64	43.5	74
1980	Dave Jennings, N.Y. Giants, NFC	94	44.8	63
	Luke Prestridge, Denver, AFC	70	43.9	57
1979	*Bob Grupp, Kansas City, AFC	89	43.6	74
	Dave Jennings, N.Y. Giants, NFC	104	42.7	72
1978	Pat McInally, Cincinnati, AFC	91	43.1	65
	*Tom Skladany, Detroit, NFC	86	42.5	63
1977	Ray Guy, Oakland, AFC	59	43.3	74
	Tom Blanchard, New Orleans, NFC	82	42.4	66
1976	Marv Bateman, Buffalo, AFC	86	42.8	78
	John James, Atlanta, NFC	101	42.1	67
1975	Ray Guy, Oakland, AFC	68	43.8	64
	Herman Weaver, Detroit, NFC	80	42.0	61

1974	Ray Guy, Oakland, AFC	74	42.2	66
	Tom Blanchard, New Orleans, NFC	88	42.1	71
1973	Jerrel Wilson, Kansas City, AFC	80	45.5	68
	*Tom Wittum, San Francisco, NFC	79	43.7	62
1972	Jerrel Wilson, Kansas City, AFC	66	44.8	69
	Dave Chapple, Los Angeles, NFC	53	44.2	70
1971	Dave Lewis, Cincinnati, AFC	72	44.8	56
	Tom McNeill, Philadelphia, NFC	73	42.0	64
1970	*Dave Lewis, Cincinnati, AFC	79	46.2	63
	*Julian Fagan, New Orleans, NFC	77	42.5	64
1969	David Lee, Baltimore, NFL	57	45.3	66
	Dennis Partee, San Diego, AFL	71	44.6	62
1968	Jerrel Wilson, Kansas City, AFL	63	45.1	70
	Billy Lothridge, Atlanta, NFL	75	44.3	70
1967	Bob Scarpitto, Denver, AFL	105	44.9	73
	Billy Lothridge, Atlanta, NFL	87	43.7	62
1966	Bob Scarpitto, Denver, AFL	76	45.8	70
	*David Lee, Baltimore, NFL	49	45.6	64
1965	Gary Collins, Cleveland, NFL	65	46.7	71
	Jerrel Wilson, Kansas City, AFL	69	45.4	64
1964	*Bobby Walden, Minnesota, NFL	72	46.4	73
	Jim Fraser, Denver, AFL	73	44.2	67
1963	Yale Lary, Detroit, NFL	35	48.9	73
	Jim Fraser, Denver, AFL	81	44.4	66
1962	Tommy Davis, San Francisco, NFL	48	45.6	82
	Jim Fraser, Denver, AFL	55	43.6	75
1961	Yale Lary, Detroit, NFL	52	48.4	71
	Billy Atkins, Buffalo, AFL	85	44.5	70
1960	Jerry Norton, St. Louis, NFL	39	45.6	62
	*Paul Maguire, L.A. Chargers, AFL	43	40.5	61
1959	Yale Lary, Detroit	45	47.1	67
1958	Sam Baker, Washington	48	45.4	64
1957	Don Chandler, N.Y. Giants	60	44.6	61
1956	Norm Van Brocklin, Los Angeles	48	43.1	72
1955	Norm Van Brocklin, Los Angeles	60	44.6	61
1954	Pat Brady, Pittsburgh	66	43.2	72
1953	Pat Brady, Pittsburgh	80	46.9	64
1952	Horace Gillom, Cleveland	61	45.7	73
1951	Horace Gillom, Cleveland	73	45.5	66
1950	*Fred (Curly) Morrison, Chi. Bears	57	43.3	65
1949	*Mike Boyda, N.Y. Bulldogs	56	44.2	61
1948	Joe Muha, Philadelphia	57	47.3	82
1947	Jack Jacobs, Green Bay	57	43.5	74
1946	Roy McKay, Green Bay	64	42.7	64
1945	Roy McKay, Green Bay	44	41.2	73
1944	Frank Sinkwich, Detroit	45	41.0	73
1943	Sammy Baugh, Washington	50	45.9	81
1942	Sammy Baugh, Washington	37	48.2	74
1941	Sammy Baugh, Washington	30	48.7	75
1940	Sammy Baugh, Washington	35	51.4	85
1939	*Parker Hall, Cleveland	58	40.8	80

*First year in the league.

ANNUAL PUNT RETURN LEADERS

Year	Player, Team	No.	Yards	Avg.	Long	TD
1981	LeRoy Irvin, Los Angeles, NFC	46	615	13.4	84	3
	*James Brooks, San Diego, AFC	22	290	13.2	42	0
1980	J. T. Smith, Kansas City, AFC	40	581	14.5	75	2
	*Kenny Johnson, Atlanta, NFC	23	281	12.2	56	0
1979	John Sciarra, Philadelphia, NFC	16	182	11.4	38	0
	*Tony Nathan, Miami, AFC	28	306	10.9	86	1
1978	Rick Upchurch, Denver, AFC	36	493	13.7	75	1
	Jackie Wallace, Los Angeles, NFC	52	618	11.9	58	0

1977	Billy Johnson, Houston, AFC	35	539	15.4	87	2
	Larry Marshall, Philadelphia, NFC	46	489	10.6	48	0
1976	Rick Upchurch, Denver, AFC	39	536	13.7	92	4
	Eddie Brown, Washington, NFC	48	646	13.5	71	1
1975	Billy Johnson, Houston, AFC	40	612	15.3	83	3
	Terry Metcalf, St. Louis, NFC	23	285	12.4	69	1
1974	Lemar Parrish, Cincinnati, AFC	18	338	18.8	90	2
	Dick Jauron, Detroit, NFC	17	286	16.8	58	0
1973	Bruce Taylor, San Francisco, NFC	15	207	13.8	61	0
	Ron Smith, San Diego, AFC	27	352	13.0	84	2
1972	*Ken Ellis, Green Bay, NFC	14	215	15.4	80	1
	Chris Farasopoulos, N.Y. Jets, AFC	17	179	10.5	65	1
1971	Les (Speedy) Duncan, Washington, NFC	22	233	10.6	33	0
	Leroy Kelly, Cleveland, AFC	30	292	9.7	74	0
1970	Ed Podolak, Kansas City, AFC	23	311	13.5	60	0
	*Bruce Taylor, San Francisco, NFC	43	516	12.0	76	0
1969	Alvin Haymond, Los Angeles, NFL	33	435	13.2	52	0
	*Bill Thompson, Denver, AFL	25	288	11.5	40	0
1968	Bob Hayes, Dallas, NFL	15	312	20.8	90	2
	Noland Smith, Kansas City, AFL	18	270	15.0	80	1
1967	Floyd Little, Denver, AFL	16	270	16.9	72	1
	Ben Davis, Cleveland, NFL	18	229	12.7	52	1
1966	Les (Speedy) Duncan, San Diego, AFL	18	238	13.2	81	1
	Johnny Roland, St. Louis, NFL	20	221	11.1	86	1
1965	Leroy Kelly, Cleveland, NFL	17	265	15.6	67	2
	Les (Speedy) Duncan, San Diego, AFL	30	464	15.5	66	2
1964	Bobby Jancik, Houston, AFL	12	220	18.3	82	1
	Tommy Watkins, Detroit, NFL	16	238	14.9	68	2
1963	Dick James, Washington, NFL	16	214	13.4	39	0
	Claude (Hoot) Gibson, Oakland, AFL	26	307	11.8	85	2
1962	Dick Christy, N.Y. Titans, AFL	15	250	16.7	73	2
	Pat Studstill, Detroit, NFL	29	457	15.8	44	0
1961	Dick Christy, N.Y. Titans, AFL	18	383	21.3	70	2
	Willie Wood, Green Bay, NFL	14	225	16.1	72	2
1960	*Abner Haynes, Dall. Texans, AFL	14	215	15.4	46	0
	Abe Woodson, San Francisco, NFL	13	174	13.4	48	0
1959	Johnny Morris, Chi. Bears	14	171	12.2	78	1
1958	Jon Arnett, Los Angeles	18	223	12.4	58	0
1957	Bert Zagers, Washington	14	217	15.5	76	2
1956	Ken Konz, Cleveland	13	187	14.4	65	1
1955	Ollie Matson, Chi. Cardinals	13	245	18.8	78	2
1954	*Veryl Switzer, Green Bay	24	306	12.8	93	1
1953	Charley Trippi, Chi. Cardinals	21	239	11.4	38	0
1952	Jack Christiansen, Detroit	15	322	21.5	79	2
1951	Claude (Buddy) Young, N.Y. Yanks	12	231	19.3	79	1
1950	*Herb Rich, Baltimore	12	276	23.0	86	1
1949	Verda (Vitamin T) Smith, Los Angeles	27	427	15.8	85	1
1948	George McAfee, Chi. Bears	30	417	13.9	60	1
1947	*Walt Slater, Pittsburgh	28	435	15.5	33	0
1946	Bill Dudley, Pittsburgh	27	385	14.3	52	0
1945	*Dave Ryan, Detroit	15	220	14.7	56	0
1944	*Steve Van Buren, Philadelphia	15	230	15.3	55	1
1943	Andy Farkas, Washington	15	168	11.2	33	0
1942	Merlyn Condit, Brooklyn	21	210	10.0	23	0
1941	Byron (Whizzer) White, Detroit	19	262	13.8	64	0

*First year in the league.

ANNUAL KICKOFF RETURN LEADERS

Year	Player, Team	No.	Yards	Avg.	Long	TD
1981	Mike Nelms, Washington, NFC	37	1,099	29.7	84	0
	Carl Roaches, Houston, AFC	28	769	27.5	96	1
1980	Horace Ivory, New England, AFC	36	992	27.6	98	1
	Rich Mauti, New Orleans, NFC	31	798	25.7	52	0

Year	Player, Team	No.	Yds	Avg	Long	TD
1979	Larry Brunson, Oakland, AFC	17	441	25.9	89	0
	*Jimmy Edwards, Minnesota, NFC	44	1,103	25.1	83	0
1978	Steve Odom, Green Bay, NFC	25	677	27.1	95	1
	*Keith Wright, Cleveland, AFC	30	789	26.3	86	0
1977	*Raymond Clayborn, New England, AFC	28	869	31.0	101	3
	*Wilbert Montgomery, Philadelphia, NFC	23	619	26.9	99	1
1976	*Duriel Harris, Miami, AFC	17	559	32.9	69	0
	Cullen Bryant, Los Angeles, NFC	16	459	28.7	90	1
1975	*Walter Payton, Chicago, NFC	14	444	31.7	70	0
	Harold Hart, Oakland, AFC	17	518	30.5	102	1
1974	Terry Metcalf, St. Louis, NFC	20	623	31.2	94	1
	Greg Pruitt, Cleveland, AFC	22	606	27.5	88	1
1973	Carl Garrett, Chicago, NFC	16	486	30.4	67	0
	*Wallace Francis, Buffalo, AFC	23	687	29.9	101	2
1972	Ron Smith, Chicago, NFC	30	924	30.8	94	1
	*Bruce Laird, Baltimore, AFC	29	843	29.1	73	0
1971	Travis Williams, Los Angeles, NFC	25	743	29.7	105	1
	Eugene (Mercury) Morris, Miami, AFC	15	423	28.2	94	1
1970	Jim Duncan, Baltimore, AFC	20	707	35.4	99	1
	Cecil Turner, Chicago, NFC	23	752	32.7	96	4
1969	Bobby Williams, Detroit, NFL	17	563	33.1	96	1
	*Bill Thompson, Denver, AFL	18	513	28.5	63	0
1968	Preston Pearson, Baltimore, NFL	15	527	35.1	102	2
	*George Atkinson, Oakland, AFL	32	802	25.1	60	0
1967	*Travis Williams, Green Bay, NFL	18	739	41.1	104	4
	*Zeke Moore, Houston, AFL	14	405	28.9	92	1
1966	Gale Sayers, Chicago, NFL	23	718	31.2	93	2
	*Goldie Sellers, Denver, AFL	19	541	28.5	100	2
1965	Tommy Watkins, Detroit, NFL	17	584	34.4	94	0
	Abner Haynes, Denver, AFL	34	901	26.5	60	0
1964	*Clarence Childs, N.Y. Giants, NFL	34	987	29.0	100	1
	Bo Robertson, Oakland, AFL	36	975	27.1	59	0
1963	Abe Woodson, San Francisco, NFL	29	935	32.2	103	3
	Bobby Jancik, Houston, AFL	45	1,317	29.3	53	0
1962	Abe Woodson, San Francisco, NFL	37	1,157	31.3	79	0
	*Bobby Jancik, Houston, AFL	24	826	30.3	61	0
1961	Dick Bass, Los Angeles, NFL	23	698	30.3	64	0
	*Dave Grayson, Dall. Texans, AFL	16	453	28.3	73	0
1960	*Tom Moore, Green Bay, NFL	12	397	33.1	84	0
	Ken Hall, Houston, AFL	19	594	31.3	104	1
1959	Abe Woodson, San Francisco	13	382	29.4	105	1
1958	Ollie Matson, Chi. Cardinals	14	497	35.5	101	2
1957	*Jon Arnett, Los Angeles	18	504	28.0	98	1
1956	*Tom Wilson, Los Angeles	15	477	31.8	103	1
1955	Al Carmichael, Green Bay	14	418	29.9	100	1
1954	Billy Reynolds, Cleveland	14	413	29.5	51	0
1953	Joe Arenas, San Francisco	16	551	34.4	82	0
1952	Lynn Chandnois, Pittsburgh	17	599	35.2	93	2
1951	Lynn Chandnois, Pittsburgh	12	390	32.5	55	0
1950	Verda (Vitamin T) Smith, Los Angeles	22	742	33.7	97	3
1949	*Don Doll, Detroit	21	536	25.5	56	0
1948	*Joe Scott, N.Y. Giants	20	569	28.5	99	1
1947	Eddie Saenz, Washington	29	797	27.5	94	2
1946	Abe Karnofsky, Boston	21	599	28.5	97	1
1945	Steve Van Buren, Philadelphia	13	373	28.7	98	1
1944	Bob Thurbon, Card.-Pitt.	12	291	24.3	55	0
1943	Ken Heineman, Brooklyn	16	444	27.8	69	0
1942	Marshall Goldberg, Chi. Cardinals	15	393	26.2	95	1
1941	Marshall Goldberg, Chi. Cardinals	12	290	24.2	41	0

*First year in the league.

POINTS SCORED — TEAM

Year	Team	Points
1981	San Diego, AFC	478
	Atlanta, NFC	426
1980	Dallas, NFC	454
	New England, AFC	441
1979	Pittsburgh, AFC	416
	Dallas, NFC	371
1978	Dallas, NFC	384
	Miami, AFC	372
1977	Oakland, AFC	351
	Dallas, NFC	345
1976	Baltimore, AFC	417
	Los Angeles, NFC	351
1975	Buffalo, AFC	420
	Minnesota, NFC	377
1974	Oakland, AFC	355
	Washington, NFC	320
1973	Los Angeles, NFC	388
	Denver, AFC	354
1972	Miami, AFC	385
	San Francisco, NFC	353
1971	Dallas, NFC	406
	Oakland, AFC	344
1970	San Francisco, NFC	352
	Baltimore, AFC	321
1969	Minnesota, NFL	379
	Oakland, AFL	377
1968	Oakland, AFL	453
	Dallas, NFL	431
1967	Oakland, AFL	468
	Los Angeles, NFL	398
1966	Kansas City, AFL	448
	Dallas, NFL	445
1965	San Francisco, NFL	421
	San Diego, AFL	340
1964	Baltimore, NFL	428
	Buffalo, AFL	400
1963	N.Y. Giants, NFL	448
	San Diego, AFL	399
1962	Green Bay, NFL	415
	Dall. Texans, AFL	389
1961	Houston, AFL	513
	Green Bay, NFL	391
1960	N.Y. Titans, AFL	382
	Cleveland, NFL	362
1959	Baltimore	374
1958	Baltimore	381
1957	Los Angeles	307
1956	Chi. Bears	363
1955	Cleveland	349
1954	Detroit	337
1953	San Francisco	372
1952	Los Angeles	349
1951	Los Angeles	392
1950	Los Angeles	466
1949	Philadelphia	364
1948	Chi. Cardinals	395
1947	Chi. Bears	363
1946	Chi. Bears	289
1945	Philadelphia	272
1944	Philadelphia	267
1943	Chi. Bears	303
1942	Chi. Bears	376
1941	Chi. Bears	396
1940	Washington	245
1939	Chi. Bears	298
1938	Green Bay	223
1937	Green Bay	220
1936	Green Bay	248
1935	Chi. Bears	192
1934	Chi. Bears	286
1933	N.Y. Giants	244
1932	Green Bay	152

YARDS GAINED — TEAM

Year	Team	Yards
1981	San Diego, AFC	6,744
	Detroit, NFC	5,933
1980	San Diego, AFC	6,410
	Los Angeles, NFC	6,006
1979	Pittsburgh, AFC	6,258
	Dallas, NFC	5,968
1978	New England, AFC	5,965
	Dallas, NFC	5,959
1977	Dallas, NFC	4,812
	Oakland, AFC	4,736
1976	Baltimore, AFC	5,236
	St. Louis, NFC	5,136
1975	Buffalo, AFC	5,467
	Dallas, NFC	5,025
1974	Dallas, NFC	4,983
	Oakland, AFC	4,718
1973	Los Angeles, NFC	4,906
	Oakland, AFC	4,773
1972	Miami, AFC	5,036
	N.Y. Giants, NFC	4,483
1971	Dallas, NFC	5,035
	San Diego, AFC	4,738
1970	Oakland, AFC	4,829
	San Francisco, NFC	4,503
1969	Dallas, NFL	5,122
	Oakland, AFL	5,036
1968	Oakland, AFL	5,696
	Dallas, NFL	5,117
1967	N.Y. Jets, AFL	5,152
	Baltimore, NFL	5,008
1966	Dallas, NFL	5,145
	Kansas City, AFL	5,114
1965	San Francisco, NFL	5,270
	San Diego, AFL	5,188
1964	Buffalo, AFL	5,206
	Baltimore, NFL	4,779
1963	San Diego, AFL	5,153
	N.Y. Giants, NFL	5,024
1962	N.Y. Giants, NFL	5,005
	Houston, AFL	4,971
1961	Houston, AFL	6,288
	Philadelphia, NFL	5,112
1960	Houston, AFL	4,936
	Baltimore, NFL	4,245
1959	Baltimore	4,458
1958	Baltimore	4,539
1957	Los Angeles	4,143
1956	Chi. Bears	4,537
1955	Chi. Bears	4,316

1954	Los Angeles	5,187
1953	Philadelphia	4,811
1952	Cleveland	4,352
1951	Los Angeles	5,506
1950	Los Angeles	5,420
1949	Chi. Bears	4,873
1948	Chi. Cardinals	4,705
1947	Chi. Bears	5,053
1946	Los Angeles	3,793
1945	Washington	3,549
1944	Chi. Bears	3,239
1943	Chi. Bears	4,045
1942	Chi. Bears	3,900
1941	Chi. Bears	4,265
1940	Green Bay	3,400
1939	Chi. Bears	3,988
1938	Green Bay	3,037
1937	Green Bay	3,201
1936	Detroit	3,703
1935	Chi. Bears	3,454
1934	Chi. Bears	3,900
1933	N.Y. Giants	2,973
1932	Chi. Bears	2,755

RUSHING

Year	Team	Yards
1981	Detroit, NFC	2,795
	Kansas City, AFC	2,633
1980	Los Angeles, NFC	2,799
	Houston, AFC	2,635
1979	N.Y. Jets, AFC	2,646
	St. Louis, NFC	2,582
1978	New England, AFC	3,165
	Dallas, NFC	2,783
1977	Chicago, NFC	2,811
	Oakland, AFC	2,627
1976	Pittsburgh, AFC	2,971
	Los Angeles, NFC	2,528
1975	Buffalo, AFC	2,974
	Dallas, NFC	2,432
1974	Dallas, NFC	2,454
	Pittsburgh, AFC	2,417
1973	Buffalo, AFC	3,088
	Los Angeles, NFC	2,925
1972	Miami, AFC	2,960
	Chicago, NFC	2,360
1971	Miami, AFC	2,429
	Detroit, NFC	2,376
1970	Dallas, NFC	2,300
	Miami, AFC	2,082
1969	Dallas, NFL	2,276
	Kansas City, AFL	2,220
1968	Chicago, NFL	2,377
	Kansas City, AFL	2,227
1967	Cleveland, NFL	2,139
	Houston, AFL	2,122
1966	Kansas City, AFL	2,274
	Cleveland, NFL	2,166
1965	Cleveland, NFL	2,331
	San Diego, AFL	2,085
1964	Green Bay, NFL	2,276
	Buffalo, AFL	2,040
1963	Cleveland, NFL	2,639

	San Diego, AFL	2,203
1962	Buffalo, AFL	2,480
	Green Bay, NFL	2,460
1961	Green Bay, NFL	2,350
	Dall. Texans, AFL	2,189
1960	St. Louis, NFL	2,356
	Oakland, AFL	2,056
1959	Cleveland	2,149
1958	Cleveland	2,526
1957	Los Angeles	2,142
1956	Chi. Bears	2,468
1955	Chi. Bears	2,388
1954	San Francisco	2,498
1953	San Francisco	2,230
1952	San Francisco	1,905
1951	Chi. Bears	2,408
1950	N.Y. Giants	2,336
1949	Philadelphia	2,607
1948	Chi. Cardinals	2,560
1947	Los Angeles	2,171
1946	Green Bay	1,765
1945	Cleveland	1,714
1944	Philadelphia	1,661
1943	Phil-Pitt	1,730
1942	Chi. Bears	1,881
1941	Chi. Bears	2,263
1940	Chi. Bears	1,818
1939	Chi. Bears	2,043
1938	Detroit	1,893
1937	Detroit	2,074
1936	Detroit	2,885
1935	Chi. Bears	2,096
1934	Chi. Bears	2,847
1933	Boston	2,260
1932	Chi. Bears	1,770

PASSING YARDAGE

Leadership in this category has been based on net yards since 1952.

Year	Team	Yards
1981	San Diego, AFC	4,739
	Minnesota, NFC	4,333
1980	San Diego, AFC	4,531
	Minnesota, NFC	3,688
1979	San Diego, AFC	3,915
	San Francisco, NFC	3,641
1978	San Diego, AFC	3,375
	Minnesota, NFC	3,243
1977	Buffalo, AFC	2,530
	St. Louis, NFC	2,499
1976	Baltimore, AFC	2,933
	Minnesota, NFC	2,855
1975	Cincinnati, AFC	3,241
	Washington, NFC	2,917
1974	Washington, NFC	2,978
	Cincinnati, AFC	2,804
1973	Philadelphia, NFC	2,998
	Denver, AFC	2,519
1972	N.Y. Jets, AFC	2,777
	San Francisco, NFC	2,735
1971	San Diego, AFC	3,134
	Dallas, NFC	2,786

Year	Team	Yards
1970	San Francisco, NFC	2,923
	Oakland, AFC	2,865
1969	Oakland, AFL	3,271
	San Francisco, NFL	3,158
1968	San Diego, AFL	3,623
	Dallas, NFL	3,026
1967	N.Y. Jets, AFL	3,845
	Washington, NFL	3,730
1966	N.Y. Jets, AFL	3,464
	Dallas, NFL	3,023
1965	San Francisco, NFL	3,487
	San Diego, AFL	3,103
1964	Houston, AFL	3,527
	Chicago, NFL	2,841
1963	Baltimore, NFL	3,296
	Houston, AFL	3,222
1962	Denver, AFL	3,404
	Philadelphia, NFL	3,385
1961	Houston, AFL	4,392
	Philadelphia, NFL	3,605
1960	Houston, AFL	3,203
	Baltimore, NFL	2,956
1959	Baltimore	2,753
1958	Pittsburgh	2,752
1957	Baltimore	2,388
1956	Los Angeles	2,419
1955	Philadelphia	2,472
1954	Chi. Bears	3,104
1953	Philadelphia	3,089
1952	Cleveland	2,566
1951	Los Angeles	3,296
1950	Los Angeles	3,709
1949	Chi. Bears	3,055
1948	Washington	2,861
1947	Washington	3,336
1946	Los Angeles	2,080
1945	Chi. Bears	1,857
1944	Washington	2,021
1943	Chi. Bears	2,310
1942	Green Bay	2,407
1941	Chi. Bears	2,002
1940	Washington	1,887
1939	Chi. Bears	1,965
1938	Washington	1,536
1937	Green Bay	1,398
1936	Green Bay	1,629
1935	Green Bay	1,449
1934	Green Bay	1,165
1933	N.Y. Giants	1,348
1932	Chi. Bears	1,013

FEWEST POINTS ALLOWED

Year	Team	Points
1981	Philadelphia, NFC	221
	Miami, AFC	275
1980	Philadelphia, NFC	222
	Houston, AFC	251
1979	Tampa Bay, NFC	237
	San Diego, AFC	246
1978	Pittsburgh, AFC	195
	Dallas, NFC	208
1977	Atlanta, NFC	129
	Denver, AFC	148
1976	Pittsburgh, AFC	138
	Minnesota, NFC	176
1975	Los Angeles, NFC	135
	Pittsburgh, AFC	162
1974	Los Angeles, NFC	181
	Pittsburgh, AFC	189
1973	Miami, AFC	150
	Minnesota, NFC	168
1972	Miami, AFC	171
	Washington, NFC	218
1971	Minnesota, NFC	139
	Baltimore, AFC	140
1970	Minnesota, NFC	143
	Miami, AFC	228
1969	Minnesota, NFL	133
	Kansas City, AFL	177
1968	Baltimore, NFL	144
	Kansas City, AFL	170
1967	Los Angeles, NFL	196
	Houston, AFL	199
1966	Green Bay, NFL	163
	Buffalo, AFL	255
1965	Green Bay, NFL	224
	Buffalo, AFL	226
1964	Baltimore, NFL	225
	Buffalo, AFL	242
1963	Chicago, NFL	144
	San Diego, AFL	255
1962	Green Bay, NFL	148
	Dall. Texans, AFL	233
1961	San Diego, AFL	219
	New York Giants, NFL	220
1960	San Francisco, NFL	205
	Dall. Texans, AFL	253
1959	New York	170
1958	New York	183
1957	Cleveland	172
1956	Cleveland	177
1955	Cleveland	218
1954	Cleveland	162
1953	Cleveland	162
1952	Detroit	192
1951	Cleveland	152
1950	Philadelphia	141
1949	Philadelphia	134
1948	Chi. Bears	151
1947	Green Bay	210
1946	Pittsburgh	117
1945	Washington	121
1944	New York	75
1943	Washington	137
1942	Chi. Bears	84
1941	New York	114
1940	Brooklyn	120
1939	New York	85
1938	New York	79
1937	Chi. Bears	100
1936	Chi. Bears	94
1935	Green Bay	96
	New York	96
1934	Detroit	59

Year	Team	Yards
1933	Brooklyn	54
1932	Chi. Bears	44

FEWEST TOTAL YARDS ALLOWED

Year	Team	Yards
1981	Philadelphia, NFC	4,447
	N.Y. Jets, AFC	4,871
1980	Buffalo, AFC	4,101
	Philadelphia, NFC	4,443
1979	Tampa Bay, NFC	3,949
	Pittsburgh, AFC	4,270
1978	Los Angeles, NFC	3,893
	Pittsburgh, AFC	4,168
1977	Dallas, NFC	3,213
	New England, AFC	3,638
1976	Pittsburgh, AFC	3,323
	San Francisco, NFC	3,562
1975	Minnesota, NFC	3,153
	Oakland, AFC	3,629
1974	Pittsburgh, AFC	3,074
	Washington, NFC	3,285
1973	Los Angeles, NFC	2,951
	Oakland, AFC	3,160
1972	Miami, AFC	3,297
	Green Bay, NFC	3,474
1971	Baltimore, AFC	2,852
	Minnesota, NFC	3,406
1970	Minnesota, NFC	2,803
	N.Y. Jets, AFC	3,655
1969	Minnesota, NFL	2,720
	Kansas City, AFL	3,163
1968	Los Angeles, NFL	3,118
	N.Y. Jets, AFL	3,363
1967	Oakland, AFL	3,294
	Green Bay, NFL	3,300
1966	St. Louis, NFL	3,492
	Oakland, AFL	3,910
1965	San Diego, AFL	3,262
	Detroit, NFL	3,557
1964	Green Bay, NFL	3,179
	Buffalo, AFL	3,878
1963	Chicago, NFL	3,176
	Boston, AFL	3,834
1962	Detroit, NFL	3,217
	Dall. Texans, AFL	3,951
1961	San Diego, AFL	3,726
	Baltimore, NFL	3,782
1960	St. Louis, NFL	3,029
	Buffalo, AFL	3,866
1959	New York	2,843
1958	Chi. Bears	3,066
1957	Pittsburgh	2,791
1956	New York	3,081
1955	Cleveland	2,841
1954	Cleveland	2,658
1953	Philadelphia	2,998
1952	Cleveland	3,075
1951	New York	3,250
1950	Cleveland	3,154
1949	Philadelphia	2,831
1948	Chi. Bears	2,931
1947	Green Bay	3,396
1946	Washington	2,451
1945	Philadelphia	2,073
1944	Philadelphia	1,943
1943	Chi. Bears	2,262
1942	Chi. Bears	1,703
1941	New York	2,368
1940	New York	2,219
1939	Washington	2,116
1938	New York	2,029
1937	Washington	2,123
1936	Boston	2,181
1935	Boston	1,996
1934	Chi. Cardinals	1,539
1933	Brooklyn	1,789

FEWEST YARDS RUSHING ALLOWED

Year	Team	Yards
1981	Detroit, NFC	1,623
	Kansas City, AFC	1,747
1980	Detroit, NFC	1,599
	Cincinnati, AFC	1,680
1979	Denver, AFC	1,693
	Tampa Bay, NFC	1,873
1978	Dallas, NFC	1,721
	Pittsburgh, AFC	1,774
1977	Denver, AFC	1,531
	Dallas, NFC	1,651
1976	Pittsburgh, AFC	1,457
	Los Angeles, NFC	1,564
1975	Minnesota, NFC	1,532
	Houston, AFC	1,680
1974	Los Angeles, NFC	1,302
	New England, AFC	1,587
1973	Los Angeles, NFC	1,270
	Oakland, AFC	1,470
1972	Dallas, NFC	1,515
	Miami, AFC	1,548
1971	Baltimore, AFC	1,113
	Dallas, NFC	1,144
1970	Detroit, NFC	1,152
	N.Y. Jets, AFC	1,283
1969	Dallas, NFL	1,050
	Kansas City, AFL	1,091
1968	Dallas, NFL	1,195
	N.Y. Jets, AFL	1,195
1967	Dallas, NFL	1,081
	Oakland, AFL	1,129
1966	Buffalo, AFL	1,051
	Dallas, NFL	1,176
1965	San Diego, AFL	1,094
	Los Angeles, NFL	1,409
1964	Buffalo, AFL	913
	Los Angeles, NFL	1,501
1963	Boston, AFL	1,107
	Chicago, NFL	1,442
1962	Detroit, NFL	1,231
	Dall. Texans, AFL	1,250
1961	Boston, AFL	1,041
	Pittsburgh, NFL	1,463
1960	St. Louis, NFL	1,212
	Dall. Texans, AFL	1,338

Year	Team	Yards
1959	New York	1,261
1958	Baltimore	1,291
1957	Baltimore	1,174
1956	New York	1,443
1955	Cleveland	1,189
1954	Cleveland	1,050
1953	Philadelphia	1,117
1952	Detroit	1,145
1951	New York	913
1950	Detroit	1,367
1949	Chi. Bears	1,196
1948	Philadelphia	1,209
1947	Philadelphia	1,329
1946	Chi. Bears	1,060
1945	Philadelphia	817
1944	Philadelphia	558
1943	Phil--Pitt	793
1942	Chi. Bears	519
1941	Washington	1,042
1940	New York	977
1939	Chi. Bears	812
1938	Detroit	1,081
1937	Chi. Bears	933
1936	Boston	1,148
1935	Boston	998
1934	Chi. Cardinals	954
1933	Brooklyn	964

FEWEST YARDS PASSING ALLOWED

Leadership in this category has been based on net yards since 1952.

Year	Team	Yards
1981	Philadelphia, NFC	2,696
	Buffalo, AFC	2,870
1980	Washington, NFC	2,171
	Buffalo, AFC	2,282
1979	Tampa Bay, NFC	2,076
	Buffalo, AFC	2,530
1978	Buffalo, AFC	1,960
	Los Angeles, NFC	2,048
1977	Atlanta, NFC	1,384
	San Diego, AFC	1,725
1976	Minnesota, NFC	1,575
	Cincinnati, AFC	1,758
1975	Minnesota, NFC	1,621
	Cincinnati, AFC	1,729
1974	Pittsburgh, AFC	1,466
	Atlanta, NFC	1,572
1973	Miami, AFC	1,290
	Atlanta, NFC	1,430
1972	Minnesota, NFC	1,699
	Cleveland, AFC	1,736
1971	Atlanta, NFC	1,638
	Baltimore, AFC	1,739
1970	Minnesota, NFC	1,438
	Kansas City, AFC	2,010
1969	Minnesota, NFL	1,631
	Kansas City, AFL	2,072
1968	Houston, AFL	1,671
	Green Bay, NFL	1,796
1967	Green Bay, NFL	1,377
	Buffalo, AFL	1,825
1966	Green Bay, NFL	1,959
	Oakland, AFL	2,118
1965	Green Bay, NFL	1,981
	San Diego, AFL	2,168
1964	Green Bay, NFL	1,647
	San Diego, AFL	2,518
1963	Chicago, NFL	1,734
	Oakland, AFL	2,589
1962	Green Bay, NFL	1,746
	Oakland, AFL	2,306
1961	Baltimore, NFL	1,913
	San Diego, AFL	2,363
1960	Chicago, NFL	1,388
	Buffalo, AFL	2,124
1959	New York	1,582
1958	Chi. Bears	1,769
1957	Cleveland	1,300
1956	Cleveland	1,103
1955	Pittsburgh	1,295
1954	Cleveland	1,608
1953	Washington	1,751
1952	Washington	1,580
1951	Pittsburgh	1,687
1950	Cleveland	1,581
1949	Philadelphia	1,607
1948	Green Bay	1,626
1947	Green Bay	1,790
1946	Pittsburgh	939
1945	Washington	1,121
1944	Chi. Bears	1,052
1943	Chi. Bears	980
1942	Washington	1,093
1941	Pittsburgh	1,168
1940	Philadelphia	1,012
1939	Washington	1,116
1938	Chi. Bears	897
1937	Detroit	804
1936	Philadelphia	853
1935	Chi. Cardinals	793
1934	Philadelphia	545
1933	Portsmouth	558

SUPER BOWL

RESULTS

Game	Date	Winner	Loser	Site	Attendance
XVI	1-24-82	SanFrancisco(NFC)26	Cincinnati (AFC) 21	Pontiac	81,270
XV	1-25-81	Oakland (AFC) 27	Philadelphia (NFC) 10	New Orleans	76,135
XIV	1-20-80	Pittsburgh (AFC) 31	Los Angeles (NFC) 19	Pasadena	103,985
XIII	1-21-79	Pittsburgh (AFC) 35	Dallas (NFC) 31	Miami	79,484
XII	1-15-78	Dallas (NFC) 27	Denver (AFC) 10	New Orleans	75,583
XI	1- 9-77	Oakland (AFC) 32	Minnesota (NFC) 14	Pasadena	103,438
X	1-18-76	Pittsburgh (AFC) 21	Dallas (NFC) 17	Miami	80,187
IX	1-12-75	Pittsburgh (AFC) 16	Minnesota (NFC) 6	New Orleans	80,997
VIII	1-13-74	Miami (AFC) 24	Minnesota (NFC) 7	Houston	71,882
VII	1-14-73	Miami (AFC) 14	Washington (NFC) 7	Los Angeles	90,182
VI	1-16-72	Dallas (NFC) 24	Miami (AFC) 3	New Orleans	81,023
V	1-17-71	Baltimore (AFC) 16	Dallas (NFC) 13	Miami	79,204
IV	1-11-70	Kansas City (AFL) 23	Minnesota (NFL) 7	New Orleans	80,562
III	1-12-69	New York (AFL) 16	Baltimore (NFL) 7	Miami	75,389
II	1-14-68	Green Bay (NFL) 33	Oakland (AFL) 14	Miami	75,546
I	1-15-67	Green Bay (NFL) 35	Kansas City (AFL) 10	Los Angeles	61,946

SUPER BOWL COMPOSITE STANDINGS

	W	L	Pct	Pts.	OP
Pittsburgh Steelers	4	0	1.000	103	73
Green Bay Packers	2	0	1.000	68	24
New York Jets	1	0	1.000	16	7
San Francisco 49ers	1	0	1.000	26	21
Miami Dolphins	2	1	.667	41	38
Oakland Raiders	2	1	.667	73	57
Baltimore Colts	1	1	.500	23	29
Kansas City Chiefs	1	1	.500	33	42
Dallas Cowboys	2	3	.400	112	85
Cincinnati Bengals	0	1	.000	21	26
Denver Broncos	0	1	.000	10	27
Los Angeles Rams	0	1	.000	19	31
Philadelphia Eagles	0	1	.000	10	27
Washington Redskins	0	1	.000	7	14
Minnesota Vikings	0	4	.000	34	95

SUPER BOWL XVI

Pontiac Silverdome, Pontiac, Michigan   January 24, 1982
Attendance: 81,270

SAN FRANCISO 26, CINCINNATI 21 —Ray Wersching's Super Bowl record-tying four field goals and Joe Montana's controlled passing helped lift the San Francisco 49ers to their first NFL championship with a 26-21 victory over AFC representative Cincinnati. The 49ers, champions of the NFC Western Division, built a game-record 20-0 halftime lead via Montana's one-yard touchdown run, which capped an 11-play, 68-yard drive; fullback Earl Cooper's 11-yard scoring pass from Montana, which climaxed a Super Bowl record 92-yard drive on 12 plays; and Wersching's 22- and 26-yard field goals. The Bengals, AFC Central Division titlists, rebounded in the second half, closing the gap to 20-14 on quarterback Ken Anderson's five-yard run and Dan Ross's four-yard catch from Anderson, who established Super Bowl passing records for completions

(25) and completion percentage (73.5 percent on 25 of 34). Wersching added early fourth-period field goals of 40 and 23 yards to increase the 49ers' lead to 26-14. The Bengals managed to score on an Anderson-to-Ross three-yard pass with only 16 seconds remaining. Ross set a Super Bowl record with 11 receptions for 104 yards. Montana, the game's most valuable player, completed 14 of 22 passes for 157 yards. Dwight Clark had four catches for 45 yards and Freddie Solomon four for 52. Cincinnati compiled 356 yards to San Francisco's 275, which marked the first time in Super Bowl history that the team that gained the most yards from scrimmage lost the game.

San Francisco (26)	Offense	Cincinnati (21)
Dwight Clark	WR	Cris Collinsworth
Dan Audick	LT	Anthony Munoz
John Ayers	LG	Dave Lapham
Fred Quillan	C	Blair Bush
Randy Cross	RG	Max Montoya
Keith Fahnhorst	RT	Mike Wilson
Charle Young	TE	Dan Ross
Freddie Solomon	WR	Isaac Curtis
Joe Montana	QB	Ken Anderson
Ricky Patton	RB	Charles Alexander
Earl Cooper	RB	Pete Johnson
	Defense	
Jim Stuckey	LE	Eddie Edwards
Archie Reese	NT	Wilson Whitley
Fred Dean	RE	Ross Browner
Dwaine Board	DE-LLB	Bo Harris
Jack Reynolds	LLB	Jim LeClair
Bobby Leopold	RLB	Glenn Cameron
Keena Turner	RLB	Reggie Williams
Ronnie Lott	LCB	Louis Breeden
Eric Wright	RCB	Ken Riley
Carlton Williamson	SS	Bobby Kemp
Dwight Hicks	FS	Bryan Hicks

SUBSTITUTIONS

San Francisco—Offense: K—Ray Wersching. P—Jim Miller. RB—Johnny Davis, Amos Lawrence, Bill Ring. WR—Mike Shumann, Mike Wilson. TE—Eason Ramson. C—Walt Downing. T—Allan Kennedy. G—John Choma. Defense: E—Lawrence Pillers. T—John Harty. LB—Dan Bunz, Willie Harper, Milt McColl, Craig Puki. DB—Rick Gervais, Lynn Thomas. DNP—Guy Benjamin (QB), Walt Easley (RB), Lenvil Elliott (RB), Saladin Martin (DB).
Cincinnati—Offense: K—Jim Breech. P—Pat McInally. RB—Archie Griffin, Jim Hargrove. WR—Don Bass, Steve Kreider, David Verser. TE—M. L. Harris. C—Blake Moore. T—Mike Obrovac. Defense: E—Gary Burley, Mike St. Clair. NT—Rod Horn. LB—Tom Dinkel, Guy Frazier, Rick Razzano. DB—Oliver Davis, Mike Fuller, Ray Griffin, John Simmons. DNP—Turk Schonert (QB), Jack Thompson (QB), Glenn Bujnoch (G).

OFFICIALS

Referee: Pat Haggerty. Umpire: Al Conway. Head Linesman: Jerry Bergman. Line Judge: Bob Beeks. Back Judge: Bill Swanson. Field Judge: Don Hakes. Side Judge: Bob Rice.

SCORING

San Francisco	7	13	0	6	— 26
Cincinnati	0	0	7	14	— 21

Super Bowl

SF —Montana 1 run (Wersching kick)
SF —Cooper 11 pass from Montana (Wersching kick)
SF —FG Wersching 22
SF —FG Wersching 26
Cin—Anderson 5 run (Breech kick)
Cin—Ross 4 pass from Anderson (Breech kick)
SF —FG Wersching 40
SF —FG Wersching 23
Cin—Ross 3 pass from Anderson (Breech kick)

TEAM STATISTICS

	San Francisco	Cincinnati
Total First Downs	20	24
First Downs Rushing	9	7
First Downs Passing	9	13
First Downs Penalty	2	4
Rushes	40	24
Yards Gained Rushing (net)	127	72
Average Yards per Rush	3.2	3.0
Passes Attempted	22	34
Passes Completed	14	25
Had Intercepted	0	2
Times Tackled Attempting to Pass	1	5
Yards Lost Attempting to Pass	9	16
Yards Gained Passing (net)	148	284
Total Net Yardage	275	356
Total Offensive Plays	63	63
Average Gain per Offensive Play	4.4	5.7
Punts	4	3
Average Distance	46.3	43.7
Punt Returns	1	4
Punt Return Yardage	6	35
Kickoff Returns	2	7
Kickoff Return Yardage	40	52
Interception Return Yardage	52	0
Fumbles	2	2
Own Fumbles Recovered	1	0
Opponent Fumbles Recovered	2	1
Total Return Yardage	98	87
Penalties	8	8
Yards Penalized	65	57
Total Points Scored	26	21
Touchdowns	2	3
Touchdowns Rushing	1	1
Touchdowns Passing	1	2
Touchdown Returns	0	0
Extra Points	2	3
Field Goals	4	0
Field Goals Attempted	4	0

FINANCIAL FACTS

Paid Attendance	81,270
Winning Player's Share	$18,000
Losing Player's Share	$ 9,000

INDIVIDUAL STATISTICS

RUSHING

San Francisco	Att.	Yds.	LG	TD
Patton	17	55	10	0
Cooper	9	34	14	0
Montana	6	18	7	1
Ring	5	17	7	0
J. Davis	2	5	4	0
Clark	1	−2	−2	0

Cincinnati	Att.	Yds.	LG	TD
Johnson	14	36	5	0
Alexander	5	17	13	0
Anderson	4	15	6	1
A. Griffin	1	4	4	0

PASSING

San Fran.	Att.	Comp.	Yds.	TD	Int.
Montana	22	14	157	1	0

Cin.	Att.	Comp.	Yds.	TD	Int.
Anderson	34	25	300	2	2

RECEIVING

San Francisco	No.	Yds.	LG	TD
Solomon	4	52	20	0
Clark	4	45	17	0
Cooper	2	15	11	1
Wilson	1	22	22	0
Young	1	14	14	0
Patton	1	6	6	0
Ring	1	3	3	0

Cincinnati	No.	Yds.	LG	TD
Ross	11	104	16	2
Collinsworth	5	107	49	0
Curtis	3	42	21	0
Kreider	2	36	19	0
Johnson	2	8	5	0
Alexander	2	3	3	0

INTERCEPTIONS

San Francisco	No.	Yds.	LG	TD
Hicks	1	27	27	0
Wright	1	25	25	0

Cincinnati
None

PUNTING

San Francisco	No.	Avg.	LG	Blk.
Miller	4	46.3	50	0

Cincinnati	No.	Avg.	LG	Blk.
McInally	3	43.7	53	0

PUNT RETURNS

San Fran.	No.	FC	Yds.	LG	TD
Hicks	1	0	6	6	0
Solomon	0	1	0	0	0

Cincinnati	No.	FC	Yds.	LG	TD
Fuller	4	0	35	17	0

KICKOFF RETURNS

San Francisco	No.	Yds.	LG	TD
Hicks	1	23	23	0
Lawrence	1	17	17	0

Cincinnati	No.	Yds.	LG	TD
Verser	5	52	16	0
Frazier	1	0	0	0
A. Griffin	1	0	0	0

SUPER BOWL XV

Louisiana Superdome, New Orleans, Louisiana   January 25, 1981
Attendance: 76,135

OAKLAND 27, PHILADELPHIA 10—Jim Plunkett threw three touchdown passes, including an 80-yarder to Kenny King, as the Raiders became the first wild card team to win the Super Bowl. Plunkett's touchdown bomb to King—the longest play in Super Bowl history—gave Oakland a decisive 14-0 lead with nine seconds left in the first period. Linebacker Rod Martin had set up Oakland's first touchdown, a two-yard reception by Cliff Branch, with a 16-yard interception return to the Eagles' 32 yard line. The Eagles never recovered from that early deficit, managing only a Tony Franklin field goal (30 yards) and an eight-yard touchdown pass from Ron Jaworski to Keith Krepfle the rest of the game. Plunkett, who became a starter in the sixth game of the season, completed 13 of 21 for 261 yards and was named the game's most valuable player. Oakland won 9 of 11 games with Plunkett starting, but that was good enough only for second place in the AFC West, although they tied division winner San Diego with an 11-5 record. The Raiders, who had previously won Super Bowl XI over Minnesota, had to win three playoff games to get to the championship game. Oakland defeated Houston 27-7 at home followed by road victories over Cleveland, 14-12, and San Diego, 34-27. Oakland's Mark van Eeghen was the game's leading rusher with 80 yards on 19 carries. Philadelphia's Wilbert Montgomery led all receivers with six receptions for 91 yards. Branch had five for 67 and Harold Carmichael of Philadelphia five for 83. Martin finished the game with three interceptions, a Super Bowl record.

Oakland (AFC)	14	0	10	3	— 27
Philadelphia (NFC)	0	3	0	7	— 10

Oak—Branch 2 pass from Plunkett (Bahr kick)
Oak—King 80 pass from Plunkett (Bahr kick)
Phil —FG Franklin 30
Oak—Branch 29 pass from Plunkett (Bahr kick)
Oak—FG Bahr 46
Phil —Krepfle 8 pass from Jaworski (Franklin kick)
Oak—FG Bahr 35

SUPER BOWL XIV

Rose Bowl, Pasadena, California   January 20, 1980
Attendance: 103,985

PITTSBURGH 31, LOS ANGELES 19—Terry Bradshaw completed 14 of 21 passes for 309 yards and set two passing records as the Steelers became the first team to win four Super Bowls. Despite three interceptions by the Rams, Bradshaw kept his poise and brought the Steelers from behind twice in the second half. Trailing 13-10 at halftime, Pittsburgh went ahead 17-13 when Bradshaw hit Lynn Swann with a 47-yard touchdown pass after 2:48 of the third quarter. On the Rams' next possession Vince Ferragamo, who completed 15 of 25 passes for 212 yards, responded with a 50-yard pass to Billy Waddy that moved Los Angeles from its own 26 to the Steelers' 24. On the following play, Lawrence McCutcheon connected with Ron Smith on a halfback option pass that gave the Rams a 19-17 lead. On Pittsburgh's initial possession of the final period, Bradshaw lofted a 73-yard scoring pass to John Stallworth to put the Steelers in front to stay, 24-19. Franco Harris scored on a one-yard run later in the quarter to seal the verdict. A 45-yard pass from Bradshaw to Stallworth was the key play in the drive to Harris's score. Bradshaw, the game's most valuable player for the second straight year, set career Super Bowl records for most touchdown passes (nine) and most passing yards (932). Larry Anderson gave the Steelers excellent field position throughout the game with five kickoff returns for a record 162 yards.

Los Angeles (NFC)	7	6	6	0	— 19
Pittsburgh (AFC)	3	7	7	14	— 31

Pitt—FG Bahr 41
LA —Bryant 1 run (Corral kick)
Pitt—Harris 1 run (Bahr kick)
LA —FG Corral 31
LA —FG Corral 45
Pitt—Swann 47 pass from Bradshaw (Bahr kick)
LA —Smith 24 pass from McCutcheon (kick failed)
Pitt—Stallworth 73 pass from Bradshaw (Bahr kick)
Pitt—Harris 1 run (Bahr kick)

SUPER BOWL XIII

Orange Bowl, Miami, Florida   January 21, 1979
Attendance: 79,484

PITTSBURGH 35, DALLAS 31—Terry Bradshaw threw a record four touchdown passes to lead the Steelers to victory. The Steelers became the first team to win three Super Bowls, mostly because of Bradshaw's accurate arm. Bradshaw, voted the game's most valuable player, completed 17 of 30 passes for 318 yards, a personal high. Three of those passes went for touchdowns—two to John Stallworth and the third, with 26 seconds remaining in the second period, to Rocky Bleier. The Cowboys scored twice before intermission on Roger Staubach's 39-yard pass to Tony Hill and a 37-yard run by linebacker Mike Hegman, who stole the ball from Bradshaw. The Steelers broke open the contest with two touchdowns in a span of 19 seconds midway through the final period. Franco Harris rambled 22 yards up the middle to give the Steelers a 28-17 lead with 7:10 left. Pittsburgh got the ball right back when Randy White fumbled the kickoff and Dennis Winston recovered for the Steelers. On first down, Bradshaw hit Lynn Swann with an 18-yard scoring pass to boost the Steelers' lead to 35-17 with 6:51 to play. The Cowboys refused to let the Steelers run away with the contest. Staubach connected with Billy Joe DuPree on an eight-yard scoring pass with 2:23 left. Then the Cowboys recovered an onside kick and Staubach took them in for another score, passing four yards to Butch Johnson with 22 seconds remaining. Bleier recovered another onside kick with 17 seconds left to seal the victory for the Steelers.

Pittsburgh (AFC)	7	14	0	14 —	35
Dallas (NFC)	7	7	3	14 —	31

Pitt —Stallworth 28 pass from Bradshaw (Gerela kick)
Dall—Hill 39 pass from Staubach (Septien kick)
Dall—Hegman 37 fumble recovery return (Septien kick)
Pitt —Stallworth 75 pass from Bradshaw (Gerela kick)
Pitt —Bleier 7 pass from Bradshaw (Gerela kick)
Dall—FG Septien 27
Pitt —Harris 22 run (Gerela kick)
Pitt —Swann 18 pass from Bradshaw (Gerela kick)
Dall—DuPree 8 pass from Staubach (Septien kick)
Dall—B. Johnson 4 pass from Staubach (Septien kick)

SUPER BOWL XII

Louisiana Superdome, New Orleans, Louisiana   January 15, 1978
Attendance: 75,583

DALLAS 27, DENVER 10—The Cowboys evened their Super Bowl record at 2-2 by defeating Denver before a sellout crowd of 75,583, plus 102,010,000 television viewers, the largest audience ever to watch a sporting event. Dallas converted two interceptions into 10 points and Efren Herrera added a 35-yard field goal for a 13-0 halftime advantage. In the third period Craig Morton engineered a drive to the Cowboys' 30 and Jim Turner's 47-yard field goal made the score 13-3. After an exchange of punts, Butch Johnson made a spectacular diving catch in the end zone to complete a 45-yard pass from Roger Staubach and put the Cowboys ahead 20-3. Following Rick Upchurch's 67-yard kickoff return, Norris Weese guided the Broncos to a touchdown to cut the Dallas lead to 20-10. Dallas clinched the victory when running back Robert Newhouse threw a 29-yard touchdown pass to Golden Richards with 7:04 remaining in the game. It was the first pass thrown by Newhouse since 1975. Harvey Martin and Randy White, who were named co-most valuable players, led the Cowboys' defense, which recovered four fumbles and intercepted four passes.

Dallas (NFC)	10	3	7	7 —	27
Denver (AFC)	0	0	10	0 —	10

Dall—Dorsett 3 run (Herrera kick)
Dall—FG Herrera 35
Dall—FG Herrera 43
Den—FG Turner 47
Dall—Johnson 45 pass from Staubach (Herrera kick)
Den—Lytle 1 run (Turner kick)
Dall—Richards 29 pass from Newhouse (Herrera kick)

SUPER BOWL XI

Rose Bowl, Pasadena, California   January 9, 1977
Attendance: 103,438

OAKLAND 32, MINNESOTA 14—The Raiders won their first NFL championship before a record Super Bowl crowd plus 81 million television viewers, the
largest audience ever to watch a sporting event. The Raiders gained a record-
breaking 429 yards, including running back Clarence Davis's 137 yards rushing, and wide receiver Fred Biletnikoff made four key receptions, which earned
him the game's most valuable player trophy. Oakland scored on three succes-
sive possessions in the second quarter to build a 16-0 halftime lead. Errol
Mann's 24-yard field goal opened the scoring, then the AFC champions put
together drives of 64 and 35 yards, scoring on a one-yard pass from Ken Stabler to Dave Casper and a one-yard run by Pete Banaszak. The Raiders increased their lead to 19-0 on a 40-yard field goal in the third quarter, but
Minnesota responded with a 12-play, 58-yard drive late in the period, with Fran
Tarkenton passing eight yards to wide receiver Sammy White to cut the deficit
to 19-7. Two fourth quarter interceptions clinched the title for the Raiders. One
set up Banaszak's second touchdown run, the other resulted in cornerback
Willie Brown's Super Bowl record 75-yard interception return.

Oakland (AFC)	0	16	3	13	— 32
Minnesota (NFC)	0	0	7	7	— 14

Oak —FG Mann 24
Oak —Casper 1 pass from Stabler (Mann kick)
Oak —Banaszak 1 run (kick failed)
Oak —FG Mann 40
Minn—S. White 8 pass from Tarkenton (Cox kick)
Oak —Banaszak 2 run (Mann kick)
Oak —Brown 75 interception (kick failed)
Minn—Voigt 13 pass from Lee (Cox kick)

SUPER BOWL X

Orange Bowl, Miami, Florida   January 18, 1976
Attendance: 80,187

PITTSBURGH 21, DALLAS 17—The Steelers won the Super Bowl for the second year in a row on Terry Bradshaw's 64-yard touchdown pass to Lynn Swann
and an aggressive defense that snuffed out a late rally by the Cowboys with an
end zone interception on the final play of the game. In the fourth quarter Pittsburgh ran on fourth down and gave up the ball on the Cowboys' 39 with 1:22 to
play. Staubach ran and passed for two first downs but his last desperation pass
was picked off by Glen Edwards. Dallas's scoring was the result of two touchdown passes by Staubach, one to Drew Pearson for 29 yards and the other to
Percy Howard for 34 yards. Toni Fritsch had a 36-yard field goal. The Steelers
scored on two touchdown passes by Bradshaw, one to Randy Grossman for
seven yards and the long bomb to Swann. Roy Gerela had 36- and 18-yard field
goals. Reggie Harrison blocked a punt through the end zone for a safety.
Swann set a Super Bowl record by gaining 161 yards on his four receptions.

Dallas (NFC)	7	3	0	7	— 17
Pittsburgh (AFC)	7	0	0	14	— 21

Dall—D. Pearson 29 pass from Staubach (Fritsch kick)
Pitt —Grossman 7 pass from Bradshaw (Gerela kick)
Dall—FG Fritsch 36
Pitt —Safety, Harrison blocked Hoopes's punt through end zone
Pitt —FG Gerela 36
Pitt —FG Gerela 18
Pitt —Swann 64 pass from Bradshaw (kick failed)
Dall—P. Howard 34 pass from Staubach (Fritsch kick)

SUPER BOWL IX

Tulane Stadium, New Orleans, Louisiana   January 12, 1975

Attendance: 80,997

PITTSBURGH 16, MINNESOTA 6—AFC champion Pittsburgh, in its initial Super Bowl appearance, and NFC champion Minnesota, making a third bid for its first Super Bowl title, struggled through a first half in which the only score was produced by the Steelers' defense when Dwight White downed Vikings' quarterback Fran Tarkenton in the end zone for a safety 7:49 into the second period. The Steelers forced another break and took advantage on the second half kickoff when Minnesota's Bill Brown fumbled and Marv Kellum recovered for Pittsburgh on the Vikings' 30. After Rocky Bleier failed to gain on first down, Franco Harris carried three consecutive times for 24 yards, a loss of 3, and a 12-yard touchdown and a 9-0 lead. Though its offense was completely stymied by Pittsburgh's defense, Minnesota managed to move into a threatening position after 4:27 of the final period when Matt Blair blocked Bobby Walden's punt and Terry Brown recovered the ball in the end zone for a touchdown. Fred Cox's kick failed and the Steelers led 9-6. Pittsburgh wasted no time putting the victory away. The Steelers took the ensuing kickoff and marched 66 yards in 11 plays, climaxed by Terry Bradshaw's four-yard scoring pass to Larry Brown with 3:31 left. Pittsburgh's defense permitted Minnesota only 119 yards total offense, including a Super Bowl low of 17 yards rushing. The Steelers, meanwhile, gained 333 yards, including Harris's record 158 yards on 34 carries.

Pittsburgh (AFC)	0	2	7	7 — 16
Minnesota (NFC)	0	0	0	6 — 6

Pitt —Safety, White downed Tarkenton in end zone
Pitt —Harris 12 run (Gerela kick)
Minn—T. Brown recovered blocked punt in end zone (kick failed)
Pitt —L. Brown 4 pass from Bradshaw (Gerela kick)

SUPER BOWL VIII

Rice Stadium, Houston, Texas   January 13, 1974

Attendance: 71,882

MIAMI 24, MINNESOTA 7—The defending NFL champion Dolphins, representing the AFC for the third straight year, scored the first two times they had possession on marches of 62 and 56 yards in the first period while the Miami defense limited the Vikings to only seven plays. Larry Csonka climaxed the initial 10-play drive with a five-yard touchdown bolt through right guard after 5:27 had elapsed. Four plays later, Miami began another 10-play scoring drive, which ended with Jim Kiick bursting one yard through the middle for another touchdown after 13:38 of the period. Garo Yepremian added a 28-yard field goal midway in the second period for a 17-0 Miami lead. Minnesota then drove from its 20 to a second-and-two situation on the Miami 7 yard line with 1:18 left in the half. But on two plays, Miami limited Oscar Reed to one yard. On fourth-and-one from the 6, Reed went over right tackle, but Dolphins middle linebacker Nick Buoniconti jarred the ball loose and Jake Scott recovered for Miami to halt the Minnesota threat. The Vikings were unable to muster enough offense in the second half to threaten the Dolphins. Csonka rushed 33 times for a Super Bowl record 145 yards. Bob Griese of Miami completed six of seven passes for 73 yards.

Minnesota (NFC)	0	0	0	7 — 7
Miami (AFC)	14	3	7	0 — 24

Mia —Csonka 5 run (Yepremian kick)
Mia —Kiick 1 run (Yepremian kick)
Mia —FG Yepremian 28

Mia —Csonka 2 run (Yepremian kick)
Minn—Tarkenton 4 run (Cox kick)

SUPER BOWL VII

Memorial Coliseum, Los Angeles, California   January 14, 1973
Attendance: 90,182

MIAMI 14, WASHINGTON 7—The Dolphins played virtually perfect football in the first half as their defense permitted the Redskins to cross midfield only once and their offense turned good field position into two touchdowns. On its third possession, Miami opened its first scoring drive from the Dolphins' 37 yard line. An 18-yard pass from Bob Griese to Paul Warfield preceded by three plays Griese's 28-yard touchdown pass to Howard Twilley. After Washington moved from its 17 to the Miami 48 with two minutes remaining in the first half, Dolphins linebacker Nick Buoniconti intercepted a Billy Kilmer pass at the Miami 41 and returned it to the Washington 27. Jim Kiick ran for three yards, Larry Csonka for three, Griese passed to Jim Mandich for 19, and Kiick gained one to the 1 yard line. With 18 seconds left until intermission, Kiick scored from the 1. Washington's only touchdown came with 7:07 left in the game and resulted from a misplayed field goal attempt and fumble by Garo Yepremian, with the Redskins' Mike Bass picking the ball out of the air and running 49 yards for the score.

Miami (AFC)	7	7	0	0 — 14
Washington (NFC)	0	0	0	7 — 7

Mia —Twilley 28 pass from Griese (Yepremian kick)
Mia —Kiick 1 run (Yepremian kick)
Wash—Bass 49 fumble recovery return (Knight kick)

SUPER BOWL VI

Tulane Stadium, New Orleans, Louisiana   January 16, 1972
Attendance: 81,023

DALLAS 24, MIAMI 3—The Cowboys rushed for a record 252 yards and their defense limited the Dolphins to a low of 185 yards while not permitting a touchdown for the first time in Super Bowl history. Dallas converted Chuck Howley's recovery of Larry Csonka's first fumble of the season into a 3-0 advantage and led at halftime 10-3. After Dallas received the second half kickoff, Duane Thomas led a 71-yard march in eight plays for a 17-3 margin. Howley intercepted Bob Griese's pass at the 50 and returned it to the Miami 9 early in the fourth period, and three plays later Roger Staubach passed seven yards to Mike Ditka for the final touchdown. Thomas rushed for 95 yards and Walt Garrison gained 74. Staubach, voted the game's most valuable player, completed 12 of 19 passes for 119 yards and two touchdowns.

Dallas (NFC)	3	7	7	7 — 24
Miami (AFC)	0	3	0	0 — 3

Dall—FG Clark 9
Dall—Alworth 7 pass from Staubach (Clark kick)
Mia—FG Yepremian 31
Dall—D. Thomas 3 run (Clark kick)
Dall—Ditka 7 pass from Staubach (Clark kick)

SUPER BOWL V

Orange Bowl, Miami, Florida   January 17, 1971
Attendance: 79,204

BALTIMORE 16, DALLAS 13—A 32-yard field goal by first-year kicker Jim O'Brien brought the Baltimore Colts a victory over the Dallas Cowboys in the final five seconds of Super Bowl V. The game between the champions of the

AFC and NFC was played on artificial turf for the first time. Dallas led 13-6 at the half but interceptions by Rick Volk and Mike Curtis set up a Baltimore touchdown and O'Brien's decisive kick in the fourth period. Earl Morrall relieved an injured Johnny Unitas late in the first half, although Unitas completed the Colts' only scoring pass. It caromed off receiver Eddie Hinton's finger tips, off Dallas defensive back Mel Renfro, and finally settled into the grasp of John Mackey, who went 45 yards to score on a 75-yard play.

Baltimore (AFC)	0	6	0	10	—	16
Dallas (NFC)	3	10	0	0	—	13

Dall—FG Clark 14
Dall—FG Clark 30
Balt—Mackey 75 pass from Unitas (kick blocked)
Dall—Thomas 7 pass from Morton (Clark kick)
Balt—Nowatzke 2 run (O'Brien kick)
Balt—FG O'Brien 32

SUPER BOWL IV

Tulane Stadium, New Orleans, Louisiana   January 11, 1970
Attendance: 80,562

KANSAS CITY 23, MINNESOTA 7—The AFL squared the Super Bowl at two games apiece with the NFL, building a 16-0 halftime lead behind Len Dawson's superb quarterbacking and a powerful defense. Dawson, the fourth consecutive quarterback to be chosen the Super Bowl's top player, called an almost flawless game, completing 12 of 17 passes and hitting Otis Taylor on a 46-yard play for the final Chiefs touchdown. The Kansas City defense limited Minnesota's strong rushing game to 67 yards and made three interceptions and two fumble recoveries. The crowd of 80,562 set a Super Bowl record, as did the gross receipts of $3,817,872.69.

Minnesota (NFL)	0	0	7	0	—	7
Kansas City (AFL)	3	13	7	0	—	23

KC —FG Stenerud 48
KC —FG Stenerud 32
KC —FG Stenerud 25
KC —Garrett 5 run (Stenerud kick)
Minn—Osborn 4 run (Cox kick)
KC —Taylor 46 pass from Dawson (Stenerud kick)

SUPER BOWL III

Orange Bowl, Miami, Florida   January 12, 1969
Attendance: 75,389

NEW YORK JETS 16, BALTIMORE 7—Jets quarterback Joe Namath "guaranteed" victory on the Thursday before the game, then went out and led the AFL to its first Super Bowl victory over a Baltimore team that had lost only once in 16 games all season. Namath, chosen the outstanding player, completed 17 of 28 passes for 206 yards and directed a steady attack that dominated the NFL champions after the Jets' defense had intercepted Colts quarterback Earl Morrall three times in the first half. The Jets had 337 total yards, including 121 yards rushing by Matt Snell. Johnny Unitas, who had missed most of the season with a sore elbow, came off the bench and led Baltimore to its only touchdown late in the fourth quarter after New York led 16-0.

New York Jets (AFL)	0	7	6	3	—	16
Baltimore (NFL)	0	0	0	7	—	7

NY —Snell 4 run (Turner kick)
NY —FG Turner 32
NY —FG Turner 30

NY —FG Turner 9
Balt—Hill 1 run (Michaels kick)

SUPER BOWL II

Orange Bowl, Miami, Florida   January 14, 1968
Attendance: 75,546

GREEN BAY 33, OAKLAND 14—Green Bay, after winning its third consecutive NFL championship, won the Super Bowl title for the second straight year
33-14 over the AFL champion Raiders in a game that drew the first $3 million
dollar gate in football history. Bart Starr again was chosen the game's most
valuable player as he completed 13 of 24 passes for 202 yards and one touchdown and directed a Packers attack that was in control all the way after building a 16-7 halftime lead. Don Chandler kicked four field goals and Herb
Adderley, all-pro cornerback, capped the Green Bay scoring with a 60-yard
run with an interception. The game marked the last for Vince Lombardi as
Packers coach, ending nine years at Green Bay in which he won six Western
Conference championships, five NFL championships, and two Super Bowls.

Green Bay (NFL)	3	13	10	7 — 33
Oakland (AFL)	0	7	0	7 — 14

GB —FG Chandler 39
GB —FG Chandler 20
GB —Dowler 62 pass from Starr (Chandler kick)
Oak—Miller 23 pass from Lamonica (Blanda kick)
GB —FG Chandler 43
GB —Anderson 2 run (Chandler kick)
GB —FG Chandler 31
GB —Adderley 60 interception return (Chandler kick)
Oak—Miller 23 pass from Lamonica (Blanda kick)

SUPER BOWL I

Memorial Coliseum, Los Angeles, California   January 15, 1967
Attendance: 61,946

GREEN BAY 35, KANSAS CITY 10—The Green Bay Packers opened the
Super Bowl series by defeating Kansas City's American Football League
champions 35-10 behind the passing of Bart Starr, the receiving of Max
McGee, and a key interception by all-pro safety Willie Wood. Green Bay broke
open the game with three second-half touchdowns, the first of which was set up
by Wood's 40-yard return of an interception to the Chiefs' 5 yard line. McGee,
filling in for ailing Boyd Dowler after having caught only three passes all season, caught seven from Starr for 138 yards and two touchdowns. Elijah Pitts ran
for two other scores. The Chiefs' 10 points came in the second quarter, the only
touchdown on a seven-yard pass from Len Dawson to Curtis McClinton. Starr
completed 16 of 23 passes for 250 yards and two touchdowns and was chosen
the most valuable player. The Packers collected $15,000 per man and the
Chiefs $7,500—the largest single-game shares in the history of team sports.

Kansas City (AFL)	0	10	0	0 — 10
Green Bay (NFL)	7	7	14	7 — 35

GB—McGee 37 pass from Starr (Chandler kick)
KC—McClinton 7 pass from Dawson (Mercer kick)
GB—Taylor 14 run (Chandler kick)
KC—FG Mercer 31
GB—Pitts 5 run (Chandler kick)
GB—McGee 13 pass from Starr (Chandler kick)
GB—Pitts 1 run (Chandler kick)

SUPER BOWL RECORDS

Compiled by Elias Sports Bureau

1967: Super Bowl I
1968: Super Bowl II
1969: Super Bowl III
1970: Super Bowl IV
1971: Super Bowl V

1972: Super Bowl VI
1973: Super Bowl VII
1974: Super Bowl VIII
1975: Super Bowl IX
1976: Super Bowl X
1977: Super Bowl XI

1978: Super Bowl XII
1979: Super Bowl XIII
1980: Super Bowl XIV
1981: Super Bowl XV
1982: Super Bowl XVI

INDIVIDUAL RECORDS

SERVICE

Most Games
- 5 Marv Fleming, Green Bay, 1967-68; Miami, 1972-74
  - Larry Cole, Dallas, 1971-72, 1976, 1978-79
  - Cliff Harris, Dallas, 1971-72, 1976, 1978-79
  - D. D. Lewis, Dallas, 1971-72, 1976, 1978-79
  - Preston Pearson, Baltimore, 1969; Pittsburgh, 1975; Dallas, 1976, 1978-79
  - Charlie Waters, Dallas, 1971-72, 1976, 1978-79
  - Rayfield Wright, Dallas, 1971-72, 1976, 1978-79
- 4 By many players

Most Games, Winning Team
- 4 By many players

Most Games, Coach
- 5 Tom Landry, Dallas, 1971-72, 1976, 1978-79
- 4 Don Shula, Baltimore, 1969; Miami, 1972-74
  - Harry (Bud) Grant, Minnesota, 1970, 1974-75, 1977
  - Chuck Noll, Pittsburgh, 1975-76, 1979-80

Most Games, Winning Team, Coach
- 4 Chuck Noll, Pittsburgh, 1975-76, 1979-80
- 2 Vince Lombardi, Green Bay, 1967-68
  - Don Shula, Miami, 1973-74
  - Tom Landry, Dallas, 1972, 1978

SCORING

POINTS

Most Points, Career
- 24 Franco Harris, Pittsburgh, 4 games (4-td)
- 20 Don Chandler, Green Bay, 2 games (8-pat, 4-fg)

Most Points, Game
- 15 Don Chandler, Green Bay vs. Oakland, 1968 (3-pat, 4-fg)

TOUCHDOWNS

Most Touchdowns, Career
- 4 Franco Harris, Pittsburgh, 4 games (4-r)
- 3 John Stallworth, Pittsburgh, 4 games (3-p)
  - Lynn Swann, Pittsburgh, 4 games (3-p)

Most Touchdowns, Game
- 2 Max McGee, Green Bay vs. Kansas City, 1967 (2-p)
  - Elijah Pitts, Green Bay vs. Kansas City, 1967 (2-r)
  - Bill Miller, Oakland vs. Green Bay, 1968 (2-p)
  - Larry Csonka, Miami vs. Minnesota, 1974 (2-r)
  - Pete Banaszak, Oakland vs. Minnesota, 1977 (2-r)
  - John Stallworth, Pittsburgh vs. Dallas, 1979 (2-p)
  - Franco Harris, Pittsburgh vs. Los Angeles, 1980 (2-r)
  - Cliff Branch, Oakland vs. Philadelphia, 1981 (2-p)
  - Dan Ross, Cincinnati vs. San Francisco, 1982 (2-p)

POINTS AFTER TOUCHDOWN
Most Points After Touchdown, Career

8	Don Chandler, Green Bay, 2 games (8 att)
	Roy Gerela, Pittsburgh, 3 games (9 att)
5	Garo Yepremian, Miami, 3 games (5 att)

Most Points After Touchdown, Game

5	Don Chandler, Green Bay vs. Kansas City, 1967 (5 att)
	Roy Gerela, Pittsburgh vs. Dallas, 1979 (5 att)

FIELD GOALS
Field Goals Attempted, Career

7	Roy Gerela, Pittsburgh, 3 games
6	Jim Turner, N. Y. Jets-Denver, 2 games

Most Field Goals Attempted, Game

5	Jim Turner, N. Y. Jets vs. Baltimore, 1969
	Efren Herrera, Dallas vs. Denver, 1978

Most Field Goals, Career

4	Don Chandler, Green Bay, 2 games (4 att)
	Jim Turner, N. Y. Jets-Denver, 2 games (6 att)
	Ray Wersching, San Francisco, 1 game (4 att)
3	Mike Clark, Dallas, 2 games (3 att)
	Jan Stenerud, Kansas City, 1 game (3 att)

Most Field Goals, Game

4	Don Chandler, Green Bay vs. Oakland, 1968
	Ray Wersching, San Francisco vs. Cincinnati, 1982

Longest Field Goal

48	Jan Stenerud, Kansas City vs. Minnesota, 1970

SAFETIES
Most Safeties, Game

1	Dwight White, Pittsburgh vs. Minnesota, 1975
	Reggie Harrison, Pittsburgh vs. Dallas, 1976

RUSHING

ATTEMPTS
Most Attempts, Career

101	Franco Harris, Pittsburgh, 4 games
57	Larry Csonka, Miami, 3 games

Most Attempts, Game

34	Franco Harris, Pittsburgh vs. Minnesota, 1975

YARDS GAINED
Most Yards Gained, Career

354	Franco Harris, Pittsburgh, 4 games
297	Larry Csonka, Miami, 3 games

Most Yards Gained, Game

158	Franco Harris, Pittsburgh vs. Minnesota, 1975

Longest Run From Scrimmage

58	Tom Matte, Baltimore vs. N.Y. Jets, 1969

AVERAGE GAIN
Highest Average Gain, Career (20 attempts)

5.3	Walt Garrison, Dallas, 2 games (26-139)
5.2	Tony Dorsett, Dallas, 2 games (31-162)

Highest Average Gain, Game (10 attempts)

10.5	Tom Matte, Baltimore vs. N.Y. Jets, 1969 (11-116)

TOUCHDOWNS
Most Touchdowns, Career

4	Franco Harris, Pittsburgh, 4 games
2	Elijah Pitts, Green Bay, 1 game
	Jim Kiick, Miami, 3 games
	Larry Csonka, Miami, 3 games

Pete Banaszak, Oakland, 2 games

Most Touchdowns, Game

2 Elijah Pitts, Green Bay vs. Kansas City, 1967
Larry Csonka, Miami vs. Minnesota, 1974
Pete Banaszak, Oakland vs. Minnesota, 1977
Franco Harris, Pittsburgh vs. Los Angeles, 1980

PASSING

ATTEMPTS

Most Passes Attempted, Career

98 Roger Staubach, Dallas, 4 games
89 Fran Tarkenton, Minnesota, 3 games

Most Passes Attempted, Game

38 Ron Jaworski, Philadelphia vs. Oakland, 1981

COMPLETIONS

Most Passes Completed, Career

61 Roger Staubach, Dallas, 4 games
49 Terry Bradshaw, Pittsburgh, 4 games

Most Passes Completed, Game

25 Ken Anderson, Cincinnati vs. San Francisco, 1982

COMPLETION PERCENTAGE

Highest Completion Percentage, Career (40 attempts)

63.6 Len Dawson, Kansas City, 2 games (44-28)
63.4 Bob Griese, Miami, 3 games (41-26)

Highest Completion Percentage, Game (20 attempts)

73.5 Ken Anderson, Cincinnati vs. San Francisco, 1982 (34-25)

YARDS GAINED

Most Yards Gained, Career

932 Terry Bradshaw, Pittsburgh, 4 games
734 Roger Staubach, Dallas, 4 games

Most Yards Gained, Game

318 Terry Bradshaw, Pittsburgh vs. Dallas, 1979

Longest Pass Completion

80 Jim Plunkett (to King), Oakland vs. Philadelphia, 1981 (TD)

AVERAGE GAIN

Highest Average Gain, Career (40 attempts)

11.10 Terry Bradshaw, Pittsburgh, 4 games (84-932)
9.62 Bart Starr, Green Bay, 2 games (47-452)

Highest Average Gain, Game (20 attempts)

14.71 Terry Bradshaw, Pittsburgh vs. Los Angeles, 1980 (21-309)

TOUCHDOWNS

Most Touchdown Passes, Career

9 Terry Bradshaw, Pittsburgh, 4 games
8 Roger Staubach, Dallas, 4 games

Most Touchdown Passes, Game

4 Terry Bradshaw, Pittsburgh vs. Dallas, 1979

HAD INTERCEPTED

Lowest Percentage, Passes Had Intercepted, Career (40 attempts)

2.13 Bart Starr, Green Bay, 2 games (47-1)
4.08 Roger Staubach, Dallas, 4 games (98-4)

Most Attempts, Without Interception, Game

28 Joe Namath, N.Y. Jets vs. Baltimore, 1969

Most Passes Had Intercepted, Career

7 Craig Morton, Dallas-Denver, 2 games
6 Fran Tarkenton, Minnesota, 3 games

Most Passes Had Intercepted, Game

4 Craig Morton, Denver vs. Dallas, 1978

PASS RECEIVING

RECEPTIONS
Most Receptions, Career
- 16 Lynn Swann, Pittsburgh, 4 games
- 15 Chuck Foreman, Minnesota, 3 games

Most Receptions, Game
- 11 Dan Ross, Cincinnati vs. San Francisco, 1982

YARDS GAINED
Most Yards Gained, Career
- 364 Lynn Swann, Pittsburgh, 4 games
- 268 John Stallworth, Pittsburgh, 4 games

Most Yards Gained, Game
- 161 Lynn Swann, Pittsburgh vs. Dallas, 1976

Longest Reception
- 80 Kenny King (from Plunkett), Oakland vs. Philadelphia, 1981 (TD)

AVERAGE GAIN
Highest Average Gain, Career (8 receptions)
- 24.4 John Stallworth, Pittsburgh, 4 games (11-268)
- 22.8 Lynn Swann, Pittsburgh, 4 games (16-364)

Highest Average Gain, Game (3 receptions)
- 40.3 John Stallworth, Pittsburgh vs. Los Angeles, 1980 (3-121)

TOUCHDOWNS
Most Touchdowns, Career
- 3 John Stallworth, Pittsburgh, 4 games
  - Lynn Swann, Pittsburgh, 4 games
- 2 Max McGee, Green Bay, 2 games
  - Bill Miller, Oakland, 1 game
  - Butch Johnson, Dallas, 2 games
  - Cliff Branch, Oakland, 2 games
  - Dan Ross, Cincinnati, 1 game

Most Touchdowns, Game
- 2 Max McGee, Green Bay vs. Kansas City, 1967
  - Bill Miller, Oakland vs. Green Bay, 1968
  - John Stallworth, Pittsburgh vs. Dallas, 1979
  - Cliff Branch, Oakland vs. Philadelphia, 1981
  - Dan Ross, Cincinnati vs. San Francisco, 1982

INTERCEPTIONS BY

Most Interceptions By, Career
- 3 Chuck Howley, Dallas, 2 games
  - Rod Martin, Oakland, 1 game
- 2 Randy Beverly, N.Y. Jets, 1 game
  - Jake Scott, Miami, 3 games
  - Mike Wagner, Pittsburgh, 3 games
  - Mel Blount, Pittsburgh, 4 games

Most Interceptions By, Game
- 3 Rod Martin, Oakland vs. Philadelphia, 1981

YARDS GAINED
Most Yards Gained, Career
- 75 Willie Brown, Oakland, 2 games
- 63 Chuck Howley, Dallas, 2 games
  - Jake Scott, Miami, 3 games

Most Yards Gained, Game
- 75 Willie Brown, Oakland vs. Minnesota, 1977

Longest Return
- 75 Willie Brown, Oakland vs. Minnesota, 1977 (TD)

TOUCHDOWNS
Most Touchdowns, Game

    1 Herb Adderley, Green Bay vs. Oakland, 1968
       Willie Brown, Oakland vs. Minnesota, 1977

PUNTING
Most Punts, Career

   17 Mike Eischeid, Oakland-Minnesota, 3 games
   15 Larry Seiple, Miami, 3 games

Most Punts, Game

    9 Ron Widby, Dallas vs. Baltimore, 1971

Longest Punt

   61 Jerrel Wilson, Kansas City vs. Green Bay, 1967

AVERAGE YARDAGE
Highest Average, Punting, Career (10 punts)

  46.5 Jerrel Wilson, Kansas City, 2 games
  41.3 Larry Seiple, Miami, 3 games

Highest Average, Punting, Game (4 punts)

  48.5 Jerrel Wilson, Kansas City vs. Minnesota, 1970

PUNT RETURNS
Most Punt Returns, Career

    6 Willie Wood, Green Bay, 2 games
       Jake Scott, Miami, 3 games
       Theo Bell, Pittsburgh, 2 games
    4 By seven players

Most Punt Returns, Game

    5 Willie Wood, Green Bay vs. Oakland, 1968

Most Fair Catches, Game

    3 Ron Gardin, Baltimore vs. Dallas, 1971
       Golden Richards, Dallas vs. Pittsburgh, 1976

YARDS GAINED
Most Yards Gained, Career

   45 Jake Scott, Miami, 3 games
   44 Theo Bell, Pittsburgh, 2 games

Most Yards Gained, Game

   43 Neal Colzie, Oakland vs. Minnesota, 1977

Longest Return

   31 Willie Wood, Green Bay vs. Oakland, 1968

AVERAGE YARDAGE
Highest Average, Career (4 returns)

  10.8 Neal Colzie, Oakland, 1 game
   8.8 Mike Fuller, Cincinnati, 1 game

Highest Average, Game (3 returns)

  11.3 Lynn Swann, Pittsburgh vs. Minnesota, 1975

TOUCHDOWNS
Most Touchdowns, Game

       None

KICKOFF RETURNS
Most Kickoff Returns, Career

    8 Larry Anderson, Pittsburgh, 2 games
    7 Preston Pearson, Baltimore-Pittsburgh-Dallas, 5 games

Most Kickoff Returns, Game

    5 Larry Anderson, Pittsburgh vs. Los Angeles, 1980
       Billy Campfield, Philadelphia vs. Oakland, 1981
       David Verser, Cincinnati vs. San Francisco, 1982

YARDS GAINED
Most Yards Gained, Career
- 207　Larry Anderson, Pittsburgh, 2 games
- 123　Eugene (Mercury) Morris, Miami, 3 games

Most Yards Gained, Game
- 162　Larry Anderson, Pittsburgh vs. Los Angeles, 1980

Longest Return
- 67　Rick Upchurch, Denver vs. Dallas, 1978

AVERAGE YARDAGE
Highest Average, Career (4 returns)
- 25.9　Larry Anderson, Pittsburgh, 2 games
- 22.5　Jim Duncan, Baltimore, 1 game

Highest Average, Game (3 returns)
- 32.4　Larry Anderson, Pittsburgh vs. Los Angeles, 1980

TOUCHDOWNS
Most Touchdowns, Game
- None

FUMBLES

Most Fumbles, Career
- 5　Roger Staubach, Dallas, 4 games
- 　Franco Harris, Pittsburgh, 4 games
- 　Terry Bradshaw, Pittsburgh, 4 games

Most Fumbles, Game
- 3　Roger Staubach, Dallas vs. Pittsburgh, 1976

RECOVERIES
Most Fumbles Recovered, Career
- 2　Jake Scott, Miami, 3 games (1 own, 1 opp)
- 　Fran Tarkenton, Minnesota, 3 games (2 own)
- 　Franco Harris, Pittsburgh, 4 games (2 own)
- 　Roger Staubach, Dallas, 4 games (2 own)
- 　Bobby Walden, Pittsburgh, 2 games (2 own)
- 　John Fitzgerald, Dallas, 4 games (2 own)
- 　Randy Hughes, Dallas, 3 games (2 opp)
- 　Butch Johnson, Dallas, 2 games (2 own)

Most Fumbles Recovered, Game
- 2　Jake Scott, Miami vs. Minnesota, 1974 (1 own, 1 opp)
- 　Roger Staubach, Dallas vs. Pittsburgh, 1976 (2 own)
- 　Randy Hughes, Dallas vs. Denver, 1978 (2 opp)
- 　Butch Johnson, Dallas vs. Denver, 1978 (2 own)

YARDS GAINED
Most Yards Gained, Game
- 49　Mike Bass, Washington vs. Miami, 1973 (opp)

Longest Return
- 49　Mike Bass, Washington vs. Miami, 1973 (TD)

TOUCHDOWNS
Most Touchdowns, Game
- 1　Mike Bass, Washington vs. Miami, 1973 (opp 49 yds)
- 　Mike Hegman, Dallas vs. Pittsburgh, 1979 (opp 37 yds)

COMBINED NET YARDS GAINED

ATTEMPTS
Most Attempts, Career
- 108　Franco Harris, Pittsburgh, 4 games
- 60　Larry Csonka, Miami, 3 games

Most Attempts, Game
- 35　Franco Harris, Pittsburgh vs. Minnesota, 1975

YARDS GAINED

Most Yards Gained, Career
- 468   Franco Harris, Pittsburgh, 4 games
- 391   Lynn Swann, Pittsburgh, 4 games

Most Yards Gained, Game
- 163   Sammy White, Minnesota vs. Oakland, 1977

TEAM RECORDS

GAMES, VICTORIES, DEFEATS

Most Games
- 5   Dallas, 1971-72, 1976, 1978-79

Most Consecutive Games
- 3   Miami, 1972-74

Most Games Won
- 4   Pittsburgh, 1975-76, 1979-80

Most Consecutive Games Won
- 2   Green Bay, 1967-68
-     Miami, 1973-74
-     Pittsburgh, 1975-76, 1979-80

Most Games Lost
- 4   Minnesota, 1970, 1974-75, 1977

Most Consecutive Games Lost
- 2   Minnesota, 1974-75

SCORING

Most Points, Game
- 35   Green Bay vs. Kansas City, 1967
-     Pittsburgh vs. Dallas, 1979

Fewest Points, Game
- 3   Miami vs. Dallas, 1972

Most Points, Both Teams, Game
- 66   Pittsburgh (35) vs. Dallas (31), 1979

Fewest Points, Both Teams, Game
- 21   Washington (7) vs. Miami (14), 1973

Most Points, Each Half
- 1st: 21   Pittsburgh vs. Dallas, 1979
- 2nd: 21   Green Bay vs. Kansas City, 1967
-            Pittsburgh vs. Los Angeles, 1980
-            Cincinnati vs. San Francisco, 1982

Most Points, Each Quarter
- 1st: 14   Miami vs. Minnesota, 1974
-            Oakland vs. Philadelphia, 1981
- 2nd: 16   Oakland vs. Minnesota, 1977
- 3rd: 14   Green Bay vs. Kansas City, 1967
- 4th: 14   Pittsburgh vs. Dallas, 1976; vs. Dallas, 1979; vs. Los Angeles, 1980
-            Dallas vs. Pittsburgh, 1979
-            Cincinnati vs. San Francisco, 1982

Most Points, Both Teams, Each Half
- 1st: 35   Pittsburgh (21) vs. Dallas (14), 1979
- 2nd: 31   Dallas (17) vs. Pittsburgh (14), 1979

Most Points, Both Teams, Each Quarter
- 1st: 14   Miami (14) vs. Minnesota (0), 1974
-            Dallas (7) vs. Pittsburgh (7), 1976, 1979
-            Oakland (14) vs. Philadelphia (0), 1981
- 2nd: 21   Pittsburgh (14) vs. Dallas (7), 1979
- 3rd: 17   Denver (10) vs. Dallas (7), 1978
- 4th: 28   Dallas (14) vs. Pittsburgh (14), 1979

TOUCHDOWNS

Most Touchdowns, Game
- 5   Green Bay vs. Kansas City, 1967
-    Pittsburgh vs. Dallas, 1979

Fewest Touchdowns, Game
 0 Miami vs. Dallas, 1972
Most Touchdowns, Both Teams, Game
 9 Pittsburgh (5) vs. Dallas (4), 1979
Fewest Touchdowns, Both Teams, Game
 2 Baltimore (1) vs. N.Y. Jets (1), 1969

POINTS AFTER TOUCHDOWN
Most Points After Touchdown, Game
 5 Green Bay vs. Kansas City, 1967
    Pittsburgh vs. Dallas, 1979
Most Points After Touchdown, Both Teams, Game
 9 Pittsburgh (5) vs. Dallas (4), 1979
Fewest Points After Touchdown, Both Teams, Game
 2 Baltimore (1) vs. N.Y. Jets (1), 1969
    Baltimore (1) vs. Dallas (1), 1971
    Minnesota (0) vs. Pittsburgh (2), 1975

FIELD GOALS
Most Field Goals Attempted, Game
 5 N.Y. Jets vs. Baltimore, 1969
    Dallas vs. Denver, 1978
Most Field Goals Attempted, Both Teams, Game
 7 N.Y. Jets (5) vs. Baltimore (2), 1969
Fewest Field Goals Attempted, Both Teams, Game
 1 Minnesota (0) vs. Miami (1), 1974
Most Field Goals, Game
 4 Green Bay vs. Oakland, 1968
    San Francisco vs. Cincinnati, 1982
Most Field Goals, Both Teams, Game
 4 Green Bay (4) vs. Oakland (0), 1968
    San Francisco (4) vs. Cincinnati (0), 1982
Fewest Field Goals, Both Teams, Game
 0 Miami vs. Washington, 1973
    Pittsburgh vs. Minnesota, 1975

SAFETIES
Most Safeties, Game
 1 Pittsburgh vs. Minnesota, 1975; vs. Dallas, 1976

FIRST DOWNS

Most First Downs, Game
 24 Cincinnati vs. San Francisco, 1982
Fewest First Downs, Game
 9 Minnesota vs. Pittsburgh, 1975
Most First Downs, Both Teams, Game
 44 Cincinnati (24) vs. San Francisco (20), 1982
Fewest First Downs, Both Teams, Game
 24 Dallas (10) vs. Baltimore (14), 1971

RUSHING
Most First Downs, Rushing, Game
 15 Dallas vs. Miami, 1972
Fewest First Downs, Rushing, Game
 2 Minnesota vs. Kansas City, 1970; vs. Pittsburgh, 1975
    Pittsburgh vs. Dallas, 1979
Most First Downs, Rushing, Both Teams, Game
 18 Dallas (15) vs. Miami (3), 1972
    Miami (13) vs. Minnesota (5), 1974
Fewest First Downs, Rushing, Both Teams, Game
 8 Baltimore (4) vs. Dallas (4), 1971
    Pittsburgh (2) vs. Dallas (6), 1979

PASSING

Most First Downs, Passing, Game
15   Minnesota vs. Oakland, 1977
         Pittsburgh vs. Dallas, 1979
Fewest First Downs, Passing, Game
1   Denver vs. Dallas, 1978
Most First Downs, Passing, Both Teams, Game
28   Pittsburgh (15) vs. Dallas (13), 1979
Fewest First Downs, Passing, Both Teams, Game
9   Denver (1) vs. Dallas (8), 1978

PENALTY

Most First Downs, Penalty, Game
4   Baltimore vs. Dallas, 1971
         Miami vs. Minnesota, 1974
         Cincinnati vs. San Francisco, 1982
Most First Downs, Penalty, Both Teams, Game
6   Cincinnati (4) vs. San Francisco (2), 1982
Fewest First Downs, Penalty, Both Teams, Game
0   Dallas vs. Miami, 1972
         Miami vs. Washington, 1973
         Dallas vs. Pittsburgh, 1976

NET YARDS GAINED RUSHING AND PASSING

Most Yards Gained, Game
429   Oakland vs. Minnesota, 1977
Fewest Yards Gained, Game
119   Minnesota vs. Pittsburgh, 1975
Most Yards Gained, Both Teams, Game
782   Oakland (429) vs. Minnesota (353), 1977
Fewest Yards Gained, Both Teams, Game
452   Minnesota (119) vs. Pittsburgh (333), 1975

RUSHING

ATTEMPTS

Most Attempts, Game
57   Pittsburgh vs. Minnesota, 1975
Fewest Attempts, Game
19   Kansas City vs. Green Bay, 1967
         Minnesota vs. Kansas City, 1970
Most Attempts, Both Teams, Game
78   Pittsburgh (57) vs. Minnesota (21), 1975
         Oakland (52) vs. Minnesota (26), 1977
Fewest Attempts, Both Teams, Game
52   Kansas City (19) vs. Green Bay (33), 1967

YARDS GAINED

Most Yards Gained, Game
266   Oakland vs. Minnesota, 1977
Fewest Yards Gained, Game
17   Minnesota vs. Pittsburgh, 1975
Most Yards Gained, Both Teams, Game
337   Oakland (266) vs. Minnesota (71), 1977
Fewest Yards Gained, Both Teams, Game
171   Baltimore (69) vs. Dallas (102), 1971

AVERAGE GAIN

Highest Average Gain, Game
6.22   Baltimore vs. N.Y. Jets, 1969 (23-143)
Lowest Average Gain, Game
0.81   Minnesota vs. Pittsburgh, 1975 (21-17)

TOUCHDOWNS
Most Touchdowns, Game
   3   Green Bay vs. Kansas City, 1967
      Miami vs. Minnesota, 1974
Fewest Touchdowns, Game
   0   By eleven teams
Most Touchdowns, Both Teams, Game
   4   Miami (3) vs. Minnesota (1), 1974
Fewest Touchdowns, Both Teams, Game
   0   Pittsburgh vs. Dallas, 1976
      Oakland vs. Philadelphia, 1981

PASSING

ATTEMPTS
Most Passes Attempted, Game
   44   Minnesota vs. Oakland, 1977
Fewest Passes Attempted, Game
   7   Miami vs. Minnesota, 1974
Most Passes Attempted, Both Teams, Game
   70   Baltimore (41) vs. N.Y. Jets (29), 1969
Fewest Passes Attempted, Both Teams, Game
   35   Miami (7) vs. Minnesota (28), 1974

COMPLETIONS
Most Passes Completed, Game
   25   Cincinnati vs. San Francisco, 1982
Fewest Passes Completed, Game
   6   Miami vs. Minnesota, 1974
Most Passes Completed, Both Teams, Game
   39   Cincinnati (25) vs. San Francisco (14), 1982
Fewest Passes Completed, Both Teams, Game
   20   Pittsburgh (9) vs. Minnesota (11), 1975

COMPLETION PERCENTAGE
Highest Completion Percentage, Game (20 attempts)
   73.5   Cincinnati vs. San Francisco, 1982 (34-25)
Lowest Completion Percentage, Game (20 attempts)
   32.0   Denver vs. Dallas, 1978 (25-8)

YARDS GAINED
Most Yards Gained, Game
   309   Pittsburgh vs. Los Angeles, 1980
Fewest Yards Gained, Game
   35   Denver vs. Dallas, 1978
Most Yards Gained, Both Teams, Game
   551   Philadelphia (291) vs. Oakland (260), 1981
Fewest Yards Gained, Both Teams, Game
   156   Miami (69) vs. Washington (87), 1973

TACKLED ATTEMPTING PASSES
Most Times Tackled, Attempting Passes, Game
   7   Dallas vs. Pittsburgh, 1976
Fewest Times Tackled, Attempting Passes, Game
   0   Baltimore vs. N.Y. Jets, 1969; vs. Dallas, 1971
      Minnesota vs. Pittsburgh, 1975
      Pittsburgh vs. Los Angeles, 1980
      Philadelphia vs. Oakland, 1981
Most Times Tackled, Attempting Passes, Both Teams, Game
   9   Kansas City (6) vs. Green Bay (3), 1967
      Dallas (7) vs. Pittsburgh (2), 1976
      Dallas (5) vs. Denver (4), 1978
      Dallas (5) vs. Pittsburgh (4), 1979

Fewest Times Tackled, Attempting Passes, Both Teams, Game
    1   Philadelphia (0) vs. Oakland (1), 1981

TOUCHDOWNS
Most Touchdowns, Game
    4   Pittsburgh vs. Dallas, 1979
Fewest Touchdowns, Game
    0   By nine teams
Most Touchdowns, Both Teams, Game
    7   Pittsburgh (4) vs. Dallas (3), 1979
Fewest Touchdowns, Both Teams, Game
    0   N.Y. Jets vs. Baltimore, 1969
        Miami vs. Minnesota, 1974

INTERCEPTIONS BY
Most Interceptions By, Game
    4   N.Y. Jets vs. Baltimore, 1969
        Dallas vs. Denver, 1978
Most Interceptions By, Both Teams, Game
    6   Baltimore (3) vs. Dallas (3), 1971

YARDS GAINED
Most Yards Gained, Game
    95   Miami vs. Washington, 1973
Most Yards Gained, Both Teams, Game
    95   Miami (95) vs. Washington (0), 1973

TOUCHDOWNS
Most Touchdowns, Game
    1   Green Bay vs. Oakland, 1968
        Oakland vs. Minnesota, 1977

PUNTING
Most Punts, Game
    9   Dallas vs. Baltimore, 1971
Fewest Punts, Game
    2   Pittsburgh vs. Los Angeles, 1980
Most Punts, Both Teams, Game
    13   Dallas (9) vs. Baltimore (4), 1971
        Pittsburgh (7) vs. Minnesota (6), 1975
Fewest Punts, Both Teams, Game
    6   Oakland (3) vs. Philadelphia (3), 1981

AVERAGE YARDAGE
Highest Average, Game (4 punts)
    48.5   Kansas City, 1970
Lowest Average, Game (4 punts)
    31.2   Washington, 1973

PUNT RETURNS
Most Punt Returns, Game
    5   Green Bay vs. Oakland, 1968
        Baltimore vs. Dallas, 1971
        Pittsburgh vs. Minnesota, 1975; vs. Dallas, 1976
Fewest Punt Returns, Game
    0   Minnesota vs. Miami, 1974
Most Punt Returns, Both Teams, Game
    9   Pittsburgh (5) vs. Minnesota (4), 1975
Fewest Punt Returns, Both Teams, Game
    2   Dallas (1) vs. Miami (1), 1972

YARDS GAINED
Most Yards Gained, Game
    43 Oakland vs. Minnesota, 1977
Fewest Yards Gained, Game
   −1 Dallas vs. Miami, 1972
Most Yards Gained, Both Teams, Game
    60 Dallas (33) vs. Pittsburgh (27), 1979
Fewest Yards Gained, Both Teams, Game
    13 Miami (4) vs. Washington (9), 1973

AVERAGE RETURN
Highest Average, Game (3 returns)
  10.8 Oakland vs. Minnesota, 1977

TOUCHDOWNS
Most Touchdowns, Game
    None

KICKOFF RETURNS

Most Kickoff Returns, Game
    7 Oakland vs. Green Bay, 1968
       Minnesota vs. Oakland, 1977
       Cincinnati vs. San Francisco, 1982
Fewest Kickoff Returns, Game
    1 N.Y. Jets vs. Baltimore, 1969
Most Kickoff Returns, Both Teams, Game
   11 Los Angeles (6) vs. Pittsburgh (5), 1980
Fewest Kickoff Returns, Both Teams, Game
    5 N.Y. Jets (1) vs. Baltimore (4), 1969
       Miami (2) vs. Washington (3), 1973

YARDS GAINED
Most Yards Gained, Game
  173 Denver vs. Dallas, 1978
Fewest Yards Gained, Game
   25 N.Y. Jets vs. Baltimore, 1969
Most Yards Gained, Both Teams, Game
  241 Pittsburgh (162) vs. Los Angeles (79), 1980
Fewest Yards Gained, Both Teams, Game
   78 Miami (33) vs. Washington (45), 1973

AVERAGE GAIN
Highest Average, Game (3 returns)
  32.4 Pittsburgh vs. Los Angeles, 1980

TOUCHDOWNS
Most Touchdowns, Game
    None

PENALTIES

Most Penalties, Game
   12 Dallas vs. Denver, 1978
Fewest Penalties, Game
    0 Miami vs. Dallas, 1972
       Pittsburgh vs. Dallas, 1976
Most Penalties, Both Teams, Game
   20 Dallas (12) vs. Denver (8), 1978
Fewest Penalties, Both Teams, Game
    2 Pittsburgh (0) vs. Dallas (2), 1976

YARDS PENALIZED
Most Yards Penalized, Game
  133 Dallas vs. Baltimore, 1971

Most Yards Penalized, Both Teams, Game
   164   Dallas (133) vs. Baltimore (31), 1971
Fewest Yards Penalized, Both Teams, Game
    15   Miami (0) vs. Dallas (15), 1972

FUMBLES

Most Fumbles, Game
    6   Dallas vs. Denver, 1978
Fewest Fumbles, Game
    0   Green Bay vs. Oakland, 1968
         Kansas City vs. Minnesota, 1970
         Oakland vs. Minnesota, 1977; vs. Philadelphia, 1981
         Los Angeles vs. Pittsburgh, 1980
         Pittsburgh vs. Los Angeles, 1980
Most Fumbles, Both Teams, Game
    10   Dallas (6) vs. Denver (4), 1978
Fewest Fumbles, Both Teams, Game
    0   Los Angeles vs. Pittsburgh, 1980
Most Fumbles Lost, Game
    4   Baltimore vs. Dallas, 1971
         Denver vs. Dallas, 1978
Most Fumbles Recovered, Game
    8   Dallas vs. Denver, 1978 (4 own, 4 opp)

TURNOVERS
(Number of times losing the ball on interceptions and fumbles.)
Most Turnovers, Game
    8   Denver vs. Dallas, 1978
Fewest Turnovers, Game
    0   Green Bay vs. Oakland, 1968
         Miami vs. Minnesota, 1974
         Pittsburgh vs. Dallas, 1976
         Oakland vs. Minnesota, 1977; vs. Philadelphia, 1981
Most Turnovers, Both Teams, Game
    10   Baltimore (6) vs. Dallas (4), 1971
         Denver (8) vs. Dallas (2), 1978
Fewest Turnovers, Both Teams, Game
    2   Green Bay (1) vs. Kansas City (1), 1967
         Miami (0) vs. Minnesota (2), 1974

AFC CHAMPIONSHIP GAME

RESULTS

Season	Date	Winner (Share)	Loser (Share)	Score	Site	Attendance
1981	Jan. 10	Cincinnati ($9,000)	San Diego ($9,000)	27-7	Cincinnati	46,302
1980	Jan. 11	Oakland ($9,000)	San Diego ($9,000)	34-27	San Diego	52,675
1979	Jan. 6	Pittsburgh ($9,000)	Houston ($9,000)	27-13	Pittsburgh	50,475
1978	Jan. 7	Pittsburgh ($9,000)	Houston ($9,000)	34-5	Pittsburgh	50,725
1977	Jan. 1	Denver ($9,000)	Oakland ($9,000)	20-17	Denver	75,044
1976	Dec. 26	Oakland ($8,500)	Pittsburgh ($5,500)	24-7	Oakland	53,821
1975	Jan. 4	Pittsburgh ($8,500)	Oakland ($5,500)	16-10	Pittsburgh	50,609
1974	Dec. 29	Pittsburgh ($8,500)	Oakland ($5,500)	24-13	Oakland	53,800
1973	Dec. 30	Miami ($8,500)	Oakland ($5,500)	27-10	Miami	79,325
1972	Dec. 31	Miami ($8,500)	Pittsburgh ($5,500)	21-17	Pittsburgh	50,845
1971	Jan. 2	Miami ($8,500)	Baltimore ($5,500)	21-0	Miami	76,622
1970	Jan. 3	Baltimore ($8,500)	Oakland ($5,500)	27-17	Baltimore	54,799
1969	Jan. 4	Kansas City ($7,755)	Oakland ($6,252)	17-7	Oakland	53,564
1968	Dec. 29	N.Y. Jets ($7,007)	Oakland ($5,349)	27-23	New York	62,627
1967	Dec. 31	Oakland ($6,321)	Houston ($4,996)	40-7	Oakland	53,330
1966	Jan. 1	Kansas City ($5,309)	Buffalo ($3,799)	31-7	Buffalo	42,080
1965	Dec. 26	Buffalo ($5,189)	San Diego ($3,447)	23-0	San Diego	30,361
1964	Dec. 26	Buffalo ($2,668)	San Diego ($1,738)	20-7	Buffalo	40,242
1963	Jan. 5	San Diego ($2,498)	Boston ($1,596)	51-10	San Diego	30,127
1962	Dec. 23	Dallas ($2,206)	Houston ($1,471)	20-17*	Houston	37,981
1961	Dec. 24	Houston ($1,792)	San Diego ($1,111)	10-3	San Diego	29,556
1960	Jan. 1	Houston ($1,025)	Los Angeles ($718)	24-16	Houston	32,183

*Sudden death overtime.

AFC CHAMPIONSHIP GAME COMPOSITE STANDINGS

	W	L	Pct.	Pts.	OP
Kansas City Chiefs*	3	0	1.000	68	31
Miami Dolphins	3	0	1.000	69	27
Cincinnati Bengals	1	0	1.000	27	7
Denver Broncos	1	0	1.000	20	17
New York Jets	1	0	1.000	27	23
Buffalo Bills	2	1	.667	50	38
Pittsburgh Steelers	4	2	.667	125	86
Baltimore Colts	1	1	.500	27	38
Houston Oilers	2	4	.333	76	140
Oakland Raiders	3	7	.300	195	199
San Diego Chargers**	1	6	.143	111	148
New England Patriots***	0	1	.000	10	51

*One game played when franchise was in Dallas (Texans). (Won 20-17)
**One game played when franchise was in Los Angeles. (Lost 24-16)
***Game played when franchise was in Boston. (Lost 51-10)

1981 AMERICAN FOOTBALL CONFERENCE CHAMPIONSHIP GAME

Riverfront Stadium, Cincinnati, Ohio   January 10, 1982
Attendance: 46,302

CINCINNATI 27, SAN DIEGO 7—Ken Anderson passed for two touchdowns to lead Cincinnati to a 27-7 victory over San Diego that provided the Bengals with their first AFC championship. Anderson completed 14 of 22 passes for 161 yards in a game that was played in minus 9 degree weather and winds of 20-35 miles per hour. After Jim Breech kicked a 31-yard field goal on the Bengals' first possession of the game, Don Bass recovered a fumble by the Chargers' James Brooks on the ensuing kickoff at the San Diego 12 yard line. On the second play, Anderson threw an eight-yard touchdown pass to M. L. Harris to provide the Bengals with a 10-0 lead. Dan Fouts and Kellen Winslow connected on a 33-yard pass play early in the second period for the Chargers' only score. Cincinnati responded with a 55-yard march, capped by Pete Johnson's one-yard run. Breech kicked a 38-yard field goal midway through the third period to increase the Bengals' lead to 20-7, and Anderson tossed his second scoring pass, a three-yarder to Bass, to finish off a 68-yard drive in the final period.

San Diego (7)	Offense	Cincinnati (27)
Charlie Joiner	WR	Cris Collinsworth
Billy Shields	LT	Anthony Munoz
Doug Wilkerson	LG	Dave Lapham
Don Macek	C	Blair Bush
Ed White	RG	Max Montoya
Russ Washington	RT	Mike Wilson
Wes Chandler	WR	Isaac Curtis
Kellen Winslow	TE	Dan Ross
Dan Fouts	QB	Ken Anderson
Chuck Muncie	RB	Charles Alexander
James Brooks	RB	Pete Johnson
	Defense	
Leroy Jones	LE	Eddie Edwards
Louie Kelcher	LT-NT	Wilson Whitley
Gary Johnson	RT-RE	Ross Browner
John Woodcock	RE-LOLB	Bo Harris
Linden King	LLB-LILB	Jim LeClair
Bob Horn	MLB-RILB	Glenn Cameron
Woodrow Lowe	RLB-ROLB	Reggie Williams
Willie Buchanon	LCB	Louis Breeden
Mike Williams	RCB	Ken Riley
Pete Shaw	SS	Bobby Kemp
Glen Edwards	FS	Bryan Hicks

SUBSTITUTIONS
San Diego—Offense: K—Rolf Benirschke. P—George Roberts. QB—Ed Luther. RB—Hank Bauer, John Cappelletti, Clarence Williams. WR—Dwight Scales. TE—Eric Sievers. C—Bob Rush. T—Sam Claphan. G—Chuck Loewen. Defense: E—Keith Ferguson, Wilbur Young. LB—Jim Laslavic, Ray Preston, Cliff Thrift. DB—Doug Beaudoin, Allan Ellis, Bob Gregor, Irvin Phillips. DNP—James Harris (QB), Scott Fitzkee (WR), Jimmy Webb (DT).
Cincinnati—Offense: K—Jim Breech. P—Pat McInally. QB—Jack Thompson. RB—Archie Griffin, Jim Hargrove. WR—Don Bass, Steve Kreider, David Verser. TE—M. L. Harris. C—Blake Moore. T—Mike Obrovac. Defense: E—Gary Burley, Mike St. Clair. NT—Rod Horn. LB—Tom Dinkel, Guy Frazier, Rick Razzano. DB—Oliver Davis, Mike Fuller, Ray Griffin, John Simmons. DNP—Turk Schonert (QB), Glenn Bujnoch (G).

OFFICIALS
Referee: Fred Silva. Umpire: Art Demmas. Head Linesman: Burl Toler. Line Judge: Walt Peters. Back Judge: Jim Poole. Field Judge: Bob Lewis. Side Judge: Dave Parry.

SCORING
San Diego	0	7	0	0 —	7
Cincinnati	10	7	3	7 —	27

Cin—FG Breech 31

Cin—M. L. Harris 8 pass from Anderson (Breech kick)
Cin—Johnson 1 run (Breech kick)
SD —Winslow 33 pass from Fouts (Benirschke kick)
Cin—FG Breech 38
Cin—Bass 3 pass from Anderson (Breech kick)

TEAM STATISTICS

	San Diego	Cincinnati
Total First Downs	18	19
First Downs Rushing	11	8
First Downs Passing	7	11
First Downs Penalty	0	0
Rushes	31	36
Yards Gained Rushing (net)	128	143
Average Yards per Rush	4.1	3.9
Passes Attempted	28	23
Passes Completed	15	15
Had Intercepted	2	0
Times Tackled Attempting to Pass	2	0
Yards Lost Attempting to Pass	12	0
Yards Gained Passing (net)	173	175
Total Net Yardage	301	318
Total Offensive Plays	61	59
Average Gain per Offensive Play	4.9	5.4
Punts	2	3
Average Distance	29.5	30.6
Punt Returns	1	0
Punt Return Yardage	7	0
Kickoff Returns	7	1
Kickoff Return Yardage	132	40
Interception Return Yardage	0	24
Fumbles	4	3
Own Fumbles Recovered	2	2
Opponent Fumbles Recovered	1	2
Total Return Yardage	139	64
Penalties	2	3
Yards Penalized	15	25
Total Points Scored	7	27
Touchdowns	1	3
Touchdowns Rushing	0	1
Touchdowns Passing	1	2
Touchdown Returns	0	0
Extra Points	1	3
Field Goals	0	2
Field Goals Attempted	2	2

FINANCIAL FACTS

Paid Attendance	46,302
Winning Player's Share	$9,000
Losing Player's Share	$9,000

INDIVIDUAL STATISTICS

RUSHING

San Diego	Att.	Yds.	LG	TD
Muncie	23	94	11	0
Brooks	6	23	9	0
Fouts	1	6	6	0
Cappelletti	1	5	5	0
Cincinnati	**Att.**	**Yds.**	**LG**	**TD**
Johnson	21	80	11	1
Anderson	5	39	13	0
Alexander	9	22	4	0
Collinsworth	1	2	2	0

PASSING

S.D.	Att.	Comp.	Yds.	Int.	TD
Fouts	28	15	185	2	1
Cin.	**Att.**	**Comp.**	**Yds.**	**Int.**	**TD**
Anderson	22	14	161	0	2
Thompson	1	1	14	0	0

RECEIVING

San Diego	No.	Yds.	LG	TD
Chandler	6	79	25	0
Winslow	3	47	33	1
Joiner	3	41	21	0
Brooks	2	5	4	0
Sievers	1	13	13	0
Cincinnati	**No.**	**Yds.**	**LG**	**TD**
Ross	5	69	19	0
Alexander	3	25	16	0
Collinsworth	2	28	16	0
Curtis	2	28	15	0
Johnson	1	14	14	0
M. L. Harris	1	8	8	1
Bass	1	3	3	1

INTERCEPTIONS

San Diego	No.	Yds.	LG	TD
None				
Cincinnati	**No.**	**Yds.**	**LG**	**TD**
Kemp	1	24	24	0
Breeden	1	0	0	0

NFC CHAMPIONSHIP GAME

RESULTS

Season	Date	Winner (Share)	Loser (Share)	Score	Site	Attendance
1981	Jan. 10	San Francisco ($9,000)	Dallas ($9,000)	28-27	San Francisco	60,525
1980	Jan. 11	Philadelphia ($9,000)	Dallas ($9,000)	20-7	Philadelphia	71,522
1979	Jan. 6	Los Angeles ($9,000)	Tampa Bay ($9,000)	9-0	Tampa Bay	72,033
1978	Jan. 7	Dallas ($9,000)	Los Angeles ($9,000)	28-0	Los Angeles	71,086
1977	Jan. 1	Dallas ($9,000)	Minnesota ($9,000)	23-6	Dallas	64,293
1976	Dec. 26	Minnesota ($8,500)	Los Angeles ($5,500)	24-13	Minnesota	48,379
1975	Jan. 4	Dallas ($8,500)	Los Angeles ($5,500)	37-7	Los Angeles	88,919
1974	Dec. 29	Minnesota ($8,500)	Los Angeles ($5,500)	14-10	Minnesota	48,444
1973	Dec. 30	Minnesota ($8,500)	Dallas ($5,500)	27-10	Dallas	64,422
1972	Dec. 31	Washington ($8,500)	Dallas ($5,500)	26-3	Washington	53,129
1971	Jan. 2	Dallas ($8,500)	San Francisco ($5,500)	14-3	Dallas	63,409
1970	Jan. 3	Dallas ($8,500)	San Francisco ($5,500)	17-10	San Francisco	59,364
1969	Jan. 4	Minnesota ($7,930)	Cleveland ($5,118)	27-7	Minnesota	46,503
1968	Dec. 29	Baltimore ($9,306)	Cleveland ($5,963)	34-0	Cleveland	78,410
1967	Dec. 31	Green Bay ($7,950)	Dallas ($5,299)	21-17	Green Bay	50,861
1966	Jan. 1	Green Bay ($9,813)	Dallas ($6,527)	34-27	Dallas	74,152
1965	Jan. 2	Green Bay ($7,819)	Cleveland ($5,288)	23-12	Green Bay	50,777
1964	Dec. 27	Cleveland ($8,052)	Baltimore ($5,571)	27-0	Cleveland	79,544
1963	Dec. 29	Chicago ($5,899)	New York ($4,218)	14-10	Chicago	45,801
1962	Dec. 30	Green Bay ($5,888)	New York ($4,166)	16-7	New York	64,892
1961	Dec. 31	Green Bay ($5,195)	New York ($3,339)	37-0	Green Bay	39,029
1960	Dec. 26	Philadelphia ($5,116)	Green Bay ($3,105)	17-13	Philadelphia	67,325
1959	Dec. 27	Baltimore ($4,674)	New York ($3,083)	31-16	Baltimore	57,545
1958	Dec. 28	Baltimore ($4,718)	New York ($3,111)	23-17*	New York	64,185
1957	Dec. 29	Detroit ($4,295)	Cleveland ($2,750)	59-14	Detroit	55,263
1956	Dec. 30	New York ($3,779)	Chi. Bears ($2,485)	47-7	New York	56,836
1955	Dec. 26	Cleveland ($3,508)	Los Angeles ($2,316)	38-14	Los Angeles	85,693
1954	Dec. 26	Cleveland ($2,478)	Detroit ($1,585)	56-10	Cleveland	43,827
1953	Dec. 27	Detroit ($2,424)	Cleveland ($1,654)	17-16	Detroit	54,577
1952	Dec. 28	Detroit ($2,274)	Cleveland ($1,712)	17-7	Cleveland	50,934
1951	Dec. 23	Los Angeles ($2,108)	Cleveland ($1,483)	24-17	Los Angeles	57,522
1950	Dec. 24	Cleveland ($1,113)	Los Angeles ($686)	30-28	Cleveland	29,751
1949	Dec. 18	Philadelphia ($1,094)	Los Angeles ($739)	14-0	Los Angeles	27,980
1948	Dec. 19	Philadelphia ($1,540)	Chi. Cardinals ($874)	7-0	Philadelphia	36,309
1947	Dec. 28	Chi. Cardinals ($1,132)	Philadelphia ($754)	28-21	Chicago	30,759
1946	Dec. 15	Chi. Bears ($1,975)	New York ($1,295)	24-14	New York	58,346
1945	Dec. 16	Cleveland ($1,469)	Washington ($902)	15-14	Cleveland	32,178
1944	Dec. 17	Green Bay ($1,449)	New York ($814)	14-7	New York	46,016
1943	Dec. 26	Chi. Bears ($1,146)	Washington ($765)	41-21	Chicago	34,320
1942	Dec. 13	Washington ($965)	Chi. Bears ($637)	14-6	Washington	36,006
1941	Dec. 21	Chi. Bears ($430)	New York ($288)	37-9	Chicago	13,341
1940	Dec. 8	Chi. Bears ($873)	Washington ($606)	73-0	Washington	36,034
1939	Dec. 10	Green Bay ($703.97)	New York ($455.57)	27-0	Milwaukee	32,279
1938	Dec. 11	New York ($504.45)	Green Bay ($368.81)	23-17	New York	48,120
1937	Dec. 12	Washington ($225.90)	Chi. Bears ($127.78)	28-21	Chicago	15,870
1936	Dec. 13	Green Bay ($250)	Boston ($180)	21-6	New York	29,545
1935	Dec. 15	Detroit ($313.35)	New York ($200.20)	26-7	Detroit	15,000
1934	Dec. 9	New York ($621)	Chi. Bears ($414.02)	30-13	New York	35,059
1933	Dec. 17	Chi. Bears ($210.34)	New York ($140.22)	23-21	Chicago	26,000

*Sudden death overtime.

NFC CHAMPIONSHIP GAME COMPOSITE STANDINGS

	W	L	Pct.	Pts.	OP
Green Bay Packers	8	2	.800	223	116
Detroit Lions	4	1	.800	129	100
Minnesota Vikings	4	1	.800	98	63
Philadelphia Eagles	4	1	.800	79	48
Baltimore Colts	3	1	.750	88	60
Chicago Bears	6	4	.600	259	194
St. Louis Cardinals*	1	1	.500	28	28
Dallas Cowboys	5	6	.455	210	182
Washington Redskins**	3	4	.429	109	180
Cleveland Browns	4	7	.364	224	253
San Francisco 49ers	1	2	.333	41	58
Los Angeles Rams***	3	7	.300	120	216
New York Giants	3	11	.214	208	309
Tampa Bay Buccaneers	0	1	.000	0	9

Both games played when franchise was in Chicago. (Won 28-21, lost 7-0)
**One game played when franchise was in Boston. (Lost 21-6)*
***One game played when franchise was in Cleveland. (Won 15-14)*

1981 NATIONAL FOOTBALL CONFERENCE CHAMPIONSHIP GAME

Candlestick Park, San Francisco, California · · · · · · · · · · · January 10, 1982
Attendance: 60,525

SAN FRANCISCO 28, DALLAS 27 — Quarterback Joe Montana's six-yard touchdown pass to wide receiver Dwight Clark with 51 seconds remaining lifted the NFC West champion 49ers to a thrilling 28-27 win over NFC East titlist Dallas. The victory gave San Francisco its first NFC championship and its initial Super Bowl appearance. With 38 seconds left, Dallas was on the San Francisco 44 yard line, but defensive end Lawrence Pillers tackled Cowboys quarterback Danny White, causing a fumble that was recovered by Jim Stuckey to end the Dallas threat. The Cowboys went up 27-21 with 10:41 to go on tight end Doug Cosbie's 21-yard touchdown pass from White. Dallas led 17-14 at halftime on Rafael Septien's 44-yard field goal, Tony Hill's 26-yard touchdown reception, and Tony Dorsett's five-yard run. San Francisco took a 21-17 edge 9:16 into the third quarter on fullback Johnny Davis's two-yard run. The Cowboys pulled to within one point on Septien's 22-yard field goal 52 seconds into the fourth period.

Dallas (27)	Offense	San Francisco (28)
Tony Hill	WR	Mike Wilson
Pat Donovan	LT	Dan Audick
Herbert Scott	LG	John Ayers
Tom Rafferty	C	Fred Quillan
Kurt Petersen	RG	Randy Cross
Jim Cooper	RT	Keith Fahnhorst
Billy Joe DuPree	TE	Charle Young
Drew Pearson	WR-TE	Dwight Clark
Danny White	QB	Joe Montana
Ron Springs	RB	Earl Cooper
Tony Dorsett	RB-WR	Mike Shumann

Defense

Ed Jones	LE	Jim Stuckey
Larry Bethea	LT-NT	Archie Reese
Randy White	RT-RE	Dwaine Board
Harvey Martin	RE-LOLB	Willie Harper
Mike Hegman	LLB-LILB	Jack Reynolds
Bob Breunig	MLB-RILB	Craig Puki
D. D. Lewis	RLB-ROLB	Kenna Turner
Everson Walls	LCB	Ronnie Lott
Dennis Thurman	RCB	Eric Wright
Charlie Waters	SS	Carlton Williamson
Michael Downs	FS	Dwight Hicks

SUBSTITUTIONS

Dallas—Offense: K—Rafael Septien. RB—James Jones, Robert Newhouse, Tim Newsome. WR—Doug Donley, Butch Johnson. TE—Doug Cosbie, Jay Saldi. T—Howard Richards, Steve Wright. Defense: E—Bruce Thornton. LB—Guy Brown, Anthony Dickerson, Angelo King, Danny Spradlin. DB—Benny Barnes, Ron Fellows, Steve Wilson. DNP—Glenn Carano (QB), Glen Titensor (G), John Dutton (DT), Andy Frederick (T), Gary Hogeboom (QB).

San Francisco—Offense: K—Ray Wersching. P—Jim Miller. RB—Walt Easley, Lenvil Elliott, Amos Lawrence, Bill Ring, Johnny Davis. WR—Freddie Solomon. TE—Eason Ramson. C—Walt Downing. T—Allan Kennedy. G—John Choma. Defense: E—Fred Dean, Lawrence Pillers. T—John Harty. LB—Dan Bunz, Bobby Leopold, Milt McColl. DB—Rick Gervais, Saladin Martin, Lynn Thomas. DNP—Guy Benjamin (QB), Ricky Patton (RB).

OFFICIALS

Referee: Jim Tunney. Umpire: Bob Boylston. Head Linesman: Ed Marion. Line Judge: Bob Beeks. Back Judge: Ray Douglas. Field Judge: Ed Merrifield. Side Judge: Dean Look.

SCORING

Dallas	10	7	0	10 — 27	
San Francisco	7	7	7	7 — 28	

SF —Solomon 8 pass from Montana (Wersching kick)
Dall—FG Septien 44
Dall—Hill 26 pass from D. White (Septien kick)
SF —Clark 20 pass from Montana (Wersching kick)
Dall—Dorsett 5 run (Septien kick)
SF —Davis 2 run (Wersching kick)
Dall—FG Septien 22
Dall—Cosbie 21 pass from D. White (Septien kick)
SF —Clark 6 pass from Montana (Wersching kick)

TEAM STATISTICS

	Dallas	San Francisco
Total First Downs	16	26
First Downs Rushing	5	6
First Downs Passing	9	17
First Downs Penalty	2	3
Rushes	32	31
Yards Gained Rushing (net)	115	127
Average Yards per Rush	3.6	4.1
Passes Attempted	24	35
Passes Completed	16	22

Had Intercepted	1	3
Times Tackled Attempting to Pass	4	3
Yards Lost Attempting to Pass	38	20
Yards Gained Passing (net)	135	266
Total Net Yardage	250	393
Total Offensive Plays	60	69
Average Gain per Offensive Play	4.2	5.7
Punts	6	3
Average Distance	39.3	35.7
Punt Returns	3	3
Punt Return Yardage	13	24
Kickoff Returns	5	6
Kickoff Return Yardage	89	107
Interception Return Yardage	0	5
Fumbles	4	3
Own Fumbles Recovered	2	0
Opponent Fumbles Recovered	3	2
Total Return Yardage	102	136
Penalties	5	7
Yards Penalized	39	106
Total Points Scored	27	28
Touchdowns	3	4
Touchdowns Rushing	1	1
Touchdowns Passing	2	3
Touchdown Returns	0	0
Extra Points	3	4
Field Goals	2	0
Field Goals Attempted	2	0

FINANCIAL FACTS

Paid Attendance	61,061
Winning Player's Share	$9,000
Losing Player's Share	$9,000

INDIVIDUAL STATISTICS

RUSHING

Dallas	Att.	Yds.	LG	TD
Dorsett	22	91	11	1
J. Jones	4	14	7	0
Springs	5	10	3	0
D. White	1	0	0	0
San Francisco	**Att.**	**Yds.**	**LG**	**TD**
Elliott	10	48	11	0
Cooper	8	35	11	0
Ring	6	27	11	0
Solomon	1	14	14	0
Easley	2	6	4	0
Davis	1	2	2	1
Montana	3	−5	2	0

PASSING

Dallas	Att.	Comp.	Yds.	Int.	TD
D. White	24	16	173	1	2
San Fran.	**Att.**	**Comp.**	**Yds.**	**Int.**	**TD**
Montana	35	22	286	3	3

RECEIVING

Dallas	No.	Yds.	LG	TD
J. Jones	3	17	10	0
DuPree	3	15	7	0
Springs	3	13	12	0
Hill	2	43	26	1
Pearson	1	31	31	0
Cosbie	1	21	21	1
Johnson	1	20	20	0
Saldi	1	9	9	0
Donley	1	4	4	0
San Francisco	**No.**	**Yds.**	**LG**	**TD**
Clark	8	120	38	2
Solomon	6	75	21	1
Young	4	45	17	0
Cooper	2	11	6	0
Elliott	1	24	24	0
Shumann	1	11	11	0

INTERCEPTIONS

Dallas	No.	Yds.	LG	TD
Walls	2	0	0	0
R. White	1	0	0	0
San Francisco	**No.**	**Yds.**	**LG**	**TD**
Leopold	1	5	5	0

AFC DIVISIONAL PLAYOFFS

RESULTS

Season	Date	Winner	Loser	Site	Attendance
1981	Jan. 3	Cincinnati 28	Buffalo 21	Cincinnati	55,420
	Jan. 2	*San Diego 41	Miami 38	Miami	73,735
1980	Jan. 4	Oakland 14	Cleveland 12	Cleveland	78,245
	Jan. 3	San Diego 20	Buffalo 14	San Diego	52,253
1979	Dec. 30	Pittsburgh 34	Miami 14	Pittsburgh	50,214
	Dec. 29	Houston 17	San Diego 14	San Diego	51,192
1978	Dec. 31	Houston 31	New England 14	New England	60,735
	Dec. 30	Pittsburgh 33	Denver 10	Pittsburgh	50,230
1977	Dec. 24	*Oakland 37	Baltimore 31	Baltimore	59,925
	Dec. 24	Denver 34	Pittsburgh 21	Denver	75,059
1976	Dec. 19	Pittsburgh 40	Baltimore 14	Baltimore	59,296
	Dec. 18	Oakland 24	New England 21	Oakland	53,050
1975	Dec. 28	Oakland 31	Cincinnati 28	Oakland	53,030
	Dec. 27	Pittsburgh 28	Baltimore 10	Pittsburgh	49,557
1974	Dec. 22	Pittsburgh 32	Buffalo 14	Pittsburgh	49,841
	Dec. 21	Oakland 28	Miami 26	Oakland	53,023
1973	Dec. 23	Miami 34	Cincinnati 16	Miami	78,928
	Dec. 22	Oakland 33	Pittsburgh 14	Oakland	52,646
1972	Dec. 24	Miami 20	Cleveland 14	Miami	78,916
	Dec. 23	Pittsburgh 13	Oakland 7	Pittsburgh	50,327
1971	Dec. 26	Baltimore 20	Cleveland 3	Cleveland	70,734
	Dec. 25	*Miami 27	Kansas City 24	Kansas City	45,822
1970	Dec. 27	Oakland 21	Miami 14	Oakland	52,594
	Dec. 26	Baltimore 17	Cincinnati 0	Baltimore	49,694
1969	Dec. 21	Oakland 56	Houston 7	Oakland	53,539
	Dec. 20	Kansas City 13	N.Y. Jets 6	New York	62,977
1968	Dec. 22	Oakland 41	Kansas City 6	Oakland	53,605
1963	Dec. 28	Boston 26	Buffalo 8	Buffalo	33,044

Sudden death overtime.

AFC DIVISIONAL PLAYOFFS COMPOSITE STANDINGS

	W	L	Pct.	Pts.	OP
Oakland Raiders	9	1	.900	292	172
Pittsburgh Steelers	6	2	.750	215	136
Houston Oilers	2	1	.667	55	84
San Diego Chargers	2	1	.667	75	69
Denver Broncos	1	1	.500	44	54
Miami Dolphins	3	4	.429	173	178
Baltimore Colts	2	3	.400	92	108
Kansas City Chiefs	1	2	.333	43	74
New England Patriots*	1	2	.333	61	63
Cincinnati Bengals	1	3	.250	72	103
New York Jets	0	1	.000	6	13
Cleveland Browns	0	3	.000	29	54
Buffalo Bills	0	4	.000	57	106

One game played when franchise was in Boston. (Won 26-8)

1981 AFC DIVISIONAL PLAYOFFS

Orange Bowl, Miami, Florida   January 2, 1982
Attendance: 73,735

SAN DIEGO 41, MIAMI 38—Rolf Benirschke's 29-yard field goal with 1:08 left in overtime gave San Diego a 41-38 victory over Miami in the highest-scoring playoff game in NFL history. Benirschke redeemed himself after missing a 27-yard attempt at the beginning of overtime. He got a second chance after Miami's Uwe von Schamann's 35-yard field goal try in overtime was blocked by San Diego's Leroy Jones. The Chargers opened a 24-0 lead in the first period, but Miami rallied to tie the game on the first series of the third period when quarterback Don Strock hit Joe Rose with a nine-yard touchdown pass. The Chargers went ahead 31-24 when quarterback Dan Fouts passed 25 yards to Kellen Winslow. The next two touchdowns were Miami's before San Diego tied the score at 38 near the end of regulation time when Fouts hit James Brooks on a nine-yard scoring pass.[1]

San Diego	24	0	7	7	3 — 41	
Miami	0	17	14	7	0 — 38	

SD —FG Benirschke 32
SD —Chandler 56 punt return (Benirschke kick)
SD —Muncie 1 run (Benirschke kick)
SD —Brooks 8 pass from Fouts (Benirschke kick)
Mia—FG von Schamann 34
Mia—Rose 1 pass from Strock (von Schamann kick)
Mia—Nathan lateral 25 from Harris, 15 pass from Strock (von Schamann kick)
Mia—Rose 15 pass from Strock (von Schamann kick)
SD —Winslow 25 pass from Fouts (Benirschke kick)
Mia—Hardy 50 pass from Strock (von Schamann kick)
Mia—Nathan 12 run (von Schamann kick)
SD —Brooks 9 pass from Fouts (Benirschke kick)
SD —FG Benirschke 29

Riverfront Stadium, Cincinnati, Ohio   January 3, 1982
Attendance: 55,240

CINCINNATI 28, BUFFALO 21—Ken Anderson fired a 16-yard touchdown pass to Cris Collinsworth with 10:39 remaining to lift Cincinnati over Buffalo and send the Central Division champion Bengals into their first AFC Championship Game. Cincinnati, making its first playoff appearance since 1975, opened a 14-0 lead in the first period, but the Bills scored the game's next two touchdowns on runs of 1 and 44 yards by Joe Cribbs. The Bengals regained the lead 21-14 on Charles Alexander's 20-yard scoring run with 6:56 left in the third period. Buffalo pulled into a 21-21 tie eight seconds into the final period on a 21-yard pass from Joe Ferguson to Jerry Butler. Anderson, who completed 14 of 21 for 192 yards, directed a 305-yard attack.

Buffalo	0	7	7	7 — 21
Cincinnati	14	0	7	7 — 28

Cin —Alexander 4 run (Breech kick)
Cin —Johnson 1 run (Breech kick)
Buff—Cribbs 1 run (Mike-Mayer kick)
Buff—Cribbs 44 run (Mike-Mayer kick)
Cin —Alexander 20 run (Breech kick)
Buff—Butler 21 pass from Ferguson (Mike-Mayer kick)
Cin —Collinsworth 16 pass from Alexander (Breech kick)

NFC DIVISIONAL PLAYOFFS

RESULTS

Season	Date	Winner	Loser	Site	Attendance
1981	Jan. 3	San Francisco 38	N.Y. Giants 24	San Francisco	58,360
	Jan. 2	Dallas 38	Tampa Bay 0	Dallas	64,848
1980	Jan. 4	Dallas 30	Atlanta 27	Atlanta	59,793
	Jan. 3	Philadelphia 31	Minnesota 16	Philadelphia	70,178
1979	Dec. 30	Los Angeles 21	Dallas 19	Dallas	64,792
	Dec. 29	Tampa Bay 24	Philadelphia 17	Tampa Bay	71,402
1978	Dec. 31	Los Angeles 34	Minnesota 10	Los Angeles	70,436
	Dec. 30	Dallas 27	Atlanta 20	Dallas	63,406
1977	Dec. 26	Dallas 37	Chicago 7	Dallas	63,260
	Dec. 26	Minnesota 14	Los Angeles 7	Los Angeles	70,203
1976	Dec. 19	Los Angeles 14	Dallas 12	Dallas	63,283
	Dec. 18	Minnesota 35	Washington 20	Minnesota	47,466
1975	Dec. 28	Dallas 17	Minnesota 14	Minnesota	48,050
	Dec. 27	Los Angeles 35	St. Louis 23	Los Angeles	73,459
1974	Dec. 22	Los Angeles 19	Washington 10	Los Angeles	77,925
	Dec. 21	Minnesota 30	St. Louis 14	Minnesota	48,150
1973	Dec. 23	Dallas 27	Los Angeles 16	Dallas	63,272
	Dec. 22	Minnesota 27	Washington 20	Minnesota	48,040
1972	Dec. 24	Washington 16	Green Bay 3	Washington	52,321
	Dec. 23	Dallas 30	San Francisco 28	San Francisco	59,746
1971	Dec. 26	San Francisco 24	Washington 20	San Francisco	45,327
	Dec. 25	Dallas 20	Minnesota 12	Minnesota	47,307
1970	Dec. 27	San Francisco 17	Minnesota 14	Minnesota	45,103
	Dec. 26	Dallas 5	Detroit 0	Dallas	69,613
1969	Dec. 28	Cleveland 38	Dallas 14	Dallas	69,321
	Dec. 27	Minnesota 23	Los Angeles 20	Minnesota	47,900
1968	Dec. 22	Baltimore 24	Minnesota 14	Baltimore	60,238
	Dec. 21	Cleveland 31	Dallas 20	Cleveland	81,497
1967	Dec. 24	Dallas 52	Cleveland 14	Dallas	70,786
	Dec. 23	Green Bay 28	Los Angeles 7	Milwaukee	49,861
1965	Dec. 26	*Green Bay 13	Baltimore 10	Green Bay	50,484
1958	Dec. 21	N.Y. Giants 10	Cleveland 0	New York	61,274
1957	Dec. 22	Detroit 31	San Francisco 27	San Francisco	60,118
1952	Dec. 21	Detroit 31	Los Angeles 21	Detroit	47,645
1950	Dec. 17	Los Angeles 24	Chi. Bears 14	Los Angeles	83,501
	Dec. 17	Cleveland 8	N.Y. Giants 3	Cleveland	33,054
1947	Dec. 21	Philadelphia 21	Pittsburgh 0	Pittsburgh	35,729
1943	Dec. 19	Washington 28	N.Y. Giants 10	New York	42,800
1941	Dec. 14	Chi. Bears 33	Green Bay 14	Chicago	43,425

Sudden death overtime.

NFC DIVISIONAL PLAYOFFS COMPOSITE STANDINGS

	W	L	Pct.	Pts.	OP
Dallas Cowboys	10	4	.714	348	242
Detroit Lions	2	1	.667	62	53
Philadelphia Eagles	2	1	.667	69	40
Cleveland Browns	3	2	.600	91	99
San Francisco 49ers	3	2	.600	134	119
Los Angeles Rams	6	5	.545	218	211
Baltimore Colts	1	1	.500	34	27
Green Bay Packers	2	2	.500	58	66
Tampa Bay Buccaneers	1	1	.500	24	55
Minnesota Vikings	5	6	.455	209	224
Chicago Bears	1	2	.333	54	75
New York Giants	1	3	.250	47	74

Washington Redskins	2	4	.333	114	118
Pittsburgh Steelers	0	1	.000	0	21
Atlanta Falcons	0	2	.000	47	57
St. Louis Cardinals	0	2	.000	37	65

1981 NFC DIVISIONAL PLAYOFFS

Texas Stadium, Irving, Texas   January 2, 1982
Attendance: 64,848

DALLAS 38, TAMPA BAY 0—NFC Eastern Division champion Dallas advanced to its fourth NFC Championship Game in the last five years behind a convincing 38-0 blanking of NFC Central champion Tampa Bay. The win tied the widest margin of victory in an NFC divisional playoff, a record that was set by the Cowboys in their 52-14 victory over Cleveland in 1967. Dallas dominated on defense by picking off four interceptions, two by Dennis Thurman, and compiling four sacks of Buccaneers quarterback Doug Williams. Dallas running back Tony Dorsett rushed 16 times for 86 yards. Dallas quarterback Danny White was 15 of 26 for 143 yards and one touchdown. Dallas managed 345 yards (212 rush, 133 pass) and yielded 222 yards (74 rush, 148 pass).

Tampa Bay	0	0	0	0 —	0
Dallas	0	10	21	7 —	38

Dall—Hill 9 pass from White (Septien kick)
Dall—FG Septien 32
Dall—Springs 1 run (Septien kick)
Dall—Dorsett 5 run (Septien kick)
Dall—Jones 5 run (Septien kick)
Dall—Newsome 1 run (Septien kick)

Candlestick Park, San Francisco, California   January 3, 1982
Attendance: 58,360

SAN FRANCISCO 38, NEW YORK GIANTS 24—The NFC Western Division titlist 49ers moved to their first National Conference Championsip Game since 1971 with a 38-24 win over wild card survivor New York Giants. San Francisco built a 24-10 halftime lead on quarterback Joe Montana's eight-yard touchdown pass to tight end Charle Young, a 58-yard touchdown pass to Freddie Solomon, Ricky Patton's 25-yard touchdown run, and Ray Wersching's 22-yard field goal. After the Giants pulled to within seven points at 24-17, the 49ers put the game out of reach on Bill Ring's three-yard touchdown run and rookie cornerback Ronnie Lott's 20-yard interception return for a touchdown. Montana was 20 for 31 for a personal high of 304 yards. Solomon caught six passes for 107 yards, and 49ers teammate Dwight Clark had five for 104.

New York Giants	7	3	7	7 —	24
San Francisco	7	17	0	14 —	38

SF —Young 8 pass from Montana (Wersching kick)
NYG—Gray 72 pass from Brunner (Danelo kick)
SF —FG Wersching 22
SF —Solomon 58 pass from Montana (Wersching kick)
SF —Patton 25 run (Wersching kick)
NYG—FG Danelo 48
NYG—Perkins 59 pass from Brunner (Danelo kick)
SF —Ring 3 run (Wersching kick)
SF —Lott 20 interception return (Wersching kick)
NYG—Perkins 17 pass from Brunner (Danelo kick)

AFC FIRST ROUND PLAYOFF GAMES

RESULTS

Season	Date	Winner	Loser	Site	Attendance
1981	Dec. 27	Buffalo 31	New York Jets 27	New York	57,050
1980	Dec. 28	Oakland 27	Houston 7	Oakland	53,333
1979	Dec. 23	Houston 13	Denver 7	Houston	48,776
1978	Dec. 24	Houston 17	Miami 9	Miami	72,445

1981 AFC FIRST ROUND PLAYOFF

Shea Stadium, New York, New York   December 27, 1981
Attendance: 57,050

BUFFALO 31, NEW YORK 27—Free safety Bill Simpson intercepted Richard Todd's pass at the 2 yard line with :02 remaining to preserve the Bills' victory. It was Simpson's ninth postseason interception, which ties an NFL playoff record. Charles Romes returned Bruce Harper's fumble on the opening kickoff 26 yards for a touchdown, then Joe Ferguson connected on scoring passes of 50 and 26 yards to Frank Lewis. A 29-yard field goal by Nick Mike-Mayer enabled Buffalo to jump off to a 24-0 lead halfway through the second period. The Jets got on the scoreboard with 2:47 remaining in the half when Todd hit Mickey Shuler on a 30-yard pass. New York closed to within 14 points at the half on Pat Leahy's 26-yard field goal. With five minutes remaining in the third quarter, Leahy connected on a 19-yarder. In the fourth quarter, on the first play following Chuck Ramsey's punt, Joe Cribbs raced 45 yards down the right sideline for the touchdown that proved to be the game winner. Frank Lewis had seven receptions for 158 yards and two touchdowns. Joe Ferguson was 17 of 34 for 268 yards, two touchdowns, and four interceptions. For the Jets, Shuler had six catches for 116 yards and one touchdown. Todd, who was intercepted four times, set playoff records for most passes (51) and most completions (28). Both records were broken by Dan Fouts of San Diego one week later.

Buffalo	17	7	0	7 — 31	
New York Jets	0	10	3	14 — 27	

Buff—Romes 26 fumble recovery return (Mike-Mayer kick)
Buff—Lewis 50 pass from Ferguson (Mike-Mayer kick)
Buff—FG Mike-Mayer 29
Buff—Lewis 26 pass from Ferguson (Mike-Mayer kick)
NYJ—Shuler 30 pass from Todd (Leahy kick)
NYJ—FG Leahy 26
NYJ—FG Leahy 19
Buff—Cribbs 45 run (Mike-Mayer kick)
NYJ—B. Jones 30 pass from Todd (Leady kick)
NYJ—Long 1 run (Leahy kick)

NFC FIRST ROUND PLAYOFF GAMES

RESULTS

Season	Date	Winner	Loser	Site	Attendance
1981	Dec. 27	N.Y. Giants 27	Philadelphia 21	Philadelphia	71,611
1980	Dec. 28	Dallas 34	Los Angeles 13	Dallas	63,052
1979	Dec. 23	Philadelphia 27	Chicago 17	Philadelphia	69,397
1978	Dec. 24	Atlanta 14	Philadelphia 13	Atlanta	59,403

1981 NFC FIRST ROUND PLAYOFF

Veterans Stadium, Philadelphia, Pennsylvania   December 27, 1981

Attendance: 71,611

NEW YORK GIANTS 27, PHILADELPHIA 21 —New York's Leon Bright and Mark Haynes scored first-quarter touchdowns that were set up by two Philadelphia kick return fumbles as the Giants beat the Eagles. New York built a 27-7 halftime lead in its first playoff appearance since 1963. Philadelphia pulled within six points with 2:51 remaining, but New York ran out the clock. Giants running back Rob Carpenter gained 161 yards on 33 carries. Scott Brunner completed 9 of 14 passes for 96 yards and three touchdowns.

New York Giants	20	7	0	0 — 27
Philadelphia	0	7	7	7 — 21

NYG—Bright 9 pass from Brunner (kick failed)

NYG—Mistler 10 pass from Brunner (Danelo kick)

NYG—Haynes recovered fumble in end zone (Danelo kick)

Phil —Carmichael 15 pass from Jaworski (Franklin kick)

NYG—Mullady 22 pass from Brunner (Danelo kick)

Phil —Montgomery 6 run (Franklin kick)

Phil —Montgomery 1 run (Franklin kick)

POSTSEASON GAME RECORDS

Compiled by Elias Sports Bureau

This is a compilation of outstanding postseason performances.

SB: Super Bowl
AFC: Championship
NFC: Championship
AFC-D: Divisional

NFC-D: Divisional
AFC-FR: First Round
NFC-FR: First Round

POSTSEASON GAME COMPOSITE STANDINGS

	W	L	Pct.	Pts.	OP
Detroit Lions	6	2	.750	191	153
Green Bay Packers	12	4	.750	349	206
Pittsburgh Steelers	14	5	.737	443	316
Kansas City Chiefs*	5	3	.625	144	147
Oakland Raiders	15	9	.625	587	435
Philadelphia Eagles	7	5	.583	219	173
Dallas Cowboys	18	13	.581	704	522
Miami Dolphins	8	6	.571	292	260
San Francisco 49ers	5	4	.556	201	198
Baltimore Colts	8	7	.533	264	262
Chicago Bears	7	7	.500	330	296
Houston Oilers	6	6	.500	168	267
New York Jets	2	2	.500	76	74
Minnesota Vikings	9	11	.450	341	382
Denver Broncos	2	3	.400	81	111
Los Angeles Rams**	9	14	.391	370	492
Buffalo Bills	3	5	.375	138	171
Cleveland Browns	7	12	.368	344	406
Washington Redskins***	5	9	.357	230	312
Atlanta Falcons	1	2	.333	61	70
Cincinnati Bengals	2	4	.333	120	136
Tampa Bay Buccaneers	1	2	.333	24	64
San Diego Chargers†	3	7	.300	186	217
New York Giants	5	14	.263	282	404
New England Patriots††	1	3	.250	71	114
St. Louis Cardinals†††	1	3	.250	65	93

*One game played when franchise was in Dallas (Texans). (Won 20-17)
**One game played when franchise was in Cleveland. (Won 15-14)
***One game played when franchise was in Boston. (Lost 21-6)
†One game played when franchise was in Los Angeles. (Lost 24-16)
††Two games played when franchise was in Boston. (Won 26-8, lost 51-10)
†††Two games played when franchise was in Chicago. (Won 28-21, lost 7-0)

INDIVIDUAL RECORDS

SERVICE

Most Games, Career
- 27　D. D. Lewis, Dallas (SB-5; NFC-9; NFC-D 12; NFC-FR 1)
- 26　Larry Cole, Dallas (SB-5; NFC-8; NFC-D-12; NFC-FR 1)
- 25　Charlie Waters, Dallas (SB-5; NFC-9, NFC-D 9, NFC-FR 1)

SCORING

POINTS
Most Points, Career
- 115　George Blanda, Chi. Bears-Houston-Oakland, 19 games (49-pat, 22-fg)
- 102　Franco Harris, Pittsburgh, 17 games (17-td)
- 86　Toni Fritsch, Dallas-Houston, 14 games (26-pat, 20-fg)

Most Points, Game
- 19　Pat Harder, NFC-D: Detroit vs. Los Angeles, 1952 (2-td, 4-pat, 1-fg)
　　　Paul Hornung, NFC: Green Bay vs. N.Y. Giants, 1961 (1-td, 4-pat, 3-fg)
- 18　By 12 players

TOUCHDOWNS
Most Touchdowns, Career
- 17　Franco Harris, Pittsburgh, 17 games (16-r, 1-p)
- 10　Fred Biletnikoff, Oakland, 19 games (10-p)
　　　Larry Csonka, Miami, 12 games (9-r, 1-p)
　　　Tony Dorsett, Dallas, 12 games (9-r, 1-p)
- 9　Lynn Swann, Pittsburgh, 15 games (9-p)

Most Touchdowns, Game
- 3　Andy Farkas, NFC-D: Washington vs. N.Y. Giants, 1943 (3-r)
　　　Tom Fears, NFC-D: Los Angeles vs. Chi. Bears, 1950 (3-p)
　　　Otto Graham, NFC: Cleveland vs. Detroit, 1954 (3-r)
　　　Gary Collins, NFC: Cleveland vs. Baltimore, 1964 (3-p)
　　　Craig Baynham, NFC-D: Dallas vs. Cleveland, 1967 (2-r, 1-p)
　　　Fred Biletnikoff, AFC-D: Oakland vs. Kansas City, 1968 (3-p)
　　　Tom Matte, NFC: Baltimore vs. Cleveland, 1968 (3-r)
　　　Larry Schreiber, NFC-D: San Francisco vs. Dallas, 1972 (3-r)
　　　Larry Csonka, AFC: Miami vs. Oakland, 1973 (3-r)
　　　Franco Harris, AFC-D: Pittsburgh vs. Buffalo, 1974 (3-r)
　　　Preston Pearson, NFC: Dallas vs. Los Angeles, 1975 (3-p)
　　　Dave Casper, AFC-D: Oakland vs. Baltimore, 1977 (OT) (3-p)

POINTS AFTER TOUCHDOWN
Most Points After Touchdown, Career
- 49　George Blanda, Chi. Bears-Houston-Oakland, 19 games (49 att)
- 38　Fred Cox, Minnesota, 18 games (40 att)
- 37　Roy Gerela, Houston-Pittsburgh, 15 games (42 att)

Most Points After Touchdown, Game
- 8　Lou Groza, NFC: Cleveland vs. Detroit, 1954 (8 att)
　　　Jim Martin, NFC: Detroit vs. Cleveland, 1957 (8 att)
　　　George Blanda, AFC-D: Oakland vs. Houston, 1969 (8 att)
- 7　Danny Villanueva, NFC-D: Dallas vs. Cleveland, 1967 (7 att)
- 6　George Blair, AFC: San Diego vs. Boston, 1963 (6 att)

Most Points After Touchdown, No Misses, Career
- 49　George Blanda, Chi. Bears-Houston-Oakland, 19 games
- 30　Rafael Septien, Los Angeles-Dallas, 10 games
- 27　Lou Groza, Cleveland, 12 games

FIELD GOALS
Most Field Goals Attempted, Career
- 39　George Blanda, Chi. Bears-Houston-Oakland, 19 games
- 27　Roy Gerela, Houston-Pittsburgh, 15 games
- 25　Toni Fritsch, Dallas-Houston, 14 games

Most Field Goals Attempted, Game

6	George Blanda, AFC: Oakland vs. Houston, 1967	
	David Ray, NFC-D: Los Angeles vs. Dallas, 1973	
5	Jerry Kramer, NFC: Green Bay vs. N.Y. Giants, 1962	
	Gino Cappelletti, AFC-D: Boston vs. Buffalo, 1963	
	Pete Gogolak, AFC: Buffalo vs. San Diego, 1965	
	Jan Stenerud, AFC-D: Kansas City vs. N.Y. Jets, 1969	
	George Blanda, AFC-D: Oakland vs. Pittsburgh, 1973	
4	By many players	

Most Field Goals, Career

22	George Blanda, Chi. Bears-Houston-Oakland, 19 games
20	Toni Fritsch, Dallas-Houston, 14 games
15	Roy Gerela, Houston-Pittsburgh, 15 games

Most Field Goals, Game

4	Gino Cappelletti, AFC-D: Boston vs. Buffalo, 1963
	George Blanda, AFC: Oakland vs. Houston, 1967
	Don Chandler, SB: Green Bay vs. Oakland, 1967
	Curt Knight, NFC: Washington vs. Dallas, 1972
	George Blanda, AFC-D: Oakland vs. Pittsburgh, 1973
	Ray Wersching, SB: San Francisco vs. Cincinnati, 1981
3	By many players

Longest Field Goal

52	Lou Groza, NFC: Cleveland vs. Los Angeles, 1951
	Curt Knight, NFC-D: Washington vs. Minnesota, 1973
50	Garo Yepremian, AFC-D: Miami vs. Cincinnati, 1973
48	George Blanda, AFC: Oakland vs. Baltimore, 1970
	Rafael Septien, NFC-D: Dallas vs. Atlanta, 1978
	Joe Danelo, NFC-D: N.Y. Giants vs. San Francisco, 1981

Highest Field Goal Percentage, Career (10 made)

83.3	Rafael Septien, Los Angeles-Dallas, 10 games (12-10)
80.0	Toni Fritsch, Dallas-Houston, 14 games (25-20)
73.3	Curt Knight, Washington, 5 games (15-11)

SAFETIES

Most Safeties, Game

1	Bill Willis, NFC-D: Cleveland vs. N.Y. Giants, 1950
	Carl Eller, NFC-D: Minnesota vs. Los Angeles, 1969
	George Andrie, NFC-D: Dallas vs. Detroit, 1970
	Alan Page, NFC-D: Minnesota vs. Dallas, 1971
	Dwight White, SB: Pittsburgh vs. Minnesota, 1974
	Reggie Harrison, SB: Pittsburgh vs. Dallas, 1975
	Jim Jensen, NFC-D: Dallas vs. Los Angeles, 1976
	Ted Washington, AFC: Houston vs. Pittsburgh, 1978
	Randy White, NFC-D: Dallas vs. Los Angeles, 1979

RUSHING

ATTEMPTS

Most Attempts, Career

384	Franco Harris, Pittsburgh, 17 games
229	Chuck Foreman, Minnesota, 13 games
225	Larry Csonka, Miami, 12 games

Most Attempts, Game

38	Ricky Bell, NFC-D: Tampa Bay vs. Philadelphia, 1979
37	Lawrence McCutcheon, NFC-D: Los Angeles vs. St. Louis, 1975
34	Franco Harris, SB: Pittsburgh vs. Minnesota, 1974

YARDS GAINED

Most Yards Gained, Career

1,488	Franco Harris, Pittsburgh, 17 games
1,000	Tony Dorsett, Dallas, 12 games
891	Larry Csonka, Miami, 12 games

Most Yards Gained, Game

206	Keith Lincoln, AFC: San Diego vs. Boston, 1963
202	Lawrence McCutcheon, NFC-D: Los Angeles vs. St. Louis, 1975

196 Steve Van Buren, NFC: Philadelphia vs. Los Angeles, 1949

Longest Run From Scrimmage

71 Hugh McElhenny, NFC-D: San Francisco vs. Detroit, 1957
70 Elmer Angsman, NFC: Chi. Cardinals vs. Philadelphia, 1947 (twice, 2 TDs)
69 Hewritt Dixon, AFC: Oakland vs. Houston, 1967 (TD)

AVERAGE GAIN

Highest Average Gain, Career (50 attempts)

6.67 Paul Lowe, L.A. Chargers / San Diego, 5 games (57-380)
5.68 Roger Staubach, Dallas, 20 games (76-432)
5.31 Otto Graham, Cleveland, 7 games (55-292)

Highest Average Gain, Game (10 attempts)

15.90 Elmer Angsman, NFC: Chi. Cardinals vs. Philadelphia, 1947 (10-159)
15.85 Keith Lincoln, AFC: San Diego vs. Boston, 1963 (13-206)
10.90 Bill Osmanski, NFC: Chi. Bears vs. Washington, 1940 (10-109)

TOUCHDOWNS

Most Touchdowns, Career

16 Franco Harris, Pittsburgh, 17 games
9 Larry Csonka, Miami, 12 games
  Tony Dorsett, Dallas, 12 games
7 Chuck Foreman, Minnesota, 13 games

Most Touchdowns, Game

3 Andy Farkas, NFC-D: Washington vs. New York, 1943
  Otto Graham, NFC: Cleveland vs. Detroit, 1954
  Tom Matte, NFC: Baltimore vs. Cleveland, 1968
  Larry Schreiber, NFC-D: San Francisco vs. Dallas, 1972
  Larry Csonka, AFC: Miami vs. Oakland, 1973
  Franco Harris, AFC-D: Pittsburgh vs. Buffalo, 1974

PASSING

ATTEMPTS

Most Passes Attempted, Career

417 Terry Bradshaw, Pittsburgh, 18 games
410 Roger Staubach, Dallas, 20 games
351 Ken Stabler, Oakland-Houston, 13 games

Most Passes Attempted, Game

53 Dan Fouts, AFC-D: San Diego vs. Miami, 1981 (OT)
51 Richard Todd, AFC-FR: N. Y. Jets vs. Buffalo, 1981
49 Joe Namath, AFC: N.Y. Jets vs. Oakland, 1968
  Billy Kilmer, NFC-D: Washington vs. Minnesota, 1976

COMPLETIONS

Most Passes Completed, Career

233 Terry Bradshaw, Pittsburgh, 18 games
223 Roger Staubach, Dallas, 20 games
203 Ken Stabler, Oakland-Houston, 13 games

Most Passes Completed, Game

33 Dan Fouts, AFC-D: San Diego vs. Miami, 1981 (OT)
29 Don Strock, AFC-D: Miami vs. San Diego, 1981 (OT)
28 Richard Todd, AFC-FR: N. Y. Jets vs. Buffalo, 1981

COMPLETION PERCENTAGE

Highest Completion Percentage, Career (100 attempts)

64.1 Ken Anderson, Cincinnati, 5 games (131-84)
61.2 Dan Pastorini, Houston, 5 games (116-71)
61.0 Bart Starr, Green Bay, 10 games (213-130)

Highest Completion Percentage, Game (20 attempts)

76.2 Sammy Baugh, NFC-D: Washington vs. N.Y. Giants, 1943 (21-16)
73.9 Ken Stabler, AFC-D: Oakland vs. Cincinnati, 1975 (23-17)
73.5 Ken Anderson, SB: Cincinnati vs. San Francisco, 1981 (34-25)

YARDS GAINED
Most Yards Gained, Career
3,508	Terry Bradshaw, Pittsburgh, 18 games	
2,791	Roger Staubach, Dallas, 20 games	
2,641	Ken Stabler, Oakland-Houston, 13 games	

Most Yards Gained, Game
433	Dan Fouts, AFC-D: San Diego vs. Miami, 1981 (OT)
403	Don Strock, AFC-D: Miami vs. San Diego, 1981 (OT)
401	Daryle Lamonica, AFC: Oakland vs. N.Y. Jets, 1968

Longest Pass Completion
93	Daryle Lamonica (to Dubenion), AFC-D: Buffalo vs. Boston, 1963 (TD)
88	George Blanda (to Cannon), AFC: Houston vs. L.A. Chargers, 1960 (TD)
86	Don Meredith (to Hayes), NFC-D: Dallas vs. Cleveland, 1967 (TD)

AVERAGE GAIN
Highest Average Gain, Career (100 attempts)
8.41	Terry Bradshaw, Pittsburgh, 18 games (417-3,508)
8.27	Joe Kapp, Minnesota, 4 games (101-835)
8.23	Bart Starr, Green Bay, 10 games (213-1,753)

Highest Average Gain, Game (20 attempts)
14.71	Terry Bradshaw, SB: Pittsburgh vs. Los Angeles, 1979
13.33	Bob Waterfield, NFC-D: Los Angeles vs. Chi. Bears, 1950 (21-280)
12.73	Earl Morrall, NFC-D: Baltimore vs. Minnesota, 1968 (22-280)

TOUCHDOWNS
Most Touchdown Passes, Career
28	Terry Bradshaw, Pittsburgh, 18 games
24	Roger Staubach, Dallas, 20 games
19	Daryle Lamonica, Buffalo-Oakland, 12 games
	Ken Stabler, Oakland-Houston, 13 games

Most Touchdown Passes, Game
6	Daryle Lamonica, AFC-D: Oakland vs. Houston, 1969
5	Sid Luckman, NFC: Chi. Bears vs. Washington, 1943
	Daryle Lamonica, AFC-D: Oakland vs. Kansas City, 1968
4	Otto Graham, NFC: Cleveland vs. Los Angeles, 1950
	Tobin Rote, NFC: Detroit vs. Cleveland, 1957
	Bart Starr, NFC: Green Bay vs. Dallas, 1966
	Ken Stabler, AFC-D: Oakland vs. Miami, 1974
	Roger Staubach, NFC: Dallas vs. Los Angeles, 1975
	Terry Bradshaw, SB: Pittsburgh vs. Dallas, 1978
	Don Strock, AFC-D: Miami vs. San Diego, 1981 (OT)

HAD INTERCEPTED
Lowest Percentage, Passes Had Intercepted, Career (100 attempts)
1.41	Bart Starr, Green Bay, 10 games (213-3)
2.29	Ken Anderson, Cincinnati, 5 games (131-3)
3.42	Joe Namath, N.Y. Jets, 3 games (117-4)

Most Attempts Without Interception, Game
47	Daryle Lamonica, AFC: Oakland vs. N.Y. Jets, 1968
39	Daryle Lamonica, AFC-D: Oakland vs. Kansas City, 1968
	Ron Jaworski, NFC-D: Philadelphia vs. Tampa Bay, 1979
35	Ron Jaworski, NFC-FR: Philadelphia vs. Atlanta, 1978

Most Passes Had Intercepted, Career
24	Terry Bradshaw, Pittsburgh, 18 games
19	Roger Staubach, Dallas, 20 games
17	George Blanda, Chi. Bears-Houston-Oakland, 19 games
	Fran Tarkenton, Minnesota, 11 games

Most Passes Had Intercepted, Game
6	Frank Filchock, NFC: New York vs. Chi. Bears, 1946
	Bobby Layne, NFC: Detroit vs. Cleveland, 1954
	Norm Van Brocklin, NFC: Los Angeles vs. Cleveland, 1955
5	Frank Filchock, NFC: Washington vs. Chi. Bears, 1940
	George Blanda, AFC: Houston vs. San Diego, 1961

George Blanda, AFC: Houston vs. Dall. Texans, 1962 (OT)
Y. A. Tittle, NFC: N. Y. Giants vs. Chicago, 1963
Mike Phipps, AFC-D: Cleveland vs. Miami, 1972
Dan Pastorini, AFC: Houston vs. Pittsburgh, 1978
Dan Fouts, AFC-D: San Diego vs. Houston, 1979
Tommy Kramer, NFC-D: Minnesota vs. Philadelphia, 1980
4   By many players

PASS RECEIVING

RECEPTIONS
Most Receptions, Career
70   Fred Biletnikoff, Oakland, 19 games
58   Paul Warfield, Cleveland-Miami, 18 games
52   Drew Pearson, Dallas, 18 games
Most Receptions, Game
13   Kellen Winslow, AFC-D: San Diego vs. Miami, 1981 (OT)
12   Raymond Berry, NFC: Baltimore vs. New York, 1958
11   Dante Lavelli, NFC: Cleveland vs. Los Angeles, 1950
     Dan Ross, SB: Cincinnati vs. San Francisco, 1981

YARDS GAINED
Most Yards Gained, Career
1,167   Fred Biletnikoff, Oakland, 19 games
1,121   Paul Warfield, Cleveland-Miami, 18 games
  903   Drew Pearson, Dallas, 18 games
Most Yards Gained, Game
198   Tom Fears, NFC-D: Los Angeles vs. Chi. Bears, 1950
190   Fred Biletnikoff, AFC: Oakland vs. N. Y. Jets, 1968
186   Cliff Branch, AFC: Oakland vs. Pittsburgh, 1974
Longest Reception
93   Elbert Dubenion (from Lamonica), AFC-D: Buffalo vs. Boston, 1963 (TD)
88   Billy Cannon (from Blanda), AFC: Houston vs. L. A. Chargers, 1960 (TD)
86   Bob Hayes (from Meredith), NFC: Dallas vs. Cleveland, 1967 (TD)

AVERAGE GAIN
Highest Average Gain, Career (20 receptions)
24.0   Harold Jackson, Los Angeles-New England, 7 games (22-529)
20.5   Frank Lewis, Pittsburgh-Buffalo, 12 games (27-553)
19.6   Tom Fears, Los Angeles, 5 games (30-587)
Highest Average Gain, Game (3 receptions)
46.3   Harold Jackson, NFC: Los Angeles vs. Minnesota, 1974 (3-139)
42.7   Billy Cannon, AFC: Houston vs. L. A. Chargers, 1960 (3-128)
42.0   Lenny Moore, NFC: Baltimore vs. N. Y. Giants, 1959 (3-126)

TOUCHDOWNS
Most Touchdowns, Career
10   Fred Biletnikoff, Oakland, 19 games
 9   Lynn Swann, Pittsburgh, 15 games
 8   John Stallworth, Pittsburgh, 14 games
Most Touchdowns, Game
3   Tom Fears, NFC-D: Los Angeles vs. Chi. Bears, 1950
    Gary Collins, NFC: Cleveland vs. Baltimore, 1964
    Fred Biletnikoff, AFC-D: Oakland vs. Kansas City, 1968
    Preston Pearson, NFC: Dallas vs. Los Angeles, 1975
    Dave Casper, AFC-D: Oakland vs. Baltimore, 1977 (OT)

INTERCEPTIONS BY

Most Interceptions, Career
9   Charlie Waters, Dallas, 25 games
    Bill Simpson, Los Angeles-Buffalo, 11 games
7   Willie Brown, Oakland, 17 games
6   Bobby Bryant, Minnesota, 14 games
    Vernon Perry, Houston, 4 games

Postseason Game Records

Cliff Harris, Dallas, 21 games
Glen Edwards, Pittsburgh-San Diego, 17 games

Most Interceptions, Game

4   Vernon Perry, AFC-D: Houston vs. San Diego, 1979
3   Joe Laws, NFC: Green Bay vs. N. Y. Giants, 1944
    Charlie Waters, NFC-D: Dallas vs. Chicago, 1977
    Rod Martin, SB: Oakland vs. Philadelphia, 1980
2   By many players

YARDS GAINED

Most Yards Gained, Career

196 Willie Brown, Oakland, 17 games
151 Glen Edwards, Pittsburgh-San Diego, 17 games
149 Bill Simpson, Los Angeles-Buffalo, 11 games

Most Yards Gained, Game

88 Walt Sumner, NFC-D: Cleveland vs. Dallas, 1969
83 Bill Simpson, NFC-D: Los Angeles vs. St. Louis, 1975
75 Willie Brown, SB: Oakland vs. Minnesota, 1976
    Vernon Perry, AFC: Houston vs. Pittsburgh, 1979

Longest Return

88 Walt Sumner, NFC-D: Cleveland vs. Dallas, 1969 (TD)
75 Willie Brown, SB: Oakland vs. Minnesota, 1976 (TD)
    Vernon Perry, AFC: Houston vs. Pittsburgh, 1976 (TD)
68 Thomas Henderson, NFC: Dallas vs. Los Angeles, 1978 (TD)

TOUCHDOWNS

Most Touchdowns, Career

3   Willie Brown, Oakland, 17 games
1   By 23 players

Most Touchdowns, Game

1   By 25 players

PUNTING

Most Punts, Career

79 Ray Guy, Oakland, 15 games
73 Mike Eischeid, Oakland-Minnesota, 14 games
69 Danny White, Dallas, 13 games

Most Punts, Game

12 David Lee, AFC-D: Baltimore vs. Oakland, 1977 (OT)
11 Ken Strong, NFC: N. Y. Giants vs. Chi. Bears, 1933
    Jim Norton, AFC: Houston vs. Oakland, 1967
10 Keith Molesworth, NFC: Chi. Bears vs. N. Y. Giants, 1933
    Riley Smith, NFC: Boston vs. Green Bay, 1936
    Len Younce, NFC: N. Y. Giants vs. Green Bay, 1944
    Curley Johnson, AFC: N. Y. Jets vs. Oakland, 1968

Longest Punt

76 Ed Danowski, NFC: N.Y. Giants vs. Detroit, 1935
72 Charlie Conerly, NFC-D: N. Y. Giants vs. Cleveland, 1950
71 Ray Guy, AFC: Oakland vs. San Diego, 1980

AVERAGE YARDAGE

Highest Average, Career (20 punts)

43.4   Jerrel Wilson, Kansas City-New England, 8 games (43-1,866)
43.10 Ray Guy, Oakland, 15 games (79-3,405)
43.06 Don Chandler, N.Y. Giants-Green Bay, 14 games (53-2,282)

Highest Average, Game (4 punts)

56.0   Ray Guy, AFC: Oakland vs. San Diego, 1980 (4-224)
52.5   Sammy Baugh, NFC: Washington vs. Chi. Bears, 1942 (6-315)
51.4   John Hadl, AFC: San Diego vs. Buffalo, 1965 (5-257)

PUNT RETURNS

Most Punt Returns, Career

24 Theo Bell, Pittsburgh-Tampa Bay, 7 games
19 Willie Wood, Green Bay, 10 games

Butch Johnson, Dallas, 13 games
18 Neal Colzie, Oakland-Miami-Tampa Bay, 9 games
Most Punt Returns, Game
7 Ron Gardin, AFC-D: Baltimore vs. Cincinnati, 1970
Carl Roaches, AFC-FR: Houston vs. Oakland, 1980
6 George McAfee, NFC-D: Chi. Bears vs. Los Angeles, 1950
Eddie Brown, NFC-D: Washington vs. Minnesota, 1976
Theo Bell, AFC: Pittsburgh vs. Houston, 1978
Eddie Brown, NFC: Los Angeles vs. Tampa Bay, 1979
John Sciarra, NFC: Philadelphia vs. Dallas, 1980
5 By many players

YARDS GAINED
Most Yards Gained, Career
221 Neal Colzie, Oakland-Miami-Tampa Bay, 9 games
208 Butch Johnson, Dallas, 13 games
196 Theo Bell, Pittsburgh-Tampa Bay, 7 games
Most Yards Gained, Game
141 Bob Hayes, NFC-D: Dallas vs. Cleveland, 1967
102 Charley Trippi, NFC: Chi. Cardinals vs. Philadelphia, 1947
101 Bosh Pritchard, NFC-D: Philadelphia vs. Pittsburgh, 1947
Longest Return
81 Hugh Gallarneau, NFC-D: Chi. Bears vs. Green Bay, 1941 (TD)
79 Bosh Pritchard, NFC-D: Philadelphia vs. Pittsburgh, 1947 (TD)
75 Charley Trippi, NFC: Chi. Cardinals vs. Philadelphia, 1947 (TD)

AVERAGE YARDAGE
Highest Average, Career (10 returns)
12.6 Bob Hayes, Dallas, 15 games (12-151)
12.4 Mike Fuller, San Diego-Cincinnati, 6 games (13-161)
12.3 Neal Colzie, Oakland-Miami-Tampa Bay, 9 games (18-221)
Highest Average Gain, Game (3 returns)
47.0 Bob Hayes, NFC-D: Dallas vs. Cleveland, 1967 (3-141)
29.0 George (Butch) Byrd, AFC: Buffalo vs. San Diego, 1965 (3-87)
25.3 Bosh Pritchard, NFC-D: Philadelphia vs. Pittsburgh, 1947 (4-101)

TOUCHDOWNS
Most Touchdowns
1 Hugh Gallarneau, NFC-D: Chicago Bears vs. Green Bay, 1941
Bosh Pritchard, NFC-D: Philadelphia vs. Pittsburgh, 1947
Charley Trippi, NFC: Chicago Cardinals vs. Philadelphia, 1947
Verda (Vitamin T) Smith, NFC-D: Los Angeles vs. Detroit, 1952
George Byrd, AFC: Buffalo vs. San Diego, 1965
Golden Richards, NFC: Dallas vs. Minnesota, 1973
Wes Chandler, AFC-D: San Diego vs. Miami, 1981 (OT)

KICKOFF RETURNS
Most Kickoff Returns, Career
19 Preston Pearson, Baltimore-Pittsburgh-Dallas, 22 games
18 Charlie West, Minnesota, 9 games
16 Clarence Davis, Oakland, 12 games
Carl Garrett, Oakland, 5 games
Larry Anderson, Pittsburgh, 6 games
Most Kickoff Returns, Game
7 Don Bingham, NFC: Chi. Bears vs. New York, 1956
6 Wallace Francis, AFC-D: Buffalo vs. Pittsburgh, 1974
Eddie Brown, NFC-D: Washington vs. Minnesota, 1976
Eddie Payton, NFC-D: Minnesota vs. Philadelphia, 1980
5 By many players

YARDS GAINED
Most Yards Gained, Career
481 Carl Garrett, Oakland, 5 games

391   Preston Pearson, Baltimore-Pittsburgh-Dallas, 22 games
387   Charlie West, Minnesota, 9 games
        Larry Anderson, Pittsburgh, 6 games

Most Yards Gained, Game

170   Les (Speedy) Duncan, NFC-D: Washington vs. San Francisco, 1971
169   Carl Garrett, AFC-D: Oakland vs. Baltimore, 1977 (OT)
162   Larry Anderson, SB: Pittsburgh vs. Los Angeles, 1979

Longest Return

97   Vic Washington, NFC-D: San Francisco vs. Dallas, 1972 (TD)
89   Nat Moore, AFC-D: Miami vs. Oakland, 1974 (TD)
87   Marshall Johnson, AFC-D: Baltimore vs. Oakland, 1977 (TD) (OT)

AVERAGE YARDAGE
Highest Average, Career (10 returns)

30.1   Carl Garrett, Oakland, 5 games (16-481)
27.9   George Atkinson, Oakland, 16 games (12-335)
24.2   Larry Anderson, Pittsburgh, 6 games (16-387)

Highest Average, Game (3 returns)

56.7   Les (Speedy) Duncan, NFC-D: Washington vs. San Francisco, 1971 (3-170)
51.3   Ed Podolak, AFC-D: Kansas City vs. Miami, 1971 (OT) (3-154)
49.0   Les (Speedy) Duncan, AFC: San Diego vs. Buffalo, 1964 (3-147)

TOUCHDOWNS
Most Touchdowns

1   Vic Washington, NFC-D: San Francisco vs. Dallas, 1972
   Nat Moore, AFC-D: Miami vs. Oakland, 1974
   Marshall Johnson, AFC-D: Baltimore vs. Oakland, 1977 (OT)

FUMBLES

Most Fumbles, Career

11   Tony Dorsett, Dallas, 12 games
10   Franco Harris, Pittsburgh, 17 games
     Terry Bradshaw, Pittsburgh, 18 games
     Roger Staubach, Dallas, 20 games
9   Chuck Foreman, Minnesota, 13 games

Most Fumbles, Game

4   Brian Sipe, AFC-D: Cleveland vs. Oakland, 1980
3   Y. A. Tittle, NFC-D: San Francisco vs. Detroit, 1957
   Bill Nelsen, AFC-D: Cleveland vs. Baltimore, 1972
   Chuck Foreman, NFC: Minnesota vs. Los Angeles, 1974
   Lawrence McCutcheon, NFC-D: Los Angeles vs. St. Louis, 1975
   Roger Staubach, SB: Dallas vs. Pittsburgh, 1975
   Terry Bradshaw, AFC: Pittsburgh vs. Houston, 1978
   Earl Campbell, AFC: Houston vs. Pittsburgh, 1978
   Franco Harris, AFC: Pittsburgh vs. Houston, 1978
   Chuck Muncie, AFC: San Diego vs. Cincinnati, 1981
2   By many players

RECOVERIES
Most Own Fumbles Recovered, Career

5   Roger Staubach, Dallas, 20 games
4   Fran Tarkenton, Minnesota, 11 games
3   Alex Webster, N.Y. Giants, 7 games
   Don Meredith, Dallas, 4 games
   Franco Harris, Pittsburgh, 17 games
   Gerry Mullins, Pittsburgh, 18 games
   Ron Jaworski, Los Angeles-Philadelphia, 10 games

Most Opponents' Fumbles Recovered, Career

4   Cliff Harris, Dallas, 21 games
   Harvey Martin, Dallas, 18 games
3   Paul Krause, Minnesota, 19 games
   Jack Lambert, Pittsburgh, 15 games
   Fred Dryer, Los Angeles, 14 games

Charlie Waters, Dallas, 25 games
Jack Ham, Pittsburgh, 15 games
2 By many players

Most Fumbles Recovered, Game, Own and Opponents'
  3 Jack Lambert, AFC: Pittsburgh vs. Oakland, 1975 (3 opp)
     Ron Jaworski, NFC-FR: Philadelphia vs. N. Y. Giants, 1981 (3 own)

YARDS GAINED
Longest Return
  93 Andy Russell, AFC-D: Pittsburgh vs. Baltimore, 1975 (TD)
  60 Mike Curtis, NFC-D: Baltimore vs. Minnesota, 1968 (TD)
  50 Lee Artoe, NFC: Chi. Bears vs. Washington, 1942 (TD)

TOUCHDOWNS
Most Touchdowns
  1 By 18 players

TEAM RECORDS

GAMES, VICTORIES, DEFEATS
Most Consecutive Seasons Participating in Postseason Games
  8 Dallas, 1966-73
     Pittsburgh, 1972-79
     Los Angeles, 1973-80
  7 Dallas, 1975-81
  6 Oakland, 1972-77
     Minnesota, 1973-78

Most Games
  31 Dallas, 1966-73, 1975-81
  24 Oakland, 1967-70, 1972-77, 1980
  23 Cleveland/Los Angeles, 1945, 1949-52, 1955, 1967, 1969, 1973-80

Most Games Won
  18 Dallas, 1967, 1970-73, 1975, 1977-78, 1980-81
  15 Oakland, 1967-70, 1973-77, 1980
  14 Pittsburgh, 1972, 1974-76, 1978-79

Most Consecutive Games Won
  9 Green Bay, 1961-62, 1965-67
  7 Pittsburgh, 1974-76
  6 Miami, 1972-73
     Pittsburgh, 1978-79 (current)

Most Games Lost
  14 Los Angeles, 1949-50, 1952, 1955, 1967, 1969, 1973-80
     N. Y. Giants, 1933, 1935, 1939, 1941, 1943-44, 1946, 1950, 1958-59, 1961-63, 1981
  13 Dallas, 1966-73, 1972-73, 1975-76, 1978-81
  12 Cleveland, 1951-53, 1957-58, 1965, 1967-69, 1971-72, 1980

Most Consecutive Games Lost
  6 N.Y. Giants, 1939, 1941, 1943-44, 1946, 1950
  5 N. Y. Giants, 1958-59, 1961-63
     Los Angeles, 1952, 1955, 1967, 1969, 1973
  4 Washington, 1972-74, 1976 (current)
     Baltimore, 1971, 1975-77 (current)
     Cleveland, 1969, 1971-72, 1980 (current)
     Miami, 1974, 1978-79, 1981 (current)

SCORING
Most Points, Game
  73 NFC: Chi. Bears vs. Washington, 1940
  59 NFC: Detroit vs. Cleveland, 1957
  56 NFC: Cleveland vs. Detroit, 1954
     AFC-D: Oakland vs. Houston, 1969
Most Points, Both Teams, Game
  79 AFC-D: San Diego (41) vs. Miami (38), 1981 (OT)

Postseason Game Records

	73	NFC: Chi. Bears (73) vs. Washington (0), 1940
		NFC: Detroit (59) vs. Cleveland (14), 1957
	68	AFC-D: Oakland (37) vs. Baltimore (31), 1977 (OT)

Fewest Points, Both Teams, Game

	5	NFC-D: Detroit (0) vs. Dallas (5), 1970
	7	NFC: Chi. Cardinals (0) vs. Philadelphia (7), 1948
	11	NFC-D: N. Y. Giants (3) vs. Cleveland (8), 1950

Most Points, Each Half

1st:	35	NFC: Cleveland vs. Detroit, 1954
		AFC-D: Oakland vs. Houston, 1969
	34	NFC: N. Y. Giants vs. Chi. Bears, 1956
	31	AFC: San Diego vs. Boston, 1963
		AFC: Pittsburgh vs. Houston, 1978
2nd:	45	NFC: Chi. Bears vs. Washington, 1940
	28	NFC: Chi. Bears vs. N. Y. Giants, 1941
		NFC: Detroit vs. Cleveland, 1957
		NFC-D: Dallas vs. Cleveland, 1967
		NFC-D: Dallas vs. Tampa Bay, 1981
	27	NFC: N. Y. Giants vs. Chi. Bears, 1934
		NFC: Chi. Bears vs. Washington, 1943
		NFC: Cleveland vs. Baltimore, 1964

Most Points, Each Quarter

1st:	28	AFC-D: Oakland vs. Houston, 1969
	24	AFC-D: San Diego vs. Miami, 1981
	21	NFC: Chi. Bears vs. Washington, 1940
		AFC: San Diego vs. Boston, 1963
		AFC-D: Oakland vs. Kansas City, 1968
		AFC: Oakland vs. San Diego, 1980
2nd:	26	AFC-D: Pittsburgh vs. Buffalo, 1974
	24	NFC-D: Chi. Bears vs. Green Bay, 1941
		NFC: Green Bay vs. N. Y. Giants, 1961
	21	NFC: Cleveland vs. Detroit, 1954
		NFC: N. Y. Giants vs. Chi. Bears, 1956
		AFC-D: Houston vs. New England, 1978
3rd:	26	NFC: Chi. Bears vs. Washington, 1940
	21	NFC-D: Dallas vs. Cleveland, 1967
		NFC-D: Dallas vs. Tampa Bay, 1981
	17	NFC: Cleveland vs. Baltimore, 1964
		NFC-D: Dallas vs. Chicago, 1977
4th	27	NFC: N.Y. Giants vs. Chi. Bears, 1934
	24	NFC: Baltimore vs. N. Y. Giants, 1959
	21	AFC: Pittsburgh vs. Oakland, 1974
		NFC: Dallas vs. Los Angeles, 1978
OT:	6	NFC: Baltimore vs. N.Y. Giants, 1958
		AFC-D: Oakland vs. Baltimore, 1977

TOUCHDOWNS

Most Touchdowns, Game

	11	NFC: Chi. Bears vs. Washington, 1940
	8	NFC: Cleveland vs. Detroit, 1954
		NFC: Detroit vs. Cleveland, 1957
		AFC-D: Oakland vs. Houston, 1969
	7	AFC: San Diego vs. Boston, 1963
		NFC-D: Dallas vs. Cleveland, 1967

Most Touchdowns, Both Teams, Game

	11	NFC: Chi. Bears (11) vs. Washington (0), 1940
	10	NFC: Detroit (8) vs. Cleveland (2), 1957
		AFC-D: Miami (5) vs. San Diego (5), 1981 (OT)
	9	NFC: Chi. Bears (6) vs. Washington (3), 1943
		NFC: Cleveland (8) vs. Detroit (1), 1954
		NFC-D: Dallas (7) vs. Cleveland (2), 1967
		AFC-D: Oakland (8) vs. Houston (1), 1969
		AFC-D: Oakland (5) vs. Baltimore (4), 1977 (OT)
		SB: Pittsburgh (5) vs. Dallas (4), 1978

Fewest Touchdowns, Both Teams, Game

 0 NFC-D: N.Y. Giants vs. Cleveland, 1950
   NFC-D: Dallas vs. Detroit, 1970
   NFC: Los Angeles vs. Tampa Bay, 1979
 1 NFC: Chi. Cardinals (0) vs. Philadelphia (1), 1948
   AFC: San Diego (0) vs. Houston (1), 1961
   AFC-D: N. Y. Jets (0) vs. Kansas City (1), 1969
   NFC-D: Green Bay (0) vs. Washington (1), 1972
 2 In many games

POINTS AFTER TOUCHDOWN
Most Points After Touchdown, Game

 8 NFC: Cleveland vs. Detroit, 1954
   NFC: Detroit vs. Cleveland, 1957
   AFC-D: Oakland vs. Houston, 1969
 7 NFC: Chi. Bears vs. Washington, 1940
   NFC-D: Dallas vs. Cleveland, 1967
 6 AFC: San Diego vs. Boston, 1963

Most Points After Touchdown, Both Teams, Game

 10 NFC: Detroit (8) vs. Cleveland (2), 1957
   AFC-D: Miami (5) vs. San Diego (5), 1981 (OT)
 9 NFC: Cleveland (8) vs. Detroit (1), 1954
   NFC-D: Dallas (7) vs. Cleveland (2), 1967
   AFC-D: Oakland (8) vs. Houston (1), 1969
 8 In many games

Fewest Points After Touchdown, Both Teams, Game

 0 NFC-D: N.Y. Giants vs. Cleveland, 1950
   NFC-D: Dallas vs. Detroit, 1970
   NFC: Los Angeles vs. Tampa Bay, 1979

FIELD GOALS
Most Field Goals, Game

 4 AFC-D: Boston vs. Buffalo, 1963
   AFC: Oakland vs. Houston, 1967
   SB: Green Bay vs. Oakland, 1967
   NFC: Washington vs. Dallas, 1972
   AFC-D: Oakland vs. Pittsburgh, 1973
   SB: San Francisco vs. Cincinnati, 1981
 3 By many teams

Most Field Goals, Both Teams, Game

 5 NFC: Green Bay (3) vs. Cleveland (2), 1965
   AFC: Oakland (3) vs. N.Y. Jets (2), 1968
   NFC: Washington (4) vs. Dallas (1), 1972
   AFC-D: Cincinnati (3) vs. Miami (2), 1973
   NFC-D: Los Angeles (3) vs. Dallas (2), 1973
 4 In many games

Most Field Goals Attempted, Game

 6 AFC: Oakland vs. Houston, 1967
   NFC-D: Los Angeles vs. Dallas, 1973
 5 By many teams

Most Field Goals Attempted, Both Teams, Game

 8 NFC-D: Los Angeles (6) vs. Dallas (2), 1973
 7 In many games

SAFETIES
Most Safeties, Game

 1 By 11 teams

FIRST DOWNS
Most First Downs, Game

 34 AFC-D: San Diego vs. Miami, 1981 (OT)
 29 AFC-D: Pittsburgh vs. Buffalo, 1974
   AFC-D: Pittsburgh vs. Baltimore, 1976

NFC-FR: Dallas vs. Los Angeles, 1980
28 AFC-D: Oakland vs. Baltimore, 1977 (OT)

Fewest First Downs, Game
6 NFC: N.Y. Giants vs. Green Bay, 1961
7 NFC: Green Bay vs. Boston, 1936
NFC-D: Pittsburgh vs. Philadelphia, 1947
NFC: Chi. Cardinals vs. Philadelphia, 1948
NFC: Los Angeles vs. Philadelphia, 1949
NFC-D: Cleveland vs. N.Y. Giants, 1958
AFC-D: Cincinnati vs. Baltimore, 1970
NFC-D: Detroit vs. Dallas, 1970
8 By many teams

Most First Downs, Both Teams, Game
59 AFC-D: San Diego (34) vs. Miami (25), 1981 (OT)
50 AFC: Oakland (28) vs. Baltimore (22), 1977 (OT)
48 NFC-D: Los Angeles (26) vs. St. Louis (22), 1975

Fewest First Downs, Both Teams, Game
15 NFC: Green Bay (7) vs. Boston (8), 1936
19 NFC: N.Y. Giants (9) vs. Green Bay (10), 1939
NFC: Washington (9) vs. Chi. Bears (10), 1942
20 NFC-D: Cleveland (9) vs. N.Y. Giants (11), 1950

RUSHING
Most First Downs, Rushing, Game
19 NFC-FR: Dallas vs. Los Angeles, 1980
18 AFC-D: Miami vs. Cincinnati,1973
AFC-D: Pittsburgh vs. Buffalo, 1974
16 NFC: Philadelphia vs. Chi. Cardinals, 1948
NFC: Dallas vs. San Francisco, 1970

Fewest First Downs, Rushing, Game
0 NFC: Los Angeles vs. Philadelphia, 1949
AFC-D: Buffalo vs. Boston, 1963
AFC: Oakland vs. Pittsburgh, 1974
1 NFC: N.Y. Giants vs. Green Bay, 1961
AFC-D: Houston vs. Oakland, 1969
NFC: Los Angeles vs. Dallas, 1975
2 By many teams

Most First Downs, Rushing, Both Teams, Game
25 NFC-FR: Dallas (19) vs. Los Angeles (6), 1980
23 NFC: Cleveland (15) vs. Detroit (8), 1952
AFC-D: Miami (18) vs. Cincinnati (5), 1973
AFC-D: Pittsburgh (18) vs. Buffalo (5), 1974
22 AFC: Miami (18) vs. Oakland (4), 1973
AFC-D: Buffalo (11) vs. Cincinnati (11), 1981

Fewest First Downs, Rushing, Both Teams, Game
5 AFC-D: Buffalo (0) vs. Boston (5), 1963
6 NFC: Green Bay (2) vs. Boston (4), 1936
NFC-D: Baltimore (2) vs. Minnesota (4), 1968
AFC-D: Houston (1) vs. Oakland (5), 1969
7 NFC-D: Washington (2) vs. N.Y. Giants (5), 1943
NFC: Baltimore (3) vs. N.Y. Giants (4), 1959
NFC: Washington (3) vs. Dallas (4), 1972
AFC-FR: N.Y. Jets (3) vs. Buffalo (4), 1981

PASSING
Most First Downs, Passing, Game
21 AFC-D: Miami vs. San Diego, 1981 (OT)
AFC-D: San Diego vs. Miami, 1981 (OT)
18 AFC-FR: N.Y. Jets vs. Buffalo, 1981
17 NFC: Baltimore vs. N.Y. Giants, 1958
NFC-D: Minnesota vs. Baltimore, 1968
NFC-D: Cleveland vs. Dallas, 1969
AFC-D: Oakland vs. Baltimore, 1977

AFC: San Diego vs. Oakland, 1980
NFC: San Francisco vs. Dallas, 1981

Fewest First Downs, Passing, Game

0 NFC: Philadelphia vs. Chi. Cardinals, 1948
1 NFC-D: N. Y. Giants vs. Washington, 1943
NFC: Cleveland vs. Detroit, 1953
SB: Denver vs. Dallas, 1977
2 By many teams

Most First Downs, Passing, Both Teams, Game

42 AFC-D: Miami (21) vs. San Diego (21), 1981 (OT)
29 NFC-D: Minnesota (17) vs. Baltimore (12), 1968
AFC: N.Y. Jets (15) vs. Oakland (14), 1968
AFC: San Diego (17) vs. Oakland (12), 1980
AFC-FR: N.Y. Jets (18) vs. Buffalo (11), 1981
28 SB: Pittsburgh (15) vs. Dallas (13), 1978

Fewest First Downs, Passing, Both Teams, Game

2 NFC: Philadelphia (0) vs. Chi. Cardinals (2), 1948
4 NFC-D: Cleveland (2) vs. N. Y. Giants (2), 1950
5 NFC: Detroit (2) vs. N. Y. Giants (3), 1935
NFC: Green Bay (2) vs. N. Y. Giants (3), 1939

PENALTY
Most First Downs, Penalty, Game

7 AFC-D: New England vs. Oakland, 1976
4 AFC: Houston vs. San Diego, 1961
AFC: Dall. Texans vs. Houston, 1962 (OT)
SB: Baltimore vs. Dallas, 1970
SB: Miami vs. Minnesota, 1973
SB: Cincinnati vs. San Francisco, 1981

Most First Downs, Penalty, Both Teams, Game

9 AFC-D: New England (7) vs. Oakland (2), 1976
7 AFC-D: Baltimore (4) vs. Oakland (3), 1977
6 AFC-D: Cincinnati (3) vs. Oakland (3), 1975
AFC-D: Baltimore (4) vs. Pittsburgh (2), 1976
AFC-D: Pittsburgh (4) vs. Denver (2), 1978
SB: Cincinnati (4) vs. San Francisco (2), 1981

NET YARDS GAINED RUSHING AND PASSING
Most Yards Gained, Game

610 AFC: San Diego vs. Boston, 1963
564 AFC-D: San Diego vs. Miami, 1981 (OT)
528 NFC-FR: Dallas vs. Los Angeles, 1980

Fewest Yards Gained, Game

86 NFC-D: Cleveland vs. N.Y. Giants, 1958
99 NFC: Chi. Cardinals vs. Philadelphia, 1948
114 NFC-D: N.Y. Giants vs. Washington, 1943

Most Yards Gained, Both Teams, Game

1,036 AFC-D: San Diego (564) vs. Miami (472), 1981 (OT)
871 AFC: San Diego (610) vs. Boston (261), 1963
858 AFC-D: Kansas City (451) vs. Miami (407), 1971 (OT)

Fewest Yards Gained, Both Teams, Game

331 NFC: Chi. Cardinals (99) vs. Philadelphia (232), 1948
332 NFC-D: N.Y. Giants (150) vs. Cleveland (182), 1950
336 NFC: Boston (116) vs. Green Bay (220), 1936

RUSHING
ATTEMPTS
Most Attempts, Game

65 NFC: Detroit vs. N.Y. Giants, 1935
61 NFC: Philadelphia vs. Los Angeles, 1949
57 NFC: Chi. Bears vs. Washington, 1940
NFC: Philadelphia vs. Chi. Cardinals, 1948
SB: Pittsburgh vs. Minnesota, 1974

Postseason Game Records

Fewest Attempts, Game

- 12   AFC-D: Buffalo vs. Boston, 1963
- 13   NFC-D: Cleveland vs. N.Y. Giants, 1958
  - AFC: Buffalo vs. Kansas City, 1966
  - NFC-D: Minnesota vs. Philadelphia, 1980
- 14   NFC: Washington vs. Chi. Bears, 1940
  - NFC: N.Y. Giants vs. Green Bay, 1961

Most Attempts, Both Teams, Game

- 109   NFC: Detroit (65) vs. N.Y. Giants (44), 1935
- 97   AFC-D: Baltimore (50) vs. Oakland (47), 1977 (OT)
- 91   NFC: Philadelphia (57) vs. Chi. Cardinals (34), 1948

Fewest Attempts, Both Teams, Game

- 45   AFC-FR: N.Y. Jets (22) vs. Buffalo (23), 1981
- 46   AFC: Buffalo (13) vs. Kansas City (33), 1966
- 48   AFC-D: Buffalo (12) vs. Boston (36), 1963
  - AFC: Boston (16) vs. San Diego (32), 1963

YARDS GAINED

Most Yards Gained, Game

- 382   NFC: Chi. Bears vs. Washington, 1940
- 338   NFC-FR: Dallas vs. Los Angeles, 1980
- 318   AFC: San Diego vs. Boston, 1963

Fewest Yards Gained, Game

- 7   AFC-D: Buffalo vs. Boston, 1963
- 17   SB: Minnesota vs. Pittsburgh, 1974
- 21   NFC: Los Angeles vs. Philadelphia, 1949

Most Yards Gained, Both Teams, Game

- 430   NFC-FR: Dallas (338) vs. Los Angeles (92), 1980
- 426   NFC: Cleveland (227) vs. Detroit (199), 1952
- 404   NFC: Chi. Bears (382) vs. Washington (22), 1940

Fewest Yards Gained, Both Teams, Game

- 90   AFC-D: Buffalo (7) vs. Boston (83), 1963
- 106   NFC: Boston (39) vs. Green Bay (67), 1936
- 128   NFC-FR: Philadelphia (53) vs. Atlanta (75), 1978

AVERAGE GAIN

Highest Average Gain, Game

- 9.94   AFC: San Diego vs. Boston, 1963 (32-318)
- 7.35   NFC-FR: Dallas vs. Los Angeles, 1980 (46-338)
- 7.23   NFC: Chi. Cardinals vs. Philadelphia, 1947 (39-282)

Lowest Average Gain, Game

- 0.58   AFC-D: Buffalo vs. Boston, 1963 (12-7)
- 0.81   SB: Minnesota vs. Pittsburgh, 1974 (21-17)
- 0.88   NFC: Los Angeles vs. Philadelpia, 1949 (24-21)

TOUCHDOWNS

Most Touchdowns, Game

- 7   NFC: Chi. Bears vs. Washington, 1940
- 5   NFC: Cleveland vs. Detroit, 1954
- 4   NFC: Detroit vs. N.Y. Giants, 1935
  - AFC: San Diego vs. Boston, 1963
  - NFC-D: Dallas vs. Cleveland, 1967
  - NFC: Baltimore vs. Cleveland, 1968
  - NFC-FR: Dallas vs. Los Angeles, 1980

Most Touchdowns, Both Teams, Game

- 7   NFC: Chi. Bears (7) vs. Washington (0), 1940
- 6   NFC: Cleveland (5) vs. Detroit (1), 1954
- 5   NFC: Chi. Cardinals (3) vs. Philadelphia (2), 1947
  - AFC: San Diego (4) vs. Boston (1), 1963
  - AFC-D: Cincinnati (3) vs. Buffalo (2), 1981

PASSING

ATTEMPTS
Most Attempts, Game
- 54   AFC-D: San Diego vs. Miami, 1981 (OT)
- 51   NFC: Washington vs. Chi. Bears, 1940
  -      AFC-FR: N.Y. Jets vs. Buffalo, 1981
- 49   AFC: N.Y. Jets vs. Oakland, 1968
  -      NFC-D: Washington vs. Minnesota, 1976

Fewest Attempts, Game
- 5   NFC: Detroit vs. N.Y. Giants, 1935
- 6   AFC: Miami vs. Oakland, 1973
- 7   SB: Miami vs. Minnesota, 1973

Most Attempts, Both Teams, Game
- 102   AFC-D: San Diego (54) vs. Miami (48), 1981 (OT)
- 96   AFC: N.Y. Jets (49) vs. Oakland (47), 1968
- 85   AFC-FR: N.Y. Jets (51) vs. Buffalo (34), 1981

Fewest Attempts, Both Teams, Game
- 18   NFC: Detroit (5) vs. N.Y. Giants (13), 1935
- 21   NFC: Chi. Bears (7) vs. N.Y. Giants (14), 1933
- 23   NFC: Chi. Cardinals (11) vs. Philadelphia (12), 1948

COMPLETIONS
Most Completions, Game
- 33   AFC-D: San Diego vs. Miami, 1981 (OT)
- 31   AFC-D: Miami vs. San Diego, 1981 (OT)
- 28   AFC-FR: N.Y. Jets vs. Buffalo, 1981

Fewest Completions, Game
- 2   NFC: Detroit vs. N.Y. Giants, 1935
  -      NFC: Philadelphia vs. Chi. Cardinals, 1948
- 3   NFC: N.Y. Giants vs. Chi. Bears, 1941
  -      NFC: Green Bay vs. N.Y. Giants, 1944
  -      NFC: Chi. Cardinals vs. Philadelphia, 1947
  -      NFC: Chi. Cardinals vs. Philadelphia, 1948
  -      NFC-D: Cleveland vs. N.Y. Giants, 1950
  -      NFC-D: N.Y. Giants vs. Cleveland, 1950
  -      NFC: Cleveland vs. Detroit, 1953
  -      AFC: Miami vs. Oakland, 1973
- 4   NFC-D: Dallas vs. Detroit, 1970
  -      AFC: Miami vs. Baltimore, 1971

Most Completions, Both Teams, Game
- 64   AFC-D: San Diego (33) vs. Miami (31), 1981 (OT)
- 45   AFC-FR: N.Y. Jets (28) vs. Buffalo (17), 1981
- 43   AFC-D: Miami (22) vs. Pittsburgh (21), 1979
  -      NFC-D: Dallas (25) vs. Atlanta (18), 1980

Fewest Completions, Both Teams, Game
- 5   NFC: Philadelphia (2) vs. Chi. Cardinals (3), 1948
- 6   NFC: Detroit (2) vs. N.Y. Giants (4), 1935
  -      NFC-D: Cleveland (3) vs. N.Y. Giants (3), 1950
- 11   NFC: Green Bay (3) vs. N.Y. Giants (8), 1944
  -      NFC-D: Dallas (4) vs. Detroit (7), 1970

COMPLETION PERCENTAGE
Highest Completion Percentage, Game (20 attempts)
- 79.2   AFC-D: Pittsburgh vs. Baltimore, 1976 (24-19)
- 77.3   NFC-D: Washington vs. N.Y. Giants, 1943 (22-17)
- 73.9   NFC-D: Green Bay vs. Los Angeles, 1967 (23-17)
  -      AFC-D: Oakland vs. Cincinnati, 1975 (23-17)

Lowest Completion Percentage, Game (20 attempts)
- 18.5   NFC: Tampa Bay vs. Los Angeles, 1979 (27-5)
- 20.0   NFC-D: N.Y. Giants vs. Washington, 1943 (20-4)
- 25.8   NFC: Chi. Bears vs. Washington, 1937 (31-8)

YARDS GAINED

Postseason Game Records

Most Yards Gained, Game
- 415 AFC-D: San Diego vs. Miami, 1981 (OT)
- 394 AFC-D: Miami vs. San Diego, 1981 (OT)
- 393 AFC: Oakland vs. N.Y. Jets, 1968

Fewest Yards Gained, Game
- 3 NFC: Chi. Cardinals vs. Philadelphia, 1948
- 7 NFC: Philadelphia vs. Chi. Cardinals, 1948
- 9 NFC-D: N.Y. Giants vs. Cleveland, 1950
- NFC: Cleveland vs. Detroit, 1953

Most Yards Gained, Both Teams, Game
- 809 AFC-D: San Diego (415) vs. Miami (394), 1981 (OT)
- 649 AFC: Oakland (393) vs. N.Y. Jets (256), 1968
- 595 NFC-D: Dallas (310) vs. Atlanta (285), 1980

Fewest Yards Gained, Both Teams, Game
- 10 NFC: Chi. Cardinals (3) vs. Philadelphia (7), 1948
- 38 NFC-D: N.Y. Giants (9) vs. Cleveland (29), 1950
- 102 NFC-D: Dallas (22) vs. Detroit (80), 1970

TACKLED ATTEMPTING PASSES
Most Times Tackled, Attempting Passes, Game
- 9 AFC: Kansas City vs. Buffalo, 1966
- 8 NFC: Green Bay vs. Dallas, 1967
- 7 NFC-D: Dallas vs. Los Angeles, 1973
- SB: Dallas vs. Pittsburgh, 1975
- AFC-FR: Houston vs. Oakland, 1980

Most Times Tackled, Attempting Passes, Both Teams, Game
- 13 AFC: Kansas City (9) vs. Buffalo (4), 1966
- 12 NFC-D: Dallas (7) vs. Los Angeles (5), 1973
- 10 AFC-FR: Houston (7) vs. Oakland (3), 1980

Fewest Times Tackled, Attempting Passes, Both Teams, Game
- 0 AFC-D: Buffalo vs. Pittsburgh, 1974
- 1 In many games

TOUCHDOWNS
Most Touchdowns, Game
- 6 AFC-D: Oakland vs. Houston, 1969
- 5 NFC: Chi. Bears vs. Washington, 1943
- NFC: Detroit vs. Cleveland, 1957
- AFC-D: Oakland vs. Kansas City, 1968
- 4 NFC: Cleveland vs. Los Angeles, 1950
- NFC: Green Bay vs. Dallas, 1966
- AFC-D: Oakland vs. Miami, 1974
- NFC: Dallas vs. Los Angeles, 1975
- SB: Pittsburgh vs. Dallas, 1978
- AFC-D: Miami vs. San Diego, 1981 (OT)

Most Touchdowns, Both Teams, Game
- 7 NFC: Chi. Bears (5) vs. Washington (2), 1943
- AFC-D: Oakland (6) vs. Houston (1), 1969
- SB: Pittsburgh (4) vs. Dallas (3), 1978
- AFC-D: Miami (4) vs. San Diego (3), 1981 (OT)
- 5 In many games

INTERCEPTIONS BY

Most Interceptions By, Game
- 8 NFC: Chi. Bears vs. Washington, 1940
- 7 NFC: Cleveland vs. Los Angeles, 1955
- 6 NFC: Green Bay vs. N.Y. Giants, 1939
- NFC: Chi. Bears vs. N.Y. Giants, 1946
- NFC: Cleveland vs. Detroit, 1954
- AFC: San Diego vs. Houston, 1961

Most Interceptions By, Both Teams, Game
- 10 NFC: Cleveland (7) vs. Los Angeles (3), 1955
- AFC: San Diego (6) vs. Houston (4), 1961

9	NFC: Green Bay (6) vs. N.Y. Giants (3), 1939
8	NFC: Chi. Bears (8) vs. Washington (0), 1940
	NFC: Chi. Bears (6) vs. N.Y. Giants (2), 1946
	NFC: Cleveland (6) vs. Detroit (2), 1954
	AFC-FR: Buffalo (4) vs. N.Y. Jets (4), 1981

YARDS GAINED
Most Yards Gained, Game
136	AFC: Dall. Texans vs. Houston, 1962 (OT)
130	NFC-D: Los Angeles vs. St. Louis, 1975
123	NFC: Green Bay vs. N.Y. Giants, 1939
	NFC-D: Cleveland vs. Dallas, 1969
	NFC: Dallas vs. Los Angeles, 1978

Most Yards Gained, Both Teams, Game
156	NFC: Green Bay (123) vs. N.Y. Giants (33), 1939
149	NFC: Cleveland (103) vs. Los Angeles (46), 1955
141	AFC-FR: Buffalo (79) vs. N.Y. Jets (62), 1981

TOUCHDOWNS
Most Touchdowns, Game
3	NFC: Chi. Bears vs. Washington, 1940
2	NFC-D: Los Angeles vs. St. Louis, 1975
1	In many games

PUNTING

Most Punts, Game
13	NFC: N.Y. Giants vs. Chi. Bears, 1933
	AFC-D: Baltimore vs. Oakland, 1977 (OT)
11	AFC: Houston vs. Oakland, 1967
	AFC-D: Houston vs. Oakland, 1969
10	In many games

Fewest Punts, Game
1	NFC-D: Cleveland vs. Dallas, 1969
	AFC: Miami vs. Oakland, 1973
	AFC-D: Oakland vs. Cincinnati, 1975
	AFC-D: Pittsburgh vs. Baltimore, 1976
	AFC: Pittsburgh vs. Houston, 1978
2	In many games

Most Punts, Both Teams, Game
23	NFC: N.Y. Giants (13) vs. Chi. Bears (10), 1933
21	AFC-D: Baltimore (13) vs. Oakland (8), 1977 (OT)
20	NFC: Green Bay (10) vs. N.Y. Giants (10), 1944

Fewest Punts, Both Teams, Game
3	AFC: Miami (1) vs. Oakland (2), 1973
5	NFC: Chi. Bears (2) vs. Washington (3), 1940
	AFC-D: Pittsburgh (1) vs. Baltimore (4), 1976
	AFC: San Diego (2) vs. Cincinnati (3), 1981
6	In many games

AVERAGE YARDAGE
Highest Average, Punting, Game (4 punts)
56.0	AFC: Oakland vs. San Diego, 1980
52.5	NFC: Washington vs. Chi. Bears, 1942
51.3	AFC: Pittsburgh vs. Miami, 1972

Lowest Average, Punting, Game (4 punts)
24.9	NFC: Washington vs. Chi. Bears, 1937
25.5	NFC: Green Bay vs. N.Y. Giants, 1962
27.8	AFC-D: San Diego vs. Buffalo, 1980

PUNT RETURNS

Most Punt Returns, Game
8	NFC: Green Bay vs. N.Y. Giants, 1944
7	NFC-D: Washington vs. N.Y. Giants, 1943

       NFC-D: Chi. Bears vs. Los Angeles, 1950
       AFC-D: Baltimore vs. Cincinnati, 1970
       NFC: Los Angeles vs. Minnesota, 1976
       AFC-FR: Houston vs. Oakland, 1980
       AFC-D: Cleveland vs. Oakland, 1980
  6 By many teams

Most Punt Returns, Both Teams, Game
 13 AFC-FR: Houston (7) vs. Oakland (6), 1980
 11 NFC: Green Bay (8) vs. N.Y. Giants (3), 1944
       NFC-D: Green Bay (6) vs. Baltimore (5), 1965
 10 In many games

Fewest Punt Returns, Both Teams, Game
  0 NFC: Chi. Bears vs. N.Y. Giants, 1941
       AFC: Boston vs. San Diego, 1963
  1 AFC: Miami (0) vs. Pittsburgh (1), 1972
       AFC: Cincinnati (0) vs. San Diego (1), 1981
  2 In many games

YARDS GAINED
Most Yards Gained, Game
 155 NFC-D: Dallas vs. Cleveland, 1967
 150 NFC: Chi. Cardinals vs. Philadelphia, 1947
 112 NFC-D: Philadelphia vs. Pittsburgh, 1947

Fewest Yards Gained, Game
 −10 NFC: Green Bay vs. Cleveland, 1965
  −9 NFC: Dallas vs. Green Bay, 1966
       AFC-D: Kansas City vs. Oakland, 1968
  −5 AFC-D: Miami vs. Oakland, 1970
       NFC-D: San Francisco vs. Dallas, 1972
       NFC: Dallas vs. Washington, 1972

Most Yards Gained, Both Teams, Game
 166 NFC-D: Dallas (155) vs. Cleveland (11), 1967
 160 NFC: Chi. Cardinals (150) vs. Philadelphia (10), 1947
 146 NFC-D: Philadelphia (112) vs. Pittsburgh (34), 1947

Fewest Yards Gained, Both Teams, Game
  −9 NFC: Dallas (-9) vs. Green Bay (0), 1966
  −6 AFC-D: Miami (−5) vs. Oakland (−1), 1970
  −3 NFC-D: San Francisco (−5) vs. Dallas (2), 1972

TOUCHDOWNS
Most Touchdowns, Game
  1 By seven teams

KICKOFF RETURNS
Most Kickoff Returns, Game
  9 NFC: Chi. Bears vs. N.Y. Giants, 1956
       AFC: Boston vs. San Diego, 1963
       AFC: Houston vs. Oakland, 1967
  8 NFC: Washington vs. Chi. Bears, 1940
       NFC: Cleveland vs. Detroit, 1957
       AFC-D: Kansas City vs. Oakland, 1968
       NFC: Los Angeles vs. Dallas, 1975
       AFC-D: Baltimore vs. Pittsburgh, 1976
       NFC-D: Chicago vs. Dallas, 1977
       AFC: Houston vs. Pittsburgh, 1978
  7 By many teams

Most Kickoff Returns, Both Teams, Game
 12 AFC: Boston (9) vs. San Diego (3), 1963
       NFC: Dallas (6) vs. Green Bay (6), 1966
       AFC-D: Baltimore (6) vs. Oakland (6), 1977 (OT)
       AFC: Oakland (6) vs. San Diego (6), 1980
       AFC-D: Miami (6) vs. San Diego (6), 1981 (OT)
       NFC-D: N.Y. Giants (7) vs. San Francisco (5), 1981

        11 In many games
Fewest Kickoff Returns, Both Teams, Game
        1 NFC: Green Bay (0) vs. Boston (1), 1936
        2 NFC-D: Los Angeles (0) vs. Chi. Bears (2), 1950
           AFC: Houston (0) vs. San Diego (2), 1961
           AFC-D: Oakland (1) vs. Pittsburgh (1), 1972
        3 In many games

YARDS GAINED
Most Yards Gained, Game
      225 NFC: Washington vs. Chi. Bears, 1940
      215 AFC: Houston vs. Oakland, 1967
      193 AFC-D: Baltimore vs. Oakland, 1977 (OT)
Most Yards Gained, Both Teams, Game
      379 AFC-D: Baltimore (193) vs. Oakland (186), 1977
      318 AFC-D: Miami (183) vs. Oakland (135), 1974
      294 AFC: Houston (215) vs. Oakland (79), 1967
Fewest Yards Gained, Both Teams, Game
       31 NFC-D: Los Angeles (0) vs. Chi. Bears (31), 1950
       32 NFC: Green Bay (0) vs. Boston (32), 1936
       46 NFC-D: Philadelphia (15) vs. Pittsburgh (31), 1947
           AFC-D: Baltimore (0) vs. Cincinnati (46), 1970

TOUCHDOWNS
Most Touchdowns, Game
        1 NFC-D: San Francisco vs. Dallas, 1972
           AFC-D: Miami vs. Oakland, 1974
           AFC-D: Baltimore vs. Oakland, 1977 (OT)

PENALTIES
Most Penalties, Game
       14 AFC-FR: Oakland vs. Houston, 1980
           NFC-D: San Francisco vs. N.Y. Giants, 1981
       12 NFC-D: Chi. Bears vs. Green Bay, 1941
           AFC-D: Pittsburgh vs. Baltimore, 1976
           SB: Dallas vs. Denver, 1977
       11 NFC: N.Y. Giants vs. Green Bay, 1944
           AFC-D: Oakland vs. New England, 1976
           AFC-D: Pittsburgh vs. Denver, 1978
           NFC-FR: Dallas vs. Los Angeles, 1980
Fewest Penalties, Game
        0 NFC: Philadelphia vs. Green Bay, 1960
           NFC-D: Detroit vs. Dallas, 1970
           AFC-D: Miami vs. Oakland, 1970
           SB: Miami vs. Dallas, 1971
           NFC-D: Washington vs. Minnesota, 1973
           SB: Pittsburgh vs. Dallas, 1975
        1 By many teams
Most Penalties, Both Teams, Game
       22 AFC-FR: Oakland (14) vs. Houston (8), 1980
           NFC-D: San Francisco (14) vs. N.Y. Giants (8), 1981
       21 AFC-D: Oakland (11) vs. New England (10), 1976
       20 SB: Dallas (12) vs. Denver (8), 1977
Fewest Penalties, Both Teams, Game
        2 NFC: Washington (1) vs. Chi. Bears (1), 1937
           NFC-D: Washington (0) vs. Minnesota (2), 1973
           SB: Pittsburgh (0) vs. Dallas (2), 1975
        3 AFC: Miami (1) vs. Baltimore (2), 1971
           NFC: San Francisco (1) vs. Dallas (2), 1971
           SB: Miami (0) vs. Dallas (3), 1971
           AFC-D: Pittsburgh (1) vs. Oakland (2), 1972
           AFC-D: Miami (1) vs. Cincinnati (2), 1973
        4 NFC-D: Cleveland (2) vs. Dallas (2), 1967

NFC-D: Minnesota (1) vs. San Francisco (3), 1970
AFC-D: Miami (0) vs. Oakland (4), 1970
NFC-D: Dallas (2) vs. Minnesota (2), 1971

YARDS PENALIZED
Most Yards Penalized, Game
- 145 NFC-D: San Francisco vs. N.Y. Giants, 1981
- 133 SB: Dallas vs. Baltimore, 1970
- 128 NFC-D: Chi. Bears vs. Green Bay, 1941

Fewest Yards Penalized, Game
- 0 By six teams

Most Yards Penalized, Both Teams, Game
- 206 NFC-D: San Francisco (145) vs. N.Y. Giants (61), 1981
- 192 AFC-D: Denver (104) vs. Pittsburgh (88), 1978
- 177 AFC-D: Oakland (93) vs. New England (84), 1976

Fewest Yards Penalized, Both Teams, Game
- 9 NFC-D: Washington (0) vs. Minnesota (9), 1973
- 15 SB: Miami (0) vs. Dallas (15), 1971
- 20 NFC: Washington (5) vs. Chi. Bears (15), 1937
  AFC-D: Pittsburgh (5) vs. Oakland (15), 1972
  SB: Pittsburgh (0) vs. Dallas (20), 1975

FUMBLES

Most Fumbles, Game
- 6 By nine teams

Most Fumbles, Both Teams, Game
- 12 AFC: Houston (6) vs. Pittsburgh (6), 1978
- 10 Chi. Bears (5) vs. N.Y. Giants (5), 1934
  SB: Dallas (6) vs. Denver (4), 1977
- 9 NFC-D: San Francisco (6) vs. Detroit (3), 1957
  NFC-D: San Francisco (5) vs. Dallas (4), 1972
  NFC: Dallas (5) vs. Philadelphia (4) 1980

Most Fumbles Lost, Game
- 4 NFC: N.Y. Giants vs. Baltimore, 1958 (OT)
  AFC: Kansas City vs. Oakland, 1969
  SB: Baltimore vs. Dallas, 1970
  AFC: Pittsburgh vs. Oakland, 1975
  SB: Denver vs. Dallas, 1977
  AFC: Houston vs. Pittsburgh, 1978
- 3 By many teams

Fewest Fumbles, Both Teams, Game
- 0 NFC: Green Bay vs. Cleveland, 1965
  AFC: Buffalo vs. San Diego, 1965
  AFC-D: Oakland vs. Miami, 1974
  AFC-D: Houston vs. San Diego, 1979
  NFC-D: Dallas vs. Los Angeles, 1979
  SB: Los Angeles vs. Pittsburgh, 1979
  AFC-D: Buffalo vs. Cincinnati, 1981
- 1 In many games

RECOVERIES
Most Total Fumbles Recovered, Game
- 8 SB: Dallas vs. Denver, 1977 (4 own, 4 opp)
- 7 NFC: Chi. Bears vs. N.Y. Giants, 1934 (5 own, 2 opp)
  NFC-D: San Francisco vs. Detroit, 1957 (4 own, 3 opp)
  NFC-D: San Francisco vs. Dallas, 1972 (4 own, 3 opp)
  AFC: Pittsburgh vs. Houston, 1978 (3 own, 4 opp)
- 6 AFC: Houston vs. San Diego, 1961 (4 own, 2 opp)
  AFC-D: Cleveland vs. Baltimore, 1971 (4 own, 2 opp)
  AFC-D: Cleveland vs. Oakland, 1980 (5 own, 1 opp)
  NFC: Philadelphia vs. Dallas, 1980 (3 own, 3 opp)

Most Own Fumbles Recovered, Game
- 5 NFC: Chi. Bears vs. N.Y. Giants, 1934

AFC-D: Cleveland vs. Oakland, 1980
4   By many teams

TURNOVERS
(Numbers of times losing the ball on interceptions and fumbles.)

Most Turnovers, Game
9   NFC: Washington vs. Chi. Bears, 1940
     NFC: Detroit vs. Cleveland, 1954
     AFC: Houston vs. Pittsburgh, 1978
8   NFC: N.Y. Giants vs. Chi. Bears, 1946
     NFC: Los Angeles vs. Cleveland, 1955
     NFC: Cleveland vs. Detroit, 1957
     SB: Denver vs. Dallas, 1977
     NFC-D: Minnesota vs. Philadelphia, 1980
7   AFC: Houston vs. San Diego, 1961
     SB: Baltimore vs. Dallas, 1970
     AFC: Pittsburgh vs. Oakland, 1975
     NFC-D: Chicago vs. Dallas, 1977
     NFC: Los Angeles vs. Dallas, 1978

Fewest Turnovers, Game
0   By many teams

Most Turnovers, Both Teams, Game
14   AFC: Houston (9) vs. Pittsburgh (5), 1978
13   NFC: Detroit (9) vs. Cleveland (4), 1954
     AFC: Houston (7) vs. San Diego (6), 1961
12   AFC: Pittsburgh (7) vs. Oakland (5), 1975

Fewest Turnovers, Both Teams, Game
1   AFC-D: Baltimore (0) vs. Cincinnati (1), 1970
     AFC-D: Pittsburgh (0) vs. Buffalo (1), 1974
     AFC: Oakland (0) vs. Pittsburgh (1), 1976
2   In many games

AFC-NFC PRO BOWL

NFC leads series, 7-5

RESULTS

Year	Date	Winner	Loser	Site	Attendance
1982	Jan. 31	AFC 16	NFC 13	Honolulu	49,521
1981	Feb. 1	NFC 21	AFC 7	Honolulu	47,879
1980	Jan. 27	NFC 37	AFC 27	Honolulu	48,060
1979	Jan. 29	NFC 13	AFC 7	Los Angeles	46,281
1978	Jan. 23	NFC 14	AFC 13	Tampa	51,337
1977	Jan. 17	AFC 24	NFC 14	Seattle	64,151
1976	Jan. 26	NFC 23	AFC 20	New Orleans	30,546
1975	Jan. 20	NFC 17	AFC 10	Miami	26,484
1974	Jan. 20	AFC 15	NFC 13	Kansas City	66,918
1973	Jan. 21	AFC 33	NFC 28	Dallas	37,091
1972	Jan. 23	AFC 26	NFC 13	Los Angeles	53,647
1971	Jan. 24	NFC 27	AFC 6	Los Angeles	48,222

1982 AFC-NFC PRO BOWL

Aloha Stadium, Honolulu, Hawaii   Sunday, January 31, 1982
Attendance: 50,402

AFC 16, NFC 13—Nick Lowery kicked a 23-yard field goal with three seconds remaining to give the AFC a 16-13 victory over the NFC. Lowery's kick climaxed a 69-yard drive directed by quarterback Dan Fouts. The NFC gained a 13-13 tie with 2:43 to go when Tony Dorsett ran four yards for a touchdown. In the drive to the game-winning field goal Fouts completed three passes, including a 23-yarder to San Diego teammate Kellen Winslow that put the ball on the NFC's 5 yard line. Two plays later, Lowery kicked the field goal. Winslow, who caught six passes for 86 yards, was named co-player of the game along with NFC defensive end Lee Roy Selmon.

NFC (13)	Offense	AFC (16)
James Lofton (Green Bay)	WR	Cris Collinsworth (Cincinnati)
Pat Donovan (Dallas)	LT	Anthony Munoz (Cincinnati)
Herbert Scott (Dallas)	LG	Doug Wilkerson (San Diego)
Rich Saul (Los Angeles)	C	Mike Webster (Pittsburgh)
Randy Cross (San Francisco)	RG	John Hannah (New England)
Mike Kenn (Atlanta)	RT	Marvin Powell (New York Jets)
Jimmie Giles (Tampa Bay)	TE	Kellen Winslow (San Diego)
Alfred Jenkins (Atlanta)	WR	Frank Lewis (Buffalo)
Joe Montana (San Francisco)	QB	Ken Anderson (Cincinnati)
Tony Dorsett (Dallas)	RB	Pete Johnson (Cincinnati)
Billy Sims (Detroit)	RB	Joe Delaney (Kansas City)
	Defense	
Ed Jones (Dallas)	LE	Mark Gastineau (New York Jets)
Doug English (Detroit)	LT	Bob Baumhower (Miami)
Randy White (Dallas)	RT	Gary Johnson (San Diego)
Lee Roy Selmon (Tampa Bay)	RE	Joe Klecko (New York Jets)
Lawrence Taylor (New York Giants)	LLB	Ted Hendricks (Oakland)
Harry Carson (New York Giants)	MLB	Jack Lambert (Pittsburgh)
Matt Blair (Minnesota)	RLB	Robert Brazile (Houston)
Roynell Young (Philadelphia)	LCB	Lester Hayes (Oakland)
Ronnie Lott (San Francisco)	RCB	Mel Blount (Pittsburgh)

Gary Fencik (Chicago)	SS	Donnie Shell (Pittsburgh)
Nolan Cromwell (Los Angeles)	FS	Gary Barbaro (Kansas City)

HEAD COACHES
NFC—John McKay (Tampa Bay)
AFC—Don Shula (Miami)

SUBSTITUTIONS
NFC—Offense: K—Rafael Septien (Dallas). P—Tom Skladany (Detroit). QB—Steve Bartkowski (Atlanta). RB—William Andrews (Atlanta), George Rogers (New Orleans). WR—Dwight Clark (San Francisco), Ahmad Rashad (Minnesota). TE—Junior Miller (Atlanta). KR—Mike Nelms (Washington). C—Jeff Van Note (Atlanta). G—R. C. Thielemann (Atlanta). T—Jerry Sisemore (Philadelphia). Defense: E—Fred Dean (San Francisco). T—Charlie Johnson (Philadelphia). LB—Frank LeMaster (Philadelphia), Jerry Robinson (Philadelphia). CB—Everson Walls (Dallas). S—Dwight Hicks (San Francisco).
AFC—Offense: K—Nick Lowery (Kansas City). P—Pat McInally (Cincinnati). QB—Dan Fouts (San Diego). RB—Earl Campbell (Houston), Chuck Muncie (San Diego). WR—Steve Largent (Seattle), Steve Watson (Denver). TE—Ozzie Newsome (Cleveland). KR—Carl Roaches (Houston). C—Joe Fields (New York Jets). G—Ed Newman (Miami). T—Leon Gray (Houston). Defense: E—Art Still (Kansas City). T—Fred Smerlas (Buffalo). LB—Randy Gradishar (Denver), Bob Swenson (Denver). CB—Gary Green (Kansas City). S—Billy Thompson (Denver).

OFFICIALS
Referee: Red Cashion. Umpire: John Keck. Head Linesman: Sid Semon. Line Judge: Dick McKenzie. Back Judge: Roy Clymer. Field Judge: Pat Mallette. Side Judge: Nate Jones.

SCORING
NFC	0	6	0	7 —	13
AFC	0	0	13	3 —	16

NFC—Giles 4 pass from Montana (kick blocked)
AFC—Muncie 2 run (kick failed)
AFC—Campbell 1 run (Lowery kick)
NFC—Dorsett 4 run (Septien kick)
AFC—FG Lowery 23

TEAM STATISTICS
	NFC	AFC
Total First Downs	12	25
First Downs Rushing	6	11
First Downs Passing	6	12
First Downs Penalty	0	2
Rushes	28	45
Net Yards Gained Rushing	116	154
Average Yards per Rush	4.1	3.4
Passes Attempted	29	30
Passes Completed	7	16
Had Intercepted	2	3
Times Tackled Attempting to Pass	3	7
Yards Lost Attempting to Pass	30	54
Net Yards Gained Passing	42	195

Total Net Yardage	158	349
Total Offensive Plays	60	82
Average Gain per Offensive Play	2.6	4.2
Punts	8	5
Average Distance	45.3	45.0
Punt Returns	3	5
Punt Return Yardage	64	40
Kickoff Returns	4	3
Kickoff Return Yardage	57	65
Interception Return Yardage	27	17
Fumbles	4	4
Own Fumbles Recovered	2	3
Opponent Fumbles Recovered	1	2
Total Return Yardage	148	133
Penalties	6	1
Yards Penalized	35	5
Total Points Scored	13	16
Touchdowns	2	2
Touchdowns Rushing	1	2
Touchdowns Passing	1	0
Touchdowns Returns	0	0
Extra Points	1	1
Field Goals	0	1
Field Goals Attempted	0	2

INDIVIDUAL STATISTICS
RUSHING

NFC	Att.	Yds.	LG	TD
Dorsett	13	39	19	1
Sims	6	23	11	0
Montana	2	19	10	0
Andrews	4	12	6	0
Rogers	2	12	6	0
Bartkowski	1	11	11	0

AFC	Att.	Yds.	LG	TD
Campbell	11	52	16	1
Johnson	9	32	7	0
Delaney	11	28	8	0
Muncie	8	28	9	1
Anderson	3	18	9	0
Fouts	1	0	0	0
Largent	1	0	0	0
Lewis	1	−4	−4	0

PASSING

NFC	Att.	Comp.	Yds.	TD	Int.
Montana	14	4	23	1	1
Bartkowski	15	3	49	0	1

AFC	Att.	Comp.	Yds.	TD	Int.
Anderson	14	8	106	0	1
Fouts	16	8	143	0	2

RECEIVING

NFC	No.	Yds.	LG	TD
Jenkins	2	33	22	0
Giles	2	20	16	1
Clark	1	23	23	0
Andrews	1	4	4	0
Rogers	1	−8	−8	0

AFC	No.	Yds.	LG	TD
Winslow	6	86	23	0
Watson	3	51	26	0
Newsome	2	28	19	0
Johnson	2	16	10	0
Largent	1	35	35	0
Lewis	1	19	19	0
Collinsworth	1	14	14	0

INTERCEPTIONS

NFC	No.	Yds.	LG	TD
Walls	2	14	12	0
LeMaster	1	13	13	0

AFC	No.	Yds.	LG	TD
Barbaro	1	17	17	0
Hendricks	1	0	0	0

1981 AFC-NFC PRO BOWL

Aloha Stadium, Honolulu, Hawaii   February 1, 1981

Attendance: 47,879

NFC 21, AFC 7—Ed Murray kicked four field goals and Steve Bartkowski fired a 55-yard scoring pass to Alfred Jenkins to lead the NFC to its fourth straight victory over the AFC and a 7-4 edge in the series. Murray was named the game's most valuable player and missed tying Garo Yepremian's Pro Bowl record of five field goals when a 37-yard attempt hit the crossbar with 22 seconds remaining. The AFC's only score came on a nine-yard pass from Brian Sipe to Stanley Morgan in the second period. Bartkowski completed 9 of 21 for 173 yards, while Sipe connected on 10 of 15 for 142 yards. Ottis Anderson led all rushers with 70 yards on 10 carries. Earl Campbell, the NFL's leading rusher in 1980, was limited to 24 on eight attempts.

AFC	0	7	0	0 — 7
NFC	3	6	0	12 — 21

NFC—FG Murray 31
AFC—Morgan 9 pass from Sipe (J. Smith kick)
NFC—FG Murray 31
NFC—FG Murray 34
NFC—Jenkins 55 pass from Bartkowski (Murray kick)
NFC—FG Murray 36
NFC—Safety (Team)

1980 AFC-NFC PRO BOWL

Aloha Stadium, Honolulu, Hawaii   January 27, 1980

Attendance: 48,060

NFC 37, AFC 27—Running back Chuck Muncie ran for two touchdowns and threw a 25-yard option pass for another score to give the NFC its third consecutive victory over the AFC. Muncie, who was selected the game's most valuable player, snapped a 3-3 tie on a one-yard touchdown run at 1:41 of the second quarter, then scored on an 11-yard run in the fourth quarter for the NFC's final touchdown. Two scoring records were set in the game—37 points by the NFC, eclipsing the 33 by the AFC in 1973, and the 64 points by both teams, surpassing the 61 scored in 1973.

NFC	3	20	7	7 — 37
AFC	3	7	10	7 — 27

NFC—FG Moseley 37
AFC—FG Fritsch 19
NFC—Muncie 1 run (Moseley kick)
AFC—Pruitt 1 pass from Bradshaw (Fritsch kick)
NFC—D. Hill 13 pass from Manning (kick failed)
NFC—T. Hill 25 pass from Muncie (Moseley kick)
NFC—Henry 86 punt return (Moseley kick)
AFC—Campbell 2 run (Fritsch kick)
AFC—FG Fritsch 29
NFC—Muncie 11 run (Moseley kick)
AFC—Campbell 1 run (Fritsch kick)

1979 AFC-NFC PRO BOWL

Memorial Coliseum, Los Angeles, California   January 29, 1979

Attendance: 46,281

NFC 13, AFC 7—Roger Staubach completed 9 of 15 passes for 125 yards, including the winning touchdown on a 19-yard strike to Dallas Cowboys teammate Tony Hill in the third period. The winning drive began at the AFC's 45 yard line after a shanked punt. Staubach hit Ahmad Rashad with passes of 15 and

17 yards to set up Hill's decisive catch. The victory gave the NFC a 5-4 advantage in Pro Bowl games. Rashad, who accounted for 89 yards on five receptions, was named the player of the game. The AFC led 7-6 at halftime on Bob Griese's eight-yard scoring toss to Steve Largent late in the secnd quarter. Largent finished the game with five receptions for 75 yards. The NFC scored first as Archie Manning marched his team 70 yards in 11 plays, capped by Wilbert Montgomery's two-yard touchdown run. The AFC's Earl Campbell was the game's leading rusher with 66 yards on 12 carries.

| AFC | 0 | 7 | 0 | 0 — 7 |
| NFC | 0 | 6 | 7 | 0 — 13 |

NFC—Montgomery 2 run (kick failed)
AFC—Largent 8 pass from Griese (Yepremian kick)
NFC—T. Hill 19 pass from Staubach (Corral kick)

1978 AFC-NFC PRO BOWL

Tampa Stadium, Tampa, Florida   January 23, 1978
Attendance: 51,337

NFC 14, AFC 13—Walter Payton, the NFL's leading rusher in 1977, sparked a second half comeback to give the NFC a 14-13 win and tie the series between the two conferences at four victories each. Payton, who was the game's most valuable player, gained 77 yards on 13 carries and scored the tying touchdown on a one-yard burst with 7:37 left in the game. Efren Herrera kicked the winning extra point. The AFC dominated the first half of the game, taking a 13-0 lead on field goals of 21 and 39 yards by Toni Linhart and a 10-yard touchdown pass from Ken Stabler to Oakland teammate Cliff Branch. On the NFC's first possession of the second half, Pat Haden put together the first touchdown drive after Eddie Brown returned Ray Guy's punt to the AFC 46 yard line. Haden connected on all four of his passes on that drive, finally hitting Terry Metcalf with a four-yard scoring toss. The NFC continued to rally and, with Jim Hart at quarterback, moved 63 yards in 12 plays for the go-ahead score. During the winning drive Hart completed five of six passes for 38 yards and Payton picked up 20 more on the ground.

| AFC | 3 | 10 | 0 | 0 — 13 |
| NFC | 0 | 0 | 7 | 7 — 14 |

AFC—FG Linhart 21
AFC—Branch 10 pass from Stabler (Linhart kick)
AFC—FG Linhart 39
NFC—Metcalf 4 pass from Haden (Herrera kick)
NFC—Payton 1 run (Herrera kick)

1977 AFC-NFC PRO BOWL

Kingdome, Seattle, Washington   January 17, 1977
Attendance: 64,752

AFC 24, NFC 14—O. J. Simpson's three-yard touchdown burst at 7:03 of the first quarter gave the AFC a lead it would not surrender, the victory breaking a two-game NFC win streak and giving the American Conference stars a 4-3 series lead. The AFC took a 17-7 lead midway through the second period on the first of two Ken Anderson touchdown passes, a 12-yarder to Charlie Joiner. But the NFC mounted a 73-yard scoring drive capped by Lawrence McCutcheon's one-yard touchdown plunge to pull within three of the AFC, 17-14, at the half. Following a scoreless third quarter, player of the game Mel Blount thwarted a possible NFC score when he intercepted Jim Hart's pass in the end zone. Less than three minutes later, Blount again picked off a Hart pass, returning it 16 yards to the NFC 27. That set up Anderson's 27-yard touchdown strike to Cliff Branch for the final score.

NFC	0	14	0	0 — 14
AFC	10	7	0	7 — 24

AFC—Simpson 3 run (Linhart kick)
AFC—FG Linhart 31
NFC—Thomas 15 run (Bakken kick)
AFC—Joiner 12 pass from Anderson (Linhart kick)
NFC—McCutcheon 1 run (Bakken kick)
AFC—Branch 27 pass from Anderson (Linhart kick)

1976 AFC-NFC PRO BOWL

Superdome, New Orleans, Louisiana   January 26, 1976
Attendance: 30,546

NFC 23, AFC 20—Mike Boryla, a late substitute who did not enter the game until 5:39 remained, lifted the National Football Conference to a 23-20 victory over the American Football Conference with two touchdown passes in the final minutes. It was the second straight NFC win, squaring the series at 3-3. Until Boryla started firing the ball the AFC was in control, leading 13-0 at the half. Boryla entered the game after Billy Johnson had raced 90 yards with a punt to make the score 20-9 in favor of the AFC. He floated a 14-yard pass to Terry Metcalf and later fired an eight-yarder to Mel Gray for the winner.

AFC	0	13	0	7 — 20
NFC	0	0	9	14 — 23

AFC—FG Stenerud 20
AFC—FG Stenerud 35
AFC—Burrough 64 pass from Pastorini (Stenerud kick)
NFC—FG Bakken 42
NFC—Foreman 4 pass from Hart (kick blocked)
AFC—Johnson 90 punt return (Stenerud kick)
NFC—Metcalf 14 pass from Boryla (Bakken kick)
NFC—Gray 8 pass from Boryla (Bakken kick)

1975 AFC-NFC PRO BOWL

Orange Bowl, Miami, Florida   January 20, 1975
Attendance: 26,484

NFC 17, AFC 10—Los Angeles quarterback James Harris, who took over the NFC offense after Jim Hart of St. Louis suffered a laceration above his right eye in the second period, threw a pair of touchdown passes early in the fourth period to pace the NFC to its second victory in the five-game Pro Bowl series. The NFC win snapped a three-game AFC victory string. Harris, who was named the player of the game, connected with St. Louis's Mel Gray for an eight-yard touchdown 2:03 into the final period. One minute and 24 seconds later, following a recovery by Washington's Ken Houston of a fumble by Franco Harris of Pittsburgh, Harris tossed another eight-yard scoring pass to Washington's Charley Taylor for the decisive points.

NFC	0	3	0	14 — 17
AFC	0	0	10	0 — 10

NFC—FG Marcol 33
AFC—Warfield 32 pass from Griese (Gerela kick)
AFC—FG Gerela 33
NFC—Gray 8 pass from J. Harris (Marcol kick)
NFC—Taylor 8 pass from J. Harris (Marcol kick)

1974 AFC-NFC PRO BOWL

Arrowhead, Kansas City, Missouri   January 20, 1974
Attendance: 66,918

AFC 15, NFC 13—Miami's Garo Yepremian kicked his fifth consecutive field goal without a miss from the 42 yard line with 21 seconds remaining to give the AFC its third straight victory since the NFC won the inaugural game following the 1970 season. The field goal by Yepremian, who was voted the game's outstanding player, offset a 21-yard field goal by Atlanta's Nick Mike-Mayer that had given the NFC a 13-12 advantage with 1:41 remaining. The only touchdown in the game was scored by the NFC on a 14-yard pass from Roman Gabriel to Lawrence McCutcheon.

NFC	0	10	0	3 —	13
AFC	3	3	3	6 —	15

AFC—FG Yepremian 16
NFC—FG Mike-Mayer 27
NFC—McCutcheon 14 pass from Gabriel (Mike-Mayer kick)
AFC—FG Yepremian 37
AFC—FG Yepremian 27
AFC—FG Yepremian 41
NFC—FG Mike-Mayer 21
AFC—FG Yepremian 42

1973 AFC-NFC PRO BOWL

Texas Stadium, Irving, Texas   January 21, 1973
Attendance: 37,091

AFC 33, NFC 28—Paced by the rushing and receiving of player of the game O.J. Simpson, the AFC erased a 14-0 first period deficit and built a commanding 33-14 lead midway through the fourth period before the NFC managed two touchdowns in the final minute of play. Simpson rushed for 112 yards and caught three passes for 58 more to gain unanimous recognition in the balloting for player of the game. John Brockington scored three touchdowns for the NFC.

AFC	0	10	10	13 —	33
NFC	14	0	0	14 —	28

NFC—Brockington 1 run (Marcol kick)
NFC—Brockington 3 pass from Kilmer (Marcol kick)
AFC—Simpson 7 run (Gerela kick)
AFC—FG Gerela 18
AFC—FG Gerela 22
AFC—Hubbard 11 run (Gerela kick)
AFC—O. Taylor 5 pass from Lamonica (kick failed)
AFC—Bell 12 interception return (Gerela kick)
NFC—Brockington 1 run (Marcol kick)
NFC—Kwalick 12 pass from Snead (Marcol kick)

1972 AFC-NFC PRO BOWL

Memorial Coliseum, Los Angeles, California   January 23, 1972
Attendance: 53,647

AFC 26, NFC 13—Four field goals by Jan Stenerud of Kansas City, including a 6-6 tie-breaker from 48 yards, helped lift the AFC from a 6-0 deficit to a 19-6 advantage early in the fourth period. The AFC defense picked off three interceptions. Stenerud was selected as the outstanding offensive player and his Kansas City teammate, linebacker Willie Lanier, was the game's outstanding defensive player.

AFC	0	3	13	10 —	26
NFC	0	6	0	7 —	13

NFC—Grim 50 pass from Landry (kick failed)
AFC—FG Stenerud 25

AFC—FG Stenerud 23
AFC—FG Stenerud 48
AFC—Morin 5 pass from Dawson (Stenerud kick)
AFC—FG Stenerud 42
NFC—V. Washington 2 run (Knight kick)
AFC—F. Little 6 run (Stenerud kick)

1971 AFC-NFC PRO BOWL

Memorial Coliseum, Los Angeles, California   January 24, 1971
Attendance: 48,222

NFC 27, AFC 6—Mel Renfro of Dallas broke open the first meeting between the American Football Conference and National Football Conference all-pro teams as he returned a pair of punts 82 and 56 yards for touchdowns in the final period to provide the NFC with a 26-6 victory over the AFC. Renfro was voted the game's outstanding back and linebacker Fred Carr of Green Bay the outstanding lineman.

AFC	0	3	3	0 —	6
NFC	0	3	10	14 —	27

AFC—FG Stenerud 37
NFC—FG Cox 13
NFC—Osborn 23 pass from Brodie (Cox kick)
NFC—FG Cox 35
AFC—FG Stenerud 16
NFC—Renfro 82 punt return (Cox kick)
NFC—Renfro 56 punt return (Cox kick)

AFC-NFC PRO BOWL RECORDS

Compiled by Elias Sports Bureau

INDIVIDUAL RECORDS

SERVICE

Most Games
9   Ken Houston, Houston (3), 1971-73; Washington (6), 1974-79
    Joe Greene, Pittsburgh, 1971-77, 1979-80

SCORING

POINTS
Most Points, Game
18   John Brockington, Green Bay, 1973 (3-td)

TOUCHDOWNS
Most Touchdowns, Game
3   John Brockington, Green Bay, 1973 (2-r, 1-p)

POINTS AFTER TOUCHDOWN
Most Points After Touchdown, Game
4   Chester Marcol, Green Bay, 1973 (4 att)
    Mark Moseley, Washington, 1980 (5 att)

FIELD GOALS
Most Field Goals Attempted, Game
6   Jan Stenerud, Kansas City, 1972
    Ed Murray, Detroit, 1981
Most Field Goals, Game
5   Garo Yepremian, Miami, 1974 (5 att)
Longest Field Goal
48   Jan Stenerud, Kansas City, 1972

RUSHING

ATTEMPTS
Most Attempts, Game
19   O. J. Simpson, Buffalo, 1974

YARDS GAINED
Most Yards Gained, Game
112   O. J. Simpson, Buffalo, 1973
Longest Run From Scrimmage
41   Lawrence McCutcheon, Los Angeles, 1976

TOUCHDOWNS
Most Touchdowns, Game
2   John Brockington, Green Bay, 1973
    Earl Campbell, Houston, 1980
    Chuck Muncie, New Orleans, 1980

PASSING

ATTEMPTS
Most Attempts, Game
28   Jim Hart, St. Louis, 1976

COMPLETIONS
Most Completions, Game
14   Norm Snead, N.Y. Giants, 1973

Highest Completion Percentage, Game (10 attempts)
    90.0   Archie Manning, New Orleans, 1980 (10-9)

YARDS GAINED
Most Yards Gained, Game
    173   Steve Bartkowski, Atlanta, 1981
Longest Completion
    64   Dan Pastorini, Houston (to Burrough, Houston), 1976

TOUCHDOWNS
Most Touchdowns, Game
    2   James Harris, Los Angeles, 1975
        Mike Boryla, Philadelphia, 1976
        Ken Anderson, Cincinnati, 1977

HAD INTERCEPTED
Most Passes Had Intercepted, Game
    5   Jim Hart, St. Louis, 1977
Most Attempts, Without Interception, Game
    26   John Brodie, San Francisco, 1971

PASS RECEIVING

RECEPTIONS
Most Receptions, Game
    6   John Stallworth, Pittsburgh, 1980
       Kellen Winslow, San Diego, 1982

YARDS GAINED
Most Yards Gained, Game
    96   Ken Burrough, Houston, 1976
Longest Reception
    64   Ken Burrough, Houston (from Pastorini, Houston), 1976

TOUCHDOWNS
Most Touchdowns, Game
    1   By many players

INTERCEPTIONS BY

Most Interceptions By, Game
    2   Mel Blount, Pittsburgh, 1977
       Everson Walls, Dallas, 1982

YARDS GAINED
Most Yards Gained, Game
    65   Ted Hendricks, Baltimore, 1973
Longest Gain
    65   Ted Hendricks, Baltimore, 1973

TOUCHDOWNS
Most Touchdowns, Game
    1   Bobby Bell, Kansas City, 1973

PUNTING

Most Punts, Game
    9   Tom Wittum, San Francisco, 1974
Longest Punt
    64   Tom Wittum, San Francisco, 1974

AVERAGE YARDAGE
Highest Average, Game (4 punts)
    49.0   Ray Guy, Oakland, 1974 (4)

PUNT RETURNS

Most Punt Returns, Game
    5 Rick Upchurch, Denver, 1980
       Mike Nelms, Washington, 1981
       Carl Roaches, Houston, 1982

Most Fair Catches, Game
    2 Jerry Logan, Baltimore, 1971
       Dick Anderson, Miami, 1974

YARDS GAINED

Most Yards Gained, Game
   159 Billy Johnson, Houston, 1976

Longest Punt Return
   90 Billy Johnson, Houston, 1976 (TD)

TOUCHDOWNS

Most Touchdowns, Game
    2 Mel Renfro, Dallas, 1971

KICKOFF RETURNS

Most Kickoff Returns, Game
    5 Les (Speedy) Duncan, Washington, 1972
       Ron Smith, Chicago, 1973
       Herb Mul-Key, Washington, 1974

YARDS GAINED

Most Yards Gained, Game
   175 Les (Speedy) Duncan, Washington, 1972

Longest Kickoff Return
   61 Mercury Morris, Miami, 1972

TOUCHDOWNS

Most Touchdowns, Game
   None

FUMBLES

Most Fumbles, Game
    3 Dan Fouts, San Diego, 1982

RECOVERIES

Most Fumbles Recovered, Game
    2 Dick Anderson, Miami, 1974 (1-own, 1-opp)
       Harold Jackson, Los Angeles, 1974 (2-own)
       Dan Fouts, San Diego, 1982 (2 own)

YARDAGE

Longest Fumble Return
   51 Phil Villapiano, Oakland, 1974

TOUCHDOWNS

Most Touchdowns, Game
   None

TEAM RECORDS

SCORING

Most Points, Game
   37 NFC, 1980

Fewest Points, Game
    6 AFC, 1971

Most Points, Both Teams, Game
   64 NFC (37) vs. AFC (27), 1980

Fewest Points, Both Teams, Game
 20 AFC (7) vs. NFC (13), 1979

TOUCHDOWNS
Most Touchdowns, Game
 5 NFC, 1980
Fewest Touchdowns, Game
 0 AFC, 1971, 1974
Most Touchdowns, Both Teams, Game
 8 AFC (4) vs. NFC (4), 1973
  NFC (5) vs. AFC (3), 1980
Fewest Touchdowns, Both Teams, Game
 1 AFC (0) vs. NFC (1), 1974

POINTS AFTER TOUCHDOWNS
Most Points After Touchdown, Game
 4 NFC, 1973
  NFC, 1980
Most Points After Touchdown, Both Teams, Game
 7 NFC (4) vs. AFC (3), 1973
  NFC (4) vs. AFC (3), 1980

FIELD GOALS
Most Field Goals Attempted, Game
 6 AFC, 1972
  NFC, 1981
Most Field Goals Attempted, Both Teams, Game
 8 AFC (5) vs. NFC (3), 1974
Most Field Goals, Game
 5 AFC, 1974
Most Field Goals, Both Teams, Game
 7 AFC (5) vs. NFC (2), 1974

NET YARDS GAINED RUSHING AND PASSING
Most Yards Gained, Game
 410 AFC, 1980
Fewest Yards Gained, Game
 146 AFC, 1971
Most Yards Gained, Both Teams, Game
 721 AFC (410) vs. NFC (311), 1980
Fewest Yards Gained, Both Teams, Game
 468 NFC (159) vs. AFC (309), 1972

RUSHING
ATTEMPTS
Most Attempts, Game
 50 AFC, 1974
Fewest Attempts, Game
 22 AFC, 1981
Most Attempts, Both Teams, Game
 80 AFC (50) vs. NFC (30), 1974
Fewest Attempts, Both Teams, Game
 55 AFC (23) vs. NFC (32), 1971

YARDS GAINED
Most Yards Gained, Game
 224 NFC, 1976
Fewest Yards Gained, Game
 64 NFC, 1974
Most Yards Gained, Both Teams, Game
 425 NFC (224) vs. AFC (201), 1976
Fewest Yards Gained, Both Teams, Game
 178 AFC (66) vs. NFC (112), 1971

TOUCHDOWNS
Most Touchdowns, Game
> 2 AFC, 1973, 1980, 1982
> NFC, 1973, 1977, 1980

PASSING

ATTEMPTS
Most Attempts, Game
> 39 NFC, 1971

Fewest Attempts, Game
> 17 NFC, 1972

Most Attempts, Both Teams, Game
> 74 NFC (39) vs. AFC (35), 1971

Fewest Attempts, Both Teams, Game
> 42 NFC (17) vs. AFC (25), 1972

COMPLETIONS
Most Completions, Game
> 20 AFC, 1980

Fewest Completions, Game
> 7 NFC, 1972, 1982

Most Completions, Both Teams, Game
> 34 AFC (17) vs. NFC (17), 1979

Fewest Completions, Both Teams, Game
> 18 NFC (7) vs. AFC (11), 1972

YARDS GAINED
Most Yards Gained, Game
> 275 AFC, 1980

Fewest Yards Gained, Game
> 42 NFC, 1982

Most Yards Gained, Both Teams, Game
> 398 AFC (275) vs. NFC (123), 1980

Fewest Yards Gained, Both Teams, Game
> 215 NFC (89) vs. AFC (126), 1972

TACKLED ATTEMPTING PASSES
Most Times Tackled Attempting Passes, Game
> 7 AFC, 1982

Fewest Times Tackled Attempting Passes, Game
> 0 NFC, 1971

Most Times Tackled Attempting Passes, Both Teams, Game
> 10 AFC (7) vs. NFC (3), 1982

Fewest Times Tackled Attempting Passes, Both Teams, Game
> 4 AFC (2) vs. NFC (2), 1978

TOUCHDOWNS
Most Touchdowns, Game
> 3 NFC, 1976

Fewest Touchdowns, Game
> 0 AFC, 1971, 1974, 1982
> NFC, 1977

Most Touchdowns, Both Teams, Game
> 4 NFC (3) vs. AFC (1), 1976

Fewest Touchdowns, Both Teams, Game
> 1 AFC (0) vs. NFC (1), 1971
> AFC (0) vs. NFC (1), 1974
> AFC (0) vs. NFC (1), 1982

INTERCEPTIONS BY
Most Interceptions By, Game
> 6 AFC, 1977

Most Interceptions By, Both Teams, Game
    7   AFC (6) vs. NFC (1), 1977

YARDS GAINED
Most Yards Gained, Game
    77   AFC, 1973
Most Yards Gained, Both Teams, Game
    99   NFC (64) vs. AFC (35), 1975

TOUCHDOWNS
Most Touchdowns, Game
    1   AFC, 1973

PUNTING

Most Punts, Game
    9   NFC, 1974
Fewest Punts, Game
    3   AFC, 1972, 1975
       NFC, 1978
Most Punts, Both Teams, Game
    15   AFC (8) vs. NFC (7), 1971
Fewest Punts, Both Teams, Game
    7   NFC (3) vs. AFC (4), 1978

AVERAGE YARDAGE
Highest Average, Game
    49.0   AFC, 1974 (4)

PUNT RETURNS

Most Punt Returns, Game
    6   NFC, 1971
Fewest Punt Returns, Game
    1   NFC, 1975
       AFC, 1978
Most Punt Returns, Both Teams, Game
    10   AFC (5) vs. NFC (5), 1981
Fewest Punt Returns, Both Teams, Game
    4   AFC (1) vs. NFC (3), 1978

YARDS GAINED
Most Yards Gained, Game
    177   AFC, 1976
Fewest Yards Gained, Game
    3   AFC, 1971
Most Yards Gained, Both Teams, Game
    263   AFC (177) vs. NFC (86), 1976
Fewest Yards Gained, Both Teams, Game
    47   AFC (8) vs. NFC (39), 1978

TOUCHDOWNS
Most Touchdowns, Game
    2   NFC, 1971

KICKOFF RETURNS

Most Kickoff Returns, Game
    6   AFC, 1971
       NFC, 1972, 1974
Fewest Kickoff Returns, Game
    1   NFC, 1971
Most Kickoff Returns, Both Teams, Game
    10   AFC (5) vs. NFC (5), 1976
Fewest Kickoff Returns, Both Teams, Game
    5   NFC (2) vs AFC (3), 1979

YARDS GAINED
Most Yards Gained, Game
200   NFC, 1972
Fewest Yards Gained, Game
6   NFC; 1971
Most Yards Gained, Both Teams, Game
293   NFC (200) vs. AFC (93), 1972
Fewest Yards Gained, Both Teams, Game
108   AFC (49) vs. NFC (59), 1979

TOUCHDOWNS
Most Touchdowns, Game
0

FUMBLES

Most Fumbles, Game
10   NFC, 1974
Most Fumbles, Both Teams, Game
15   NFC (10) vs. AFC (5), 1974

RECOVERIES
Most Fumbles Recovered, Game
10   NFC, 1974 (6 own, 4 opp)
Most Fumbles Lost, Game
4   AFC, 1974

YARDS GAINED
Most Yards Gained, Game
60   AFC, 1974

TOUCHDOWNS
Most Touchdowns, Game
None

TURNOVERS
(Number of times losing the ball on interceptions and fumbles.)
Most Turnovers Game
8   AFC, 1974
Fewest Turnovers, Game
1   AFC, 1972, 1976, 1978, 1979
NFC, 1976, 1980
Most Turnovers, Both Teams, Game
12   AFC (8) vs. NFC (4), 1974
Fewest Turnovers, Both Teams, Game
2   AFC (1) vs. NFC (1), 1976

CHICAGO ALL-STAR GAME

RESULTS

Pro teams won 31, lost 9, tied 2
The game was discontinued after 1976.

Year	Date	Winner	Loser	Attendance
1976	July 23	Pittsburgh 24	All-Stars 0	52,895
1975	Aug. 1	Pittsburgh 21	All-Stars 14	54,103
1974		No game was played		
1973	July 27	Miami 14	All-Stars 3	54,103
1972	July 28	Dallas 20	All-Stars 7	54,162
1971	July 30	Baltimore 24	All-Stars 17	52,289
1970	July 31	Kansas City 24	All-Stars 3	69,940
1969	Aug. 1	N.Y. Jets 26	All-Stars 24	74,208
1968	Aug. 2	Green Bay 34	All-Stars 17	69,917
1967	Aug. 4	Green Bay 27	All-Stars 0	70,934
1966	Aug. 5	Green Bay 38	All-Stars 0	72,000
1965	Aug. 6	Cleveland 24	All-Stars 16	68,000
1964	Aug. 7	Chicago 28	All-Stars 17	65,000
1963	Aug. 2	All-Stars 20	Green Bay 17	65,000
1962	Aug. 3	Green Bay 42	All-Stars 20	65,000
1961	Aug. 4	Philadelphia 28	All-Stars 14	66,000
1960	Aug. 12	Baltimore 32	All-Stars 7	70,000
1959	Aug. 14	Baltimore 29	All-Stars 0	70,000
1958	Aug. 15	All-Stars 35	Detroit 19	70,000
1957	Aug. 9	N.Y. Giants 22	All-Stars 12	75,000
1956	Aug. 10	Cleveland 26	All-Stars 0	75,000
1955	Aug. 12	All-Stars 30	Cleveland 27	75,000
1954	Aug. 13	Detroit 31	All-Stars 6	93,470
1953	Aug. 14	Detroit 24	All-Stars 10	93,818
1952	Aug. 15	Los Angeles 10	All-Stars 7	88,316
1951	Aug. 17	Cleveland 33	All-Stars 0	92,180
1950	Aug. 11	All-Stars 17	Philadelphia 7	88,885
1949	Aug. 12	Philadelphia 38	All-Stars 0	93,780
1948	Aug. 20	Chi. Cardinals 28	All-Stars 0	101,220
1947	Aug. 22	All-Stars 16	Chi. Bears 0	105,840
1946	Aug. 23	All-Stars 16	Los Angeles 0	97,380
1945	Aug. 30	Green Bay 19	All-Stars 7	92,753
1944	Aug. 30	Chi. Bears 24	All-Stars 21	48,769
1943	Aug. 25	All-Stars 27	Washington 7	48,471
1942	Aug. 28	Chi. Bears 21	All-Stars 0	101,100
1941	Aug. 28	Chi. Bears 37	All-Stars 13	98,203
1940	Aug. 29	Green Bay 45	All-Stars 28	84,567
1939	Aug. 30	N.Y. Giants 9	All-Stars 0	81,456
1938	Aug. 31	All-Stars 28	Washington 16	74,250
1937	Sept. 1	All-Stars 6	Green Bay 0	84,560
1936	Sept. 3	All-Stars 7	Detroit 7 (tie)	76,000
1935	Aug. 29	Chi. Bears 5	All-Stars 0	77,450
1934	Aug. 31	Chi. Bears 0	All-Stars 0 (tie)	79,432

1982 ROSTER OF OFFICIALS

No.	Name	Position	College
115	Ancich, Hendi	Line Judge	Harbor College
112	Austin, Gerald	Side Judge	Western Carolina
22	Baetz, Paul	Back Judge	Heidelberg
14	Barth, Gene	Referee	St. Louis
59	Beeks, Bob	Line Judge	Lincoln
17	Bergman, Jerry	Head Linesman	Duquesne
110	Botchan, Ron	Umpire	Occidental
101	Boylston, Bob	Umpire	Alabama
43	Cashion, Red	Referee	Texas A&M
16	Cathcart, Royal	Side Judge	UC Santa Barbara
24	Clymer, Roy	Back Judge	New Mexico State
27	Conway, Al	Umpire	Army
61	Creed, Dick	Side Judge	Louisville
78	Demmas, Art	Umpire	Vanderbilt
45	DeSouza, Ron	Line Judge	Morgan State
74	Dodez, Ray	Head Linesman	Wooster
31	Dolack, Dick	Field Judge	Ferris State
6	Dooley, Tom	Referee	Virginia Military
102	Douglas, Merrill	Side Judge	Utah
5	Douglas, Ray	Back Judge	Baltimore
12	Dreith, Ben	Referee	Colorado State
33	Everett, John	Line Judge	Illinois
87	Ferguson, Dick	Side Judge	West Virginia
39	Fette, Jack	Line Judge	No College
57	Fiffick, Ed	Umpire	Marquette
111	Frantz, Earnie	Head Linesman	No College
71	Frederic, Bob	Referee	Colorado
62	Gandy, Duwayne	Side Judge	Tulsa
50	Gereb, Neil	Umpire	UC Berkeley
72	Gierke, Terry	Head Linesman	Portland State
15	Glass, Bama	Line Judge	Colorado
85	Glover, Frank	Head Linesman	Morris Brown
4	Gosier, Wilson	Line Judge	Fort Valley State
34	Graf, Fritz	Field Judge	Western Reserve
23	Grier, Johnny	Field Judge	D.C. Teachers
63	Hagerty, Ligouri	Head Linesman	Syracuse
40	Haggerty, Pat	Referee	Colorado State
96	Hakes, Don	Field Judge	Bradley
104	Hamer, Dale	Head Linesman	California State, Pa.
42	Hamilton, Dave	Umpire	Utah
105	Hantak, Dick	Back Judge	S.E. Missouri
88	Harder, Pat	Umpire	Wisconsin
66	Hawk, Dave	Side Judge	Southern Methodist
46	Heberling, Chuck	Referee	Washington & Jefferson
19	Hensley, Tom	Umpire	Tennessee
11	Jacob, Vince	Side Judge	No College
54	Johnson, Jack	Line Judge	Pacific Lutheran
114	Johnson, Tom	Head Linesman	Miami, Ohio
97	Jones, Nathan	Side Judge	Lewis & Clark
60	Jorgensen, Dick	Referee	Wisconsin
106	Jury, Al	Back Judge	San Bernardino Valley
107	Kearney, Jim	Back Judge	Pennsylvania
67	Keck, John	Umpire	Cornell College
25	Kelleher, Tom	Back Judge	Holy Cross
73	Knight, Pat	Back Judge	Southern Methodist
65	Kragseth, Norm	Head Linesman	Northwestern
120	Lane, Gary	Side Judge	Missouri

68	Leimbach, John	Umpire	Missouri
18	Lewis, Bob	Field Judge	No College
49	Look, Dean	Side Judge	Michigan State
90	Mace, Gil	Side Judge	Westminster
82	Mallette, Pat	Field Judge	Nebraska
26	Marion, Ed	Head Linesman	Pennsylvania
9	Markbreit, Jerry	Referee	Illinois
94	Marshall, Vern	Line Judge	Linfield
116	McCallum, Chuck	Field Judge	Michigan State
48	McCarter, Gordon	Referee	Western Reserve
95	McElwee, Bob	Referee	Navy
41	McKenzie, Dick	Line Judge	Ashland
108	McLaughlin, Bob	Head Linesman	Xavier
76	Merrifield, Ed	Field Judge	Missouri
35	Miles, Leo	Head Linesman	Virginia State
117	Montgomery, Ben	Line Judge	Xavier
81	Moss, Dave	Umpire	Dartmouth
55	Musser, Charley	Field Judge	North Carolina State
10	Myers, Tom	Umpire	San Jose State
83	O'Brien, Bill	Field Judge	Indiana
51	Orem, Dale	Line Judge	Louisville
77	Orr, Don	Field Judge	Vanderbilt
64	Parry, Dave	Side Judge	Wabash
44	Peters, Walt	Line Judge	Indiana State, Pa.
92	Poole, Jim	Back Judge	San Diego State
58	Quinby, Bill	Side Judge	Iowa State
53	Reynolds, Bill	Line Judge	West Chester State
80	Rice, Bob	Side Judge	Denison
98	Rosser, Jimmy	Back Judge	Auburn
29	Sanders, J.W.	Back Judge	Southern Illinois
70	Seeman, Jerry	Referee	Winona State
109	Semon, Sid	Head Linesman	Southern California
7	Silva, Fred	Referee	San Jose State
20	Sinkovitz, Frank	Umpire	Duke
3	Smith, Boyce	Line Judge	Vanderbilt
119	Spitler, Ron	Field Judge	Panhandle State
91	Stanley, Bill	Field Judge	Redlands
38	Swanson, Bill	Back Judge	Lake Forest
37	Toler, Burl	Head Linesman	San Francisco
52	Tompkins, Ben	Back Judge	Texas
32	Tunney, Jim	Referee	Occidental
93	Vaughan, Jack	Field Judge	Mississippi State
36	Veteri, Tony	Head Linesman	No College
79	Ward, Ed	Side Judge	Southern Methodist
28	Wedge, Don	Back Judge	Ohio Wesleyan
89	Wells, Gordon	Umpire	Occidental
99	Williams, Banks	Back Judge	Houston
8	Williams, Dale	Head Linesman	Cal State-Northridge
84	Wortman, Bob	Field Judge	Findlay
75	Wyant, Fred	Referee	West Virginia

FIGURING THE 1983 NFL SCHEDULE

As soon as the final game of the 1982 NFL regular season has been completed, you'll be able to determine each of the 28 NFL team's 1983 schedules.

The schedules are based on a formula initiated for the 1978 season that uses the team's won-lost-tied percentage from the current season as the primary guide.

The first item necessary is the final standings. Teams are listed by their division according to won-lost-tied percentage in 1982.

If two teams in the same division finish with identical won-lost-tied percentages, the following steps will be taken until the tie is broken:

1. Head-to-head (best won-lost-tied percentage in games between the clubs).
2. Best won-lost-tied percentage in games played within the division.
3. Best won-lost-tied percentage in games played within the conference.
4. Best won-lost-tied percentage in common games, if applicable.
5. Best net points in division games.
6. Best net points in all games.
7. Strength of schedule.
8. Best net touchdowns in all games.
9. Coin toss.

The tie-breaking procedure changes slightly if three or more clubs in the same division finish with the same won-lost-tied percentage (if two clubs remain tied after a third club is eliminated during any step, the tie-breaker reverts to Step 1 of the two-club format):

1. Head-to-head (best won-lost-tied percentage in games among the clubs).
2. Step 2 of two-club format.
3. Step 3 of two-club format
4. Best won-lost-tied percentage in common games.
5. Step 5 of two-club format.
6. Step 6 of two-club format.
7. Step 7 of two-club format.
8. Step 8 of two-club format.
9. Coin toss.

After you have the correct final standings, record them on the chart on page 394 and proceed with the scheduling.

The 16-game regular season schedule of any NFL team is determined by one of the following three formulas:

A. First- through fourth-place teams in a five-team division (AFC East and West, NFC East and Central).
   1. Home-and-home round-robin within the division (8 games).
   2. One game each with the first- through fourth-place teams in a division of the other conference. In 1983, AFC East will play

NFC West, AFC Central will play NFC Central, and AFC West will play NFC East (4 games).

3. The first-place team plays the first- and fourth-place teams in the other divisions within the conference. The second-place team plays the second- and third-place teams in the other divisions within the conference. The third-place team plays the third- and second-place teams in the other divisions within the conference. The fourth-place team plays the fourth- and first-place teams in the other divisions within the conference (4 games).

This completes the 16-game schedule.

B. First- through fourth-place teams in a four-team division (AFC Central and NFC West):

1. Home-and-home round robin within the division (6 games).
2. One game with each of the fifth-place teams in the conference (2 games).
3. The same procedure that is listed in step A2 (4 games).
4. The same procedure that is listed in step A3 (4 games).

This completes the 16-game schedule.

C. The fifth-place teams in a division (AFC East, AFC West, NFC East, NFC Central):

1. Home-and-home round robin within the division (8 games).
2. One game with each team in the four-team division of the conference (4 games).
3. A home-and-home with the other fifth-place team in the conference (2 games).
4. One game each with the fifth-place teams in the other conference (2 games).

This completes the 16-game schedule.

The "1983 Opponent Breakdown" included in the chart on page 395 does not include the round-robin games within the division. Those are automatically on a home and away basis. The dates and sites of all games will be announced by the NFL.

1982 NFL STANDINGS

AFC

EAST AE
1 _____
2 _____
3 _____
4 _____
5 _____

CENTRAL AC
1 _____
2 _____
3 _____
4 _____

WEST AW
1 _____
2 _____
3 _____
4 _____
5 _____

NFC

EAST NE
1 _____
2 _____
3 _____
4 _____
5 _____

WEST NW
1 _____
2 _____
3 _____
4 _____

CENTRAL NC
1 _____
2 _____
3 _____
4 _____
5 _____

YOUR FAVORITE TEAM'S 1983 SCHEDULE

Team Name _____

_____ _____
_____ _____
_____ _____
_____ _____
_____ _____
_____ _____
_____ _____
_____ _____

1983 OPPONENT BREAKDOWN

AFC EAST-AE

AE-1		AE-2		AE-3		AE-4		AE-5	
NW-1	NW-2	NW-1	NW-2	NW-1	NW-2	NW-1	NW-2	AC-2	AC-1
NW-3	NW-4	NW-3	NW-4	NW-3	NW-4	NW-3	NW-4	AC-4	AC-3
AC-1	AC-4	AC-2	AC-3	AC-3	AC-2	AC-4	AC-1	AW-5	AW-5
AW-4	AW-1	AW-3	AW-2	AW-2	AW-3	AW-1	AW-4	NC-5	NE-5

AFC CENTRAL-AC

AC-1		AC-2		AC-3		AC-4	
NC-1	NC-2	NC-1	NC-2	NC-1	NC-2	NC-1	NC-2
NC-3	NC-4	NC-3	NC-4	NC-3	NC-4	NC-3	NC-4
AE-4	AE-1	AE-3	AE-2	AE-2	AE-3	AE-1	AE-4
AW-1	AW-4	AW-2	AW-3	AW-3	AW-2	AW-4	AW-1
AE-5	AW-5	AW-5	AE-5	AE-5	AW-5	AW-5	AE-5

AFC WEST-AW

AW-1		AW-2		AW-3		AW-4		AW-5	
NE-1	NE-2	NE-1	NE-2	NE-1	NE-2	NE-1	NE-2	AC-1	AC-2
NE-3	NE-4	NE-3	NE-4	NE-3	NE-4	NE-3	NE-4	AC-3	AC-4
AE-1	AE-4	AE-2	AE-3	AE-3	AE-2	AE-4	AE-1	AE-5	AE-5
AC-4	AC-1	AC-3	AC-2	AC-2	AC-3	AC-1	AC-4	NE-5	NC-5

NFC EAST-NE

NE-1		NE-2		NE-3		NE-4		NE-5	
AW-1	AW-2	AW-1	AW-2	AW-1	AW-2	AW-1	AW-2	NW-2	NW-1
AW-3	AW-4	AW-3	AW-4	AW-3	AW-4	AW-3	AW-4	NW-4	NW-3
NW-1	NW-4	NW-2	NW-3	NW-3	NW-2	NW-4	NW-1	NC-5	NC-5
NC-4	NC-1	NC-3	NC-2	NC-2	NC-3	NC-1	NC-4	AE-5	AW-5

NFC CENTRAL-NC

NC-1		NC-2		NC-3		NC-4		NC-5	
AC-1	AC-2	AC-1	AC-2	AC-1	AC-2	AC-1	AC-2	NW-1	NW-2
AC-3	AC-4	AC-3	AC-4	AC-3	AC-4	AC-3	AC-4	NW-3	NW-4
NE-1	NE-4	NE-2	NE-3	NE-3	NE-2	NE-4	NE-1	NE-5	NE-5
NW-4	NW-1	NW-3	NW-2	NW-2	NW-3	NW-1	NW-4	AW-5	AE-5

NFC WEST-NW

NW-1		NW-2		NW-3		NW-4	
AE-1	AE-2	AE-1	AE-2	AE-1	AE-2	AE-1	AE-2
AE-3	AE-4	AE-3	AE-4	AE-3	AE-4	AE-3	AE-4
NE-4	NE-1	NE-3	NE-2	NE-2	NE-3	NE-1	NE-4
NC-1	NC-4	NC-2	NC-3	NC-3	NC-2	NC-4	NC-1
NE-5	NC-5	NC-5	NE-5	NE-5	NC-5	NC-5	NE-5

BALTIMORE COLTS

AFC Eastern Division
Address: P.O. Box 2000, Owings Mills, Md. 21117
Telephone: 301-356-9600
President-Treasurer: Robert Irsay
Vice President: Harriet Irsay
Vice President-General Counsel: Michael G. Chernoff
General Manager: Ernie Accorsi
Controller: Elizabeth H. Moses
Director of Player Personnel: Fred Schubach
Pro Personnel Director: Bob Terpening
Head Coach: Frank Kush
Assistant Coaches: Zeke Bratkowski, Bud Carson, Gunther Cunningham,
  Hal Hunter, Richard Mann, Roger Theder, Bob Valesente, Rick Venturi,
  Mike Westhoff
Public Relations Director: Walt Gutowski
Marketing Coordinator: Marty Goldman
Assistant Public Relations Director: Marge Blatt
Community Relations Director: Lenny Moore
Administrative Assistant: Greg Gladysiewski
Assistant Business Manager: James Irsay
Ticket Manager: Bill Roberts **Assistant:** Carol Martin
Trainer Emeritus: Ed Block
Trainer: John Lopez **Assistant Trainer:** John Kasik
Equipment Manager: Rex Patterson
Stadium: Memorial Stadium (60,714) **Surface:** Grass
Stadium Address: 33rd and Ellerslie Streets, Baltimore, Md. 21218
Colors: Royal Blue, White & Silver
Training Camp: Goucher College, Towson, Md. 21204

1982 SCHEDULE

Preseason

Aug. 7	vs. Minnesota at Canton, OH (HOF)	1:30
Aug. 14	**New York Giants**	8:00
Aug. 21	vs. Atlanta (Tempe, Arizona)	8:00
Aug. 28	at Pittsburgh	6:00
Sept. 4	at Chicago	6:00

Regular Season

Sept. 12	**New England**	2:00
Sept. 19	at Miami	4:00
Sept. 26	**New York Jets**	4:00
Oct. 3	at Detroit	1:00
Oct. 10	**Buffalo**	2:00
Oct. 17	at Cleveland	1:00
Oct. 24	**Miami**	2:00
Oct. 31	**Tampa Bay**	2:00
Nov. 7	at New England	1:00
Nov. 14	**Oakland**	2:00
Nov. 21	at New York Jets	1:00
Nov. 28	at Buffalo	1:00
Dec. 5	**Cincinnati**	2:00
Dec. 12	at Minnesota	12:00
Dec. 19	**Green Bay**	2:00
Dec. 26	at San Diego	1:00

BUFFALO BILLS

AFC Eastern Division
Address: One Bills Drive, Orchard Park, N.Y. 14127
Telephone: 716-648-1800
President: Ralph C. Wilson, Jr.
Vice President in Charge of Administration: Stew Barber
Vice President: Patrick J. McGroder, Jr.
Vice President in Charge of Football Operations and Head Coach: Chuck Knox
Assistant Coaches: Tom Catlin, Jack Donaldson, George Dyer, Chick Harris, Ralph Hawkins, Miller McCalmon, Steve Moore, Ray Prochaska, Kay Stephenson
Director of College Scouting: Norm Pollom
Vice President-Public Relations: L. Budd Thalman
Ticket Director: Jim Cipriano
Assistant Public Relations Director: Dave Senko
Trainers: Ed Abramoski, Bud Tice
Stadium: Rich Stadium (80,020) **Surface:** AstroTurf
Stadium Address: One Bills Drive, Orchard Park, N.Y. 14127
Colors: Scarlet Red, Royal Blue, White
Training Camp: Fredonia State University College, Fredonia, N. Y. 14063

1982 SCHEDULE

Preseason

Aug. 14	at Dallas	8:00
Aug. 21	**Chicago**	6:00
Aug. 27	at Washington	7:30
Sept. 4	**Detroit**	6:00

Regular Season

Sept. 12	**Kansas City**	1:00
Sept. 16	**Minnesota** (Thursday)	8:30
Sept. 26	at Houston	12:00
Oct. 3	**New England**	1:00
Oct. 10	at Baltimore	2:00
Oct. 18	at New York Jets (Monday)	9:00
Oct. 24	**Detroit**	1:00
Oct. 31	at Denver	2:00
Nov. 7	**New York Jets**	4:00
Nov. 14	at New England	1:00
Nov. 21	**Miami**	1:00
Nov. 28	**Baltimore**	1:00
Dec. 5	vs. Green Bay (Milwaukee)	12:00
Dec. 12	**Pittsburgh**	1:00
Dec. 19	at Tampa Bay	1:00
Dec. 27	at Miami (Monday)	9:00

CINCINNATI BENGALS

AFC Central Division
Address: 200 Riverfront Stadium, Cincinnati, Ohio 45202
Telephone: 513-621-3550
President: John Sawyer
General Manager: Paul E. Brown
Head Coach: Forrest Gregg
Assistant Coaches: Hank Bullough, Bruce Coslet, Lindy Infante,
  Dick LeBeau, Jim McNally, Dick Modzelewski, George Sefcik, Kim Wood
Assistant General Manager: Michael Brown
Business Manager: John Murdough
Director of Public Relations: Allan Heim
Director of Player Personnel: Pete Brown
Ticket Manager: Bill Hedgecock
Trainer: Marv Pollins
Equipment Manager: Tom Gray
Stadium: Riverfront Stadium (59,754) **Surface:** AstroTurf
Stadium Address: 200 Riverfront Stadium, Cincinnati, Ohio 45202
Colors: Orange, Black, White
Training Camp: Wilmington College, Wilmington, Ohio 45177

1982 SCHEDULE

Preseason

Aug. 13	at Kansas City	7:35
Aug. 20	vs. Green Bay (Milwaukee)	7:30
Aug. 28	**Detroit**	7:00
Sept. 3	**Washington**	7:30

Regular Season

Sept. 12	**Houston**	1:00
Sept. 19	at Pittsburgh	1:00
Sept. 27	at Cleveland (Monday)	9:00
Oct. 3	**Miami**	1:00
Oct. 10	at New England	1:00
Oct. 17	at New York Giants	1:00
Oct. 24	**Dallas**	9:00
Oct. 31	**Pittsburgh**	1:00
Nov. 7	**Washington**	1:00
Nov. 14	at Houston	12:00
Nov. 21	at Philadelphia	1:00
Nov. 28	**Oakland**	1:00
Dec. 5	at Baltimore	2:00
Dec. 12	**Cleveland**	1:00
Dec. 20	at San Diego (Monday)	6:00
Dec. 26	**Seattle**	1:00

CLEVELAND BROWNS

AFC Central Division
Address: Tower B, Cleveland Stadium, Cleveland, Ohio 44114
Telephone: 216-696-5555
President: Arthur B. Modell
Assistant to the President: Paul Warfield
Vice President-Director of Public Relations: Nate Wallack
Vice President and General Counsel: James N. Bailey
Treasurer-Controller: Gordon Helms
Director of Operations: Denny Lynch
Director of Publicity: Kevin Byrne
Director of Programs and Promotions: John Minco
Head Coach: Sam Rutigliano
Assistant Coaches: Dave Adolph, Len Fontes, Jim Garrett, Paul Hackett, Rod Humenuik, Rich Kotite, John Petercuskie, Tom Pratt, Dave Redding, Joe Scannella, Marty Schottenheimer
Director of Player Personnel: Bill Davis
Director of Pro Scouting: Alan Webb
Special Scouts: Dave Beckman, Chuck Garcia, Tom Heckert, Tim Miner, Mike Nixon
Film Coordinator: Ed Ulinski
Ticket Director: Bill Breit
Trainer: Leo Murphy
Equipment Manager: Charles Cusick
Stadium: Cleveland Stadium (80,322) **Surface:** Grass
Stadium Address: West 3rd Street, Cleveland, Ohio 44114
Colors: Seal Brown, Orange, White
Training Camp: Lakeland Community College, Mentor, Ohio 44094

1982 SCHEDULE

Preseason

Aug. 14	at Detroit	7:00
Aug. 19	**Los Angeles**	7:30
Aug. 28	at New Orleans	7:00
Sept. 4	at Oakland	6:00

Regular Season

Sept. 12	at Seattle	1:00
Sept. 19	**Philadelphia**	1:00
Sept. 27	**Cincinnati** (Monday)	9:00
Oct. 3	at Washington	1:00
Oct. 10	at Oakland	1:00
Oct. 17	**Baltimore**	1:00
Oct. 24	at Pittsburgh	1:00
Oct. 31	**Houston**	1:00
Nov. 7	**New York Giants**	1:00
Nov. 14	at Miami	4:00
Nov. 21	**New England**	1:00
Nov. 25	at Dallas (Thanksgiving)	3:00
Dec. 5	**San Diego**	1:00
Dec. 12	at Cincinnati	1:00
Dec. 19	**Pittsburgh**	1:00
Dec. 26	at Houston	12:00

DENVER BRONCOS

AFC Western Division
Address: 5700 Logan Street, Denver, Colo. 80216
Telephone: 303-623-8778
Chairman of the Board: Edgar F. Kaiser, Jr.
General Manager: Grady Alderman
Director of Player Personnel: John Beake
Coordinator of College Scouting: Carroll Hardy
Head Coach: Dan Reeves
Assistant Coaches: Marvin Bass, Joe Collier, Rod Dowhower, Jerry Frei, Stan Jones, Richie McCabe, Nick Nicolau, Fran Polsfoot, Bob Zeman
Director of Public Relations: Charlie Lee
Publicity Director: Jim Saccomano
Assistant to the Chairman of the Board: Rick Schloss
Treasurer: Robert M. Hurley
Ticket Manager: Gail Stuckey
Equipment Manager: Larry Elliott
Trainer: Steve Antonopulos
Stadium: Denver Mile High Stadium (75,123) **Surface:** Grass (PAT)
Stadium Address: 1900 West Eliot, Denver, Colo. 80204
Colors: Orange, Blue, White
Training Camp: University of Northern Colorado, Greeley, Colo. 80521

1982 SCHEDULE

Preseason

Aug. 14	at Los Angeles	7:00
Aug. 21	**Miami**	7:00
Aug. 28	**Minnesota**	7:00
Sept. 4	vs. New York Jets (Giants Stadium)	8:00

Regular Season

Sept. 12	**San Diego**	2:00
Sept. 19	**San Francisco**	2:00
Sept. 26	at New Orleans	12:00
Oct. 3	**Pittsburgh**	2:00
Oct. 10	at New York Jets	4:00
Oct. 17	at Houston	12:00
Oct. 24	**Oakland**	2:00
Oct. 31	**Buffalo**	2:00
Nov. 7	at Seattle	1:00
Nov. 14	at Kansas City	12:00
Nov. 21	**Seattle**	2:00
Nov. 28	at San Diego	1:00
Dec. 5	**Atlanta**	2:00
Dec. 12	at Los Angeles	1:00
Dec. 19	**Kansas City**	2:00
Dec. 26	at Oakland	1:00

HOUSTON OILERS

AFC Central Division
Address: Box 1516, Houston, Tex. 77001
Telephone: 713-797-9111
President: K. S. (Bud) Adams, Jr.
Executive Vice President-General Manager: Ladd K. Herzeg
Assistant General Manager: Mike Holovak
Head Coach: Ed Biles
Assistant Coaches: Andy Bourgeois, Ray Callahan, Bob Gambold, Ken
 Houston, Elijah Pitts, Dick Selcer, Jim Shofner
Marketing Director: Rick Nichols
Media Relations Director: Bob Hyde
Business Manager: Lewis Mangum
Ticket Coordinator: David Fuqua
Head Trainer: Jerry Meins
Assistant Trainer: Joel Krekelberg
Strength & Conditioning Coach: Bill Allerheligen
Equipment Manager: Gordon Batty
Stadium: Astrodome (Baseball Configuration—47,690,
 Football Configuration—50,496) **Surface:** AstroTurf
Stadium Address: Loop 610, Kirby and Fannin Streets, Houston, Tex. 77202
Colors: Scarlet, Columbia Blue, White
Training Camp: Angelo State University, San Angelo, Tex. 76901

1982 SCHEDULE

Preseason

Aug. 12	**New Orleans**	7:00
Aug. 22	**New York Jets**	12:00
Aug. 28	**Tampa Bay**	8:00
Sept. 4	at Dallas	8:00

Regular Season

Sept. 12	at Cincinnati	1:00
Sept. 19	**Seattle**	3:00
Sept. 26	**Buffalo**	12:00
Oct. 3	at New York Jets	1:00
Oct. 10	at Kansas City	12:00
Oct. 17	**Denver**	12:00
Oct. 24	**Washington**	12:00
Oct. 31	at Cleveland	1:00
Nov. 7	at Pittsburgh	1:00
Nov. 14	**Cincinnati**	12:00
Nov. 21	**Pittsburgh**	12:00
Nov. 28	at New England	1:00
Dec. 5	at New York Giants	1:00
Dec. 13	**Dallas** (Monday)	8:00
Dec. 19	at Philadelphia	1:00
Dec. 26	**Cleveland**	12:00

KANSAS CITY CHIEFS

AFC Western Division
Address: One Arrowhead Drive, Kansas City, Mo. 64129
Telephone: 816-924-9300
Owner: Lamar Hunt
President: Jack Steadman
Vice President and General Manager: Jim Schaaf
Head Coach: Marv Levy
Assistant Coaches: Rick Abernethy, Tom Bresnahan, Ted Cottrell,
   Walt Corey, Kay Dalton, Frank Gansz, J. D. Helm, Don Lawrence, Rod Rust
Director of Player Personnel: Les Miller
Director of Research & Development: Ron Waller
Treasurer: Roger Peyton
Secretary: Jim Seigfried
Stadium Manager: Bob Wachter
Ticket Manager: Joe Mazza
Public Relations Director: Bob Sprenger
Assistant Director of Public Relations: Gary Heise
Promotions Director: Russ Cline
Director of Sales: David Smith
Trainer: Wayne Rudy
Assistant Trainer: Dave Kendall
Equipment Manager: Bobby Yarborough
Stadium: Arrowhead (78,067)   **Surface:** Tartan Turf
Stadium Address: One Arrowhead Drive, Arrowhead Stadium, Kansas City,
   Mo. 64129
Colors: Red, Gold
Training Camp: William Jewell College, Liberty, Mo. 64068

1982 SCHEDULE

Preseason

Aug. 13	**Cincinnati**	7:35
Aug. 21	at New Orleans	7:00
Aug. 28	**Miami**	7:35
Sept. 4	at St. Louis	6:00

Regular Season

Sept. 12	at Buffalo	1:00
Sept. 19	**San Diego**	12:00
Sept. 23	**Atlanta** (Thursday)	7:30
Oct. 3	at Seattle	1:00
Oct. 10	**Houston**	12:00
Oct. 17	at San Diego	1:00
Oct. 24	**New York Jets**	12:00
Oct. 31	**Seattle**	12:00
Nov. 7	at Oakland	1:00
Nov. 14	**Denver**	12:00
Nov. 21	at New Orleans	12:00
Nov. 28	at Los Angeles	1:00
Dec. 5	at Pittsburgh	1:00
Dec. 12	**Oakland**	3:00
Dec. 19	at Denver	2:00
Dec. 26	**San Francisco**	12:00

MIAMI DOLPHINS

AFC Eastern Division
Address: 3550 Biscayne Boulevard, Miami, Fla. 33137
Telephone: 305-576-1000
President: Joseph Robbie
Vice President-General Manager: J. Michael Robbie
Vice President-Head Coach: Don Shula
Vice President: Joe Thomas
Director of Player Personnel: Chuck Connor
Director of Pro Personnel: Charley Winner
Assistant Director of Player Personnel: Steve Crosby
Assistant Coaches: Bill Arnsparger, Steve Crosby, Wally English, Tom Keane, John Sandusky, Mike Scarry, Carl Taseff
Director of Public Relations: Bob Kearney
Ticket Director: Gordon Cramer
Controller: Howard F. Rieman
Trainers: Bob Lundy, Junior Wade
Equipment Manager: Danny Dowe
Stadium: Orange Bowl (75,459) **Surface:** Grass (PAT)
Stadium Address: 1501 N.W. Third Street, Miami, Fla. 33125
Colors: Aqua, Orange
Training Center: 16400-D N.W. 32nd Avenue, Miami, Fla. 33054

1982 SCHEDULE

Preseason

Aug. 14	**Washington**	8:00
Aug. 21	at Denver	7:00
Aug. 28	at Kansas City	7:35
Sept. 3	**New York Giants**	8:00

Regular Season

Sept. 12	at New York Jets	4:00
Sept. 19	**Baltimore**	4:00
Sept. 26	at Green Bay	12:00
Oct. 3	at Cincinnati	1:00
Oct. 10	**Detroit**	4:00
Oct. 17	**New England**	1:00
Oct. 24	at Baltimore	2:00
Oct. 31	at Oakland	1:00
Nov. 8	**San Diego** (Monday)	9:00
Nov. 14	**Cleveland**	4:00
Nov. 21	at Buffalo	1:00
Nov. 29	at Tampa Bay (Monday)	9:00
Dec. 5	**Minnesota**	1:00
Dec. 12	at New England	1:00
Dec. 18	**New York Jets** (Saturday)	12:30
Dec. 27	**Buffalo** (Monday)	9:00

NEW ENGLAND PATRIOTS

AFC Eastern Division
Address: Schaefer Stadium, Route 1, Foxboro, Mass. 02035
Telephone: 617-543-7911
President: William H. Sullivan, Jr.
Executive Vice President: Charles W. Sullivan
General Manager: Francis J. (Bucko) Kilroy
Assistant General Manager: Patrick Sullivan
Director of Player Development: Dick Steinberg
Executive Director of Player Personnel: Darryl Stingley
Head Coach: Ron Meyer
Assistant Coaches: Tommy Brasher, Cleve Bryant, LeBaron Caruthers,
  Steve Endicott, Lew Erber, Jim Mora, Bill Muir, Dante Scarnecchia,
  Steve Sidwell, Steve Walters
Director Marketing: Miceal Chamberlain
Director Media Relations: Tom Hoffman
Director, Pro Scouting: Bill McPeak
Director, Public Affairs: Claudia Smith
Personnel Scouts: George Blackburn, Joe Mendes, Pat Naughton,
  Bob Teahan
Stadium Manager: Billy Sullivan III
Film Manager: Ken Deininger
Ticket Manager: Kevin Fitzgerald
Assistant Director, Media Relations: Dave Wintergrass
Trainer: Tom Healion
Equipment Manager: George Luongo
Stadium: Schaefer Stadium (61,297)   **Surface:** Super Turf
Stadium Address: Route 1, Foxboro, Mass. 02035
Colors: Red, Blue, White
Training Camp: Bryant College, Smithfield, R.I. 02917

1982 SCHEDULE

Preseason

Aug. 14	vs. Pittsburgh (Knoxville)	7:30
Aug. 20	at Philadelphia	6:00
Aug. 28	at Dallas	8:00
Sept. 4	**Green Bay**	1:00

Regular Season

Sept. 12	at Baltimore	2:00
Sept. 19	**New York Jets**	1:00
Sept. 26	**Seattle**	1:00
Oct. 3	at Buffalo	1:00
Oct. 10	**Cincinnati**	1:00
Oct. 17	at Miami	1:00
Oct. 24	**St. Louis**	1:00
Oct. 31	at New York Jets	1:00
Nov. 7	**Baltimore**	1:00
Nov. 14	**Buffalo**	1:00
Nov. 21	at Cleveland	1:00
Nov. 28	**Houston**	1:00
Dec. 5	at Chicago	12:00
Dec. 12	**Miami**	1:00
Dec. 19	at Seattle	1:00
Dec. 26	at Pittsburgh	1:00

NEW YORK JETS

AFC Eastern Division
Address: 598 Madison Avenue, New York, N.Y. 10022
Telephone: 212-421-6600
Chairman of the Board: Leon Hess
President-Chief Operating Officer: Jim Kensil
Secretary and Administrative Manager: Steve Gutman
Head Coach: Walt Michaels
Assistant Coaches: Bill Baird, Ralph Baker, Bob Fry, Joe Gardi,
  Bob Ledbetter, Pete McCulley, Larry Pasquale, Dan Sekanovich,
  Joe Walton
Director of Public Relations: Frank Ramos
Assistant Director of Public Relations: Ron Cohen
Director of Facilities Operation: Tim Davey
Traveling Secretary: Mike Kensil
Ticket Manager: Bob Parente
Director of Player Personnel: Mike Hickey
Pro Personnel Director: Jim Royer
Talent Scouts: Joe Collins, Don Grammer, Sid Hall, Marv Sunderland
Film Director: Jim Pons
Trainer: Bob Reese
Assistant Trainer: Pepper Burruss
Equipment Manager: Bill Hampton
Stadium: Shea Stadium (60,372) **Surface:** Grass
Stadium Address: Flushing, N.Y. 11368
Colors: Kelly Green, White
Training Center: 1000 Fulton Avenue, Hempstead, N.Y. 11550
Telephone: 516-538-6600

1982 SCHEDULE

Preseason

Aug. 14	at Green Bay	7:00
Aug. 22	at Houston	12:00
Aug. 28	at New York Giants	8:00
Sept. 4	**Denver** (Giants Stadium)	8:00

Regular Season

Sept. 12	**Miami**	4:00
Sept. 19	at New England	1:00
Sept. 26	at Baltimore	4:00
Oct. 3	**Houston**	1:00
Oct. 10	**Denver**	4:00
Oct. 18	**Buffalo** (Monday)	9:00
Oct. 24	at Kansas City	12:00
Oct. 31	**New England**	1:00
Nov. 7	at Buffalo	4:00
Nov. 14	at Pittsburgh	1:00
Nov. 21	**Baltimore**	1:00
Nov. 28	**Green Bay**	1:00
Dec. 6	at Detroit (Monday)	9:00
Dec. 12	**Tampa Bay**	1:00
Dec. 18	at Miami (Saturday)	12:30
Dec. 26	at Minnesota	12:00

OAKLAND RAIDERS

AFC Western Division
Address: 7850 Edgewater Drive, Oakland, Calif. 94621
Telephone: 415-562-5900
General Partners: Al Davis, E. W. McGah
Managing General Partner: Al Davis
Executive Assistant: Al LoCasale
Director of Operations: Ron Wolf
Head Coach: Tom Flores
Assistant Coaches: Sam Boghosian, Willie Brown, Chet Franklin,
   Larry Kennan, Earl Leggett, Charlie Sumner, Tom Walsh, Ray Willsey
Director of Player Personnel: Bob Mischak
Director of College Personnel: Tom Grimes
Director of Pro Personnel: Steve Ortmayer
Pro Scout: Joe Madro
Business Manager: Ken LaRue
Publications Director: Bill Glazier
Ticket Manager: George Glace
Controller: Steve Ballard
Trainer: George Anderson
Equipment Manager: Richard Romanski
Stadium: Oakland-Alameda County Coliseum (54,615)   **Surface:** Grass
Stadium Address: Hegenberger Road and Nimitz Freeway,
   Oakland, Calif. 94621
Colors: Silver, Black
Training Camp: El Rancho Tropicana, Santa Rosa, Calif. 95401

1982 SCHEDULE

Preseason

Aug. 14	at San Francisco	12:00
Aug. 21	at Detroit	7:00
Aug. 28	**Green Bay**	6:00
Sept. 4	**Cleveland**	6:00

Regular Season

Sept. 12	at San Francisco	1:00
Sept. 19	at Atlanta	1:00
Sept. 26	at San Diego	1:00
Oct. 3	**New Orleans**	1:00
Oct. 10	**Cleveland**	1:00
Oct. 17	at Seattle	1:00
Oct. 24	at Denver	2:00
Oct. 31	**Miami**	1:00
Nov. 7	**Kansas City**	1:00
Nov. 14	at Baltimore	2:00
Nov. 22	**San Diego** (Monday)	6:00
Nov. 28	at Cincinnati	1:00
Dec. 5	**Seattle**	1:00
Dec. 12	at Kansas City	3:00
Dec. 18	**Los Angeles** (Saturday)	1:00
Dec. 26	**Denver**	1:00

PITTSBURGH STEELERS

AFC Central Division
Address: Three Rivers Stadium, 300 Stadium Circle, Pittsburgh, Pa. 15212
Telephone: 412-323-1200
Chairman of the Board: Arthur J. Rooney, Sr.
President: Daniel M. Rooney
Vice President: John R. McGinley
Vice President: Arthur J. Rooney, Jr.
Head Coach: Chuck Noll
Assistant Coaches: Rollie Dotsch, Tony Dungy, Dick Hoak, Jon Kolb,
   Tom Moore, George Perles, Woody Widenhofer
Director of Public Relations: Ed Kiely
Traveling Secretary: Jim Boston
Controller: Dennis P. Thimons
Publicity Director: Joe Gordon
Assistant Publicity Director: John Evenson
Director of Player Personnel: Dick Haley
Assistant Director of Player Personnel: William Nunn, Jr.
Talent Scout-West Coast: Bob Schmitz
Pro Talent Scout: Tom Modrak
College Talent Scout: Joe Krupa
Director of Ticket Sales: Geraldine R. Glenn
Trainer: Ralph Berlin
Equipment Manager: Anthony Parisi
Stadium: Three Rivers Stadium (54,000)   **Surface:** Tartan Turf
Stadium Address: 300 Stadium Circle, Pittsburgh, Pa. 15212
Colors: Black, Gold
Training Camp: St. Vincent College, Latrobe, Pa. 15650

1982 SCHEDULE

Preseason

Aug. 14	vs. New England (Knoxville)	7:30
Aug. 21	at New York Giants	8:00
Aug. 28	**Baltimore**	6:00
Sept. 4	**Philadelphia**	6:00

Regular Season

Sept. 13	at Dallas (Monday)	8:00
Sept. 19	**Cincinnati**	1:00
Sept. 26	**New York Giants**	1:00
Oct. 3	at Denver	2:00
Oct. 11	**Philadelphia** (Monday)	9:00
Oct. 17	at Washington	1:00
Oct. 24	**Cleveland**	1:00
Oct. 31	at Cincinnati	1:00
Nov. 7	**Houston**	1:00
Nov. 14	**New York Jets**	1:00
Nov. 21	at Houston	12:00
Nov. 28	at Seattle	1:00
Dec. 5	**Kansas City**	1:00
Dec. 12	at Buffalo	1:00
Dec. 19	at Cleveland	1:00
Dec. 26	**New England**	1:00

SAN DIEGO CHARGERS

AFC Western Division
Address: San Diego Jack Murphy Stadium, P.O. Box 20666,
  San Diego, Calif. 92120
Telephone: 714-280-2111
President: Eugene V. Klein
General Manager: John R. Sanders
Assistant General Manager: Paul (Tank) Younger
Assistant to the President: Jack Teele
Head Coach: Don Coryell
Assistant Coaches: Tom Bass, Marv Braden, Earnel Durden, Dave Levy,
  Jerry Smith, Jim Wagstaff, Larrye Weaver, Chuck Weber, Ernie Zampese
Administrative Assistant, Player Personnel: John Trump
Chief Scout: Aubrey (Red) Phillips
Director of Public Relations: Rick Smith
Business Manager: Pat Curran
Director of Advertising/Promotions: Rich Israel
Assistant Director of Public Relations: Rodney Knox
Director of Ticket Operations: Gary McCauley
Controller: Frances Beede
Trainer: Ric McDonald
Equipment Manager: Sid Brooks
Stadium: San Diego Jack Murphy Stadium (52,675) **Surface:** Grass
Stadium Address: 9449 Friars Road, San Diego, Calif. 92108
Colors: Blue, Gold, White
Training Camp: University of California-San Diego, La Jolla, Calif. 92037

1982 SCHEDULE

Preseason

Aug. 16	**Chicago**	7:00
Aug. 21	**Dallas**	6:00
Aug. 28	**San Francisco**	6:00
Sept. 4	at Los Angeles	7:00

Regular Season

Sept. 12	at Denver	2:00
Sept. 19	at Kansas City	12:00
Sept. 26	**Oakland**	1:00
Oct. 3	at Atlanta	1:00
Oct. 10	**Seattle**	1:00
Oct. 17	**Kansas City**	1:00
Oct. 24	at Seattle	1:00
Oct. 31	**Los Angeles**	1:00
Nov. 8	at Miami (Monday)	9:00
Nov. 14	**New Orleans**	1:00
Nov. 22	at Oakland (Monday)	6:00
Nov. 28	**Denver**	1:00
Dec. 5	at Cleveland	1:00
Dec. 11	at San Francisco (Saturday)	1:00
Dec. 20	**Cincinnati** (Monday)	6:00
Dec. 26	**Baltimore**	1:00

SEATTLE SEAHAWKS

AFC Western Division
Address: 5305 Lake Washington Boulevard, Kirkland, Wash. 98033
Telephone: 206-827-9777
Majority Ownership: Elmer J. Nordstrom, Representative
General Manager: John Thompson
Assistant General Manager: Mark Duncan
Head Coach: Jack Patera
Assistant Coaches: Jack Christiansen, Andy MacDonald, Frank Lauterbur, Howard Mudd, Jerry Rhome, Jackie Simpson, Rusty Tillman
Director of Football Operations: Mike McCormack
Director of Non-Football Operations: Don H. Andersen
Publicity Director: Gary Wright
Director of Player Personnel: Dick Mansperger
Director of Pro Scouting: Chuck Allen
Business Manager: Bob Anderson
Ticket Manager: James Nagaoka
Assistant to the General Manager: Mike Keller
Trainers: Bruce Scott, Jim Whitesel
Equipment Managers: Walt Loeffler, Terry Sinclair
Stadium: Kingdome (64,757) **Surface:** AstroTurf
Stadium Address: 201 South King Street, Seattle, Wash. 98104
Colors: Blue, Green, Silver
Training Camp: Eastern Washington University, Cheney, Wash. 99004

1982 SCHEDULE

Preseason

Aug. 13	**St. Louis**	7:30
Aug. 21	at Minnesota	7:30
Aug. 28	at Los Angeles	7:00
Sept. 3	**San Francisco**	7:30

Regular Season

Sept. 12	**Cleveland**	1:00
Sept. 19	at Houston	3:00
Sept. 26	at New England	1:00
Oct. 3	**Kansas City**	1:00
Oct. 10	at San Diego	1:00
Oct. 17	**Oakland**	1:00
Oct. 24	**San Diego**	1:00
Oct. 31	at Kansas City	12:00
Nov. 7	**Denver**	1:00
Nov. 14	at St. Louis	12:00
Nov. 21	at Denver	2:00
Nov. 28	**Pittsburgh**	1:00
Dec. 5	at Oakland	1:00
Dec. 12	**Chicago**	1:00
Dec. 19	**New England**	1:00
Dec. 26	at Cincinnati	1:00

ATLANTA FALCONS

NFC Western Division
Address: Suwanee Road at I-85, Suwanee, Ga. 30174
Telephone: 404-588-1111
Chairman of the Board: Rankin M. Smith, Sr.
President: Rankin Smith, Jr.
Executive Vice President: Eddie LeBaron
General Manager: Tom Braatz
Corporate Secretary: Taylor Smith
Chief Financial Officer: Jim Hay
Head Coach: Leeman Bennett
Assistant Coaches: Jerry Glanville, Mike McDonnell, Wayne McDuffie, John North, Jimmy Raye, Doug Shively, Jim Stanley, Bill Walsh, Dick Wood
Director of Pro Personnel: Bill Jobko
Ticket Manager: Bill Brokaw
Assistant Ticket Manager: Ken Grantham
Public Relations Director: Charlie Dayton
Assistant Public Relations Director: Bob Dickinson
Head Trainer: Jerry Rhea
Assistant Trainer: J. L. Shoop
Equipment Manager: Whitey Zimmerman
Scouts: Bob Cegelski, John Jelacic, Bob Riggle, Bill Striegel
Assistant Equipment Manager: Horace Daniel
Stadium: Atlanta-Fulton County Stadium (60,748) **Surface:** Grass
Stadium Address: 521 Capitol Avenue S.W., Atlanta, Ga. 30312
Colors: Red, Black, White, Silver
Training Camp: Suwanee Road at I-85, Suwanee, Ga. 30174

1982 SCHEDULE

Preseason

Aug. 14	**Minnesota**	8:00
Aug. 21	vs. Baltimore (Tempe, Arizona)	8:00
Aug. 27	**Philadelphia**	8:30
Sept. 3	at Tampa Bay	7:00

Regular Season

Sept. 12	at New York Giants	1:00
Sept. 19	**Oakland**	1:00
Sept. 23	at Kansas City (Thursday)	7:30
Oct. 3	**San Diego**	1:00
Oct. 10	at Los Angeles	1:00
Oct. 17	at Detroit	1:00
Oct. 24	**San Francisco**	1:00
Oct. 31	at New Orleans	12:00
Nov. 7	at Chicago	12:00
Nov. 15	**Philadelphia** (Monday)	9:00
Nov. 21	**Los Angeles**	1:00
Nov. 28	**St. Louis**	1:00
Dec. 5	at Denver	2:00
Dec. 12	**New Orleans**	4:00
Dec. 19	at San Francisco	6:00
Dec. 26	**Green Bay**	1:00

CHICAGO BEARS

NFC Central Division
Corporate Headquarters and Tickets Address: 55 E. Jackson Blvd.,
 Chicago, Ill. 60604
Halas Hall (Coaching Staff, Personnel, Public Relations): 250 N.
 Washington, Lake Forest, Ill. 60045
Telephone: 312-663-5100 (Administrative, Tickets), 312-295-6600
 (Halas Hall)
Chairman of the Board, President, CEO: George S. Halas
Executive Vice President-General Manager: Jim Finks
Vice President: Ed McCaskey
Head Coach: Mike Ditka
Assistant Coaches: Jim Dooley, Dale Haupt, Ed Hughes, Hank Kuhlmann,
 Jim LaRue, Ted Plumb, Buddy Ryan, Dick Stanfel
Assistant to General Manager: Bill McGrane
Director, Collegiate Scouting: Jim Parmer
Director, Pro Scouting: Bill Tobin
Stadium Operations-Admissions Director: George Arneson
Business Manager: Rudy Custer
Treasurer: Jerry Vainisi
Public Relations Director: Patrick McCaskey
Film Director: Mitch Friedman
Trainer: Fred Caito
Physical Coordinator: Clyde Emrich
Equipment Manager: Ray Earley
Stadium: Soldier Field.(65,077) **Surface:** AstroTurf
Stadium Address: 425 McFetridge Place, Chicago, Ill. 60605
Colors: Burnt Orange, Navy Blue, White
Training Camp: Halas Hall, Lake Forest, Ill. 60045

1982 SCHEDULE

Preseason

Aug. 16	at San Diego	7:00
Aug. 21	at Buffalo	6:00
Aug. 28	**St. Louis**	6:00
Sept. 4	**Baltimore**	6:00

Regular Season

Sept. 12	at Detroit	1:00
Sept. 19	**New Orleans**	12:00
Sept. 26	at San Francisco	1:00
Oct. 3	**Minnesota**	12:00
Oct. 10	**Green Bay**	12:00
Oct. 17	at St. Louis	12:00
Oct. 24	**Tampa Bay**	12:00
Oct. 31	at Green Bay	12:00
Nov. 7	**Atlanta**	12:00
Nov. 14	at Tampa Bay	1:00
Nov. 21	**Detroit**	12:00
Nov. 28	at Minnesota	12:00
Dec. 5	**New England**	12:00
Dec. 12	at Seattle	1:00
Dec. 19	**St. Louis**	12:00
Dec. 26	at Los Angeles	1:00

DALLAS COWBOYS

NFC Eastern Division
Address: 6116 North Central Expressway, Dallas, Tex. 75206
Telephone: 214-369-8000
Chairman of the Board: Clint W. Murchison, Jr.
President-General Manager: Texas E. Schramm
Head Coach: Tom Landry
Assistant Coaches: Ermal Allen, Neill Armstrong, Al Lavan, Alan Lowry,
  John Mackovic, Jim Myers (assistant head coach), Dick Nolan,
  Gene Stallings, Ernie Stautner, Jerry Tubbs, Bob Ward
Vice President-Personnel Development: Gil Brandt
Vice President-Treasurer: Don Wilson
Vice President-Administration: Joe Bailey
Administrative Assistant: Dan Werner
Director of Public Relations: Doug Todd
Assistant Public Relations Director: Greg Aiello
Ticket Manager: Kay Lang
Trainers: Don Cochren, Ken Locker
Equipment Manager: William T. (Buck) Buchanan
Cheerleaders Director: Suzanne Mitchell
Stadium: Texas Stadium (65,101) **Surface:** Texas Turf
Stadium Address: Irving, Tex. 75062
Colors: Royal Blue, Metallic Blue, White
Training Camp: California Lutheran, Thousand Oaks, Calif. 91360

1982 SCHEDULE

Preseason

Aug. 14	**Buffalo**	8:00
Aug. 21	at San Diego	6:00
Aug. 28	**New England**	8:00
Sept. 4	**Houston**	8:00

Regular Season

Sept. 13	**Pittsburgh** (Monday)	8:00
Sept. 19	at St. Louis	12:00
Sept. 26	at Minnesota	12:00
Oct. 3	**New York Giants**	3:00
Oct. 10	**Washington**	12:00
Oct. 17	at Philadelphia	4:00
Oct. 24	at Cincinnati	9:00
Oct. 31	at New York Giants	4:00
Nov. 7	**St. Louis**	12:00
Nov. 14	at San Francisco	1:00
Nov. 21	**Tampa Bay**	12:00
Nov. 25	**Cleveland** (Thanksgiving)	3:00
Dec. 5	at Washington	4:00
Dec. 13	at Houston (Monday)	8:00
Dec. 19	**New Orleans**	3:00
Dec. 26	**Philadelphia**	3:00

DETROIT LIONS

NFC Central Division
Address: Pontiac Silverdome, 1200 Featherstone Road, Box 4200, Pontiac, Mich. 48057
Telephone: 313-335-4131
President-Owner: William Clay Ford
Executive Vice President-General Manager: Russell Thomas
Head Coach and Director of Football Operations: Monte Clark
Director of Player Personnel: Tim Rooney
Assistant Coaches: Maxie Baughan, John Brunner, Don Doll, Fred Hoaglin, Ed Khayat, Joe Madden, Ted Marchibroda, Mel Phillips, Larry Seiple
Controller: Charles Schmidt
College Scouts: Jerry Neri (Western Area), Joe Bushofsky (Eastern Area), Dick Dierking (Central Area)
Director of Public Relations: Don Kremer
Publicity Assistant: Brian Muir
Ticket Manager: Fred Otto
Trainer: Kent Falb
Strength and Conditioning: Gary Wade
Equipment Manager: Dan Jaroshewich
Stadium: Pontiac Silverdome (80,638)   **Surface:** AstroTurf
Stadium Address: 1200 Featherstone Road, Pontiac, Mich. 48057
Colors: Honolulu Blue, Silver
Training Camp: Oakland University, Rochester, Mich. 48063

1982 SCHEDULE

Preseason

Aug. 14	**Cleveland**	7:00
Aug. 21	**Oakland**	7:00
Aug. 28	at Cincinnati	7:00
Sept. 4	at Buffalo	6:00

Regular Season

Sept. 12	**Chicago**	1:00
Sept. 19	at Los Angeles	1:00
Sept. 26	**Tampa Bay**	1:00
Oct. 3	**Baltimore**	1:00
Oct. 10	at Miami	4:00
Oct. 17	**Atlanta**	1:00
Oct. 24	at Buffalo	1:00
Nov. 1	at Minnesota (Monday)	8:00
Nov. 7	at Philadelphia	1:00
Nov. 14	**Green Bay**	1:00
Nov. 21	at Chicago	12:00
Nov. 25	**New York Giants** (Thanksgiving)	12:30
Dec. 6	**New York Jets** (Monday)	9:00
Dec. 12	at Green Bay	12:00
Dec. 19	**Minnesota**	1:00
Dec. 26	at Tampa Bay	1:00

GREEN BAY PACKERS

NFC Central Division
Address: 1265 Lombardi Avenue, Green Bay, Wis. 54303
Telephone: 414-494-2351
Chairman of the Board: Dominic Olejniczak
President, CEO: Robert Parins
Vice President Tony Canadeo
Secretary: John Torinus
Treasurer: John S. Stiles
Head Coach: Bart Starr
Assistant Coaches: Lew Carpenter, Ross Fichtner, Pete Kettela,
   John Marshall, John Meyer, Bill Meyers, Ernie McMillan, Dick Rehbein,
   Bob Schnelker, Richard Urich
Assistant to the President: Bob Harlan
Assistant to the President: Tom Miller
Green Bay Ticket Director: Mark Wagner
Public Relations Director: Lee Remmel
Director of Player Personnel: Dick Corrick
Director of Pro Personnel: Burt Gustafson
Film Director: Al Treml
Trainer: Domenic Gentile
Equipment Manager: Bob Noel
Stadiums: Lambeau Field (56,189); Milwaukee County Stadium (55,958)
Stadium Addresses: 1265 Lombardi Avenue, Green Bay, Wis. 54303;
   Hwy. 1-94, Milwaukee, Wis. 53214 **Surfaces:** Grass
Colors: Green, Gold
Training Camp: St. Norbert College, DePere, Wis. 54115
        (Practices at Lambeau Field, Green Bay)

1982 SCHEDULE

Preseason

Aug. 14	**New York Jets**	7:00
Aug. 20	**Cincinnati** (Milwaukee)	7:30
Aug. 28	at Oakland	6:00
Sept. 4	at New England	1:00

Regular Season

Sept. 12	**Los Angeles** (Milwaukee)	12:00
Sept. 20	at New York Giants (Monday)	9:00
Sept. 26	**Miami**	12:00
Oct. 3	**Philadelphia** (Milwaukee)	12:00
Oct. 10	at Chicago	12:00
Oct. 17	**Tampa Bay**	12:00
Oct. 24	at Minnesota	12:00
Oct. 31	**Chicago**	12:00
Nov. 7	at Tampa Bay	1:00
Nov. 14	at Detroit	1:00
Nov. 21	**Minnesota** (Milwaukee)	12:00
Nov. 28	at New York Jets	1:00
Dec. 5	**Buffalo** (Milwaukee)	12:00
Dec. 12	**Detroit**	12:00
Dec. 19	at Baltimore	2:00
Dec. 26	at Atlanta	1:00

LOS ANGELES RAMS

NFC Western Division
Business Address: 2327 W. Lincoln Ave., Anaheim, Calif. 92801
Ticket Office: Anaheim Stadium, 1900 State College Blvd., Anaheim,
Calif. 92806
Telephone: 714-535-7267 or 213-585-5400
President: Georgia Frontiere
Vice President, Finance: John Shaw
Administrator, Football Operations: Jack Faulkner
Director, Marketing: Les Marshall
Director of Operations: Dick Beam
Director of Player Personnel: John Math
Head Coach: Ray Malavasi
Assistant Coaches: Clyde Evans, John Hadl, Paul Lanham, Herb Paterra,
Jim Ringo, Fritz Shurmur, Jack Snow, Jim Vechiarella, Fred Whittingham
Director of Public Relations: Jerry Wilcox
Assistant Director of Public Relations: Geno Effler
Trainers: Gary Tuthill, George Menefee
Equipment Manager: Don Hewitt
Stadium: Anaheim Stadium (69,007) **Surface:** Grass
Stadium Address: 1900 State College Blvd., Anaheim, Calif. 92806
Colors: Royal Blue, Gold, White
Training Camp: Cal State-Fullerton, Fullerton, Calif. 92634

1982 SCHEDULE

Preseason

Aug. 14	**Denver**	7:00
Aug. 19	at Cleveland	7:30
Aug. 28	**Seattle**	7:00
Sept. 4	**San Diego**	7:00

Regular Season

Sept. 12	vs. Green Bay (Milwaukee)	12:00
Sept. 19	**Detroit**	1:00
Sept. 26	at Philadelphia	1:00
Oct. 3	at St. Louis	12:00
Oct. 10	**Atlanta**	1:00
Oct. 17	at San Francisco	1:00
Oct. 24	**New Orleans**	1:00
Oct. 31	at San Diego	1:00
Nov. 7	at New Orleans	12:00
Nov. 14	**New York Giants**	1:00
Nov. 21	at Atlanta	1:00
Nov. 28	**Kansas City**	1:00
Dec. 2	**San Francisco** (Thursday)	6:00
Dec. 12	**Denver**	1:00
Dec. 18	at Oakland (Saturday)	1:00
Dec. 26	**Chicago**	1:00

MINNESOTA VIKINGS

NFC Central Division
Address: 9520 Viking Drive, Eden Prairie, Minn. 55344
Telephone: 612-828-6500
President: Max Winter
Vice President-General Manager: Mike Lynn
Head Coach: Bud Grant
Assistant Coaches: Jerry Burns, Tom Cecchini, Bob Hollway,
  Jed Hughes, Bus Mertes, John Michels, Floyd Reese, Les Steckel
Director of Administration: Harley Peterson
Director of Operations: Jeff Diamond
Ticket Manager: Harry Randolph
Director of Football Operations: Jerry Reichow
Director of Player Personnel: Frank Gilliam
Head Scout: Ralph Kohl
Assistant Head Scout: Don Deisch
Director of Public Relations: Merrill Swanson
Assistant Public Relations Director: Kernal Buhler
Trainer: Fred Zamberletti
Equipment Manager: Dennis Ryan
Stadium: Hubert H. Humphrey Metrodome (62,212) **Surface:** SuperTurf
Stadium Address: Sixth St. and 11th Ave. S., Minneapolis, Minn. 55415
Colors: Purple, White, Gold
Training Camp: Mankato State University, Mankato, Minn. 56001

1982 SCHEDULE

Preseason

Aug. 7	vs. Baltimore at Canton, OH (HOF)	1:30
Aug. 14	at Atlanta	8:00
Aug. 21	**Seattle**	7:30
Aug. 28	at Denver	7:00
Sept. 3	**New Orleans**	7:30

Regular Season

Sept. 12	**Tampa Bay**	12:00
Sept. 16	at Buffalo (Thursday)	8:30
Sept. 26	**Dallas**	12:00
Oct. 3	at Chicago	12:00
Oct. 10	at Tampa Bay	1:00
Oct. 17	**New Orleans**	12:00
Oct. 24	**Green Bay**	12:00
Nov. 1	**Detroit** (Monday)	8:00
Nov. 7	at San Francisco	1:00
Nov. 14	at Washington	1:00
Nov. 21	vs. Green Bay (Milwaukee)	12:00
Nov. 28	**Chicago**	12:00
Dec. 5	at Miami	1:00
Dec. 12	**Baltimore**	12:00
Dec. 19	at Detroit	1:00
Dec. 26	**New York Jets**	12:00

NEW ORLEANS SAINTS

NFC Western Division
Address: 944 St. Charles Ave., New Orleans, La. 70130
Telephone: 504-525-0792
Owner: John W. Mecom, Jr.
President: Eddie Jones
Vice President-Administration: Fred Williams
Director of Football Operations: Harry Hulmes
Head Coach/General Manager: O. A. (Bum) Phillips
Assistant Coaches: Andy Everest, King Hill, John Levra, Carl Mauck, Lamar McHan, Russell Paternostro, Wade Phillips, Harold Richardson, Joe Spencer, Lance Van Zandt, John Paul Young, Willie Zapalac
Director of Player Negotiations: Pat Peppler
Director of Scouting: Bob Whitman
Director of Public Relations: Greg Suit
Assistant Director of Public Relations: Rusty Kasmiersky
Ticket Manager: Don Johnson
Controller: Bob Landry
Director of Marketing: Barra Birrcher
Administrative Assistant: Jack Cherry
Trainer: Dean Kleinschmidt
Equipment Manager: Dan Simmons
Stadium: Louisiana Superdome (71,330) **Surface:** AstroTurf
Stadium Address: 1500 Poydras Street, New Orleans, La. 70112
Colors: Old Gold, Black, White
Training Camp: Dodgertown, Vero Beach, Fla. 32960

1982 SCHEDULE

Preseason

Aug. 12	at Houston	7:00
Aug. 21	**Kansas City**	7:00
Aug. 28	**Cleveland**	7:00
Sept. 3	at Minnesota	7:30

Regular Season

Sept. 12	**St. Louis**	12:00
Sept. 19	at Chicago	12:00
Sept. 26	**Denver**	12:00
Oct. 3	at Oakland	1:00
Oct. 10	**San Francisco**	12:00
Oct. 17	at Minnesota	12:00
Oct. 24	at Los Angeles	1:00
Oct. 31	**Atlanta**	12:00
Nov. 7	**Los Angeles**	12:00
Nov. 14	at San Diego	1:00
Nov. 21	**Kansas City**	12:00
Nov. 28	at San Francisco	1:00
Dec. 5	**Tampa Bay**	12:00
Dec. 12	at Atlanta	4:00
Dec. 19	at Dallas	3:00
Dec. 26	**Washington**	12:00

NEW YORK GIANTS

NFC Eastern Division
Address: Giants Stadium, East Rutherford, N.J. 07073
Telephone: 201-935-8111
President: Wellington T. Mara
Vice President-Treasurer: Timothy J. Mara
Vice President-Secretary: Raymond J. Walsh
General Manager: George Young
Assistant General Manager: Terry Bledsoe
Head Coach: Ray Perkins
Assistant Coaches: Bill Austin, Bill Belichick, Romeo Crennel, Ron Erhardt,
  Fred Glick, Pat Hodgson, Lamar Leachman, Bob Lord, Bill Parcells
Controller: John Pasquali
Director of Player Personnel: Tom Boisture
Director of Pro Personnel: Ernie Adams
Director of Media Services: Ed Croke
Director of Promotions: Tom Power
Director of Special Projects: Victor Del Guercio
Box Office Treasurer: Jim Gleason
Trainers: Ronnie Barnes, Dave Barringer, John Dziegiel, John Johnson
Equipment Manager: Ed Wagner, Jr.
Stadium: Giants Stadium (76,891) **Surface:** AstroTurf
Stadium Address: East Rutherford, N.J. 07073
Colors: Blue, Red, White
Training Camp: Pace University, Pleasantville, N.Y. 10570

1982 SCHEDULE

Preseason

Aug. 14	at Baltimore	8:00
Aug. 21	**Pittsburgh**	8:00
Aug. 28	**New York Jets**	8:00
Sept. 3	at Miami	8:00

Regular Season

Sept. 12	**Atlanta**	1:00
Sept. 20	**Green Bay** (Monday)	9:00
Sept. 26	at Pittsburgh	1:00
Oct. 3	at Dallas	3:00
Oct. 10	**St. Louis**	1:00
Oct. 17	**Cincinnati**	1:00
Oct. 25	at Philadelphia (Monday)	9:00
Oct. 31	**Dallas**	4:00
Nov. 7	at Cleveland	1:00
Nov. 14	at Los Angeles	1:00
Nov. 21	**Washington**	4:00
Nov. 25	at Detroit (Thanksgiving)	12:30
Dec. 5	**Houston**	1:00
Dec. 11	**Philadelphia** (Saturday)	12:30
Dec. 19	at Washington	1:00
Dec. 26	at St. Louis	12:00

PHILADELPHIA EAGLES

NFC Eastern Division
Address: Philadelphia Veterans Stadium, Broad Street and Pattison
   Avenue, Philadelphia, Pa. 19148
Telephone: 215-463-2500
President: Leonard H. Tose
General Manager: Jim Murray
Head Coach: Dick Vermeil
Assistant Coaches: John Becker, Chuck Bednarik (honorary), Fred
   Bruney, Marion Campbell, Chuck Clausen, Dick Coury, Sid Gillman,
   George Hill, Ken Iman, Lynn Stiles, Jerry Wampfler
Business Manager: Jim Borden
Legal Counsel: Susan Fletcher
Director of Public Relations: Jim Gallagher
Public Relations Assistant: Chick McElrone
Sales and Marketing: Sam Procopio
Ticket Manager: Hugh Ortman
Director of Player Personnel: Carl Peterson
Assistant Director of Player Personnel: Jackie Graves
Player Personnel Consultant: Herman Ball
Talent Scouts: Bill Baker, Jim Katcavage, Phil Neri
Trainer: Otho Davis
Equipment Manager: Rusty Sweeney
Stadium: Philadelphia Veterans Stadium (72,204) **Surface:** AstroTurf
Stadium Address: Broad Street and Pattison Avenue,
   Philadelphia, Pa. 19148
Colors: Kelly Green, White, Silver
Training Camp: West Chester State College, West Chester, Pa. 19380

1982 SCHEDULE

Preseason

Aug. 14	at Tampa Bay	7:00
Aug. 20	**New England**	6:00
Aug. 27	at Atlanta	8:30
Sept. 4	at Pittsburgh	6:00

Regular Season

Sept. 12	**Washington**	1:00
Sept. 19	at Cleveland	1:00
Sept. 26	**Los Angeles**	1:00
Oct. 3	vs. Green Bay (Milwaukee)	12:00
Oct. 11	at Pittsburgh (Monday)	9:00
Oct. 17	**Dallas**	4:00
Oct. 25	**New York Giants** (Monday)	9:00
Oct. 31	at St. Louis	12:00
Nov. 7	**Detroit**	1:00
Nov. 15	at Atlanta (Monday)	9:00
Nov. 21	**Cincinnati**	1:00
Nov. 28	at Washington	1:00
Dec. 5	**St. Louis**	1:00
Dec. 11	at New York Giants (Saturday)	12:30
Dec. 19	**Houston**	1:00
Dec. 26	at Dallas	3:00

ST. LOUIS CARDINALS

NFC Eastern Division
Address: 200 Stadium Plaza, St. Louis, Mo. 63102
Telephone: 314-421-0777
Chairman of the Board, CEO: William V. Bidwill
President: Bing Devine
Director of Pro Personnel: Larry Wilson
Treasurer: Charley Schlegel
Head Coach: Jim Hanifan
Assistant Coaches: Chuck Banker, Tom Bettis, Don Brown, Rudy Feldman, Harry Gilmer, Dick Jamieson, Tom Lovat, Leon McLaughlin, Floyd Peters, Emmitt Thomas
Director of Player Personnel: George Boone
Media Coordinator: Marty Igel
Director of Community Relations: Adele Harris
Ticket Manager: Steve Walsh
Trainer: John Omohundro
Assistant Trainer: Jim Shearer
Equipment Manager: Bill Simmons
Assistant Equipment Manager: Mark Ahlmeier
Stadium: Busch Memorial Stadium (51,392) **Surface:** AstroTurf
Stadium Address: 200 Stadium Plaza, St. Louis, Mo. 63102
Colors: Cardinal Red, White, Black
Training Camp: Eastern Illinois University
Charleston, Ill. 61920

1982 SCHEDULE

Preseason

Aug. 13	at Seattle	7:30
Aug. 21	at San Francisco	6:00
Aug. 28	at Chicago	6:00
Sept. 4	**Kansas City**	6:00

Regular Season

Sept. 12	at New Orleans	12:00
Sept. 19	**Dallas**	12:00
Sept. 26	at Washington	1:00
Oct. 3	**Los Angeles**	12:00
Oct. 10	at New York Giants	1:00
Oct. 17	**Chicago**	12:00
Oct. 24	at New England	1:00
Oct. 31	**Philadelphia**	12:00
Nov. 7	at Dallas	12:00
Nov. 14	**Seattle**	12:00
Nov. 21	**San Francisco**	3:00
Nov. 28	at Atlanta	1:00
Dec. 5	at Philadelphia	1:00
Dec. 12	**Washington**	12:00
Dec. 19	at Chicago	12:00
Dec. 26	**New York Giants**	12:00

SAN FRANCISCO 49ERS

NFC Western Division
Address: 711 Nevada St., Redwood City, Calif. 94061
Telephone: 415-365-3420
President: Edward J. DeBartolo, Jr.
Head Coach-General Manager: Bill Walsh
Vice President-Administration: John McVay
Director of Marketing and Community Affairs: Ken Flower
Assistant Coaches: Norb Hecker, Milt Jackson, Billie Matthews, Bobb McKittrick, Bill McPherson, Ray Rhodes, George Seifert, Chuck Studley, Al Vermeil, Sam Wyche
Public Relations Director: George Heddleston
Public Relations Assistant: Jerry Walker
Publicity Assistant: Delia Newland
Business Manager: Keith Simon
Ticket Manager: Ken Dargel
Co-Trainers: Hal Wyatt, Lindsy McLean
Equipment Manager: Chico Norton
Stadium: Candlestick Park (61,185) **Surface:** Grass
Stadium Address: San Francisco, Calif. 94124
Colors: Forty Niner Gold and Scarlet
Training Camp: Sierra Community College, Rocklin, Calif. 95677

1982 SCHEDULE

Preseason

Aug. 14	`Oakland	12:00
Aug. 21	**St. Louis**	6:00
Aug. 28	at San Diego	6:00
Sept. 3	at Seattle	7:30

Regular Season

Sept. 12	**Oakland**	1:00
Sept. 19	at Denver	2:00
Sept. 26	**Chicago**	1:00
Oct. 4	at Tampa Bay (Monday)	9:00
Oct. 10	at New Orleans	12:00
Oct. 17	**Los Angeles**	1:00
Oct. 24	at Atlanta	1:00
Oct. 31	at Washington	1:00
Nov. 7	**Minnesota**	1:00
Nov. 14	**Dallas**	1:00
Nov. 21	at St. Louis	3:00
Nov. 28	**New Orleans**	1:00
Dec. 2	at Los Angeles (Thursday)	6:00
Dec. 11	**San Diego** (Saturday)	1:00
Dec. 19	**Atlanta**	6:00
Dec. 26	at Kansas City	12:00

TAMPA BAY BUCCANEERS

NFC Central Division
Address: One Buccaneer Place, Tampa, Fla. 33607
Telephone: 813-870-2700
Owner: Hugh F. Culverhouse
President: Hugh F. Culverhouse
Vice President-Head Coach: John H. McKay
Vice President: Joy Culverhouse
Secretary/Treasurer: Ward Holland
Director of Administration: Herbert M. Gold
Assistant to the President: Phil Krueger
Assistant Coaches: Boyd Dowler, Frank Emanuel, Wayne Fontes,
  Abe Gibron, Jim Gruden, Bill Johnson, Bill Nelsen, Howard Tippett
Director of Public Relations and Promotions: Bob Best
Assistant Director of Public Relations: Rick Odioso
Assistant Director of Promotions: Jim Rowe
Director of Ticket Operations: John Sheffield
Assistant Director of Ticket Operations: Terry Wooten
Director of Player Personnel: Ken Herock
Pro Personnel Scout: Jack Bushofsky
College Personnel: Craig Fertig, Bill Groman, George Saimes
Controller: Ed Easom
Trainer: Tom Oxley
Assistant Trainer: Scott Anderson
Equipment Manager: Pat Marcuccillo
Stadium: Tampa Stadium (72,128) **Surface:** Grass
Stadium Address: N. Dale Mabry, Tampa, Fla. 33607
Colors: Florida Orange, White with Red Trim
Training Camp: One Buccaneer Place, Tampa, Fla. 33607

1982 SCHEDULE

Preseason

Aug. 14	**Philadelphia**	7:00
Aug. 21	**Washington**	7:00
Aug. 28	at Houston	8:00
Sept. 3	**Atlanta**	7:00

Regular Season

Sept. 12	at Minnesota	12:00
Sept. 19	**Washington**	4:00
Sept. 26	at Detroit	1:00
Oct. 4	**San Francisco** (Monday)	9:00
Oct. 10	**Minnesota**	1:00
Oct. 17	at Green Bay	12:00
Oct. 24	at Chicago	12:00
Oct. 31	at Baltimore	2:00
Nov. 7	**Green Bay**	1:00
Nov. 14	**Chicago**	1:00
Nov. 21	at Dallas	12:00
Nov. 29	**Miami** (Monday)	9:00
Dec. 5	at New Orleans	12:00
Dec. 12	at New York Jets	1:00
Dec. 19	**Buffalo**	1:00
Dec. 26	**Detroit**	1:00

WASHINGTON REDSKINS

NFC Eastern Division
Address: Redskin Park, P.O. Box 17247, Dulles International Airport,
  Washington, D.C. 20041
Telephone: 703-471-9100
Chairman of the Board-Chief Operating Executive: Jack Kent Cooke
President: Edward Bennett Williams
Senior Vice President: Gerrard T. Gabrys
Board of Directors: Jack Kent Cooke, John Kent Cooke, Lawrence
  Lucchino, W. Jarvis Moody, Robert A. Schulman, William A. Shea,
  Edward Bennett Williams
General Manager: Bobby Beathard
Assistant General Managers: Bobby Mitchell, Dick Myers
Head Coach: Joe Gibbs
Assistant Head Coach: Dan Henning
Assistant Coaches: Don Breaux, Joe Bugel, Bill Hickman,
  Larry Peccatiello, Richie Petitbon, Wayne Sevier, Warren Simmons,
  Charley Taylor, LaVern Torgeson
Director of Player Personnel: Mike Allman
Director of Pro Scouting: Kirk Mee
Director of College Scouting: Dick Daniels   **Scout:** Charles Casserly
Public Relations Director: Joe F. Blair
Assistant Public Relations Director: Charles M. Taylor
Ticket Manager: George Christophel
Head Trainer: Lamar (Bubba) Tyer   **Assistants:** Joe Kuczo, Keoki Kamau
Equipment Manager: Jay Brunetti
Stadium: Robert F. Kennedy Stadium (55,045)   **Surface:** Grass (PAT)
Stadium Address: East Capitol Street, Washington, D.C. 20003
Colors: Burgundy, Gold
Training Camp: Dickinson College, Carlisle, Pa. 17013

1982 SCHEDULE

Preseason

Aug. 14	at Miami	8:00
Aug. 21	at Tampa Bay	7:00
Aug. 27	**Buffalo**	7:30
Sept. 3	at Cincinnati	7:30

Regular Season

Sept. 12	at Philadelphia	1:00
Sept. 19	at Tampa Bay	4:00
Sept. 26	**St. Louis**	1:00
Oct. 3	**Cleveland**	1:00
Oct. 10	at Dallas	12:00
Oct. 17	**Pittsburgh**	1:00
Oct. 24	at Houston	12:00
Oct. 31	**San Francisco**	1:00
Nov. 7	at Cincinnati	1:00
Nov. 14	**Minnesota**	1:00
Nov. 21	at New York Giants	4:00
Nov. 28	**Philadelphia**	1:00
Dec. 5	**Dallas**	4:00
Dec. 12	at St. Louis	12:00
Dec. 19	**New York Giants**	1:00
Dec. 26	at New Orleans	12:00

1982 PRESEASON SCHEDULE

(All times local)

FIRST WEEK
SATURDAY, AUGUST 7
Baltimore vs. Minnesota at Canton, Ohio .... (ABC) 1:30
THURSDAY, AUGUST 12
New Orleans at Houston 7:00
FRIDAY, AUGUST 13
Cincinnati at Kansas City 7:35
St. Louis at Seattle 7:30
SATURDAY, AUGUST 14
Buffalo at Dallas 8:00
Cleveland at Detroit 7:00
Denver at Los Angeles 7:00
Minnesota at Atlanta 8:00
New York Jets at Green Bay 7:00
New York Giants at Baltimore 8:00
Oakland at San Francisco .... (CBS) 12:00
Philadelphia at Tampa Bay 7:00
Pittsburgh vs. New England at Knoxville 7:30
Washington at Miami 8:00
MONDAY, AUGUST 16
Chicago at San Diego 7:00

SECOND WEEK
THURSDAY, AUGUST 19
Los Angeles at Cleveland 7:30
FRIDAY, AUGUST 20
Cincinnati vs. Green Bay at Milwaukee .... (ABC) 7:30
New England at Philadelphia 6:00
SATURDAY, AUGUST 21
Atlanta vs. Baltimore at Tempe, Arizona 8:00
Chicago at Buffalo 6:00
Dallas at San Diego .... (CBS) 6:00
Kansas City at New Orleans 7:00
Miami at Denver 7:00
Oakland at Detroit 7:00
Pittsburgh at New York Giants 8:00
St. Louis at San Francisco 6:00
Seattle at Minnesota 7:30
Washington at Tampa Bay 7:00
SUNDAY, AUGUST 22
New York Jets at Houston .... (NBC) 12:00

THIRD WEEK
FRIDAY, AUGUST 27
Buffalo at Washington 7:30
Philadelphia at Atlanta .... (ABC) 8:30
SATURDAY, AUGUST 28
Baltimore at Pittsburgh 6:00
Cleveland at New Orleans 7:00

Detroit at Cincinnati	7:00
Green Bay at Oakland	6:00
Miami at Kansas City	7:35
Minnesota at Denver	7:00
New England at Dallas	8:00
New York Jets at New York Giants	8:00
St. Louis at Chicago	6:00
San Francisco at San Diego (NBC)	6:00
Seattle at Los Angeles	7:00
Tampa Bay at Houston	8:00

FOURTH WEEK
FRIDAY, SEPTEMBER 3

Atlanta at Tampa Bay	7:00
New Orleans at Minnesota	7:30
New York Giants at Miami (NBC)	8:00
San Francisco at Seattle	7:30
Washington at Cincinnati	7:30

SATURDAY, SEPTEMBER 4

Baltimore at Chicago	6:00
Cleveland at Oakland	6:00
Denver at New York Jets at Giants Stadium	8:00
Detroit at Buffalo	6:00
Green Bay at New England	1:00
Houston at Dallas (CBS)	8:00
Kansas City at St. Louis	6:00
Philadelphia at Pittsburgh	6:00
San Diego at Los Angeles	7:00

1982 REGULAR SEASON SCHEDULE

(All times local. CBS and NBC television doubleheader games
to be announced.)

FIRST WEEK
Sunday, September 12 (NBC-TV doubleheader)
1.	Atlanta at New York Giants	1:00
2.	Chicago at Detroit	1:00
3.	Cleveland at Seattle	1:00
4.	Houston at Cincinnati	1:00
5.	Kansas City at Buffalo	1:00
6.	Los Angeles vs. Green Bay at Milwaukee	12:00
7.	Miami at New York Jets	4:00
8.	New England at Baltimore	2:00
9.	Oakland at San Francisco	1:00
10.	St. Louis at New Orleans	12:00
11.	San Diego at Denver	2:00
12.	Tampa Bay at Minnesota	12:00
13.	Washington at Philadelphia	1:00

Monday, September 13
14.	Pittsburgh at Dallas	(ABC)	8:00

SECOND WEEK
Thursday, September 16
15.	Minnesota at Buffalo	(ABC)	8:30

Sunday, September 19 (CBS-TV doubleheader)
16.	Baltimore at Miami	4:00
17.	Cincinnati at Pittsburgh	1:00
18.	Dallas at St. Louis	12:00
19.	Detroit at Los Angeles	1:00
20.	New Orleans at Chicago	12:00
21.	New York Jets at New England	1:00
22.	Oakland at Atlanta	1:00
23.	Philadelphia at Cleveland	1:00
24.	San Diego at Kansas City	12:00
25.	San Francisco at Denver	2:00
26.	Seattle at Houston	3:00
27.	Washington at Tampa Bay	4:00

Monday, September 20
28.	Green Bay at New York Giants	(ABC)	9:00

THIRD WEEK
Thursday, September 23
29.	Atlanta at Kansas City	(ABC)	7:30

Sunday, September 26 (NBC-TV doubleheader)
30.	Buffalo at Houston	12:00
31.	Chicago at San Francisco	1:00
32.	Dallas at Minnesota	12:00
33.	Denver at New Orleans	12:00
34.	Los Angeles at Philadelphia	1:00
35.	Miami at Green Bay	12:00

36.	New York Giants at Pittsburgh		1:00
37.	New York Jets at Baltimore		4:00
38.	Oakland at San Diego		1:00
39.	St. Louis at Washington		1:00
40.	Seattle at New England		1:00
41.	Tampa Bay at Detroit		1:00

Monday, September 27

| 42. | Cincinnati at Cleveland | (ABC) | 9:00 |

FOURTH WEEK
Sunday, October 3 (CBS-TV doubleheader)

43.	Baltimore at Detroit		1:00
44.	Cleveland at Washington		1:00
45.	Houston at New York Jets		1:00
46.	Kansas City at Seattle		1:00
47.	Los Angeles at St. Louis		12:00
48.	Miami at Cincinnati		1:00
49.	Minnesota at Chicago		12:00
50.	New England at Buffalo		1:00
51.	New Orleans at Oakland		1:00
52.	New York Giants at Dallas		3:00
53.	Philadelphia vs. Green Bay at Milwaukee		12:00
54.	Pittsburgh at Denver		2:00
55.	San Diego at Atlanta		1:00

Monday, October 4

| 56. | San Francisco at Tampa Bay | (ABC) | 9:00 |

FIFTH WEEK
Sunday, October 10 (NBC-TV doubleheader)

57.	Atlanta at Los Angeles		1:00
58.	Buffalo at Baltimore		2:00
59.	Cincinnati at New England		1:00
60.	Cleveland at Oakland		1:00
61.	Denver at New York Jets		4:00
62.	Detroit at Miami		4:00
63.	Green Bay at Chicago		12:00
64.	Houston at Kansas City		12:00
65.	Minnesota at Tampa Bay		1:00
66.	St. Louis at New York Giants		1:00
67.	San Francisco at New Orleans		12:00
68.	Seattle at San Diego		1:00
69.	Washington at Dallas		12:00

Monday, October 11

| 70. | Philadelphia at Pittsburgh | (ABC) | 9:00 |

SIXTH WEEK
Sunday, October 17 (CBS-TV doubleheader)

71.	Atlanta at Detroit		1:00
72.	Baltimore at Cleveland		1:00
73.	Chicago at St. Louis		12:00
74.	Cincinnati at New York Giants		1:00
75.	Dallas at Philadelphia		4:00
76.	Denver at Houston		12:00
77.	Kansas City at San Diego		1:00
78.	Los Angeles at San Francisco		1:00

79.	New England at Miami		1:00
80.	New Orleans at Minnesota		12:00
81.	Oakland at Seattle		1:00
82.	Pittsburgh at Washington		1:00
83.	Tampa Bay at Green Bay		12:00

Monday, October 18

| 84. | Buffalo at New York Jets | (ABC) | 9:00 |

SEVENTH WEEK

Sunday, October 24 (NBC-TV doubleheader)

85.	Cleveland at Pittsburgh		1:00
86.	Dallas at Cincinnati	(ABC)	9:00
87.	Detroit at Buffalo		1:00
88.	Green Bay at Minnesota		12:00
89.	Miami at Baltimore		2:00
90.	New Orleans at Los Angeles		1:00
91.	New York Jets at Kansas City		12:00
92.	Oakland at Denver		2:00
93.	St. Louis at New England		1:00
94.	San Diego at Seattle		1:00
95.	San Francisco at Atlanta		1:00
96.	Tampa Bay at Chicago		12:00
97.	Washington at Houston		12:00

Monday, October 25

| 98. | New York Giants at Philadelphia | (ABC) | 9:00 |

EIGHTH WEEK

Sunday, October 31 (CBS-TV doubleheader)

99.	Atlanta at New Orleans		12:00
100.	Buffalo at Denver		2:00
101.	Chicago at Green Bay		12:00
102.	Dallas at New York Giants		4:00
103.	Houston at Cleveland		1:00
104.	Los Angeles at San Diego		1:00
105.	Miami at Oakland		1:00
106.	New England at New York Jets		1:00
107.	Philadelphia at St. Louis		12:00
108.	Pittsburgh at Cincinnati		1:00
109.	San Francisco at Washington		1:00
110.	Seattle at Kansas City		12:00
111.	Tampa Bay at Baltimore		2:00

Monday, November 1

| 112. | Detroit at Minnesota | (ABC) | 8:00 |

NINTH WEEK

Sunday, November 7 (NBC-TV doubleheader)

113.	Atlanta at Chicago		12:00
114.	Baltimore at New England		1:00
115.	Denver at Seattle		1:00
116.	Detroit at Philadelphia		1:00
117.	Green Bay at Tampa Bay		1:00
118.	Houston at Pittsburgh		1:00
119.	Kansas City at Oakland		1:00
120.	Los Angeles at New Orleans		12:00
121.	Minnesota at San Francisco		1:00

122.	New York Giants at Cleveland	1:00
123.	New York Jets at Buffalo	4:00
124.	St. Louis at Dallas	12:00
125.	Washington at Cincinnati	1:00

Monday, November 8

| 126. | San Diego at Miami | (ABC) | 9:00 |

TENTH WEEK
Sunday, November 14 (CBS-TV doubleheader)

127.	Buffalo at New England	1:00
128.	Chicago at Tampa Bay	1:00
129.	Cincinnati at Houston	12:00
130.	Cleveland at Miami	4:00
131.	Dallas at San Francisco	1:00
132.	Denver at Kansas City	12:00
133.	Green Bay at Detroit	1:00
134.	Minnesota at Washington	1:00
135.	New Orleans at San Diego	1:00
136.	New York Giants at Los Angeles	1:00
137.	New York Jets at Pittsburgh	1:00
138.	Oakland at Baltimore	2:00
139.	Seattle at St. Louis	12:00

Monday, November 15

| 140. | Philadelphia at Atlanta | (ABC) | 9:00 |

ELEVENTH WEEK
Sunday, November 21 (CBS-TV doubleheader)

141.	Baltimore at New York Jets	1:00
142.	Cincinnati at Philadelphia	1:00
143.	Detroit at Chicago	12:00
144.	Kansas City at New Orleans	12:00
145.	Los Angeles at Atlanta	1:00
146.	Miami at Buffalo	1:00
147.	Minnesota vs. Green Bay at Milwaukee	12:00
148.	New England at Cleveland	1:00
149.	Pittsburgh at Houston	12:00
150.	San Francisco at St. Louis	3:00
151.	Seattle at Denver	2:00
152.	Tampa Bay at Dallas	12:00
153.	Washington at New York Giants	4:00

Monday, November 22

| 154. | San Diego at Oakland | (ABC) | 6:00 |

TWELFTH WEEK
Thursday, November 25 (Thanksgiving Day)

| 155. | Cleveland at Dallas | (NBC) | 3:00 |
| 156. | New York Giants at Detroit | (CBS) | 12:00 |

Sunday, November 28 (NBC-TV doubleheader)

157.	Baltimore at Buffalo	1:00
158.	Chicago at Minnesota	12:00
159.	Denver at San Diego	1:00
160.	Green Bay at New York Jets	1:00
161.	Houston at New England	1:00
162.	Kansas City at Los Angeles	1:00
163.	New Orleans at San Francisco	1:00

164.	Oakland at Cincinnati	1:00
165.	Philadelphia at Washington	1:00
166.	Pittsburgh at Seattle	1:00
167.	St. Louis at Atlanta	1:00

Monday, November 29

| 168. | Miami at Tampa Bay | (ABC) 9:00 |

THIRTEENTH WEEK

Thursday, December 2

| 169. | San Francisco at Los Angeles | (ABC) 6:00 |

Sunday, December 5 (CBS-TV doubleheader)

170.	Atlanta at Denver	2:00
171.	Buffalo vs. Green Bay at Milwaukee	12:00
172.	Cincinnati at Baltimore	2:00
173.	Dallas at Washington	4:00
174.	Houston at New York Giants	1:00
175.	Kansas City at Pittsburgh	1:00
176.	Minnesota at Miami	1:00
177.	New England at Chicago	12:00
178.	St. Louis at Philadelphia	1:00
179.	San Diego at Cleveland	1:00
180.	Seattle at Oakland	1:00
181.	Tampa Bay at New Orleans	12:00

Monday, December 6

| 182. | New York Jets at Detroit | (ABC) 9:00 |

FOURTEENTH WEEK

Saturday, December 11

| 183. | Philadelphia at New York Giants | (CBS) 12:30 |
| 184. | San Diego at San Francisco | (NBC) 1:00 |

Sunday, December 12 (NBC-TV doubleheader)

185.	Baltimore at Minnesota	12:00
186.	Chicago at Seattle	1:00
187.	Cleveland at Cincinnati	1:00
188.	Denver at Los Angeles	1:00
189.	Detroit at Green Bay	12:00
190.	Miami at New England	1:00
191.	New Orleans at Atlanta	4:00
192.	Oakland at Kansas City	3:00
193.	Pittsburgh at Buffalo	12:00
194.	Tampa Bay at New York Jets	1:00
195.	Washington at St. Louis	12:00

Monday, December 13

| 196. | Dallas at Houston | (ABC) 8:00 |

FIFTEENTH WEEK

Saturday, December 18

| 197. | Los Angeles at Oakland | (CBS) 1:00 |
| 198. | New York Jets at Miami | (NBC) 12:30 |

Sunday, December 19 (NBC-TV doubleheader)

199.	Atlanta at San Francisco	6:00
200.	Buffalo at Tampa Bay	1:00
201.	Green Bay at Baltimore	2:00
202.	Houston at Philadelphia	1:00
203.	Kansas City at Denver	2:00

204.	Minnesota at Detroit	1:00
205.	New England at Seattle	1:00
206.	New Orleans at Dallas	3:00
207.	New York Giants at Washington	1:00
208.	Pittsburgh at Cleveland	1:00
209.	St. Louis at Chicago	12:00

Monday, December 20

| 210. | Cincinnati at San Diego | (ABC) | 6:00 |

SIXTEENTH WEEK
Sunday, December 26 (CBS-TV doubleheader)

211.	Baltimore at San Diego	1:00
212.	Chicago at Los Angeles	1:00
213.	Cleveland at Houston	12:00
214.	Denver at Oakland	1:00
215.	Detroit at Tampa Bay	1:00
216.	Green Bay at Atlanta	1:00
217.	New England at Pittsburgh	1:00
218.	New York Giants at St. Louis	12:00
219.	New York Jets at Minnesota	12:00
220.	Philadelphia at Dallas	3:00
221.	San Francisco at Kansas City	12:00
222.	Seattle at Cincinnati	1:00
223.	Washington at New Orleans	12:00

Monday, December 27

| 224. | Buffalo at Miami | (ABC) | 9:00 |

POSTSEASON GAMES

Sunday, January 2	NFL First Round Playoffs (CBS and NBC)
Saturday, January 8	AFC and NFC Divisional Playoffs (NBC and CBS)
Sunday, January 9	AFC and NFC Divisional Playoffs (NBC and CBS)
Sunday, January 16	AFC Championship Game (NBC) NFC Championship Game (CBS)
Sunday, January 30	Super Bowl XVII at Rose Bowl, Pasadena, Calif. (NBC)
Sunday, February 6	AFC-NFC Pro Bowl at Honolulu, Hawaii (ABC)

1982 NATIONALLY TELEVISED GAMES
(All games also carried on CBS Radio Network.)

REGULAR SEASON

Monday, September 13	Pittsburgh at Dallas (night, ABC)
Thursday, September 16	Minnesota at Buffalo (night, ABC)
Monday, September 20	Green Bay at New York Giants (night, ABC)
Thursday, September 23	Atlanta at Kansas City (night, ABC)
Monday, September 27	Cincinnati at Cleveland (night, ABC)
Monday, October 4	San Francisco at Tampa Bay (night, ABC)
Monday, October 11	Philadelphia at Pittsburgh (night, ABC)
Monday, October 18	Buffalo at New York Jets (night, ABC)
Sunday, October 24	Dallas at Cincinnati (night, ABC)
Monday, October 25	New York Giants at Philadelphia (night, ABC)
Monday, November 1	Detroit at Minnesota (night, ABC)

Monday, November 8	San Diego at Miami (night, ABC)
Monday, November 15	Philadelphia at Atlanta (night, ABC)
Monday, November 22	San Diego at Oakland (night, ABC)
Thursday, November 25 (Thanksgiving)	Cleveland at Dallas (day, NBC)
	New York Giants at Detroit (day, CBS)
Monday, November 29	Miami at Tampa Bay (night, ABC)
Thursday, December 2	San Francisco at Los Angeles (night, ABC)
Monday, December 6	New York Jets at Detroit (night, ABC)
Saturday, December 11	Philadelphia at New York Giants (day, CBS)
	San Diego at San Francisco (day, NBC)
Monday, December 13	Dallas at Houston (night, ABC)
Saturday, December 18	Los Angeles at Oakland (day, CBS)
	New York Jets at Miami (day, NBC)
Sunday, December 19	Atlanta at San Francisco (night, ABC)
Monday, December 20	Cincinnati at San Diego (night, ABC)
Monday, December 27	Buffalo at Miami (night, ABC)

AFC-NFC INTERCONFERENCE GAMES

(Sunday unless noted; all times local.)

September 12	Oakland at San Francisco	1:00
September 13 (Monday)	Pittsburgh at Dallas	8:00
September 16 (Thursday)	Minnesota at Buffalo	8:30
September 19	Oakland at Atlanta	1:00
	Philadelphia at Cleveland	1:00
	San Francisco at Denver	2:00
September 23 (Thursday)	Atlanta at Kansas City	7:30
September 26	Denver at New Orleans	12:00
	Miami at Green Bay	12:00
	New York Giants at Pittsburgh	1:00
October 3	Baltimore at Detroit	1:00
	Cleveland at Washington	1:00
	New Orleans at Oakland	1:00
	San Diego at Atlanta	1:00
October 10	Detroit at Miami	4:00
October 11 (Monday)	Philadelphia at Pittsburgh	9:00
October 17	Cincinnati at New York Giants	1:00
	Pittsburgh at Washington	1:00
October 24	Dallas at Cincinnati	9:00
	Detroit at Buffalo	1:00
	St. Louis at New England	1:00
	Washington at Houston	12:00
October 31	Los Angeles at San Diego	1:00
	Tampa Bay at Baltimore	2:00
November 7	New York Giants at Cleveland	1:00
	Washington at Cincinnati	1:00
November 14	New Orleans at San Diego	1:00
	Seattle at St. Louis	12:00
November 21	Cincinnati at Philadelphia	1:00
	Kansas City at New Orleans	12:00
November 25 (Thursday)	Cleveland at Dallas	3:00
November 28	Green Bay at New York Jets	1:00
	Kansas City at Los Angeles	1:00
November 29 (Monday)	Miami at Tampa Bay	9:00
December 5	Atlanta at Denver	2:00

	Buffalo vs. Green Bay at Milwaukee . . .	12:00
	Houston at New York Giants	1:00
	Minnesota at Miami	1:00
	New England at Chicago	12:00
December 6 (Monday)	New York Jets at Detroit	9:00
December 11 (Saturday)	San Diego at San Francisco	1:00
December 12	Baltimore at Minnesota	12:00
	Chicago at Seattle	1:00
	Denver at Los Angeles	1:00
	Tampa Bay at New York Jets	1:00
December 13 (Monday)	Dallas at Houston	8:00
December 18 (Saturday)	Los Angeles at Oakland	1:00
December 19	Buffalo at Tampa Bay	1:00
	Green Bay at Baltimore	2:00
	Houston at Philadelphia	1:00
December 26	New York Jets at Minnesota	12:00
	San Francisco at Kansas City	12:00

MONDAY NIGHT GAMES AT A GLANCE

(All times local; televised by ABC and broadcast by CBS Radio.)

September 13	Pittsburgh at Dallas	8:00
September 20	Green Bay at New York Giants	9:00
September 27	Cincinnati at Cleveland	9:00
October 4	San Francisco at Tampa Bay	9:00
October 11	Philadelphia at Pittsburgh	9:00
October 18	Buffalo at New York Jets	9:00
October 25	New York Giants at Philadelphia	9:00
November 1	Detroit at Minnesota	8:00
November 8	San Diego at Miami	9:00
November 15	Philadelphia at Atlanta	9:00
November 22	San Diego at Oakland	6:00
November 29	Miami at Tampa Bay	9:00
December 6	New York Jets at Detroit	9:00
December 13	Dallas at Houston	8:00
December 20	Cincinnati at San Diego	6:00
December 27	Buffalo at Miami	9:00

SUNDAY-THURSDAY NIGHT GAMES AT A GLANCE

(All times local; televised by ABC and broadcast by CBS Radio.)

Thursday, September 16	Minnesota at Buffalo	8:30
Thursday, September 23	Atlanta at Kansas City	7:30
Sunday, October 24	Dallas at Cincinnati	9:00
Thursday, December 2	San Francisco at Los Angeles	6:00
Sunday, December 19	Atlanta at San Francisco	6:00

NOTES

NOTES

NOTES

NOTES

NOTES

NOTES

NOTES

NOTES

NOTES

NOTES

NOTES

NOTES

NOTES